...KLEY PUBLISHING GROUP
...y the Penguin Group
...oup (USA) Inc.
...a Street, New York, New York 10014, USA
...oup (Canada), 90 Eglinton Avenue East, Suite 700, Toronto, Ontario M4P 2Y3, Canada
...of Pearson Penguin Canada Inc.)
...oks Ltd., 80 Strand, London WC2R 0RL, England
...oup Ireland, 25 St. Stephen's Green, Dublin 2, Ireland (a division of Penguin Books Ltd.)
...oup (Australia), 250 Camberwell Road, Camberwell, Victoria 3124, Australia
...of Pearson Australia Group Pty. Ltd.)
...ooks India Pvt. Ltd., 11 Community Centre, Panchsheel Park, New Delhi—110 017, India
...oup (NZ), 67 Apollo Drive, Rosedale, North Shore 0632, New Zealand
...of Pearson New Zealand Ltd.)
...ooks (South Africa) (Pty.) Ltd., 24 Sturdee Avenue, Rosebank, Johannesburg 2196,
...ica

...Books Ltd., Registered Offices: 80 Strand, London WC2R 0RL, England

...ANTATION

...ey Book / published by arrangement with the author

...G HISTORY
...Publishing trade edition / April 2002
...mass-market edition / July 2009

...nt © 2002 by Chris Kuzneski, Inc.
...from The Lost Throne by Chris Kuzneski copyright © 2009 by Chris Kuzneski, Inc.
...ver photos: Wrought Iron Gate © Agence Images/Beateworks/Corbis; Path © Yossan/
...Spanish Moss © Philip Gould/Corbis; Rusty Chain © Nathan Griffith/Corbis. Stepback
...xpresses at Sunset © David Muench/Corbis Edge.
...sign by Diana Kolsky.
...ext design by Kristin del Rosario.

0-425-22237-9

®
...oks are published by The Berkley Publishing Group,
...f Penguin Group (USA) Inc.,
...Street, New York, New York 10014.
...® is a registered trademark of Penguin Group (USA) Inc.
...ign is a trademark of Penguin Group (USA) Inc.

...THE UNITED STATES OF AMERICA
...7 6 5 4

"CHRI... P9-DML-551
completely understands what makes for a good story:
action, sex, suspense, humor, and great characters."

—Nelson DeMille

THE PLANTATION

"INGENIOUS . . . Chris Kuzneski's writing has the same kind of raw power as the early Stephen King."

—James Patterson,
New York Times bestselling author

"EXCELLENT! High stakes, fast action, vibrant characters, and a very, very original plot concept. Not to be missed!"

—Lee Child,
New York Times bestselling author

"RIVETING . . . Kuzneski displays a remarkable sense of suspense and action . . . will leave readers breathless and up much too late! Don't miss it!"

—James Rollins, *USA Today* bestselling author

"POWERFUL . . . A great plot twist. Right from the opening scenes, the book takes off, and all I can say is hang on for the ride."

—Douglas Preston, *New York Times* bestselling author

"GRAPHIC . . . Becomes more sinister with each turn of the page."

—James Tucker, bestselling author of *Tragic Wand*

"ACTION-PACKED . . . The twists and turns of a Stephen King chiller . . . will keep you on the edge of your seat."

—M. J. Hollingshead,
author of *The Inspector's Wife*

"WOW! . . . Powerful stuff. It's a gripping novel that smells of gunpowder and reeks of heroism, with a beautiful girl, some crazed characters, and lots of sadistic revenge . . . Kuzneski has written a sick, sensational yarn. I can't wait for the next one."

—Thom Racina, *USA Today* bestselling author

THE
PLANTATI

CHRIS KU

BERKLEY

Foreword

A few years ago I nearly gave up. Like many writers, I had a tough time breaking into the industry. Agents ignored me, and publishers rejected me. My life was like a bad country song, only I didn't have a mullet. To make matters worse, my savings were almost gone, which meant I was *this* close to doing something desperate—like getting a "real" job.

Back then, the only thing that stood between me and the workforce was a novel I had just written called *The Plantation*. It featured two main characters that I really liked, Jonathon Payne and David Jones, and a plot that was pretty original. In hindsight, maybe *too* original. At least that's what I was told in several rejection letters. Editors and agents loved the book but weren't sure how to market it. And in the book business, that is the kiss of death. No marketing means no sales. No sales means no book deal. And no book deal means it's time to search the want ads.

Thankfully, I came across an article about a company called iUniverse and a new type of technology called print on demand. Simply put, copies of a book could be printed *after* a book order was placed, thereby eliminating large print runs that a struggling writer like myself couldn't afford.

Suddenly I had the freedom to print a small quantity of books that I could sell to family and friends. And if I was really lucky, total strangers would buy it, too.

Long story short, my plan worked. I sold enough copies out of the trunk of my car to ward off starvation, plus it gave me the confidence to take things one step further. I figured since readers loved *The Plantation*, maybe writers would as well. So I wrote letters to many of my favorite authors, asking if they'd be interested in reading my book. Incredibly, most of them agreed to help, and before long they were writing letters to me, telling me how much they enjoyed it. And I'm talking about famous authors like James Patterson, Nelson DeMille, Lee Child, Douglas Preston, and James Rollins. Each of them willing to endorse my novel.

Seriously, how cool is that?

Anyway, even though I had their support, I still didn't have a publisher. But all of that changed when Scott Miller, an agent at Trident Media, bought one of my self-published copies in a Philadelphia bookstore and liked it enough to e-mail me. At the time I had a folder with more than one hundred rejection letters, yet the best young agent in the business bought my book and contacted me. Not only did I get a royalty from his purchase, but I also got the perfect agent.

By then I had written my next novel, a religious thriller called *Sign of the Cross*, which Scott wanted to shop immediately since *The Da Vinci Code* was dominating the bestseller lists at that time. It proved to be a wise decision. Within months, he had sold the American rights to Berkley and the foreign rights to more than fifteen publishers around the world.

Finally, I could throw away the want ads.

Next up was *Sword of God*, which became my second international bestseller. In my mind, it was book three in the Payne/Jones universe. But to most readers, it was only book two because *The Plantation* was never released by a major publisher.

That is, until now.

Several years have passed since I wrote the first draft of

The Plantation. The original version was much longer and contained several mistakes that rookie writers tend to make. With the help of my good friend Ian Harper, I tried to eliminate as many of those as possible—while keeping the plot intact. After a lot of tweaking, I'm thrilled with the final product.

To me, *The Plantation* is my first love. It's the book that allowed me to write for a living.

Hopefully, you'll fall in love with it, too.

CHAPTER 1

Thursday, July 1st
Icy River, Colorado
(122 miles southwest of Denver)

ROBERT Edwards hurdled the fallen spruce but refused to break his frantic stride.

He couldn't afford to. They were still giving chase.

After rounding a bend in the path, he decided to gamble, leaping from the well-lined trail into the dense underbrush of the forest. He dodged the first few branches, trying to shield his face from their thorny vegetation, but his efforts were futile. His reckless speed, coupled with the early-morning gloom, hindered his reaction time, and within seconds he felt his flesh being torn from his cheeks and forehead. The coppery taste of blood soon flooded his lips.

Ignoring the pain, the thirty-two-year-old struggled forward, increasing his pace until the only sounds he heard were the pounding of his heart and the gasping of his breath. But even then, he struggled on, pushing harder and harder until he could move no farther, until his legs could carry him no more.

Slowing to a stop, Edwards turned and scanned the timberland for any sign of his pursuers. He searched the ground, the trees, and finally the dark sky above. He had no idea where they had come from—it was like they'd just materialized out of the night—so he wasn't about to overlook anything. Hell, he wouldn't have been surprised if they'd emerged from the underworld itself.

Their appearance was *that* mystifying.

When his search revealed nothing, he leaned against a nearby boulder and fought for air. But the high altitude of the Rockies and the blanket of fear that shrouded him made it difficult to breathe. But slowly, the pungent aroma of the pine-scented air reached his starving lungs.

"I . . . made . . . it," he whispered in between breaths. "I . . . fuckin' . . . made . . . it."

Unfortunately, his joy was short-lived.

A snapping twig announced the horde's approach, and without hesitation Edwards burst from his resting spot and continued his journey up the sloped terrain. After a few hundred feet, he reached level ground for the first time in several minutes and used the opportunity to regain his bearings. He studied the acreage that surrounded him, looking for landmarks of any kind, but a grove of bright green aspens blocked his view.

"Come on!" He groaned. "Where . . . am . . . I?"

With nothing but instinct to rely on, Edwards turned to his right and sprinted across the uneven ground, searching for something to guide him. A trail, a rock, a bush. It didn't matter as long as he recognized it. Thankfully, his effort was quickly rewarded. The unmistakable sound of surging water overpowered the patter of his own footsteps, and he knew that could mean only one thing. Chinook Falls was nearby.

Edwards increased his speed and headed for the source of the thunderous sound, using the rumble as a beacon. As he got closer, the dense forest that had concealed the dawn abruptly tapered into a grass-filled clearing, allowing soft beams of light to fall across his blood-streaked face. Suddenly the crystal clear water of the river came into view. It wasn't much, but to Edwards it was a sign of hope. It meant that things were going to be all right, that he had escaped the evil presence in the woods.

While fighting tears of joy, the athletic ski instructor scurried across the open field, hoping that the campground near the base of the falls would be bustling with early-morning activity, praying that someone had the firepower to stop the advancing mob.

Regrettably, Edwards never got a chance to find out.

Before he reached the edge of the meadow, two hooded figures dressed in black robes emerged from a thicket near the water's edge, effectively cutting off his escape route. Their sudden appearance forced him to react, and he did, planting his foot in the soft soil and banking hard to the left. Within seconds he'd abandoned the uncovered space of the pasture and had returned to the wooded cover of the thick forest. It took a moment to readjust to the darkness, but once he did, he decided to climb the rocky bluff that rose before him.

At the top of the incline, Edwards veered to his right, thinking he could make it to the crest of the falls before anyone had a chance to spot him. At least that was his plan. He moved quickly, focusing solely on the branches that endangered his face and the water that surged in the distance. But his narrow focus prevented him from seeing the stump that lay ahead. In a moment of carelessness, he caught his foot on its moss-covered roots and instantly heard a blood-curdling snap. He felt it, too, crashing hard to the ground.

In a final act of desperation, Edwards struggled to his feet, pretending nothing had happened, but the lightning bolt of pain that exploded through his tattered leg was so intense, so agonizing, he collapsed to the ground like a marionette without strings.

"Shit!" he screamed, suddenly realizing the hopelessness of his situation. "Who the hell are you? What do you want from me?!"

Unfortunately, he was about to find out.

CHAPTER 2

Mars, Pennsylvania
(13 miles north of Pittsburgh)

THE alarm clock buzzed at 10:00 A.M., but Jonathon Payne didn't feel like waking up. He had spent the previous night hosting a charity event—one that lasted well past midnight—and now he was paying for his lack of sleep. Begrudgingly, after hitting the snooze button twice, he forced himself out of bed.

"God, I hate mornings," he moaned.

After getting undressed, the brown-haired bachelor twisted the brass fixtures in his shower room and eased his chiseled, 6'4", 230-pound frame under the surging liquid. When he was done, he hustled through the rest of his morning routine, threw on a pair of jeans and a golf shirt, and headed to his kitchen for a light breakfast.

He lived in a mansion that he'd inherited from his grandfather, the man who raised Payne after the death of his parents. Even though the house was built in 1977, it still had the feel of a brand-new home due to Payne's passion for neatness and organization, traits he had developed in the military.

Payne entered the U.S. Naval Academy as a member of the basketball and football teams, but it was his expertise in hand-to-hand combat, not man-to-man defense, that eventually got him recognized. Two years after graduation, he was selected to join the MANIACs, a highly classified special operations unit composed of the best soldiers the Marines, Army, Navy, Intelligence, Air Force, and Coast Guard could find. Established at the request of the Pentagon, the MANIACs' goal was to complete missions that the U.S. government couldn't afford to publicize: political assassinations, antiterrorist acts, etc. The squad was the best of the best, and their motto was fitting. *If the military can't do the job, send in the MANIACs.*

Of course, all of that was a part of Payne's past.

He was a working man now. Or at least he tried to be.

THE Payne Industries complex sat atop Mount Washington, offering a breathtaking view of the Pittsburgh skyline and enough office space for 550 employees. One of the executives—a vice president in the legal department—was exiting the glass elevator as Payne was stepping in.

"Morning," Payne said.

"Barely," the man replied, as he headed off for a lunch meeting.

Payne smiled at the wisecrack, then made a mental note to dock the bastard's wages. Well, not really. But as CEO of his family's company, Payne didn't have much else to do, other than showing up for an occasional board meeting and using his family name to raise money for charities. Everything else, he left to his underlings.

Most people in his position would try to do more than they could handle, but Payne understood his limitations. He realized he wasn't blessed with his grandfather's business acumen or his passion for the corporate world. And even though his grandfather's dying wish was for Payne to run the company, he didn't want to screw it up. So while people with MBAs made the critical decisions, Payne stayed in the background, trying to help the community.

The moment Payne walked into his penthouse office, his elderly secretary greeted him. "How did last night's event go?"

"Too late for my taste. Those Make-A-Wish kids sure know how to party."

She smiled at his joke and handed him a stack of messages. "Ariane just called. She wants to discuss your plans for the long weekend."

"What? She *must* be mistaken. I'd never take a long weekend. Work is *way* too important!"

The secretary rolled her eyes. Payne had once taken a vacation for Yom Kippur, and he wasn't even Jewish. "D.J. called, too. In fact, he'd like you to stop down as soon as you can."

"Is it about a case?" he asked excitedly.

"I have no idea, but he stressed it was *very* important."

"Great! Give him a call and tell him I'm on my way."

With a burst of adrenaline, Payne bypassed the elevator and headed directly to the stairs, which was the quickest way to Jones's office during business hours. When he reached his best friend's floor, he stopped to admire the gold lettering on the smoked glass door.

DAVID JOSEPH JONES
Private Investigator

He liked the sound of that, especially since he'd helped Jones achieve it.

When Payne inherited the large office complex from his grandfather, he gave Jones, a former lieutenant of his, a chance to live out his dream. Payne arranged the necessary financing and credit, gave him an entire floor of prime Pittsburgh real estate, and provided him with a well-paid office staff. All Payne wanted in return was to be a part of his friend's happiness.

Oh, and to assist Jones on all of his glamorous cases.

Plus he wanted business cards that said *Jonathon Payne, Private Eye*.

But other than that, he just wanted his friend to be happy.

Payne waved at Jones's receptionist, who was talking on the phone, and entered the back office. Jones was sitting behind his antique desk, a scowl etched on his angular face. He had short hair, which was tight on the sides, and cheeks that were free from stubble.

"What's up?" Payne asked. "Trouble in Detectiveland?"

"It's about time you got here," Jones barked. His light mocha skin possessed a reddish hue that normally wasn't there. "I've been waiting for you all morning."

Payne plopped into the chair across from Jones. "I came down as soon as I got your message. What's the problem?"

Jones exhaled as he eased back into his leather chair. "Before I say anything, I need to stress something to you. What I'm about to tell you is confidential. It's for your ears only. No one, and I mean *no one*, is allowed to know anything about this but you. All right?"

Payne smiled at the possibilities. This sounded like something big. He couldn't wait to hear what it was. Maybe a robbery, or even a murder. Jones's agency had never handled a crime like that. "Of course! You can count on me. I promise."

Relief flooded Jones's face. "Thank God."

"So, what is it? A big case?"

Jones shook his head, then slowly explained the situation. "You know how you have all those boxes of gadgets near my filing cabinets in the storage area?"

"Yeah," Payne replied. He'd been collecting magic tricks and gizmos ever since he was a little boy. His grandfather had started the collection for him, buying him a deck of magic playing cards when Payne was only five, and the gift turned out to be habit-forming. Ever since then, Payne was hooked on the art of prestidigitation. "What about 'em?"

"Well," Jones muttered, "I know I'm not supposed to mess with your stuff. I know that. But I went in there to get some paperwork this morning, and . . ."

"And what? What did you do?"

"I saw a pair of handcuffs in there, and they looked pretty damn real."

"Go on," Payne grumbled, not liking where this was going.

"I brought them back here and tried to analyze them. You know, figure them out? And after a while, I did. I figured out the trick."

"You did?"

"Yeah, so I slipped them on to test my theory, and . . ."

Payne stared at D.J. and smiled. For the first time, he realized his friend's hands had been hidden from view during their entire conversation. "You're handcuffed to the desk, aren't you?"

Jones took a deep breath and nodded sheepishly. "I've been like this for three freakin' hours, and I have to take a leak. You know how my morning coffee goes right through me!"

Laughing, Payne jumped to his feet and peered behind the desk to take a look. "Whoa! That doesn't look comfortable at all. You're all twisted and—"

"It's not comfortable," Jones interrupted. "That's why I need you to give me a hand."

"Why don't you just break off the handle? Or aren't you strong enough?"

"It's an antique desk! I'm not breaking an antique desk!"

Payne smiled. "Wait a second. I thought you could pick any lock in the world."

"With the proper tools, I can. But as you can plainly see, I can't reach any tools."

"I see that," Payne said, laughing. "Fine. I'll give you some help, but . . ."

"But what?" Jones snapped as his face got more flushed. "Just tell me the secret to your stupid trick so I can get free. I'm not in the mood to joke here."

"I know. That's why I don't know how to tell you this. I've got some bad news for you."

"Bad news? What kind of bad news?"

Payne patted his friend on his arm, then whispered, "I don't own any fake handcuffs."

"What? You've got to be kidding me!" Jones tried pulling free from the desk, but the cuffs wouldn't budge. "You mean I locked myself to my desk with a real set of cuffs? Son of a bitch!"

"Not exactly something you'll put on your private eye résumé, huh?"

Jones was tempted to curse out Payne but quickly realized that he was the only one who could help. "Jon. Buddy. Could you please get me some bolt cutters?"

"I could, but I'm actually kind of enjoying—"

"Now!" Jones screamed. "This isn't a time for jokes! If my bladder gets any fuller, I'll be forced to piss all over your office building! I swear to God, I will!"

"Okay, okay. I'm going." Payne bit his lip to keep from laughing. "But before I leave . . ." He placed his hand on the cuffs, and with a flick of his wrist, he popped off the stainless steel device—a trick he'd learned from a professional escape artist. "I better grab my handcuffs so I know what type of bolt cutters to get."

Jones stared in amazement as his best friend walked across the room. "You bastard! I thought you said they were real?"

Payne shrugged. "And I thought you promised not to mess with my stuff."

CHAPTER 3

PAYNE'S schedule was free until an afternoon meeting, so he decided to return his girlfriend's message in person.

Ariane Walker had recently been named the youngest vice president in the history of the First National Bank of Pittsburgh, an amazing accomplishment for a twenty-eight-year-old female in the boys' club of banking. She was born and raised in nearby Moon Township, a fact that she and Payne were often kidded about since he grew up in Mars, Pennsylvania. Both of them took it in stride. Normally, they just replied that their relationship was out of this world, and they meant it. They'd been dating for over a year and had *never* had a fight—at least none without pillows.

As Payne strolled to Ariane's office, a journey he tried to make a few times a week, he peered down at Pittsburgh's gleaming skyline and smiled. Even though he grew up disliking the place, a city that used to be littered with steel mills, industrial parks, and the worst air this side of Chernobyl, his opinion had slowly changed. In recent years Pittsburgh had undergone an amazing metamorphosis, one that had transformed it from an urban nightmare to one of the most scenic cities in America.

First, the steel industry shifted elsewhere, leaving plenty of land for new businesses, luscious green parks, and state-of-the-art sports stadiums. Then Pittsburgh's three rivers—the Allegheny, the Monongahela, and the Ohio—were dredged, making them suitable for recreational use and riverfront enterprises. Buildings received face-lifts. Bridges received paint jobs. The air received oxygen. This mutt of a city was given a thorough bath, and a pure pedigree had somehow emerged, one that had been voted "America's Most Livable City."

"Hey," Ariane said the moment Payne knocked on her open office door. "I called you earlier. You get my message?"

"Yep, and since I had nothing else to do, I figured I'd pay my favorite girl a visit."

"I don't know where she is right now, so I guess I'll have to do until she gets back."

Payne sighed as he moved closer. "Oh well, I guess you're better than nothing."

The chestnut-haired executive grinned and gave him a peck on the cheek. "We've got to make this quick, Jonathon. With a long weekend coming up, I've got a lot of work to do."

"But you still have tomorrow off, right? Or am I going to have to buy the bank and fire you?"

"Oh, how romantic!" she teased. "No, that won't be necessary. Once I leave here at five, I'm officially free until Tuesday morning. The next one hundred and eleven hours are all yours."

"And I'm gonna use every one of them. I swear, woman, I don't get to see you enough."

"I feel the same way, *man*. But one of us has to work, and I know it's not going to be you."

Payne grimaced. "It certainly doesn't look like you're working too hard. I mean, here you are, a highly paid bank official, and instead of doing something productive, you're sitting at your desk, undressing me with your eyes."

Ariane blushed slightly. "Please!"

"And now you're begging for me. Damn, get a hold of your passion. You're embarrassing yourself."

She smacked him on the arm and ordered him to calm down. "What is it that you want?"

"Hey, you called me. Remember?"

"Please don't remind me of my bold and desperate act."

"I can't help it that you're easy."

"That's true," she joked. "I think I get that from my grandmother. She used to run a brothel, you know."

"Really?"

"No, not really." She laughed at the thought. "So, what are we going to do tonight?"

Payne shrugged. "Some of the new holiday movies come out today. I guess we could grab some dinner and catch a flick."

"Your treat?"

"I don't know," he scoffed. "You claim I don't even have a job. Why should I pay?"

Ariane faked a growl. "That wasn't a question, Jonathon. That was an order. Your treat!"

He loved it when she called him Jonathon. He really did. For some reason she was the first person he'd ever met that made it sound sexy. With anyone else, the name gave him flashbacks to the days when his parents were alive and he was just a boy. Jonathon was the name his mother used when he was in trouble. Like the time he accidentally ran over the neighbor's cat with a lawn mower. The cat's tail healed quickly, but Payne's ass was sore for weeks.

"Of course it's my treat!" He laughed. "I pay for all the women I'm currently dating."

"Well, we can talk about your hookers later. In the meantime, do you have time to take me out to lunch? I think this place could do without me for a little while."

"It would be my pleasure," he said, smiling.

Within minutes, they were strolling hand in hand above

the city, enjoying the summer sun and each other's company. In fact, they were so lost in their own little world that neither of them noticed the black van that started following them the moment they left the bank.

CHAPTER 4

Longview Regional Hospital
Longview, Colorado
(109 miles southwest of Denver)

TONYA Edwards sat in the ob-gyn's office, nervously waiting for her test results. Normally, Tonya was an optimistic person, someone who always looked at the bright side of life, but a first-time pregnancy has a way of changing that. Anxiety and fear often replace calm and joy, and as she waited for her doctor, the tension gnawed away at her very large stomach.

When the exam room door finally opened, Tonya wanted to jump up to greet the doctor, but it was physically impossible. She just wasn't in the condition to make any quick movements.

"How are you feeling, Tonya?" asked the middle-aged doctor as he pulled a chair next to her. "Any better?"

"Not really, Dr. Williamson. I'm still nauseous, and I have a slight headache."

"And how's the little fellow doing today?"

She grinned and patted her belly. "Robert Jr. is doing fine. He's been kicking up a storm while I've been waiting for the results, though."

"Well, I've got good news for both of you. Everything looks perfect. No problems at all."

Relief flooded Tonya's face. After taking a deep breath,

her lips curled into a bright smile. "That is such good news, doc. You wouldn't believe how worried I've been."

"Actually," he said, "I probably would. I've been doing this for many years, and I've seen this happen many times before. Tension tends to bring on flulike symptoms. First-time mothers have it pretty rough. Especially someone like you. Since you no longer have your own mother to talk to, you really don't have anyone to help you through this. Sure, Robert is there, but this is all new to him, too. And he certainly has no idea about the physical changes that you're going through, now does he?"

Tonya smiled as she wiped the moisture from her eyes. "He's kind of clueless on the physical stuff. In fact, I had to tell him how he got me in this condition to begin with."

Dr. Williamson let out a loud laugh. "Well, I must admit I expected him to know at least that much."

"Oh, don't get me wrong. Robert is a wonderful husband, and he's going to make a great dad, but you're right. He's clueless when it comes to my body and this baby."

"I'm sure he's doing the best he can, so take it easy on him."

When her appointment was over, Tonya waddled down the corridor toward the elevators. After pushing the down button, she leaned against a nearby wall and rested.

"Are you all right?" asked a man in a powder blue nurse's outfit.

The voice startled her. "What? Ah, yeah, I'm fine. Just tired."

"How many months are you?"

She laughed as she touched her belly. "Eight down, one to go."

"I bet you're excited, huh?"

Tonya nodded her head. "I don't know what I'm looking forward to the most: having a baby or getting my body back to the way it used to be."

The black man grinned. "Well, I admire you women. You go through so much in order to bring something so precious into the world. I got to hand it to you."

"Well, somebody's got to do it, and it certainly isn't going to be a man."

He nodded. He couldn't agree with her more. "So, what were you doing here?"

"I just had an appointment with Dr. Williamson. He wanted to run a few tests to make sure I'm fine."

"And everything went well, I hope?"

"Perfect."

"Good," the man said. "I'm glad to hear it."

As he finished his statement, the elevator door slid open, revealing an empty car. Tonya took a few steps forward, but she appeared a little unsteady on her feet.

"Wow," she muttered. "I really don't feel very good."

The man grimaced, then patted her on the arm. "I'll tell you what. If you hold the door for me, I'll get something that will help you out. Okay?"

She stared at him, a look of confusion on her face.

"Just trust me, all right?"

Tonya nodded, holding the door open button. The man jogged halfway down the hall and grabbed a wheelchair that had been abandoned in the corridor. Pushing it as quickly as he could, the man returned to the elevator. "Your chariot, madam."

She smiled and settled her wide frame into the seat. "Normally you wouldn't catch me in one of these for a million bucks, but to be honest with you, I think the rest will do me good."

"I was heading outside anyway, so it would be my pleasure to assist you to the parking lot."

"Thanks," Tonya said. "I appreciate it."

As the elevator door slid shut, the smile that had filled the man's face during the entire conversation quickly faded. Reaching into his pocket, he grabbed the hypodermic needle that he had prepared ten minutes earlier and brought it into view. After removing the cap, the man inched the syringe toward the exposed flesh of the unsuspecting woman.

"Don't worry, Tonya," he whispered. "The baby won't feel a thing."

Before she had a chance to question his comment or the use of her name, he jabbed the needle into her neck and watched her succumb to the potent chemical. The elevator door opened a moment later and he wasted no time pushing the sleeping woman through the lobby, right past the security staff at the front desk.

"Is she all right?" asked one of the guards.

"Dead tired," he answered as he rolled her toward the black vehicle that waited outside.

LATER that night, Payne and Ariane went to the movies. Unfortunately, the theater was so packed they were actually relieved when the film ended.

"Well, what do you think?" he asked as they walked outside. "Did you like it?"

"Like what?"

"Um, the movie we just saw."

Ariane smiled, giggling at her atypical behavior. "I'm sorry. I should've been able to figure that out. I've got a slight headache from that darn crowd. I guess I'm kind of out of it right now."

"No problem, as long as you aren't trying to back out of tomorrow."

"No chance there, mister. In fact, I think I have our entire weekend planned."

"Oh, you do, do you? Well, what do I have to look forward to?"

Ariane glanced at him and smiled. "I figured we can start off tomorrow morning with breakfast and a round of golf. Then, when I'm done kicking your butt, we can grab some lunch before heading back to your pool for some skinny-dipping and a variety of aquatic activities that will never be in the Olympics."

"I don't know." Payne laughed. "The TV ratings would

go through the roof if the Olympics used some of the events that I have in mind."

She blushed slightly. "Then on Saturday, if you're not too tired, I figured we can work on perfecting our routines."

Payne threw his arm around her shoulder and pulled her close. "That sounds pretty good to me. But one question still remains: What's on the itinerary for tonight?"

Ariane frowned. "Nothing but sleep. As I mentioned, I've got a slight headache, and I think it has to do with a lack of rest. If it's okay with you, I just want to go home and snooze."

"Sure, that's fine." In truth, he was disappointed, but he didn't want to make her feel guilty. "I guess I'll just go home and do some paperwork. You know me. My job always comes first."

CHAPTER 5

Friday, July 2nd
Plantation Isle, Louisiana
(42 miles southeast of New Orleans)

THE cross was ten feet high, six feet wide, and built with a sole purpose in mind. The carpenter had used the right kind of wood, soaked it in the ideal fuel, and planted it into the ground at the appropriate angle. The Plantation had one shot to do this right, and they wanted it to go smoothly. It would set the perfect tone for their new guests.

"Torch it," Octavian Holmes snarled through the constraints of his black hood. The wooden beams were set aflame, and before long fiery sparks shot high into the predawn sky, illuminating the row of cabins that encircled the grass field.

Ironically, the image brought a smile to Holmes's shrouded face. As a child, he had witnessed a similar scene, a cross being burned in his family's front yard, and it had evoked a far different reaction. It had terrified him. The bright glow of the smoldering wood. The sharp stench of smoke. The dancing specters in white hoods and sheets. The racial taunts, the threats of violence, the fear in his father's eyes. All of it had left an indelible mark on his young psyche, a scar that had remained for years. Now things were different. He was no longer a scared boy, cowering with his family, seeking strength and protection. Now the roles were reversed. He built the cross. He lit the flame. And he controlled the guest list.

Finally, a chance to exorcise some of his personal demons.

Over the roar of the blaze, he continued his commands. "Bring the prisoners into formation!"

A small battalion of men, dressed in long black cloaks and armed with semiautomatic handguns, burst into the cramped huts and dragged the blindfolded captives toward the light of the flames. One by one, the confused prisoners were placed into a prearranged pattern—three lines of six people—and ordered to stand at attention while facing the cross. When the leader of the guards was finally happy with the setup, he let his superior know. "We're ready, sir."

"Good," Holmes replied as he settled into his black saddle. "Drop your hoods!"

In unison, the entire team of guards covered their faces with the thick black hoods that hung loosely from the back of their cloaks. When they were done, they looked like Klansmen in black robes. Their eyes were all that remained uncovered, and they burned like glowing embers in the Louisiana night.

"It's time to show them our power!"

With sharp blades in hand, the guards charged toward the prisoners and swiftly cut small holes in the white cotton bags that had been draped over the heads of the captives.

"Ladies and gentlemen," Holmes barked as he trotted his stallion to the front of his guests. "Welcome to the Plantation."

He paused dramatically for several seconds before continuing his monologue. "I'm sure each of you would like to see your new surroundings, but there is something blocking your sight. It is called duct tape, and it will be quite painful when you pull it off. . . . Don't worry. Your eyebrows will eventually grow back." Holmes laughed quietly. "I realize that your hands are currently bound, but I'm quite confident you'll be able to remove the tape without our assistance."

Slowly and painfully, the prisoners removed the adhesive

strips from their faces, tearing flesh and hair as they did. Then, once their eyes had adjusted to the light from the intense fire, they glanced from side to side, trying to observe as much as they could. The sudden realization that each person was a part of a large group gave some captives comfort and others anxiety.

"Impressive!" Holmes shouted in mock admiration. "I'm quite pleased with the guts of this group. Normally my prisoners are weeping and praying to me for mercy, but not you guys. No, you are too strong for that." He clapped sarcastically, slamming the palms of his black leather gloves together. "Now that you've dazzled me with your inner strength, it's time for me to show you how weak you really are. While you are guests on my plantation, there are strict rules that you must follow. Failure to follow any of them will result in severe and immediate punishment. Do I make myself clear?"

The prisoners remained quiet, too scared to speak.

"My God! I must be going deaf! Why? Because I didn't hear a goddamned word from any of you." He rode his horse between the lines of prisoners. "Let's try this again, but this time I want you to scream, *Yes, Master Holmes!*" He glared at the captives. "Are you ready? Failure to follow my rules will result in severe and immediate punishment. Do I make myself clear?"

Fewer than half of them answered. An act of disobedience that pissed off Holmes.

"Yesterday you had the right to do what you wanted, say what you wanted, think what you wanted. But all of that is gone now. Your freedom has faded into the air, like smoke from this burning cross." The prisoners glanced at the clouds of ash that slowly rose into the darkness. "You are no longer members of a free society. You are now possessions. You got that? And as my possessions, you are now governed by the rules that I'm about to share with you. Failure to comply with *anything* will result in swift and decisive action on my part. Do you understand?"

"Yes, Master Holmes," mumbled most of the crowd.

Holmes shook his head in disgust, disappointed that he

would have to damage some of his property so early in the proceedings. "Bring out the block," he ordered.

Two guards ran to the side of the field and lifted a four-foot wooden cube onto a small cart. Then, as the prisoners stared in confusion, the guards dragged the large chunk of wood to the front of the crowd.

"Thank you," Holmes said as he climbed off his horse. "Before you hustle off, I'd like you to do me a favor."

"Yes, sir!" the guards said in unison.

"Do you see the tall man at the end of the front row?" Holmes pointed at Paul Metz, a father of two from Missouri. "Please bring him to me."

"Me?" Paul shrieked as he was pulled from the line and dragged to the front of the group. His family, who'd been standing next to him, trembled with fear. "What did I do?"

"So you *can* talk! See, I wasn't sure if you had the ability to speak until now. Why? Because a moment ago I asked the group to answer a question, and no sound came from your lips."

"I answered, I swear."

Holmes slammed his gloved hand onto the wooden block, and the sound echoed above the roar of the fire. "Are you calling me a liar?"

"No," Paul sobbed. "But I swear, I answered you. I yelled my response."

"Oh, you yelled your response, did you? I was staring right at you, focusing solely on you, and I saw nothing! No sound, no head movement, not a goddamned thing!"

"I screamed, I swear."

Holmes shrugged his shoulders at the claim. He had no desire to argue with a prisoner. It would set a very bad precedent. "Put your hands on the block," he said calmly.

"What?"

Holmes responded to the question by slapping Paul in the face. "Don't make me tell you again. Put your hands on the fucking block."

He closed his eyes and eased his bound hands onto the wood. He quivered as he did.

"Now, choose a finger."

Paul opened his eyes and stared into the hooded face of his captor. "Please, not that," he begged softly.

In a second flash of rage, Holmes threw a savage punch into Metz's stomach, knocking the breath from him. On impact, Paul collapsed to the ground in front of the wooden block.

"Choose a finger or lose them all."

From his knees, Paul reluctantly placed his hands on the chopping board, then extended the pinkie of his left hand. As he wiggled it, announcing his choice, he sobbed at the impending horror. "This one, Master Holmes."

Holmes smiled under his hood, enjoying his moment of omnipotence. This was the type of respect he would demand from all of his prisoners. And if they failed to comply, he would make sure that they had a very unpleasant stay.

"Now," he shouted at the transfixed crowd, "I would like you to observe the following." With the viselike grip of his left hand, he grabbed Paul's wrist and pinned it painfully to the wood. "This man chose to ignore a direct order from me, and because of that, he will be severely punished."

With his right hand, Holmes grabbed his stiletto, then paused to enjoy the surreal nature of the moment. In the presence of the dancing flames, the length of the five-inch steel shaft gleamed like Excalibur in the regal hands of King Arthur. The crowd gaped in awe at the spectacle they were witnessing. Wailing from his knees, Paul waited for his punishment to be executed.

"Let this be a lesson to you all!"

With a quick downward stroke, Holmes rammed the razor-sharp blade into Paul's knuckle, just below his fingernail, immediately severing the tip. A flood of crimson gushed from it, glistening in the firelight. Paul screamed in agony while trying to pull his damaged hand off the block, but Holmes was too strong for him. After lifting the knife again, he plunged the blade into Paul's finger a second time, severing it just below the middle knuckle.

"Stop!" Alicia Metz shrieked above her husband's wails.

A guard instantly silenced her with a ferocious backhand.

"Not yet!" Holmes answered. He pulled the embedded blade from the block again, and this time buried it into the edge of Paul's palm, dislodging the last section of his little finger with a sickening pop.

"Why?" she sobbed as she slumped to the ground. "Why are you doing this? What have we done to deserve this?"

Holmes glanced at the three chunks of finger that sat on the chopping block in front of him and smiled, admiring his handiwork. "I'm sick of her babbling. Gag her."

Two guards grabbed the fallen woman and wrapped her mouth in duct tape.

"Anything else, sir!"

"Yes," Holmes sneered. "Get this man some gauze. It seems he's had an accident."

CHAPTER 6

The Kotto family estate
Lagos, Nigeria
(Near the Gulf of Guinea coast)

HANNIBAL Kotto stared into his bathroom mirror and frowned at the flecks of gray that had recently emerged. Although he was fifty-one years old, he didn't look it. In fact, people always assumed that he was ten years younger than he actually was.

After opening his plush purple curtains, Kotto gazed across the man-made moat that encircled his majestic grounds and observed a team of workers as they pulled weeds from his impeccably maintained gardens. All of them were new employees, and he wanted to make sure that they were following his orders. Unfortunately, before he had an opportunity to evaluate their performance, his phone rang. "Damn," he muttered. "There's always something."

Kotto reached into the pocket of his robe and pulled out his cellular phone. "Kotto here."

"Hannibal, my dear friend, how are things in Nigeria?"

For the first time that day, Kotto smiled. It had been a while since he'd spoken with his business partner, Edwin Drake, and that was unusual. They normally spoke a few times a week. "Things are fine. How about South Africa? Is Johannesburg still in one piece?"

"Yes, and I still own most of it." Drake, an Englishman who made the majority of his money in African diamond mines, laughed. "However, with the civil unrest in this bloody city, my holdings are not as impressive as they used to be."

"That is a shame, but a common drawback to life in Africa. Governments come, and governments go. The only thing that's constant is conflict."

"A more accurate statement has never been spoken."

Kotto smiled. "Tell me, Edwin, where have you been hiding? I thought maybe you were getting cold feet about our recent operation."

"Not at all. I couldn't be happier with our partnership. The truth is I had some last-minute family business to attend to in London, and I honestly didn't want to call you from there. I never trust those bloody hotels. You can never tell who's listening."

After a few minutes of small talk, Kotto steered the conversation to business. "I was wondering what you thought of the last shipment of snow you received. Was it to your liking?"

"*Snow*? Is that what we're calling it now? I like the sound of that."

"I'm glad. I felt we needed a code name for the merchandise, and I hate the term they use in South America."

"You're right. *Snow* is so much simpler to say than *cargo blanco*."

"Exactly. And since both of us speak English, I figured an English word was appropriate."

"Why not something Nigerian? Couldn't you come up with something colorful from your native tongue?"

Kotto laughed loudly. He always got a kick out of the white man's unfamiliarity with Africa. "Edwin, I *did* come up with a word from my native tongue. English is the official language of Nigeria."

"Really? I didn't know that. I'm sorry if I offended you."

"It's all right. I'm used to your ignorance by now," Kotto teased. "But I hope you realize I don't walk the streets of Lagos in a loincloth while carrying my favorite spear."

Drake couldn't tell if his friend was lecturing or joking until he heard Kotto laugh. "Hannibal, I must admit you had me going for a while. I thought I hit a nerve."

"Not at all. I just thought a moment of levity was in order before we continued our business."

"Yes, it was rather pleasant. Thank you."

"So, what did you think of your last shipment of snow? Did it meet the expectations of your buyers?"

"In some ways yes, and in some ways no."

Kotto frowned. It wasn't the answer he was hoping for. "What do you think needs to be improved?"

"Honestly, the overall quality. I think my buyers were hoping for something better than the street product that I sold them. They wanted something purer. You know, upper-class snow."

"Well," he replied, "the last batch was just a trial run. From what I understand, the next shipment we receive will be the best yet."

CHAPTER 7

WITH such a diverse group—an equal mix of young and old, male and female—there appeared to be no link between the prisoners of the Plantation. But Harris Jackson knew that wasn't the case. He knew the reason that these people had been pulled from their lives and brought to this island. He understood why they were being humiliated, abused, and tortured. And he relished the fact that they were stripped of their homes, their possessions, and their pride. All of it made sense, and he was going to enjoy his authority over them for as long as it lasted.

In the flickering firelight, Jackson stared at the seventeen people in front of him and savored how each of them was shaking, literally trembling with fear. God, how he loved that! It made him feel indestructible. "Ladies and gentlemen, my name is Master Jackson, and my job on this island is leader of the guards. When you address me, you shall use the name *Master Jackson* or *sir*. Nothing else is acceptable. Nothing else will be tolerated."

Under his black hood, he smiled. When he'd worked as a lawyer during his short-lived legal career, he loved addressing the jury—trying to get them to listen, hoping to catch their eye, convincing them to believe—and for some reason, his orientation speech made him think back to his days in the courtroom. The days before his disbarment.

"As you can probably tell, none of you were given an opportunity to change your clothes after you received your invitation to the Plantation. Some of you are filthy, and some of you are clean. A few of you are dressed warmly, and others are not." He stared at Susan Ross, a sixteen-year-old who'd been abducted from a community pool in Florida, and appreciated the way her teenage body looked in her bikini. He made a mental note to pay her a visit later. "In an attempt to make everybody equal, I'd like each of you to disrobe."

Despite his command, nobody moved. They just stared straight ahead in absolute shock.

Like Holmes before him, Jackson shook his head in disappointment. "What a shame! I assumed that each of you had a pretty good understanding of your situation by now. I figured the Ginsu display from earlier was going to keep you in line for the rest of your visit." Jackson shrugged his broad shoulders as he walked toward the prisoners. "I guess I was wrong."

Jackson stopped in front of Susan, his six-foot frame towering above her. "I'm looking for a volunteer," he roared in the voice of a drill sergeant. "And I think *you* will do nicely."

Despite her cries of protest, he lifted her half-naked, 110-pound body over his shoulder and carried her toward the chopping block. Two guards offered to assist him, but he quickly ordered them to stay back. He was enjoying himself far too much to let them share in the fun. When he reached the wooden cube, he set her gently on the ground, then put her in a stranglehold so she couldn't run away.

"What do you want from me?" she cried through the cloth of her white hood.

"You'll find out soon enough," he whispered into her left ear. "And I must admit I'm looking forward to it." He pushed his groin against the small of her lower back, and she immediately felt his excitement start to grow. "Can you feel how hard I am? That's because of you, you know. All because of you."

Susan tried squirming free of his grip, but Jackson was simply too strong for her. As she tried to pull away, he laughed at her feeble attempts.

"Are you done?" he asked in a civil tone.

After one more try, she nodded her head.

"Good, because I'm dying to begin."

Like a tarantula, Jackson's black fingers crawled down her nubile flesh, gradually creeping across her firm stomach, then sliding under her bathing suit. "Do you like my magic fingers?" he whispered. "Do you like when I touch you?"

Before she could respond, he lifted her off the ground and forced her to stand on the bloody chopping block. Within seconds, her bare feet were coated with the red fluid that had gushed from Paul Metz's finger.

"As I told you a moment ago, I would like each of you to take off your clothes. Apparently, you're not as threatened by me as you were by Master Holmes. Now, because of your ignorance, this young girl has to suffer."

"Please don't hurt me," she sobbed. "I was being good. I didn't do anything wrong. I was being good."

With a mischievous smile, he placed his dark hand on the back of her leg and slowly, sexually, stroked her inner thigh. "I know, my dear, but it's not my doing. You should fault your fellow inmates for ignoring my instructions. They're more to blame than I." His hand crept higher and higher on her smooth leg until it stopped on her ass. "Remember, I'm not to blame for this. Bear me no ill will."

Taking his stiletto from the folds of his cloak, Jackson slowly raised the blade behind the unsuspecting female, inching it toward his target. The sharp steel glistened in the light of the raging fire.

"I want you to kneel for me," he purred. "And I want you to take your time."

Without a word of complaint, the girl dropped to her

knees. His unblinking eyes followed the curvature of her cheeks on their downward path. When she reached the block, he heard her groan as she sank into the cherry liquid that coated the surface. The sound brought a smile to his lips.

"Now raise your hands above your head, and hold them there."

She did as she was told, and her movement electrified him—her unquestioning compliance literally made his heart race faster.

"Remember," he breathed, "no ill will."

Jackson placed his hand on the girl's bare back and searched for the perfect spot to make his incision. Once he found it, he lifted the knife to her flesh, tracing the ridges of her spine with the broad side of his cold, metal blade. As he did, he noticed the emergence of goose bumps, not only on her skin but on his as well. Gathering his emotions, Jackson inched the stiletto to the midsection of her back, the spot directly between her shoulder blades, then paused.

This was where the cut would be made.

Turning the blade to the appropriate angle, Jackson gazed at the crowd to make sure that they were watching. They were. The entire throng was focused on the hypnotic movements of his knife, like he was an ancient Mayan priest preparing for a ritual sacrifice. Pleased by the attention, he redirected his gaze to his target.

"It's time!" he whispered.

With a quick slash, Jackson sliced the strap of her bikini top. Then, before she had an opportunity to flinch, he carved her swimsuit bottom as well, exposing her entire body to the audience and the humid Louisiana night.

A wave of humiliation flooded over the girl. She tried to cover herself by crouching into a tiny ball on the wooden cube, but Jackson wouldn't allow it. He yanked her from her bloody perch and forced her to retake her position with the rest of the prisoners.

He would've preferred to wrap her in his arms but knew this was no time to be playing favorites. He had to treat everyone the same in order to set the rules, in order to get their respect.

Besides, he'd have a chance to make things up to her later—when they were alone.

CHAPTER 8

**Wexford, Pennsylvania
(11 miles north of Pittsburgh)**

DESPITE the early hour, Jonathon Payne managed to smile as he drove to Ariane's apartment. Normally a grin wouldn't make an appearance on his lips until much closer to noon, but since he was spending the entire day with her, he woke up in an atypically good mood.

Years of predawn calisthenics had soured his opinion of the morning.

Dressed in khaki shorts and a white golf shirt, Payne pulled his Infiniti SUV into the crowded lot outside of her building. After parking, he walked under the maroon awning that covered the complex's entrance and pressed the button to be let in. When she didn't reply, he tried the system a few more times before he walked back to the parking lot to make sure that her car was in her assigned space. It was there, and in his mind that meant she was definitely home.

Slightly frustrated, Payne strolled back to the intercom system and tried the buzzer again, yet nothing changed. He was still unable to get her attention.

Come on, he thought. *I know you're scared to face me on the golf course, but this is ridiculous.*

Standing in the entryway, pondering what to do next, he noticed a thin strip of duct tape sticking to the frame near the automatic lock of the security door. Moving closer, he realized that the tape started outside the frame and ran inside the building, purposely keeping the door open.

"Oh," Payne mumbled, figuring the intercom system must be broken.

Thankful to be inside, he jogged up the carpeted stairs to the second floor and noticed that the thick fire door at the top of the steps was propped open with a large stick.

Without giving it much thought, Payne continued his journey down the hallway toward Ariane's apartment. That's when he noticed something he couldn't dismiss. A piece of duct tape had been placed over the peephole of her door. Tape that wasn't there when he dropped her off the night before.

Suddenly, a wave of nausea swept through Payne's stomach. He wasn't sure why, but he knew that something had happened to Ariane.

Payne pounded on her door loudly, hoping that she had overslept or had been in the bathroom when he was buzzing her. But somehow he knew that wasn't the case. He knew that something was wrong. Very seriously wrong.

"Ariane!" he yelled. "It's Jon. Open the door!"

When his pleas went unanswered, Payne reached into his pocket and pulled out his cell phone. He hit the speed dial and watched as her name and number appeared on the screen. "Come on! Answer the damn phone!"

After four rings, Payne heard a click on the line. It was her voice mail.

Payne cursed as he waited to leave his message. "Ariane, if you're screening your calls or you're still in bed, pick up the phone." There was no response. "I'm really worried about you, so *please* call me on my cell as soon as you hear this message, okay?"

He hung up the phone, worried. "Think, goddamn it, think! Where could she be?"

Payne racked his brain for possibilities, but couldn't

think of any logical explanations. Most stores weren't open at that hour, and even if they were, she would have taken her car to get there. Most of her friends would still be sleeping or getting ready for work, so they wouldn't have picked her up. And her family lived out of state, so she wasn't with them.

No, something had happened to Ariane. He was sure of it.

PAYNE wasn't the type of guy who waited around for news. He was the aggressor, a man of action. Someone who followed his instincts, despite the odds. In the military, his gut feelings were so accurate that they were treated with reverence, like a message from God.

And in this case, he sensed that time was precious.

Without delay, Payne took a step back and launched his right leg toward the door. His foot met wood with a mighty *thump*. It echoed down the hallway like a gunshot. The sturdy frame splintered in several places as the door swung open with so much force that the lower hinge snapped a bolt. Adrenaline was a wonderful thing.

In his former career, Payne would've been armed and whispering orders into his headset. But today he was alone and empty-handed, worried about what he might find inside.

Cautiously, he walked into Ariane's apartment. The place was immaculate. No overturned tables, no broken lamps. And most importantly, no dead bodies. Payne wasn't sure what he was expecting to see, but he felt a certain sense of relief when he found nothing.

The only damage he noticed was the damage that he had done himself.

Taking a deep breath, Payne realized that he needed a second opinion. And when he needed help, he turned to his best friend. Payne hit his speed dial and waited for Jones to answer.

"Yeah?" Jones croaked, obviously sleeping in on his day off.

"D.J., it's Jon. Something's happened, and I need your help."

That was all that Jones needed to hear.

FIFTEEN minutes later, Jones pulled up next to Payne's SUV and studied the parking lot, but nothing seemed out of place. "Have you heard from her?"

Payne shook his head as he jogged over to Jones's car.

"Don't worry. That doesn't mean something bad has happened. I'm sure there are a thousand possibilities that could explain where she is, so tell me everything you can. I'm sure we can figure something out."

Payne nodded while shaking his friend's hand. "I appreciate you coming over so early. I feel better just having you here."

"No problem. It's the least I can do for free office space."

Payne smiled, but his body language told the real story. He was scared. "You know how I used to get gut feelings back when we were in the MANIACs?"

Jones nodded. "Your gut saved my ass more often than Preparation H."

"I don't know why, but I'm getting the same bad feeling right now. I know that something's happened to Ariane. I don't know what, but something."

"Jon, listen. We've been out of the military for a while now, so the tuning fork in your stomach is bound to be rusty. Right? Besides, you're not used to being awake at this time of day, so I'm sure your system is out of whack."

Reluctantly, Payne agreed.

"Why don't you fill me in on everything, and we can come up with some kind of solution."

Payne nodded. "I walked Ariane to her door last night. She had a headache and said she needed to get some sleep. We made plans for this morning, then I went home."

"You didn't stay the night?"

"If I had, do you think I'd be out here?" he snapped.

"Sorry, I just—"

"No," Payne apologized. "I'm the one who should be sorry. I didn't mean to yell at you. It's just, I don't know. . . ." He paused for a minute, trying to gather his thoughts. "I would've stayed the night, but she had a headache and thought it would be best if she got some rest."

"So, you didn't have a fight or anything?"

Payne shook his head. "I was supposed to pick her up at seven thirty. We were going to grab a light breakfast, then head straight for the golf course. She told me that she'd made an eight thirty tee time."

"Fine. Now walk me through this morning."

"I woke up early and showed up on time. I tried buzzing the intercom, but there was no reply. Next I checked the lot, and her car is here." Payne pointed toward it. "I went back to the front door, and that's when I noticed the duct tape."

"What duct tape?" The two of them walked to the entryway, and Jones studied the way the tape had been placed over the lock. "Well, if something has happened to her—and I'm not saying that it has—I doubt we're dealing with professionals."

"Why do you say that?"

"Look at the placement of the tape. Instead of running the strip over the lock in a vertical fashion, they placed it horizontally, allowing us to see it."

"And in your opinion, is this lack of professionalism good or bad news?"

Jones shrugged. "To be honest with you, it could be either. If something has happened to Ariane—and it's still a big *if* in my mind—then there's a good chance that other mistakes have been made as well. And that'll increase our opportunity to find her."

"That sounds good to me. So, what's the bad news?"

"If this isn't a professional job, there's a better chance that someone will panic, and if that happens . . ." Jones didn't have the heart to finish the sentence.

"Understood," Payne grunted. "Let me show you upstairs."

The two men jogged to the second floor. Jones shook his

head when he saw the stick used as a door prop. "Definitely not professionals," he muttered as they walked toward Ariane's front door. "You tried calling her, right? Maybe she's just sleeping and can't hear the door from her bedroom."

"Trust me, she's not in her bedroom."

"How can you be so sure?"

"I went *into* her bedroom."

"You had your key with you?"

Payne shook his head. "Not exactly."

Jones noticed the splintered door frame before he reached Ariane's apartment. The door hung there, slightly tilted, like it had been battered by a tropical storm.

"Let me guess," Jones quipped. "Hurricane Payne."

"She wouldn't answer the door."

Jones shrugged as he walked inside. "Seems like a reasonable response."

"Listen," Payne said, "I realize everything I've showed you is marginal at best. But this is the thing that really got me going." He pointed to the tape that covered Ariane's peephole. It was the same type of tape that covered the lock on the front door. "There's nothing innocent about this. And I guarantee that this tape wasn't here last night. No way in hell."

Jones grimaced. It did seem suspicious. But he didn't touch it, just in case there were fingerprints on it. "What kind of security system does her apartment have? Didn't you pay to have it upgraded?"

"Yeah, they installed alarms on all the windows and the two doors. I also had a camera mounted inside the peephole, but they must've known about that."

"Not necessarily. Just because they put tape on the door doesn't guarantee that they knew about the camera. They could've been trying to prevent her from seeing into the corridor. Shoot, for all we know, maybe her neighbor across the hall was doing something illegal, and he wanted to guarantee his privacy."

"But how does that explain the fact that she's missing?"

"I have no idea," Jones admitted. "But I'm trying to keep

as many options open as possible. Have you tried talking to her neighbors? Maybe they saw something."

"I was reluctant to bug them so early, but now that it's after eight o'clock and you're beginning to see my point of view, I'm willing to try anything."

Jones nodded his approval. "Why don't you handle this floor while I head downstairs?"

"Fine. But if you find anything, please let me know immediately."

"Will do," he assured Payne. "And Jon? Keep the faith. We'll find her."

CHAPTER 9

KNOCKING on each door, Payne started with Ariane's neighbor across the hall and slowly made his way down the corridor. Everyone that he talked to was friendly and immediately knew who Ariane was—females of her beauty tended to stand out. Unfortunately, no one saw or heard anything out of the ordinary. And no one could account for the duct tape over the front lock.

After speaking to the last of her neighbors on the second floor, Payne heard Jones running up the stairs in an obvious state of excitement.

"I think I've got a witness," Jones exclaimed. "He's waiting downstairs in the hall." Within seconds, the two men were standing in front of the open door of apartment 101. "Mr. McNally, this is Jonathon Payne, Ariane's boyfriend. Jon, this is Mr. McNally."

Payne shook the hand of the elderly man while trying to observe as much as he could. McNally appeared to be in his mid-eighties, walked with the aid of a metal cane, and closely resembled Yoda from *Star Wars*—minus the green color. His apartment was cluttered with heirlooms and antiques, yet for some reason a framed *Baywatch* poster of

Pamela Anderson hung near the entrance to his kitchen. "Mr. McNally, D.J. tells me that you might've seen something that could help me find Ariane?"

"Who the hell is D.J.?" the old man snapped. "I didn't talk to any bastard named D.J."

Jones looked at Payne and grimaced. "Sir? Remember me? I talked to you about two minutes ago. My name's David Jones, but my friends call me D.J."

"What the hell kind of person has friends that refuse to use his real name? You kids today. I just don't understand your damn generation."

"Sir, I don't mind. D.J. is just a nickname."

"A nickname?" he shrieked. "You think that's a nickname? Horseshit! It's just two capital letters. Why don't you just use B.S. as your nickname instead? Because that's what your nickname is: bullshit! When I was growing up, people used to have nicknames that said something about them, like Slim or Cocksucker, not pansy names like D.J."

"Sir," Payne interrupted, "I don't mean to be rude, but I was wondering what you saw this morning. David said you saw something that could help me find my girlfriend."

"Your girlfriend? Who's your girlfriend?"

Payne rolled his eyes in frustration. This was getting nowhere. "Ariane Walker. She lives upstairs in apartment 210."

McNally pondered the information for a few seconds before his face lit up. "Oh! You mean the brunette with the dark eyes and the nice cha-chas? Yeah, I saw her bright and early, about an hour ago. She was wearing a red top and a short skirt. It was so small I could almost see her panties." The elderly man cackled in delight as he pondered his memory of the beautiful girl. "That gal's a real looker."

Payne couldn't agree with him more. She was the prettiest woman he had ever seen. The first and only person who had literally left him speechless, which was unfortunate since he was in the middle of a speech at the time.

A few years back, Payne had volunteered to speak to a group of convicted drunk drivers about the tragic death of his parents. The goal of the program was to make recent offenders listen to the horrors of the crime in order to make them think twice about ever drinking and driving again. Payne was in the middle of reliving his nightmare—describing the devastation he felt when he was pulled from his eighth-grade algebra class and told about the death of his parents—when his eyes focused on Ariane's. She was standing off to the side, watching and listening with complete empathy. In a heartbeat, he could tell that she'd been through the same horror, that she'd lost a loved one in a similar nightmare. It didn't matter if it was a brother, sister, or lover. He knew that she *understood.*

Payne managed to finish his heart-wrenching tale without incident, but when he started his conclusion, he found himself unable to take his eyes off of her. He knew he was there to make a point, but suddenly he was unable to focus. There was just some quality about her, something pure and perfect that made him feel completely at ease. In his mind, something good had finally come from their loss. His parents' accident and her parents' accident had brought them together.

And the realization stole his ability to speak.

"Jon?" D.J. whispered. "Do you have some questions for Mr. McNally, or do you want me to ask him?"

Payne blinked a few times, which brought him back to the moment at hand. Turning toward the elderly man, he said, "Where did you see Ariane?"

"In my bedroom," McNally muttered.

Payne and Jones exchanged confused glances, trying to figure out what the man meant. "Ariane was in your bedroom?"

The man cackled again. "If she was in my bedroom, do you think I'd be out here talking to you bozos? Hell, no! I'd be popping Viagra like it was candy corn."

"Then why did you mention your bedroom?" Jones asked.

McNally inhaled before replying. "Do I have to spell everything out for you whippersnappers? I was in my bedroom when I saw her outside my window with a bunch of fellows. And let me tell you . . ." He tapped Payne on his chest. "You need to get your woman on a leash because she looked pretty darn snookered. They were practically dragging her."

"She was being dragged by a bunch of guys? What did they look like?"

McNally pondered the question for a few seconds, then pointed at Jones.

"They were black?" Payne asked.

"No, you dumb ass, I mean they were butt ugly and had stupid nicknames! Of course I mean they were black."

"Could you tell us anything else? Were they tall? Short? Fat? Anything?"

"They were black. That's it. Everything about them was black. Black clothes, black hoods, black shoes. I don't even know how many there were because they looked like shadows, for God's sake. Shoot, they even drove a black van."

Payne grimaced at the news. "Did you happen to see a license plate on the van?"

"As a matter of fact, I did!" McNally declared. "It was the only thing that wasn't black."

"You saw it? What did it say?"

"I have no damn idea," he answered. "The numbers were just a big ol' blur. But I do know one thing. The plate was from Louisiana."

Skepticism filled Payne's face. "How do you know that?"

"I got me a lady friend that lives down in Cajun country, and every year I visit her for Mardi Gras. When the van first pulled up, I saw the Louisiana plate and thought maybe she was coming here for a little lovin', but obviously, when I, um . . ." The old man furrowed his brow as he tried to remember his train of thought. "What was I talking about again?"

"Actually," Jones lied, "you had just finished. Is there anything else that you can tell us about this morning?"

"I'm kind of constipated. But I ate some prunes, so I'm hoping—"

"That's not what he meant," interrupted Payne. Even though he was sympathetic to McNally's advancing age, he didn't have the time to listen to him ramble about his bowel movements. "David wanted to know if you had anything else to tell us about Ariane?"

McNally pondered the question, then shook his head.

"Well, I'd like to thank you for your information." Jones handed McNally a business card, then helped him back inside his apartment. "If you think of anything else, please don't hesitate to call me."

Once Jones returned to the hall, he said, "I have to admit things are looking worse for Ariane, but I don't think we can go to the cops quite yet."

"Why not? You heard what he said. A group of guys dragged her to their van early this morning, and no one's heard from her since."

"True, but Mr. McNally is not exactly what you would call an ideal witness. Don't get me wrong, I don't think he's lying or anything, but you have to admit he lost touch with reality a couple of times during our conversation."

"Shit!" Payne thought they had enough information to go on, but Jones knew a lot more about police procedures than he did. "So what do you recommend?"

"Honestly, I think we should go upstairs and snoop around Ariane's apartment a little more. Plus we can see if the peephole video camera recorded anything before they covered the lens."

CHAPTER 10

INSIDE the plantation house, Theo Webster stared at his computer screen as he scrolled through page after page of painstaking research. After removing his wire-rimmed glasses, Webster rubbed his tired eyes and stretched his skinny 5'8" frame. The track lighting above him reflected off the ebony skin that covered his ever-growing forehead and highlighted the dark bags that had recently surfaced under his drooping eyelids.

After cracking his neck, Webster settled back into his seat and resumed his research, studying the in-depth genealogy of the island's most recent arrivals. As he scrutinized Mike Cussler's family, Webster heard a creak in a floorboard behind him.

"Shit," he muttered as he reached inside his oaken desk.

Without looking Webster fumbled through various items until his hand made contact with his gun. Slipping his fingers around the polymer handle, Webster slowly pulled the .38 Special from his desk while staring at his computer screen.

The floorboard whined again, but this time the sound was several feet closer.

It was time to make his move.

In a sudden burst, Webster dropped to the hardwood floor and spun toward his unsuspecting target. The move stunned the trespasser so much that he dropped the cup of coffee he was carrying and shrieked like a wounded girl.

The pathetic wail brought a smile to Webster's face. "Gump, what the hell are you doing sneaking up on me? Don't you know we have nearly two dozen prisoners on this island that would like to see me dead? You got to use your head, boy! God gave you a brain for a reason."

Bennie Blount lowered his head in shame, and as he did, his elaborate dreadlocks cascaded over his dark eyes, making him look like a Rastafarian sheepdog. "I sorry 'bout that. I was just trying to bring you something to wakes you up."

Webster glanced at the brown puddle that covered the floor and grimaced. "Unless you have a straw, I think it's going to be tough for me to drink."

The 6'6" servant stared at the steaming beverage for several seconds before his face broke into a gold-toothed smile. "For a minute, I thought you be serious, but then I says to myself, Master Webster ain't no dog. He ain't gonna drink his drink from no floor, even with a straw!"

"Well, that's awfully clever of you, but before I congratulate you too much, why don't you run into the other room and get a mop?"

"That's a mighty good idea, sir. I guess I shoulda thought of it since it's my job to clean and all." Blount slowly backed away from the spill as he continued to speak. "Don't ya worry now."

Blount had been hired by the Plantation for his strong work ethic and knowledge of the local swamps. Nicknamed Gump for his intellectual similarities to Forrest Gump, the dim-witted character from the movie bearing his name, Blount lived in the guest wing of the white-pillared mansion. During the course of the day, he spent most of his time cooking and cleaning, but twice a week he was allowed to journey to the mainland for food and supplies.

When Blount returned to Webster's office, he was disappointed to see his boss working again. He liked talking to his superiors whenever he could, even though they often got upset when he interrupted their top-secret duties.

"Gump," Webster asked without turning around, "what are we having for breakfast?"

The question brought a smile to his lips, and his gold teeth glistened in the sunlight. "Well, I figure since this be a big week for y'all, I should fix a big Southern meal likes my momma used to make. I makes eggs 'n' bacon 'n' ham 'n' grits 'n' biscuits 'n' fresh apple butter, too. Oooooooweeeeee! I think my mouth is gonna water all day!"

Webster nodded his head in appreciation, at least until Blount's statement sank in. He turned from his computer and faced the dark-skinned servant. "What exactly did you mean when you said this was a big week for us? What do you know about this week?"

With the soiled mop in his hand, he shrugged. "Not much, sir, but I can tell somethin's up. There be an excitement in the air that's easier to smell than the magnolias in May. I figured maybe it's your birthday. Or maybe it's 'cause the Fourth of July is coming!"

Webster studied Blount as he spoke, and it appeared that he was telling the truth. "I think it's just the holiday that has everybody excited," he lied. "I know I'm looking forward to it."

"Well, I be, too! In fact, I was wondering if I can go to the city for the fireworks show on Saturday night. I don't know why they on the third, but they is!"

"Let me ask the other guys at breakfast, then I'll let you know. But as far as I'm concerned, that's fine with me."

"Thank ya, Master Webster! Thank ya! That'd be nice of ya!" Blount picked up his bucket and backed toward the open door. "Oh! Speaking of breakfast, I almost forgets to tell ya that it's ready to eat."

CHAPTER 11

ARIANE'S place appeared to be in order, with the exception of her splintered door. An off-white sofa sat against the wall to the left and faced a tasteful entertainment center that held a television, stereo, and DVD player. A leather chair rested in the corner of the room under a halogen lamp.

Jones walked to the security panel near the front door and pushed the button for a system check. Within seconds, the unit beeped and a digitized voice filled the room. "The crime alert system is operational. Current status is deactivated. Push one to activate the system."

"The unit is working, which means she probably turned it off to answer the door. Either that or she forgot to turn it on last night."

Payne shook his head. "When I walked her to the door last night, I made sure she got in and turned the system on before I left. In fact, I always wait until the damn thing beeps."

"Then she turned it off for some reason. And my guess is to open the door."

Payne swallowed deeply while opening the tiny black box that was mounted to the inside of Ariane's front door.

He removed the recordable DVD from the peephole surveillance system and carried it to the player. "I don't know if we'll see anything, but it's worth a look."

After slipping the disc inside, he hit play and waited for it to begin.

"How does this thing work?" Jones asked.

"It's activated by movement in the hallway. That way it doesn't record hour after hour of nothing." Payne pointed to the black screen to show Jones what he meant. "Since the opening is blocked, the camera interpreted that as someone standing directly in front of the door." Payne glanced at his watch, then looked at the electronic counter on the DVD player. "What time did Mr. McNally say he saw Ariane?"

"He said it was about an hour before we talked to him."

"Well, I got here about seven thirty, and there was no black van in the parking lot, so I'd guess we're talking about seven or seven fifteen, right?"

Payne skipped back several minutes until his own face filled the screen.

"When was that filmed?" Jones asked.

Payne studied the image and recognized the clothes he'd worn the previous evening. "That was from last night, but I'm not sure if it was before or after my date with Ariane." The faint beeping of the security system could be heard through the TV's speaker as Payne's image turned and walked away from the door. "See, I told you she set the damn system last night. I told you!"

Jones started to defend himself when a figure flashed across the screen. "Whoa! What was that?"

"I don't know," Payne said as he hit the pause button, then frame advance.

The picture crept by at a sluggish pace. After several seconds of nonaction, a gloved hand emerged from the right side of the screen. Moving an inch at a time, the arm eventually reached the lens of the peephole, and once it did, the picture immediately went black.

"Damn!" Payne cursed. "Not a goddamned thing!"

"Be patient." Jones grabbed the remote from Payne and

slowly rewound the image to the moment before the tape was applied to the door. "Just because we didn't see a face doesn't mean it's a total loss. There's more here than you think."

"Like what?"

"What color was the man who put the tape on the door?"

Payne stared at the screen. "I can't tell. He's wearing black gloves and long black sleeves."

"True," Jones muttered as he placed his finger on the image. "But look closer. There's a gap where the glove ends here, and the sleeve begins there."

Payne moved closer to the screen and stared. "I'll be damned! You're right. I can see the edge of each garment."

"You thought they overlapped because of his skin. Whoever put the tape on the door is black. Not coffee and cream like me, but pure black. I'm talking *hold the milk, hold the sugar, hold the freakin' water* black."

"Hey," Payne interrupted. "What's that on his arm?"

"Where?"

"Right between the glove and sleeve. Is that a tattoo?"

Jones crouched in front of the TV and considered the question. Unfortunately, the image was too dark to see things conclusively. "Hang on a sec. Let me change the brightness on the TV. It might help."

Payne stared at the screen as it brightened. "It might be a tattoo, but I honestly don't know."

"Don't worry. I know a way we can find out. I have a computer program at my office that lets me blow up video images, alter color schemes, manipulate contrast, and so on. I'll take the disc over there and see if I can learn anything else."

"Sounds good to me." Payne reached for the eject button, but before he pressed it, Jones grabbed his arm.

"Listen," he said in a sympathetic voice, "I wasn't going to mention this, but I have to be upfront with you. There's still one thing we need to check. I was going to wait until later, but I feel you deserve to be with me when it's done."

"What are you talking about? What do you need to check?"

Jones placed his hand on Payne's broad shoulder and squeezed. "The peephole camera records image and sound, right? I mean, we heard the alarm system beeping, didn't we?"

"Yeah, so?"

Jones swallowed hard. "The video of what happened this morning is obviously unwatchable because of the duct tape, but there's a good chance that we might be able to hear this morning's events after the peephole was blocked."

"Oh, God, you're right! Put it on!"

"Jon, keep in mind if something did happen to Ariane, it might be painful to—"

"Put it on! I've got to know what happened."

Jones nodded, then hit the appropriate button on the remote. After several seconds of silence, the faint sound of a doorbell could be heard from the blank TV screen. It was followed by a loud, rhythmic knock.

"You're early," Ariane complained. "I'm still getting ready."

A brief silence followed her comment before a faint giggle emerged from the speaker.

"First you're early, now you're covering the peephole!"

Beeps from the security system chimed in the tape's background.

"I'll tell you what, Jonathon, I'm going to kick your butt all over the golf course. There's no doubt about that!"

Her comment was followed by the click of a deadbolt, the twist of the door handle, and—

Jones pushed the pause button and glanced at Payne, whose face was completely ashen. "Are you sure you want to hear this?"

"Yeah," Payne muttered, his voice trembling with emotion. He didn't really want to, but if he was going to help Ariane, he knew he had no choice. "Play the disc."

"Are you sure?"

Payne shook his head from side to side. "But play it anyways."

With the touch of a button, Ariane screamed like a banshee, sending chills through Payne and Jones. As her wail echoed through the room, it was quickly replaced by heavy footsteps, muffled squeals, and then the most frightening sound of all.

Silence.

CHAPTER 12

WHILE Holmes, Jackson, and Webster had breakfast in the mansion, Hakeem Ndjai, an unmerciful man who'd been hired as the Plantation overseer, took control of the captives.

Even though he was a valuable part of the Plantation team, his foreign heritage excluded him from the decision-making hierarchy. He had been handpicked by Holmes, who had heard several stories of Ndjai's unwavering toughness in Nkambé, Cameroon, where Ndjai had been an overseer on a cacao plantation. Like most workers from his country, he had labored in unbearable conditions for virtually nothing—his average income was only $150 per year—so when Holmes offered him a job in America, Ndjai wept for joy for the first time in his life.

But that was several months ago, and Ndjai was back to his old ways.

In a cold growl, Ndjai reinforced the instructions that Jackson and Holmes had given during their cross-burning party, but he did it with his own special touch. "I am the overseer of this Plantation, and out of respect for my job, you shall refer to me as *sir*. Do I make myself clear?"

"Yes, sir!" the naked group shouted.

"Each of you has been brought here for a reason, and that reason will eventually be revealed. Until that time, you will become a part of the Plantation's working staff, performing the duties that will be assigned to you." Ndjai signaled one of the guards, who ran forward, carrying a silver belt that shone in the sun. "While you are working, you will be positioned on various parts of our land, and at some point, you might be tempted to run for freedom."

He smiled under his dark cloak. "It is something I do not recommend."

Ndjai grabbed the metal belt and wrapped it around a cement slab that rested near the bloodstained chopping block. After clicking the belt in place, he handed the cement to a nearby guard, who immediately carried it fifty yards from the crowd.

"When you are given your uniforms, you will have one of these belts locked to your ankle. It cannot be removed by anyone but me, and I will not remove it for any reason during your stay on this island." He reached into the pocket of his robe and pulled out a tiny remote control. He held the gadget in the air so everyone could see it. "This is what you Americans call a deterrent."

With a push of a button, the cement block erupted into a shower of rubble, sending shards of rock in every direction and smoke high into the air.

"Did I get your attention?" he asked. "Now imagine what would have happened if your personal anklet were to be detonated. I doubt much of you would be found."

A couple of the guards snickered, but Ndjai silenced them with a sharp stare. He would not tolerate disrespect from anybody.

"I know some of you will try to figure out how your anklets work, and some of you will try to disarm them. Well, I will tell you now: Your efforts will fail! We have buried a small number of transmitters throughout the Plantation. If at any time your anklet crosses the perimeter, your personal bomb will explode, killing you instantly. Is that clear?"

"Yes, sir."

"Oh, one more thing. If your device is detonated, it will send a signal to the anklets that are being worn by several other prisoners, and they will be killed as well. Do you understand?"

They certainly did, and the mere thought of it made them shudder.

CHAPTER 13

JONES returned to his scenic office and locked himself in his massive technology lab. The room cost a staggering amount of money and was filled with high-tech equipment that many police departments would love to have. The most important piece of hardware was the computer, but it was the instrument that cost Jones the least. Built by Payne Industries, the computer was a scaled-down version of the system used at FBI headquarters in Langley, Virginia, and had been given to Jones as an office-warming gift.

Placing the surveillance disc into the unit, Jones quickly broke the footage into manageable data files. He was then able to select a precise frame from the video and put it on his screen in microscopic clarity.

"What should I look at first?" he mumbled to himself.

Then it dawned on him. He wanted to examine the assailant's right wrist to see if the black mark was, in fact, a tattoo.

Jones scrolled through a number of frames until he found the scene that fit his specific needs. The suspect's arm was centered perfectly on the monitor, and the gap between the glove and the sleeve was at its widest. Then he zoomed in and sharpened the image.

A few seconds later, Jones smiled in triumph when an elaborate tattoo came into view. The three-inch design was in the shape of the letter *P*, and it started directly below the palm of the suspect's hand. The straight edge of the symbol was in the form of an intricately detailed sword, the blade's handle rising high above the letter's curve. At the base of the drawing, small drops of blood fell from the weapon's tip, leaving the impression that it had just been pulled from the flesh of a fallen victim. Finally, dangling from each side of the sword was a series of broken chains, which appeared to be severed near the left and right edge.

As Jones printed several copies of the image, his speakerphone buzzed, followed by the voice of his secretary. "Mr. Payne is on line one."

With a touch of a button, Jones answered his call. "Jon, any news?"

"I was about to ask you the same thing. I went to the police like you suggested and filled out the appropriate paperwork. It turns out that I knew a few of the officers on duty. They assured me that Ariane would get top priority."

"Even though she's only been gone a few hours?"

"Her scream on the surveillance tape and Mr. McNally's testimony have a lot to do with it. Normally, they'd wait a lot longer before they pursued a missing person, but as I said, the evidence suggests foul play."

"Did they give you any advice?"

"I wouldn't call it *advice*. I think a warning would be more accurate. These cops know me, so they automatically assumed that I would do something stupid to get in their way. Why would they think that?"

Jones smiled. The cops had pegged him perfectly. Payne was definitely the intrusive type. "Instead of giving you the obvious answer, let me tell you what I discovered." He described the image in detail, then filled him in on a theory. "I think we're looking for a Holotat."

"A Holo-what?"

"Holotat."

Payne scrunched his face. "What the hell is that?"

"Back in World War Two, German guards used to tattoo their prisoners with numbers on their wrists in order to keep track of them. After the war, the people who survived these camps had a constant reminder of the Holocaust, marks that eventually became a source of inspiration."

"What does that have to do with Ariane?"

"About five years ago, members of Los Diablos, a Hispanic gang from East L.A., decided it would be cool if they tattooed their brothers in a similar fashion, marking them on their wrists. Before then, gangs used to get their tattoos on their arms, chests, or back, but suddenly this trend caught on. Holocaust tattoos, known as Holotats, started popping up everywhere."

"And you think the *P* tattoo is a Holotat gang emblem?"

Jones nodded his head. "That's what it looks like to me. Of course, I could be wrong. It could be a jailhouse tat or the initial of his girlfriend, but my guess would be a Holotat."

Payne considered the information, and a question sprang to mind. "You said it might be his girlfriend's initial. Does that mean we're sure it's a guy?"

"That would be my guess. The thickness of the wrist suggests a masculine suspect, but to be on the safe side, I wouldn't completely rule out a female. Of course, she'd have to be a Sasquatch-looking bitch."

Payne laughed for the first time in a long time. He felt better knowing that Jones was helping him through this. "So, what now?"

"Why don't you come down here? I have a few more tests I want to run on the video. But I want you to look at the tattoo to see if you notice anything that I didn't."

"Sounds good to me. I'll be there in a few minutes."

IT took Payne nearly an hour to reach Mount Washington, and the drive was a miserable one. Holiday traffic was starting to pick up even though it was only midday. Payne used his master key to enter Jones's technology lab and found his friend hard at work on the computer.

"Any new developments?" Payne asked as he picked up a printout of the tattoo and studied it.

"There wasn't much visual data to work with on the disc, so I focused on the audio. I know it's hard to believe, but sound can tell you so much."

"You mean like her scream?"

"No, I mean like background noise. You know, stuff that's there, but isn't really obvious."

"Such as?"

Jones walked to the far side of the room and tapped his hand on a small metallic unit. "I call this device the Listener, and for the last half hour, it's been our best friend."

Payne crossed the room for a closer look and watched as Jones typed a specific code into the unit's keypad. The Listener responded by extending its front tray six inches forward.

"This unit was designed to analyze sound and place it into specific categories. Since we were dealing with a stable environment with little background noise I had the machine focus on a couple of things. The first was her voice. I wanted to see if I could understand what she tried to say after her initial scream."

"You mean when her voice got garbled."

"Yeah. My guess is they were probably gagging her at the time, but I was hoping the machine might be able to isolate the sound and clean it up for us."

"Did it work?"

"Actually, it worked beautifully. Unfortunately, it won't help our cause very much."

"Why not? What did she say?"

Jones picked up the transcript and read it aloud. "She said, 'Help me. Somebody help me.' "

Payne closed his eyes as Ariane's words sank in. He had managed to stay relaxed while Jones explained the features of his computer equipment, but now that the focus of the conversation was back on Ariane, Payne felt the nausea return. What would he do if he couldn't track her down? Or worse yet, if someone had already killed her?

"Jon?" Jones said. "Are you okay? I asked you a question."

Payne opened his eyes and turned to his friend. "Sorry. What was that?"

"I wanted to know if you told the cops how many people were involved."

He thought for a moment, then shook his head. "I told them that Mr. McNally saw more than one person, but wasn't sure how many."

"Well, thanks to the Listener, I'd say that there were probably three of them."

Payne sat up in his chair. "How did you figure that out?"

"Simple. I programmed the device to filter out everything but the footsteps, and after listening to the disc, I could hear three distinct sets. But, as they were leaving, I could only hear two."

"You mean someone stayed inside Ariane's apartment?"

Jones shook his head. "At first, that's what I thought, too, but as I listened to the disc again, I noticed a scratching noise in the background. I filtered out all the other sounds, isolating the scratch, and this is what I got." He pushed his mouse button once, and a rough grating sound emerged from his system's speakers. "What does that sound like to you?"

"Feet dragging on a carpet?"

"Bingo!" Jones was impressed that his friend had figured it out so quickly. It had taken him several minutes to come up with a hypothesis. "Remember what McNally said? It looked like your girlfriend was snookered because they were practically carrying her to the van? Well, my guess is she was drugged or knocked out. The three sets of footsteps that the Listener originally detected were Ariane and the two assailants. They broke into her place, gagged her, drugged her, then dragged her out. That's the only thing that fits."

"But I thought you said there were three guys involved. Where was the third guy while the abduction was going on?" Before Jones had a chance to answer, the solution popped into Payne's head. "Oh, shit! They probably needed a driver to stay outside in the van."

Jones nodded. "That's what most criminals would do."

CHAPTER 14

PAYNE and Jones gathered all of the information they'd accumulated and took it directly to the police. When they entered the local precinct, Payne headed for Captain Tomlin's office. He had met Tomlin a year earlier at a charity golf event that Payne Industries had sponsored, and they had stayed in touch since.

"Do you have a minute?" Payne asked as he tapped on Tomlin's glass door. The captain, who had curly hair and thick arms, waved him in. "Have you ever met David Jones?"

Tomlin introduced himself, shaking Jones's hand with a powerful grip. "Jon has told me all about you. I almost feel like we've met. I understand that you served under him in special ops."

"Yeah," Jones answered as he took a seat next to Payne. "We relied on each other so much we ended up attached in the real world."

"That happens all the time. There's something about life in the military that draws soldiers together—a kindred spirit that bonds all warriors."

Payne winced at the suggestion. "I don't know about that crap. I think D.J. stuck with me so I could get him a job."

Jones nodded. "To be honest, he's right. I actually can't stand the bastard."

Tomlin laughed loudly. "So, I take it from your comedy that Ariane's all right? Where was that gal hiding?"

The comment drained the humor from the room.

"Don't let our joking fool you," Jones declared. "It's just our way of dealing with things. The truth is we're still looking for her."

Payne held up his cell phone, showing it to Tomlin. "I'm having all of my calls forwarded. If she tries to contact any one of my lines, it'll ring here."

"Good, then you won't have to sit at home, killing time."

Payne took a deep breath and nodded. To him, waiting was the hardest part. "How are things on your end? Did you have a chance to send any officers to her apartment?"

"I sent a small crew over. Unfortunately, we didn't notice anything new. You guys must've done a pretty thorough job this morning."

"We did," Payne said. "I hope we didn't step on any toes by entering the scene."

"Heavens no. I would've done the same thing if a loved one of mine was involved in something like this. Of course, my answer as a police officer would've been different if I didn't know you. But you're professionals, so I trust your judgment when it comes to a crime scene."

Jones stood from his chair and handed the captain all of the information he had acquired from Ariane's DVD. "We did get some data on one of the suspects that entered the apartment. He had an elaborate tattoo on his right wrist. Looks like a Holotat to me."

Tomlin pulled a close-up of the tattoo from the large stack of papers and studied it. "It could be, but very few gangs in Allegheny County use them. They're a lot more common on the West Coast and down south."

"That makes sense," Payne said, "since this person's probably from Louisiana."

Tomlin furrowed his brow. "I'm not so sure of that. If I were a criminal, I wouldn't use my own van as a getaway vehicle. And if I did, you can bet I wouldn't use my own license plate. I'd bet there's a good chance we're going to get a report of a stolen plate or an abandoned black van somewhere in the area. And when we do, we can go from there."

That wasn't what Payne wanted to hear. He was hoping the captain supported his theory on the van's origin. When he didn't, he felt an unexpected burst of betrayal. "What are you saying, that these clues are a waste of time?"

"No, I'm not saying that at all. Every little bit helps. However, I'm not going to blow smoke. I respect you way too much for that."

"Good! Then tell me where we stand. I need to know."

Tomlin leaned back in his chair and searched for the appropriate words. "In a standard kidnapping, there's little we can actually do until we get some kind of ransom demand. Sure, we'll continue to search for evidence and witnesses, but without some kind of break, the odds of us finding her *before* they call are pretty slim."

Jones glanced at his friend and waited to see if he was going to speak, but it was obvious he was done talking for the moment. "Captain? In your opinion, do you think this abduction was done for money?"

Tomlin didn't want Payne to feel responsible for the kidnapping, but there was no denying the obvious. "To be honest, that would be my guess. Payne Industries is a well-known company, and Jon is recognized as one of the wealthiest men in the city. Since Ariane doesn't have a history with drugs or any other criminal activities, I can think of no other reason for her abduction."

"Thank you for your honesty," Payne said. Then, to the surprise of Jones and Tomlin, he stood up and headed for the door. "If you find anything at all, please let me know."

"I promise," Tomlin called out. "The same goes for you. Call me day or night."

* * *

WHEN they reached the parking lot, Jones questioned Payne. "Jon, what's going on? First you snapped at the man, then you bolted from his office without even saying goodbye. What's going on in that head of yours?"

Payne shrugged. "I'm not really sure. But I'll tell you one thing. I'm not going to sit at home, waiting for some ransom demand."

"I kind of assumed that. You aren't exactly the sit-on-your-ass type."

Payne nodded as he pondered what to do next. Even though he valued Captain Tomlin's advice, there was something about his opinion that bothered him. He couldn't place his finger on why, but he knew he didn't agree with Tomlin's assessment of the black van.

While thinking things through, Payne pulled from the crowded police lot and turned onto a busy side street. He maneuvered his vehicle in and out of traffic until he got to McKnight Road, one of the busiest business districts in the area. As he stopped at a red light, Payne reached across Jones's lap and pulled a small book out of the Infiniti's glove compartment.

"What's that?" Jones asked.

"It's my address book. I'm checking to see if I know anyone from Louisiana. I figure maybe a local would know something about the Holotat. You don't know anyone down there, do you?"

"Sorry. My roots are up north, just like yours. Why, do you have someone in mind?"

"No, but—" The light turned green, and as it did, the word *green* clicked in Payne's mind. "I'll be damned! I just thought of someone from New Orleans."

"Who?"

"Did I ever introduce you to Levon Greene?"

Jones's eyes lit up with excitement. Levon Greene was an All-Pro linebacker for the Buffalo Bills before a devastating knee injury knocked him from the NFL. Before getting chop-blocked by Nate Barker, a guard with the San Diego

Chargers, Greene was a fan favorite. He was known throughout the country for his tenacity and his colorful nickname, taken from a famous Bob Marley song. "The Buffalo Soldier? You know the Buffalo Soldier?"

Payne nodded. "He lived in Pittsburgh for a year after the Bills cut him. The Steelers signed him and kept him on their injured list for over a season. Our paths crossed on more than one occasion on the b-ball courts. He liked to play hoops for therapy."

"But that doesn't mean you *know* him. I see Steelers and Pirates all of the time, but that doesn't mean they're my boys."

"True, but I know Levon." He handed Jones the address book and told him to look for a phone number. Jones quickly flipped to the *G*s and was stunned when he saw Greene listed.

"Holy shit! You do know him."

"I told you I knew him. What's Levon's home number?"

Jones glanced at the page for the requested information. "You don't have a home number. You only have a cell listed."

"Yeah, that makes sense. When he gave me his info, he was just getting ready to move back to New Orleans and didn't know his new number."

"He was moving to Louisiana, and he gave you his number? What, were you guys dating or something?"

Payne laughed. "Jealous?"

Jones shook his head and grinned. He'd always been amazed at Payne's ability to keep his sense of humor in the most tragic of times. Sure, his buddy would have the occasional flare-up and reveal his true emotions during a crisis, but on the whole Payne was able to conceal his most personal feelings under a facade of levity.

Originally, when the two first met, Jones had interpreted Payne's frivolity as a lack of seriousness, and he actually resented him for it. After a while, though, he learned that Payne's sense of humor was simply his way of dealing with things. He realized that Payne never mocked the tragedy of a situation. Instead, he tried to use humor as a way of coping with the fear and adrenaline that would otherwise overwhelm him. It was a good trick, and eventually Jones and several other MANIACs learned to do the same thing.

"Seriously, what's the deal with you two? Have you known him long?"

"I met him in North Park playing basketball. We were on the same team, and the two of us just clicked on the court. He was rehabbing his knee, so he couldn't move like he used to on the football field. But he was strong as an ox. He set some of the most vicious screens I have ever seen in my life, and most of the time he did it to get me open jumpers."

Jones laughed at the description of Greene. "It sounds like Levon plays hoops with the same intensity he showed in the NFL."

"Hell, yeah! Even though we were in the park, he had a serious game face on. In fact, some people were afraid to play against the guy."

"I bet, but that still doesn't explain why he gave you his number."

"We ended up making it a daily thing. We'd meet at the courts at the same time every day, and we'd take on all comers. Kicked some serious ass, too. Unfortunately, right before Steelers camp started, he failed his physical and was released from the team. But he told me if I was ever in New Orleans I should give him a call."

"Wow, I'm kind of surprised. I thought I knew most of your friends, and now I find out you've been keeping a celebrity from me. So, are there any movie star chums that I should know about?"

"Did I ever tell you about my three-way with the Olsen twins?"

Jones laughed at the comment. "What are you going to do about Levon?"

"It's not what I'm going to do. It's what you're going to do." Payne handed him his cell phone. "I want you to dial his number for me."

"You want me to call Levon Greene? This is so cool!" Jones dialed the phone, then looked at Payne when it started to ring. "What should I say to him?"

Payne snatched the phone from Jones's grasp. "Not a damn thing. He's my friend, not yours."

"You are such a tease!"

Payne was still laughing when Greene answered the phone. "Who's this?"

"Levon, I don't know if you'll remember me. My name is Jonathon Payne. I used to run ball with you at North Park when you were living up in Pittsburgh."

"White dude, nice jump shot?"

"Yeah, that's me."

"Yo, man, wazzup? I haven't heard from your ass in a long time. How ya doin'?"

"I'm fine, and you? How's the knee?"

Greene winced. It was one topic that he didn't like dwelling on. "Still not a hundred percent, but it's better than it used to be. I'm still hoping some team needs a run-stuffing linebacker and gives me a look in camp. But I don't know. It's getting kind of late."

"Well, they'd be crazy not to take you, Levon. You're as fierce as they come."

"Thanks, man. I appreciate it. So, wazzup? Why the call out of the blue? Are you coming to New Orleans? I got a big-ass house. I can hook you up with a room. Won't charge you much, neither," he joked.

Payne wasn't sure what he was hoping to find out from Greene, but he figured the only way to learn anything was to be up-front with the man. "Actually, Levon, the reason I called is an important one. You know how I told you I was doing fine?"

"Yeah?"

"Well, I lied. Something's going on up here, and I was hoping you could give me a hand."

"I don't loan people money, man. You're gonna have to ask someone else."

Payne grinned. If Greene knew how much money Payne actually had, Levon might be asking him for a loan. "No, it's not about cash. Nothing like that. I promise."

"What is it then? What's the deal?"

Payne exhaled, trying not to think about Ariane. "I was hoping to get some information about a gang that might be operating in Louisiana, and I figured since you play a lot of street ball, you might be able to find something out on the courts."

"Is that all you need? Shit! No problem, man. What's the name of the posse?"

"Actually, that's what I was hoping you could tell me."

"All right, but you gotta give me something to go on, 'cause there's a lot of motherfuckin' gangs down here. And every day a new crew pops up."

"Damn," Payne mumbled. He had been naively hoping that New Orleans was a one-gang town. "Do any of the gangs have Holotats? You know, tattooed gang emblems on their wrists?"

"Hell, yeah. A lot of crews do. Just tell me what it looks like, and I'll tell you what I know."

"The letter *P*, with a bloody knife sticking out of it."

Greene thought about the information for a moment, then responded. "Off the top of my head, there's nothing I can think of. But if you give me some time, I can ask around. If anything turns up, I'll let you know immediately."

"That sounds great," Payne replied. "And I'd really appreciate anything you can come up with. It's a matter of life or death."

"Give me an hour, and I'll give you a buzz at this number. I know a couple of brothers that know about this type of shit. Let me get ahold of them, then I'll get ahold of you."

"Levon, thank you! I'll be awaiting your call."

Jones, who'd overheard the entire conversation, questioned Payne the minute he hung up the phone. "So, he's going to hook you up?"

"He's going to try."

"And what if he does? What are you gonna do?"

Payne smiled as he put his hand on Jones's shoulder. "How does Fourth of July in New Orleans sound to you?"

CHAPTER 15

The Kotto Distribution Center
Ibadan, Nigeria
(56 miles northeast of Lagos)

MOST aspects of the sprawling complex were recognized as legitimate. Hundreds of Nigerian-born workers came to the center each day to unload massive shipments of cacao, palm oil, peanuts, and rubber that had been brought in from Hannibal Kotto's various businesses. Because of these ventures and the numerous employment opportunities that he offered, Kotto's name was known and respected throughout Africa.

And it was this respect that allowed him to take advantage of the system.

As he sat behind his mahogany desk, Kotto waited for his assistant to give him the go-ahead to start the conference call. When the woman nodded, Kotto knew that everybody was ready.

"Gentlemen," he said into the speakerphone, "I realize that English is not the strongest language for all of you, but since I'm dealing with several clients at once, I feel it is the most appropriate selection." Kotto took a sip of Oyo wine, a local beverage made from the sap of palm trees, then continued. "In order to give everybody a sense of who they'll be bidding against, I'd like each of you to name the country that you're representing. Each of you has been assigned an auction number. When your number is called, please tell the group where you are from."

As Kotto's assistant read the numbers, heavily accented voices emerged from the speakerphone, each announcing his country of origin. Algeria, Angola, Cameroon, Ethiopia, Kenya, Libya, Namibia, and the Democratic Republic of the Congo were all represented.

"If you were listening," Kotto stated, "I am sure each of you realizes that Africa is the only continent that Mr. Drake and I are dealing with. We've had several offers from Asia and South America as well, but we're not ready to deal with their politics. At least, not yet."

"When do you expect to broaden the operation?" asked the Ethiopian delegate.

"That's a decision we haven't made. If all continues to go well, there's the possibility of expansion within the next few months." Kotto took another sip of wine while waiting for further questions. When none came, he changed the course of the discussion. "I realize that some of you were disappointed with the last shipment. Mr. Drake and I discussed the issue, and I apologize for any problems it might've caused. I would like to assure you that you will have no such problems with the next delivery. It is the best quality we've ever prepared."

The Kenyan spoke next. "What will that do to the price? I imagine we will have to pay more for the increase in caliber, will we not?"

Kotto grinned. "I would imagine, like in any business, that an increase in quality will cause an increase in price, but to what extent the price will rise, we'll find out shortly."

JONES settled into the soft leather seats of the Payne Industries jet and closed his eyes for a moment of retrospection. During his military career, he'd been on hundreds of life-threatening missions, but this was the first time he'd ever felt hopeless before a flight. For one reason or another, he knew he was completely unprepared for what he was about to do.

And it was a feeling that he didn't like.

When he was a member of the MANIACs, they were always given advanced reconnaissance before they were dropped into enemy territory. Maps, guides, safe houses, and specific objectives were always provided before they were put into danger. But not today. No, on this mission Jones was willing to ignore every protocol he had ever been taught because his best friend needed his help. He was flying to a city he'd never visited to look for a girl who probably wasn't there, and the only thing they had to go on was a tattoo of the letter *P*.

"This is crazy," he said to himself.

As he opened his eyes, he saw Payne hang up the phone at the front of the cabin and return to his seat, which was across the aisle from Jones.

"Go on. Get it off your chest," Payne said, knowing his friend wasn't happy.

"Are you sure this trip is wise? I mean, don't you think it's a little bit impulsive?"

"Not really. As I told you before, Levon talked to some of his boys in the city, and they assured him that Holotats are used by several of the local gangs."

"Yeah, but that doesn't guarantee that Ariane is going to be down there. For all we know, the gang could have members in cities across America like the Bloods or the Crips. It could be a local thug from the Hill District that we're looking for. Heck, the *P* could stand for *Pittsburgh*."

"True, but that doesn't explain the Louisiana license plate, now does it?"

Jones shook his head. He wasn't really sure how to explain that. "But don't you think that this is jumping the gun? We have no idea what we're getting ourselves into."

Payne smiled. If he didn't know better, he would've assumed that his friend was afraid of flying. "What's troubling you, D.J.? We've been to thousands of places that are more dangerous than New Orleans, and I've never seen you act like this."

"Well, I've never felt like this," Jones admitted. "I don't

know how to explain it, but I can tell we're about to walk into a hornet's nest. And the fact that we weren't allowed to bring any weapons into the airport makes me feel unprotected."

"I figured you'd feel that way. That's why I just gave Levon another call. Since he has a number of contacts on the street, I assumed that he'd have some gun connections."

"Does he?"

"He said he'd see what he could do, but I think that's his way of saying he'll get it done."

A few hours later, the jet landed on an auxiliary runway at Louis Armstrong International Airport in Kenner, Louisiana, which spared Payne and Jones from dealing with the hassle of the main terminal. After grabbing their bags from the plane, they walked to the nearest rent-a-car agency, where they picked up the fastest rental available, a Ford Mustang GT convertible.

The airport was only fifteen miles west of the Crescent City, so the drive to New Orleans was a short one. Following Interstate 10 all the way into Orleans Parish, Payne followed the directions Greene had given him. Before long they were navigating the streets of the central business district.

As Payne and Jones expected, the contrast between the tourist areas and the outlying neighborhoods was disheartening. Hurricane Katrina had ravaged the entire city in August 2005, and since that time most of the governmental funds had been funneled into the city's businesses and infrastructure, not the residential sections or suburbs. In many ways, the reasoning was sound. Tourists were the lifeblood of the region, and the only way to get them to return was to restore the areas that they wanted to visit.

One of those places was the Spanish Plaza, the spot where they would meet Greene.

Donated by Spain in 1976 as a bicentennial gift, the plaza was one of four foreign squares that paid tribute to the roles that France, Italy, England, and Spain played in the history and culture of New Orleans. The focal point of the site was a man-made geyser, encircled by an elaborate cut-stone deck and illuminated by a rainbow of lights that lined the scenic monument.

As Payne and Jones strolled down the plaza's steps, they saw Greene, wearing a pair of white Dockers and an ice blue Tommy Hilfiger shirt, looking even larger than he did during his NFL playing days.

"Levon," Payne called as he neared his friend. "Thanks for meeting me."

Greene, 6'3" and 275 pounds of muscle, stood from the bench where he'd been resting his knee. "No problem, my man." He grabbed Payne's hand and pulled him close, bumping his shoulder while patting him on the back with his free hand. It was a greeting that was quite common in the sports world. "You're looking good. You still playin' ball?"

"Not as much as I used to. But I manage to work out whenever I can. Of course, I still have a long way to go before I'm a badass like you."

Greene smiled and turned his attention to Jones. "By the way, my name's Levon Greene. And you are?"

Jones grabbed Greene's hand and replicated the greeting Greene had given Payne—except Jones did it with much more vigor. He was thrilled to meet one of his biggest sports heroes. "I'm David Jones, a friend of Jon's and a big fan of yours."

"That's always nice to hear, especially since I'm a huge fan of yours as well. I can hardly believe that I'm actually talking to the lead singer of the Monkees!"

Payne couldn't help but laugh. He occasionally teased Jones about his name's similarity to Davy Jones, and it was something that D.J. couldn't stand. However, Payne had a feeling that the remark would produce a much different reaction coming from Greene.

"Oh, I get it!" Jones said as he playfully punched Greene on his arm. "The Monkees! That's pretty damn funny. I bet I used to look a lot whiter on TV, huh?"

Greene laughed, then returned his attention to Payne. "Have you guys eaten yet? There are a number of places in this city where we can get traditional Louisiana food, like jambalaya or gumbo. Or, if you prefer, we can just head over to the French Quarter for a beer and some naked breasts. Trust me, whatever you want, I can deliver. Just name it, and it's yours."

Payne glanced at Jones, then back at Greene. He'd been less than forward with Greene on the phone and decided it was time to give him a few details about their mission. "Levon, I have to tell you something. This isn't going to be a pleasure trip. We're down here for one reason and one reason only: to find out about your local gangs."

Greene grimaced, confused. "Man, what is it about this damn tattoo that brought you guys down here? What could possibly be so important?"

Jones noticed the anguish on Payne's face, so he decided to answer for him. "Early this morning Jon's girlfriend was kidnapped from her apartment building. On the surveillance video, we noticed the tattoo that Jon described on one of the criminals. There was a witness who saw his girlfriend thrown into the back of a van that had Louisiana plates. We're down here to try and find her."

Greene grunted. "Damn, I had no idea. What did the police say?"

"Not much," Jones answered. "They're doing everything they can in Pittsburgh, but until we receive a ransom demand or find some conclusive evidence about the gang, they aren't willing to contact the FBI or any other law enforcement agency."

"So, you two are here to snoop around? What are you planning to do to get her back?"

With determination in his eyes, Payne rejoined the conversation. "Whatever it takes."

CHAPTER 16

BECAUSE of his size, Greene claimed the shotgun seat of the cramped Mustang, forcing Jones to sit in the back. Normally Jones would've bitched and moaned about losing his front-seat status, but since Greene would've needed the flexibility of a Russian gymnast to contort his 275-pound frame into the backseat, Jones didn't mutter a single complaint.

After getting into the car, Greene spoke first. "I was able to purchase the artillery that you guys wanted, but it cost me a pretty penny. If you want, we can pick it up now."

Payne agreed, and Greene directed him to the nearby parking garage where his black Cadillac Escalade was parked. The SUV was equipped with a gas-guzzling 400-plus-horsepower engine, limousine-tinted windows, and enough speakers and subwoofers to register a 3.5 on the Richter scale. "This here is my pride and joy," Greene exclaimed. "It was the last extravagant gift I bought myself before my injury. Ain't she sweet?"

"She's a nice ride, and it certainly looks like you take care of her."

Greene nodded as he opened his hatch. "My daddy always used to say, if you take care of your car, your car will take care of you."

Jones slid up next to the ex-linebacker and glanced inside the spacious cargo hold. "My God, your trunk's bigger than the seat you're making me ride around in."

Payne rolled his eyes at Jones's remark. "What did you get for us, big man?"

"You said you needed some reliable handguns, so I picked you up a couple of Glocks. I didn't know which model you'd prefer, so I got a 19 and a 27. The 19 uses standard nine-millimeter ammo, which many people like. Personally, I prefer the 27. In fact, it's the kind I carry for protection. It's chambered in forty-caliber Smith & Wesson, which I think is ballistically better than the nine-millimeter."

Payne smiled his approval as he picked up the charcoal gray Glock 27 from Greene's cargo hold. The ridged polymer handle fit snugly into his experienced hand, and as he held it up to the overhead lights, he stared at the gun with the wide-eyed fascination of a kid with a new toy. "You made a nice choice. No external safeties to worry about. It's light, dependable. Perfect."

"I guess that means I'm stuck with the 19, huh?" Jones didn't have a problem with the weapon, but after riding in the cramped backseat, he was in the mood to complain about something. "Did you get us anything else?"

Greene leaned into the trunk and pulled out a large maroon suitcase. As he fiddled with the case's combination lock, he spoke. "You told me that money wasn't an object and that you needed a couple of weapons with some serious firepower, right? Well, I hope this is what you had in mind." Greene opened the case, revealing a Heckler & Koch MP5 K submachine gun and a Steyr AUG assault rifle.

Jones reacted quickly, grabbing the MP5 K before Payne could get his hands on it. "My, my, my! What do we have here? German-made, three-round burst capability, nine hundred rounds a minute. A nice piece of hardware."

"That's not all," Greene declared. "I picked up the optional silencer as well."

"Great!" Payne said. "That means he can kill a librarian without disturbing any readers."

"Not that I'd *ever* kill a librarian," Jones assured him. "They're special people."

Greene ignored their banter, focusing on Payne instead. "Jon, this Steyr AUG is one of the best assault rifles on the market. It has an interchangeable barrel, so you can use it accurately from a distance like a sniper or up close like a banger. And the cartridges—five-point-five-six by forty-five millimeters—can be bought in department stores, for God's sake! It's very versatile."

Payne picked up the rifle and attached the scope with the skill of a soldier. Once it was in place, he held the eyepiece to his face and put a fire alarm across the garage in his sight. He held the weapon steady, sucked in a deep breath, then paused. "Bang!" he mouthed before dropping the AUG to his side. "You're right. This is a fine choice, and all the weapons appear to be in pretty good shape. What did the purchase run you?"

Greene pulled a handwritten invoice out of his pocket and gave it to Payne.

Payne glanced at the sheet and smiled. "What kind of a street dealer writes out receipts? Does he have a return policy if we're not completely satisfied?"

"Actually, I wrote the stuff down so I wouldn't forget. I'm not that strong with numbers."

"Me, either," Payne admitted. "That's why I try to avoid them at work."

"Oh, yeah? What do you do for a living?"

"I'm the CEO of a multinational conglomeration. We specialize in everything from new technologies to clothes to food products."

Greene laughed in a disbelieving tone. "Okay, whatever. If you don't want to tell me, that's fine. Besides, I'm too hungry to worry about it. Why don't we get out of here?"

Jones agreed. "Sounds good to me. Should we take one car or two?"

"Why don't we take two?" Payne said. "There's a good chance that we're going to be putting ourselves in danger before the end of the night, and I'm not comfortable asking

Levon to help us any more than he already has. It's one thing to ask him for guns and a place to stay, but it's entirely different to put his life in danger for two guys he barely knows."

"Yeah, you're probably right," Jones seconded. "Things could get a little bit nasty if we meet up with the wrong people."

"Come on, D.J., let's put our stuff in the back of the Mustang, then we can follow Levon to dinner." Jones nodded, then walked toward the car with a handful of weapons.

"Hold up a fuckin' minute!" Greene roared. "I can't believe you had an entire conversation about me and didn't bother to ask my opinion. What kind of Yankee bullshit is that?"

"Yankee bullshit?" Payne muttered. "I don't remember talking about baseball."

"I don't think you did. He must've misheard you. The acoustics down here aren't that great."

"Enough already! Would you guys please shut up before I'm forced to use a Glock on your ass? Damn!" Greene shook his head in disgust as he walked toward Payne and Jones. "Listen, I realize that I don't know you guys very well, but I'll be honest with you: This shit intrigues me. When I was still playing ball, I used to live for the adrenaline rush that I got on game day. The crowd calling my name, the speakers blasting my Bob Marley theme song, the feel of a quarterback sack. Man, those were the days."

Greene's eyes glazed slightly as he thought back to his All-Pro seasons with the Bills.

"Unfortunately, that shit has changed. Since Barker blew out my fucking knee, I haven't been able to get too excited about anything. I've done my best to rehab and run and lift, but the truth is, my career is probably done."

"So, what are you saying?" Payne asked.

"For the first time in almost three years, I can feel the adrenaline pumping again. When you called and told me that you wanted me to round up some weapons, I nearly got a hard-on. Then, when you told me the reason for your visit, I got even more excited—an excitement I haven't felt in a long time. Anyway, I guess this is what I'm saying: If you don't mind, I'd like to come along for the ride. I'd like to help you find your girlfriend."

Payne turned to Jones and grinned. He'd been hoping Greene would offer his services. "I don't know, man. I just don't know. D.J., what do you think?"

"Well, a New Orleans native with street connections might come in handy, and his nickname is the Buffalo Soldier after all."

"Good point." Payne smiled and shook Greene's hand. "Okay, Levon, you're on. But if at any time you feel like we're leading you somewhere you don't want to go, just say the word and we'll understand."

Jones nodded his head. "Yeah, there's no sense getting killed in a fight where you have nothing to gain."

"That sounds pretty fair," Greene exclaimed. "But before we begin, I need to ask for one small favor."

"You got it," Payne said. "Just name it."

"Well, since there's a good chance that you might die on this trip, I was hoping you could pay me for the guns before you got killed."

CHAPTER 17

ROBERT Edwards lay on the dirt floor of the small cabin, trying to hold back tears. He had never felt more exhausted in his entire life, yet the waves of agony that engulfed his body hindered his ability to slip into a painless sleep.

His face was still scarred and scabbed from his unsuccessful escape attempt through the Colorado woods on Thursday morning. The flesh on his back was sunburned and slashed from the numerous whippings he had received in the field as punishment for alleged misbehavior. His hands were sore from pulling weeds, and his arms ached from crawling through the untilled soil.

But all of that paled in comparison to the pain that he felt in his injured left leg.

The swelling in Robert's foot and ankle was so severe that his limb no longer looked like a normal appendage, but instead appeared to be a severe birth defect or some kind of laboratory mutation. The bloated and deformed leg had turned such a deep shade of purple that its hue bordered on black instead of the peach color of his uninjured leg. And enough blood had pooled in the lower extremity that the subsequent pressure was cutting off his foot's circulation.

His toes were ice-cold, and his foot tingled as if it were on the verge of falling asleep. Robert knew something needed to be done, but his limited knowledge of first aid was not advanced enough to deal with the severity of his injury. Without ice or an analgesic to reduce the pain and swelling, he did the only thing that he could. He elevated his leg by resting it on the cabin's lone bench.

As he closed his eyes, trying to get the rest that his body required, he heard the rattling of the cabin's lock. He turned his head and watched the door inch open. He stared at it with unblinking eyes until he recognized the shadow that slid into the room. It was Master Holmes, and he was holding a sledgehammer.

"What's that for?" Robert cried. "I've done everything you've asked of me! I haven't caused any problems!"

"That's not what I've heard," Holmes growled. "My guards assured me that you were lagging behind in the field, you needed assistance on more than one occasion, and you objected to being beaten. Those sound like serious problems to me."

"I swear I was doing my best! The pain in my leg was unbearable, and it slowed me down at times, but I never quit. I never gave up. I swear to God I did everything I could! Please don't hit me. I swear I'll get better. Oh, God, I swear!"

Holmes considered Robert's plea, then shrugged as he moved closer. "But I don't see *how* you can get better. You claim you were doing your best today, but my guards told me that your efforts weren't good enough. If you were already doing your best, I don't see how you could improve."

Robert tried to sit up, but he was unable to budge his leg. "I promise I'll get better. Just give me a painkiller and I could work harder. I just need something for the pain."

Holmes shook his head and sneered. "It's always something with you. This morning you were complaining to the guards. Now you're claiming you can do anything if we get you some drugs. As far as your pain goes, I don't give a fuck! Pain is something everyone must deal with, and those that deal with it the best will succeed the most. Obviously, you're one of those people that can't cope."

"I can, Master Holmes. I swear I can cope with the pain."

Holmes grinned as he tightened his grip on the wooden handle. "All right," he stated, lifting the sledgehammer high above Robert's head. "Let's see if you can deal with this!"

Screaming like a medieval warrior, Holmes shifted his weight forward and swung the mallet's iron head. Robert raised his hands and tried to deflect the blow, but his reflexes were too slow and Holmes's efforts were too determined. The hammer smashed into the bridge of Robert's nose, splintering the delicate bones of his face, not stopping until the cold steel collided with the blood-soaked floor.

"Can you handle that?" Holmes mocked. "Or do you need something for the pain?"

Gasping for air, Robert opened his eyes and lifted his head from the floor with a terrified shriek. He gazed around the room, searching for Holmes with every ounce of energy that remained in his body, but the powerful man was nowhere to be found. The tiny cabin was empty, except for the sound of a feminine voice that was urging him to lie down.

"Honey," Tonya Edwards pleaded as she stroked her husband's damp hair, "you were just dreaming! It was just a bad dream."

Robert tried to catch his breath as he glanced at his wife's face, but the image of Holmes's hammer still lingered. The dream had been so intense, so real, that his entire body was dripping with perspiration and his heart was pounding with urgency.

"Shhh," she begged, "let me take care of you."

It took a moment to settle him down, but Robert finally did as she requested. He eased his weary head to the cabin's floor, then stared into Tonya's dark eyes, searching for answers. "How did you get in here? How did you find me?"

Tonya continued to stroke her husband's hair, doing everything in her power to calm him. "You collapsed when the guards brought you back from the field, and they didn't want you to die. They brought me here to help you. I've been waiting for you to wake up ever since."

Robert's eyes filled with tears as he tried to make sense of it all. The abduction, the brutality, the labor. What had he done to deserve this? He had never lived the life of a saint, but he had never done anything to warrant this. He had never killed, robbed, or harmed anyone. In fact, he had never purposely hurt anybody in his entire life. And what about his wife? Why was she here? She was pregnant, for God's sake! What could she have possibly done to merit her imprisonment on the Plantation?

"Sweetie, did you hear me?" Tonya sobbed. "Can you hear what I'm saying?"

Robert did his best to focus on her lips, yet he had no idea what she had said. "How did you get in here?" he repeated, not remembering his earlier question.

She swallowed deeply, trying to stay strong for him. "The guards brought me in to take care of you. They want me to try and fix your leg."

"But you're not a doctor."

Tonya smiled, and the small movement of her lips temporarily lifted his spirits. "I know I'm not a doctor, but I'm the only person who's allowed to help. The guards told me what needed to be done, but I didn't want to do it until you woke up. I wanted to get your approval first."

"My approval?" Robert didn't like the sound of that. If it was a simple medical procedure like putting on a bandage, Tonya would've done it while he was asleep. Since she wanted to ask his permission, he knew it was something serious. "What do you have in mind?"

Tonya clambered to her feet—a difficult task because of her pregnancy—and waddled to the bench where her husband was currently elevating his leg. Carefully, she sat next to his swollen limb, trying not to jostle the bench with her body weight. Then, with the tenderness of a new mother, she placed her left hand on his injured ankle.

"Robert, the guard told me you have a displaced fracture. That means your bone was broken and the pieces shifted away from each other."

"The guard told you? Is he a doctor?"

His wife shook her head as she pointed to his leg. "No, he's not a doctor, but if you look at it, it's kind of obvious." Tonya took a deep breath before continuing. "Your leg's pointing straight ahead, but your foot is turned way to the right."

Robert didn't need to look at his injury. The severity of his pain let him know that something was seriously wrong. "How are you supposed to fix it?"

Tonya gulped before answering. "The guard told me if you want the bone to heal properly, I need to . . . um . . . straighten it out."

He was going to ask how she was going to do that, but he knew the answer. She had to twist his foot until everything was aligned in his leg. "Do you trust his advice?"

She nodded. "Remember when I slipped on the ice and broke my finger two years ago? The first thing the doctor did was pop it back into place. That way, it was able to grow back together." She bent her right index finger back and forth. "And see? It turned out just fine."

Robert agreed with her logic. If he wanted the ability to walk without a limp, he knew that something needed to be done immediately. "Do you think you can handle this? I know how squeamish you can be."

"Yeah, I can handle it," she said, smiling. It was a smile that said, *If I'm doing it for you, I can handle anything.*

Robert appreciated the sentiment. "I want you to promise me something, though. When you do this, do it quick, like removing a Band-Aid. Just make one decisive move and get it over with, okay?"

"You got it." Tonya stared at him, wanting to say something to her husband, but the appropriate words escaped her. "Are you ready?"

"Not really." He laughed through gritted teeth, "but I have a feeling I could never be ready."

She grinned, admiring his courageous sense of humor. "I think this will be easier if we did it on the flat ground. That way, I'll be able to anchor your upper leg with my body weight."

Robert closed his eyes as his wife lifted his swollen limb off of the bench and lowered it to the cabin's dirt floor. He winced as she placed it on the hard ground, but the pain wasn't nearly as bad as he had expected. "So far, so good."

Tonya leaned forward and gently kissed her husband on his forehead. After whispering soft words of encouragement, she turned away from him, resting her weight on his left knee, anchoring his upper leg in place. Without stopping to think, she leaned toward his broken limb and grabbed his foot. Then, with a quick burst, she rotated his foot to the left. The violent twist filled the cabin with a series of sounds—first the grotesque snap of his leg as his bones shifted back into place, then the heart-stopping shriek of a man in agony.

It was a sound that would be repeated by several prisoners in the coming days.

CHAPTER 18

THE last thing on Payne's mind was dinner, but Greene insisted that they stop for something to eat. They had to, he said. His stomach demanded it. As a compromise, Payne pulled into the first drive-through he could find and ordered several ham and cheese po'boys, a local specialty.

"So," said Payne as they waited for their food, "where to next?"

Greene thought about it for several seconds. "The first thing we're gonna have to do is talk to some of my boys from the Quarter. They'd be more aware of things on the street than me."

"What kind of things?" Jones asked.

"Everything. If it happens in the city, they'll know about it. They'll be able to fill you in on the tattoo you're looking for. Plus, if you're lucky, they might be able to tell you something about the kidnapping. Of course, since that didn't happen down here, details might be limited."

Payne considered Greene's words carefully. "Will your friends be willing to talk to us?"

Greene shrugged. "That's something I don't know. Most of the time, they're pretty receptive about helping me, but in your case, I don't know. You have two things working against you."

"And those are?"

"You're white, and you're from the North. Some people down here don't take kindly to those two things."

Payne nodded. "I can understand that, and I figured as much. But at the same time, I have two things that will help my cause."

"Like what?" Greene asked.

"First of all, I have you guys on my side, and since both of you are black, that might help us with some of the bigger racists we come across."

"That's true, but it might not be enough."

"And secondly," he said as he laid a thick wad of cash on the dashboard, "I'm willing to spend my entire fortune if it helps get Ariane back."

Greene eyed the stack of bills that sat before him and grinned. "You know, I think you'll get along with my boys just fine!"

"I had a feeling I would."

"But before we go anywhere, there are still a few ground rules I'm gonna have to insist on before we meet my people."

Payne scooped up his money and nodded. "I'm listening."

"This is my hometown, the place I've chosen to live for the rest of my life. So I don't want you doing anything that's going to hurt me after you guys leave. That means I don't want you roughing up any of my contacts, and I don't want you making me look bad in any way. I have a reputation to uphold in this city, and I don't want it tarnished. Okay?"

Payne and Jones agreed to his conditions.

"And finally, if I'm going to help you out, you need to promise me one more thing: absolutely no police involvement of any kind."

"Why not?" Jones asked, slightly suspicious.

"The people that we'll be dealing with aren't exactly friends of the law, and if word gets out that I'm teaming up with the local authorities, then my sources will dry up. And trust me, that won't help you find the girl, and it won't help me after you've left."

"No cops, no problem," replied Payne, who was willing to agree to just about anything. "Now, unless there's something else, can we get this show on the road?"

AFTER arranging a meeting with his best source, Greene directed his friends through the narrow streets of the Vieux Carré, the historic neighborhood also known as the French Quarter.

"Some people get confused when they come down here because the term French Quarter is misleading," Greene said. "Most of the architecture around here is Spanish in design, built in the eighteenth century. Most of the original French settlement was burned during a rebellion a little more than two hundred years ago. And thankfully, much of it survived Katrina."

From the backseat, Jones glanced at the buildings and noticed nothing but bars, strip clubs, and T-shirt shops, and none of them looked very old. "Levon? Are you telling me that Spain had nude dancing back in the seventeen hundreds?"

Greene laughed. "If they did, I doubt the conquistadors would've ever left. No, this is the one part of the French Quarter that has been ruined by modern-day greed. If you want to experience the true character of this area, you need to explore the side streets. That's where you'll find the flavor of the early settlers."

Payne suddenly looked at Greene in a whole new light. He always knew that Greene was intelligent, but he never realized the ex-linebacker had a passion for history. In the past, their playground conversations never got beyond street basketball and life in the NFL. "I have to admit, Levon, I'm kind of surprised. You never seemed to be the type of person who cared about the events of early America. Now you sound like a tour guide."

"I'm not sure if that's supposed to be a compliment or not."

"Yes," he assured Greene, "it's a compliment."

"Thanks. I guess ever since I hurt my knee I've had the opportunity to do a lot of things that I wouldn't have done earlier in my career. One of those things is historical research. I've been reading a lot of books on the past, trying to picture what life used to be like down here before the nineteen hundreds. As you can imagine, it was a much different place."

Payne nodded as they pulled up in front of the Fishing Hole, a nightclub where the marquee boasted "the Prettiest Girls in *Nude* Orleans." After parking, the three men walked to the front door and were quickly greeted by a bouncer who recognized Greene. With a slight nod, he allowed the trio to enter the club for free. Payne and Jones followed Greene into the smoke-filled lobby and were immediately taken aback by the first thing they saw: the couch dance room.

Similar in design to the orgy rooms of the Roman Empire, the room consisted of ten couches scattered around a spacious chamber. For a twenty-dollar tip, a naked vixen led an eager man to one of the black leather couches. During the course of a song, she would attempt to seduce him by rubbing, sliding, and grinding against his fully clothed body. Her goal was simple: convince him to purchase another song. And it wasn't a tough sale. Mix horny men with inexpensive alcohol, naked women, and heavy petting, and there's a better chance that a guy will file for bankruptcy before saying no to a beautiful stripper.

Strolling between the couches, Payne and Jones gaped at the erotic scene that unfolded around them while Greene chuckled with childlike delight.

"It's kind of hypnotic, isn't it?" asked Greene. "I always enjoy watching the crowd that stands along the walls. You'll see an awful lot of perverts with their hands in their pockets, if you know what I mean."

Both men knew what he meant, but that didn't mean they wanted to watch it.

"What are we doing here?" Payne asked. "Is it for the

scenery, or did we come here to meet somebody in particular?"

"Actually, both. The main guy I wanted you to speak to is the owner of this club. And since I didn't want you fellas to come to New Orleans without having a chance to experience Bourbon Street, I told him that we would meet him here. I hope that doesn't bother you."

Jones continued to stare at the naked females and shook his head. "Nope, doesn't bother me at all. In fact, I'm tempted to borrow twenty bucks."

Payne grabbed Jones by the arm and pulled him into the hallway. "Come on, D.J., get your mind in the game. If we start to lose focus, we could miss something important."

"Sorry," Jones muttered, his face flushed with embarrassment. "But the only time I see stuff like this is late night on Cinemax."

Greene led Payne and Jones through a back corridor, and before long they were strolling through the dancers' dressing room. Surprisingly, none of the undressed women were bothered by the men's presence. When they reached the back corner of the room, Greene spoke to the security guard who stood outside of a private office. "Let Terrell know I'm here. He's expecting me." The guard quickly opened the thick metal door to get authorization from the club's owner but noticed that he was on the phone.

"It'll be one minute, Mr. Greene. Mr. Murray is finishing up a call."

Greene nodded, then returned his attention to Payne and Jones. It was time to supply them with some background information on the man they were about to meet. "Terrell Murray is one of the most influential men in New Orleans, even though you'll rarely hear his name mentioned in high society. He tends to stay out of politics and high finance and prefers to deal with the seedier side of the city—strip clubs, prostitution, gambling, and so on. Very few things of an illegal nature get done in Orleans Parish without his permission or knowledge, so there is a very good chance that he'll be able to point us in the right direction."

Payne nodded. "And I take it you'll do all of the talking?"

"Since he doesn't know you, he won't help you. Fortunately, he's an avid football fan and has a place in his heart for me, so I'll be able to ask him anything that you guys want to know. I obviously understand the basics of your case, so I'll get him to talk about the tattoo and the kidnapping, but is there anything else you want to find out?"

Payne shook his head before they were led into Murray's private office.

The well-lit room was immaculately maintained and outfitted with French Neoclassical furniture from the late seventeen hundreds—definitely not what Payne and Jones were expecting to find. Four Louis XVI chairs, possessing the classic straight lines of the period, encircled a round wooden table that sat in the middle of the hardwood floor. Gold trim lined the walls, ceilings, and picture frames of the chamber, matching a chandelier that dangled above the sitting area. The room's artwork was obviously influenced by the Roman Empire, a motif that reflected the French's interest in the designs of the ancient cities of Pompeii and Herculaneum. A marble bust of Tiberius, the second emperor of Rome, sat proudly on a pedestal in the far corner.

An elderly black man, dressed in a pale gray suit and an open-collared shirt, stood from his seat behind his Louis XVI desk and greeted his visitors with a warm smile. "Please come in. Make yourself at home."

"Thank you," Payne replied as he soaked in the office's decor. "This is an impressive setup you have here. It's like a museum."

Murray shook Payne's hand and thanked him for the compliment. "First of all, enough with the formalities. If you're a friend of Levon's, there's no need to call me *sir*. Please, my name is Terrell." Payne nodded in understanding. "And as far as this room is concerned, antiques are a hobby of mine. I own a number of shops on Royal Street, but I'm afraid I deny my customers the opportunity to buy the best items. I tend to keep them for myself."

"And you've done a wonderful job," Jones added. "You truly have."

"Good, I'm glad you like it." Murray motioned for the men to be seated in the Louis XVI chairs and eagerly joined them. "So, Levon, what brings you here on a Friday night to see an old man like me? I know it can't be companionship because most of the lovely ladies of the club would be more than willing to go home with you."

Greene smiled at the thought. "Actually, I've come for your knowledge of the city. My friends and I are in search of a particular gang that operates in the area, and we were hoping that you could point us in the right direction."

Murray furrowed his wrinkled brow before speaking. "And am I to guess the name of the gang, or would you like to give me that information?"

"That's one of the reasons I came to you. The only thing we know is the design of their Holotat. It's in the shape of the letter *P* and uses a bloody dagger in the image."

"Yes," Murray replied with the blank face of a gambler. "I know that tattoo, and its appearance is a recent one to this city. Unfortunately, I know little about the men who wear them. I am sorry I cannot tell you more."

Without saying a word, Payne turned toward Greene and pleaded for him to dig deeper. Payne sensed that the old man was holding something back, and Greene picked up on the nonverbal request to continue.

"Terrell, I know that you try to stay out of other people's business, but in this case, I'm hoping you'll make an exception. Earlier today a man bearing that Holotat burst into the apartment of Jon's girlfriend and abducted her. So far, there's been no ransom demand and very little police activity. We're afraid if we don't do something immediately we may be too late. Please, any lead that you can give us would be appreciated."

Murray considered Greene's plea for several stress-filled seconds before nodding. "Above Rampart Street near St. Louis Cemetery #1, there is a small tattoo shop. It is operated by a man known as Jamaican Sam. He's the most popular skin artist in the area, and I would bet he's the man responsible for designing that Holotat. Go to him, and see where it leads you."

CHAPTER 19

Galléon Township Docks
Galléon, Louisiana
(37 miles southeast of New Orleans)

THE driver of the Washington Parish ambulance stopped near the narrow dock, then made a three-point turn in the gravel driveway. Once the vehicle pointed away from the Gulf of Mexico, he backed it carefully to the edge of the secluded pier. Satisfied with its positioning, he turned off the motor and stepped under the wharf's lone streetlight.

Tension was evident on his face.

While listening to the lapping water, he checked his watch and realized he was a few minutes early. To kill time, he pulled a cigarette from his pocket and lit it with a paper match. He took a deep drag, then blew a puff of smoke into the nighttime air.

This would be his last delivery for a while, and for that he was quite thankful. He didn't know why, but he'd grown more and more anxious with each mission that he'd completed for the Plantation. At first, he blamed his uncomfortable feelings on the recent death of his aunt. He assumed her passing had caused some sort of subconscious guilt since his after-hours duties centered on the shipment of cadavers for medical experiments. But lately, his concerns were a little more tangible. Snippets of overheard conversations, copies of phony death certificates, and deliveries that were scheduled for the dead of night.

All of which made him nervous.

But that was only part of it. What freaked him out more than anything were the sounds. On more than one occasion, he could've sworn he heard noises coming from the back of his ambulance—loud thumps emerging from the sealed containers, muffled screams leaking from the crates of the dead. God, the thought of it made him shudder.

To calm down, he took another drag on his cigarette and stared at the warm waters of the gulf. Something about this didn't seem right.

As he continued to wait, he pondered his role as a deliveryman, thinking back to the day he was first hired. A well-dressed black man spotted him washing his ambulance and asked him if he was interested in making some extra cash. The man claimed he was operating a private medical center off the coast in Breton Sound and was looking for the quickest way to deliver his research from Lakefront Airport to his new facility. Since emergency vehicles were given special privileges on the roadway, he felt that an ambulance would be the most efficient mode of transportation. Plus, he pointed out, he was looking for someone who would be comfortable around dead bodies and felt a medical worker would be perfect.

The driver glanced at his watch again and realized he still had a few minutes until the workers from the Plantation would arrive. If he hurried, he figured he could sneak into the back of his ambulance and investigate the crates that had been loaded for him at the airport.

"Screw it," he said aloud.

He emphasized his statement by slamming his cigarette into the water.

With quiet determination, he opened the door of the ambulance and climbed across the front seat. Sliding through the narrow entryway, he crept into the back and quickly grabbed the paperwork that had been attached to the top of the first wooden container. It read:

WALKER, ARIANE
28 YEARS OLD
WEXFORD, PA
JULY 2

Wow, he thought to himself. She died earlier today. That's pretty quick for someone to be moved across state lines.

He continued to flip through the documents, hoping to find a cause of death or the reason she was going to be examined, but the sheets were filled with numbers and other data that he was unable to comprehend.

Taking a deep breath, he glanced at his watch again. They would be here soon. And the last thing he wanted was to be caught snooping. Not only would they refuse to pay him, but he realized he might end up in one of the coffins as well.

AFTER leaving the ambulance, the small boat navigated the narrow channel of the cypress swamp, carefully avoiding any logs or stumps that would puncture its bow. As it eased against the moss-covered dock, the captain of the vessel tossed a rope to one of the guards, who quickly attached it to its anchoring post.

The craft was now secured.

Octavian Holmes emerged from the shadows of the stern and shouted terse orders to the men on cargo duty. The workers, dressed in black fatigues and carrying firearms, hauled the two wooden crates to a waiting truck. Once Holmes climbed into the back of the vehicle, the driver started the motor and maneuvered the shipment through the thick camouflage of the island's foliage. A short time later, the flatbed truck burst from the claustrophobic world of leaves into the neatly manicured grounds of the Plantation.

"Stop here," Holmes growled with authority.

The workers lifted the wooden crates from the vehicle and placed them on the charred remains of the burned cross. As Holmes watched closely, they tore into the crates with crowbars and within seconds the boxes were reduced to shreds. Cautiously, the men lifted the two unconscious prisoners from the dismantled containers and placed them in the cool grass.

"They're all yours, sir."

Holmes nodded while studying the paperwork of his new arrivals. Satisfied, he bent over to examine their sleeping forms and immediately liked what he saw. The first captive was an elderly man with a strong jaw, thinning white hair, and a deep surfer's tan. He was in amazing physical shape for his age, possessing great muscle tone despite his seventy-one years of life. His wrists were thick, his shoulders broad, and his stomach carried little flab.

"Jake Ross," he mumbled as he nudged the man's hip. "I bet you're still a pit bull, huh?"

When he was done with the senior citizen, he turned his attention to the drugged female, and her beauty instantly overwhelmed him. Her chestnut hair flowed over her rosy cheeks, cascading down her neck and onto her slender shoulders like a tropical waterfall. Her bosom, concealed under a bright red golf shirt, danced with each life-sustaining breath, and the image stirred something deep within Holmes. Her legs, tanned and athletic, were in full view since her white skirt had been torn during her cross-country journey. But even in rest, they possessed the fragile grace of a master ballerina's.

And her face—her gorgeous face—was the most beautiful he had seen in a very long time.

After catching his breath, Holmes dropped to his knees and kissed the girl on her lips. "Ariane Walker," he whispered, "it's a pleasure to have you on my island."

With a smile on his face, Holmes scooped her off of the turf and gently folded her frame over his left shoulder. As her arms dangled against his muscular back, he carried the unconscious girl toward her cabin with little effort. His eighteen years of work as a mercenary, which required stamina, strength, and discipline, guaranteed a level of physical conditioning that few men could ever hope to achieve. His missions had taken him through the severe warmth of the equator, the extreme cold of the Arctic Circle, and all the milder climates in between. In the process, he had learned how to survive anything that this world was capable of throwing at him.

And because of that, invincibility radiated from him like heat from a flame.

When he reached Ariane's cabin, he paused briefly, letting one of the guards unlock the exterior deadbolt. "You go in first," Holmes ordered. "Make sure her roommates are facing the wall in the back corner of the room." The guard did what he was told, threatening Tonya and Robert Edwards until they were properly positioned.

"All clear, sir."

Holmes walked into the cabin and eased Ariane onto the hard ground. Then, before either captive could see his face, he turned from the room and disappeared into the dark night, leaving Tonya to take care of another family member.

This time, her unconscious baby sister.

CHAPTER 20

Saturday, July 3rd

IN New Orleans, St. Louis Cemeteries #1 and #2 are referred to by locals as "cities of the dead." Designed in the eighteenth century, both graveyards feature elaborate aboveground vaults and French inscriptions that are both poetic and charming. Unfortunately, a nighttime visit to either burial ground is liable to add to the body count of the sacred lands. Located west of Louis Armstrong Park, this area is known as one of the most dangerous in the city. Gangs and criminals control the territories to the north of Rampart Street, and they use the popularity of the graveyards to ambush unsuspecting tourists.

Before leaving the safety of their Mustang, Payne, Jones, and Greene gazed at the terrain like antelopes surveying a water hole. They carefully searched the shadows of the land, looking for predators that lay in wait, hunting for a clear passage to their intended destination. When they were satisfied, they crept cautiously from their vehicle.

"If I'm not mistaken," Greene stated, "the tattoo shop should be right ahead of us."

The men continued their walk in silence until they found

a small shop with a flickering neon sign that said *Sam's Tattoos* in the window. Like most tattoo parlors, this one stayed open after midnight to cater to the bar crowd. Glancing at a historical plaque that was fastened to the building's front, Greene pushed the door aside. Chimes from a small bell announced their presence.

A tall white man, dressed in an elaborately tie-dyed shirt and baggy denim shorts, emerged from behind a wall of dangling beads and greeted his customers with a nod of his head. As he did, his braided orange hair fell across his pale green eyes while his shaggy beard bunched up in the folds of his neck. Tattoos covered the tanned flesh of his arms and legs.

"What can I do for you dudes?" he asked in the syntax of a stoner.

As Payne studied the employee, he realized it looked like a box of Skittles had thrown up on the guy. "We're looking for a man named Jamaican Sam. Can you tell us where to find him?"

"Dude! You're in luck. Sam, I am!"

The three men looked at each other in confusion. They were expecting their contact be a little more Jamaican and a little less Dr. Seuss.

"You mean you're the owner?" Payne asked. "You don't look like I pictured you."

"Is it the nickname, dude? People always get thrown by my nickname." The three men nodded at the walking rainbow. "Damn! I gotta get me a new nickname."

Jones knew he was going to regret asking it, but for the sake of curiosity, he had to know. "How did you get the name Jamaican Sam?"

"Well, dude, the Sam part was easy because, you see, that's my name. But the Jamaican part, well, that's a little more complex. A couple years ago, a bro from the islands came in to get some ink done. I did this bitchin' drawing of a naked hottie and put it on his back. Once I was finished, he was pretty stoked. In a heavily accented voice, the dude said, 'Ja makin' Sam's name known t'roughout da city, mon!' Well, some customers overheard it, and they lumped *ja makin'* with the *Sam*, so people started calling me Jamaican Sam." He punctuated his story with a huge grin. "Pretty sweet, eh?"

As fascinating as the story was, Payne didn't come to this part of town to learn Sam's history. He had more important things to find out—things that could possibly save his girlfriend. "I don't mean to be rude, but I was hoping you could give us some help."

With his left hand, Sam brushed his braided orange locks from his eyes. "Like I said in the beginning, what can I do for you dudes?"

"Actually, you can help me with a tattoo. I recently saw an elaborate design on this guy on the bus. The moment I saw it, I knew I wanted to have it. I just knew it! Unfortunately, before I had a chance to ask him where he got it done, we arrived at his stop and he disappeared. Do you think you could tell me who drew it for him?"

Sam shook his head violently, trying to clear his head. "Hold up. Let me see if I understand your quandary. You spotted a slammin' tat, and you expect me, even though I've never seen it, to picture it in my mind and tell you who did it? That's some challenge, dude."

"But can you do it?" Payne demanded.

It took thirty seconds for Sam to reply, but he finally shrugged his shoulders. "I don't see why not. But it'll cost ya twenty bucks." Payne handed him the money, and Sam quickly stuffed the bill into his multicolored boxers, which could be seen above the waistline of his shorts. "What did this Picasso look like?"

"It was in the shape of the letter *P*. The straight part of the *P* was a dagger, and—"

"Whoa!" Sam gasped, sounding like Keanu Reeves. "Was there, like, blood dripping from the dagger?"

Payne stared at the guy—he couldn't have been older than twenty-two—and nodded. "So, you're familiar with it?"

Sam walked over to his counter and flipped through a picture album of some of his most impressive designs. When he reached the page he was looking for, he handed the book to Payne. "The tat you're looking for is one of mine. How cool is that? Kind of a small globe, eh?"

"Yeah," Jones grunted, who suddenly didn't like the precision of Terrell Murray's off-the-cuff recommendation. "Way too small for my taste."

Payne picked up on Jones's tone and instinctively touched the gun that he'd concealed under the flap of his shirt. "What can you tell me about its design?"

Sam scratched his bright orange beard for a moment, pondering his position, then shook his head from side to side. "It just ain't worth it, dude." He reached into his boxer shorts and withdrew Payne's twenty dollars. "You can take your money back. I've got nothing for ya."

Payne looked at the money with disapproval. He wasn't willing to touch something that had been stored in Sam's underwear. Nor was he about to let him off the hook that easily. "A deal's a deal. You accepted the cash, now it's time to give me some info."

"Sorry, dude, but I just can't do that!" Sam laid the money on the counter and slowly backed away. "I made a previous deal with a group of brothers that requested my work for that particular job. I told them my lips were *el sealed-o* if anyone asked me about that tat."

"How many people were in the group?" Jones asked.

Sam shrugged, then let out a weasely little laugh. "Sorry, bro. I don't remember getting any money from you, so I don't owe you any info. You dig?"

Payne grinned at Sam and waited for the orange-haired freak to return his smile. When he did, Payne pulled his firearm into view and nestled it under the artist's hairy chin. "First, you referred to a bunch of black men as 'brothers,' and then you referred to my friend as your 'bro.' Now you're going to test my patience even further by refusing to answer a simple question? Sorry, bro, that's not the way my friends and I operate."

"Wait a second," Sam gulped, as the color drained from his face. "Did you guys come in together? Oh, dude, I didn't know that! If I had known that, I wouldn't have been so shady!"

Payne nodded, but refused to lower his gun. "Tell us about this group, Sam, before my finger gets a twitch and I add some red to your obnoxious shirt."

"Well, a bunch of brothers . . . uh, I mean, Africans came here a couple weeks ago—"

Jones quickly corrected him. "The appropriate term is African Americans."

"No, dude, not in this case. These dudes were African."

Payne raised an eyebrow. "Continue."

"Anyways," Sam stuttered, "they were looking for a Holotat. They told me the name of their gang and what they were looking for, then left the rest up to me. They gave me some cash and told me to have a tat design by the next day." Sam pointed to the picture in the album. "This is what I came up with, dude. Honest!"

"What was the name of the gang?" Payne demanded.

"Dude, I can't tell ya that. I just can't."

Payne pushed the barrel of his gun even harder against Sam's throat, and as he did, he noticed Sam start to tremble with fear. "Sammy? I have a policy that prevents me from killing the mentally challenged, but since we're in a hurry, I might be willing to make an exception."

Sam took a trouble-filled breath, then answered. "I've got a problem, dude. When the group got their tats, they threatened to kill me if I told anyone about their posse. Now, here you are, and you're threatening to kill me if I *don't* tell you about their posse. Well, you don't have to be Alex Trebek to see that I'm in jeopardy."

"Jeez," Payne said. "That jeopardy comment was pretty funny."

"Did you like that?" Sam asked, hoping to lighten the mood. "I just made that up."

"You did?" Payne grunted. "Well, unless you want it to be the last clever thing you say, I think you should start talking. What's the name of the gang?"

Sam closed his eyes in thought. After thinking about all

of the consequences, he figured it was better to possibly die later than to definitely die now. "The Plantation Posse."

Payne lowered his weapon. "And what can you tell us about this Posse?"

"I don't know," Sam mumbled. "They were young, black, and very athletic-looking."

"Wow," Greene remarked. "You just described every team in the NBA. You gotta do better than that."

"And some of the guys had thick African accents."

"Come on!" he objected. "My NBA comment is still accurate."

Sam glared at the ex–football star. After a moment, a flash of recognition crossed his face. "Whoa, dude, I know you. I know who you are!"

Greene cursed under his breath. He knew going into this partnership that there was a good chance that he was going to be recognized. Now it was just a matter of how he was going to handle it. "Who I am is not important, you box-of-crayons-looking motherfucker! What *is* important is my boy's question. What did these guys look like?"

The rage in Greene's voice was enough to silence Sam. There was no way he wanted to piss off the Buffalo Soldier. "Okay, dude, I'll tell you anything you want to know, just don't hurt me! I've got a low threshold for pain."

Greene nodded. "I appreciate your honesty. In return, I promise not to test that threshold. But instead of talking to me, I want you to talk to my friends. Okay? And while you're telling them everything that they need to know, I'm gonna go in the back and use your bathroom." He turned toward Payne and Jones, looking for permission. "That is, if you guys can handle things alone for a couple of minutes."

Payne patted Greene on his shoulder. "Thanks, I think we can take over from here."

"While you're back there," Jones added quietly, "check to see if anybody is hiding or if there's another way into this place. I'm not in the mood for any surprises."

Greene hustled into the back and did what was requested.

"Things look fine," he yelled to Payne and Jones. "There's nothing back here that can hurt you."

Payne grinned as he leaned against the counter. "Sorry, Sam. Since you're all out of allies, it appears that you're kind of stuck. You have no choice but to tell us about the Posse."

"Dude, I swear, I can't describe them any better than I have. The only thing in my brain is their black clothes and the large roll of bills they were toting. Other than that, nothing!"

Payne nodded, beginning to believe Sam's claim. He realized that it would be tough for anyone to remember specific details about a group of men who had visited him several weeks ago, especially if they were foreigners. One face would blend in with the next. "Fine, let's get off their appearance. Why don't you tell me about the tattoo? What did the image symbolize?"

Sam scratched his beard while studying the picture from his album. "Well, dude, the *P* obviously stands for *Plantation Posse*, but I bet you figured that out, huh?"

"Come on," Payne mumbled. "Tell us something that might actually be useful."

"Fine!" Sam growled. "I'll tell you what you want to know, but I'm warning you dudes, you're forcing me to sign my own death warrant. My blood's gonna be on your hands!"

And in a blink of an eye, Sam's words became prophetic.

CHAPTER 21

THUNDER echoed from across the street as the sniper pulled the trigger on his rifle. His first shot shattered the window of the tattoo shop, sending thousands of knifelike shards in every direction. As they fell to the floor in a melodic song, the bullet entered the right eye of its victim, obliterating Sam's brain and skull in a single flash.

Without pausing to think, Payne and Jones reacted to the situation like it was an everyday occurrence. Their experiences with the MANIACs had prepared them for far worse. Payne dashed for cover in the front corner of the shop, which was away from the broken window and allowed him to take a clean shot at anyone who entered the front door. Meanwhile, Jones headed in the opposite direction, taking refuge behind the front counter.

"Are you all right?" Jones yelled as he pulled out his Glock.

"I'm not perfect, but I'm better than Sam."

Jones glanced around the corner and stared at the near-headless victim. Crimson gushed from the gaping hole where his face used to be. Hair, brain, and bone clung to the back wall like chunky spaghetti sauce.

"We're dealing with a serious weapon, Jon. Whatever it is tore right through his skull."

Payne surveyed the scene before offering his summation of the kill. "From the looks of it, the shooter has an elevated position."

"Why do you say that?"

"Look at the window if you can. The top is the only part that's broken, and the only way a bullet can do that and hit a man in the head is if it was discharged from above."

Jones nodded in agreement. "If that's the case, this wasn't a drive-by. The bastard's probably on a roof or in a tree. No way we'll be able to nail him from this angle."

"You're probably right. That's why we're going to have to go outside and get him."

Jones put his finger in his ear and tried to unclog it. "Sorry, I must've misheard you. Did you say we should go out there and get him?"

"Yes, princess, that's what I said."

The statement didn't sit well with Jones. "But we don't know what we're up against! Hell, we don't know a damn thing, and you want us to go outside with our weapons blazing? Am I Butch or Sundance?"

Payne chuckled at Jones's reaction. He expected something more soldierly from an ex-MANIAC. "Wow, wait until I tell the fellas about this at our next squad reunion. They won't believe how quickly you've lost your nerve!"

"I haven't lost my nerve, Jon. I've gained common sense. What good is it to go outside and face a sniper?"

"What good? Going out there could save Ariane's life!"

"How do you figure?"

"Think about it! Why was Sam killed? What purpose could that have served?"

Jones shrugged. "I don't know. Somebody wanted to keep him quiet."

"Exactly! Sam must've known something, and it must've been pretty damn important."

"Like what?"

"I have no idea. Maybe he could identify someone, or has

a billing address in his files, or maybe, just maybe, he knew something about Ariane. Truthfully, I don't know. But if we don't go outside, our odds of getting an answer go down considerably. And you know it!"

"Shit," Jones grumbled, realizing what Payne had in mind. "You're hoping to take this guy alive, aren't you?"

Payne nodded. "How else is he going to be useful?"

Jones knew that Payne was right, that they needed to talk to the guy, but he also realized the level of danger that would be involved. If the sniper was still outside, he was probably waiting for them to make a move. And the moment they did— *bang!* Because that's how snipers operated. They patiently waited for their targets to do something stupid, then they took full advantage.

"So, are you coming or not?" Payne asked in a less than pleasant tone. "'Cause if you aren't, I gotta start looking for a new best friend."

"Ah, man, why did you have to go there? Anytime you need a favor, you always pull out the best-friend card. Fine, I'll help you out, but I'm not doing this because of your stupid threat. I'm doing this because I need the exercise."

Payne grinned in appreciation. "The first thing we need to do is figure out how we're going to get out of here. Since the door is glass, he'll pick us off before we even open it. We'll need to find a different exit."

"How about the window? If I knock out the bottom half, we could slip behind one of the cars outside with little exposure time. Plus, it'll let this guy know we're armed."

"Sounds good. But before we go, let me get the lights. The less this guy sees, the better."

Jones liked the idea. Darkness would improve their odds even more. "Can you reach 'em from there, or are you going to have to shoot 'em out?"

Payne leaned out from his hiding place and stared at the small panel of switches near the door. It would take some doing, but he felt he could reach the buttons without risking his life.

"No problem," he lied. "Piece of cake."

Moving quickly, Payne dropped to his hands and stomach and crawled across the vinyl floor. He did his best to avoid the broken glass, but since there were chunks of it everywhere, he found himself bleeding immediately.

"Looking good," Jones whispered as he peered out from behind the counter. "In about two feet, you'll be directly under the switch. Okay, stop."

Payne tilted his head back and tried to reach the metal panel above him, but the damn thing was a foot too high. That meant he'd have to leave the safety of the floor to reach it. Of course, the advantage he'd gain with darkness outweighed the risk of going for the lights. While keeping his torso parallel to the floor, he stretched his bloody hand upward, inching it slowly along the wall until he felt the cold surface of the switch.

"Let's see if you like the dark," Payne said as he turned off the lights.

The gunman replied with a blitzkrieg that tore through the tiny shop. Glass, wood, and plaster erupted into the air as the sightless sniper relied on blind luck and sheer volume to hit his targets. A second wave followed quickly, which shattered the front door and showered the room with a stream of razor-sharp confetti, but Payne remained calm, keeping his face covered and his body against the base of the thick front wall.

"I guess not," he sneered.

When the violence subsided, Payne risked a quick peek into the back of the shop. Things were blurry at first because of the lack of light and a cloud of dust, but after a few seconds, he realized the counter that shielded Jones had taken more hits than a hippie at Woodstock.

"D.J.," Payne whispered, "are you all right?"

"Yeah, and very lucky. I don't know how that last batch missed me."

"Me, either." Payne glanced around the shop and realized they couldn't stay there much longer. "We have to get out of here. If we stay put, he's going to hit us eventually."

Jones agreed. "He did us a favor by knocking out the

door and window. If you want, I can fire a few clearing shots so you can bolt outside."

Payne nodded. Even though Jones wouldn't be aiming at the sniper, he would minimize the risk of return fire, which would allow him to slip outside. Of course, the drawback to the plan was the possibility of more than one gunman. If someone was waiting near the door, he'd shoot Payne rather easily.

But it was a chance they had to take.

"Are you ready?" Payne asked as he peered through the darkness. "On the count of three, shoot through the window as I head for the door."

"You got it."

"One," Payne whispered as he adjusted the Glock in his sweaty right hand.

"Two," muttered Jones as he peered at his glassless target.

"Three!" they yelled in unison.

With a burst of adrenaline, Payne leapt from the ground and sprinted out the door while Jones aimed his gun at the window and fired. Or at least tried to. Unfortunately, nothing came out when he squeezed the Glock's trigger, which left his friend in a very precarious position.

The concrete under Payne's feet exploded in wispy puffs of smoke as the gunman opened fire from the roof across the street. With nowhere else to go, Payne cut sharply to his right and dove behind the closest car he saw, a maneuver that tore most of the skin from his knees. In Payne's mind, it was a fair trade. He definitely preferred scabs to bullet holes.

"Are you all right?" Jones called from inside.

"I'm fine!" Payne snarled. "Where the hell was my cover fire?"

"Sorry. I had a misfire. The damn gun wouldn't shoot."

"What do you mean it wouldn't shoot? You have to pull the trigger, you know."

Jones grinned, countering the insult with a fact that Payne had overlooked. "Don't be mad at me, be mad at the source. Remember, you got your gun from the same place as me."

Growling softly, Payne focused his attention on the weapon in his hand. If it had the same malfunction as Jones's, he wouldn't have a chance against the sniper. The truth was he had slim odds to begin with, but with a broken firearm, he would be in serious trouble.

"Shit," he mumbled to himself. There was only one way to find out.

Payne pointed his Glock toward the building across the street and squeezed the trigger. But nothing happened. No explosion. No discharge. Just a quiet click.

In situations like this, Payne was taught to use a simple corrective technique known as "tap, rack, bang." He tapped the bottom of the handle to make sure his magazine was properly engaged. Then he racked the gun, ejecting the misfired round and chambering the next one. Finally, he pulled the trigger again, hoping to hear a bang.

But in this case, the only sound he heard was another click.

"Well?" Jones called from inside the shop. He had tried the same technique without any luck.

"We're so screwed we should be wearing condoms."

Jones grinned. "Don't give up hope yet. What kind of shot is this guy? Any good?"

Payne glanced at the holes in the sidewalk and sighed at the damage that had been done. "Not really. If he was, I wouldn't be talking to you right now."

"And he's probably working alone, huh?"

"If he wasn't, his partner would've nailed me by now."

"If that's the case, then what are we afraid of? Are we going to let some redneck knock off two of this country's best soldiers, or are we going to come up with a plan to take this guy out?"

"If I was a betting man, I'd put my money on the redneck."

"I'm serious! We've been in several situations worse than this, and we've always made it out."

Payne grunted as he stared at his broken Glock. "Fine, let's list everything that we have, and maybe a plan will become obvious."

Jones nodded. "As far as I can tell, we have two defective handguns and . . ."

"And?" Payne muttered, hoping that he was forgetting something important.

"And that's about it! As far as I can tell, we have two broken Glocks."

Payne leaned his head against the Chevy Celebrity that protected him and groaned. Their current inventory wouldn't stop a mugger, let alone a well-placed sniper. "Is there anything else in there that can be used? A gun behind the counter? A telephone? A flashlight?"

"Oh, shit!" Jones suddenly shrieked. "I just thought of something big!"

"Oh, yeah? What's that?"

"Levon!"

The answer stunned Payne. Somehow he had completely forgotten about Greene. "Holy hell! Why don't you see where that badass is hiding?"

"Be back in a flash."

Payne snuggled up against the car the best he could, trying to conceal his body under the maroon frame. He realized if the sniper attempted a ground assault, the only way he could protect himself was by hiding under the car. Thankfully, before that was necessary, Payne detected a sound in the far-off distance. At first he wasn't sure if he was imagining it or not, but after a few seconds of listening, he knew that he wasn't. It was the wail of sirens, and they were headed his way.

"Jon?" Jones shouted from the back of the shop. "Is that what I think it is?"

Payne peered underneath the Chevy and saw several squad cars pulling onto his street. "Yes, Mr. Jones, the cavalry has arrived!"

"Thank God."

"You said it." Payne leaned back on the sidewalk, his

legs still underneath the car for protection. "By the way, how's Levon doing?"

Instead of shouting his response, Jones scrambled out of the store and took a seat next to his friend. Once he was safely behind the car, he turned toward Payne and looked him dead in the eye. "You're not going to believe this. You're really not."

"What now?"

"I don't even know how to start, but . . ." Jones struggled for the right words to break the news to his friend. "Levon is gone."

Payne sat upright, the color draining from his face. "Oh, my God! How did he—"

"No," Jones said as he grabbed Payne's arm. "He's not *dead* gone. He's *gone* gone. I don't know how he did it, but that slippery son of a bitch managed to escape."

CHAPTER 22

AS the police pulled to a screeching stop in front of Sam's Tattoos, Payne stared at Jones, trying to determine if his best friend was serious. After several seconds, Payne decided that he was. "Levon has disappeared?"

"Yep. He's gone."

Payne shook his head in disbelief. "How is that possible? He's, like, eight feet tall and weighs five hundred pounds, yet you managed to lose him in an empty room."

"That's what I said."

"I thought you were supposed to be a professional detective."

"I am. And in my professional opinion, I'm telling you he's not in there."

Payne leaned closer to Jones and tried to smell his breath. "Have you been drinking?"

Jones grinned. "I wish I was."

Payne was about to reply, but before he had a chance, a booming voice shattered the stillness of the night.

"We see you behind the car," announced a patrolman through his bullhorn. "Put your hands where we can see them and come out very slowly."

The two of them did as they were told and were frisked by a team of gun-toting officers.

"Gentlemen," barked Sergeant Rutherford, the lead officer at the scene, "I'm sure you realize y'all have a lot of explaining to do."

Rutherford was in his mid-forties and possessed the face of an ex-boxer. His nose was crooked, his teeth were fake, and his face was dotted with several scars. His thick black hair was splashed with gray, but his police hat covered most of it.

"Before I throw you guys in cuffs and haul your asses to the station, you need to tell me what happened here."

Payne cleared his throat and began to speak before Jones had a chance to say anything. "My buddy and I just flew in to New Orleans earlier tonight for a little R & R. We rented a car, got something to eat, and decided to do something out of the ordinary. A local told us that Jamaican Sam drew the best tattoos in the whole darn state—"

"A lovely state, I might add."

"It sure is, D.J. Anyway, we decided to come here to check out his craftsmanship."

"We were impressed. Very colorful stuff."

"But we were here for less than ten minutes when somebody shot Sam from across the street."

"We think from that rooftop there," Jones said, pointing. "With a sniper rifle."

"We wanted to fight back."

"But we didn't have any weapons."

Payne nodded. "I hid in the corner for protection, and D.J. dove behind the counter."

"When I was back there, I found two guns. I tossed one to Jon and kept the other for myself."

"We tried to use them when the madman started shooting at us."

"But neither of them worked."

"I left mine on the sidewalk," Payne volunteered.

"And mine is inside."

"You can check for yourself. Neither of them is capable of firing a round."

"Yep," Jones seconded. "I squeezed the trigger, but it wouldn't make a bang or nothing."

Payne paused in thought. "Anything else you can think of?"

Jones shook his head. "Nope. I think that covers it."

Payne nodded in agreement. "That's about all we've got, sir. Hopefully that makes your report pretty easy to write."

Rutherford studied the two men and smiled. He wanted to comment on the conversation but was simply too fascinated to speak. Even though Payne's and Jones's statements were coming from two different voices, it was like they were coming from the same mind. When Payne started a sentence, Jones finished it. If Jones started, Payne ended it. Rutherford had been on the job for over twenty years and had never seen anything like it.

"Okay," the cop muttered as he emerged from his trance. "We'll take a look around and see if your story checks out. If it does, y'all have nothing to worry about. I'll have you back on your vacation by sunrise. However, if it doesn't, then you might be staying here in our state"—Rutherford turned his head toward Jones and smirked—"pardon me, our *lovely* state, for a lot longer than you were planning. In the meantime, why don't you guys show me some ID? That'll give me a chance to see if y'all have escaped from a mental health facility, which is a distinct possibility in my book."

AFTER examining the scene for an hour, Rutherford decided that Payne and Jones were telling the truth. But before he let them go, he decided to discuss the facts with his second in command. "Richie, can you think of any reason to hold these two any longer?"

The second cop, white and overweight, glanced at his notes and shook his head. "Nah. From what we've found, these guys couldn't have been the shooter. The bullet that killed Sam matched the size of the casings from the roof across the street. The two Glocks found at the scene have no serial numbers, probably bought by Sam for protection. And just like the guys said, the damn things appeared to be unfired. We couldn't smell discharge."

"On top of that," Rutherford added, "the two suspects are covered in cuts and scratches, which were probably caused by flying glass. That means they were in the shop when the shooting started."

"Yep, and the initial 911 call mentioned a sniper as well."

"What about their histories? Any warrants?"

"We checked their backgrounds, and neither of them have any prior convictions. Both of them have military academy educations, and both are currently employed by a reputable company, Payne Industries. In fact, the white guy in your car is CEO of the corporation."

"You mean it's *his* corporation?" Rutherford asked.

"Yes, sir. He's the head honcho. Flew down here on his private jet."

"I'll be damned. What the hell is a rich corporate type doing in a New Orleans ghetto in the middle of the damn night?"

"Apparently getting a tattoo."

Rutherford laughed at the suggestion. "Kind of unlikely, huh?"

"Yeah, but I'll be honest with you. I don't think he flew all the way down here to kill Jamaican Sam, either. A rich man like that doesn't commit his own crimes. A millionaire pays to have them done for him."

Rutherford nodded. "True, but we've already decided that Payne and Jones didn't kill anyone, right? So what brings them here at this hour?"

"Drugs?"

"I doubt it. I ordered a background check on Jamaican Sam Fletcher, and he had no record other than a few busts for marijuana. The guy was a smoker, not a seller. The cops that patrol this neighborhood claim he ran a clean place. In fact, his artwork was so admired by the local gangs that thugs went out of their way to protect him."

"Where does that leave us?"

Rutherford didn't want to admit it, but he had no choice. "Honestly, it leaves us without a case. We can't charge these two without just cause, and we can't prove that these guys did anything wrong. We could hold them for twenty-four hours of questioning if we wanted to, but I guarantee that Payne would have a fancy-pants lawyer down here in the blink of an eye causing a big stink about something. No, thank you! It just wouldn't be worth it."

"Then we're kinda forced to let them go, huh?"

"It looks that way, but that doesn't mean we're gonna forget 'em."

The cop looked at his superior and grinned. "What do you have in mind? Some kind of tail?"

Rutherford laughed at the suggestion. "Nothing that drastic, at least not yet. I'm gonna do some digging when I get back to the station and see if I can turn up anything that makes sense. If I do, I'll nail these guys before they know what hit 'em." Rutherford groaned as he stared at the captives in the back of his squad car. "Let 'em loose, but tell 'em I want to have a brief chat with them before they leave."

While waiting for the duo, Rutherford leaned against a nearby building, ready to verbally pounce on the men at the first opportunity. Payne and Jones barely had time to stretch their legs before the veteran cop started his lecture.

"Gentlemen," he said sternly, "y'all should know better than to be roaming this type of neighborhood in the middle of the night. Violence is pretty common here, and the idiot that told you to visit Sam's shop at night should've known better. Y'all are lucky to be alive."

Payne nodded his head in agreement as he walked toward the sergeant. "Thanks to you, we are. If you guys didn't show up when you did, we would've been killed by the sniper for sure."

"Don't thank me," admitted the cop. "Thank the person who called 911. He was the one that made us aware of the shooting."

"Actually, I'd like to. Is the guy around?"

Rutherford shrugged while staring at the crowd that had

gathered across the street. "Probably, but I don't know where to find him. He used a pay phone to report the incident, but refused to leave his name."

Jones smiled to himself, wondering if Levon Greene was the person who'd made the call. If he had, they probably owed the Buffalo Soldier their lives. "If you manage to find out who it was, thank him for us, okay?"

Rutherford shook Jones's hand and smiled. "You got it." Then he turned to shake Payne's. "In the meantime, stay out of trouble, all right? Keep in mind if I hear your names mentioned at the station in connection with any other suspicious events during your vacation in New Orleans, I might be forced to reconsider your involvement. Do I make myself clear?"

Both men nodded even though they realized that their trouble was far from over.

In fact, it was just beginning.

CHAPTER 23

LIGHTNING bolts. The pain felt like lightning bolts surging through her brain.

Ariane did her best to ignore it—tried to open her eyes, tried to fight through the jackhammer that thumped inside her skull—but the agony was overwhelming. God, she wondered, what's wrong with me? She'd never felt this bad before. Ever. She'd suffered through hangovers, migraines, and a skiing accident that left her with a severe concussion, but in all her years, she had never come close to feeling like this.

Hell, it felt like she was giving birth through her nose. The pain was *that* intense.

To escape the pounding, Ariane was tempted to fall back asleep. She figured if she got a little more rest she'd have to feel a whole lot better than she did now. Then, if all went well, she'd roll out of bed like she had planned and whip Jonathon's butt in a round of golf.

Golf? Wait a second. Something about that didn't seem right. She tried to figure it out, struggled to put her snippets of memory together in an orderly fashion, but was unable to. She could vaguely remember waking up and brushing her teeth and getting a shower and . . . the door. Something about the door. She could remember someone pounding on her door.

Or was the pounding in her head?

Wow! She honestly didn't know. The details were hazy, like a painful childhood incident that had suddenly crept back into her consciousness. Why couldn't she remember the door? What was it about her door?

Ariane tried to open her eyes, fought to pry her lids apart, but the pain was too intense. Wave after wave crashed inside her head, causing her to lurch forward into the fetal position. As she did, the maelstrom surged toward her gut, inducing the worst muscle spasms of her life. To her it felt like her innards were exploding upward. Like her gallbladder, liver, and intestines were inching their way toward her mouth, swimming ever so slowly up the back of her throat on a viscous river of bile.

"What's wrong with me?" she called out, hoping God would provide her with an answer.

"Shhh," a motherly voice replied. "Just relax. The pain will soon pass. I promise."

The sound of a strange voice sent shock waves through Ariane.

"Who are you?" she shrieked, now trying to open her eyes with twice the urgency of before. "What are you doing in my bedroom?"

The voice sighed at the query. "You're not in your bedroom."

That was news to Ariane. She honestly couldn't remember leaving her apartment. "I'm not? Where am I, then? What's wrong with me?"

"I'm not sure where we are. I wish I knew. And as to what's wrong with you, you're having a reaction to the drugs. But don't worry, it'll pass quickly."

"Drugs?" Ariane mumbled.

"Yeah, sis, I said drugs." The female paused to let the information sink in.

Sis? Did she say *sis*? Why the hell would this person call her *sis*?

Oh, God! The reason suddenly dawned on her.

"Tonya? Is that you?"

Tonya Edwards looked down at Ariane and attempted to smile. "Of course it's me—unless you have another sister that you've been hiding."

"No, but . . ." The presence of her pregnant older sister only added to Ariane's confusion. Tonya lived in Colorado. What in the world was she doing in Pittsburgh? "Why are you here? Is something wrong?"

It was the understatement of the year.

"Yeah, sis, I'd say something is wrong."

Ariane swallowed, the bitter taste of bile still in her mouth. "Is it the baby?"

"The baby, Robert, you, me. Pretty much everything." Tonya tried to lower herself to the floor, but her belly prevented it. "I'm not sure why, but our family's been kidnapped."

SLIGHTLY banged up but happy to be alive, the two friends walked to their rented Mustang in total silence. As they strolled past the ancient cemetery, Payne shuddered slightly, realizing how close he'd come to his own funeral. If the sniper had been a little more accurate, Payne and Jones would've been returning to Pittsburgh in wooden crates, not in the comfort of a private jet.

"You're awfully quiet," Jones said, studying his silent friend. "Are you all right?"

Payne nodded as he slid into the car. "As good as can be expected."

After strapping himself in, Payne allowed his mind to drift back to the incident at the tattoo shop. Even though the shooting was unexpected, Payne knew that Ariane's kidnappers were bound to become aware of his presence. But the big question was, how? How did they find out about him so quickly? Was there a spy at the airport? At the Fishing Hole? Or was the late-night gunplay an unlucky coincidence? Maybe Sam's death had been ordered several days before, and the sniper just happened to show up at the same time they did. Sam was the first one eliminated, so maybe he was the number one priority of the hit. Maybe the Plantation Posse, or some unrelated gang, had been planning to silence him for an entirely different reason. Even though it seemed unlikely, it was a possibility.

Shit, in New Orleans, anything was possible. One trip to Mardi Gras would prove that.

"By the way," Jones asked, "where are we going? Or are you planning on driving around this city until someone starts shooting at us again?"

"That's not what I had in mind, but now that you mention it, that's better than anything I can come up with."

"Stumped already?"

"I wouldn't say stumped, but I'm pretty confused. There are simply too many variables floating around in my mind right now. And I can't figure out which ones are important."

"I was thinking the same thing. There are lots of questions and very few answers."

"You're right about that. However, two things are bothering me more than anything else. I can't figure them out for the life of me."

"And they are?"

"Number one, if Ariane was kidnapped for money, why the hell would the Posse try to kill me? I'm the one with the bank account. Why eliminate me? My death would instantly take away their chance of a big payday."

Jones nodded. It was a thought that hadn't entered his mind. "You're right. That's a pretty big issue, one that I can't answer. What's number two? Maybe I can help you with that."

"That one's even more confusing. Where the hell is Levon?"

CHAPTER 24

BECAUSE of his size and the weapon he carried, Levon Greene showed no fear as he walked through Louis Armstrong Park. Like most American cities, New Orleans had a policy against large, gun-toting black men walking in its city parks after midnight. But Greene knew he was in no danger of being stopped since most cops were at Sam's Tattoos, trying to solve that shooting.

As he emerged from the darkness of the tree-lined sidewalks, Greene tucked his pistol in the waistband of his Dockers, concealing it completely under his shirt. Despite the early-morning hour, up-tempo funk leaked from Donna's Bar and Grill, a famous jazz club off of St. Ann Street. A group of well-dressed men and women waited to show the bouncer their IDs. Greene didn't have the patience to linger in line, so he shook the hand of the starstruck guard and slipped inside without delay.

Celebrity had some privileges.

Since the sniper had prevented him from using the bathroom at Sam's, Greene quickly made his way to the rear of the club while trying to conceal his identity from as many people as he could. He simply didn't have time to sign autographs for anyone at the moment. There were more pressing matters on his mind—and his lower colon—to deal with. After making his way into the restroom, Greene found himself angered by his phone, which started to ring the moment he turned the lock on his stall door.

"Who's this?" he demanded.

"This is D.J.," Jones said, relieved. "Are you all right?"

The call was completely unexpected, like hearing the voice of a ghost, and it took Greene a moment to catch his breath. "Am *I* all right? I think the better question is, are *you* all right? I thought you were dead for sure! I can't believe you're alive! Did Jon make it, too?"

"He's fine. He's sitting next to me."

"I'll be a son of a bitch," Greene muttered. From the number of bullets fired, he assumed nobody in the front of the shop could've survived. And if someone had, he figured they'd be bleeding all over intensive care by now. "How about Sam? Did he make it?"

"I'm afraid not. The first shot took him out clean. He didn't have a chance."

"What about the next one hundred shots? What the hell did they hit?"

"Everything but us," Jones admitted. "I guess our military training helped us escape."

"Training? What kind of training teaches you to dodge bullets? Are you guys fucking ninjas?"

"I swear I never fucked a ninja in my life." Jones chuckled, hoping that Greene understood his joke. "The truth is, luck played a bigger role in our safety than I'm willing to admit."

"Man, how lucky can two guys get?"

"Speaking of lucky, how did you get out of there? I could've sworn we left you in Sam's bathroom. When we went to save you, you weren't in there. How did you pull that one off?"

Greene smiled as he thought about his easy escape, but it

was a secret that he wasn't ready to share. He wanted Payne and Jones to ponder the mystery for a little while longer. "I'll tell you in a little bit, okay? But I'm in a public restroom as we speak, and I don't know if there are people in the other stalls listening."

"What did you do? Flush yourself to another part of the city?"

Greene laughed. "No, nothing like that, but you'll have to wait a few more minutes for the details. Where are you guys now?"

Jones asked Payne for details. "We're somewhere in the French Quarter. Jon thinks it's called Conti Street."

"That's pretty close to me." Greene gave Jones directions to Donna's Bar and Grill and told him that he'd be waiting outside when they got there. "But first," he insisted, "I've got some urgent business to attend to, and I'm not willing to do it while we're on the phone."

THE Mustang stopped in front of the crowded club and pulled away with its new passenger. As the car picked up speed, Greene greeted Payne and Jones, warmly shaking their hands. "Military? You guys never told me you were in the military. What branch were you in?"

Payne answered first. "I went to the Naval Academy. After that I got selected by the government to work on a special forces unit."

"That's where I met him," Jones added. "I was assigned to the same team as Jon, even though I was from the Air Force. And we've been side by side ever since."

"I'll be damned," Greene muttered. "I'm sitting here with two Rambos. No wonder you guys were able to escape the tattoo parlor. I'm surprised you didn't kill the shooter in the process. What, are you guys rusty or something?"

"Actually, we wanted to get the bastard but weren't able to because of you."

Greene looked at Payne, confused. "Because of me? What did I do?"

"It's what you didn't do. You didn't get us guns that worked."

"They didn't work? What do you mean they didn't work?"

Jones jumped into the fray. "Just like he said. We pulled our triggers several times, and nothing came out. Like a guy with a vasectomy."

Payne grinned at the analogy. "Tell me more about your gun dealer. Has anything like this ever happened before?"

"No," Greene assured them. "He's got a first-class rep on the streets."

"Maybe so, but his faulty products almost got us killed." Payne slowed to a stop at a red light and turned toward Greene. "I'd love a chance to meet this guy. You know, to see if I get a good feeling about him. Do you think you could set something up?"

Greene glanced at Payne and shrugged. "I could, but it won't do you any good. You guys already met him, and you trusted him just fine."

"Terrell Murray?" Payne asked. "The owner of the Fishing Hole?"

Greene nodded. "The one and only."

"Why didn't you mention that before we talked to him?" Jones demanded.

"Terrell is very hush-hush about his activities. Sure, he owns and operates some skin clubs, but those things are legal and can't get him into trouble. What he refuses to do, though, is flaunt the things that could get him busted. If he sells something illegal, he deals with a restricted list of clientele, and if they betray him, he cuts them off immediately. That's why I purchased the weapons by myself and why I didn't mention his name earlier. Can you understand that?"

"Sure," Payne admitted. "That makes plenty of sense to me. So, why tell us now? If Terrell is so secretive, why risk his confidence by mentioning his name?"

"Sometimes you gotta betray one trust to gain another."

Payne and Jones pondered the comment, nodding their

heads in admiration. For an ex-jock, Greene possessed a pretty good understanding of human nature.

"And besides," he continued, "when we go to get your refund, I want you to do the talking. I'd feel safer if you pissed him off instead of me."

CHAPTER 25

AS they drove to the Fishing Hole, Jones patiently waited for Greene to answer the question that he'd asked earlier, but it was apparent that Greene had completely forgotten about it—or was trying to avoid it. "Levon, since you're out of the john now, can you please tell me how you managed to escape from Sam's? That's been bugging me for the past hour."

Payne glanced at Jones and smiled. "You must've been reading my mind. I was getting ready to ask him the same thing."

Realizing that he was the center of attention, Greene grinned mischievously, his eyes twinkling like a small child's at a birthday party. When he could hold it in no longer, he blurted the secret. "I went through the back wall."

Jones laughed in a disbelieving tone. "Who are you, the Kool-Aid guy? I don't remember seeing any Negro-shaped holes in the back room."

But Greene stuck by his story. "How hard did ya look?"

"Pretty damn hard."

"Apparently not hard enough, because I got my ass out."

Payne joined Greene in laughter. "He's got you there,

Sherlock. I guess you aren't the infallible detective after all."

Jones leaned forward to object. "Yeah, but—"

"Actually," Payne interrupted, "why don't you let him explain things? Maybe you can learn a thing or two from the big man."

Jones rolled his eyes while he waited for Greene to begin.

"Thank you, Jon. I'd love to help him out. When I got into the back, I did as you asked. I looked for anything suspicious, but there was nothing there but a bathroom and a closet."

"Right," Jones blurted. "That's what I found, too."

"So, like I said, I went into the bathroom to take care of my business, and—*boom! crash!*—I heard a gunshot then glass breaking in the front. I wanted to come out to check on things, but my pants were around my ankles, and that slowed me down a bit."

"I bet it did," Jones muttered.

"By the time I got my pants up, I heard a number of shots. Glass was breaking, walls were shattering, chaos! At that point, I assumed you guys were dead. I mean, come on! How was I supposed to know that you were commandos in a former life? Anyway, I figured I needed to get out of the place without going out the front door, right? I remembered from when I walked into the shop that there was a historical landmark plaque on the front wall, and it said the building used to be a part of the Underground Railroad."

"Seriously?" Jones asked.

Greene nodded. "Like I told you guys, I've been doing a lot of research on my hometown, and one of the things that fascinates me was New Orleans' role in the slave trade. A number of ports on the Gulf of Mexico were notorious for bringing slaves into this country, but at the same time, a number of ports were used to smuggle slaves out. Shit, there was so much diversity in this city during the eighteen hundreds that people often confused slaves with their masters. In fact, there was one period, in 1803, when ownership of New Orleans passed from Spain to France to the United

States in less than a month's time. If a city doesn't even know what country it belongs to, how's it gonna keep track of the people?"

Jones tried to absorb all of the information. Historical facts and local folklore normally fascinated him, but in this case, he wanted to get to the important stuff. He wanted to know how Greene got out of the damn shop without being seen. "Levon, not to be rude, but—"

"I know, I know. You want to know how I did it. Fine, I'll tell you. The landmark plaque clicked in my mind, and I remembered going on a tour or two where there was a trap-door or a hidden set of steps that allowed fugitives to slip out of the place undetected. And guess what?"

Payne answered. "You found something."

"Exactly! The rear wall of the closet was actually a door. A well-concealed door."

"Once you got outside, did you try to get the shooter?"

"To be honest with you, no. My nickname is the Buffalo Soldier, but I don't have much experience with killing people. And the truth is, I thought you guys were already dead."

"We probably should've been," Jones admitted. "A well-trained gunman would've picked us off clean. *If* that was his goal."

Greene frowned. "What does that mean? You don't think he was aiming for you?"

"At this point, we don't know. What would be the purpose of killing Jon if he hasn't paid a ransom yet? If the kidnappers want his millions, they better not kill him. Right?"

The comment took Greene by surprise. "You've got millions? I thought you were some kind of unemployed street baller. You really got that many bucks in the bank?"

"I have a nice nest egg, yeah."

"I'll be damned! A rich Rambo! What the hell did you do? Auction your soldiering skills to the highest bidder? Or did you just sell a stolen warhead?"

"Nothing that dramatic. When my grandfather died, he left the family business to me."

"Like a family restaurant or something?"

Payne shrugged, trying not to brag. "Something like that."

Greene nodded his approval. "As I was saying, I didn't have the expertise to take out the shooter, so I did the next best thing. I called the cops."

"So, that was you!" Jones said, happy that Greene had come through for them. "The police said someone had reported the crime to 911, but they weren't willing to give a name."

"I told you, I don't like dealing with the cops. Plus, I don't want to read tomorrow's newspaper and see my name linked to a bad part of town. That wouldn't be good for my image."

"Amen!" said Payne as he thought about the irony of Greene's statement. "Now let's go inside this strip club and bitch to the owner about the defective guns that you bought for us."

DESPITE the approach of daylight, the Fishing Hole was still crawling with semiaroused men and naked women, a sight that surprised Payne and Jones. Neither man was a huge fan of the skin club scene, so they weren't aware that most dancers usually did their best business just before closing time—due to the horniness and intoxication of their fans.

"Let me see if Terrell's still here," Greene stated. "It's nearly four A.M., so there's a good chance he's already gone home for the night."

"Should we go with you?" Jones wondered.

"Probably not. Terrell's pretty skittish around new people. If the three of us go charging back there, he's liable to get pissed. And trust me, you don't want to see him pissed."

Payne nodded while receiving a skeptical glance from Jones. Once Greene had entered the club's back corridor, Jones spoke up. "What's your gut say about Terrell Murray?"

"It's undecided. Earlier tonight he seemed pretty hospitable, but it could've been an act. I find it pretty suspicious that he sold us defective weapons and recommended our visit to Sam's shooting gallery within a twenty-four-hour period. That's a pretty big coincidence, don't you think?"

"But what would he gain from our deaths? Like you mentioned, if the kidnappers want your money, they need to keep you alive."

"I know. That's why my gut is undecided. I don't know why he'd want to eliminate us. Shoot, maybe all of this was just a fluke."

Jones pondered Murray's role as he watched the Fishing Hole's crowd. "You know, maybe he doesn't want to kill us. Maybe he has to."

"How so?"

"In a perfect world, the people who took Ariane would want to take your money, but maybe our presence in New Orleans has everyone spooked. Maybe the kidnappers figure it's better to cut their losses before they get caught. You know, live to play another day."

"Possibly," Payne admitted. It was a thought that hadn't crossed his mind. "But to be honest with you, I didn't get the sense that Murray was surprised by our visit. If he is, in fact, the ringleader of this crime, you'd think that our appearance would've flustered him."

"You're right, but if Levon had mentioned our names when he purchased the guns earlier in the day, Murray would've had plenty of time to gather his senses. Right?"

"Right."

"And get faulty weapons for us."

"Yep."

"And arrange our death."

"I see what you're saying. But for some reason that last part just doesn't seem to click. If Murray wanted us dead and he knew that we had broken guns, then why didn't he have someone walk into Sam's shop and shoot us at close range?"

"That's a good point. So where does that leave us?"

Payne shrugged. "Confused and very tired. I'm sure there's something staring us in the face, but I can't think of it."

"Then let's get out of here," Greene said from behind. His approach had been so silent he startled both Payne and

Jones. "Terrell's not here, so I think our refund is going to have to wait."

"That's okay," Jones muttered. "I think all of us could use some sleep before we face our next round of confrontations."

Payne nodded. "Trust me, my gut tells me that there are some big ones headed our way."

CHAPTER 26

WITH the help of several guards, Hakeem Ndjai ordered the captives out of their cabins at the first sign of daylight. He led the bruised and battered group across the dew-covered grass to the far end of the field. The walk was a brisk one, forcing the prisoners to maintain a pace that they were barely able to keep, but at no point were they tempted to complain since their journey was far better than the backbreaking labor that Ndjai usually put them through. Furthermore, a complaint would have resulted in a swift and vicious beating at the hands of the guards.

Not exactly the way the prisoners wanted to start their day.

When they neared the tree-lined edge of the field, Ndjai ordered the group to stop, then waited for everyone to gather around him. After clearing his throat, the African native spoke to the prisoners, lecturing in his thick accent on the torture device that they were about to see, an invention that he had constructed himself.

"What I am about to show you is a contraption that I was never allowed to use on the cacao plantations of Cameroon because the landowners felt it was too destructive to the morale of the workers. Thankfully, Master Holmes views things differently and has given me permission to use some of my toys on the people that need to be disciplined the most." Ndjai paused, staring into the scared eyes of his prisoners. "I like to call it the Devil's Box."

Ndjai started walking again, leading the group along the edge of the forest, taking them even further from the cabins where they spent their terror-filled nights.

As their journey continued, the sights, sounds, and smells of nature were more prevalent than on the cultivated land near the plantation house. Ducks, geese, and brown pelicans waddled on the marsh's edge, carefully avoiding the foxes that guarded the land and the alligators that patrolled the water of the swamps. White-tailed deer darted among the fallen timber like a scene from a Disney movie, while nutrias scoured for food on the hard ground. Doves, egrets, and wild turkeys squawked and sang in the dense groves of oak trees to their left, which dripped with thick blankets of Spanish moss. Small pockets of flowers—lilies, orchids, honeysuckle, jasmine, and azaleas—dotted the terrain, filling the air with a sweet fragrance that overpowered the horrid stench that covered the skin and clothes of the prisoners, temporarily giving the group a reason for hope.

But five more minutes of hiking ended that.

The soft sounds of nature that had calmed them a moment before had been replaced by the distant howl of a man. The echoing scream was muffled at first, but it slowly increased in volume and intensity with every step that the group took.

"A little farther," Ndjai said as he enjoyed the sound of torture. "Then you will see why my friend is so unhappy."

With tired legs and shortness of breath, the group mounted a man-made slope that had been built decades earlier to prevent flooding. A few of the prisoners struggled with the climb, stumbling on the loose sand and gravel that covered the mound, but the guards showed them no mercy, flogging the fallen captives across their backs with punishing blows from their braided whips. The loud cracks of cowhide, followed by the sharp shrieks of pain, only added to the horrific sound of terror that came from the crest of the hill. In unison, the combination of cruelty, agony, and torment created a noise that was so sinister, so evil, that some of the guards shielded their ears from the heinous symphony.

When the last captive reached the top of the ridge, Ndjai ordered the prisoners to study his invention. He wanted their full attention when he explained the torture device. But his command wasn't necessary. Members of the pilgrimage had never been more wide-eyed in their entire lives. The concentration of each person was focused solely on the wooden cube that had been anchored into the hilltop. Trembling, they waited for a detailed explanation of Ndjai's masterpiece, the Devil's Box.

Standing four feet tall and four feet wide, the cube did not appear threatening at first glance. Made out of thick slabs of oak, the device was secured in place by a number of sturdy metal cables that had been pounded into the rocky turf. The outside surface of the box had been sanded to a smooth finish, then painted with several coats of black waterproof sealant, giving the device the look of a giant charcoal briquette. The box was solid on all sides but one; the center of the top layer had been carved in an intricate lattice pattern, allowing fresh air into the cube without giving the occupant any view except of the hot sun above.

"I know what you are thinking. The Devil's Box does not appear dangerous, but do not let its simplicity fool you. It can be nasty in so many ways. And if you do not believe me, you can always ask Nathan." Ndjai put his face above the box and laughed. "Isn't that right, Nathan? You thought you were tough when you were out here, but now that you have been in there for a while, you do not feel very tough, do you?"

The prisoner answered with a torture-filled grunt, but his words were indecipherable.

"You will have to excuse Nathan. He has been in my box since long before your arrival on the Plantation, and it seems dehydration has swollen his tongue to twice its normal size. Unfortunately, that makes words very difficult to pronounce." Ndjai turned his attention back to Nathan. "Isn't that right? You are a little bit thirsty, aren't you? Well, you should have thought of that before you hurt one of my bosses, you stupid man!"

The guards laughed in amusement as they watched the taunting continue.

"But do not worry. I will not let you die of thirst. I will keep you like this for as long as I possibly can, teetering on the edge of life and death."

Once again the captive screamed in agony, but this time with a far greater intensity. It caused each prisoner to shiver with fear and hatred for the man who had put him there.

"Before you get the wrong idea," Ndjai continued, "and start to think that this device is simply used to bake the bad attitude out of a troubled inmate, let me point out your error. The Devil's Box is not used for dehydration, even though I must admit the severe loss of fluids is a pleasant side effect to my invention. In fact, that is why I painted it black to begin with, to draw in the intense heat of the sun. You would be surprised at how uncomfortable a person can get when they run out of liquid."

He moved closer to the group so they could see the emotion on his face.

"In the beginning you feel an unquenchable thirst, but from there the human body falls apart quite quickly. The tongue starts to balloon, followed by the drying of the throat lining and nasal passages, making it difficult to talk or even breathe. Lips start to crack, and skin starts to separate, painfully pulling apart with the slightest movement of any kind. Intense cramps surface in your arms and legs, causing spasms of agony that you cannot stop. Your bladder swells from the lack of moisture in your body, making you suffer through the severe urge to urinate, but the joke is on you because there is no liquid in your system to squeeze out. From there your kidneys fail, followed by the rest of your body, including your brain. All in all, not a pleasant way to go."

Ndjai caught his breath while enjoying the horrified look of the crowd that surrounded him—children clinging to their parents, strangers holding hands for comfort and unity, fear and desperation in the eyes of everyone. It was a sight that he truly loved.

"But as I pointed out to you, dehydration is not the main intent of the Devil's Box. It is merely a bonus, heightening the effects of its original purpose. And what purpose is that, you may ask. Well, let me tell you. The purpose is agony!"

Ndjai approached the box again, but this time one of the guards handed him a plastic container that was no larger than a carton of tissues.

"When we put Nathan in here several weeks ago, he was covered in cuts and scratches, wounds that I personally administered with the aid of a metal-tipped whip. Since that time his body has been unable to heal the torn flesh because of his severe thirst and his lack of a balanced diet. In fact, I would guess that his wounds are in worse shape now than the day I created them due to the infections that have developed. Tsk-tsk. It is really a shame. Nathan used to be such a large man. We even had a difficult time squeezing him inside the box because of his girth. But now, due to his lengthy stay in my device, he has been sapped of his size and strength—like Superman in a kryptonite cage!"

Ndjai grinned as he held the small container above the opening in the top of the box, taunting the imprisoned man by swooshing the object back and forth. This increased the intensity of Nathan's screams, turning his moans and wails into terrified shrieks of torment. The sound, which filled the air with a sense of dread, quickly brought gooseflesh to everyone on the ridge.

"One of the most difficult things to deal with in the Devil's Box is the loneliness. The heat is bad, the thirst is horrible, but the solitude is what gets you. Without companionship, the mind tends to wander, leaving sanity behind while looking for ways to amuse itself. It is a terrible thing, but it eventually happens to each of my victims."

Ndjai peeled open the container's cover and slowly started dumping its contents into the box.

"Since I worry about my friend's sanity, I do my best to occupy him with tangible things. Instead of allowing his mind to drift into a fantasy world, where it is liable to get lost, I try to keep his brain focused on real-life issues. Each day it is something new, and each problem gets more and more difficult for Nathan to solve. You are probably wondering, what is today's problem?" He laughed softly while answering his own question. "Fire ants!"

Ndjai drained the container into the Devil's Box, glancing through the cube's tiny slits to see how Nathan handled it. His intense screams proved that he wasn't happy.

"As you can tell from his reaction, the sting of the fire ant is very painful. The poison is not life threatening—unless, of course, a person gets stung by several dozen ants in a short period of time. Did you hear that, Nathan? Do not let them sting you, if you can help it!"

Ndjai chuckled as he redirected his attention to the group. "Unfortunately, his task might be difficult. You see, fire ants are actually drawn to the taste of blood, and since he has a number of open wounds, they are going to get pretty wound up, like sharks in a sea full of chum. Oh, well, look on the bright side. If he is able to eat the ants before they eat him, he will get his first dose of protein since his capture."

The guards smiled at the remark, showing their approval of Ndjai's presentation.

"At this point of my lecture, I am sure you are wondering why I brought you up here to start this day. That is what you are wondering, isn't it? Well, the reason is quite simple. I wanted to show you how good you currently have it." Ndjai paused for a moment to let that comment sink in. "Is the heat of the summer sun intense? Sure it is. Is working all day in the field tough? Definitely. Is sleeping on the ground of your cabin uncomfortable? Of course."

Moving closer to the group, Ndjai narrowed his eyes to tiny slits. "But keep this in mind. If you mess with me or my staff, I will make things so much worse for you. I will make your stay a living hell."

CHAPTER 27

DRAPED in a Tulane University blanket, Payne opened his eyes and gazed around the room. Wearing nothing but boxers, he had spent the night on Greene's couch but barely got any sleep. Thoughts of Ariane had kept him awake way past daybreak.

Payne felt much better after a quick shower. His body was reenergized, and his mind was suddenly clear. Some people needed caffeine in the morning, but Payne relied on a bar of soap. After getting dressed, he looked for Jones, finding him downstairs in the living room.

"What time is it?" Payne asked.

"Almost noon. I would've woken you up earlier, but I know you didn't sleep much."

"You got that right."

"Don't worry. Levon and I were busy while you were getting your beauty rest."

"Doing what?"

"Discussing last night. And after careful analysis, we came to the conclusion that Levon messed up bad."

"How so?"

"He neglected to tell us something about our guns. Something important."

"Such as?"

"They were loaded with dummy bullets."

Payne shook his head as he sat on the couch next to Jones. "How did *that* slip his mind?"

"Apparantly, on the rare occasion that Terrell sells a weapon to a new customer, he likes to load them with dummy bullets—substituting sand for powder. That way his weapons can't be used to rob him."

"And Levon knew this?"

Jones nodded. "But since he was buying the guns for us, Levon assumed that they'd be loaded with regular ammo."

"You realize his assumption could've gotten us killed."

"You're right, and he knows it. The big baby's been pouting all morning."

"Why? There's nothing he can do about it now. Besides, it's not like we could've saved Sam, even if our guns had worked."

"That's what I told him, but he's still taking it hard."

"Don't worry, he'll be fine once I talk to him. Speaking of which, where is he?"

"At Terrell's. While you were sleeping, he made an appointment to get us some new guns. This time, loaded with *real* bullets."

"That should help. When will he be back?"

Jones pointed to a nearby security monitor. "Actually, I think that's him now."

Payne glanced at the screen and saw an Escalade pull through the front gate. A minute later, Greene walked through the front door.

"Guys!" Greene shouted. "Where are you?"

Payne and Jones made their way to the foyer, anxious to see why Greene was so excited.

"What's gotten into you?" Jones asked. "You seem happier than before."

"That's 'cause I am! You know how I went to get you

guns? Well, I came back with more than that. Something *much* better."

"I hope you didn't buy a missile, because Jon doesn't carry that much cash."

"No." Greene laughed. "I got some news on the Posse!"

"On the Posse?" Payne demanded. "How did that happen?"

"Well, I went to the Fishing Hole to talk to Terrell about the dummy bullets. I figured if I bitched enough I could get him to cut us a deal on some new guns. Unfortunately, he was on the phone when I rolled in, and his boys said he'd take a while to finish. So instead of waiting by his office, I strolled out front to check out the talent. And that's when I saw him!"

"Him?" Jones asked. "What the hell were you doing watching a guy dance?"

Greene rolled his eyes. "The guy I saw was a customer."

"Was he cute?"

"Anyway," Greene said, ignoring Jones's teasing, "I saw this guy leaning against one of the brass railings, his hand and arm just dangling over the side. And guess what I noticed?"

Payne guessed. "A Posse tattoo."

"Give that man a prize! Can you believe my luck?"

"Did you talk to him?"

"I tried, but he saw me staring at his wrist. I don't know how he noticed me—I mean, I was being really careful—but he did. Next thing I know, he's whispering something to the buckwheat next to him, then bolting from the club. Thankfully, the buckwheat at the bar knew everything we needed to know. Well, not everything, but he knew a lot."

"And trust me," Jones said, "I want to hear every last word. But first, you've got to explain something for me. You keep saying *buckwheat*. What the hell does that mean?"

"Sorry, man, it's a Southern term. You remember that Little Rascals character, Buckwheat? You know, the one that Eddie Murphy played on *Saturday Night Live*?"

"O-tay," Jones chuckled, using Murphy's famous expression. "I remember."

"Well, there are brothers around this part of the country that are *really* rural. Nappy-looking hair, old work clothes, messed-up backwater language. Well, we call those brothers buckwheats. And trust me, this guy was a buckwheat and a half. Fucked-up dreadlocks, gold teeth, taller than me. Shit, I almost felt bad for the punk."

"Buckwheat, huh? I'll have to remember that term."

"Guys!" Payne yelled, unable to wait any longer. "What did he tell you, Levon?"

"Sorry, Jon." Greene gathered his thoughts before continuing. "I went up to him all cool-like, just watching the girls for a while. After a couple of minutes, he turns to me and starts talking. As luck would have it, he recognized me from my playing days, and we started bullshitting about football. After this goes on for five minutes or so, I decided to push my luck. I asked him about the guy with the tattoo."

"And what did he tell you?"

"He said he worked with the guy. He wouldn't give me many details but said all the brothers he worked with had the same kind of tattoo. It was a requirement for their job."

Jones frowned. "I didn't know gangbangers had jobs, other than shooting each other."

Greene shrugged. "Apparently, these guys do."

"Or," Payne added, "maybe they aren't bangers. Maybe the tattoo isn't what we think it is. Maybe it isn't a Holotat."

"Well, that gets me to the next part. This guy is pretty quiet about his friend, but he's unable to shut up about himself. He keeps rambling on about his job and stuff. He says he cooks and cleans for a bunch of people every day, and the only time they let him leave is to pick up supplies. Then he mentions the guy with the tattoo is the one who brought him to New Orleans. I guess he's the buckwheat's driver or something."

Jones groaned. "They're not from New Orleans? That's gonna make our job a lot more difficult. Or did this guy let the name of the town slip?"

"Nah, I wasn't that lucky. I asked him where he worked and what kind of place it was, but he got rattled. Said it was top-secret stuff. Said he could get into all kinds of trouble from the state if he blabbed about it."

Payne frowned. "From the state? What does that mean?"

"You've got me," Greene admitted. "Louisiana might be a little backward, but I've never heard of any state workers getting inked for employment. Or any top-secret facilities that would hire a dumb-ass buckwheat like this guy."

"What kind of place was he talking about?"

"I don't know, Jon. I asked him, but he said he had to shut up. I even offered to buy him a drink for his trouble, but he quickly turned me down. He said he had to buy a bunch of supplies before it got too late, that he wanted to get his work done before the fireworks started."

Jones raised an eyebrow. "Fireworks? Isn't it a day early for that?"

"You'd think so, huh? But the local shows are gonna be held on the third this year. So if you fellas want to see fireworks in New Orleans, you better be looking at the sky to-night."

Payne didn't care for fireworks—the loud bangs and bright lights brought back memories of Iraq. But due to the circumstances of that night's show, he was suddenly a fan. "I'm sure I'm asking for a miracle here, but did this guy happen to say where he'd be watching the fireworks? Because I'll tell ya, I'd love to talk to him."

Greene smiled at the inquiry. Not a sly smirk, but a big, *I got a secret* grin. "As a matter of fact, he did. He'll be watching them at Audubon Park."

CHAPTER 28

PAYNE dropped off his friends on opposite ends of the park, then focused his attention on finding a nameless witness in a sea of sixty thousand people. Sure, he realized his chances were slim, but he knew he had three things going for him—his target's unique appearance (very tall, gold teeth, and more dreadlocks than a Bahamas barbershop), his unwavering determination to find Ariane, and his two kick-ass partners.

Together, they made the Three Musketeers look like Girl Scouts.

With cell phone in hand, Payne parked his car on the Tulane University campus, then jogged for several blocks until he reached the spacious grounds that he had been assigned. Greene had told him that the center of Audubon Park would be packed with partygoers, but when Payne arrived, he was greeted by the exact opposite. The scenic grove was empty.

Confused, he pulled his gun and inched along the concrete walkway, suspiciously searching the green boughs above him for signs of a potential ambush. A cracking branch. A glint of color. The smell of human sweat. Yet the only thing he noticed was insects, dozens of chirping insects wailing their sum-mertime song. Next he examined the massive trunks of the live oak trees that surrounded him, the decorative cast-iron benches that lined the sidewalks, and the Civil War fountain in the center of the park. But everything in the vicinity seemed clear.

Too clear for his liking.

Puzzled by the lack of activity, Payne paused for a mo-ment and considered what to do next. He was tempted to call Greene for advice, but before he did, he heard the faint sound of horns seeping through the trees several hundred yards to the south. Relieved, he strolled toward the music and eventually found the scene that Greene had described. Thousands of drunken revelers frolicked on the banks of the Mississippi River, enjoying the hell out of the city's Third of July extravaganza.

"Damn," Payne grumbled. "This place looks like Go-morrah."

Clowns with rainbow-colored wigs trudged by on stilts while tossing miniature Tootsie Rolls to every child in sight. A high-stepping brass band blared their Dixieland sound as they strutted past an elaborate barbecue pit that oozed the smoky scent of Cajun spareribs and grilled andouille. Ven-dors peddled their wares, ranging from traditional plastic necklaces to fluffy bags of red, white, and blue cotton candy. And a group of scantily clad transsexuals, dressed as Uncle Samanthas, pranced in a nearby circle, chanting, "We are gay for the USA."

But Payne ignored it all. With a look of determination on his face, he blocked out the kaleidoscope of diversions that pleaded for his attention—the gleaming streaks of light as kids skipped by with sparklers, the sweet smell of funnel cakes that floated through the air, the distant popping of fire-crackers as they exploded in the twilight like Rebel cannons on the attack—and remained focused on the only thing that mattered: finding the Plantation witness.

Unfortunately, Payne had little experience when it came to tracking civilians on American soil. He was much more accustomed to finding soldiers in murky swamps than buck-wheats at carnivals, but after giving it some thought, he realized his basic objective remained the same.

He needed to locate his target as quickly and quietly as possible.

To do so, he tried mingling with the locals, slyly shifting his gaze from black man to black man as he made his way through the festive crowd. But his efforts to blend in were almost comical. No matter what he attempted, the scowl on his face made him stand out from the lively cast of characters that surrounded him. He tried smiling and nodding to the people that he passed, but the unbridled intensity on his face made him look like a serial killer.

After making a few children cry, Payne realized he needed to change his approach. Drastically. So instead of trying to hide in the crowd, he decided to stand out in it, making his anxiety work for him instead of against him.

Why be cautious when there was no risk in being bold? The Plantation witness had never seen his face, so it made little sense for Payne to slink through the crowd, hiding. He figured, why not approach every Rastafarian in sight and just talk to him? To do so, he simply needed an excuse, one that would allow him to talk to strangers without raising their suspicion. But what could he use? What could he ask anyone that would seem so harmless that a person wouldn't flinch at the query? The question needed to be simple, yet something that explained the frazzled look on his face, a look with so much intensity that it actually scared kids.

Kids! That was it! He could pretend he'd lost his kids. He could move from person to person, pretending to look for his lost kids, while actually searching for the Plantation witness. Heck, in the few seconds it took for a person to respond to his query, Payne could study the man's face, hair, teeth, and height. And if that wasn't enough, Payne could listen to the man's voice and see if it possessed the backwater accent of a buckwheat.

Damn! Payne thought to himself. The plan was ingenious.

It was bold, daring, creative . . . and completely unsuccessful.

Payne talked to every black man he saw, every single one, but most of them turned out to be way too short to be his suspect. And the few he found who actually stood over Greene's height of 6'4" didn't have the Fort Knox dental work or the redneck speech pattern that Greene had described. In fact, nobody in the crowd even came close.

Yet Payne remained undeterred. He had waited his entire life to find someone like Ariane—intelligent, witty, beautiful—so he wasn't about to give up hope after an hour. If it was necessary, he would stay in New Orleans for the rest of his life, spending every cent of his family's fortune, searching for the one witness that could bring her back into his arms.

But as it turned out, none of that was necessary.

His best friend was having a lot more luck on the eastern end of the park.

Payne hardly noticed it at first. The sound was too soft, too timid, to be heard above the cacophony of the boisterous crowd. But when it repeated itself a second and third time, it grabbed his attention. It was his cell phone.

"Hello?" he mumbled.

"Jon, it's D.J. You're not going to believe this, but I nabbed the bastard!"

"You what?"

"You heard me! I found him!"

A huge smile formed on Payne's lips. "Are you serious? I was beginning to think this was a waste of time."

"Me, too," Jones admitted. "But I got the Bob Marley wannabe right here." There was a brief pause on the line before he spoke again. "Say something, you little prick."

For a minute, Payne thought he was being scolded. Then he heard a meek squeal on Jones's end of the phone. "Howdy, sir. How is you?"

The accent brought a smile to Payne's lips. "What's your name?"

"Bennie Blount."

"Well, Bennie, it's nice to meet you. Now do me a favor and put my friend back on."

Jones got on the line a second later. "Polite sucker, isn't he?"

Payne ignored the question. "Where are you? I want to chat with this guy *now*."

"We're near the main road, about five minutes from the basketball courts where you dropped me off. How about you?"

"Not too far." Payne paused to collect his thoughts. "Listen, get to the courts as quietly as possible. I don't want our conversation to draw a crowd, and the courts should be deserted."

"No problem. And I'll give Levon a buzz on my way there."

"No," he growled. "I'll call Levon. I want you to keep two hands on this guy at all times."

Jones laughed at the indirect order. "Don't worry, Jon. This boy ain't going anywhere. I've got a gun shoved in his back. Plus, I'm using his hair as a leash."

Payne chuckled at the image. "Well, don't hurt him too much, you big bully. I want Bennie to be talkative, not comatose, when I meet him."

After calling Greene, Payne ran to the basketball courts, hoping to survey the territory before his partners arrived. As he'd hoped, the courts were completely deserted. Plus they were far enough from the festivities to attract unwanted attention, which would come in handy if they had to pacify Bennie with force.

As for the area itself, it was divided into two contrasting regions. Three concrete basketball courts with tattered nets and bent rims sat off to the left, next to a jungle gym and an old swing set that had clearly seen better days. A sandbox sat dormant, decorated with a number of sandcastles that crumbled like many of the structures in the surrounding neighborhood.

Meanwhile, the second region was in impeccable shape. Finished in smooth black asphalt and recently painted with bright white lines, the full-length basketball court was tournament ready. It was surrounded on all sides by metal bleachers and a large barbed wire fence, designed to keep the ball in and vandals out. To get inside the compound, a person normally had to file past an armed park guard, but on this night, the only people who were armed were Payne and his friends.

"Yo, Jon!" called a voice in the night.

Payne turned from his perch on the metal bleachers and saw the massive form of Levon Greene jogging toward him. "Over here, Levon."

Greene lumbered closer, a limp fairly obvious in his stride. "Where is he? I want to make sure you got the right guy."

Payne shrugged as he watched Greene enter the main gate and approach the bleachers. "D.J. was the one who found him, but he hasn't shown up yet. I hope he didn't run into any problems."

"None at all," Jones bellowed from the shadows. Payne and Greene whipped their heads sideways, searching for the source of the sound. "I was just waiting to make a big entrance."

Payne struggled to see him, but after a while, two dark faces emerged from the night.

"Gentlemen," Jones announced, "let me introduce you to our new best friend and a future witness for the prosecution, Mr. Bennie Blount."

CHAPTER 29

PAYNE had seen thousands of people in his life, folks from dozens of different lands and cultures, yet despite all of his experiences, he could not remember seeing a more unique character than Bennie Blount.

Standing 6'6" with an elaborate web of dreadlocks that added an additional three to five inches of puffiness to the top of his head, Blount looked like an exaggerated stick figure, created in the mind of a warped cartoonist. He lacked muscle mass of any kind; instead, he resembled a limbo pole turned vertically, topped off with a poorly crocheted black wig. Gold front teeth were the only remarkable thing about his face, and his dark eyes revealed absolutely nothing, like the lifeless props often found in a taxidermist's shop.

"How'd you find him?" Payne asked as he watched them enter the court.

"It wasn't very tough," Jones joked. "Some kids were using him to break open a piñata."

Payne smiled despite the seriousness of the situation. "And does our new friend know why you've brought him here?"

"Not yet." Jones released Blount's hair and pushed him forward. "I figured you'd want to provide him with all the details."

Payne nodded as he walked toward the witness. "Do you know why you're here?"

Blount raked the dreadlocks from his eyes with his E.T.-like fingers, then responded. "I gets the feeling it ain't to play basketball."

"You got that right," Greene growled from the bleachers. "You're lucky I'm resting my knee, or I'd come down there and kick the shit out of you."

Blount trembled as he cowered from the angry voice. "Mr. Greene, is that you? My lord, that is you! Did I do somethin' bad that I don't remember?"

"It's not what you did," Payne interjected, "it's what you didn't do. You failed to tell Levon the things that he wanted to know during your earlier conversation."

Blount glanced at Payne and frowned. "Do I knows ya, sir? I don't mean to be rude none, but ya don't looks like someone I knows."

"My name's Jonathon Payne, and we talked on the phone a few minutes ago." He pointed to Jones before continuing. "And that over there is David Jones."

Blount instinctively massaged the top of his sore scalp. "Oh, yes, I knows him. We's already been introduced."

Payne tried not to laugh as he pictured Jones using Blount's hair as a leash. "Bennie, as I mentioned, the reason that Mr. Greene is angry with you is because of your behavior earlier today at the Fishing Hole."

"But I didn't do nothin' wrong! I didn't drinks too much or cause no problems! Mr. Murray warns me about touching the gals, and I swears I didn't do none of that today! I swears!"

"That's not what I'm talking about. Mr. Greene is upset because you weren't willing to answer his questions about the man with the tattoo. He asked you some simple questions, and you refused to answer."

Blount glanced at Greene and shivered slightly. "Is that

why you's mad at me, Mr. Greene? 'Cause I wasn't in a talkin' mood?"

"I gave you an autograph, Bennie, and you weren't willing to give me any information. That was kind of disappointing."

"More like rude," Jones chimed in. "You should be ashamed, Bennie."

"Real ashamed," Payne added.

As Blount considered his actions and studied the men that surrounded him, guilt flooded his face. "I'm so sorry, Mr. Greene! I didn't know that it meant that much to ya! If I'd known things was that important, I'd've told ya everything I known. I promise I woulda!"

Grinning, Payne slowly reached out his hand and placed it on Blount's rail-thin shoulder. "Well, Bennie, maybe it's not too late to make amends. If you act nicely, I bet Mr. Greene would give you a second chance. In fact, I know he would."

"Does ya think so, Mr. Payne?"

"I know so, Bennie." Payne stepped aside, allowing Blount to get a full view of Greene. "Go ahead, Bennie. Apologize to my friend."

Blount lowered his head in shame and looked at Greene's feet as he spoke. "Mr. Greene, I swears I didn't do nothin' wrong on purpose. If you gives me one mo' chance, I promise I make things up to ya!"

Greene sighed deeply, as if he actually had to weigh the consequences of Blount's apology. "All right, kid. I'll let this one slide. But you better tell us everything that we want to know, or I'll never forgive you. Ever!"

Blount's face erupted into a wide smile. "Anything, Mr. Greene. Just ask it and I'll tells ya. I promise, Mr. Greene. I don't wants ya to be mad at me. Really I don't!"

Greene grinned with satisfaction, enjoying every moment of this mini drama. "I'm glad, Bennie. That's what I was hoping you'd say."

"Me, too," Payne interjected. He led Blount to the metal bleachers and asked him to sit down. "I've got a number of questions that I'd like to ask you, Bennie, and some of them might seem a little bit strange. But trust me, each of them is really important to me and my friends."

"Okay," he mumbled, slightly confused.

"First of all, what can you tell me about your friend with the tattoo? How do you know him?"

"Ya mean the *P* tattoo? I met him at work, Mr. Payne. Most of the people have it."

"And where do you work, Bennie?"

Blount paused for a second, not sure if he should answer the question.

"Come on, Bennie," Greene urged. "You promised you'd help us."

"That's true, I did. But it's not as easy as that, sir. Ya see, I promised other peoples that I wouldn't talk about this none."

Greene moved forward on the bleachers, flexing his massive arms as he did. "But those other people can't hurt you right now, can they?"

Blount gulped. "I guess you's right. The place is called the Plantation."

The word piqued the interest of all three men, yet Greene was the first to speak. "The Plantation? What exactly is the Plantation?"

Blount gazed at Greene. It was obvious that the Plantation was one of the things he wasn't supposed to talk about, but all it took was one glare from Greene and he started to speak. "The Plantation is the name of the place that I be working. It's a special jail that the state put in less than a year ago."

"A jail? What kind of jail?" Payne demanded.

"The *secret* kind."

"What the hell is a *secret* jail?"

Blount exhaled. "You know, the kind that people is sent to for special crimes."

Payne grimaced. This was getting nowhere. "Special crimes? What the hell are they?"

"You know," he whispered, "the kind that people ain't suppose to talk about."

Payne glanced at Jones, looking for an explanation, but it was obvious that he was just as confused. "Bennie? Can you please tell me what type of people commit special crimes?"

"Not really, Mr. Payne. There've been too many people for me to keep track of over the past months."

"Men? Women? Old? Young?"

"Yes, sir. All of them."

"Is there anything else that you can tell us about this place?"

Blount considered the question for a moment, then brushed the hair from his face. "Yes, Mr. Payne, there be one more thing I could tell you about the people at the Plantation."

"And what's that, Bennie?"

Blount pointed a long, bony finger at Payne. "All the people look like you."

It took a moment for Blount's comment to sink in, but once it did, none of the men knew how to respond. After a moment of silence, Jones spoke. "All of the people look like him? You mean everybody at the Plantation is ugly?"

The joke brought a smile to Blount's face. "That's not what I meant, sir. What I be tryin' to say is they white. Everybody at the jail is white."

"Levon?" Payne said in a soft voice. "Do you have any idea what he's talking about?"

"I wish I did, but I'm clueless." Greene turned his attention to Blount. "Bennie? What do you mean everybody's white? You're telling me there aren't any black people at the Plantation?"

"No, I ain't sayin' that. There be plenty of black people at the jail. All the workers be black."

"What?!" Jones demanded. "The prisoners are white and the guards are black? Holy parallel universe, Batman!"

Payne glanced at his friend. Sometimes he wondered if Jones was still a teenager. "Bennie, don't you think that's a little bit strange? Why are all of the prisoners white?"

"I don't know, sir, 'cause I ain't in charge of no prisoners. I just be in charge of the taters and grits. My bosses don't allow me to get near the people. They keeps me far away."

"And why do you think that is, Bennie?"

"My bosses tell me it be for my safety, but sometime I don't know. I just don't know."

"Why's that?" Payne wondered. "Why do you doubt them?"

"'Cause some of the prisoners ain't that scary. I ain't afraid of no girls, and I sure as heck ain't afraid of no kids."

Nausea quickly built in Payne's belly. "Kids? What kind of kids, Bennie?"

"White ones."

"No, that's not what I meant. How old are the kids?"

"Well," Blount mumbled, suddenly realizing he had probably already revealed too much information, "it be hard to say. I ain't too good at guessin' no ages."

Payne moved closer, trying to intimidate Blount with his proximity. "This isn't the time to quit talking. How old are the damn kids?"

"I don't know," he whined. "I really don't. I just know that some of them have to be young 'cause I have to make them different chow. I have to cut up their food 'cause they don't got big teeth yet."

"Jesus," Payne groaned. That meant the Posse had kidnapped kids under the age of five. "And you don't find that strange? Come on, Bennie, you can't be that dumb! What kind of prison holds toddlers?"

Blount lowered his head in disgrace, too embarrassed to answer the question.

"Levon," Jones whispered, trying to take the focus off of Bennie, "what do you think? Could a place like this exist?"

Greene chuckled at the thought. "A state-run facility with black guards and white inmates? Hell, no! The government couldn't get away with a place like that in Louisiana. There are way too many David Dukes down here to oppose it."

"How about privately?" Payne wondered. "Do you think a black-run facility, one that imprisons and punishes white people, could secretly exist in this state?"

"Now that's another story." Greene sighed, closing his eyes as he did. "Racial tension has always been a huge concern in this state. For one reason or another, there are still thousands of people that are upset about the Civil War. I know that sounds ridiculous to a Northerner, but trust me, it's true. White supremacists run some towns, while black militants control others. Then, to complicate things further, there are places in this state that no one controls. The swamps, the forests, the bayou. Shit, I guarantee you there are entire communities in Louisiana that don't know what year it is—or even care. Those are the areas where a place like the Plantation could exist. No visitors, no cops, no laws. That's where a place like that could *thrive*."

The possibility didn't make Payne happy. He had secretly hoped that Bennie Blount was a simpleton who mumbled to strangers about fictitious places in order to get attention, but that seemed less likely now. If someone like Greene was willing to believe that the Plantation could exist, then there was a good chance that it actually did.

And if that was the case, then it was up to Payne to find it.

CHAPTER 30

**Sunday, July 4th
Independence Day**

THE leaders of the Plantation had waited several years for
this day to come, and now that their plan had come to frui-
tion, they could barely contain their enthusiasm. The special
ceremony they had planned was originally slated to begin
an hour before dawn, the same time they had held the symbolic ritual of the burning cross, but now that their big day
was actually here, they realized that their adrenaline wouldn't
let them wait another four hours.

Their big announcement would have to be pushed forward.

Holmes notified Hakeem Ndjai, who told the rest of the
guards. Within minutes, the Plantation's tattooed battalion
began assembling the prisoners into formation, forcing the
tired captives into a very specific order:

GROUP ONE:	GROUP TWO:	GROUP THREE:
The Metz and Ross families	The Potter and Cussler families	The Edwards and Walker families

Before Holmes, Jackson, and Webster made their appearance, the guards double-checked the prisoners, making sure

everyone was where they were supposed to be.

Then, like a shadow through a sea of black, Master Holmes and his raven-colored steed charged through the night. The only thing announcing their presence was the sound of hooves tearing up the soft turf in rhythmic bursts and the occasional crack of a leather whip against the horse's dark flesh. The sound brought chills to the recently flogged prisoners.

Once he reached the three groups, Holmes stared through the holes of his black hood and sighed. "Well, well, well! What do we have here? A bunch of frightened white people! The sight warms my heart!" He turned his attention to Ndjai. "Is everyone here, Hakeem?"

"Everyone except Master Jackson and Master Webster."

Holmes nodded as he thought back to the days when he was the scared victim, when he watched members of the Ku Klux Klan ride in on horseback and terrorize his family with burning crosses and threats of violence. Shit, he could still remember the pounding of his heart and the knot in his gut. The way he trembled while clinging to his mom for safety.

"Will they be joining us?" Ndjai asked.

Holmes nodded, refusing to take his eyes off of the prisoners. He loved the way they quivered in the firelight. "My friends wouldn't miss it for the world."

BLOUNT gawked at the interior of Greene's mansion as he walked down the hallways, glancing into every room he passed. He had never been in such a large house before and wanted a chance to snoop around. Unfortunately, his hosts had other ideas.

"Bennie!" Payne shouted. "Where are you hiding? Levon got off the phone five minutes ago, and we've been waiting for you ever since!"

"I sorry, Mr. Payne!" He jogged toward the sound of Payne's voice. "I guess I gots a little bit lost when I left the toilet. I sorry!"

Payne grinned at Blount's lanky form and easygoing country manner. "That's all right. But if we're gonna finish our preparations, we've got to get back to work." He threw his arm around Blount's shoulder and squeezed. "And you're our star!"

The concept made him smile. "Let's gets to it then! I been waitin' my whole life to be a star!" Blount and Payne joined Greene and Jones at the massive dining room table. Maps and sketches were scattered all over the wooden surface. "So tells me, what does ya need to know?"

Jones, who possessed the strongest background in military strategy, glanced at the information in front of him. He had graduated from the U.S. Air Force Academy, where he had studied computers at the Colorado Springs campus. After receiving the highest score in Air Force history on the MSAE, the Military Strategy Acumen Examination, he earned his entrance into the MANIACs after a short stint in the military police. Once in the MANIACs, he served several years under Payne, planning a variety of successful missions.

"Now that we know about the Plantation itself, we need to talk about points of entry. How are we supposed to get onto the island?"

Blount answered. "The only way to gets onto the island is from the western dock. Cypress swamps is gonna block every other way to this place."

"Then tell me about the west. What do we have to worry about before the dock?"

"There be a clean path, right down the middle, and you needs to follow it to avoid trouble. If you goes to one side of the path, boom! You hits some stumps. If you goes to the other side, boom! You hits some trees. But, if you stays in the middle—"

"Boom! The guards see us coming and blow our asses out of the water."

Blount laughed at Jones's comment. "That's right! We's gonna be gator stew!"

"If that's the case," Jones continued, "how do you recommend us getting there? If we can't use the dock without being seen, how can we get there undetected?"

"Why does you want to make this so complicated, Mr. Jones? There ain't no reason to find no back door when the front door is working just fine."

"But I thought you said that there'll be guards at the western dock."

"Yep," he chuckled, "but the guards won't be expectin' what I has in mind."

"And what is that?"

Payne and Jones listened to Blount's idea and liked what they heard. Even though they had won dozens of military awards, had planned intricate missions through several of the world's most hostile countries, and had been in charge of the most elite fighting force in America's history, they were forced to admit that Bennie Blount, a dreadlocked, slow-talking buckwheat from the bayou, had bested their military minds by devising the perfect plan all by himself.

And most importantly, it was simple enough that even he couldn't screw it up.

DANCING slightly with every hill and crevice, the headlights of the all-terrain vehicles looked like giant fireflies as they skimmed across the landscape of the Plantation. When the motors could finally be heard, the three groups of prisoners turned and watched the arrival of the two men. Wearing black hoods and thick cloaks, Jackson and Webster soared through the darkness, looking like supernatural beings on a mystical quest, their ebony robes flapping in the great rush of air. It was the type of entrance that nightmares were made of.

After stopping his vehicle, Jackson climbed off his ATV and walked toward Holmes, who was impatiently sitting on his steed. "Sorry we took so long. Right after you left, we got a phone call that we had to deal with."

"Is everything all right?" Holmes asked.

Jackson nodded. "It seems that we're going to be getting a few more captives, but it's nothing to worry about."

Even though he wanted to hear about the new arrivals, Holmes realized this wasn't the time or place. He had more important things to deal with, like his announcement. "People, you have already met Master Jackson and myself. Now, it's time to meet the real brains of the Plantation. I want you to say hello to Master Webster."

Despite their hatred of the man, the group screamed in unison. "Hello, Master Webster!"

Webster laughed under his hood. When he'd started this mission of revenge, he had dreamed of this moment, but now that it was here, he no longer knew how to react. His reality had somehow intersected with his dream world, and he could no longer discern which was which.

"Soon the sun will rise on the Fourth of July. Independence Day. A day to celebrate the freedom of this great nation." Webster took a deep breath while staring at the attentive crowd, wondering if they would understand the irony of their situation. "Unfortunately, some Americans weren't given their freedom in 1776. In fact, thousands of men and women from the United States weren't given their emancipation until after the Civil War had concluded. Yet we as a nation celebrate our independence on this day and this day alone. Ironic, isn't it? A country celebrates its freedom on a day when only half of us were freed!"

He cleared his throat as the prisoners thought about his words.

"Wait! You want irony? Independence means freedom from control and restrictions. That's the basic concept, right? So what's the opposite of independence? Slavery! Back in the days, white people used to refer to slaves as indentured servants. Did you know that? That was the politically correct way to say *slaves*! *Indentured servants*. Has a nice ring to it, huh? Well, what does that term mean? If you're indentured, it means that you're bound to work for someone, literally forced to be a servant. *Forced*. In other words, slavery!"

Webster could tell that his guests were getting confused, so he simplified things for their benefit. "I'm sure you're wondering, what's so ironic about that? Well, look the two terms up in the dictionary, and guess what you'll find? The two words sit next to each other. First, you'll see indenture, then you'll see independence! Side by side, one after the other! Two words with completely different meanings, yet they're neighbors in the English language. Pretty damn amazing!" He shook his head at the irony. "And if you think about it, it's kind of like us. We're independent, but all of you are indentured!"

Holmes laughed loudly. He had never seen Webster so animated.

"And that brings us to the moment we've all been waiting for. The answer to the number one question on each of your minds . . . Why are you here?"

Under his dark hood, Webster smiled at the prisoners.

"That's what you're wondering, isn't it? Why you've been selected to join us at the Plantation? Why, out of all of the people in America, did we bring you unlucky bastards here?"

He smiled again, loving the tension in the slaves' faces.

"Why, you ask? We did it because of your past!"

CHAPTER 31

THE boat inched from the private dock, slowly making its way through the dark water that surrounded Plantation Isle. Dressed in a black robe, the muscular figure tied a rope around the white man's wrist, making sure that the knot was tight enough to pass inspection. He tested it twice just to be sure, and each time his handiwork held in place. Then, sliding toward the back of the boat, the black man repeated the process. After wrapping the thick cord around the next prisoner's arms, he completed his knot with a series of quick jerks, pulling the extra slack from the restraint with a firm tug.

"Watch it! That hurts!"

Levon Greene sneered at Jones, then yanked the rope even harder. "We're playing for keeps, D.J., and if that means you have to suffer a little bit, then so be it."

"Yeah," Payne seconded over the rumble of the boat's motor. "You didn't hear me complain when Levon tied me up, did you?"

"No," Jones cracked, "but you've always liked that kinky stuff."

After his comment, the joking stopped, giving everyone a chance to think about their duties. Since so much of the plan revolved around Blount, a simpleminded twenty-four-year-old, Payne was more concerned than usual. He turned to examine the eyes of the boat's captain and could tell the dreadlocked servant was very uptight.

"Bennie," Payne said, "we'll only get one shot at a surprise attack, so we need *everything* to go perfectly. If you don't mind, I'd like to talk about your plan one more time."

"Yes, sir. That's fine. I don't wanna be doing nothin' that gets no one hurt—especially me!"

"Don't worry!" Greene said as he moved next to Blount. "This will go smoothly."

Remarkably, as Payne stared at the pair, he suddenly realized that they were a study in contrasts. Even though both men were black, their appearances couldn't have been more different. Greene was thick and defined, muscle stacked upon muscle, veins literally bulging through his skin. His head was shaved, his nose was broad, and his teeth were pearly white. If he were a tree, he'd be the biggest, baddest oak in all the land.

Blount, on the other hand, looked like a sapling gone bad. His limbs sprouted from a thin torso and appeared too feeble to support even the smallest amount of weight. His face, long and narrow, was topped with a haircut that resembled a rotting fern, black stems and roots tangled in every direction. And his gold teeth were straight out of the Mr. T School of Dentistry.

"Like I told you earlier," Greene said, "as long as you stay by my side, you're not going to get hurt. I promise."

Blount smiled, but the action seemed forced. "If you says so, Mr. Greene."

"Yes," he asserted, "I say so."

When Payne was done watching their conversation, he turned his attention to the back of the boat. "Hey, D.J., come up here so we can discuss some things. I want to make sure everyone knows what's going to happen."

Jones hustled forward and took a seat.

"When we pull up to the western dock, Bennie said we should expect two guards. As long as we don't look suspicious, that's all we'll have to deal with. Unfortunately, if we don't make this look believable, they'll radio for backup, and our mission will get ugly before it even starts."

Payne glanced at Blount and saw confusion in his eyes.

"Do you know what I mean by believable, Bennie?"

"I think so, Mr. Payne. You just want me to play Bennie. Right?"

Payne grinned. Things couldn't be any easier. "That's correct. But I need to remind you of one little detail that you keep forgetting. You have to stop calling me Mr. Payne. I doubt that the prisoners are referred to in such a polite manner."

Blount smiled, and this time it seemed more sincere. "You's definitely right about that. I ain't even referred to in that polite a manner, and I works here."

Payne nodded, turning his attention to Greene. "Obviously, you have the most important role of all. You have to make the guards believe that you're one of them and you're bringing two new prisoners to the island. Bennie claims that your black cloak is similar to the ones they wear, but it's not a perfect match. So don't let them get a good look at it. Always keep moving, okay?"

"Don't worry. I will."

"And make sure your hood is up. If they're sports fans and they see your face, the game's over. They'll immediately know you're not a guard. Then, once we get past the dock, you'll need to borrow one of their vehicles to take Bennie's supplies to the main house and us to the holding area. But before we get there, you'll cut our ropes and leave us in the woods. That'll give us a chance to do some recon."

Jones asked, "When will we get our weapons?"

Payne answered. "One of Bennie's boxes has our guns. We'll take what we need and stash the rest in the trees. We don't want to be bogged down until we know what we're up against."

He turned back to Blount. "Bennie, this is when you execute your part of the plan. I want you to go into the house and start breakfast. While you're making food for the guards, I want you to mix in the drug that I gave you. Pour half the bottle in the coffee, the other half in the scrambled eggs. That way, everyone's bound to get some, whether they're eating or not."

"Okay, Mr. Payne, I will. . . . Oops! I mean, okay, prisoner."

Blount smiled with pride. He thought he'd done a good thing by remembering his line, but his momentary blunder would've been enough to get everyone killed.

"Keep working on it, Bennie." Payne sighed, praying that Blount would improve before the big show actually started. "Where was I? Oh, yeah, within ten minutes of breakfast, everyone should be unconscious. That's when D.J. and I will make our move. We'll emerge from the woods in serious S & D mode."

Greene frowned. He was unfamiliar with the term. "S & D mode?"

"We'll search for the prisoners and destroy anything that gets in our way."

"You mean, you's gonna kill people?" Blount asked.

Payne nodded. He'd already gone over this at Greene's house and during the car ride to the dock, and he didn't feel like discussing it again. Unfortunately, he didn't have a choice. He had to keep Blount as calm as possible. "We don't want to, Bennie, but we might have to. That's just the way it is. Sometimes, the only way to help one group is to hurt another, and that's the situation we're facing. In order to help my girlfriend and the innocent people on this island, we might have to hurt some of the guards. We'll do everything in our power not to, but if it's us against them, they're the group that has to lose. I won't settle for anything less."

"Okay," he whined. "I guess you's right. Just try not to hurt me."

"You got it, Bennie." Payne smiled at Blount, then settled into his seat for the next portion of the plan.

BECAUSE of his frequent trips to the Plantation, Blount knew the appropriate channel through the cypress swamp.

He carefully navigated the boat toward the moss-covered poles of the wooden dock until he could see the two guards.

"Is that you, Gump?" asked one of the guards as he stared at the captain of the boat. "We were expecting you a while ago."

"Yeah," said the other. "Did the fireworks run late or something?"

Before Blount could answer, Greene moved to the front of the boat and spoke for him. "It wasn't the damn fireworks!" he growled. "There's been a security breach! Now quit your small talk and take our damn line before there's trouble. I have two prisoners on board."

The guards glanced at the large figure in the black cloak and jumped to attention. After dropping their guns to the ground, they ran to the dock, offering their assistance in any way possible. Greene nodded at them, tossing them the boat's rope. The two guards snared the line and carefully pulled the craft against the side of the dock.

"It looks like they're buying it," Jones whispered. "We might pull this off."

Payne nodded slightly, but for some reason, he wasn't nearly as confident. His gut told him there was something fishy, and it wasn't just the stench from the murky water of the swamp. "I hate to say this, D.J., but—"

The confidence drained from Jones's eyes. "Don't tell me! Your gut?"

Payne nodded. But before he could explain, Greene approached the duo and ordered them to be quiet. "Things are going well. Don't blow it by talking."

Greene followed his command by forcing Payne off of the boat and onto the shore while one of the guards did the same with Jones. Once both of them were on the ground, Greene turned to the workers and spoke. "Bennie and I will watch them while you get me a truck. There are a lot of supplies out there, so start moving."

"Yes, sir!" they blurted, running to complete their tasks.

Greene smiled at Blount, then glanced at the two captives at his feet. "How was that? Was I authoritative enough for you?"

Jones tried rolling onto his back, but his bound hands hindered his effort. In a strange way, he looked like an upside-down turtle that had trouble flipping over. "You sounded good to me, but I'm not the one you need to worry about. Ask Jon what he thinks. He's worried about something."

Greene turned his attention to Payne. "Is there something we need to talk about before the guards get back?"

"Not really," he groaned. "I can wait until they return, if you'd like."

"What do you mean by that?"

"I mean, you're just going to tell them anyway."

The smile faded from Greene's lips as his bewilderment grew. In order to sort things out, he lowered his black hood and knelt on the ground next to Payne. As he did, his bad knee cracked several times. "What are you talking about?"

"Yeah," Jones demanded. "What the hell are you talking about?"

Payne wanted to look Jones in the eyes, but the position of their bodies made it impossible. "D.J., I'm sorry to tell you this, but if my guess is correct, Levon is one of them."

CHAPTER 32

HOLMES and Jackson had planned on speaking to the prisoners, but since Webster was doing such an eloquent job, they allowed him to continue his lecture.

"Independence Day is a holiday that is supposed to symbolize freedom in this country. Freedom? In America? What a joke! A country that turned its back on my people, black people, for decade after decade believes in freedom? My black brothers and sisters were smuggled into America in the hulls of slave ships in the most unsanitary of conditions, brought here like cattle, then purchased by white men for their own personal use. And you call that freedom?"

The prisoners listened, trembling.

"Take a look around you! This plantation was built several decades before the Civil War. Nice, isn't it? It's probably hard to imagine, but the people who worked this soil were my ancestors. My *actual* ancestors! That's right! Through painstaking research, I have traced my family tree back to this plantation. Isn't that amazing? My forefathers worked this land! They slept here, ate here, and raised families in the tiny cabins that surround us!"

Webster shook his head at the thought, rage boiling inside of him.

"And because of you, my family was forced to die here, too!"

A slight murmur rippled through the crowd. What did Webster mean by *that*?

"For the past few days, you have been subjected to unpleasantries. Long hours in the hot sun, a scarcity of food and water, nothing to sleep on but the hard ground itself. But guess what? That pales in comparison to the hardships that my relatives had to endure. Back in the eighteen hundreds, slaves were forced to live in these tiny cabins year-round. Ten, twelve, sometimes as many as fifteen people were thrown together into one cabin and forced to make do, huddling in the center of the dirt floor for warmth. And if they bitched, they were beaten!

"During the rainy season, the ground became so saturated with water that the moisture would rise up into their cabins, forcing them to sleep in the mud. Like animals! These were my ancestors, for God's sake, and they were treated like beasts! Meanwhile, the Delacroix family, the white bastards that owned this property, slept in the comfort of the plantation house. They didn't work, but they lived like kings! Do you know what my relatives got to eat? At the beginning of every week, each person was given three and a half pounds of bacon from the smokehouse and enough corn to make a peck of cornmeal. That's it! For the entire week! Just bacon, cornmeal, and water for every meal, for a lifetime!"

Webster paused to catch his breath.

"And what about punishment? Do you actually think we've been rough on you? The punishment that occurred in the nineteenth century was far more brutal than anything we've implemented here. Back in the old days, slave drivers used to whip their niggers until they could see *ribs*. The gashes on their backs were so wide and deep you could see their lungs! Have we done anything like that to you? Anything that brutal? Tell me, have we?"

Despite his point-blank questions, the crowd remained silent. They were way too frightened to talk. But that didn't matter to Webster. He viewed the slaves' silence as insubordination, which needed to be dealt with. Turning toward Master Holmes, he said, "Can you believe that? They don't respect me enough to answer. Maybe you better show them what I mean about discipline."

Holmes grinned savagely under his black hood. He'd been on his best behavior since the finger-chopping incident, but now that Webster was encouraging him, he figured he could slide back to his sadistic ways.

He stepped forward, searching for a target, staring at the scared faces in the moonlight. Who should he choose? Which person would be the most beneficial to their cause? Then he saw him, the perfect victim. He was the finest specimen in Group One. A middle-aged male, father of Susan and two other brats. What was his name? Ross. Jimmy Ross. Yes, he would do nicely. An impeccable sacrifice.

Devastate the strong and the weak will crumble!

With unblinking eyes, Holmes focused on him, quietly selecting him as his prey. And Ross knew it. Holmes didn't even say a word, yet Jimmy dropped to his knees in fear. His entire body trembled with trepidation.

"Pick up the coward," Holmes growled.

And the guards obliged, pouncing on Ross like hungry wolves before they dragged him to the front of the crowd. Then, just as quickly as they had attacked, they backed away, leaving Ross at the feet of his master, with nothing between the two but a palpable wall of hate.

"Master Webster?" Holmes continued. "Why don't you tell our guests about the white man's temple? I think they'd enjoy that tale."

Webster readjusted his glasses, grinning. "In the nineteenth century, the white man considered his body sacred. It was a divine and holy temple that was not to be defiled by the dirty black man. Sure, it was fine for Massah to sleep with all the good-looking black women of the plantation. Famous men like Thomas Jefferson were reputed to have fathered many biracial children during their day. But if a Negro ever touched a white man for *any* reason, the slave could legally be killed. Can you believe that? The courts actually allowed it! Of course, that didn't make much financial sense to the slave owner, so it was rarely done. I mean, why murder someone who is doing your chores? So the white man was forced to come up with a better punishment than death."

Jimmy Ross gulped, waiting for Master Holmes to make a move. But the black man didn't budge. He stood like a statue, not blinking, not breathing. Silent. Completely silent. Listening to the words of his friend.

"No one knows where the idea of the post first came from, but its popularity spread across the Southern states during the early part of the eighteen hundreds. In fact, it spread like wildfire."

Suddenly, without warning, Holmes burst from his trance and lunged in Ross's direction. The prisoner instinctively flinched, raising his hands to protect himself, but it was a grave mistake.

"You tried to hit me!" Holmes screamed, stopping six inches short of Ross. "You white piece of shit! You tried to hit me!"

"I didn't, Master Holmes. I swear! I—"

"I don't give a fuck what you swear! I'm in charge of your sorry ass, so your words mean shit to me! If I say you tried to hit me, then you tried to hit me!" Holmes turned toward his guards. "Get me the post, now! I need to teach this cocksucker a lesson!"

"In fact," Webster continued, as if he was narrating an evil documentary, "even if the threat was an implied one—a swing that never landed, a tip of a cap to a white woman, or a hand being lifted for protection—slave owners were encouraged to administer this punishment."

The guards carried a six-foot wooden post, approximately six inches in diameter, to the front of the group and slammed it into the ground. After straightening it with a careful eye, they drove the long peg into the pliable turf with several swings of a sledgehammer. Once it was anchored in the ground, the device was ready for use.

"Now get him!" Holmes ordered.

The guards clamped onto Jimmy's arms much rougher than they had before and slammed him against the post. Then, before Jimmy could move, the larger of the guards forced Jimmy's cheek against the rough wooden surface, holding his face against the post with as much strength as possible. And Holmes was pleased by the sight.

While watching Jimmy tremble, Holmes slid in behind him while pulling a claw hammer out of the folds of his dark cloak. The sight of the savage tool brought a smile to his lips. Even though he enjoyed chopping fingers, there was nothing Holmes enjoyed more than the post. The fear. The blood. The disbelief in his victim's eyes. He loved it! For one reason or another, it satisfied something inside of him that most people couldn't understand.

The desire to be violent.

Reaching into his pocket, Holmes fumbled for a nail. Four inches in length, silver in color, sharpened to a perfect point. He lifted the tiny spike behind Jimmy Ross's head, then studied it with a suspicious eye. It was so small, yet capable of producing so much pain. God, it was beautiful. Holmes breathed deeply, thinking of the impending moment of impact. The smile on his face got even broader.

"The post," Webster said, "was a two-step process. Step one was the attachment phase. In order to prevent a messy scene later, the slave needed to be attached to the post in the most appropriate fashion. According to the journals that I've read, there was one method in particular that was quite popular."

Holmes raised the tip of the metal spike and ran it through the back of Jimmy's hair, tracing the ridges of his skull, looking for the proper insertion point. Once it was located, Holmes lifted his hammer, slowly, silently. The crowd, realizing what was about to be done, gasped with fear and shouted pleas of protest, but to Holmes, the murmur of shock sounded like a beautiful chorus, only adding to his enjoyment.

With a flick of his wrist, Holmes shoved the nail through the elastic tissue of Jimmy's outer ear, piercing the cartilage with a sickening snap. Before Jimmy could even yelp in pain, Holmes followed the attack with a swift swing of the hammer, driving the nail deep into the wood, anchoring the ear to the post.

After a moment of shock, Jimmy screamed in agony, then made things far worse for himself by trying to pull his head away from the wood. It was a horrible mistake. The more he pulled, the more flesh he tore, causing sharp waves of pain to surge through his skull. Blood trickled, then gushed down the side of his face. Warm rivulets of crimson flowed over his whiskered cheek, adding gore to the already vicious attack.

And the sight of it was too much for his family to endure.

In the crowd, Jimmy's sixteen-year-old daughter, Susan, fainted from the gruesome scene. The image of her battered father was simply too much for her to handle. Tommy and Scooter, his two boys, vomited, then dropped to their knees in a series of spasmodic heaves. They had never seen anything that horrible in their young lives.

Unfortunately, the brutal part was yet to come.

With his left forearm, Holmes slammed Ross's face against the post. "Stop your fuckin' squirming," he grunted. "You're just causing more pain."

"Okay," Ross sobbed, willing to do anything to stop the agony. "Okay!"

"I promise if you stop moving, I'll let you go. I'll free you from the post."

"All right, whatever you say!" He took an unsteady breath, wanting to believe the vicious man. "I will. I swear! I'll stay still."

Holmes nodded. Things were so much easier to complete with a calm victim.

"Good," he hissed, "because your squirming is ruining my souvenir!"

From the constraints of his belt, Holmes unsheathed his

stiletto, slipping the five-inch blade behind Ross's head. Then, while calming his victim with words of reassurance, Holmes lowered the razor-sharp edge to the tip of Jimmy's ear, pausing briefly to enjoy the scene. He truly loved this part. The quiet before the storm. The silence before the screams. There was something about it that was so magical, so fulfilling, that he couldn't put it into words.

Finally, when the moment felt right, Holmes finished the job. He removed the ear with a single slice, severing the cartilage from the side of Jimmy's head in one swift slash, like a movie on the life of Vincent Van Gogh.

A wave of pain crashed over Jimmy, knocking him to the ground. Blood oozed from his open wound, flooding his neck and shoulder with a sea of red. That, coupled with his loud screams, caused his wife to break from formation. She rushed to his side, crying, hoping to administer as much first aid as possible, but there wasn't much she could do.

Her husband was missing his ear, and she didn't have a sewing kit.

"The second part of this punishment, as I'm sure you've noticed, was the removal of the ear," Webster said. "As a sign of the white man's power, it was left hanging on the post right outside the slaves' cabins for several days. Not surprisingly, it was an effective way to get the master's message to his slaves. *If you do something wrong, you will pay for it in agony!*"

Holmes stared at his souvenir, left dangling from the pole like a freshly slaughtered pig. "And that, my friends, is how the Listening Post was born."

CHAPTER 33

PAYNE wasn't sure about Greene until that very moment, but one look into his eyes told him everything he needed to know. The Buffalo Soldier was a member of the Posse.

"Were you always with them, or did they get to you after we showed up in New Orleans?"

Jones's eyes widened when he heard Payne's proclamation. "What are you talking about?"

But Payne ignored him. "Just answer me that, Levon. From the beginning or just recently? I've got to know. To me, it'll make all the difference in the world."

Greene continued to stare at Payne, no emotions crossing his face.

"Come on, Levon, just one little answer. Which was it? Before we arrived, or after?"

Greene refused to dignify the question, and to Jones, the silence was maddening. Because of his current position, he couldn't see what was going on. "Bennie!" he called, trying to get involved in the conversation. He strained his neck, trying to find the dreadlocked servant. "Bennie! Help a brother out! Kick me closer to the action! Anything!"

"Be quiet," Payne ordered. "If my guess is correct, Bennie's one of them, too, so he won't help you. He's on Levon's side."

Jones's eyes got even larger. He had no idea where any of Payne's theories were coming from, but the mere possibility that they were true was mind-blowing. "Bennie? Levon? Guards? Will somebody tell me what the hell is going on? I'm supposed to be the detective here. Someone throw me a crumb."

Payne shook his head. "D.J., just shut up and listen. Levon's about to tell us everything."

Greene glanced at Jones, then returned his gaze to Payne. "I can't believe you, man. How can you think that after all the things I've done for you? I showed you my city. I let you sleep in my house. I let you eat my food—"

Payne interrupted him. "You gave us faulty guns. You tried to have us shot. You kidnapped my girlfriend. . . . Should I go on?"

"No," Greene growled, "you shouldn't. I've heard all that I'm gonna take. You called me up, and I went out of my way to help you guys. And this is how you're gonna repay me? You accuse me of trying to have you killed? Get fucking real!"

In a burst of rage, Greene kicked a nearby rock, then stormed away in anger. But that was fine with Payne, because it gave him a chance to talk to Jones.

"Do you believe me?" he asked.

Jones tried to shrug. "I know you too well not to believe you, but I'd love to hear something that supports your theory."

Payne nodded. "Bennie? Do you want to fill him in, or should I?"

Blount glanced at the two men near his feet, then stared at Greene in the distance. "I thinks you better do the talkin'. I don't wanna make Mr. Greene mad at me."

Payne smiled. Blount was a hard man to read, but if Payne's theory about Greene was correct, then Blount had to know more than he was willing to reveal. He simply had to.

"Okay, Bennie, have it your way. I'll do all of the talking. . . . Remember how things started bugging me on the boat? How my gut knew something was wrong? Well, it was the guards. The guards acted wrong when we showed up."

Jones scrunched his face. "The guards? I could barely see the guards from the boat, but you could tell that they did something wrong? What, are you psychic or something?"

"When we pulled up to the dock, they approached the boat expecting Bennie. They called to him, asking about the fireworks. Remember? But before Bennie could say anything, Levon told them about a security problem and started giving orders. Right?"

Jones nodded his head.

"What did they do after that?"

"They jumped to attention."

"And then?"

Jones thought back, trying to remember. He knew the guards ran onto the dock, following Greene's instructions, but he couldn't recall anything else. "I give up. Tell me."

"What did they do with their guns?"

It took a moment, but the solution eventually popped into his head. "I'll be damned. They threw them to the ground, didn't they?"

"Even though Levon should've been a stranger to these guys, he tells them that there's a security problem, and they throw away their guns. How in the hell does that make any sense? Come on, even mall security guards would know better than that! Unless . . ."

"Unless they were told what to expect ahead of time."

"That's what I figured."

Jones nodded, admiring his friend's theory. "I have to admit, that's pretty good. In fact, I'd give you a round of applause, but . . ."

"You can't because we let Levon tie us up?"

"Exactly."

"Probably not the brightest thing in the world that we could've done, huh?"

"Nope. Probably not."

"Right up there with being handcuffed to the desk, isn't it?"

Jones smiled. The last few days had suddenly become cyclical. "So, did you have doubts about Levon before the guards?"

"Nope. The guards woke me up, but then I started to think back over the past couple of days. The broken guns, his rule against police involvement, his escape through Sam's secret door, his discovery of Bennie, and so on. I figured all of that was too coincidental to be a coincidence."

"Yeah, you're probably right. Detective work should never be *this* easy. I mean, two days ago, we were in Pittsburgh with a license plate and a tattoo as our only clues, and here we are on the threshold of finding Ariane. Please! Things were too simple."

"To be honest, I wasn't one hundred percent sure about Levon until I mentioned it to him. There was a look in his eye that told me everything. He looked like a big ol' dog that was caught sleeping on the couch—guilt all over his face!"

"It wasn't guilt," Greene remarked. He had circled in behind them, trying to acquire as much information as possible. "It was shock. I couldn't believe that you caught onto me. I thought I'd done everything right."

"Don't kick yourself." Payne sighed. "It was the guards' fault. They ruined the entire scene. They should be fired immediately."

"I concur," Jones echoed. "In fact, I think you have a big future in acting, just like that other ex–football player from Buffalo. Hmm? What was his name? O.J. something."

"Nah, Levon's too good for that! He decided to skip O.J.'s second career and went right to his third . . . a life of crime!"

Jones laughed. Then, using the melody and the accent of the classic Bob Marley song, he began to sing. "He's just a Buffalo Convict . . . works for da Posse! He took a bunch of steroids . . . now he's their boss-y!"

"That was clever," Greene admitted. "Very clever indeed."

Jones gave him a big wink. "Thank you, Louisiana! I'll be here all week!"

"Actually, you will be. Might not be alive the whole time, but we'll worry about that later."

Payne twisted his head and glanced at Jones. "I don't know about you, but I'm going to worry about that now."

"Damn." Greene laughed. "You guys don't stop. I thought your black humor was just an act, but you guys are even like this in the darkest of situations."

Payne ignored the comment, opting to change the subject. "Hey, Levon? I gotta know. Did you sell us out before we came to New Orleans or after?"

A grin crossed Greene's lips. Since his cover was blown, he figured the answer to one question wouldn't do too much damage to his ruined reputation. He crouched to his knees so he could stare Payne in the eyes. The kindness that had been present during the past few days had been replaced by a cold, hard glare.

"Jon, if it makes you feel any better, I've been involved with the Plantation from the very beginning. And just so you know, if you had told me why you needed my help during your initial phone call, I wouldn't have invited you down here. Can you imagine my surprise when you finally told me why you were in town? I almost shit myself! But at that point, what was I to do? You were digging, and I had to stop you. It's as simple as that."

"Then why not kill us? Why take the time to lure us here?"

"Well, as you mentioned, I did try to kill you. I didn't want to personally pull the trigger, but I set things up at Sam's. Unfortunately, the damn sniper screwed that up. After that it would be too suspicious if you were killed somewhere else in the city this weekend. I figured getting you off the mainland was a better way to take care of things."

"And what about Ariane? Why did you bring her here?"

Greene sighed. He was getting bored with the inquisition and knew that the rest of his partners were waiting for him. "I'm afraid that's a question that will have to wait. They're about to make a big announcement, and I don't want to ruin their surprise."

CHAPTER 34

THE ringing telephone brought a smile to Harris Jackson's face. He'd been expecting a call for several minutes now, and when it didn't come, his anxiety began to rise. But now that the call was here, he was finally able to relax.

"Master Jackson, this is Eric down at the dock. Bennie and Master Greene just left our area, and they're headed your way."

"And the prisoners?"

"They're tied up and docile. I don't think they'll be causing you any problems."

"Good," sighed Jackson. Since Payne and Jones had been a nuisance in New Orleans, he figured they might continue the trend on the island, especially since he'd learned of their military background. But now that he knew they were under control, he felt a whole lot better about their presence at the Plantation. "Very good indeed!"

"What's good?" asked an eavesdropping Holmes.

Jackson hung up his cellular phone. "The two prisoners will be here shortly. No problems."

Holmes patted Jackson on the back. "Nice work, Harris. It seems your guards have everything under control."

"It seems that way, but we'll find out for sure in a moment." Jackson pointed to the truck as it emerged from the trees of the outer grounds. "Why don't you tell Ndjai to keep the captives busy while I check into things? Come on down when you're done."

Holmes agreed and went on his way.

"Master Webster!" Jackson shouted. "Join me for a minute, would you?"

The two men walked cautiously toward the truck, not knowing what to expect. When they saw the huge grin on Greene's face, they knew that things were fine. Holmes joined them a short second later, and the three of them finished the trip in unison.

"Gentlemen," Greene crowed, "Bennie and I should win an Oscar for this. We just put on a spectacular performance."

"Bennie helped out?" Jackson asked.

"He practically carried it by himself! You should've seen the performance he put on. Unbelievable! His acting is even better than his cooking." Greene signaled for Blount to get out of the truck, and he willingly obliged. "Come out here and take a bow. You deserve it!"

"We heard you did a great job!"

"Congratulations, Bennie!"

Blount was flabbergasted. He had never been treated nicely by his bosses before. "Thanks," he mumbled, barely smiling. He simply didn't know how to react to their compliments.

"So," Greene asked, "what are we going to do with them now?"

"You mean the new arrivals?" Holmes glanced into the flatbed of the truck and saw Payne and Jones, bound. "You know 'em better than we do. What do you think should be done?"

Greene considered the question, but it was obvious that he already had a plan in mind.

"For the time being, we need to keep Payne and Jones as far away from the other prisoners as possible. We don't want them mentioning my name or our location to anyone. Then, after you guys make your big announcement, I think it would be best if my friends were eliminated. I figure, why take any unnecessary chances with men like these?"

ONCE the foursome had finished their discussion, they walked back to the prisoners and allowed Webster to finish his speech. Earlier, he had prepared the captives for his announcement by lecturing them on the concepts of freedom, slavery, and punishment, yet there was no way that they could be ready for what he was about to reveal.

"The concept of the Plantation came to me several years ago, back when I was in college. As part of my major, I was required to take a class in American history. The topic we were discussing was the Civil War, and somehow my white professor managed to talk during the entire class without mentioning black people. In my opinion, the Civil War was fought over the concept of slavery, and that white bastard managed to steer clear of the topic. After class I approached him and asked him about his oversight. I figured he'd tell me that an upcoming lecture would be devoted to slavery, or I'd get to learn about the topic in a future reading. But do you know what he had the audacity to say? He said, *'Over the years, the impact of slavery in this country has become greatly overrated.'* Can you believe that? We're talking about the main cause of the Civil War, and my professor tells me that it was overrated! Well, right then and there, I knew what I wanted to do with my life. I decided to devote my life to the promotion of black history, emphasizing the cruel history of slavery in our so-called Land of the Free.

"But how does one do that? I wasn't really sure, but I knew I needed to get America's attention. That's why I immediately ruled out papers, studies, or projects. Why? Most people won't pay attention to academics. What I needed was something spectacular, something unforgettable, something that would get this issue noticed. But what?

"Before I made my decision, I thought it was best if I did

some extensive research on the topic. I read books and journals and manuscripts and diaries—anything that I could find about the topic of slavery—and before long, one common theme stood out: plantations! Everything I read about slavery in America mentioned plantations as the focal point. Plantations were the place where slaves lived, worked, birthed, and died. It's where they escaped from when they could and returned when they were caught. For better or worse, plantations were the center of the black man's world!

"Now, before you get bored with my ramblings, let's move on to the good stuff. How does any of this involve you? I'm sure you're asking that question right now. Why is this bastard making us stand in a field in the middle of the night to listen to this lecture? That's what you're thinking, isn't it? You don't think there's anything in this world that I could tell you that would justify your being here. You think I'm just some kind of thug who abducted you and your families on a whim. That's what you're thinking, isn't it?"

Webster paused to let the tension build. He wanted to see the confusion and misery in his captives' eyes as it continued to grow.

"Then each of you is about to receive the shock of your lives, because you were selected for a specific purpose!"

Harris Jackson moved forward, taking over the lecture. "During Master Webster's research, he was able to compile some extensive genealogy, an actual list of black family trees. Why is this significant? Because it was nearly impossible to do. Unlike white people, whose history is well documented in public records, the history of the black man is often shrouded in obscurity. Slaves rarely had last names, marriages weren't officially recognized, kids were often sold or given away as gifts. Shit, these were just a few of the drawbacks that Master Webster had to overcome in order to complete his work."

Octavian Holmes grinned. "And that's what brings us to you. Why are you here? It's the question you've been wondering for a very long time. Trust me, I know. I've seen it in your eyes. 'Why me?' you constantly wonder. 'Why us?' you plead! 'There has to be a mistake,' you assure us! 'We've done nothing wrong!'"

Holmes grimaced, his eyes narrowing to slits. "No! There have been no mistakes! Each and every one of you is guilty of crimes against the black race! Crimes that you are in the process of being punished for!"

The captives glanced at each other, panicked. The sound of Holmes's voice told them that he truly believed what he said. Holmes actually believed that they were guilty of something terrible.

"Group One," Holmes shouted as he pointed toward them, "step forward!" Members of the Metz and Ross families glanced at each other, then reluctantly inched ahead. "Jake Ross, age seventy-one, make yourself known."

The old man emerged from the center of the pack.

"You are the father of Alicia and Jimmy Ross, are you not?"

Jake Ross nodded his balding head. "Yes, Master Holmes, I am."

"After marrying Paul Metz, Alicia gave birth to Kelly and Donny Metz. Is that correct?"

"Yes, sir," Jake agreed. "They're my grandkids."

"And your son, Jimmy? He married Mary DaMico, and she eventually gave life to Susan, Tommy, and Scooter. Right?"

Jake was mystified by the line of questioning, but he still answered. "Yes, sir."

"Now tell me, what was your grandfather's last name on your father's side?"

"It was Ross, same as mine. The Ross name has lasted for several generations now."

Holmes winced when he heard the pride in Jake's voice. The tone actually made him want to vomit. "According to our research, the Ross family first surfaced in America shortly before the 1800s. They settled in Massachusetts, but slowly migrated south as this country expanded in that direction.

Eventually, your great-great-grandfather purchased a large chunk of land in Georgia, where he grew peanuts to the ripe age of eighty-one."

Jake wasn't sure what Holmes was getting at, but he could tell that it was something big. "Yes, sir. That sounds about right."

Holmes nodded contentedly. The Plantation had located the right family.

"Group Two," Harris Jackson shouted, "step forward!" The Potter family took an immediate stride toward Jackson. "Richard Potter, as the oldest member of your family, I would like to speak to you!"

Richard groaned softly, then stepped ahead. "That's me, sir."

"If I am correct, you are fifty-eight and have three kids, Andy, Darcy, and Jennifer. Andy married Sarah Goldberg, and they have a three-year-old daughter named Courtney."

"Yes, sir."

"Your one daughter married Mike Cussler, and your other daughter, Jennifer, is single."

"Yes, sir. That's correct."

"Do either of your daughters have kids?"

"No, sir. Not yet."

Jackson was fairly certain that they were childless, but if they'd had any kids out of wedlock, he wanted to know about them, too. "Where did your maternal grandparents come from?"

"Mississippi, sir. I lived there myself until my parents died."

"Yes, I know." Jackson moved closer to the man, hoping to scare him with his proximity. "What did they do for a living?"

"They were farming people, sir. Cotton, mostly."

"And what was the name of their farm? Do you recall?"

"Yes, sir. I was forced to sell it after my folks died. It was called Tanneyhill Acres. Named after my mother's side of the family."

Jackson glanced at Holmes and nodded. Both of them were pleased with what they had learned. So far, Webster had made no mistakes in his research.

"I guess that leaves me," Webster muttered. "Group Three, step ahead and join the others."

Ariane Walker moved forward and was quickly followed by her sister, Tonya, and her injured brother-in-law, Robert Edwards.

"Since each of you is fairly young, you might not be able to help me with the questions that I would like answered. Therefore, I will give you a brief rundown on your family's history. If you disagree with anything I say, please let me know."

The three nodded, not knowing whose family he was referring to.

"Ariane, you're the closest, so you will be the spokesperson. Two years ago your sister married Robert Edwards from Richmond, Virginia, and she is currently carrying their first child. Your parents, each of them an only child, died in a car crash. Each of your grandparents died at an early age, before you were even born. You have no cousins, aunts, or uncles. It's just the three of you and the fetus on the way. Is that correct?"

Ariane agreed with everything. "Yes, sir."

"Excellent," he mumbled. "Your father's parents were raised in a coastal town in North Carolina, but your father's grandparents had roots that extended much deeper south. In fact, they stretched all the way to Louisiana."

Ariane shrugged. "If you say so. I've never had the chance to research my family. As you've pointed out, most of my family is already dead."

Webster smiled. "And they're lucky they are. Because if they weren't, they'd be standing here right next to you!"

The statement made Ariane wince. She knew her presence had something to do with her family's background, but what? Her parents were both law-abiding citizens. Her sister was never in trouble, so it couldn't have anything to do with her. And as far as she could tell, her brother-in-law was one of the sweetest guys in the world. So what the hell could it be?

"I can tell by your face, Ariane, that you are deeply confused. Your face is flushed. Your eyes are darting. Anger is boiling inside."

In a moment of reckless courage, Ariane decided to voice her feelings. "Yes, sir, I'm angry. As far as I can tell, my family's done nothing wrong, yet we're here, suffering in this field for no apparent reason. So, if you would be so kind, I was wondering if you could tell me why! Why are we here? What possible explanation could you give me that would explain why we're here?"

Ariane could tell from Webster's eyes that she had spoken too harshly. In order to soften the request, she continued.

"That is, if you'd like to tell me, Master Webster, sir."

Webster glared at the girl for a tense moment, then eventually grinned. "As fate would have it, we were just getting ready to tell the entire group that very thing. And for that, you are quite lucky. Otherwise, I would've been forced to punish you severely."

Ariane nodded, relieved.

"Master Holmes?" Webster continued. "Would you care to tell old man Ross and the rest of his family why they are here?"

For a brief moment, Holmes thought back to his own childhood, one that was filled with racial threats against his family. This was finally his chance to pay the white man back for crimes against his ancestors, to get even for generations of pain and abuse. "With pleasure."

Holmes turned toward the seventy-one-year-old slave and grinned. "During our research, we stumbled across a fact that I found quite interesting. We located the name of the man who was responsible for much of the pain in my family's history. My ancestors, after they were forced to come to America in the belly of a wooden ship, were sold to a peanut farmer in rural Georgia. There, they worked, day after day, under some of the most horrible conditions imaginable. And what does any of that have to do with you? Their owner's name was Daniel Ross, and he was your great-great-grandfather!"

Jake's head spun as he took in the news. Even though he knew his family had a farm in the South, the thought that they had once owned slaves never crossed his mind. It should've, since it was a typical practice of the time, but it never did.

"And Group Two!" Jackson growled. "We've already discussed your heritage, but I left something out. Before your family owned and operated a warm and cuddly farm, they ran one of the strictest cotton plantations in the entire South. The Tanneyhill Plantation was known for its harsh guards and inhumane treatment of slaves. In fact, some modern-day black historians refer to it as the Auschwitz of Mississippi."

Richard Potter took a deep gulp as he waited for Jackson to finish.

"For the record, many of my kin were murdered on that plantation. Their innocent blood dripped from the hands of your relatives, and I will never forgive or forget."

Richard and the rest of his family lowered their eyes in shame. Even though they were never part of the horrendous events of the Tanneyhill Plantation, they still felt guilt for the actions of their ancestors. They had no reason to, because it was a different time, a time when they weren't even alive, but the feelings surfaced nonetheless.

"And that brings us to you, Ariane!" Webster glanced at Tonya and Robert, then looked around the land of the Plantation. "Remember how I told you that your ancestors stretched way down to Louisiana? Well, guess what? Your family, formerly named Delacroix, used to own this piece of land that we're currently standing on."

The color drained from Ariane's face. She had no idea if the information was accurate or not, but she knew that Webster believed it.

"That's right! The family that you claimed was so innocent used to own this plantation and all of the people that worked on it. A group of workers that included my ancestors!"

Breathing heavily, Webster moved closer to Ariane and whispered, "That's why you're here. To make up for their sins by giving us your lives."

CHAPTER 35

AFTER leaving the announcement ceremony, Hakeem Ndjai checked on Payne and Jones. The guards assured him that neither man had put up a fight while they were being transported, and both of them had been switched from rope restraints to handcuffs, as ordered. The news pleased Ndjai. Because of the prisoners' background, Ndjai realized that these two men would pose a special problem if they ever escaped from custody, a situation he'd rather not deal with.

Payne had been locked in the smallest cabin on the Plantation, one that was usually reserved for solitary confinement of the island's troublemakers. It possessed a low-beamed ceiling, a rock-covered floor, eight square feet of living space, and the lingering odor of urine and vomit. All things considered, it was like the hazing room of a typical fraternity house.

Jones, on the other hand, was given the Taj Mahal of slave cabins, a room usually used by the guards. A narrow mattress filled the left-hand corner of the room, nestled between a sink and a small lamp that had been mounted to the thick wooden wall. A white porcelain toilet sat next to the basin, giving Jones a luxury that no other captive was afforded. To make up for it, though, they'd strapped an explosive to his leg, the same device used on the other slaves.

"Hakeem?" called a voice from behind.

Ndjai turned and was surprised to see Levon Greene approaching. He wasn't used to seeing him on the Plantation. "Yes, Master Greene? Is there a problem?"

Greene shook his head. "I need to have a word with David Jones. Can you let me see him?"

The African nodded, inserting the key into the cabin's lock. "I will be outside. Just call if you need me."

"Don't count on it," he said dismissively. "This boy's all mine."

Greene pushed the door open with confidence and scanned the room for the captive, who was resting comfortably in the corner of the room, his hands bound behind him.

Sitting up on the makeshift bed, Jones spoke. "Levon, is that you?"

Greene nodded. "Are the guards treating you all right?"

"I'm still waiting for room service, but other than that, I can't complain. How about yourself?" Jones paused for a second. So much had happened during the last couple of hours, he wasn't sure if Greene's presence was good or bad. "Oh, yeah! That's right! You're one of them, you bastard!"

He ignored the insult. "I came to get you out of here."

Jones's eyes widened in the dim light. "Excuse me?"

"You heard me. I came to get you out. Let me see your hands."

This wasn't something that Jones was expecting. When Payne had first warned him about Greene, he was skeptical. He couldn't believe that the Buffalo Soldier was playing for the enemy. But after thinking things over, it started to make sense. The broken guns, Sam's death, Greene's escape. Everything fit into place. Greene had been pulling their strings from the very beginning, treating them like wealthy tourists in a game of three-card monte. And now this. One minute he's Benedict Arnold, the next he's a hero. "Are you serious?"

"You heard me. Turn around and let me see your hands. Be quick about it!"

Despite his skepticism, Jones leapt off the mattress and turned his back to Greene. "What's going on? What are you doing?"

"This!"

With a quick burst, Greene forearmed Jones in the back of the head, sending him face-first into the corner of the cabin. Before Jones could gather his senses, Greene pounced on top of him, pummeling him with a series of vicious blows to his ribs and kidneys. Punch after punch, elbow after elbow, landed solidly on Jones's back, causing him to gasp in agony.

"You have to be the most gullible brother I've ever met! Did you actually think I was gonna set you free?" Greene punched Jones again, landing another blow to the back of his head. "What good would it do if I let you go? As far as I can tell, you've already chosen a life of captivity. David Jones, house nigger for Jonathon Payne!"

Greene chuckled as he stood. "Of all the people in this world, I hate your kind the most. You've been given so many advantages that other brothers would kill for, yet you squander them by working for a white man. You take his charity. You call him boss. You kiss his ass!"

He cleared his throat and spit a giant wad of saliva on the barely conscious Jones. "You make me sick. Absolutely sick!"

The large man turned and walked back toward the door. When he opened it, he was surprised to see Ndjai standing nearby.

"Is everything all right?" Greene asked.

The African glanced past his boss and looked at Jones, who appeared to be a few blows short of a coma. "Did he cause you any problems?"

Greene glanced at his hands for a moment, then smiled. "My knuckles are sore, but other than that, things went fairly well."

Ndjai nodded his head in understanding. "Is there anything else I can do for you?"

"Yes. I understand that you currently have my good friend Nathan in the Devil's Box."

His eyes lit up with pride. "Yes, sir! Would you like to see him now?"

Greene shook his head. "How's he doing? I don't want him to die, you know."

"Yes, sir, I am quite aware of that. We monitor his health frequently, and he is very much alive. He is a little bit swollen from a run-in with some fire ants, but other than that, he is fine."

"Can he talk?"

"Not very well. He is too dehydrated to speak."

Greene pondered things, then grinned. "Pump him full of fluids over the next few hours. I want to talk to him later today, and it won't be fun if I can't understand him. All of the others had a chance to speak to their guests, and I want the same opportunity with mine."

"Yes, sir."

"One more thing. Why don't you move Payne to the Devil's Box while you're taking care of Nathan? It's supposed to be such a lovely day. I would hate to keep him away from the summer heat. He is a guest, you know."

Ndjai smiled at the possibility.

Let the torture begin.

CHAPTER 36

PAYNE had always loved the sun. Whether he was golfing, swimming, or reading, he always tried to catch as many rays as possible. He couldn't explain why, but there was something about the sunshine that made him feel good about himself, something that made him feel healthy.

Those views quickly changed as he baked in the Devil's Box.

"What the hell was I thinking?" he moaned. "Winter is so much better than this."

With his uncovered forearm, Payne tried to wipe the large beads of sweat that had formed on his cheeks and forehead. Unfortunately, since his hands were shackled to a metal loop in the floor, it was impossible, requiring the flexibility of a triple-jointed circus freak.

"Snow, ice, hypothermia. That stuff sounds *so* good!"

When Payne was initially dragged across the length of the island and up the slope of the hill, he wasn't sure what to expect. The possibility of a lynching entered his mind, but for some reason, he had a hunch that the Plantation was more about torture than death. He wanted to ask the guards who were towing him, but the four men weren't speaking English, mumbling instead in an African dialect.

After reaching the hill's summit, Payne was actually relieved when he saw the Devil's Box. No guillotine, no electric chair, no gas chamber. Just a box, a simple four-foot wooden box that had been anchored to the ground. Shoot, he figured, how bad could it be?

Then they opened it.

The figure that emerged was something from a horror movie, a grotesquely deformed zombie breaking from the constraints of his wooden tomb. Haggard and obviously dehydrated, the man's skin practically hung from his bones, like a suit that was two sizes too large. Payne wanted to turn from the scene—no sense getting a mental picture of the personal horror that was to come—but he knew it would be a mistake. He had to study the prisoner, investigate the guards, analyze the device. He needed to know what may be in store for him, if there were any loopholes in the system. It was the only way he could plan an escape.

The first thing Payne noticed was the prisoner's size. Despite his malnutrition, the man was quite large. It took three guards to lift his massive frame from the tiny device, and even then it took a concerted effort. In fact, the prisoner was so big, Payne was amazed that the guards had been able to squeeze him into the cube to begin with. His limbs seemed too thick, too long to contort into such a confined space, but it brought Payne some optimism. He figured if they could fit the giant in there, then there should be plenty of room to maneuver.

Once hauled from the box, the victim tried to stand on his own, but it was a foolish mistake. He had been imprisoned far too long to stand unaided. Atrophy and disorientation took over, forcing him to the ground with a sickening thud, his once-proud body melting into the rocky soil that surrounded him.

The memories of the tortured man, shivering and trembling at the feet of the guards, made Payne flinch. So much so that it snapped him back to the real world.

He had been in the device for several hours, and the intense heat of the Louisiana sun was already forcing his mind to wander. And he knew things would only get worse as time wore on. The more he sweat, the more dehydration would occur. The more dehydration, the higher his body temperature. The more heat, the more illusions. And so on. It was a vicious ride, one that he desperately wanted to avoid.

"Hello!" he yelled, hoping to find a savior. "Can anybody hear me?"

But the only reply was the sound of the breeze as it coyly danced around the Devil's Box.

Payne leaned his head against the oaken interior and stared at the bright sky above. The tiny slits of the lid's lattice pattern gave him a limited view of the world, but he wasn't about to complain. He figured things could be worse. He could be rotting in a freshly dug grave right about now. Still, his current situation didn't offer much hope.

At least until he heard the sound.

At first, Payne thought it was his imagination playing tricks on him, his lack of liquid causing the synapses of his brain to misfire. A heat-induced hallucination. But then he heard it a second time. And a third. Each more clear than the last. The sound, like a memory coming into focus, grew more distinct with each occurrence. Hazy, then muffled, then clear.

It was footsteps, the sound of footsteps.

Someone was coming.

Payne stretched his neck as far as it could reach, trying to peer through the intricate grate of the Devil's Box. But the tiny slits in the device prevented it.

"Who's there?" Payne called. "Hey, I'm in the box. Can you give me a hand?"

But there was no reply. In fact, the only sound that he heard was the whistling wind as it whipped over the crest of the hill, which was baffling to Payne. He knew he had heard movement only seconds before. No doubt about it. Someone was definitely out there.

In order to listen effectively, Payne turned his head to the left and placed his ear against the grate. From this position he hoped to hear things clearer, praying that it would somehow make a difference. And it did. Despite the constant rumble of the wind, Payne was able to hear the sound again. But what the hell was it? It was loud, then quiet. Close, then distant. It sounded like breathing, labored breathing, like a fat man's in aerobics class.

"Hello," Payne yelled, his voice cracking from thirst. "Who's out there? I want to know who I'm talking to."

After a short pause, the movement started again, this time with calculated strides. But instead of approaching the box, the footsteps circled it, like a hawk examining its prey, patiently waiting for its moment to strike. Payne took a deep gulp, pondering the possibilities.

What the hell was going on?

To find out, he shoved his ear closer to the grate, his lobe actually sticking through one of the air holes in the box. Someone was out there. Payne could hear him. Breathing and footsteps, nothing but breathing and footsteps. Why wouldn't he say something? Someone was circling the device, faster and faster, building himself into a frenzy. What was this guy doing? Payne strained to catch a glimpse of him, struggled for any clue, but the only thing he could hear was breathing and footsteps, multiple footsteps.

Then it dawned on him.

"Oh, shit!" he screamed, pulling his head from the lid a split second before the attack.

The beast, a snarling mixture of teeth and sinew, landed on top of the box. Drool sprayed from its mouth like it was a rabid coyote. Hoping to get inside, the animal clawed and chewed at the sturdy lid, but the device held firm.

For the first time all day, Payne was happy to be inside the box. He was actually thrilled that the contraption was so damn sturdy. Crouching as low as he could, he tucked his head between his legs like a passenger anticipating an airplane crash. As he did, he felt the creature's saliva coating the back of his neck with drop after drop of slobber.

"Close your mouth, you drooling bitch!"

With his heart pounding furiously, Payne twisted his neck, hoping to identify the animal without getting in harm's way. He wasn't sure if it was a wolf or a dog, but it was, without question, the sleekest animal he had ever seen. Covered in a sheer white coat, the level back and lean muscular frame of the creature glistened in the bright sun as it frantically clawed at the Devil's Box, trying to rip Payne into tender, bite-sized morsels. Its face, thin and angular, revealed a full set of spiked teeth, each quite capable of inflicting serious damage, and a pink nose, one of the few instances of color on the entire beast. The most prominent of its features, besides its ferocity and propensity for drool, were its ears. Long and light pink, they stood at attention like an antenna on an old TV.

As the attack continued, Payne gained confidence in the cube's sturdiness, which allowed him to take a relaxing breath. If the animal had somehow entered the box, Payne realized he would've been screwed. Since his hands were bolted to the floor and his legs were severely restricted, he wouldn't have had a chance to defend himself.

"Bad doggie!" Payne yelled, cowering from the lid. "Go home! Return to Satan!"

Surprisingly, the command worked. Just as quickly as the attack had started, it stopped. The animal suddenly leapt from the box and scurried away.

Payne's eyes grew wide from the surprising turn of events. He had never expected his request to work. In fact, he'd said it simply in jest. "Wow! Is my breath that bad?"

Before he could answer his own question, a voice interrupted him.

"Hello, Mr. Payne. How are you doing today?" The words were English, but they were tinted with an African accent.

Payne looked above but couldn't tell where the voice was coming from. He strained his neck in all directions but was unable to see who approached. "God? Is that you?"

"Master Greene told me you were somewhat of a jokester. I guess he was right."

Payne grimaced. "Actually, I'm not *somewhat* of a jokester. I *am* a jokester! There's a big difference, my African friend."

Hakeem Ndjai leaned his face over the top of his box and smiled, revealing a set of decaying teeth that had been neglected for some time. "Yes, I guess you are a jokester. Quite comical, especially for someone in your predicament."

"By the way, I meant to talk to you about that. You know, you have to do something about this box of yours. Your wooden-mesh roof is seriously messing up my sunlight. If I'm not careful, it's going to look like I tanned my face in a waffle iron."

Ndjai grinned. "All you have to do is write down your request and put it in the suggestion box at the main house. Oh, I forgot! You are unable to get to the house. Too bad! I guess you will just have to deal with it."

Payne sighed. "I guess so."

"Now, if we are done with the fun and games, I would like to ask you a question. How did you enjoy your introduction to my pet?"

"Your pet? You mean the albino pit bull? Oh, yeah, it was swell. I bet it's great around kids. Just make sure you get a head count beforehand."

Ndjai sat on the edge of the black device and chuckled. "Surprisingly, he is wonderful around children. He is only hostile when I want him to be. That is why he backed away from the box when I called him. He is very obedient."

"You called him? Damn! I was hoping it obeyed *my* commands. That would make my escape so much easier."

"Yes"—he laughed—"I guess it would. Unfortunately for you, Tornado only listens to me."

"Tornado? That's a pretty stupid name for a dog. How the hell did you come up with that?"

Ndjai sneered. "If you did not notice, Tornado circles his prey again and again until he is ready to attack. It is how he whips himself into a frenzy."

"Boy, that's kinda weird, don't you think? Why not call him Dizzy? That's a good name for a dog. Or how about Retardo? That seems to fit. I mean, let's be honest, how smart can the dog be if it has to run in a loop to attack?"

"Quite intelligent," Ndjai argued. "Ibizan hounds are some of the smartest dogs in the world. They were originally bred for Spanish royalty."

"Well, some of them might be smart, but I don't think yours qualifies. Did you get it at a clearance sale? Because that would explain a lot."

Ndjai stood from the box. He wasn't used to arguing with his prisoners. Normally, they were too scared to even speak. "You have a lot of nerve for someone who is about to die. Trust me, I will make sure you go slowly and painfully."

"You mean, like your teeth? You know, if you started brushing now, you might be able to save the last few you have left." Payne's words hit his mark, and Ndjai responded by slamming his fist into the top of the box. "What? Was it something I said? If so, why don't you let me out of here and kick my ass like a real man? Then again, you'd probably have to run around me like your fucked-up mutt. By the time you were done, you'd be too dizzy to hit me."

Ndjai took a deep breath, finally understanding the game that the prisoner was trying to play. Payne wanted Ndjai to become so infuriated that he'd do something irrational, like opening the box to get at him. It was a nice try, but Ndjai was too smart for that.

"Do not worry about my aim, Mr. Payne. If I were to let you out of your cage—something I am not going to do—I would be able to strike you. In fact, let me prove my accuracy."

Payne sat up in the box, trying to view the exhibition that Ndjai was going to put on for him. Unfortunately, as it turned out, it was a show in which he was forced to participate.

With a grin on his face, Ndjai climbed on top of the cube and lowered the zipper on his pants. "The reason for my visit, Mr. Payne, was to give you your daily dose of water, but seeing how uncooperative you have been, I have decided to alter your menu."

A sudden stream of golden liquid fell from above, surging through the slits of the cube like a warm waterfall. By lowering his head and closing his eyes, Payne did his best to avoid the downpour, but his restricted mobility prevented much success.

"What do you think of my aim now?"

Payne wanted to answer, desperately wanted to scream insults at the sadistic guard, but he couldn't risk saying a word. The possibility of the yellow liquid seeping past his cracked lips and into his mouth was far too great. Besides, he knew that he would somehow escape from the Devil's Box and make Ndjai pay for his actions.

And when he did, he would pay for them with his life.

CHAPTER 37

IT was hard for Ariane to believe, but her seemingly perfect life was spiraling out of control. Two days earlier, she was a successful bank executive, preparing to spend a relaxing holiday with the man she loved. The only activities on her itinerary were golfing, swimming, and fooling around. No business. No stress. Just pleasure. She'd been looking forward to it all summer and had done everything in her power to plan the perfect weekend.

Unfortunately, her plans were altered.

In a matter of forty-eight hours, she'd been drugged, kidnapped, and smuggled to Louisiana, where she was being tortured for the sins of relatives she'd never even known existed. Her days, which used to be filled with meetings and paperwork in an air-conditioned office, were now occupied with grueling field labor and the stinging crack of leather whips in the sweltering Southern sun.

If it wasn't for her inner strength, a trait that was tested and fortified when her parents died several years before, she would have broken down. As it was, she stubbornly clung to hope, realizing that things were never as bad as they seemed.

Well, almost never.

Her current situation offered little hope, and because of that she decided to push her luck. While pulling weeds from the untilled ground, Ariane glanced around the spacious field, searching for someone to talk to. She knew that conversation of any kind was forbidden by the guards, but she had the feeling if she didn't do something soon, there was a very good chance she was going to end up dead. And she wasn't about to let that happen without a fight.

A young woman, no more than eighteen years old, stood fifty feet away from Ariane, busily plucking rocks from the dark brown dirt. She tried to signal the girl from a distance, hoping to catch her eye, but the teen remained focused on her task.

Undaunted by the threat of punishment, Ariane moved her wicker basket to the east, carefully approaching the teenager.

"Hello," she mumbled under her breath. "My name's Ariane."

The athletic-looking girl was stunned at first, surprised that someone had the guts to speak under the close watch of the guards. After suppressing her shock, she whispered back.

"Kelly Metz." She wiped the dirt from her hands on her orange work pants, then brushed the brown hair from her eyes. "Where you from?"

Ariane glanced around. The closest guard was over one hundred feet away. "Pittsburgh. What about you?"

"Farrell, Missouri." As she spoke, she continued ripping rocks from the soil. "Heard of it?"

Ariane shook her head. There was no sense speaking when a gesture would do. "How old are you?"

Now it was Kelly's turn to be cautious. Like a student trying to cheat on a test, she made sure the coast was clear. "Seventeen." She carefully checked a second time, then continued. "Are you new? I don't remember seeing you in the field before."

"I think I got here yesterday. I'm not sure, though. Everything's kind of foggy."

Kelly nodded in understanding. "The drugs'll wear off, you know. Don't worry. Just hang in there. You'll get through this."

Ariane smiled at the optimism. She found it amazing that a girl Kelly's age was holding up so well in such adverse conditions. "You here alone?"

Kelly searched for the guards. They were busy hassling one of the male slaves. "Me and my family are a part of Group One. Ten of us in all."

Ariane thought back to earlier in the day, back when it was still dark. If she remembered correctly, Kelly was in Master Holmes's group. "Are you the one with the cute little brother?"

For the first time in a long time, Kelly wanted to laugh. "I've heard my brother called a lot of things, but certainly never cute." She looked over her shoulder, paranoid. "The cute one is Scooter. He's my cousin."

"But you have a brother, don't you?"

"Yeah," she whispered. "His name's Donny."

Something about Kelly's voice worried Ariane. She wasn't sure why, but she could tell something was wrong. She quickly looked for the nearest guard, who was still occupied with the men. "What's going on, Kelly? Is something wrong with your brother?"

She brushed the hair from her face one more time. "He's not what you would call tough. I get the feeling that he isn't holding up too well."

Ariane found that hard to believe. If Donny was anything like his sister, he was probably cutting down trees with his bare hands. "Are you sure? 'Cause you seem to be doing great."

"I play sports year-round, so physical stuff doesn't bother me. Donny, on the other hand, is in the band. The most exertion he gets is playing his trumpet."

"So, he's breaking down physically?"

"And mentally. My dad was tortured the first night we were here. I think that got to him."

Ariane tried to picture the members of Group One. She

distinctly remembered a middle-aged man with a bandaged hand. "What did they do to him?"

Kelly took a deep breath. "They cut off his finger. He didn't even do anything wrong, but they still chopped it off. Probably to prove that they were in charge."

Ariane was surprised that Kelly was handling it so well. Ariane knew there was no way she could have witnessed a loved one tortured and remained so calm—especially back when she was a teenager.

"How about your cousins? Have you talked to them?"

"Not really, but I can tell Susan's on the edge. She's real close to losing it."

"Which one is Susan?"

"She's a year younger than me. She's petite, blond hair. Very pretty."

Ariane tried to place the girl in her mind but couldn't. Too many faces, too little time.

"She was abused on the same night as my dad. Master Jackson cut off all of her clothes in front of everybody. I think that rattled her something good."

"He cut off her clothes? What did he do that for?"

Kelly shrugged. "She was wearing a bikini, so she kind of stood out."

"And you think she's in bad shape?"

She nodded. "I don't think she's gonna make it."

DESPITE her best effort, it took Ariane over an hour to cross the field—her basket of weeds and the guards' careful scrutiny made her movement difficult—but in time she eventually made her way to Susan Ross.

As she approached the teen, the first thing she noticed were her eyes. They were striking, the color of the perfect summertime sky. But it was more than their light blue hue that made them stand out. It was also the tears.

Apparently, Kelly Metz was right. Her cousin was close to losing it.

Ariane inched closer, hoping to comfort the girl with a

word or two, but the move backfired. Susan sensed Ariane's approach and tensed with fear.

"Get away from me!" she shrieked. "Just leave me alone!"

The outburst stopped Ariane in her tracks. She assumed the plea was loud enough to be heard by the guards, and the last thing in the world she wanted to do was attract their attention. She had seen how rough they were with the other slaves and desperately wanted to avoid that.

"Calm down," Ariane whispered. "You don't have to be afraid of me. I just wanted to see how you're doing."

"I'm fine!" she screeched, not giving a damn if the guards heard her or not. "Are you happy? Now get away from me!"

Ariane was flabbergasted by Susan's behavior, but under the circumstances she was willing to cut the kid some slack. "You've got to be quiet."

She glanced over her shoulder, half expecting a stampede of guards to be headed her way, and felt a great sense of relief when she realized their attention was still focused on the men.

"I realize you don't know me and probably don't trust me, but your cousin Kelly sent me over here to check on you."

The frightened girl stared at Ariane coldly. Her body language and icy glare suggested that trust was no longer in her vocabulary.

"You know, I saw you and Scooter at the ceremony this morning. He sure is a cutie."

Susan blinked a few times but didn't respond.

"How old is he?"

She licked her parched lips, giving the question some thought. "Eight."

Ariane grinned, relieved that the girl was willing to talk. "Well, he's just about the cutest eight-year-old I've ever seen. He looks like a little athlete."

Susan nodded, but refused to comment.

"How's he holding up? He seems like he's doing pretty well considering the circumstances."

She shrugged, never shifting her eyes from Ariane's face.

"And you? What about you? How are you doing?"

Susan breathed deeply, sucking in the air through her dry mouth. "What do you want? There has to be some reason you're talking to me. You don't even know me."

Ariane smiled warmly. "Like I said, your cousin wanted me to check on you."

The answer didn't sit well with Susan. "Then why didn't Kelly come over here herself? Why'd she send you?"

Ariane moved closer, hoping her proximity would lower the volume of Susan's voice. "No reason. I'm trying to talk to as many people as possible, and when I talked to your cousin, she mentioned that she was worried about you."

"She's worried about *me*? That would be a first from my family."

"Come on! Don't be silly. Your family's worried about you. They've got to be."

The statement brought a new batch of tears to the teen's eyes. "You don't know my family very well, do you? None of them have even asked how I'm doing. Not one of them."

"Well, I'm asking you. How are you doing, Susan?"

"How the hell do you think I'm doing? Every time I turn around one of the guards is touching me. Last night I saw my dad's ear get cut off. And when I do get to see my family, all my parents care about are my younger brothers. I mean, would it kill them to ask how I am?"

Ariane couldn't believe what she was hearing. Despite the gravity of their situation, Susan was showing signs of sibling jealousy. How petty could someone be? "Don't take it personally. I'm sure your parents are paying them more attention because they feel they need it. You're older. They probably figure you can handle things by yourself."

Susan wiped the moisture from her face. "Great! You're on their side, too."

"It's not about sides. It's about—"

"Just get away from me! I don't want to hear it."

"Susan."

"Get away from me!" she repeated louder. "I don't want to talk to you!"

Ariane pleaded for her to calm down, but the teen refused to listen. "Susan, if you keep making noise, the guards are going to come over and punish us."

"Good! At least that'll get you away from me!"

"Susan, I'm just trying to help."

"I told you. I don't want your help." Susan picked up her wicker basket and began walking away. "And if you follow me, I'll scream for the guards. I swear to God. I'll scream."

Despite the threat, Ariane was tempted to run after her. In her mind, she figured Susan wasn't a bad kid. She was just a traumatized teen, one who was looking for someone to cling to. And if Ariane could be that person, she'd love to be able to help.

Unfortunately, the Plantation wasn't the best place to make friends, so Ariane's act of kindness would have to wait for another day. That is, if both of them could last that long.

CHAPTER 38

AFTER waking from his nap in the plantation house, Master Jackson strolled into the field to check on the current group of slaves. As leader of the guards, he had many important duties at the Plantation, but most of them occurred before guests were even brought to the island. Jackson was in charge of training the guards, a task he shared with Ndjai since several of the men were straight off the boat from Africa. If it hadn't been for the language barrier, Jackson would've preferred training the guards by himself, but as it was he didn't really have a choice. He was forced to work with Ndjai, even though the African gave him the creeps.

Ironically, Jackson often elicited the same reaction from women, sending off a dangerous vibe that females instinctively disliked. It hadn't always been like that. The bad vibe was more of a recent thing for Jackson. As a youngster, he'd been very effective with the fairer sex. He was suave, polite, and romantic. But all of that changed in a heartbeat, one misstep that altered Jackson's life and his attitude toward women—and white people—forever.

He'd been a young associate at one of New Orleans's top law firms, and as his friends used to say, he had the world by its balls. He was handsome, intelligent, and personable. People often confused him with Wesley Snipes, but he was quick to point out their mistake. No, he used to tell them, my name is Harris Jackson, and before long, people will say *he* looks like *me*. And he believed it, too. Jackson was on the fast track to success, and he knew in his heart that he was ultimately destined for greatness.

Until he met her.

A month before that fateful day, Jackson left his law firm to start his own business. The Harris Jackson Sports Agency. He figured that with his legal mind, quick wit, and black skin, he would be able to land professional athletes by the dozen. And he was right. Within two weeks, he had signed Levon Greene, a friend of his from college, and soon after several other stars in the world of sports started using his services.

As a token of his appreciation, Jackson invited his newest clients to New Orleans for a gala celebration and arranged everything that he needed to have a successful party: food, alcohol, strippers, and rap stars. Unfortunately, when he made the party arrangements, he didn't count on the presence of a she-devil. Sure, she looked like a harmless exotic dancer—shoulder-length blond hair, great face, see-through dress—but underneath that beautiful exterior lived the heart of the Antichrist.

At the end of the evening, she begged Jackson for a ride home, and before he could say no, she was riding him in his limo. At the time, he figured it was just a one-night stand, a meaningless night of sex with a drunken vixen, but it turned into something more. It became the event that ended his career. Unbeknownst to Jackson, the girl was young. Too young. An uninvited sixteen-year-old who had snuck into the party to meet some of the celebrities. After sobering up, she regretted her actions and quickly told the cops everything that had occurred. The liquor, the nudity, the sex, everything. In a flash, Jackson was arrested, convicted, and disbarred. Before he knew it, his legal career was over, and all because of some white bitch.

After his release from prison, Jackson realized that he needed to experience the sweet taste of revenge if he was ever going to put the past behind him, and he figured the Plantation was the perfect way to do that. One white whore had taken everything that he'd ever worked for, and in his mind, this was his opportunity to get even with her and everyone like her.

Theo Webster had academic reasons for the Plantation.

Octavian Holmes had a childhood trauma to overcome.

But Harris Jackson had something different. He was in it for personal revenge.

As he scrutinized the female slaves in the dying sunlight, he tried to choose the one he wanted to play with the most. But it was a tough process, a lot tougher than the last group that had been brought to the Plantation. In order to prepare for Webster's special group of slaves, the Plantation Posse abducted twenty-five homeless people for a trial run back in May. After practicing their kidnapping and transportation techniques on the vagrants, the Posse ironed out the kinks in the slaves' housing setup. They perfected the guards' work schedules and corrected any glaring errors in management strategy, guaranteeing that the real group of slaves would be handled as efficiently as possible.

Unfortunately for Jackson, the homeless group had only one good-looking female, a down-on-her-luck runaway, so he didn't have many playmates to choose from. But the current crop of slaves was different. As far as he could tell, there were five females in the bunch that would please him immensely. They were young, pretty, and white—just how he liked them. It was just a matter of time before he chose the one that he wanted to break first.

After figuring out the girls' names, Jackson spoke to one of the guards and told him to round up the following slaves: Kelly Metz, Jennifer Potter, Sarah Potter, Susan Ross, and Ariane Walker. As far as he was concerned, the other females were too old or too pregnant to mess with.

"Ladies," he said to the five, "I'm sure you're wondering why I've pulled you away from your work. Well, I'll explain that in good time. First of all, a question: How have you enjoyed working in this wicked heat?"

Not surprisingly, the women were too scared to speak.

"Ah," he sighed. "It seems that you have forgotten the policy that was established on day one. When I ask a question, you respond, or you will pay the price."

He looked at Susan, who trembled at his presence. She remembered how he had treated her on that first night: the sharp edge of his stiletto as it slid against her flesh, his erect penis as he rubbed it against the small of her back, his threatening words. The memory of it all made her wince in agony.

"So, let me ask you again. How have you enjoyed the heat?"

"We haven't liked it," Ariane admitted. "Not one bit."

The comment made Jackson grin. "Thank you! Even though no one else had the courage to speak, I'm sure each of you agrees with Miss Walker's statement."

The women nodded their heads.

"Finally, a sign of life!"

Jackson moved forward, glancing at the bodies and the faces of the slaves, looking for the tiniest of imperfections. Sarah and Ariane were older than he usually preferred, but they did have the nicest figures of the five. Full breasts, great legs, firm bodies. And Ariane definitely had the prettiest face. Shit, she could be a model if she wanted to be. Unfortunately, he knew that neither of them was a virgin. Good-looking women don't reach their age without screwing someone. And for Jackson, that was a turnoff. He preferred his victims innocent and pure, like the other three girls in front of him.

He wanted the opportunity to ruin them for the rest of the world.

He wanted a chance to destroy a piece of their life, just like that whore had done with him.

"What I'm about to offer to you might sound too good to be true, but it's an opportunity that is steeped in tradition. Plantations used to have house slaves, people that assisted inside the house instead of in the field. They cooked and cleaned and provided indoor services that were requested.

As payment they were given a bed to sleep in and a bath to soak in."

Jackson studied the faces of the women, trying to predict which one would jump at the chance. "Now, keeping in mind that this house has air-conditioning, I need one of you to volunteer for the position."

The females glanced at each other. Each of them had a feeling what the job was really about. Everyone, that is, but Susan Ross. After a momentary delay, she stepped forward.

"I'll do it," she said. "Take me."

"Splendid!" he remarked. In his mind, he figured that she would be the one to volunteer. Of all the females, she was the one who had struggled the most in the field. The tears in her eyes were another sign that she was looking for a way out. "Guards, take her inside so she can get cleaned up. I'll be in shortly to give her further instructions."

But as the guards moved toward the sixteen-year-old, Ariane did as well.

"Susan," she pleaded, "don't do it! This is about sex!"

Jackson jumped forward, viciously slapping Ariane in the mouth. "Get back in line, bitch, before I have you whipped."

"She's just a kid. If you need someone to abuse, take me. At least I can handle it."

"Oh, sure," Susan complained, not absorbing the extent of Jackson's ulterior motives. "Use my age against me to take my spot inside. First you talk to me in the field, and now this. That's just great!"

The moment the words sank in, Ariane took a step backward. She knew that Jackson was going to strike her again. He didn't have a choice. She had broken one of his major rules, and he would have to punish her. And he didn't let her down.

Jackson closed his fist into a ball and swung viciously, connecting with Ariane's face just above her jawline. It was a savage blow, one that knocked her unconscious before she even hit the ground. Then, as she lay there, he kicked her once in the stomach just to prove to the other women that he was still in control.

"Guards, while you're at it, take her in the house, too. Now that she's broken one of my commandments, we're gonna have to dispose of her. But before we do, I think she can provide all of us with some entertainment."

CHAPTER 39

THEO Webster answered the phone, smiling. If there was one thing in the world he could count on, it was Hannibal Kotto's punctuality. "Hannibal, it's nice to hear from you again. How are things in Nigeria?"

"They would be much better if America finally wised up and set its clocks to Nigerian time. It would make my sleeping habits much more routine."

Webster laughed. "I'll see what I can do. In the meantime, tell me about the auction."

"As I hoped, the winning bid exceeds your minimum price."

"By how much?"

Kotto smiled and told him the number.

"Holy shit," Webster mumbled as he did some calculations in his head. He had twenty-three units of snow on the Plantation. Throw in some extra cash for Tonya Edwards, the pregnant one, and they were going to make a lot more money than he had ever expected.

"How soon can you make the shipment?"

"The sooner the better."

"Excellent," Kotto said. "I'll notify the buyers at once."

Webster hung up the phone, stunned. The dollar amount that Kotto had quoted was beyond Webster's wildest dreams. Actually, in the very beginning, the concept of cash had never even entered his thoughts. He wanted to establish the Plantation for revenge, not money. He planned to smuggle people onto his island and treat them the way his ancestors had been treated. In his mind it would teach white people about the horrors of slavery while striking a blow for the black culture. Of course, since he'd never been an athletic person, he knew he needed help to make his plan a reality. He could control the bureaucracy by himself, but he needed someone to handle the brutality, someone who had been trained for it. But who?

While looking for assistance, Webster solicited the advice of Harris Jackson, his ex-roommate from college. Jackson wasn't very supportive of the idea at the time—this was before his legal problems had occurred—but he suggested the name of a client who might be willing to help. And it was the perfect recommendation.

Until that point, Octavian Holmes had made a good living as a mercenary, offering his military expertise to the highest foreign bidder, but he'd reached the point in his life where he was looking for a change of pace—guerrilla warfare in South America and jungle tactics in Africa were quickly losing their appeal. He was thinking about running a training camp for militia types or opening his own shooting range, but he'd never gotten around to it.

When Webster first called, Holmes was immediately intrigued with the idea. The concept of slavery was one that had always fascinated him, and the chance to actually participate in it was too great to pass up. Unfortunately for Webster, Holmes wasn't willing to do it for free. To coordinate something as large as the Plantation, Holmes wanted to be compensated in an appropriate fashion. But Webster didn't have that type of cash. He was willing to pay what he could, but it simply wasn't enough to please a professional soldier like Holmes. So, before it even got started, the Plantation had hit a snag, a problem that threatened its existence.

But not to worry. Holmes came up with a logical solution that saved the day. Why not make money while getting revenge? That way, they could get profits and vengeance at the same time.

It sounded good to Webster, but he wasn't quite sure how it would work.

Holmes quickly clued him in. He told Webster about an African who had hired him for some military exercises in Nigeria. The man's name was Hannibal Kotto, and he was reputed to be as powerful as he was wealthy. Holmes claimed that Kotto was loved and respected throughout Africa despite his tendency to operate outside the letter of the law. In fact, while Holmes was in Lagos, he had heard rumors of a white slavery ring that Kotto was attempting to start.

The concept intrigued Webster. If the rumors were true, then he would be able to take his slavery idea to a whole new level. Instead of just kidnapping and torturing white folks for revenge, he could actually sell them to the motherland for money. It would be the original slave trade, but in reverse: whites going to a black land instead of blacks going to a white one.

After checking with his sources, Holmes discovered that the rumors about Kotto were true. In fact, he had already laid the foundation for the business. Kotto and Edwin Drake, an Englishman who lived in Johannesburg, had cultivated a long list of African entrepreneurs who were interested in buying white-skinned slaves. Even though Africans could hire black servants at a minimal price, the idea of having a white slave was too compelling to pass up. To them, a white slave would be a status symbol, like owning a Mercedes or a Ferrari. *If I'm rich, I can hire a servant, but if I'm super rich, I can buy a white one.* On top of that, many men planned on using white women as concubines, fair-skinned mistresses to have at their disposal.

Still, the concept wasn't perfect.

After several failed experiments, Kotto and Drake realized it was difficult to find a reliable supplier of whites. Sure, the two men wanted to make money off of the slave trade, but neither of them wanted to get his hands dirty. They wanted someone else to do the hard stuff. Furthermore, even though there were thousands of white people scattered across Africa, neither man wanted to make enemies on the African continent. Kotto said it would be like defecating in his own backyard. In his mind, if they were going to get white people, they were going to have to smuggle them in from places where the two men had few ties: Australia, Europe, and North America.

And that's when the Plantation organizers stepped in and offered their services.

They were the suppliers. Kotto and Drake were the distributors.

A partnership was forged.

CHAPTER 40

IF there'd been food in his stomach, Payne was confident that he would've vomited; the strong stench of urine that engulfed him pretty much guaranteed that. But as it was, Payne was only forced to deal with dehydration, severe hunger pains, and intermittent episodes of dry heaves.

"Now I know what Gandhi must've felt like," he croaked, his throat burning from the act of speaking. Yet it didn't matter to Payne. He would continue to speak all night if he had to. It was the best way to stay in touch with reality. "Gandhi probably didn't smell like piss, though."

Payne leaned his head against the box, a position he had been in all day, when his right hamstring started to cramp again. He hastily tried stretching, doing anything to prevent the muscle contractions from striking, but the shackles on the floor made it impossible to move. He would be forced to ride out the wave of agony until the spasm passed.

As Payne suffered, Bennie Blount peered into the hole of the Devil's Box. "You ain't got enough *possium* in your body. That's why you crampin' like that."

The voice stunned him, yet Payne quickly replied. "No," he groaned. "I'm cramping like this because I'm locked in a

Rubik's Cube in the middle of a heat wave, not because I didn't eat enough bananas."

"I don't know. I still think it's the *possium*."

Payne continued fighting through his cramp, in no mood to discuss the merits of potassium. "Nothing personal, but I have a policy about talking to traitors."

Blount turned on a small flashlight and placed it under his chin. He wanted Payne to see his face as he talked. "I sorry about that, Mr. Payne, but I didn't have no choice. I wasn't allowed off the island unless I agreed to do it, and I really wanted to see the fireworks. . . . As it be, I didn't even get to see 'em."

Payne shook his head in pity. Blount was just a helpless pawn in this, caught up in something that he didn't know how to control or escape from. And even though Blount worked for the Plantation, Payne could tell he wasn't as sadistic as the others.

"Hey, Bennie, I don't want to get you into trouble, but I was hoping you could give me a hand."

"You mean free ya? They'd never trust me with the key. I'd probably lose it."

"That's okay. I don't need a key. There are other things you could do for me."

Blount lowered his face to the top of the box. "Like what?"

"Some food and drink would be nice."

Blount frowned, then suddenly stood from his perch.

Payne could hear the servant walking away and was afraid that he was abandoning him for a second time. "Bennie? What's wrong? Come back! Where are you going?"

The servant's face filled the top of the box one more time. "I wasn't going nowhere. When ya mentioned you could use some vittles, it helped me remember something. The reason I came up here was to bring ya some chow, but with all the talking I forgot to gives it to ya."

Food! Mouthwatering food! Payne couldn't believe his luck. The image of a thick, juicy steak suddenly popped into his mind, causing his stomach to rumble like a subwoofer. "Thank you, Bennie. I'm starving."

"First things first. I heard what Master Ndjai did to ya, and I thought ya could use a bath." The dreadlocked servant held up a big pot of liquid, explaining what he had in mind. "Now, don't ya be drinking this stuff while I pour it on ya. This ain't normal water."

"What the hell is it then?"

"Don't ya be worrying none. I mixed up an old family recipe, one that we use to bathe babies when they be young. Not only will it makes ya clean, but it'll make ya smell like an infant."

"Thanks, but I already smell like piss."

Blount smiled. "That's not what I meant. You be smellin' April fresh when I done with ya. I promise." He carefully tipped the pot until the liquid flowed over Payne, surging through the grate like a great flood, washing away the stale scent of urine and the lingering stench of sweat.

"I'll be damned!" Payne chuckled, suddenly feeling a lot better. He took a deep whiff, breathing in the fragrance. "You're right. I smell like the goddamn Snuggle Bear. What's in that stuff? It smells great!"

Blount's smile quickly faded. "Trust me, Mr. Payne. You don't wants to know. I know it made me sick the first time I found out. Yuck!"

Although he was curious about the secret ingredient, Payne quickly changed subjects. "Bennie, now that I'm clean, what do you have for me to eat?"

"I gots ya lots of stuff, but the most important stuff be the liquids. We gots to get ya full of fluid or you's gonna melt away like lard in a skillet."

Payne attacked his meal with zeal, smiling the entire time. Bennie Blount, the dreadlocked servant from the bayou, had saved his life—if only for the time being. Technically, Blount had only provided Payne with food, juice, and a much-needed shower, but in reality he had given Payne something even more important than sustenance. He had given him hope. "Bennie, I can't thank you enough. I can't even begin to ex-plain how much I needed that."

Blount grinned as he tidied the area around the box. He

needed to make sure that there was no sign of his visit, or he'd get in serious trouble. "Well, I be feelin' bad about the trick that we played on you and Mr. Jones. I figure it be the least I can do."

"Speaking of D.J., how's he doing?"

Blount took a deep breath, pausing ever so slightly. "I don't mean to scare ya none, but I heard that Master Greene roughed him up somethin' fierce."

"What?"

"Before ya get too worried, I didn't get a chance to find out if that be true or not, but I just thought it be best if I done told ya what I had heard."

Payne considered the information. If it was true, it would make things doubly difficult.

"Where's he being held? Is he in the main house?"

"No, sir. He be in a utility cabin near the slaves. It kinda stands out from the others, though, since it has plumbing and be much larger than the rest."

"Is there any way you can visit him? You know, to bring him food and first aid?"

Blount shook his head. "Not without them knowing. The cabin is guarded, and it be locked from the outside. Since I ain't got no key, I can't get in with no permission. And I don't think I be gettin' any."

"Is there any chance of him getting out? A window? A trapdoor? Anything?"

"You be watchin' too much TV! There ain't no such thing as trapdoors in the real world."

Payne immediately thought of Levon Greene's escape from the tattoo parlor, but he didn't have time to explain it to Blount. "So, there's no way in or out without the key, right? How about Ariane? Is she still in the same place as before?"

Blount wrinkled his face in discomfort. When he originally briefed Payne and Jones about the Plantation, he had given them bogus information. It was all a part of Greene's master plan of deception. "I been wantin' to talk to ya about that. You see, the stuff that I done told you before was a little off."

Payne leaned his head against the Devil's Box and groaned. "How off?"

"Kinda completely off."

"Bennie," he said.

"I be sorry, but Master Greene wasn't about to let me tell ya the real stuff. He's one of the bosses of this place, so I didn't have no choice."

"Yeah, but . . ." Payne stopped his complaint in midsentence. He suddenly remembered that Blount had just saved his life, so there was no way he was going to make him feel worse about his earlier actions. "Okay, Bennie, you're probably right. You didn't have a choice. But I'd certainly appreciate it if you filled me in now."

Blount nodded. "We gotta be quick, though. I don't want to be gone too long from the kitchen. I might be missed."

"Fair enough."

"So, what do ya need to know?"

Payne grimaced. There were tons of things that he wanted to learn about the island, but before the opportunity passed, he needed Blount's assistance on something else. "Bennie, I know you've done a lot of nice things for me, and I really appreciate them all. But there's something I need that's even more important than information."

Blount brushed the braided hair from his face, gazing into the box. "Like what?"

"Well, I was wondering if you could scratch me."

"Huh?"

"I was hoping you could scratch me. I've been in here for a pretty long time, and I got a number of itches all over my body that I can't reach, so . . ."

"You's being serious, ain't ya?"

Payne nodded, trying to look as pathetic as possible.

"You's crazy! I want to help ya and all, but I ain't touchin' no man. Besides, there ain't no way my arms can fit in that thing. The holes on the top be too skinny."

Payne sighed, making sure that Blount could hear his disappointment. "Come on, Bennie, there has to be something you can do. These itches are driving me crazy! Every time I move, it feels like something is crawling on me—especially down there. It's horrible!"

Blount examined the grate of the box, but his suspicions were correct. There was no way for him to get his arm inside. "Why don't ya do it yourself?"

"If I could, I would. But as you can see, my hands are bound to the floor. I can't even crack my knuckles, let alone scratch myself."

Blount peered closer, shining the light inside. "Yeah, your hands is bound good. Unless . . ."

"Unless what?"

"Unless I can do somethin' with your hands."

Payne tried not to smile, but it was tough. Blount had just suggested the one thing that Payne was hoping for. In fact, it was the only reason that Payne had bitched to begin with. "Jeez, Bennie, what do you think you can do?"

Blount examined the shackles from several angles. Then he peered at the outside of the box. "You be in handcuffs, right? And the handcuffs is bolted to the floor?"

"That's right."

"And if I release the bolt from the floor, you'll still gonna be in cuffs, won't ya?"

Payne pretended to contemplate things. "Yeah. That sounds about right."

"And you can scratch yourself with cuffs, can't ya?"

"Definitely! And it wouldn't be like you were freeing me. I'd still be locked in this thing."

Blount mulled over the situation. He didn't want to do anything that would give away his role in this. "All right. I think I can unscrew the bolt from the outside. Once you pull your cuffs from the hook, I be putting the bolt right back. That way it looks like you did it on your own."

Payne lowered his head and smiled. The servant didn't realize it, but he had given Payne much more than an opportunity to scratch.

He had given him a way to escape.

CHAPTER 41

DAVID Jones had no idea where his best friend was being held or what was being done to him, but the racial overtones of the island suggested he was probably in bad shape.

Despite the pain in his ribs and back, Jones squirmed until his hands, which had been bound behind him, were stretched beyond his feet and repositioned near his stomach. Though his hands were still bound, he had a lot more freedom to move about the cabin and search for a way out. He quickly probed the floor, walls, and ceiling, but each of them proved to be solid. After several minutes, it became apparent that his only option was the heavily guarded front door. Made of oak and finished with a light lacquer, the door was thick, too thick to knock down. It sat in a matching oak frame and was sealed from the outside with a steel dead-bolt lock.

Frustrated, Jones lay on his mattress and pondered his situation. "What would MacGyver do?" he wondered aloud, referring to the TV character who had a penchant for creative solutions. "He'd probably make a grenade out of chocolate pudding and blow up the door."

He chuckled as he said it, but as he stared at the door

over his outstretched feet, two things became apparent. One, a doorway explosion was within the realm of possibility. And two, he wouldn't have to build a device because the guards had actually given him one.

The idiots had strapped it to his leg.

Forgetting the pain in his back and ribs, Jones leaned forward to study his anklet. The mechanism, attached below his shin, was encased in a silver, metallic shell that was no thicker than his hand. The gadget was streamlined and carried little weight; that meant the technology was pretty advanced.

Unless this is a dummy, he thought to himself.

Since the latest in incendiary gear was bound to be expensive, Jones wondered if the Posse had the finances to spend so much money on deterrents. If they didn't, he figured they might be tempted to put dummy devices on the legs of their captives. To him, it made sense. The prisoners would undoubtedly accept the guards' explanation of the anklets, and because of that they'd be too scared to run away or attempt to remove them.

To find out what he was dealing with, Jones looked for the safest way to penetrate the metal casing. He carefully explored the outside of the shell, realizing that there were only two practical choices. He could pick the lock on the front of the anklet, a difficult task without the proper tools, or he could pry the case open with some kind of wedge. The second option seemed the easier of two, but it also seemed much riskier. Even though there was a thin seam that ran along the top of the mechanism, one that could be pried apart with some effort, Jones figured it was bound to be booby-trapped. Most high-tech explosives were.

That meant he had to pick it.

The question was, how? If he had his lock-picking kit with him, Jones could open the clasp in less than a minute. Without it he had no idea how long the process would take— if he could do it at all. In order to try, he had to find something slender enough to fit in the lock but sturdy enough not to break. Jones scoured the walls for stray tacks or nails, but it was pretty obvious that there were none. Next, he examined his bed, hoping that there were iron springs on the inside, but the mattress was made of foam.

"Shit!" he grumbled. "What can I use?"

Jones glanced around the room for several seconds before his statement finally sank in.

He could use a part from the toilet.

With a burst of energy that masked his pain, he rushed to the porcelain throne and removed the back lid. Peering inside, he was glad to see the water in the tank was semiclear, tainted slightly with the orange residue of rust but better than he'd expected. Wasting no time, he plunged his shackled hands into the fluid, hastily searching for a tool that would fit into the lock of his anklet. After several seconds, Jones found the best possibility. The floater lever, which was shaped like an eight-inch-long barbecue skewer, was thin and made out of a hard plastic.

Dropping to his knees, Jones turned off the main water valve with a few rotations of his wet hands, then lowered the handle on the commode. With a quick flush, the murky liquid exited the tank, filling the white bowl like a wet tornado before dropping out of sight. Jones climbed to his feet, grunting slightly as he did, then removed the plastic rod with a twist.

Wasting no time, Jones closed the lid on the toilet seat and sat down. After taking a deep breath, he crossed his legs, bringing the anklet as close to his face as possible. Then, with his hands chained, he tried sliding the slender piece into the lock.

Thankfully, it fit.

With his limited view of the anklet, Jones couldn't identify the type of lock he was dealing with. He knew it could be opened with a key, that much was certain, but he wasn't sure about its internal safeguards. If it was a spring lock, he was confident he could pop it rather quickly. Spring locks have very few safeties, making them a criminal's dream. They can often be picked with a credit card or another thin object in a matter of seconds. If, however, the lock was tubular, then Jones was out of luck. The multiple pins of the cylinder and the dead-bolt action of the cam would require something more sophisticated than a sharpened piece of plastic.

Working like a surgeon, Jones jiggled the floater lever back and forth until he got a feel for the internal mechanism of the lock. A smile crept over his face when he realized what he was dealing with. It was a spring lock, just as he had hoped. After wiping his hands on his shirt, he slowly manipulated the lock in a circular fashion until it popped open with a loud click.

"Damn!" he said to himself. "Why are women never around when I do something cool?"

After sliding the device off of his leg, Jones was able to study the casing of the anklet in greater detail. The shell was silver in color, shiny and quite reflective, yet possessed an abrasive texture that was rough to the touch. It carried very little weight—one or two pounds at the most—but was durable, holding up to the rigors of his probing. The alloy was unfamiliar to him, possibly a mixture of titanium and a lesser-quality metal, but definitely expensive.

Too expensive for it to be a hoax.

"Ladies and gentlemen, we've got ourselves a bomb."

Now that he knew what he was dealing with, he had to decide the best way to use it. Sure, he could strap the explosive to the door and blow the sucker off its hinges, but what would that get him? Probably killed, that's what. The moment he ran outside, the guards would be all over him.

No, in order to escape, Jones needed a way to take out the guards and the door at the same time. But how? Jones went to work on the device as he planned a scenario in his head.

CHAPTER 42

EVEN though Payne was still trapped in the Devil's Box, he felt good about his situation. His hunger was gone, his thirst had vanished, and he smelled kind of pretty. As soon as Bennie left the hill, Payne went to work on his shackles.

When his hands were bound to the floor, there was no way for him to remove his handcuffs. The thick bolt had prevented it. But as soon as it was disengaged, he was able to use the maneuver that he'd learned from Slippery Stan, an escape artist whom he befriended while at a magic exhibit. Unlike most magicians, escape artists rarely use optical illusions in their trade. Instead, they learn to manipulate their bodies to escape from straitjackets or multiple layers of chains. And in the case of handcuffs, Payne was taught to turn his hands and wrists at a very precise angle, which allowed him to slide from the restraints like a hand from a glove.

Of course, the cuffs were only half the battle. The next part of Payne's escape would be more difficult, and he knew it: In order to get from the box itself, he had to rely on outside help. He wasn't sure where that was going to come from—perhaps Bennie, or a guard, or even an escaped captive—but he knew he was stuck until someone showed up.

And it took nearly an hour before someone did.

The instant Payne heard movement outside he slid his hands under his chains, hoping to maintain the appearance of captivity.

"Are you still alive?" asked Ndjai with his thick African accent. "I bet you are bored up here all by yourself." He lowered his face to the grate, smiling with his nasty teeth. "Do not worry. I have some company for you."

The wheels in Payne's head quickly started to spin. Was it Jones, Ariane, or maybe even Bennie? None of the possibilities pleased Payne, and the grimace on his face proved it. "Who is it?" he croaked, trying to pretend he was dehydrated. "Who's out there with you?"

"The question should not be *who*. The question should be *what*."

Payne scrunched his face in confusion. He couldn't hear Tornado's panting so he knew it wasn't him. In fact, he didn't hear anything except Ndjai's laughter. "Okay, *what* is out there?"

"A couple of playmates to keep you company."

Payne didn't like the sound of that. "I appreciate the offer, but I'm actually all right. I've kind of enjoyed the solitude."

"Is that so? You might get bored later, and I would hate for you to think of me as a bad host." Ndjai lifted a large shoe box above the grate then shook it a few times. An angry squeal emerged from the cardboard structure. The creature, whatever it was, did not like to be jostled. "Hmmm, he sounds mad. I hope you will be able to calm him down."

"I hope so, too."

Ndjai rested the cardboard container on the top of the box. "Then again, that might be tough for you to do. My little friend tends to get upset around the other playmate that I brought for you." Ndjai lifted a large duffel bag into the air, then set it down with a loud thump. "You see, this second guy is hungry, and when he is hungry, he has a nasty habit of wanting to eat the first guy, which makes the first guy nervous."

"Wait," Payne mumbled. "Am I the first guy or the second guy? You went so fast I got confused. Please say that again."

The African was ready to explain when he realized that Payne was making another joke, a reaction he hadn't expected. "I must admit, I admire your courage. Too bad it is a weak attempt to mask the fear underneath."

"It wasn't weak," Payne argued. "I thought it was a pretty good effort on my part."

Ndjai ignored the comment, moving to the business at hand. "So, Mr. Payne, I will now give you a choice. Which would you prefer first? The bag or the box?"

"Well, it'd be a lot easier if you told me what they contained."

"But that would take away the mystery."

"Who cares? Mysteries are overrated. I prefer comedies."

Ndjai laughed. "In that case, let us do something fun. How about both at once?"

With a gloved hand, Ndjai reached inside the small box and tried to grab the animal.

Payne listened closely, trying to figure out what Ndjai had in store for him, but all he could hear was the scratching of sharp claws and tiny squeals of anguish from the trapped creature. "I would like to introduce you to the plantation rat, a breed that is indigenous to Louisiana."

Holding it by its tail, Ndjai dangled the rodent above the Devil's Box. Payne, who'd never heard of the species, marveled at its size. It was sixteen inches in length, not including its tail, and must have weighed close to two pounds. It had a short snout, small ears, and was covered in coarse fur.

"Is that your son?" Payne asked.

"No, that is your new roommate."

"Then I expect this and next month's rent in cash, plus I'll need him to sign a few waivers. Can the squirrel write?"

Ndjai smiled while lowering the rat to the box's grate. As he did, the rodent squirmed, trying to free itself from the

Ndjai's grasp. To punish the rat for its escape attempt, Ndjai squeezed its tail quite hard, causing the creature to snap its teeth and brandish its claws in anger.

"You are going to have fun with him. He is not very happy."

Payne shrugged. "That makes two of us."

With his free hand, Ndjai reached into his pocket and removed a full set of keys. After choosing the correct one, Ndjai inserted the key into the lock and opened it with a soft click. He removed the padlock with his left hand while dangling the shrieking rat with his right. "Are you ready?" he asked as he threw open the lid of the Devil's Box.

"Actually, I was about to ask you the same thing."

Before Ndjai could react, Payne leapt from his crouched position and struck his captor on the bridge of his nose. The African stumbled backward, dropping the rat into the box as he staggered, but Payne couldn't have cared less. Before the rodent could attack, Payne pounced from the wooden cage, landing next to Ndjai, who raised his hands in defense but could do little against Payne. With a quick burst, he pummeled Ndjai with several shots to his face, beating him repeatedly until blood gushed from his nose and mouth.

Once the African had submitted, Payne grabbed his legs and dragged him roughly toward the box. "Let's see how you like this thing. Maybe you can get the rat to calm down."

He pulled Ndjai to his feet and bent him over the edge of the box, dangling his upper body inside. The rat, still angry from before, reacted instantly, jumping and nipping at the crimson liquid that dripped from Ndjai's face.

"Oh, isn't that cute! I think he likes you."

Payne punctuated his comment by dumping Ndjai upside down next to the appreciative rat and slamming the lid shut. As he reached for the lock, he suddenly noticed Ndjai's duffel bag out of the corner of his eye.

"Well, well, well! What other toys did Santa bring for me?"

Payne tried lifting the bag with one hand but was caught

off guard by its weight. "Wow, I can't even imagine what's in here. But that's okay, since you're such a fan of mysteries."

After emptying the bag into the Devil's Box, Payne closed the lid and broke the key in the lock. Then, as he pocketed Ndjai's key ring, Payne took a moment to watch the terrified rat as it scurried over Ndjai, both of them trying to avoid the jaws of the angry python.

CHAPTER 43

MOVING silently in the darkness, Payne glided across the open fields of the Plantation, constantly searching for guards. Since he was unaware of Ariane's current location, he decided to head straight for Jones, hoping that his friend was in good enough health to assist him. If he wasn't, Payne realized he would have to handle the Posse by himself. He had faced longer odds in the military, so he knew he was capable of doing it again, but all things considered, he'd love to have his former lieutenant by his side.

When the cabins finally came into view, rising out of the flat ground like wooden stalagmites, Payne dropped to his belly and scouted for patrol patterns and sniper placements. He watched for several minutes, studying the tree lines and roofs, the bushes and walkways, but he was unable to detect any movement.

His hazel eyes continued to scan the darkened landscape, probing every crevice and shadow of the compound, but the waning crescent moon and the lack of overhead lights made it difficult to see from his distance. Reluctantly, he moved closer.

Payne sprang from his stomach and charged forward at

top speed, the breath barely escaping his mouth, his feet rarely creating a sound. It was as if he was moving on a cushion of air that silenced each of his strides, softening the impact of his steps as he hustled across the hard turf. After closing the gap to forty feet, Payne found cover behind a large rock, pausing for a moment to feed his hungry lungs. When his breath returned, he carefully peeked over the boulder and searched the immediate area for patrolmen.

"Come out, come out, wherever you are," he mumbled softly.

But no one did. The grounds were devoid of Posse members, leaving the front door of the nearest cabin without protection.

Taking a deep breath, Payne placed his hand in his pocket and removed Ndjai's keys so they wouldn't jingle when he ran. Next, after looking around one last time, he sprinted forward, heading straight toward the cabin that was closest to him. Upon reaching it, he crouched near the ground and made himself as small a target as possible while double-checking the terrain. When he was sure that no one was around, he shoved the first key in the lock, but it didn't work. The same problem occurred with the next key, and the one after that, and the one after that. Finally, on his fifth attempt, with sweat dripping off his forehead from tension and physical exertion, he found the one that did the job.

With a sigh of relief, Payne opened the door as quietly as he could and slid into the cabin with nary a sound. It took his eyes a moment to adjust to the darkened interior of the room, but when they finally focused, he realized his mission had just become a whole lot easier.

He had been hoping to find Ariane or Jones.

Instead, he had hit the mother lode.

STILL in handcuffs, Jones opened the silver shell of the explosive and carefully probed the interior of the bomb for booby traps. He found several. If he had removed the anklet's casing without care, the device would've exploded in his face, triggered in a millionth of a second by a series of trip wires that protected the outer core of the mechanism.

Thankfully, he noticed them in time.

After neutralizing the safeguards, Jones dug deeper, examining the high-tech circuitry that filled the unit. "I'll be damned," he said, impressed. He had never seen a portable explosive filled with so much modern technology: data microprocessors, external pressure sensors, satellite uplink antennae—which he broke off—and digital detonation switches. The kind of stuff that couldn't be bought at Radio Shack. "This is some serious shit!"

Using the sharpened lever from the toilet, Jones continued to explore, searching under the electronic hardware for the actual explosive. In order to take out the door, Jones needed to understand how much force the device was capable of producing. He assumed that the component was filled with a relatively stable explosive, something that could handle sudden movements and exposure to body heat or static electricity, but he wasn't sure what. C-4, a commonly used plastic explosive, was a possibility, so were RDX, TNT, and pentolite. Because of the high-tech craftsmanship of the anklet, Jones figured that the manufacturer would use something newer, sexier. Perhaps a synthetic hybrid.

When Jones finally discovered what he was dealing with, he gaped in fascination. The device was unlike anything he had ever seen before. Two vials, three inches in length, sat tucked underneath the circuitry. Each plastic cylinder was filled with a liquid—one red, the other clear. They were connected to a third vial, which was twice as wide as the others, through a series of slender plastic tubes. Each one was color-coded and approximately the width of a pencil.

The cylinders, the liquids, the tubes. All of them were new to Jones.

"What the hell am I supposed to do with this?"

As the words left his mouth, his problems actually worsened because he heard the distinct sound of keys rattling directly outside. Someone was about to enter the cabin.

Jones hastily looked around for a hiding place but found

nowhere to stash the equipment. The mattress was probably his best possibility, but Jones knew if he was forced to sit on the bed, there was a chance that his weight could detonate the device, and the thought of shrapnel being launched up his ass was a bit unsettling.

Finally, with no other options in mind, Jones scooped up as many parts as he could and ran toward his bed. After setting the explosive on the floor, he turned his mattress on its side and angled it across the back corner of the room like a child's fort. He figured, if he timed things just right, he could throw the explosive at the guard the moment he entered the room, then duck behind the bed for protection.

The knob twisted with a squeak.

Jones knew the plan wasn't perfect, but he also realized that this could be his only chance to escape. That was why he was willing to risk everything on this plan. His entire life on one moment.

The door swung open.

Making things tougher, Jones had to throw the explosive with his hands bound together, forcing him to use an overhead soccer toss. And on top of that, his ribs still ached from the beating that Greene had given him earlier.

A man wearing black fatigues entered the cabin.

Jones had no choice. This had to be done.

In one swift motion, he launched the explosive at the dark figure and dropped to the floor behind his protective foam shield. In anticipation of a powerful blast, he covered his face and ears, curling into the fetal position against the back corner of the room. He was lucky he did. The cylinders ruptured on contact, creating a bright ball of flame that tore across the cabin in a tidal wave of heat and light. Thunder ripped through the enclosed space with the ferocity of a jackhammer, stinging Jones's ears despite the presence of his hands. Shards of metal sliced through the mattress, narrowly avoiding the exposed flesh of his back.

Slightly dazed from the jolt, Jones peeked over the tattered barrier to see how much damage had been done. Large streaks of red and orange danced from the far wall toward the unprotected surface of the beamed ceiling. Billowy puffs of smoke filled the enclosed space, making it tough for him to breathe. The door, shaken free from the concussion of the blast, sat unhinged and heavily dented, covered in debris and awash in flames. And the guard was . . .

Wait, where was the guard?

Jones knew he'd hit him—he *had* to have hit him, didn't he?—so, despite the crackling flames that raged throughout the cabin, he climbed over the mattress and searched for a body. It didn't matter that the fire was quickly becoming an inferno, shooting tiny embers into the air like bottle rockets. He *needed* to find the guard. He had to get the man's gun and take his keys. He had to question the bastard about Payne and Ariane before it was too late.

Hell, he had to do something to even the odds.

Unfortunately, the blaze was making his mission impossible. The smoke grew thicker and blacker every second, limiting his vision to a scant few feet. And the heat was so intense that Jones felt like he was standing in the core of an active volcano, one that was getting angrier by the minute. But still he searched, heroically digging through scraps of plastic and wood, hunting for the guard until he could take no more, until the hair on his arms literally started to sear like ants under a magnifying glass.

At that point he decided to flee the firestorm before he fried in its wake.

Covering his eyes with both hands, Jones ran from the burning cabin, shielding his head from the flames as he burst through the smoldering doorway. The nighttime air brought him instant relief, but he wasn't able to enjoy it. Jones realized that the Posse would be there any moment to investigate, and when they arrived he needed to be long gone. Using the orange glow of the cabin as his torch, he probed the area for cover, but his plans to flee were quickly altered. Before he found a hiding place, Jones noticed the guard sprawled on the nearby sod, a weapon sitting on the ground next to him.

No time to waste.

He rushed to the man's side and grabbed his TEC-DC9 pistol. Then, in a moment of greed, he frisked him, looking for anything that could help, and as he did he made a startling discovery.

The injured man was Payne.

CHAPTER 44

BECAUSE of the black fatigues and face paint that Payne had found in the first cabin, he looked like a Posse member in the darkness. It wasn't until Jones stared at Payne's face in the light of the fire that he recognized his best friend.

"Is there a reason you tried to blow me up?" Payne asked. He staggered to his feet, shaken from the powerful blast but injury free.

"I thought you were a guard," Jones argued.

"If you don't want to hang out anymore, that's fine! But you don't have to blow me up."

Payne shook his head in mock anger, then jogged away from the cabin. He knew the Posse would be arriving shortly, and he didn't want to be there when they did. Once they were far enough away from the scene, he turned back toward Jones and unlocked his handcuffs.

"What was that stuff anyway? It had some serious kick."

"Some kind of high-tech chemical explosive. Some African guy with bad teeth strapped the sucker to my leg to prevent my escape."

"Hakeem did that?" The thought of Ndjai in the Devil's

Box made him laugh. "Locking a soldier in a wooden cabin with a firebomb? Pretty good thinking on his part, huh?"

"That was more than just a firebomb. That was a first-rate piece of hardware. I'm not sure what we've stumbled onto, but the Posse isn't hurting for cash. Not with that kind of technology lying around."

"You don't know the half of it. Let me show you what I found."

Payne led Jones to the first cabin that he had explored. Instead of containing prisoners like he thought it would, it was filled with military accoutrements: rifles, pistols, ammunition, explosives, detonators, camouflage paint, etc. All labeled and packed in crates for shipping.

"Whoa!" Jones glanced at the gear, smiling. There was enough equipment to start a war. "This is some kind of collection."

Payne corrected him. "This is more than a collection. This is a business."

"They deal arms? Where'd they get this stuff?"

"Where do you think?" Payne pointed to one of the invoices on the wall. The initials *T.M.* were highlighted at the top. "Does that ring any bells?"

Jones glanced at the sheet. "Terrell Murray? Mr. Fishing Hole?"

"You got it." Payne strolled through the stacks of weapons, looking to add to his personal stock. He needed as much firepower as possible if he was going to rescue Ariane and the others.

"What are you saying? The Posse sells Terrell all of his weapons?"

Payne shook his head. "From the looks of Murray's office, he's too established to be buying from a new group like the Posse. So I'm guessing it's the other way around. The Posse gets their guns from Terrell."

Jones furrowed his brow while glancing through the crates. "But why would they need to buy all of this stuff? I mean, this is like an armory."

"Not *like* an armory. It *is* an armory. If my guess is correct, the Posse doesn't own these weapons. They're probably just holding them for Terrell as a favor. Remember what Levon said? Nothing goes on in New Orleans without Murray's involvement."

Jones pulled a Steyr AUG assault rifle from a crate. "Boy, this looks familiar, huh?" It was identical to the one that Greene had supposedly purchased from Murray. "So this is where Levon got his stuff? That son of a bitch! I can't believe he played us like that! I can't wait until I see him again. I really can't."

"Well, you'll have to wait a while. The first thing we have to do is find Ariane. Once I know she's all right, we can get as much revenge as we want."

Jones nodded, thinking mainly of Greene. "Who do you have in mind?"

Payne walked toward the cabin door. "There are too many on my list to name."

CHAPTER 45

OCTAVIAN Holmes roared through the trees on his ATV while two truckloads of guards followed closely behind. Out of all the men on the Plantation, Holmes was the best equipped to handle military situations, since he was a professional soldier. He had worked for nearly two decades as a mercenary, renting out his services to a variety of causes, but this was the first time his skills would be used to protect something of his own.

The Plantation was a part of him. He would not let it be destroyed. Not if he could help it.

Holmes stopped his vehicle near the burning cabin and watched his men attack the blaze. There was little hope of saving the structure since fire equipment was very scarce on the island, but they needed to prevent the flames from spreading. The other cabins were nearby and susceptible to damage.

As Holmes watched their effort, he sensed a presence sneaking up behind him. He turned quickly, raising his gun as he did, but his effort was unnecessary. It was Jackson and Webster, checking out the damage.

"Any ideas?" Holmes asked calmly.

Webster nodded, slightly nervous. "It was the new guys. I was in my office and saw one enter the door with a key. Moments later it blew up."

Holmes frowned. "Which of you lost your keys?"

Both men showed Holmes their personal sets, proving they weren't to blame.

"Fine. Where's Hakeem? He's the other possibility."

Webster shrugged. "I tried paging him on the radio, but he didn't answer the call. I tried all of you the moment I saw the guy enter the cabin, but there was nothing else I could do from my office. I swear, I did my best."

"Theo, don't worry about it." Holmes's voice possessed a scary type of calm. His presence was almost stoic. "You aren't here to do the dirty work. You're here to handle our finances. We'll handle the rest."

Holmes moved closer to the blaze, still examining it. There was something about the flames that interested him. The way they moved. The way they danced. He had seen it before. "Theo? You saw the explosion, right? Tell me, what did it look like?"

"It was a big, mushroom-type blast. A big flash of light burst from inside. Flames spread quickly across the door and roof. An unbelievable amount of thick, black smoke."

Holmes grinned at the description. Things finally made sense. "Well, if my guess is correct, we don't have to worry about escapees. The blast you described sounds like one of the anklets was detonated."

Webster disagreed. "Actually, I saw both of them survive. One of them went in, but two of them came out."

Holmes's grin grew wider. That meant the prisoners had discovered a way to remove the anklet without getting killed. The thought of two worthy adversaries piqued his interest. He'd take great pleasure in hunting them down. "What do you know about these men?"

Jackson answered. "Levon said they were ex-soldiers. They called themselves the Crazy Men or something weird like that. If you talk to him, I'm sure he can tell you more. He babysat the bastards for two days."

"Crazy Men?" Holmes had never heard of a group that went by that name, and he considered himself an expert on the military. "Could it have been something else? Perhaps the MANIACs?"

"Yeah, that was it. Have you heard of them?"

"Yeah," Holmes muttered as the smile on his face disappeared. "I've seen their work. They're clean. Real clean. Some of the guys I worked with called them the Hyenas."

"Hyenas? Why's that?"

"They liked to ravage their victims. I mean, rip 'em to fucking shreds from very close range. Then they'd leave the scene in packs, laughing, like their job was the easiest thing in the world." Holmes shivered at the thought, an equal mixture of fear and excitement surging through him. After all these years, he would finally get to see how good he was. "They're the best-prepared soldiers in the world."

"Come on, how tough can they be?" Jackson asked naively. "We've got dozens of armed men, and we're fighting against these guys in a confined space, right?"

Holmes nodded gravely. The stories he had heard about the MANIACs bordered on legend. "True, but if these guys are who you claim, we might be outnumbered."

AFTER stealing gear from the armory, Payne and Jones hustled into the nearby trees to establish their attack strategy. Unfortunately, their planning would be difficult since they still lacked one major piece of information: Ariane's current location.

Payne updated his friend on everything he'd learned about the guards and the landscape. Then he filled him in on what he didn't know. "I searched a few of the cabins before I reached you. All of them were empty."

"Empty? Then where is everybody? Bennie said there were twenty to twenty-five captives."

"I didn't check all the cabins, but none of them are being guarded. Therefore, either the prisoners are being kept elsewhere, or they've been moved off the island."

"Or," Jones added, "there are several people in one cabin. In the old days, slaves used to sleep ten to a room, and I have a feeling the Posse isn't trying to make their guests comfortable."

Payne nodded in agreement. "So tell me, what should we do?"

Jones smiled at the question. "I thought you'd never ask."

For as long as they'd known each other, this was how their partnership worked. Payne would name a place, and Jones would lead him there. It didn't matter if it was a top-secret mission into Cuba or a beer-filled trip to a Steelers game, Jones was the navigator. He was the planner. A strategy prodigy. It was his specialty. He was the best there was.

Payne, on the other hand, was the finisher. The closer. The military's equivalent of a baseball relief pitcher. He would come in when everything was on the line and finish the job. In truth, it was rarely pretty. Most of the time his work was bloody, even borderline savage. But things always worked out in the end. Always.

Give him a quest, and he'd make it a conquest. Guaranteed.

Together, they were an unstoppable duo.

Let the games begin.

CHAPTER 46

THERE was no reason for the duo to wage battle in the open fields where a lucky shot could take them out. No, it was better to do their dirty work in the dark underbrush of the island, where they could control the game. The woods would be their playground. Search and kill, jungle style.

Without speaking, Payne and Jones communicated their ideas through hand signals. It wasn't traditional sign language, but for them it was just as effective. They knew exactly what the other meant without saying a word, and that was critical. During night runs, sound was the biggest enemy.

On the other hand, sound could also be quite useful, the ultimate ally. By making a noise on purpose, a soldier could divert his enemy's attention. The crash of a thrown rock could confuse a tracker. A snapping twig or a well-placed scream could quickly draw attention away from an endangered colleague. And occasionally, it could be used as a lure, a way to bring several people into an area at one time. It was a difficult thing to accomplish, but when done right, it was very effective.

Cows to the slaughterhouse, as Payne liked to say.

Eventually, this was the technique that Jones settled on.

In order to make it work, they placed some charges near a small clearing that they found in the middle of a thick grove. A boulder, partially buried on a nearby plateau, would be used as the duo's nest. The goal was to draw as many men as possible into the open area below the large stone before Payne and Jones used their elevated position to commence target practice.

After climbing the bluff, Jones settled into position next to Payne. Normally, they would've spread far apart, attempting to surround their victims in hopes of cutting off their escape routes, but in this case it was completely unnecessary. This assault would be child's play, a complete bloodbath. Two experienced soldiers facing a team of untrained men was as lopsided as a battle could get. Besides, the landscape didn't allow them to fan out over a wide range. The terrain dictated that both of them sit in the crow's nest from the get-go.

When Payne was ready, he glanced at Jones and nodded. It was time to begin.

BOOM!!! An explosion shook the earth, and a flash of light brightened the nearby sky. Everyone near the burning cabin flinched and turned their heads toward the trees. The prisoners were apparently in the woods. Holmes gave orders to pursue them.

Tat-tat-tat-tat-tat!!! Payne and Jones squeezed off a few rounds for additional attention, plus they wanted to make sure that their weapons were functional. The last time they'd used Terrell Murray's guns they were very disappointed with the results.

BOOM!!! A second charge exploded. Payne and Jones tried to lure the guards to a specific spot in the woods. They couldn't afford to have any strays sneaking up behind them. It would ruin their plans and cost them their lives. No, they needed everyone to appear in the open area below the boulder, right where the guards would be most vulnerable.

BOOM!!! The last of the small charges was detonated. Neither Payne nor Jones wanted the woods to be too bright when the guards arrived. They wanted a soft glow, just enough light to see their targets, but not enough light to give away their own location. Candlelight to kill by.

"Do you hear that?" Payne whispered as he screwed the silencer onto his MP5K. His weapon was capable of spitting out nine hundred rounds a minute, and now that its silencer was in place, it would make less noise than an iPod.

Jones smiled. He heard several footsteps approaching through the grove. "Here come the first contestants on *The Price Is Life.*"

Nodding, Payne focused on the area below, but he wouldn't fire his submachine gun until the small pocket of space was completely filled with guards. He needed to make sure he could get everyone at once.

One by one, the black men emerged from the trees. Two, then five, then ten. Thirteen in total. Unlucky thirteen. They glanced around, looking for the source of the commotion, but found nothing. They stood there, confused, unable to choose their next move, for none of them had the experience or the authority to take control.

"Like cows to the slaughterhouse," Jones mumbled, stealing Payne's line.

Payne nodded again, his face devoid of emotion. "Moooooo!"

Pfffft! Pfffft! Pfffft! Pfffft! The guns hissed, spraying in silence.

Pfffft! Pfffft! Pfffft! Pfffft! Their venom flew, striking its mark.

There wasn't any time for the guards to react or fire back. Hell, they never even knew what hit them. One minute they were standing, searching for the escaped prisoners. The next they were sprawled on the ground, marinating in each other's blood.

There were no screams, no tears, and no pleas of mercy. Death had been silent and swift.

ANTICIPATING an easy victory, Jackson and Webster followed the guards at a leisurely pace. Thirteen men against two. With odds like that, they figured it would be a massacre, an absolute slaughter. And it was—just not in their favor. When they arrived at the scene, they found nothing but bodies. All of them black. All of them dead. Victims of gunfire. Head shots. Heart shots. Limbs tattered. Pistols still holstered. Rifles unfired. The smell of war lingered in the air. Crimson poured from gaping wounds, flooding the forest's floor. Death was everywhere.

And Webster couldn't handle it.

When he realized what had happened, he dropped to his knees and vomited. It was the first time that he'd seen a corpse outside of a funeral home, so the sight of the baker's dozen was too much for him to handle. He was the brains, not the brawn. He took no part in the actual torture and disposal of the bodies. All of that was outside of his realm.

"They killed them! They killed them all!" He staggered to his feet, wanting to confront Jackson, but was unwilling to walk among the gory remains of his fallen comrades. "Octavian was right! These guys are the best! Look what they did to your guards! Just look!!"

"Be quiet!" Jackson whispered sternly. "They might still be around."

The thought hadn't crossed Webster's mind. The killers could be in the trees, watching him at that very moment. He gagged as more vomit rose from his belly.

Jackson rolled his eyes in disgust. He didn't have time to babysit. He needed to focus all of his attention on the battle site. He needed to look for clues while the trail was still warm. "Don't worry. I might not have their training, but I can be a warrior if I have to be."

As Jackson finished speaking, his radio squawked, causing him to flinch in fear.

The incoming voice said, "This is Octavian. What's going on out there?"

Jackson whispered. "Dead. Everyone's dead. Payne and Jones killed them all. Theo and I showed up one minute behind the guards, and we found corpses. Thirteen fuckin' corpses. Blood everywhere. No sign of the prisoners, but our guys are dead!"

"You're sure."

Jackson kicked one of the men in front of him. He didn't move. "Yep."

Holmes felt his pulse quicken and noticed the hairs on his arms stand at attention. Thirteen kills in less than ten minutes. My lord, these guys *were* good. "What did they use for weapons?"

"Guns," Jackson answered. "I don't know what kind, but they have rapid-fire capability. I don't see any shells near the guards, so I guess they didn't have time to fire back."

"Where the hell did they get weapons like—"

Holmes stopped before he finished his statement. Nervously, he glanced at the cabin on the far end of the row. The door looked closed from a distance, but there was only one way to know for sure.

"Guards!" he shouted. Two men left the burning cabin and ran to his side. "Check the armory and tell me if anything's missing!"

The men saluted crisply, then ran off.

As he watched them approach the storage shed, Holmes felt the tension rise in his body. If Payne and Jones had located the artillery, there was a good chance that they'd stolen enough equipment to wipe out the entire island. Instead of seizing the Plantation one guard at a time, they could do it one acre at a time.

Within seconds, the guards reached the cabin and studied the partially opened door. The armory had been violated. Drawing their weapons, the two men kicked the door aside and prepared to fire at the perpetrators. It was the last move they would ever make. Because of their inexperience, the men failed to notice the wire that had been tied to the base of the door. When they bumped the cord, it triggered a fragmentation grenade, which exploded in their faces. The fragger, designed to launch razorlike pieces of metal over an extended area of space without the impact of a large explosion, tattered the men with shrapnel, killing both men instantly.

Holmes grimaced as he heard the muffled blast, followed by the guards' silence. The sounds proved what he already knew in his gut. The Plantation's artillery had been compromised.

"Damn!" he muttered.

He wasn't the least bit concerned about his men, but he was worried about the missing weapons. It was going to make his job much harder to accomplish.

He grabbed his radio once again. "Harris? Theo? Are you there?"

"What do you need?" Jackson whispered. He was walking through the trees with Webster, trying not to make a sound. "We're on our way back now."

"That's probably a good idea. Not to alarm you, but Payne and Jones got into Terrell's gear. There's no telling what other surprises they have in store for us."

"What do you mean by surprises?"

"I don't know," Holmes admitted. He still needed to get someone inside of the armory to check the inventory. "Land mines, flame throwers, grenades, rocket launchers. Shit, they could have anything."

Without responding, Jackson and Webster increased their stride significantly.

CHAPTER 47

WHEN Greene saw the site of the explosion, it hit him like a punch in the gut. It was Jones's cabin, and there was nothing left of it. The wooden frame had collapsed, succumbing to the intense heat of the fire. Debris, spread from the power of the initial blast, littered the manicured yard. Clouds of smoke lingered in the air, making it tough to breathe or even see.

"Damn," he muttered as he removed his mask and cloak. "This can't be good."

Holmes, Jackson, and Webster saw Greene's approach and rushed to his side. Before they even said a word, Greene tried to assess the severity of the situation but was unable to do so because of their wide range of emotions. Holmes had the cold glare of a terrorist. Blank face, intense eyes, neither a frown nor a smile on his lips. He had seen this type of shit before and wasn't fazed by it. Jackson, though not as polished as Holmes, was still under control. His eyes showed some concern, like a sick man waiting for test results in a hospital, but he did his best to mask it with a broad grin. This was his first combat, and overall, he was holding up well.

Then there was Webster. He was the complete opposite of the other two men. In fact, if he had been a horse, Elmer's would've been negotiating for his glue rights. His face was pale and sweaty. His body trembled. And his eyes were as big as pancakes. If not for the tragic possibilities of the situation, Greene would've laughed at him.

Hell, he was tempted to do it anyway.

"Why are you here?" Webster asked. "Who's watching the boat of prisoners?"

"Don't worry about it. The passengers are chained and surrounded by water. They aren't going anywhere." Greene turned toward Holmes. He knew this was the man who would give him the facts he was looking for. "What happened?"

"Your friend blew up the cabin and managed to escape in the process."

"Jones escaped? How is that possible? Where was Hakeem when this happened?" The three men looked at each other but didn't respond. "Shit, where's Hakeem now?"

Holmes shrugged. "We don't know, but we're assuming he's dead. He's been missing for quite some time, and Theo saw one of the prisoners with his set of keys. We figure that—"

"Prisoners?" Greene blurted. "Are we talking plural?"

Holmes nodded. "It seems your other friend, Payne, unlocked the cabin door before Jones blew it up. At least that's what we've pieced together. Theo watched the escape from the house and thinks Jones made the bomb from his anklet."

All eyes turned to Webster, who just stared at the flames in the distance.

Holmes shook his head at Webster's high level of anxiety. "I'm still trying to figure out why they blew up the cabin. It just doesn't make sense to me. I mean, why blow it up if you have a set of keys to get out quietly? Wouldn't the explosion just draw attention to your escape?"

Greene considered the question. "Maybe that's what they wanted. Maybe they blew the cabin up for attention. You know, draw us to this part of the Plantation for some reason." He paused as he fleshed out the theory in his mind. "What were the other blasts I heard?"

"Actually," Jackson answered, "you may be on to something there. Three charges were set off in the trees for just that purpose. Your friends lured thirteen of my guards to a spot in the woods, then waited for their arrival. When they showed up . . ." He finished his statement by running his thumb across the base of his throat in a slashing motion.

"They killed all thirteen?" Greene asked. "How the hell did they do that?"

Webster groaned, and Jackson cleared his throat. Neither of them wanted to tell Greene about the carnage they had witnessed. But Holmes didn't mind talking. In fact, he wanted Greene to know what kind of trouble he'd brought to the island. "It seems our escapees aren't your average, everyday army grunts. These are two very talented men, special forces plus."

Greene furrowed his brow. "Special forces plus? What does that mean?"

"It means that they're the best. They're capable of doing anything they want."

"Anything?" said a doubtful Greene. He'd fought Jones a few hours before, and his opponent barely put up a fight. He certainly didn't think of him as a killer. "Come on, they're just men! Two injured men! How tough can they be?"

"You don't understand. I've known about the MANIACs for a very long time. These guys aren't human. They're machines. Military supermen."

"Get real!" Greene laughed. "Don't you think you're exaggerating just a little bit?"

Holmes's face finally showed some emotion—not much, just a slight flare-up in his eyes. "Exaggerating? They slipped out of bondage, located Terrell's armory, stole a shitload of weapons, killed thirteen guards in the woods and two with a booby trap, then mysteriously disappeared into the night. Now you tell me, do these guys sound normal to you?"

Greene took a deep breath. He didn't want to admit it,

but from Holmes's description it did seem like Payne and Jones were pretty talented. Hell, he'd underestimated them at Sam's Tattoos and they had escaped. Maybe these guys *were* something to worry about.

"So, they're still out there, huh?"

"Yeah," Holmes answered. "They're still on the loose, doing God knows what."

"And what about Payne's girlfriend? Where's she? She's our insurance policy, you know."

Holmes turned toward Jackson. "Didn't you have her in your possession?"

"She's in the guest bedroom. I left her tied to the bed."

"Jesus!" Greene growled. "You left her in the house this entire time by herself, and you didn't say anything! She's what they want!"

The thought of Ariane's escape made Greene tense with fear. She was his best chance at safety, and he knew it. As long as he had her, he had lots of bargaining power.

"We better get the bitch before they find her. If we lose her, we're in deep shit."

Holmes nodded in agreement. "I'll come with you, Levon. I think we should bring the young blonde out of the house as well. The less spread out we are, the better."

WITH a hollow reed in his mouth and a bag on his shoulder, Payne took a breath of fresh air and slipped into the warm water of the gulf. He wouldn't have to swim far, but the distance he'd travel would be done underwater in complete darkness, so the reed would guarantee a supply of oxygen if he needed it.

Using his hands as his only guide, Payne swam blindly through the intricate web of wooden poles that supported the western dock, making his way toward the heavily guarded boat. After circumnavigating the bow, he breathed through his reed and continued forward, hugging the underbelly of the ship as he successfully wove through a series of ropes before he emerged along the edge of the stern.

The toughest part was over. He was where he needed to be.

WHILE peering through the scope of his Heckler & Koch PSG1 semiautomatic sniper rifle, Jones swung his gun from side to side, searching for targets. He found several. It was a good thing that his weapon offered a deadly combination of precision and speed, or he wouldn't have a chance against so many men. And if he failed to complete his mission, Payne would probably die.

Thankfully, he had plenty of experience dealing with pressure.

The first blast echoed in the night as the bullet struck the guard. His skull exploded in a mixture of blood, brain, and bone. Before the victim's partners could react, Jones lined up his second target and repeated his performance.

Another shot. Another corpse. Blood everywhere.

Shot three eliminated one more guard. Shot four did the same.

And for some reason, the guards weren't hiding. They just stood there, scanning the trees for the source of the gunfire, hoping to see the discharge in the distant night. Jones couldn't believe his luck and their stupidity, but he was going to take advantage of both while they lasted.

"*Adios.*" Guard five, killed.

"*Sayonara.*" Guard six, dead.

If he'd had the chance, Jones would've continued shooting all night, but a few of the guards finally wised up and dashed into the woods to find him. That was his cue to leave. Before he departed, though, Jones blasted a few shots into the water—his signal for Payne to begin—then slipped deeper into the trees for safety.

He had done his part. Now it was up to his partner.

AND Payne was ready.

He'd been waiting for several seconds in the water, trying

to remain completely silent near the stern, but now that Jones had signaled him, he knew he could spring into action. Using a rope that hung from the deck, Payne quickly scaled the back edge of the ship. He slipped his hand into his shoulder bag and grabbed his Glock. The powerful handgun, fitted with a silencer and a full clip of ammo, would allow him to kill with stealth. And that was crucial. He couldn't risk drawing attention to himself before he had a chance to leave the area.

As water dripped off his damp clothes, Payne crept around the small boat, looking for the enemy. One stood by the instrument panel, his back facing the water. Another rested by the bow. And neither sensed the presence sneaking up behind them.

Pffft! the Glock whispered.

Pffft! Pffft! Both men were dead.

The prisoners saw the guards fall and immediately turned toward the sound of the muffled gunshots. Payne, covered in slime and water, raised his finger to his lips to silence them.

"I'm one of the good guys," he whispered.

Ten mouths dropped in wonderment. They couldn't believe that someone had found them.

"Are there any other guards on board?"

Ten people shook their heads in unison before a masculine voice rose from the back of the crowd. "Jon? Is that you?"

The sound of Payne's name made his heart leap. He realized it wasn't Ariane—the voice was too deep to be hers—but the question meant someone else on board knew him. But who? He frantically searched through the faces, looking for the source of the sound, but couldn't figure it out until the man spoke again.

"Jon Payne?"

Payne nodded and moved closer to the man, desperately trying to recognize him, but the guy's battered appearance made it difficult. Bruises covered his face and neck. Blood and dirt covered everything else. A makeshift splint was tied to his leg. "Do I know . . . Robbie?"

Robert Edwards, Ariane's brother-in-law, nodded his head with joy. He tried to stand up, but his ankle prevented it. "Oh, my God! I can't believe it's you."

"Yeah, it's me," he gasped. The reunion with Edwards was so unexpected that Payne didn't know what else to say. "What are you doing here?"

"I was kidnapped. We were all kidnapped." Edwards clutched Payne's hand to make sure he wasn't dreaming. "And what about you? What are you doing here?"

"I heard the island served a nice buffet." Joking was the only way he could reel his emotions back to where they needed to be. "Actually, I'm searching for Ariane. Is she here?"

Edwards nodded. "Not on the boat, but somewhere on the island. I haven't seen her today, though." He took a deep breath of air. "I haven't seen Tonya, either. I hope to God she's all right. The baby, too."

Payne winced. He had no idea that Ariane's entire family was on the Plantation. What kind of bastards would drag a family, one with a pregnant woman, into this type of situation?

"Do you have any idea where they are?"

"I don't know," he sobbed. "They might be in the cabins, but I don't know."

"No, they aren't. I already checked there." Payne glanced at the other nine slaves. "Does anyone know where the others are?"

All of the prisoners shook their heads.

"Damn!" He had hoped that someone would be able to direct him to Ariane, but it was obvious that the two groups had been kept apart. "One last question, can you tell me how many captives I should be looking for?"

Edwards shrugged. "Ten, maybe more. They rotated us around quite a bit."

"Okay, I'll take it from here. But before I leave, I'd like to make a small suggestion. Why don't you guys go home? Does that sound all right to you?"

Ten sets of eyes got misty.

Payne continued, "Before you can leave, we need to get rid of those bombs on your legs."

"But how?" shrieked one of the women. "The lead guard said they would explode if we tried to take them off. He said all of them would burst, one after another."

"And he was right. They would've exploded if you pried them off." Payne reached into his shoulder bag and retrieved Ndjai's keys. "That's why we'll use this instead."

The lady smiled in gratitude as he handed her the anklet key.

"Carefully remove the bombs, then place them gently in this bag when you're done."

While waiting for the bag to be filled, Payne walked over to the boat's instrument panel, assuming that he'd have to hot-wire it. He was pleasantly surprised to see a key in the ignition. "Hey, Robbie, how are your navigational skills? Are you any good?"

"Not too bad. I've taken you water skiing a few times, remember?"

Payne should've remembered. He and Ariane had visited Edwards in Colorado on more than one occasion. "That's right. Good, then I'm making you the captain." He placed his arm around the injured man and helped him to the wheel. "I want you to pull out of here very slowly."

"Slowly?" called out one of the kids. "Why slowly?"

Payne didn't have time to explain, but he knew he'd better do it anyway. The last thing he needed was a mutiny on the escape vessel.

"The area around the island is surrounded by fallen trees. It's a pretty thick swamp, clogged with all kinds of logs. If he goes too fast and hits one, the boat could sink." He smiled for the child's benefit. "And that would be bad."

The kid nodded his head in agreement.

Payne turned back to Edwards. "When you steer, make sure you have some people looking out into the water. They can help you avoid some of the larger obstacles. Got it?"

"Jon, I want to help," he assured him. "But Tonya is still here. I'm not going anywhere without her."

"Trust me," Payne said, "I'd feel the same way if I were you. But with your injury, you're in no shape to fight. Hell, you're not even in shape to walk. So I need you to stay on this boat and help all of these people get to safety. If you do that for me, I'll do everything in my power to rescue your wife. . . . Okay?"

Edwards nodded reluctantly. "What should I do when we get to the sea? Do you have backup waiting for us?"

"No, there's no backup. It's just me and my partner on this mission, no one else."

The looks on the prisoners' faces said it all. They couldn't believe that Payne and Jones had done so much—and risked so much—on their own.

"Once you hit the gulf, open it up to full speed and go north toward the closest set of lights. Don't stop for anyone unless it's the Coast Guard. When you hit land, call the police, NASA, anyone! The sooner I get some help around here the better."

CHAPTER 48

THE leaves and branches would have covered Jones completely, if not for the small gap near his eyes. It was the only spot that he risked showing, for it gave him his only view of the world. And if his mission was to be a success, Jones needed to know when someone was coming.

The shadow lurking in the distance told him that somebody was.

As he waited, Jones wrapped his fingers around the polymer handle of his gun, readying himself for action. If possible, he would eliminate the target from his current hiding place. If necessary, Jones was prepared to do it on the move. It was the first thing he learned with the MANIACs. Be ready for *anything.*

Jones watched as the shape moved closer, slipping past the tall trees with a graceful stride, using the darkness of the woods to his advantage. The lack of moonlight made things difficult, but in time Jones learned to distinguish his target from his surroundings. He wore black clothes, black leather boots, and a mask. A gun dangled from his right hand.

A grin appeared on Jones's face.

The more guards he killed, the better. It would make

things easier when they rescued Ariane and the other prisoners. So far, by his count, he had been a part of twenty deaths—thirteen in the ambush, six more on the boat, at least one at the armory—and the number would continue to grow. Hell, number twenty-one was currently approaching.

Without making a sound, Jones shifted his weight slightly, sticking the barrel of his gun through his thick bed of camouflage. He would fire when he had a clean shot and not a second before. No sense wasting a bullet on a maybe.

"Come to Papa," Jones whispered. "Take another step. Come on. Come on!"

His target finally came into view, no more than fifteen feet in front of him.

But before Jones had a chance to squeeze the trigger, the man whistled softly—a sound that had a meaning only to Jones. This man wasn't a guard. It was Payne.

"Jon," he called softly.

Covered in dark mud from the swamp, Payne glanced around, hunting for the source of the sound. He was supposed to rendezvous with Jones in this part of the woods, but his friend's concealment techniques made him undetectable. There was no way he would find Jones unless he accidentally stepped on him.

"Ollyollyoxenfree."

A large chunk of the forest's floor moved as Jones climbed to his knees. To Payne, it looked like an elevator rising from the Earth's core.

"You're lucky you whistled. I was going to try to kill you for the second time today."

Payne shrugged. It seemed like everyone was trying to kill him. "Actually, you're the lucky one. If you'd killed me, you'd have to fly coach on the way home."

"Good point. How'd the boat mission go?"

"Just like you planned. I took out the remaining guards without any problems and got the boatload of slaves off the island."

"That's great, isn't it?" Jones studied Payne's face and could tell he wasn't happy. "What's wrong? We just saved several lives. You should be thrilled."

"Not only did we save several lives, but we knew one of the survivors."

Jones's eyes widened with surprise. "Ariane was on the boat?"

Payne shook his head. "The Posse kidnapped her entire family. Her brother-in-law, Robbie, was one of the captives on board."

"What?" He had met Ariane's family on several occasions. "Was Tonya on the boat, too?"

"No. They still have her somewhere, and if you remember, she's pregnant." Payne paused as he thought about the situation. He knew Tonya was very close to her due date. "That is, if all this trauma hasn't brought on childbirth."

Jones could tell his buddy was hurting—it might be a future nephew or niece that he was talking about—so he tried to get Payne's mind back on the mission. "What did you learn about the others?"

"Not much, but something strange is going on. That boat was filled with families. Moms, dads, kids. These weren't strangers picked at random. These groups were chosen on purpose."

"But why?"

"I don't know."

"And where were they taking them?"

"I don't know that, either."

Jones forced a chuckle. "Shit, you don't know too much, do you?"

"I guess not," Payne admitted. "But I do know this. If ten of the captives were on the verge of leaving this place, then there's a good chance that the second group will be leaving shortly."

"If that happens, our odds of finding them goes down significantly."

"You got that right." Payne checked the ammo in his

Glock. "So tell me, Mr. Jones, you're the brilliant military strategist. What do you recommend we do?"

"That's easy. Let's go save some people."

HOLMES and Greene were ready to enter Ariane's room when Jackson's voice emerged from Holmes's radio. They had left Jackson five minutes before, and he was already calling.

"What the hell do you want now?" Holmes barked.

"Well, hello to you, too!" Jackson replied. "Sorry to disturb you, but we just heard a bunch of gunshots by the western dock."

"Damn!" Greene cursed. "They're going after the boat!" In the back of his mind, he was glad that he'd left his babysitting job when he did. He didn't want to face Payne and Jones until the odds were more in his favor. "We have to stop these guys before they ruin everything."

"How do we do that?" Holmes demanded. He had the most military experience of any of them, but he was clueless when it came to Payne and Jones. They were playing in a different league. "You know these guys better than I do. Do they have any flaws that we can exploit?"

Without speaking, Greene pointed to the door in front of him. As far as he knew, their only weakness lay inside the room.

Holmes considered the information, then pushed the button on his radio. "Harris, we're coming out with the two girls. In the meantime, gather up all the guards and arm them with the best weapons we have. As soon as I get outside, we're gonna storm the dock."

"You got it!" Jackson's voice was a mixture of excitement and concern. "I'll see ya soon."

Greene raised his eyebrows in surprise. "Do you think an all-out attack is gonna work on these guys? Won't they see us coming a mile away?"

"Definitely, but that's exactly what I want. I'll have our guys make as much noise as possible, and I guarantee that Payne and Jones will try to slip through a crack and come to the house." Holmes pointed to the door. "If she means as much to them as you say, they're just killing time until we leave the home front open. As soon as we make a move, they'll seize the opportunity."

Greene nodded in agreement. The plan made perfect sense. "So, while the guards are in the weeds, what are we gonna do with her?"

Holmes grinned sadistically. "We'll use her to set a trap of our own."

CHAPTER 49

JUST as Holmes had expected, Payne and Jones could hear the guards approaching, but it wasn't because of their military training. All it took was a good set of ears, for the African guards did everything in their power to make as much noise as possible. They'd been told to drive Payne and Jones toward the dock site, where they'd eventually be trapped against the water. Their technique might've been successful if they were hunting a man-eater or some other type of game. But Payne and Jones were far more intelligent than a lion. Much more dangerous, too.

"Uh-oh," Jones joked. "I think somebody's coming."

Using the night as their ally, the ex-MANIACs slipped past the squadron of guards without difficulty. They had the opportunity to kill a few men if they had wanted to, but they decided the risk wasn't worth it. They figured it was probably better if the guards continued their search in the woods while they crept unnoticed toward the main house. No sense rattling their cage if they didn't have to.

Once the duo reached the edge of the plantation house grounds, Jones asked Payne to stop. He had something on his mind, and he needed to voice it before it was too late.

"You realize, of course, that there's a very good chance that this is a setup."

"Yep."

"And if Ariane is inside, she's probably surrounded by armed guards."

"Mm-hmm."

"And there's a pretty good chance that we'll get killed doing this."

Payne frowned. "You think so?"

"No, but I wanted to make sure you were listening. You tend to block me out sometimes."

"What was that?"

Jones laughed. "Okay, let's do this."

The two men hustled to the nearest cabin and used it as temporary shelter. Then, by repeating the process several times, they slowly made their way up the row of cabins until they found themselves crouching near the blackened remains of Jones's blast site.

"Now what?" Payne asked.

From this point on, he knew their cover was limited. With the exception of a few oak trees covered in Spanish moss, there was nothing between their current position and the house.

"Front door or back?"

Jones studied the outside of the plantation house and shrugged. He'd never been inside the white-pillared mansion and had no idea what kind of security it had. Everything from here on out would be blind luck.

"It's your girlfriend, you decide."

Payne didn't even bother to reply as he made his way toward the rear of the house. Jones stayed close behind, scouting for potential trouble as he did. When they reached the back of the structure, they noticed something that made their choice a good one. Bennie Blount was sticking his head out of a downstairs window, trying to get their attention.

"Pssst," he called. "Over here!"

The duo raised their weapons in unison, then hustled over to Blount.

"What the hell are you doing?" Payne demanded.

"I was waiting for you. I watched your approach behind the cabins and saw you pause by the burned shed. That's when I realized you were coming to the house."

Payne and Jones looked at each other, puzzled. Something didn't seem right about Blount, but they couldn't figure out what it was.

"How'd you see us from that far away?" Jones wondered. "It's pretty dark out here, and you're in the back of the house."

"Security cameras. The Plantation has them everywhere."

"Cameras?" Payne's interest was piqued. He realized that they could be quite useful if he used them properly. "Where are they?"

"All over. I can't tell you where, though, because they're very well concealed. I wouldn't have even known about them if I didn't break into the security office to hunt for you guys. That's when I saw all of the monitors."

Payne glanced at Jones and grimaced. Something was wrong, definitely wrong. He could sense it. He couldn't quite put his finger on it, but it was there, like a word on the tip of his tongue. Jones noticed it, too, and he showed his displeasure by frowning. Something was up.

"Gentlemen," Blount said, grinning, "is something amiss? You seem strangely distressed by our conversation. Perhaps it was something I said?"

Finally, both men figured it out. Blount was no longer talking in the backwater language of a buckwheat. He was using the proper diction of a scholar instead.

"What the . . . ?" Payne couldn't believe what he was hearing. "You sneaky son of a bitch!"

"Now, don't be goin' on like that about my mama. She ain't no bitch, I tell ya!"

Jones's mouth fell wide open. He'd been completely fooled by Blount's act. As he stood there staring at the dread-locked servant, he couldn't help but feel foolish. "The Academy Award for Best Actor in a Criminal Conspiracy goes to—"

Payne cut him off. They didn't have time for humor at the moment.

"Bennie, or whatever the hell your name is, look me in the eyes and tell me which side of this war you're on." Payne raised his gun and put it under Blount's chin. "I ain't shittin' you. Tell me right now, or you'll die like the rest of the Posse."

Jones laughed to himself. "You best tell him, Master Bennie. He ain't bluffin' none."

Blount responded in perfect English. "I'm with you guys, I swear! I'm not part of the Posse. I've just been biding my time and gathering information. I swear to God!"

"Information for what?" Payne demanded, pressing the gun deeper into Blount's throat.

"Tells him, Bennie! Master Payne gots himself a nasty temper and an itchy trigga finga. And that ain't no good combination."

Blount shuddered as Jones's words sank in. "I've been gathering information for the authorities. I'm trying to get this place shut down, but I can't do it in both continents without the proof to back it up. No one will listen to me until then."

"What do you mean, *both continents*?"

"The Plantation isn't just a torture site. It's a lot more complicated than that." Blount tried to swallow, but the gun pressed against his throat made it difficult. "This is business, big business! The Posse has ties all over the world, and if I want to shut everything down, I have to learn the names of the other people. That's the only way to do it properly. Get everybody at once."

Payne looked into Blount's eyes, and he appeared to be sincere. But in this case, *appeared* was the operative word. For the longest time, Blount had appeared to be an uneducated country boy, and Payne had trusted him completely. Now Blount appeared to be telling the truth a second time, and he was asking Payne to believe him again. But how could he? Blount was such an incredible actor there was no way Payne could separate his bullshit from reality.

"I'm still not sold. You're going to have to tell me something to convince me."

"Like what?" he whimpered. "I'll tell you anything, just don't kill me!"

Jones stepped forward. "What kind of business is the Posse in?"

"You guys should know. You're holding some of their products in your hands."

"Guns?" Payne remarked. "But that doesn't make sense. Why bring all of these innocent people to this island if you're going to smuggle guns? There has to be more than that."

"There is," he grunted. "But you're going to like that even less."

Payne's eyes flared with anger, causing the pressure on his gun to increase. "Why's that, Bennie? Why am I not going to like it?"

"Because you're white."

"Okay, you racist bastard, what does that have to do with anything?"

"Hey, I'm not racist, but the Posse is."

Payne smirked. "No shit! I kind of figured that out. What does racism have to do with the Posse's business? Racism can't be sold, you know."

Blount stared Payne directly in the eyes. He wanted to make sure that Payne recognized the truth of his words. "That's true, but slaves *can* be sold. White slaves."

The concept made Payne shiver. If Blount was telling the truth, it meant that these people weren't just being tortured. They were being broken—housebroken—for their new masters. "And how do you know this?"

"I just know! I've been walking around this place for several weeks and have heard stuff. Everybody treated me like an idiot, so they tried to talk over me. Nobody knew that I could put all of the pieces of the puzzle together. But I could. I've just been waiting for the right moment." Blount took a breath. "And that moment is here. It's finally here!"

"Why's that?" Jones wondered.

"Because of you two. You've killed most of the Plantation guards, you have the masters running for their lives, and as far as I can tell, you got rid of the cargo ship. This is the time to finish them off! We can end the Posse right here, right now."

"And why should we trust you?" Payne demanded. "You already dicked us once."

"But I couldn't help that! I couldn't risk blowing my cover to help you out. I couldn't! I tried to make it up to you, though. You know that! If it wasn't for me, you would've died in the box."

Payne shook his head. "You're going to have to do better. I wouldn't have been in that damn box if it wasn't for you."

"I know you don't trust me, but without my help you won't be able to save your girlfriend from a life of slavery. I can help you find her, and you know it. But we can't wait much longer."

The comment staggered Payne. With all of the fighting and arguing that was going on, Payne had forgotten about the one thing that mattered most: Ariane.

"How can you help?"

"I know the island much better than you. I can be your guide and an extra gun. Whether you know it or not, Ariane means an awful lot to me, too."

Payne pressed the gun even harder into Bennie's neck. He interpreted Blount's comment as some kind of sexual insult.

"Why is that, you skinny bastard? And trust me, if your answer isn't a good one, I'll splatter your dreadlocks all over the wall!" Payne took a deep breath to control his fury, but it didn't work. He was still fuming. "Why is Ariane important to you?"

"Why?" he stuttered. "Because she's my cousin."

CHAPTER 50

ARIANE could hear heavy footsteps in the hall, but she had no idea who was out there until the door burst open. Two large figures entered the room.

"Well, well, well." Greene laughed. "If it isn't the troublemaker's bitch!"

Holmes followed him into the room. "All tied up and lookin' good! If we had a little more time, I'd be tempted to play with her."

Greene shook his head. "Unfortunately, we don't. And all because of Payne."

The sound of his name made her heart beat faster. "Is he here?" she tried to ask, but it came out mumbled.

"Wow, I think she's trying to talk." Holmes stared at her jaw, which had been broken by Harris Jackson. "A good-looking bitch who can't talk. It's like a dream come true."

"Tease her later," Greene suggested. "We gotta move before the two soldier boys find us."

Two soldier boys? The sound was music to her ears. That meant Jones was probably with Payne, which only made sense. They did everything together, especially when it came to the military. But how in the world did they find her so quickly?

Were they brought to the island the same time as her, or did they find her on their own?

Truthfully, it didn't matter. As long as they knew where she was, she had a chance.

"Okay," Holmes said. "I'm going to untie you from the bed now, but I expect you to be on your best behavior. Understood?"

Ariane nodded, even though it hurt her jaw to do so.

Holmes reached for the knot near her left wrist, but before he got ahold of it, a frantic voice came out of his radio. "Jesus! Is that Jackson? What does he want now?"

"Don't worry about it," Greene muttered. "You take care of the girl. I'll take care of Harris." Greene pushed the reply button on his own radio. "Harris? Is that you?"

"Levon," Jackson answered, "we've got a major problem here!"

Greene frowned. "What's going on?"

"I went down to the dock to check on the boat and . . . it's gone!"

"What are you talking about?"

"All the guards are dead, and the boat is gone!"

"What about the slaves?" Greene demanded. "Where are the slaves?"

"They're gone, too! I don't know how, but the boat is gone!"

"Fuck!" Greene shouted. "I don't believe this!"

Ariane watched Greene carefully, waiting to see what he was going to do next. She sensed that he might take his anger out on her. Thankfully, that never came to pass.

"What should we do?" he asked Holmes.

Holmes shrugged as he unfastened Ariane's rope. "Your call."

Greene gave it some thought before answering. "Just wait for us at the dock. We'll be there shortly. And try to find Theo if you can. I think it would be best if we all stuck together."

"Sounds good," Jackson replied. "Make it quick. I'm in the open down here."

Greene turned off his radio. "I can't believe this shit! How can two guys cause this many problems?"

Holmes grinned at the comment. "You'd be surprised what two men can accomplish if they put their minds to it. . . . Like us, for instance."

"What are you getting at?"

"I realize you've known Harris and Theo forever, but under the circumstances, we need someone to take the blame for all of this. If the feds get a couple of suspects in custody, they won't be as likely to hunt for anyone else. At least not immediately."

Greene's interest was piqued. "What are you proposing?"

"How much would it bother you if we left them behind? Why don't we get off this island while we still have a chance?"

"Interesting," Greene muttered. However, after giving it some thought, he detected a flaw in the plan. "But we can't leave them here."

"Why not? We have the opportunity to flee, and you're not willing to seize it because of them. My God! They'd leave your ass behind in a minute!"

"Wait a second!" he yelled back. "I don't mind leaving them, but we can't. They'll name us, say we were the force behind everything, and preach their innocence. I guarantee they'll frame their stories to suit their needs, and because of Harris's knowledge of the law, they'll come out sitting pretty. Hell, they might even be given immunity to testify against us."

Holmes grimaced at the thought. "Damn, you're right. So what do you recommend?"

Greene smiled at Ariane, then glanced at his new partner. "We should leave the island ASAP. But before we do, we need to silence Theo and Harris—permanently."

BLOUNT'S comment was absurd, completely asinine. Perhaps the most outrageous, preposterous, nonsensical thing that Payne had ever heard. But that was why he was tempted to believe it. It wasn't the type of thing that someone would make up to save his own ass.

"Okay, Bennie, my interest is aroused. But I promise you, if I smell bullshit at any point of your explanation, *boom!* Understood?"

Blount nodded. "As you know, I'm not a dumb hick, but I *am* a local. My family has lived in these parts for generations. In fact, when this place was owned and operated by the Delacroix family, my ancestors worked the land as slaves."

Payne signaled for him to speed it up.

"For the past few years I've been working on my master's degree at LSU and recently started work on my thesis. I planned to show the effect that the abolition of slavery had on black families, using my family tree as an example."

"And?"

"A few months ago, I came to this island to look around. This place had been abandoned for the longest time, and I thought a few photos would look good in my project."

"What happened?"

"I bumped into a team of black men doing all kinds of work. I assumed that someone had bought the estate after Hurricane Katrina and was going to move in. So I went up to a brother to ask him a few questions about the new owner and discovered that he couldn't speak English. Actually, none of them could. These guys were right off the boat from Africa."

Jones asked, "Everyone?"

Blount nodded, then turned his attention back to Payne. "I didn't want to get anybody into trouble, including myself, so I left quickly. It's a good thing, too, because if one of the owners had seen me, I would've never been allowed to come back later."

"Why'd you want to come back?"

"I wanted to see what they were going to do to the place, and I thought it could help my research. You see, during the course of my studies, I came across a family journal from the 1860s. It was like finding gold. It gave me a firsthand account of slave life on this plantation from a distant grandmother. Simply fascinating stuff."

"I'm sure," Payne said, "but I'm beginning to get impatient here."

"You want me to get to Ariane, don't you?"

"Is it that obvious?"

Blount nodded. "During the course of the journal, my distant grandmother admits to having an affair with Mr. Delacroix, her master. She said she did it for special treatment, but eventually, it turned into more than that. She fell in love with Delacroix and allowed him to impregnate her on several occasions. Shortly after that, the Civil War ended and the journal entries stopped."

"That's it?" Payne demanded. "What does any of that have to do with Ariane?"

"At the time, I didn't know, but I was determined to talk with someone from the Delacroix family so I could get a look at their family tree. I figured if I was a direct descendant of Mr. Delacroix, then I would technically be related to all of his white offspring."

Payne started to see where this was going, and his eyes filled with acceptance. He knew that Blount was telling the truth and couldn't wait to see how Ariane fit in.

"I went to the local courthouse and tried to find his relatives, but every path I found ended in death. I swear, the Delacroix family must've been cursed because everyone in that family died so young. Anyway, when I came back here to look around again, I hoped the new owners had bought the property from a distant relative of mine and would be willing to give me an address."

"Makes sense," Payne added.

"But when I came back, I got the shock of my life. The old plantation was back in business. Not just as a farm, but as an *actual* plantation. Crops in the ground and slaves in the field, but this time, unlike the 1800s, the slaves were white."

"What did you do?" Jones wondered as he watched for unwanted company.

"I tried to leave. I wanted to tell somebody what I saw out here, but before I could get my boat out of the swamps, a big man named Octavian Holmes blocked my passage and demanded information from me at gunpoint. I didn't want to tell him the truth, obviously. If he knew that I had been digging around, he would've killed me. So I decided to play dumb. At that moment, I became a buckwheat by the name of Bennie Blount."

"Go on," Payne said.

"I convinced Master Holmes that I'd be useful around here. I could cook, clean, and show him around the local swamps. One thing led to another, and he decided to hire me. I figured it was perfect. I could roam around the Plantation while I got to the bottom of things."

"Did you?"

Blount nodded. "Up until recently, the Posse was bringing random groups of people onto the island, mostly homeless people. They'd beat them, train them, then ship them overseas for big money. It's a lucrative business. But all of that changed with this last group of slaves. The people that were selected were no longer random. These people were brought here for a reason. They were brought here for revenge."

"What kind of revenge?"

"Revenge for the black race. Theo Webster, the brains behind the operation, traced the roots of the Plantation's four founders and determined their family origins. Three of the men came from slave backgrounds, but Levon Greene didn't. His family came to America after slavery had been abolished. Anyway, Webster determined the names of the slave owners that had once owned the ancestors of the other three men. Then, tracing their family trees to the present day, he located the modern-day relatives of those slave owners."

"And the people that were kidnapped were the relatives?"

Blount nodded. "Ariane and her sister are distant relatives of Mr. Delacroix, my great-great-great-great-grandfather. That's why they were brought here, and that's why I'm related. I realize it doesn't make her my first cousin, but she is my relative. I even have the data to back it up."

Payne shook his head. "Don't worry. I actually believe you."

"Great," muttered a relieved Jones. "Now that this Ebony

and Ivory reunion is over, do you mind if we get out of here? We got some people to save and not much time to do it."

Payne lowered his gun from Blount's chin. He was finally convinced that Bennie was on his side to stay. "Mr. Blount, would you please show us the way inside the house?"

Bennie grinned. It was the first time in his life that a white man had ever called him mister.

CHAPTER 51

WHEN the truck arrived at the western dock, Harris Jackson breathed a sigh of relief. Even though he realized he wasn't safe until Payne and Jones were caught, he felt a lot better with Holmes and Greene by his side.

"Hey, Harris," Holmes called, "where's Theo? I thought he was supposed to meet us here."

"He'll be here any minute. He said he had to go to the house for something."

Holmes nodded as he searched the dock for a trace of the missing boat. There were no clues except for a number of dead guards that littered the ground.

"These guys are good," he admitted.

"So, what are we gonna do?" Jackson wondered. "The boat's gone, half the slaves have escaped, and Payne and Jones are still running around killing our men. Is there any way we can salvage this?"

Greene gave Holmes a quick smile before speaking. "Sure we can. Remember, that's the reason we wore our masks at all times. None of the slaves can identify our faces, so they won't be able to give the cops our description. Once we leave this place, we're home free."

A flash of panic crossed Jackson's mind. He had revealed his face to Ariane Walker and Susan Ross when he tied them up inside the house.

Holmes noticed the tension in Jackson's eyes. "What's wrong? You look upset."

"I took my mask off in the bedrooms, and two of the whores saw my face."

"You idiot!" Greene blurted. "Thinking with your wrong head again, huh?"

Annoyed, Jackson took a step toward Greene. Even though Greene outweighed him by sixty pounds, he wasn't about to back down. He had to stand his ground now, or Greene would tease him forever. "What's your problem, man? Why do you have to ride me so damn hard?"

"Because I feel like it."

"And why's that? What's your problem with me?"

Greene stood his ground, reveling in the thought of a confrontation. "Here's my problem. I'm fed up with all your perverted games, your groping and raping. That shit is wrong, and it's gotta stop."

"Oh, yeah? And who's gonna stop me?"

"Who's gonna stop you?" Greene smiled at Holmes. They had discussed this moment back at the house, and Greene had volunteered for the duty. "Me, my Glock, and I."

Greene pulled his trigger and the thunderous blast echoed off the water and the surrounding trees. The bullet struck Jackson in his forehead and plowed into his brain with the finesse of a bulldozer. Then, as if in slow motion, Jackson slumped to the edge of the dock and hung there for just a second before he tumbled into the water with a loud splash.

"Nice shot," Holmes remarked. His nonchalant tone suggested that Greene had just made a free throw in a game of HORSE. "Try to keep your elbow in more. It'll improve your accuracy."

"Thanks. I'll have to remember that the next time I kill someone."

Holmes glanced at his watch and realized time was running short. "That might be sooner than you think. We have to take care of Webster before we leave. Why don't you give him a call and see what's keeping him?"

Greene nodded. The adrenaline from killing Jackson surged through him, practically making him giddy. "Breaker, breaker, one nine," he said, laughing. "Theo, do you read me?"

There was a slight delay before Webster answered. "I'm here, Levon."

"Where's here, Theo? We've been waiting for you at the dock."

Another pause. "I'm up at the house. I figured we'd have to flee, and I wanted to pack a few things before we left."

"No problem." This would work out well for Holmes and Greene. They needed to stop by the house before they left the island anyway. "I'll tell ya what, why don't we swing by the mansion and help you out with your things?"

Relief filled Webster's voice. "That would be great. I wasn't looking forward to going down to the dock by myself. I'm not very good with guns."

A wide grin returned to Greene's face. "Don't worry, Theo. I am."

PAYNE patted Webster on his head, then took the radio from his hands. "You did great. You sounded very natural."

But he refused to speak. Instead, he slumped in his chair and pouted about getting caught.

"What now?" Jones asked as he chewed on his first food in what felt like days. "We got them coming here, but what are we going to do with them when they arrive?"

Payne flicked Webster on his ear. "I say we make a trade. I'll gladly give up Theo here if they give us Ariane. As far as I'm concerned, anything we get after that will be icing."

Jones swallowed a mouthful of apple and decided it was the best goddamned piece of fruit he had ever eaten. "Speaking of icing," he said as he searched the pantry for anything that resembled cake. A box of Twinkies was the only thing he could find. "Once we get Ariane to safety, will we have time to hunt down Levon?"

"I don't care what we do as long as you understand that she's the number one priority here. After that, I'll back you on anything that your heart desires."

"Cool," he mumbled as he stuffed half a Twinkie into his mouth.

While Jones chewed the yellow cake, Blount entered the kitchen from the security office. "They'll be here any second. I just saw 'em pull their truck onto the road from the dock."

Webster stared at Blount in disbelief. It was the first time he'd heard Bennie speak normally.

"What kind of truck?" Payne wondered.

"Flatbed. Both guys are in the front, but it appears they have some hostages in the back."

Payne prayed one of them was Ariane. "Were they guys or girls?"

Blount shrugged. "Kind of looked like females, but don't quote me on it."

Jones continued eating Twinkies as he ran several different scenarios through his mind. Finally, he came across one that he liked. "Okay, fellas, this is how we'll play it. Instead of picking these guys off from a distance—which I could do with my eyes closed—I think it'd be best if we dealt with them up close and personal."

"Why's that?" Payne demanded.

"First of all, if I kill these guys long-range, there's no one to stop their speeding truck. I mean, the last thing we want is for Ariane to smash into a tree with a bomb strapped to her leg."

"Good point."

"Secondly, I get the feeling Holmes has been running things, and if that's the case, it'd be foolish to kill him without interrogating him first. There's no telling where he has slaves stored, and if we shoot him, there's a chance we won't be able to find them for a very long time."

Payne groaned at the possibilities. "Isn't a face-to-face confrontation kind of risky?"

"Definitely. And if you'd prefer, I'm still willing to pick these guys off with a scope. Of course, keep this in mind: Ariane *might* be one of those hidden slaves."

THEY drove straight to the house, across the grass of the main yard. Once they had stopped, Holmes honked the horn, hoping Webster would come to the front door. It worked. He immediately swung the door open, sticking his head out of the narrow crack.

"Can you guys come inside and give me a hand? I'm not strong enough to carry this stuff."

Greene looked at Holmes and frowned. He didn't have a clean shot from his current position, and by the time he raised his weapon, Webster would be able to duck inside the house.

"Before we do," Greene countered, "we want you to give us a hand with something."

"Really? What do you need?"

Greene glanced at Holmes and shrugged. He hadn't thought that far ahead.

Holmes jumped to his rescue with the first thing that popped into his head. "The guards have Payne and Jones cornered by the swamp, and we need help flushing 'em out. You're the smartest guy here, so we figured you could come up with something."

A grimace filled Webster's face. He didn't know what to make of Holmes's comment, but he realized something strange was going on. "Guys, I'd hate to waste my time going all the way down to the swamp for nothing. Are you sure you have them cornered?"

"Oh, yeah," Greene claimed. "We got 'em trapped all right. I made the identification myself. Now we just need some help flushing 'em out."

Payne, who was hiding behind the door, sensed Webster's

desire to make a break for the truck, so he tightened his grip on him before he could move.

"Don't even think about it," he whispered. "Tell them you can't leave until they come inside and give you a hand. Insist if you have to."

Webster obeyed. "Guys, I can't help you right now. I've got other things to worry about *inside*." He tilted his head toward the door in an effort to signal Holmes and Greene, but they didn't understand what he was pointing to. "I think it would be best if you gave me a hand."

Greene growled softly as he watched Webster twitch his head. He couldn't believe how swiftly he was becoming unglued. "I don't know what your deal is, but we need you in the truck right now. Time is running out, so let's go."

"Come on!" Holmes shouted. "We need your help immediately!"

Webster tried to move toward the truck but wasn't strong enough to tear away from Payne. In fact, the only thing that he managed to do was piss him off.

"Do that again and I'll bite off your fucking ear."

"Come on," Holmes repeated. "Let's go! Now!"

"I can't come," Webster assured him. "I'd like to, but I can't. I really can't."

Greene had heard enough. The cops were probably on their way, and the only thing that stood between him and freedom was a 150-pound computer geek. Angrily, Greene threw his door open and climbed out. "I'm sick of this. Come out here now before you really piss me off."

He accented his statement with a slam of the truck door.

And that was what Jones and Blount had been waiting for. They quietly opened their windows on the second floor of the plantation house and thrust their weapons outside. Once they had settled into comfortable positions, they aimed their guns at their targets. Jones focused on Greene. Blount pointed at Holmes, who remained inside the truck.

After counting to five, Payne threw the front door open while using Webster as a shield. "Show me your hands!" he shouted. "Show me your fucking hands!"

Greene stopped dead in his tracks and slowly raised his two closed fists into the air.

"Surprised to see us?" Jones teased from above. "You must be, since we're currently trapped down by the swamps. That's why you're turning white, isn't it?"

"Something like that."

"Don't turn too white," Payne muttered, "or someone around here might make you a slave."

Greene tried to take a breath, but his chest was too tight to inhale. "What do you guys want?"

"Revenge!" Jones shouted as he cracked his neck. "A shitload of revenge!"

Payne wrapped his arm around Webster's neck and pulled him closer. "You know what I want. I want Ariane."

"Then this is your lucky day," Greene assured him. "She's in the back of our truck with another girl. Why don't you come over and see for yourself?"

Payne shook his head. "No, thanks. I kind of like it where I'm standing now. But my partner can take a look. Hey, D.J.?"

"Yeah, chief."

"Can you see into the back of the truck?"

"Sure can. Looks like a couple of chicks to me. Not sure who they are, though. They're tied up, and their heads are covered."

"Do they look alive?"

"They sure do. I see lots of squirming."

Payne returned his attention to Greene. "So, what's next?"

"You're obviously in control. You've got a gun pointed at my heart, and your arm wrapped around Theo's neck. You tell me, how do you want to resolve this?"

"I say we shoot him," Jones suggested. "Then we can just take the girls."

Greene chuckled. "Oh, you could do that, but if you shoot me, Octavian is gonna speed off before you have a chance to grab them."

"No, he won't," Blount yelled. "Before he travels ten feet, I'll pump him like a porn star."

Greene glanced at the other end of the house and saw Blount's unobstructed view of Holmes. "That's a pretty colorful image, especially from a hick like yourself. That English of yours sounds remarkably better."

"Thanks. I borrowed your *Hooked on Phonics* tape."

Greene smiled, trying to remain as calm as possible. He had played football in front of millions of fans on TV, so he was used to keeping his nerves during times of pressure. "Hey, Octavian! Do you have a clear shot at Ariane?"

Holmes thrust his muscular arm out the back of the cab and pointed his gun at the tied-up hostages. "Definitely! There's not much that can stop a bullet from three feet away."

"That's true," Payne remarked. "But the same can be said about my distance. And I promise you, I won't miss."

"I believe you," Greene said. "But you know what? I've got a strange feeling that you're not going to shoot me. You know why? 'Cause if you do, a lot of people are gonna die!"

"Really! And how do you expect to pull that off?"

"Oh, it's not what I'm gonna *pull.* It's what I'm gonna *push!*"

Greene lowered his left hand and revealed the tiny detonator that he'd been concealing in his palm. "One touch of this button, and every anklet on this island goes *boom!*"

He accented his statement by making the sound of a large explosion, then followed it with a defiant smile. "So, let me ask you again. How do you want to resolve this?"

Payne remained stoic, showing Greene the ultimate poker face. He didn't laugh, grin, or frown. "It's simple, as far as I'm concerned. I get my girl, and you get your bitch." He tightened his grasp on Webster's neck. "Simple swap."

"What's to prevent you from shooting us the minute you get her?"

"Nothing," Payne admitted. "But what prevents you from doing the same? Remember, you're the one with the history of reneging."

"That's right," Jones cracked. "You're a re-*nigger.*"

Greene allowed his eyes to float upward. He saw nothing

but the barrel of Jones's gun. "You know if you weren't black, I'd kick your ass for that comment."

"Yeah, but you'd put me in handcuffs before you even tried."

Greene lowered his gaze back to Payne. "So, you want to make a trade, huh? Tell me how to do it, and I shall oblige."

"First of all, I need to make sure that's Ariane."

Greene clicked his tongue a few times in thought. "That's gonna be tough. She's currently gagged, and I'm not about to let you near her."

"Not a problem, Levon. Just let me see her face. If it's her, we can continue. If it isn't, D.J. is going to show you his Lee Harvey Oswald impersonation."

"Don't worry," Greene assured him. "You can trust me on this one. I'll remove her hood, and you'll see that it's her. Okay? Just don't shoot me."

As Greene strolled toward the rear of the truck, he studied the upstairs window out of the corner of his eye. He hoped that Jones would relax for just a moment, giving him enough time to make his move, but Jones was too good of a soldier to slip up. The barrel of his gun followed Greene wherever he went.

"That's far enough," Jones ordered. He was afraid that Greene would sneak to the far side of the truck, and if he did, he would no longer have a clean shot at him. "Climb into the bed from the back bumper. If you flinch, you die!"

"Bennie," Payne called, "how's your shot at the driver?"

"Clear."

"Stay on him, Bennie. Never let him leave your sight."

Greene stepped onto the back bumper as directed, then pulled himself up with a quick tug of his arm. After stepping over the hatch, he moved toward Ariane, keeping his eyes on Jones while looking for a chance to get free.

"D.J.," Payne shouted, "you still got him?"

"No problem. In fact, I'm tempted to take him now, just for the hell of it."

Despite the boast, Payne felt uneasy about the situation.

There was something about the cocky look in Greene's eyes that made him nervous. Payne wasn't sure what was going on, but his gut told him that something bad was about to happen. As a precaution, he moved forward, keeping the hostage directly between himself and Greene.

"Do this nice and slow," Payne ordered. "No mistakes."

Greene nodded as he pulled Ariane into a sitting position. Next, he placed his right hand on the hood that was tied around her neck while crouching down behind her.

"D.J.?" Payne screamed.

"Don't worry. On your command, I can put a hole in his brain."

Payne felt temporarily better, but his anxiety returned when Greene started working on the rope around her throat. "Careful!"

"You gotta chill," he growled. "If I hurt her, you'll hurt Theo. And trust me, I don't want you to do that. Why? Because I want to do it myself!"

Using Ariane as a shield, Greene pulled a gun from the back of his belt and fired two shots toward Payne. As he did, Holmes punched the gas pedal hard, sending Ariane and Greene tumbling backward in a tangle of body parts, an act that kept Jones from shooting. Sure, he could've fired, but the risk of hitting Ariane was simply too high for his taste. Instead, he figured he'd rely on his backup.

"Bennie," Jones screamed, "get the driver!"

But Blount reacted too late. He fired a number of shots at the front windshield, yet the only thing that hit Holmes was shards of broken glass.

Jones cursed as the truck continued forward. He did his best to stop it by shooting at the back right tire, but the angle of the flatbed protected it like armor. He shifted his aim to the rear window, hoping to nail the driver in the back of the head, but Holmes made a sudden turn toward the side of the house.

"Son of a bitch!" Jones yelled. He couldn't believe that so many unexpected things had happened. Greene's hidden gun, his lack of compassion for Webster, the detonator, and Ariane's unintentional interference. Jones abandoned his position and ran toward the front steps, where he came across Blount in the hallway. The two of them sprinted down the stairs together, hoping to hit the truck with a long-distance shot, but when they burst out the front door, they noticed something that changed their priorities.

Two bodies were sprawled on the columned porch.

One was Webster; the other was Payne.

Both were covered in blood, and neither was moving.

CHAPTER 52

WHILE Blount ran for a first-aid kit, Jones tended to Payne, carefully probing his unconscious friend. Unfortunately, Payne's black clothes made it tough to find his injuries.

"Bennie! Get out here! I need your help!"

Blount returned a moment later, medical supplies in hand.

"Help me get his shirt off. I need to figure out where he was hit."

Expecting the worst, they carefully cut off the bloodied garment, exposing Payne's chiseled but scarred torso. Thankfully, his chest and stomach were free of new wounds.

"The blood must've been Webster's," Blount said, relieved.

"Not all of it." Jones pointed to a gaping hole in Payne's arm. One of Greene's bullets had torn through Webster's body and embedded itself in Payne's left biceps. "It's not life threatening, but I have to patch him up before he bleeds too much."

"What do you need me to do? Get you some towels? Boil some water?"

Jones frowned. "He's not having a baby. He's been shot."

Blount nodded. "Does that mean I can't do anything?"

"Actually, you can. I won't leave Jon until I treat him, but the moment he wakes up he'll want to find Ariane. Can you find us some transportation?"

"Consider it done."

While waiting for Blount's return, Jones tried to focus on Payne. Under these conditions, there wasn't much he could do other than sterilize the wound and wrap it, but he realized that might be enough to save Payne's life. Right now the two biggest concerns were blood loss and infection. A good field dressing would stop either from happening.

As Jones prepared the bandages, Payne opened his eyes. Still groggy, he blinked a few times, absorbing his surroundings. He studied Jones as he scoured through the first-aid kit.

"Excuse me, Miss Nightingale? I think you need to reapply your makeup."

A smile crossed Jones's lips. He didn't care what Payne said as long as he was able to talk. "How are you feeling?"

"Not great." He blinked a few times, trying to remember what happened. "I think my arm hurts."

"That might have something to do with the bullet that's in it. And when you fell, I think you hit your head on the steps. That's why you blacked out."

Payne winced as he touched the back of his head. A large bump was emerging from his scalp. "Where's Ariane?"

Jones frowned. He didn't want to upset his friend before his wound was treated, but he wasn't willing to lie. "To be honest, Jon, I don't know. They all got away."

"What?" He immediately tried to sit up, but Jones restrained him. "How did that happen? I thought you had a shot at Levon."

"I did, but Ariane blocked it. When the truck started to move, she tumbled on top of him. I couldn't risk pulling the trigger."

"What about the driver? Did he get hit?"

"Bennie hit the front windshield more than once, but Holmes kept driving." He paused for a moment as he considered the events. "I don't know if he hit him or not."

Payne took a deep breath, trying to calm his rage. He wasn't mad at Jones or Blount—considering the circumstances, they'd done their best—but he was upset at the unfortunate turn of events. Ariane was within reach, but he had blown his chance to retrieve her.

"We have to catch them before they leave the island. If they get away, there's no telling where they'll go."

Jones saw the desperation on Payne's face. It showed in the color of his cheeks and the glare in his eyes. But that wasn't all he noticed. He could also see his pain. There was something about the tightness of his jaw and the grimace on his lips that revealed Payne's physical agony.

"Let's take care of you first. Then we'll worry about them."

"D.J., I'm fine." He tried to sit up a second time, but Jones pushed him down again.

"Jon, we can't chase them until we get a vehicle, and Bennie's getting us one right now. So just calm down and let me patch you up while we wait for our limo."

Jones cleaned and wrapped the wound in less than five minutes. Then, as he put the last layer of elastic tape around the sterile gauze, he heard the rumble of an approaching motor. He gazed across the field, trying to identify the motorist, but was unable to.

"We better take cover."

Both men climbed to their feet and waited in the nearby bushes until they spotted Blount. They realized it was him when they saw his dreadlocks flapping in the breeze. As he pulled up on an ATV, Payne and Jones reemerged on the porch.

"Jon! You're okay!"

"Yeah, I'm all right." He glanced at the green and black Yamaha Grizzly and realized it was too small for three people. "Is this all you could find?"

"Actually, there are two more where I found this. If one of you comes with me, we can figure out a way to bring them both back."

Jones looked at Payne. "Let me go. You should rest up."

"No arguments from me."

As Blount and Jones sped away, Payne scanned the immediate vicinity, making sure that no one was watching from the trees. When he was confident that he was alone, he walked toward Webster, staring at his face. In the aftermath of the shooting, he never thought to ask about Webster's condition—he just assumed that he was dead—but one glance proved that he wasn't. Even though his eyes were closed and his lips were blue, blood pulsated from the two wounds that were visible in his upper torso.

Blood flow meant that Webster's heart was still beating.

Payne crouched next to him and examined his injuries, but Webster's wounds were too severe to be fixed with a Band-Aid. There was nothing Payne could do except offer him comfort—something he was reluctant to do, considering his role in Ariane's abduction.

"Theo," he said in a soothing voice, "can you hear me?"

Unexpectedly, Webster opened his eyes.

"Hey," Payne whispered, "how are you feeling?"

"P-p-p—" Webster was trying to say something, but his lack of strength made it difficult to pronounce the words. "Come . . . here."

Before he moved closer, Payne checked Webster for weapons—the last thing he needed was a knife in his gut. But Webster was unarmed. "I'm here, Theo."

"Paw . . . paw," he stuttered. "Paw . . ."

He looked into Webster's eyes. They were glassy and starting to droop. Payne knew he didn't have much time left. "Theo, you have to repeat that. I can't understand you."

"Paw . . . paw . . . it," he managed to mutter. "Paw . . . it."

"*Paw it*? What does that mean? Theo? What's *paw it*?"

But this time there was no reply.

The bastard died before he could finish his final message.

ON the eastern side of the island, far from the plantation house and the western dock, lay a small inlet, filled with warm water from the nearby gulf. At first glance, it seemed like an impassable marsh. Bald cypress trees clogged the waterway in sporadic groves. Jagged stumps and fallen timber, remnants of Hurricane Katrina, rose from the water like icebergs, waiting to shred any boat that dared to float by. But appearances were sometimes misleading. In this case, the water wasn't impassable. It was actually a path to freedom.

"Where the hell are we going?" Greene screamed from the back of the truck. "There's nothing back here but swampland."

Holmes answered cryptically. "It seems that way, doesn't it?"

"So why are we going here?"

"You'll see soon enough."

Greene didn't like the sound of that, but he realized he didn't have much choice. Holmes was currently in control of the situation, and he was just along for the ride. "Fine, but keep something in mind. I'm armed."

"I know that, Levon. And so do Theo and Harris."

Greene grinned as he thought about his two fallen partners, but his smile turned to a grimace when he felt the truck slowing. "Why are we stopping?"

"I want to show you something," he said through the back window. "But before I do, I think you and I need to reach some kind of an understanding."

Greene instinctively raised his gun. "The ball's in your court, huckleberry. Just make your move, and we can dance."

"I'm not talking about violence. I'm talking about our partnership. If we're going to stick together, we need to discuss what each of us is able to contribute."

"Contribute? What exactly does that mean?"

Holmes got out of the truck to explain. "For this to work, each of us has to contribute something of value. I, for instance, am going to get us off of this island and out of the country. Once we get to Africa, I'll be able to provide us with a wide network of contacts that will set us up with fake identities and a place to stay." He paused for a few seconds to let Greene absorb all of the information. "What about you?"

"Me? What the hell *can* I contribute? All my money is tied up in my house and this place, and I'm gonna have to abandon both of them."

"True, but you'll be able to get some of your cash back."

Greene grimaced. "How do you figure?"

"You never did anything illegal in your house, did you?"

"No."

"Then the FBI won't be able to take it. When Payne and Jones tell them that you were involved, they'll be able to search your house, but they won't be able to seize it. A year from now you'll be able to sell it through a local Realtor and have all of the money wired overseas. Several million, if I'm not mistaken."

Greene hadn't thought of that, and the realization that he still had some assets made him happy. "But this investment is down the tubes, right?"

"Not necessarily. If you play your cards right, you might be able to collect insurance money."

"Insurance money? For what? The burned log cabin? My deductible is more than that thing was worth."

Holmes shook his head. He'd planned for this contingency from day one. "I'm not talking about the cabin. I'm talking about the entire house. You'll be able to collect on that."

Greene raised his eyebrows. "How do you figure? With the exception of a bullet hole or two, that place is in great shape."

"If you want an explanation, just follow me." Holmes walked into a grove of trees and removed a small metal box from underneath an azalea. "Take a look inside. It'll answer most of your insurance questions."

Greene held the box with childlike fascination. He couldn't imagine what Holmes had stored so far away from the house in a tiny crate. "Actually, I'm not really in a trusting mood." He laughed. "Why don't you open it?"

Holmes grabbed the box and pulled out a small radio transmitter, one that was commonly used for mining detonations. "Think about it, Levon. We wore masks the entire time we were here, but we didn't always wear gloves. Our fingerprints are all over that house. If we don't do something about it, the FBI will be able to gather enough evidence to put us at the top of their hit list." He shook his head decisively. "And there's no way I'm gonna let that happen."

"But won't it happen anyway? With Payne, Jones, and Blount still alive, won't they be able to tell the FBI everything?"

"Yeah, but without physical evidence, there's no way they'll be able to convince an African government to extradite us. At least that's what Harris told me. He said the testimony of witnesses won't mean dick in a situation like that. Plus, if you follow all of the safeguards that I'm going to teach you, the American government won't even know where we are. We'll disappear from their radar forever."

Greene smiled. He liked the sound of that. "What about the money? Won't they find me when I try to collect on my house?"

"Not a chance. Theo set up a number of offshore accounts using the names of bogus corporations. If you use them to filter all of the funds, the FBI won't be able to touch you."

"Are you sure? That sounds risky, especially without Theo to walk me through it."

"Hey, it's your money, not mine. But if I were in your shoes, I'd try to collect every cent that I could. If you don't, you're gonna be forced to work for the rest of your life."

Greene grimaced at the thought. He was accustomed to a life of luxury and didn't relish the thought of returning to the workforce—especially the one in Africa.

"Either way," Holmes continued, "I'm blowing this joint up. The explosives are set, and I can do it with a touch of a button."

"Bullshit," Greene growled. "I paid for it, so *I* get to blow it up. At least I'll get some enjoyment out of this place."

Holmes smiled. He was glad Greene wasn't going to fight him on this. "Good! You can do it in a minute, but before you do you still need to answer my earlier question. I need to know what you're gonna contribute to this partnership."

Greene rolled his eyes. "You're obviously looking for something, so just tell me. What do you need from me? Money?"

Holmes nodded. "I was expecting us to make millions off the current batch of slaves." He turned back toward the truck and pointed to Ariane and Susan. "Now we're down to two. Granted, they're exceptional and will get top dollar, but it won't be enough to live on for the rest of my life. That's why I want some guarantees from you, right here, right now."

"Octavian, if you expect me to give you millions, you can fuck off. But if we're talking about a reasonable settlement for getting me to safety, then there's no problem. We're good."

Holmes extended his hand, and Greene shook it eagerly.

"There is one thing, though, that confuses me. As far as I can tell, we still have almost a dozen slaves left in storage. Why don't we take them with us? It would net us a lot of cash."

Holmes signaled for Greene to follow him again, and he did so willingly. The two men walked ten feet farther into the woods, where Greene saw their getaway vehicle buried under some brush. It was a hydroplane, capable of seating no more than four people at one time.

"If we had a way to transport them, I'd be all for it. But at this point, we'll have to settle for what we have. My boat for escape and your money to live on."

CHAPTER 53

SEVERAL minutes passed before Blount and Jones returned to the house with three ATVs. Blount drove his unattached while Jones lagged behind, towing the third one.

"What took you guys so long?" Payne asked. "I thought maybe you ran into trouble."

Jones shook his head. "It just took a while to figure out a towing system."

"Well, while you were busy playing engineer, I was stuck here talking to Webster. You should've told me he was still alive before you left."

Blount and Jones exchanged glances, then looked at the dead body near the porch. Webster was lying in the same position as before. "Jon, are you feeling all right? You took a blow to the head. I think you might be hallucinating."

Payne denied the suggestion. "I'm fine, D.J. My arm hurts, but my head's fine."

"You talked to him?"

"Yes!"

"And he talked back?"

"Yes! He was alive, for God's sake. I swear!"

"You know," Blount admitted, "we never checked. I think both of us just assumed that he was dead."

"He wasn't dead," Payne insisted. "I'm telling you, he was alive."

Jones removed the towing cable while he considered Payne's statement. "So, what did Lazarus have to say? Is the light as bright as they claim?"

Payne ignored the sarcasm and answered the first question. "That's the strange part. He kept repeating the same thing over and over, but it didn't make any sense."

Intrigued, Blount spoke. "Maybe it will make sense to me. What did he say?"

Payne frowned as he thought back on the urgency of Webster's statement. "*Paw it.* He kept repeating the phrase *paw it.* Does that mean anything to you?"

"Not off the top of my head, but give me a second."

"Are you sure he didn't say *Rosebud*?" Jones joked, recalling the mysterious word whispered in the famous death scene of the movie *Citizen Kane*. "Maybe *Paw It* was the name of his sled."

"I doubt it," Blount countered. "Louisiana isn't known for its snow. Heck, I can't even remember the last time I had to put my hands in my pockets, let alone a pair of gloves."

Blount's statement triggered a smile on Payne's face. In a moment's time, he had gone from confused to enlightened, and all because of Bennie. "I'll be damned! I think I got it."

"Got what?" Jones questioned.

"The point of the message! I bet Webster was trying to say *pocket* but couldn't pronounce it! I bet he has something in his pocket that he wanted me to see!"

Blount was the closest to the body, so he reached into the dead man's clothes, looking for anything of value. Even though it was soaked with blood and tattered with holes, he probed the garment for clues, trying to avoid the liquid that saturated it.

"Nope," he said. "Nothing."

"If you want to be completely thorough," Payne added, "check to see if he's wearing an undershirt with a pocket. He might've kept something there for safekeeping."

Blount slowly unbuttoned Webster's dress shirt, pulling back the blood-soaked garment like he was peeling a bright red apple. Once he exposed the undershirt, he placed his hand on the pocket and felt for anything of value. "I think there's something in here!" With newfound excitement, Blount reached into the pocket's inner lining and removed a portable hard drive, which was two inches long and a half inch wide. "I'll be damned! You were right! He wanted you to go into his pocket."

Jones, who'd just finished his work on Payne's ATV, rushed over to Blount's side. He was eager to see what had been found.

Blount stared at the object in the dim light. A look of absolute joy engulfed his face. "It's his computer drive. One day I overheard him talking about it. I walked into his office while he was on the speakerphone. He said if anything ever happened to him, he wanted the guy on the phone to search through his belongings and look for his travel drive." Blount showed it to Payne and Jones. "He said the drive would contain financial records that were crucial to their business."

Blount stared at the drive for a few more seconds then handed it to Jones. "The other guy, whoever he was, asked him what type of records he was referring to, but Theo assured him that the information would only be important if he died."

Jones studied it, making sure that the blood from Webster's wounds hadn't seeped inside. "Well, if Bennie's right, then we hit the jackpot, because one of these drives can hold a couple gigabytes of information. There's no telling what we might get from it."

Payne smiled, finally understanding the significance of the find. If they were lucky, they had just acquired the evidence they needed to nail anyone who was associated with the Posse. Holmes, Greene, Jackson, Terrell Murray, and the slave buyers themselves.

All of them could be linked to the crimes of the Plantation through Webster's data.

AS he drove the truck across the island, Octavian Holmes shook his head at his own stupidity. He couldn't believe that Greene had convinced him to trade passengers for their journey to freedom. They already had enough money to live on for the rest of their lives. If they had left the Plantation immediately, they would have escaped from the island. So why take the chance of getting caught? To him, it just didn't make any sense.

But Greene was passionate about it. In fact, he wouldn't take no for an answer. "I'm not leaving this place without *my* prisoner," he had said. "Without him, I'm not giving you a cent."

And that had done it. Holmes's greed had taken control of his common sense and convinced him to switch Susan for Nathan. He was threatening his own life, his freedom, everything, for some extra cash. Holmes shook his head repeatedly, thinking of the mistake he was making.

"You're a greedy bastard!" he said to himself.

As he pulled his truck to a screeching halt, Holmes studied the concrete shed in front of him. It appeared to be in the same condition that he'd left it in. The door was still locked from the outside, the ground was unblemished with fresh footprints, and Ndjai's dog could be heard patrolling inside. Just like it should be.

The sound of Susan's whimpering and Holmes's jingling keys caused the dog to erupt with even more ferocity than before. The barking, which had been relatively restrained, was replaced by bloodthirsty howls as the canine flung itself against the door in an attempt to strike. Time after time, the creature repeated the process, hoping to quench its cravings with a savage battle, trying to get at the intruder before he had a chance to step inside.

The dog's effort made Holmes smile.

"Hey, Tornado, it's your Uncle O. How are ya doing?"

The Ibizan hound, which had been bred with a larger breed in order to increase its size and strength, responded quickly, going from a ferocious killer to a friendly pet in less than a second. "That's a good boy. Your daddy trained you well, didn't he?"

Holmes cracked the door slightly, allowing Tornado to smell his hand.

The inside of the structure was filled with darkness and the overwhelming stench of imprisonment, created by the bodily functions of eleven terrified prisoners. There weren't windows, vents, or toilets, which meant the unsanitary conditions were bound to get worse as the hours passed. The majority of the room was enclosed by a large cage, made from thick barbed wire and massive wooden posts, that had been placed there for two reasons: to keep the slaves from the exit and to keep Tornado away from the slaves.

Before he stepped into the room, Holmes grabbed a flashlight from above the door and shined the light into the huddled group of prisoners. He moved the beam from slave to slave, studying the dirty faces until he saw the man he was looking for. The chosen one.

Nathan was standing in the back corner of the room, far from the others, his face covered in layers of coarse facial hair. If it wasn't for the prisoner's 6'5" frame, Holmes never would've recognized him. He was a shell of his former self. His body weight had dropped by at least fifty pounds in the preceding weeks, and his face was haggard. But his failing health was easily explained. He had arrived long before the current crop of slaves and had spent most of his time within the sadistic world of the Devil's Box. It had taken longer than anyone had expected, but the harsh treatment had eventually broken him.

One look into his eyes revealed it. Nathan was no longer the same man.

The peculiar thing, though, was the reason that they had brought him to the Plantation. He wasn't kidnapped because of his ancestry or his race. He was there to fulfill one man's obsession with revenge, nothing more, and as long as the

Plantation continued to flourish, his imprisonment would never end.

And thanks to Levon Greene's orders, Nathan had never been told why.

CHAPTER 54

EVEN though he had a hole in his left biceps the size of a quarter, Payne wasn't about to give up. If he was going to rescue Ariane, he knew he had to endure whatever physical pain he was feeling. He simply had to, for he realized the agony in his arm could never approach the sorrow he would feel if he lost Ariane forever.

The body mends quickly. The mind and heart do not.

"Bennie," Payne groaned over the roar of his motor, "where do you think they took her?"

Blount started his ATV, the lead vehicle in the pack, then answered. "One day when I was exploring the island, I found a boat hidden in the weeds. I'm not sure if the Posse put it there, but I think there's a chance they did. It was in pretty good shape."

Jones started the middle Yamaha, completing the thundering chorus of engines. "That sounds like a good place to start."

With a twist of their accelerators, the three machines sprang into action, tearing up the soft ground in long strips and tossing it high into the air. After getting accustomed to his controls, Payne increased his speed until he was nearly even with Blount, choosing a position near Bennie's right shoulder. Jones, on the other hand, swung wide and settled on the opposite side, hoping to protect Blount from any outside threats.

But there was nothing he could do to prevent the explosion.

Instantaneously, a loud blast overpowered the roar of the ATV motors as an invisible force slammed into the backs of the bewildered drivers. In a moment of confusion, the three men skidded to a stop then turned to locate the source of the shock wave. It was the plantation house, and it glowed like Mount Vesuvius.

As they stared at the destruction, a second explosion tore through the remnants of the eighteenth-century structure, sending antique meteorites in all directions. Fireballs sprang into the air like popcorn, spreading the inferno to the nearby trees and cabins, igniting them like they were made out of gasoline.

"The detonation was too precise to be an accident," Payne screamed over the din of the blast. "That means either the house was on a timer or the explosion was set off by hand. And if it's the latter, that means our friends are still on the island."

Blount and Jones turned from the fireworks display and studied the surrounding terrain, using the glowing nighttime sky as a giant spotlight.

"Is that the truck over there?" Blount shouted.

Jones looked in the direction that Bennie was pointing and identified the object. "I don't know if it's the truck we want, but it's definitely a truck." Like a sheriff from the Wild West, he patted the weapon that hung from his hip. "Let's saddle up, fellas, and teach them boys a lesson."

DESPITE Tornado's barking and the loud rumble of the truck engine, Holmes heard the house's detonation and stopped to investigate. Looking back, he saw the bright orange flames as they shot toward the sky and felt the concussion of the blast as its shock wave rolled across the island like an invisible stampede.

With a smile on his face, Holmes climbed from the vehicle and strolled toward the back of the truck. Tornado emerged from the front seat as well, and the two of them gazed at the light. "Did you like that, boy?"

The dog remained silent, staring at the horizon.

"You liked that, didn't you?"

Tornado answered with a low, menacing growl. Then, after a few seconds of displeasure, it began pacing back and forth across the grass of the open field.

Holmes stared at Tornado with fascination. The only time he had seen the dog act this way was when Ndjai was preparing him for an attack. "Hey, fella, it's gonna be all right. The fire isn't gonna hurt you. It's too far away to bother us."

A guttural moan emanated from the dog's throat as it continued its movement. Back and forth. Back and forth. Again and again.

"What's spooking you, boy?"

As if answering the question, Tornado hopped onto the truck and growled at the nearby trees.

"What's wrong, boy? Is there something . . . ?"

Then Holmes heard it. Softly, just below the whisper of the wind, there was a rumble. It wasn't the sound of fire as it devoured the evidence of the plantation house. No, the sound was more man-made—like a machine. Like an engine that was headed his way.

Without delay, Holmes jumped behind the wheel of the truck and hit the accelerator. Driving as quickly as the terrain would allow, he glanced in his sideview mirror and searched the darkness for his enemies' approach. He hoped that they wouldn't be back there. He prayed that he was just being paranoid. But the mirror gave him indisputable proof.

The MANIACs were behind him, and they were gaining ground.

"Son of a bitch!" He turned back and looked at Tornado,

who was still growling fiercely at the noise. "Hang on, boy. This could get messy."

"DAMN!" Blount shouted from the lead ATV. "I think he saw us!"

Payne nodded, even though he had no idea what Blount had screamed. All of Payne's concentration was focused on the driver of the truck. Not Blount, the explosion, nor the pain in his arm. Everything—every thought, every breath, every beat of his heart—was devoted to the man that threatened Ariane. Payne would make him pay for his transgressions.

But he had to catch him first.

Little by little, second by second, Payne gained ground on the vehicle. He wasn't sure how it was possible—the pickup truck had more horsepower and quicker acceleration than his ATV—but he was getting closer.

"I'm gonna make my move," Blount yelled. "I'm gonna cut him off."

Jones nodded in understanding as Blount pulled ahead like a marathon runner using his final kick. Five feet, then ten. His lead lengthened while his dreadlocks flapped in the wind like a tattered flag. Jones stared in amazement as Blount inched closer and closer to the truck.

"He's gonna catch him!" Jones shouted. "Holy shit, he's gonna catch him!"

HOLMES looked in his sideview mirror with great displeasure. Even though he drove the fastest vehicle, the trio was still gaining on him. "Come on, truck! What's wrong with you?"

He pressed the gas pedal even harder, but it was already on the floor. There was nothing else he could do to increase his speed.

"Tornado!" he called through the back window. "Attack those men!"

The dog, who'd been watching the approach of the four-wheelers, barked in response. After locking its gaze on the nearest target, Tornado obtained top speed in three quick strides, then launched itself from the back of the truck with as much force as its legs could generate. The dog flew through the air like a white missile, aiming its sleek and powerful body at the closest threat it could find: Bennie Blount.

Tornado crashed into his face with such force that it shattered Blount's nose and cheekbones on contact, knocking him from his vehicle at a nasty angle. As he fell to the ground, his leg snagged on the underside of the handlebar, forcing his vehicle to turn sideways. The awkward movement was too extreme for his Yamaha to handle, causing the Grizzly to flip over in a series of exaggerated somersaults until the spiraling vehicle burst into a massive ball of flames.

Luckily for Blount, he was thrown free of the ATV before the explosion occurred, but his broken body skidded helplessly until it came to a stop in Jones's path.

Reacting quickly, Jones leaned hard to the left, slipping past his ally by less than a foot. Unfortunately, as he surged around Blount, he found himself heading for a different catastrophe. Blount's out-of-control vehicle, still tumbling in a pronounced spin, sprang sideways and landed squarely in front of him. The two ATVs smashed together with a metallic scream, launching Jones over the handlebars of the Grizzly and onto the hard ground beyond the fiery wreck.

Payne saw the accident out of the corner of his eye—the gruesome collision of the two vehicles and his best friend's violent spill—but realized there was nothing he could do to help. As much as he wanted to return to the crash and offer his assistance, he knew he couldn't afford to. It pained him to be so selfish, so uncaring toward Jones, but he realized if he turned around now, he might lose track of Ariane forever. And he just couldn't risk that possibility.

* * *

DESPITE the thick layer of fog that clouded his mind, Bennie Blount was able to recall many details of the accident. The truck, the ATV, the vicious impact of the dog.

God, he suddenly realized, it was a miracle that he was even alive.

While giving his body a moment to recuperate, Blount tried to clear the cobwebs in his brain but was unable to snap out of his accident-induced haze. His head throbbed with every beat of his pounding heart, and his vision came and went at unannounced intervals, making it all but impossible to concentrate. He tried to focus on something simple—the names of his family members, his childhood home, what he ate for dinner—but his concentration was distracted by the warm sensation that slowly engulfed his face.

The feeling, unlike anything he had ever experienced, started in his cheeks and gradually crawled toward his eyes at a slow rate. At first, Blount wasn't sure what was causing it. A swarm of insects? The blowing wind? A hallucination? But in time, he realized what was happening. His entire face was filling with fluid.

As he lay there, twisted and grotesquely mangled, Blount could feel his cheeks as they swelled at a hideous rate. Blood flooded his taste buds as the copper-flavored liquid surged from his nose like a waterfall and drained into his open mouth below. It quickly filled with the warm fluid. As it did, he tried to purge it with a quick burst of air but realized that he was unable to. Unfortunately, he had bitten his tongue during his fall, and the severed tip floated in his mouth like a dead fish in a crimson pond.

Blount tried to roll onto his side by using his arms and hands, but nothing happened. His limbs didn't respond, and he remained stationary. Next, he tried to pull his knees to ward his chest, hoping to see or detect movement of any kind, but his legs remained planted on the ground. In a final test, Blount tried to wiggle his fingers and tap his feet, but they remained lifeless.

He wanted to prove that he was making a mistake, that he was simply overreacting and wasn't paralyzed, but his body was unwilling to cooperate.

Sadly, it kept letting him down, over and over again.

CHAPTER 55

DESPITE the agony in his arm, Payne managed to close the gap between himself and the surging truck to less than five feet. Once he matched the truck's speed, Payne pulled his right leg from the ATV and placed his foot on the vehicle's seat. After doing the same with his other leg, Payne found himself steering the Yamaha in a catcher's stance, a position that would allow him to leap onto the back of the truck.

But Holmes wasn't about to let that happen.

Using his passenger-side mirror, Holmes spotted Payne in pursuit. In an effort to thwart him, Holmes swerved the truck violently to the left, trying to shake free of the high-speed pest, but Payne adjusted quickly, gliding adjacent to the right edge of the pickup. Without delay, Holmes whipped the steering wheel to the right, trying to flatten Payne with the violent impact of the two vehicles, but the maneuver back-fired.

Since Payne was anticipating Holmes's move, he used the truck's approach to his advantage, jumping from the Yamaha a split second before impact occurred. Holmes laughed when he heard the metallic crunch of the two vehicles and glanced in his mirror to examine the wreckage, but the darkness prevented him from grasping what had really happened. The only thing he could see was the spiraling glow of the ATV's headlight as it turned over in a series of violent flips.

"It was nice bumping into you!" Holmes howled.

Little did he know that Payne was still along for the ride.

THE initial sound came from behind, and it made Blount's heart leap with fear. It wasn't a distinct noise like a bark or a howl, but Blount still knew what had produced it. It was Tornado, the hound from Hades. The bloodthirsty dog had paralyzed him and was coming back for more.

Blount knew if he remained stationary he wouldn't stand a chance against the blood-crazed beast. The dog would pin him to the ground with its thick, muscular body and thrash him to death with its razor-sharp teeth. He had seen the animal in action during its training sessions with Ndjai, so he knew what it was capable of doing. If he was to survive, Blount needed to get to his feet and find some kind of weapon to defend himself. But how? He couldn't run or even twitch. What chance did he stand against something like Tornado?

Realizing he couldn't put up a fight, Blount tried to scream for help, hoping that Payne or Jones would hear him, but his severed tongue and mouthful of blood restricted his effort. Instead of a shout, all that he could produce was a muffled whimper. And no one was close enough to hear it except Tornado, who heard the plea and sprang forward to investigate.

IF he had wanted to, Payne could have killed Holmes immediately—all it would take was a bullet to the back of his head—but there was a slight problem with that approach: Who was going to stop the truck? The vehicle was going too fast to stop on its own, and since Payne was in the back of it, the thought of it ramming into a tree or plunging into a swamp wasn't appealing.

No, if Payne was going to take out Holmes, he had to do it from close range with a great deal of finesse. It was the only way to guarantee his own safety.

Payne pulled the Glock from his belt and studied the back of the truck, hoping to find something useful. The bed was bare except for a tool chest, a tire, and a thick military blanket. Payne thought for a moment, trying to figure out how he could use any of these things to his advantage, when an idea hit him. He could use the blanket to obscure Holmes's vision.

With a quick tug, Payne slid the blanket across the bed and readied it for use. All he needed to do was toss it over the front of the—

"Oh, my God!" Payne mumbled.

He stared at the object on the other side of the truck and couldn't believe what he was seeing. How had he been so blind when he first climbed aboard? How could he have missed such a large lump under the blanket? It just didn't seem possible.

But there it was. Or more accurately, there he was. The captive who'd been pulled from the Devil's Box before Payne had been placed inside. The man was handcuffed, unconscious, and lying no more than five feet away.

Payne crawled across the truck bed and tried to examine him, hoping he was still clinging to life. His skin was red and blistered, not only from severe sunburn but also from insect bites. Even though his eyes were responsive, they were lethargic—possibly from dehydration or an illness of some kind.

"Hang in there," Payne whispered.

He glanced at the open terrain of the surrounding field and realized that he needed to make his move immediately. He didn't want to abandon the sick prisoner, but if he struck now, he knew there was no chance of the truck slamming into anything solid.

"Everything's going to be fine."

Stretching the blanket in his two hands, Payne crawled toward Holmes. Although pain ripped through his biceps as he worked, he realized that he had to use his left arm to complete the job. There was no other choice.

Taking a quick breath to ease his agony, Payne thrust his arms through the broken back window and arched the blanket over the face of the stunned driver. Holmes instantly released the steering wheel and used both of his hands to tear at the thick blanket, but Payne wasn't about to give in. In fact, he felt like a rodeo champion clinging for life on the back of an angry bull.

"Stop the truck!" he demanded. "If you want to live, stop the truck now!"

Holmes responded by pushing on the gas pedal even harder while screaming, "Fuck you!" through the rough cloth of the blanket.

The vehicle's speed continued to increase until Payne yanked on the blanket again, this time in a series of rapid bursts. "I . . . said . . . stop . . . the . . . truck . . . *now*!"

Realizing that he had to do something, Holmes finally gave in to the request, but not in the way that Payne had been hoping for. Instead of easing his foot from the gas pedal, Holmes slammed on the brakes as hard as he could, trying to free himself from his captor. The sudden shift in the truck's momentum did the trick. Payne flipped over the top of the roof like a drunken gymnast, legs and arms flailing in every direction while trying to stop his slide. But nothing could prevent him from tumbling in front of the screeching truck.

WHILE shaking off the effects of the ATV crash, Jones pulled himself to a sitting position and studied his immediate surroundings. He saw two four-wheelers, both of them damaged and overturned, and the closest one to him was on fire. Using the light from the blaze, Jones checked himself for blood but was surprised to find very little. He had an assortment of scrapes and bruises, but he didn't have any open gushers like he had feared.

After rubbing his eyes for several seconds, Jones climbed

to his feet and looked for the other driver. He wasn't quite sure who he was looking for—his head was still groggy from the accident—but reasoned if there were two vehicles, there should be two bodies.

At least, that seemed to make sense in his current state.

Jones wandered to his left and stared at the flaming wreckage, making sure that no one was on fire. "Hello? Can anybody hear me?"

There was no response.

Jones limped to the second ATV, the one that he'd been driving, and pushed it over onto its wheels. Although it was dented and scratched, Jones didn't notice any major damage. There were no obvious leaks or stray parts lying on the ground, and despite the collision the wheels seemed to be intact.

"Takes a licking and keeps on—"

A deep growl broke Jones's concentration. He immediately stared in the direction of the noise and searched for the source.

"Hello?" he shouted, but this time with a little more apprehension.

Once again, there was no response.

As he studied the darkness, Jones placed his hand on his belt and felt for the cold touch of his gun. He was thankful when his fingers curled around the rough texture of the handle. It gave him a burst of confidence.

"Who's out there?" he demanded.

Another growl. Softer, angrier.

Jones took a few steps forward, holding his gun directly in front of him. He was in no mood for games and planned on punishing the first person he came across. "If you're out there, I recommend you answer me. Otherwise, I have a bullet with your name on it."

He took another step, moving closer to the source of the sound. The light of the fire helped show him the way. In fact, he relied on it.

"I'm telling you!" he warned. "You're really pissing me—"

But Jones wasn't able to finish his statement. In fact, he nearly choked on the words as he tried to say them.

Bennie Blount was sprawled on the ground, twisted and contorted in a puddle of his own blood. Hovering above him, like a monster from another world, was Tornado, its face and claws dripping with the liquid that surged from the open wounds it had created.

When the animal saw Jones, it lifted its head and growled in an effort to protect its dinner, and when it did, chunks of flesh dropped from its mouth and fell onto the red dirt below.

The bloody display made Jones nauseous, yet it only added to his determination.

He instantly raised his Glock and pointed it at the snarling beast.

Bang! The first shot entered the animal midshank, knocking it away from Blount amidst a series of yelps. But Jones refused to stop. He wouldn't be content until this creature had died.

Bang! The next bullet ripped through Tornado's hip, sending a spurt of blood into the air and onto the ground where the dog collapsed with a loud thud.

Bang! Bang! Bang! Tornado danced spasmodically as Jones pummeled its body with shot after well-aimed shot, making sure that this beast would never breathe again.

Jones sneered. "Tell Cujo I said hello."

CHAPTER 56

WHEN Payne opened his eyes, he was unable to see anything except two blazing orbs of light, one shining on either side of him. He tried leaning forward, using his good arm to lift him from the ground, but the front bumper of the truck restricted his movement.

"Wow!" he gasped, noticing that most of his body was underneath the frame of the vehicle. "Thank God for tall wheels."

Using the grille for support, Payne scrambled backward, freeing himself from the undercarriage as quickly as possible. He realized he didn't have time to plan anything elaborate—Holmes would be looking to strike hastily—so Payne decided to follow his gut. And it told him to attack.

With quiet confidence, Payne lowered his right hand to his hip and grabbed his Glock. As his finger curled around the trigger, Payne glanced under the motionless vehicle, looking for Holmes's feet. If he had seen them, he would've blasted them immediately, but Payne's search turned up empty.

That meant that Holmes was either inside the truck or on it.

Since the front windshield was missing, Payne knew he'd have an unobstructed shot if Holmes was in the front seat. He realized, though, that the windowless space would be far more beneficial to his opponent. The gap would give Holmes more room to maneuver inside the cab and an extra way to escape. But Payne wasn't about to let *that* happen.

No, the only way that Holmes was going to get away was through Payne, not through a window. Unfortunately, that was what Holmes had in mind.

While recovering from the sneak attack, Holmes noticed Payne's silhouette on the ground ahead, created by the headlights. The shadow gave Holmes all the information he was looking for: Payne was still alive and directly in front of the truck.

Without delay, Holmes slammed his foot on the gas, launching the truck forward at full speed. Payne, using his well-honed instincts, sensed what was about to happen before it actually did. With mongooselike quickness, Payne fell backward onto the hard ground. A split second later, the truck roared above him, its high undercarriage protecting Payne from injury.

The instant the truck had passed, Payne flipped onto his belly and burst forward like a sprinter at the start of a race, but he quickly realized that the vehicle was too far ahead for him to catch it. Stopping immediately, he aimed his Glock at the truck's back tire and discharged three quick rounds in succession. The second and third bullets hit their mark, piercing the right wheel and causing Holmes to temporarily lose control of the truck. The vehicle fishtailed, skidding sideways on the dew-filled grass, but Holmes didn't panic. He coolly compensated for the loss of air pressure, allowing the back end to straighten itself out, then continued forward as fast as the vehicle could carry him.

"WHERE the hell have you been?" Levon Greene growled. He had been standing by the boat for several minutes, impatiently waiting for Holmes's return. "I was getting ready to leave you."

With a look of annoyance on his face, Holmes stepped from the heavily damaged truck. "Where the hell have I been? I've been doing your dirty work, that's where I've been!" He opened the back of the truck with a slam, then climbed onto the tailgate. "If it wasn't for your selfishness, we'd already be far from this place, somewhere in the gulf by now. But no! You just had to have your pet slave, didn't you?"

Greene moved forward, glancing into the back of the truck. He wanted to make sure that Holmes had returned with Nathan. "He's gonna fetch you a lot of money, so I don't know what you're so pissed about."

Holmes glanced down at the slave and gave him a swift kick in the midsection. He was completely fed up with Greene's shit, and he needed to take it out on somebody.

"You don't know what I'm pissed about? Well, let me tell you! You brought two MANIACs to my island, then when they got loose, you ran and hid while I was forced to deal with them!" Holmes pulled the slave toward the back of the truck and waited for Greene to take him. "I mean, this is *your* guest, not mine. So why did I have to risk my life to get him?"

Greene shook his head at Holmes's ignorance. "Because I'm the one with money. If your name was on the bank account, then I'd be doing stuff for you. But I'm the one with the cash, so you're the one with the job."

PAYNE knew he had a lot of ground to make up—probably too much to do on foot—so he decided to take a chance. He wasn't sure if his four-wheeler had survived the vicious jolt from Holmes' truck, but he decided to run back to the crash site and find out. Thankfully, the gamble paid off. The Grizzly had overturned, but it worked just fine.

After putting it on its wheels, Payne jumped on the ATV and rocketed ahead with a touch of the accelerator. The green and black vehicle reached top speed as Payne urged the machine to catch Holmes. If Ariane was taken from the island, he knew the odds of finding her would go down significantly. It wouldn't be an impossible task—hell, Payne would devote his entire life and all of his resources to finding her—but he knew it would be quite difficult.

"Come on!" he implored, digging his heels into the ATV. "Go faster!"

But the vehicle was going as fast as it could, vibrating rapidly from the strain. The darkened scenery of the Plantation whipped by in a blur. The trees, rocks, and animals were all a part of the landscape that Payne ignored. His full concentration, every thought in his throbbing head, was focused on the love of his life and the bastards that had taken her away.

Oh, they would pay. They would fucking pay!

But he had to catch them first.

IT wasn't until the hydroplane eased into the warm water of the inlet that Holmes was finally able to relax. Until that moment, he was certain that Payne or Jones would appear at the last possible moment to foil his escape. But as he glided from the marsh's rugged shoreline, his anxiety started to fade.

He had faced two MANIACs in battle and lived to brag about it.

As the boat moved farther into the swamp, passing groves of cypress trees and several curious alligators, Greene noticed the difference in Holmes's appearance. His partner's face no longer looked haggard, and his body no longer looked beaten. In fact, he actually seemed to lose years as the boat continued forward.

"What's your deal?" he wondered. "You look like a new man."

"Feel like one, too." A full smile crossed his lips for the first time in hours. "My gut told me we weren't gonna make it. I don't know why, but something warned me about Payne and Jones."

"What did it say?"

"It told me that they were gonna be our downfall." Holmes took his eyes off the water and cast a paranoid glance back at the shore. "But I guess I was wrong, huh? We beat Mr. Payne-in-the-Ass once and for all."

Greene stood from his seat and looked back as well, but the hydroplane had traveled so far he could barely see the shoreline through the trees. "What does your gut tell you now?"

Holmes pondered the question as he increased the boat's speed. There was a faint glow in the water up ahead that he had a theory about. "Actually, it tells me that we're gonna make it to Africa, and something good is going to happen along the way."

"Along the way?" Greene questioned. "Why do you say that?"

Holmes extended his finger forward, causing Greene to glance in front of the hydroplane. When his eyes focused on the scene, he couldn't believe their good fortune.

Paul and Donny Metz were standing on a fallen cypress tree, trying to push the boat into the center of the channel, but their effort was completely useless. The duo, weakened from days of labor in the field, didn't have the strength to disengage the boat by themselves, and Robert Edwards didn't have enough experience with the craft to assist them.

No, the slaves weren't about to free themselves from the tree, and now that Holmes and Greene had stumbled upon them, they wouldn't be getting free at all.

PAYNE tried to follow the truck's tire marks in the grass, but the rocky terrain near the eastern shore of the island limited his tracking ability.

Once he was on his own, forced to locate Holmes with nothing to guide him, he decided to scan the swamps in both directions, hoping to stumble upon a clue. With each passing minute, he knew the chances of finding Ariane on the island were getting smaller and smaller, but he refused to give up hope while there was still fuel in his gas tank and ground to cover.

It wasn't until he saw Holmes's truck, slowly sinking into the soft mud of the marsh, that he knew he was too late to make a difference.

The Posse had escaped from the Plantation.

"Son of a bitch!" he screamed while punching the leather seat in frustration. "I can't believe I let them escape!" He took a deep breath, trying to calm down, but it didn't work. The extra oxygen simply made him more agitated than before. "Fuck! Fuck! *Fuck!*"

After a moment of contemplation, Payne moved from his four-wheeler to the edge of the swamp. He was tempted to wade out to the sinking truck to search for clues, but the splashing of nearby gators quickly eliminated the thought.

"Think, goddamn it, think! What can I do?"

Unfortunately, there was nothing he could do except watch the vehicle—and his chances of finding Ariane—slowly disappear.

CHAPTER 57

JONATHON Payne glared at the special agent across the table. He had already answered more questions in the past few hours than he had during his entire time at the Naval Academy, and it was starting to try his patience. He was more than willing to assist the FBI with their investigation, but enough was enough. It was time to speed up the process.

Payne stood from his chair and glanced at the large mirror that dominated the wall in front of him. If he was correct, the people in charge of the investigation were standing behind the glass, watching him give his testimony about the Plantation.

"That's it," he announced. "I've reached my limit. I've done nothing wrong, yet I'm being treated like a criminal. I'm not saying another word until one of you assholes comes into this room and answers a few questions for me. Do you understand? Not another word until I get some answers!"

Payne accented his request by slamming his hand against the two-way glass—his way of driving home the intensity of his message.

His point got through because less than a minute later the door to the conference room opened and the local director of operations walked in.

Chuck Dawson was a distinguished-looking man in his mid-fifties, and the power of his position showed in the confidence of his stride and the wisdom of his weathered face. He greeted Payne with a firm handshake and studied him for a moment before telling the other agent to leave the room. It would be easier to get things done alone.

"How's the arm feeling, Mr. Payne? Can I get you something for it?"

Payne glanced at his injured biceps and shrugged. It wouldn't get better without surgery, and he didn't have time for a trip to the hospital. "A beer would be nice. You know, for the pain."

Dawson smiled at the comment. "If I had some in my office, I'd offer you a cold one. But I was thinking more along the lines of bandages or a pillow."

"Nah, your doctors patched me up pretty well when I first came in. I don't think I'm ready for the golf course yet, but I'll be okay for our chat."

"If that changes, be sure to let me know. I don't want anything to happen to a national hero while you're under my care."

Payne raised his eyebrows in surprise. The recent line of questioning suggested that he was more of a suspect than a hero. He had been drilled on everything from the murder of Jamaican Sam to his possible involvement with the Posse, and now he was being praised? "On second thought, I might need a hearing test. I could've sworn you just called me a hero."

"I did," Dawson asserted. He opened the folder that he had carried into the room and glanced at its information. "From what I can tell, you and David Jones saved the lives of eleven prisoners—actually twelve if you include Tonya Edwards's baby—while killing more than twenty criminals in the process. At the same time, you managed to prevent the future abduction of countless others by shutting down an organization that we didn't even know existed until yesterday."

Dawson spotted Payne trying to read the FBI data and hastily closed the folder.

"That makes you a hero in my book."

Payne leaned back in his chair. "Well, Chuck, that seems a bit surprising. I don't feel like a hero. In fact, I feel like a second-class citizen around here. What's up with all the questions and accusations?"

Dawson smiled, revealing a perfect set of teeth. "Come on, Jon. You're ex-military. You know the way things work."

"Yeah, you like to burn up a bunch of manpower by asking tons of worthless questions just so you have something to put in your files."

The FBI director shrugged. "It's the government's way."

Payne grinned at the comment. "Well, at least you're willing to admit it's worthless. That's more than the last agent was willing to do."

"Don't be putting words into my mouth. I never said it was worthless. The questions weren't worthless. . . . Okay, I admit some of them were a little far-fetched, but they weren't without worth. We often gather more information from a person's reaction to a question than we do from their actual answer."

Payne rolled his eyes. He couldn't believe his entire morning had been wasted on psychological games. There were so many other things he could have been doing with his time. "And that's why you've been harassing me? To see if my answers and facial expressions were consistent during the baiting process?"

"Something like that. But it isn't just self-consistency that we look for. We also check your claim against the claims of others."

"Like D.J.?"

"And Bennie Blount, and the slaves, and anyone else we can dig up. We make sure that everything checks out before we're willing to accept things at face value. It's the only way to guarantee in-depth analysis."

"Well, Chuck, now that I've passed your little test, would you please answer some questions for me? I've been trying to get some information all morning, but I keep getting shot down by your flunkies."

Dawson nodded. His men had been instructed to keep Payne in the dark, but now that they were confident in Payne's innocence, he was willing to open up. "As long as the questions don't involve confidential data, I'd be happy to fill you in. Fire away!"

It was a poor choice of expressions, but Payne was willing to overlook the faux pas if it meant getting some answers. "You just mentioned Bennie Blount. How's he doing?"

"Mr. Blount is in serious but stable condition. He lost a lot of blood from the crash and the animal attack, but your buddy did a great job keeping him alive until help arrived."

"What about his legs? Is he going to be able to walk again?"

Dawson shrugged. "I'm not a doctor, so I don't know all the facts. From what I was told, he did sustain a spinal cord injury. They don't think it's a devastating one, so, God willing, he'll be as good as new after some rest and rehab."

Payne closed his eyes in thought. For some reason, Payne was always more devastated by his partners' injuries than his own. "And what about the twenty-plus prisoners we saved? Are they all right?"

"Maybe I should ask you the same question. Are *you* all right?"

"What's that supposed to mean?"

"Twenty-plus prisoners? You must have double vision or something. Like I mentioned before, you helped save the lives of eleven captives."

"Yeah, I heard you. There were eleven people on the island when you showed up and ten on the boat that I set free several hours before. If my math is correct, that would mean over twenty."

"Shit," Dawson mumbled. He suddenly realized that Payne hadn't been informed about the missing vessel. "I'm sorry to tell you this, but we never found the slave boat that you and your partner talked about. The Coast Guard is currently conducting an all-out search of the gulf, but as of right now, we don't know what happened to it."

"You've gotta be shitting me!"

"I wish I was. But it hasn't turned up."

Payne tried to process the new information as quickly as possible, but it threw him for a temporary loop. "So the slave boat could be on the bottom of the gulf? What about Robert Edwards? Did you find Robert Edwards anywhere?"

Dawson shook his head. "He's one of the missing slaves. His wife and future baby are fine, but he's still unaccounted for."

Payne tried to make sense of the information. When he left the island, he thought he had rescued everyone except for Ariane and the unknown captive from the truck, but now he realized that he might have sent a boatload of inexperienced sailors to a watery grave.

"Jon?" Dawson whispered in a comforting voice. "Not to change the subject, but when you pounded on the mirror and called me an asshole, you implied you had a bunch of questions. Did you want me to answer anything else, or is that all for now?"

It took Payne a moment to gather himself. "With the new information that you just gave me, one suddenly leaps to mind."

"Go ahead, fire away."

Payne wished he'd stop using that expression. "How in the hell did you find us? I thought the people on the boat must've told you about the Plantation, but since they're still missing I guess they couldn't have been the ones."

Dawson nodded. "A couple of planes noticed the house explosion from the air. They, in turn, notified the local authorities. Eventually, word filtered down to us."

"And you've had no luck finding the missing slaves? What about Levon Greene and Octavian Holmes? Any luck with them?"

Dawson shook his head. "We put out an APB and flooded the airports and local islands with their pictures. Unfortunately, if they decided to head south, we'll have little chance of finding them. Hell, a guy in a sailboat can fart and propel himself to Mexico from here. We're that close to the border. It makes things kind of tough for us."

ONCE Payne was excused from the conference room, he rode the elevator to the main lobby, where he met up with Jones. The two greeted each other with a firm handshake, then walked into the bright sunlight of the Crescent City.

"How'd the questioning go?"

Jones smirked like an uncaught shoplifter. "Just peachy, and you?"

"Not too bad. When things started to get sticky, I made a big fuss, and they immediately backed down." Jones's smirk must've been contagious because it quickly spread to Payne's lips. "Did they ask you anything about the hard drive?"

Jones patted the pocket of his T-shirt and laughed. "Nope. And to be honest with you, I forgot to mention it." He stopped on the sidewalk and pretended to turn around. "Do you think I should go back and tell them? Because I could—"

"Nah, I doubt it's important. The damn thing is bound to be blank."

"Yeah, you're right. It probably won't tell us where to look for Ariane, or Levon, or the other slave owners. And even if it did, it's not like we'd care."

"Not at all," he growled. "Not one bit."

THE property in Tampico, Mexico, had been in Edwin Drake's family for four decades, but he never had any use for it until recently. After several years of dormancy, the land was now critical to Drake's slave exportation business. It served as a makeshift airport in the middle of nowhere, a place where they could load people without interference.

The boat of slaves, piloted by Octavian Holmes, reached the Tampico coast just before dawn and was greeted by two trucks full of dark-skinned guards, all chosen from Kotto's plantations in Nigeria. The Africans loaded six slaves into each truck, then drove them to Drake's property, which sat ten miles northwest of the Mexican city. When they arrived at the camp, the slaves were quickly herded into a containment building. They were stripped, hosed, deloused, and clothed, before being fed their first meal in over a day.

The slaves were then examined by Kotto's personal physician, who treated each of their injuries with urgency—these people were Kotto's property, after all—making sure that every wound was cleaned and every infection was attended to. After certifying and documenting the health of each person, the doctor gave the slaves the immunization shots they would require for their trip to their new home, Africa.

Once the medical details were taken care of, the slaves were led to Drake's homemade airfield. There the guards checked the names and ages of each.

Doubting the ability of the foreign guards, Levon Greene double-checked the list of passengers. He realized these twelve people would generate a huge payday and knew how far that money could go in Africa, so this wasn't the time to make any mistakes.

"How do things look?" Holmes asked, no longer worried about Payne or Jones. "Are the dirty dozen ready for their trip to the motherland?"

Greene nodded. "As ready as they're ever gonna be."

Holmes smiled. "To help their transition, we've selected *Roots* for their in-flight movie."

CHAPTER 58

Wednesday, July 7th
Ibadan National Railyards
Ibadan, Nigeria
(56 miles northeast of Lagos)

THE dark-skinned American looked both directions, making sure that the busy rail station was free of incoming traffic. When he was satisfied, he continued his journey forward, lifting his white cotton robe away from the grease-covered tracks. After crossing the congested railyard, he turned left, walking parallel to the far rail while trying to conceal the limp in his gait. It was the only thing about him that was the least bit conspicuous. Other than that, he blended in perfectly, resembling the rest of the peasants as they rode the trains home after a hard day of work.

"May the peace, mercy, and blessings of God be upon you," said a passing Muslim.

"And also with you," he replied in Yoruba, one of the common languages in Ibadan.

With a watchful eye, the American continued forward, searching for the designated meeting spot. He had already completed his reconnaissance of the neighborhood—checking the security around the Kotto Distribution Center, studying the building blueprints, looking for weak spots in the perimeter of the industrial plant. Overall, he was happy with his findings, but his opinion mattered little in the greater scheme of things. He was simply a pawn in a very complex game, one that he knew very little about.

But that was about to change.

At the rendezvous point, he glanced in all directions, making sure that he wasn't being followed. Everything looked clear to his well-trained eyes. Smiling confidently, he knocked on the railcar five times, the agreed-upon signal to gain access to the boxcar that had been commandeered for the current operation.

"Who is it?" called a high-pitched voice from inside.

This wasn't a part of standard protocol, but the dark-skinned man was more than willing to play along. It helped to lessen the tension of the moment. "Domino's Pizza."

"Your delivery took more than thirty minutes. I expect a large refund."

The American grabbed his crotch with both hands. "Open the door, lady. I've got your large refund, right here!"

The cargo door slid open, revealing a white soldier in full black camouflage. "Oooh," he exclaimed in a feminine voice. "And what a big refund it is!"

Both men laughed as the black soldier climbed into the railcar.

"Any problems with your recon?" asked one of the soldiers inside.

"None, except for my damn gun." He reached under his robe, removing the weapon that had been strapped to his leg. "I need to get a new leg holster or something. This thing cut off my circulation within ten minutes, and I've been limping ever since."

"Bitch, bitch, bitch!" teased a familiar voice from the back of the car. His view was obstructed by a large stack of crates, but he knew exactly who he was listening to. "You were bitching when I first trained you, and you're still bitching now. Haven't you grown up yet?"

A grin appeared on Lieutenant Shell's face. He removed his cap as a sign of respect and looked for his former commander. "I'll be damned! What are you doing here?"

"Listening to you bitch! I thought I taught you to be

tougher than that. Complaining about a cramp? Pathetic! Take two Midols and get back to work."

The two men hugged briefly, a touching reunion between MANIACs past and present.

"It's great to see you, sir. It really is. But I have to admit, ya look like shit! What happened?"

With scabs all over his face and body, Payne glanced at his left arm, dangling lifelessly in its sling. "This is what happens when you reach your mid-thirties. Your body starts to fall apart."

"Don't let him fool you," Jones interjected, moving from his hiding place on the other side of the boxcar. "He got into a disagreement with an exotic dancer, and she kicked his ass. Breast to the face . . . breast to the face . . . high heel to the nuts . . . knockout!"

Shell laughed like a little kid as he rushed to D.J.'s side. It had been a long time since they'd spoken, and the smiles on their faces revealed their love and admiration for one another. It was the type of bond that developed when two people had been through hell together—the type of stuff that the MANIACs were known for.

"How are you doing, Rocky?"

"Pretty damn good," Shell declared. He hadn't heard his nickname since Payne and Jones had left the squad. "But I'd like the right to change my opinion. I mean, if you guys are here, then something big is about to go down. Right?"

He looked at Jones, then Payne. He noticed anxiety in both sets of eyes, something that was atypical for them.

"Damn," he groaned. "How big are we talking about?"

"Pretty big," Payne admitted. He tried to smile to lessen the tension, but his effort was less than successful. "And quite personal."

The comment piqued Shell's interest. "Personal? As in, off-the-books personal? As in, the-government-doesn't-know-we're-here-but-who-gives-a-rat's-ass-about-them-anyway personal?"

Payne nodded, looking forward to Shell's response.

"Halle-fucking-lujah! Military missions are always so

boring. It's about time we got the old gang back together and had some fun!"

Jones nodded in agreement but wasn't nearly as enthusiastic. "You're right, it's been way too long. But I don't know if *fun* is the right word to describe this mission."

"Oh, yeah?" Shell laughed, still not understanding the sensitive nature of the assignment. "Then what word would you use?"

Payne took a step forward, intensity returning to his face. It was a look that Shell had seen several times before. One that meant it was time for business. "The word I'd use is *desperate*."

"Desperate?"

Payne nodded. "And once I tell you why I called you here, you'll understand why."

"You called us here?" Shell asked, dumbfounded. "How did you pull that off? Nobody's supposed to know where we are, yet you somehow managed to track us down? Don't get me wrong, it's great to see ya, but that doesn't make much sense to me."

Captain Juan Sanchez, the MANIACs current leader, cleared his throat. "It doesn't have to make sense to you, as long as it makes sense to me."

Shell sprang to attention. "Yes, sir. Sorry, sir."

Sanchez winked at Payne, his former team leader. "But since you'll bitch the rest of the night if I don't tell you, I'll be a nice guy and let you in on the secret."

"Thank you, sir. I'm all ears, sir."

"As luck would have it, I stay in touch with Captain Payne on a regular basis, which is apparently more than you. He gave me a call and briefed me on his current situation. Soon after, I offered to give up our much-needed R & R in order to help. That is, of course, if it's all right with you."

"Once a MANIAC, always a MANIAC!" Shell shouted passionately.

"You're damn right!" Sanchez growled. He quickly turned his attention from his second in command to the man he had served under for several years. "Captain Payne, at this time I would like to offer you control of the finest, fiercest fighting force ever to walk the face of this fucking planet. We are the MANIACs, and we will follow you and fight with you until death—their death—so help me, God!"

Payne nodded in appreciation.

It had taken a while, but he finally realized that everything would be all right.

THE Qur'an, the spiritual text of Islam, required all Muslim adults to pray five times a day—at dawn (*fajr*), noon (*zuhr*), midafternoon (*asr*), sunset (*maghrib*), and night (*isha*)—to prove their unyielding faith and uncompromising devotion to Allah. Unfortunately, these sessions were not assigned to a specific hour, making prayer time a difficult thing to agree upon among modern-day Muslims. In order to rectify this problem, most Islamic communities utilized a muezzin to climb the minaret of the local mosque and announce the beginning of each prayer session. When his voice was heard, echoing loudly throughout the streets of the city, all Muslims were expected to stop what they were doing and drop to their knees in prayer.

These breaks were their holy time, moments of forgiveness and thanks. But in Payne's mind, it was also their biggest weakness. It gave him five daily opportunities to catch the enemy with their guard down. Literally. And he planned to exploit it for all it was worth.

As nighttime crept over Nigeria, the MANIACs snuck along the outer perimeter of the eight-block Kotto Distribution Center, using the shadows as their cover while waiting for their signal to start the assault. Although Payne had showed them the advantages of this unconventional approach, the twelve soldiers didn't like the lengthy exposure time that they would have in the field. They were used to invading, dominating, and leaving, but rarely waiting. But in this case, they agreed that the benefits of their master plan far outweighed the negatives. In fact, if all went well, they knew their battle with Kotto's men would be over within seconds, making it the easiest mission they'd ever been on.

Unfortunately, it didn't feel very easy while they waited.

Dressed in black and trying to blend in with the landscape, the soldiers were unable to relax. They were nervous and eager, excited and scared, but not relaxed. Too many things could go wrong for them to be relaxed, especially since the start signal was in the hands of a stranger they had never worked with before.

No, not Payne. All the MANIACs followed his advice like scripture.

In actuality, they were waiting for the muezzin, the Islamic crier. They would go on his call, during the Muslims' moment of weakness—when the sun kissed the horizon and the guards least expected violence.

The voice rang out like a tormented wail, soaring from the largest mosque in the city to the smallest homes in the neighborhoods below. The muezzin's impassioned plea, like a hypnotic command from Allah himself, sent people dropping to the ground, causing all Muslims to set aside their nightly activities in order to give thanks.

And the MANIACs took advantage of it.

"Gracias," said Payne, who was thankful for the opportunity to burst into the complex with a silenced Heckler & Koch MP5 K in his hands. He knew when he reached his assigned territory, a small section in the center where the hostages were supposedly kept, that all of Kotto's guards would be on the floor, praying toward the distant land of Mecca. And once he found them, he would use them for target practice.

Payne was trailed by Jones, Shell, and Sanchez, and their path met no resistance along the way. No guards, no workers, no noise. The place was an industrial ghost town, and the lack of activity unnerved Payne. In confusion, he drew a large question mark in the air.

Responding in the silent language of the MANIACs, Shell touched his watch, made a counterclockwise motion with his finger, pointed to his eyes, then to the room straight ahead. That meant when he had come through earlier, he had seen the guards in the next room.

Payne nodded in understanding.

If Shell's reconnaissance was accurate, the massacre was about to commence, and it would take place in the chamber they were facing. Their goal was to eliminate as many guards as possible—the plant workers were already out of the building, so they didn't have to worry about innocent by-standers getting hit—and rescue the slaves from captivity.

After taking a deep breath, Payne calmly pointed to his watch, his foot, and then his own backside before glancing back at his partners. The unexpected signal brought smiles to their faces. In MANIAC-speak, it meant it was time to kick some ass.

The four men moved forward, looking for the best pos-sible opportunity to begin their assault. And as they'd hoped, that moment occurred the instant they walked in the door. Ten guards, all assembled in the tiny area, were spread across the floor in prayer. Each was kneeling on an individual straw mat while facing Mecca.

And unluckily for Kotto's men, that direction was away from the door.

Wasting no time, Payne and Shell crept to the left while Jones and Sanchez slid to the right. Then, once everyone was in position, Payne looked at his friends and nodded. It was his signal to commence the assault.

Pfffft! Pfffft! Pfffft! Pfffft!

Fury rained upon the guards like a judgment from God, splattering their innards all over the room like a slaughter-house floor. The tiny bursts of gunfire, muffled by the si-lencers, continued at a rapid pace until the MANIACs were confident that Kotto's men were dead.

Then, just to be safe, Shell and Sanchez fired some more.

No sense in taking any chances.

When target practice was over, Jones treaded through the carnage, inspecting bodies as he moved. Crouching near the door, he examined the spring lock and chose the proper pick.

"The infrared that we used earlier showed that this room was full of people. From what we could tell, there was no sign of weapons. Hopefully, they're who we're looking for."

Payne nodded anxiously, praying that Ariane was inside and unharmed.

It had been nearly a week since he had last kissed her, since he had held her in his arms and confessed his love to her. It was the first thing he was going to do when he saw her. He was going to grab her and tell her how much he cared, how much she meant to him, how lonely he had been without her. She was his world, and he was going to make damn sure she knew it.

"Got it," Jones whispered.

The sound of his partner's voice brought Payne back to reality. He moved to the left of the entrance, wrapped his finger around his trigger, and waited for Jones to turn the handle.

With a flick of his wrist, Jones swung the door open and calmly waited against the outside wall for an outburst of violence. Payne and the others waited, too, knowing that inexperienced guards often charged forward to investigate the unknown. But when the four men heard nothing—no footsteps, voices, or gunshots—they realized they were either facing an elite team or no one at all.

Payne did his best to raise his injured arm and slowly counted down for his men.

Three fingers. Two fingers. One finger. Showtime.

The MANIACs entered with precision. Jones slid in first, followed closely by Payne and the others. With guns in a firing position, the men scoured the room for potential danger, but none was present. The only thing they saw was a scared group of hostages, gagged and tied up in the center of the floor.

"Is there anyone in here?" Jones demanded. "Did they set any traps?"

The heads of the hostages swung from side to side.

Shell and Sanchez didn't take their word for it, though.

They carefully searched the corners, the walls, and the exposed pipes of the twenty-by-twenty-foot metallic room, which had the feel of a submarine mess hall, but found nothing that concerned them.

When Shell gave the word, Jones grabbed his radio and spoke rapidly, ordering the next wave of MANIACs to enter the facility.

But Payne ignored all of that. His mind was on one thing and one thing only: Ariane.

He moved into the group of hostages and instantly recognized their faces from the boat. He couldn't wait to ask them how they managed to get caught—the last thing he knew they were motoring away from the island—but that would have to wait until after he found Ariane.

Shit! Where was she? Why couldn't he find Ariane?

Out of nowhere, the face of Robert Edwards appeared in the crowd, and Payne rushed to his side. He removed his gag and asked, "Are you okay?" But before he got a response, he continued. "Have you seen Ariane?"

"No," Edwards said. "Have you seen Tonya? Have you seen my Tonya?"

At that moment, Payne could've kicked himself. Here he was worrying about his own needs when he should've been more concerned with the needs of the slaves. They were the ones who had been through the bigger ordeal. Compared to them, he'd been through nothing.

"Tonya's fine, just fine. And the baby's still inside her, right where it should be."

Relief flooded Edwards's face. "Where *he* should be. We're having a boy."

Payne smiled at the information. "Right where *he* should be."

"And Tonya? Where is she now?"

"Don't worry. She's safe. She's in New Orleans at FBI headquarters, giving a statement. And before I left town, I got her an appointment with the best obstetrician in the state. He promised me that she'd be in good hands."

"Thank God," Edwards muttered.

Payne gave him a moment to collect his thoughts and count his blessings before he continued his questioning. "Robbie, I don't mean to be rude, but . . ."

"You want to know about Ariane."

"Have you seen her?"

Edwards nodded. "She was on the plane with the rest of us, but once we landed, the two big guys grabbed her and a male slave and took them somewhere else."

"Two big guys? Was it Holmes and Greene?"

"Yeah. They grabbed her as soon as we landed."

Payne couldn't believe the news. Why did they single her out from all the others? Was it because of him? Were they planning on torturing her because of his interference? That would be a tough thing for him to handle.

"Do you have any idea where they took her?"

Unfortunately, Edwards stared at him blankly, unable to offer a single suggestion.

CHAPTER 59

WITH trepidation, Ariane moved toward the large man. They had shared a boat to Mexico, a plane to Nigeria, and a train to Lagos, but he had failed to utter a single word during the entire journey—not even when he was handcuffed, drugged, or beaten. It was like his body was there, but his mind wasn't. She hoped to change that, though. She wanted to undo the damage that had been done to him. That is, if he would let her.

"I'm not going to hurt you," she whispered. "I promise I'm not going to hurt you like those other guys. I just want to know your name." She studied his face, hoping to see a blink or a smile, but there was no sign of interaction on his part. "My name's Ariane. What's yours?"

Nothing.

"I heard some of the guards refer to you as Nathan. Is that your real name, or did they just make it up?"

Still nothing.

"I like the name Nathan," she said. "So many people are named Mike or Scott that it gets monotonous. But not Nathan. That's a name that people will remember, like you. You're a big guy that people will remember, so you should have a memorable name." She gazed into his eyes, but they remained unresponsive. "What about my name? Ariane? Do you like it? I do, for the same reason that I like yours. It's different. In fact, I've never met another Ariane in my entire life. How about you? Have you ever met an Ariane before?"

For an instant, he shifted his eyes to hers, then looked away. It wasn't much, but it was so unexpected she almost took a step back in surprise.

"Well, I guess that means you haven't." She grabbed his hand and shook it. "Now you can never say that again because we just officially met."

A large smile crossed her dry lips as she tried to decide what she wanted to say next. "I'd ask for your last name, but I have a feeling that might take a little bit longer. Besides, we don't want to get too personal. This is our first date after all."

LEVON Greene sat on the edge of his bed, trying to block out the events of the past few days, but too much had happened for him to forget. Jackson and Webster were dead, murdered by his own hand. The Plantation was history, blown to bits with the touch of a button. And worst of all, he was a fugitive on the run, unable to return to the only country where he'd ever wanted to live.

Greene tried to analyze things, tried to figure what went wrong with Webster's full-proof scheme, and he kept coming up with the same answer: Payne and Jones. It was their fault. Everything could be traced back to them. If Greene had just shot them when they met at the Spanish Plaza or killed them while they slept at his house, none of this would have happened. The Plantation would still be in business, the second batch of slaves would be in Africa, and Greene would be enjoying a hot bowl of jambalaya in one of his favorite restaurants.

"Fuck," he mumbled in disgust. "I can't believe I let this happen."

With a scowl on his face, he trudged from his bedroom,

looking for something to alleviate his boredom. Kotto and all of his servants were already in bed, sleeping peacefully in their air-conditioned rooms, but Greene was still on New Orleans time, unable to rest because of the difference between the two continents.

Limping down the marble staircase, he heard the far-off mumble of an announcer's voice. He followed the sound to Kotto's living room.

"Couldn't sleep?" Holmes asked while glancing up from the game on the plasma TV.

A smile returned to Greene's lips. "It's late afternoon in Louisiana. My body won't be ready for bed for another ten hours."

Holmes nodded in understanding. As a mercenary, he had been forced to work in several different countries, so he knew about the inconveniences of travel. "Don't worry, Levon. Your internal clock will adjust to the sun. You should be fine by the end of the week."

Greene sat on the couch across from Holmes. "What about the other stuff? When will I get used to that?"

"Like what?"

"Food, culture, language, girls . . ."

"Oh." He laughed. "You mean all the stuff that makes life worth living. That will take a little bit longer, but if you're flexible, you'll learn to adapt. Every country has its advantages and disadvantages—if you know where to look."

"I'll believe it when I see it," Greene said while rubbing his knee.

Holmes instinctively glanced at Greene's left leg, staring at the gruesome scars that covered it. "Does your knee still trouble you?"

Greene didn't like talking about it, but he realized Holmes was the only American friend he had left. "The pain comes and goes, but the instability is constant. As I start to get older, my joint will deteriorate even more, meaning I'll have to get knee replacement surgery . . . Something to look forward to in my old age, I guess."

Holmes realized there was nothing he could say, so he decided to change the subject. "Levon, I've been meaning to ask you a question for a while now, and since this is the first time we've ever talked about your knee, I was wondering if I could ask it."

Greene looked at Holmes, studying his face. He knew what Holmes was going to ask even before he asked it. "You want to know about Nathan."

"If you don't mind talking about it."

"No problem. You brought him here for me."

"True, but I don't want to overstep—"

"It's fine. What do you want to know?"

A thousand questions flooded Holmes's mind. "Everything."

Greene smiled as he thought about it. He'd waited nearly three years to get back at Nate Barker, the player who had ended his magnificent football career. Thirty-three months of pain, rehab, and nightmares. One thousand days of planning and plotting his personal revenge.

"I started thinking about Barker as soon as they wheeled me off the field. It was amazing. There I was, in unbelievable pain, listening to the gasps of horror from the crowd as they replayed the incident over and over on the scoreboard, but for some reason, a great calm settled over me. You could actually see it during the TV telecast. One minute I was writhing in agony, the next minute I was serene."

Greene shook his head at the memory. To him, it felt like it had happened yesterday. "The team doctor assumed that I had gone into shock, but I'm telling you I didn't. The truth is I started thinking about Nate Barker. The bastard who did this to me was responsible for getting me through my agony. I'm telling you, one thought, and one thought alone, allowed me to get through my pain. It was the thought of revenge."

"So you knew right away that you wanted to get even?"

"Hell, yeah! He took away my livelihood. He took away my leg. You're damn right I wanted to get even. And do you know what? I've never regretted it. From the moment we seized him to the moment I locked him in the cage downstairs, I've never looked back. In fact, I view his kidnapping as the crowning achievement of my life."

A bittersweet smile appeared on Greene's lips.

"Nate Barker ruined my life. Now I'm getting a chance to ruin his."

THE loud ringing startled Kotto, causing him to flinch under his purple comforter. Nightmares had gotten the best of him lately, so he'd been sleeping in a state of uneasiness.

The damn phone just about killed him.

After turning on a nearby light, he realized what was happening and grabbed the cell phone off his nightstand. Few people had his number, so he knew that the call had to be important.

"Kotto," he mumbled, slightly out of breath.

"Hannibal?" Edwin Drake shrieked. "Thank God you're alive! When I heard the news, I thought perhaps they had gotten you, too."

"What in the hell are you talking about? Do you know what time it is?"

"Time! I can't believe you're worried about time! There are so many other things that we need to be concerned with."

Kotto glanced at his clock. It was after midnight. He would much rather be sleeping. "Have you been drinking, Edwin? You're not making any sense."

"Sense? *I'm* not making sense? You're the chap who isn't making sense—especially since the incident happened in Ibadan!"

The fog of sleep lifted quickly. There was only one thing in Ibadan that Drake would be concerned with, and the thought of an incident sent shivers down Kotto's spine.

"My God, what has happened?"

"You mean, you haven't heard? It happened at your place, for God's sake!"

"What did? What's wrong?"

"The slaves . . . they're gone!"

The four words hit Kotto like a lightning bolt, nearly stopping his heart in the process.

"Gone?" he croaked as his chest tightened. "How is that possible?"

"Don't ask me! I sent one of my men to inspect the snow, and when he got there, there was no snow! They were gone!"

"But that's not possible! If the slaves had escaped, I would've been told. My guards would've called me! These were my best men. They would've called me immediately."

Drake remained silent as he thought about the ramifications. "If those were your best men, then we are in trouble. Very grave trouble."

"Why?"

"Because your guards are dead."

Lightning bolt number two hit, causing pain in his chest and left arm.

"Dead? My men are dead?"

Drake nodded gravely. "Quite."

"And you're sure of this?"

"Of course I'm sure! I wouldn't be so panicked if I wasn't sure!" Drake tried taking a breath, but his chest was tight as well.

"I'm sorry to doubt you, but it just seems so unlikely . . . What should we do?"

"That is why I'm calling. We need to figure out some kind of plan. I am on my plane, and I'll be arriving there shortly. I was going to check the plant myself, but since you're still alive, I shall tell my pilot to land in Lagos instead of Ibadan. It will be easier to talk if we're face-to-face."

"I'll have my car and several guards meet you at the airport."

"I appreciate the gesture," Drake said, "but I doubt it will be necessary. Who in their right mind would plan a second attack so quickly after their first?"

* * *

JONES smirked as he continued to monitor Kotto's conversation from a nearby car. "These guys don't know us very well, do they?"

"No," Payne growled. "We'll have to make sure we introduce ourselves."

CHAPTER 60

EDWIN Drake opened the front door to Kotto's home without knocking. He had no time to be polite at this hour of the evening. All of his hard work was crumbling, and he was determined to save it before irreparable damage had occurred.

"Hannibal," he called, "where are you?"

The Nigerian rushed from the living room, where he'd been briefing Holmes and Greene on the slaves, and met Drake in the front parlor.

"Edwin," he said as he shook the man's hand. "I'm so sorry that this is necessary. I truly am. Obviously, I'm just as shocked about the incident as you are."

"I somehow doubt that," he replied coolly. "It seems that you have been keeping secrets."

The comment caught Kotto off guard. "Secrets? I have no secrets from you."

"No? I find that hard to believe, with the information I've just acquired. Who is Jonathon Payne, and why have you been keeping him from me?"

Octavian Holmes heard the name as he emerged from

the other room and decided to answer for Kotto. "Payne's our biggest problem. Now, before I respond to your other question, I've got an even better one for you. Who the fuck are you?"

Drake was ready to spout a nasty comeback until he saw Holmes's size. When he saw an even larger figure behind Holmes, he decided it would be best to play nice. "I'm Edwin Drake, Hannibal's financial partner. And you are?"

"Octavian Holmes, Hannibal's main supplier of slaves." He glanced over his shoulder and pointed to his large shadow. "This here is Levon Greene. He's *my* financial partner."

"Ah, the American footballer. I've heard about you." Drake studied the two men and realized he wanted to stay on their good sides. "It's certainly a pleasure to meet our U.S. connection. I'm glad to see that Hannibal wasn't exaggerating when he told me that our snow was in some rather capable hands. Now that I see you two, I realize he was right."

Kotto remained silent for a brief moment, waiting to see if Holmes responded to the obvious attempt at flattery. When he didn't, Kotto decided to ease the tension. "Edwin has flown in from South Africa in order to discuss the Ibadan incident."

"And to see how you're doing," Drake added. "I know that you've lost a lot of men. You must be in shock."

Kotto was more stunned by Drake's quick change in tone than by the incident itself. It had gone from accusatory to sympathetic in a matter of seconds. "I was shocked at first, but now that I've had some time to think about it, I'm fine. Saddened, but fine."

"Good," Drake stated. "I'm glad to—"

"Enough with the small talk," Holmes ordered. "You said something about Hannibal keeping secrets from you. What did you mean by that?"

Drake's complexion got whiter than normal. He wasn't used to being bossed around. "As I was saying, I just received some information from the States, and it seems you failed to let me know everything about the Plantation. You told me that there was some trouble, but you never told me that it was blown up."

All eyes shifted to Kotto, who squirmed under the sudden spotlight. "I wasn't keeping it from you, Edwin. I was just waiting for the appropriate moment to tell you. I didn't want to tell you on the phone. We've already discussed the danger of that. Besides, I wanted to design a backup plan and have it in place before I broke the news to you. I figured it would ease the shock of it all."

"Actually, it did quite the opposite. Instead of having time to make preparations, I am now forced to deal with everything at once. The Plantation, the missing slaves, the murdered guards! That is a bloody lot to recover from."

"I see that now. But obviously I couldn't have foreseen the incident at Ibadan. There was no way of knowing that they would find us so quickly."

Drake winced at the statement. "What do you mean by *they*? Who are *they*?"

"They," Holmes answered, "would be Jonathon Payne and David Jones. They single-handedly wiped out the Plantation. Once I heard the details of Ibadan, I assumed that they were behind that as well."

"I really doubt that," Drake uttered. "Maybe they were behind things at the Plantation—you were there, so you would know—but I don't see how they could've handled the Ibadan massacre. There was a variety of shell casings found, not just from one weapon but from several. And unless these are the type of men that would tote five weapons apiece, they couldn't have done it alone. They needed plenty of help to pull that off."

"Damn," Holmes mumbled under his breath. "I hope . . ."

"What?" Kotto demanded. "What do you hope?"

Holmes glanced at Kotto, then at Greene, and both of them were surprised by the look in his eyes. The air of confidence that used to ooze from Holmes was gone. No longer did he carry himself like he was invincible. In fact, his face seemed to suggest fear.

"I hope I'm wrong about this, but this sounds like the MANIACs."

THE semitropical landscape gave the soldiers many hiding places as they made their way across Kotto's yard. They had already eliminated a few of his guards and several of his security cameras; now they were going for his power supply. Once the electricity was cut, they would storm the house under a cloak of darkness.

"What can you see?" Payne asked Sanchez through his headset.

The captain of the MANIACs was in the midst of an infrared scan of the house, trying to determine the current number of occupants. When he was through, he lowered the high-tech device and spoke into his radio.

"I can't see anyone, sir. It's like the place is empty."

"No one?"

"That's affirmative, sir."

Payne and Jones winced, trying to figure out where everyone was. The house had been under surveillance for the last several hours, so they knew there should be people. A lot of people.

Jones whispered, "If you can't see anyone upstairs, scan the basement. Maybe there's someone down there."

"I'll try, but the moat around the house might interfere. It doesn't see well through water."

Payne crept closer to the house, trying to stay as low as possible. There was no sense risking his life before they knew if Ariane was inside. "Try closer to the drawbridge. The water might be shallower there."

"You got it."

Payne and Jones waited patiently while Sanchez attempted to get a better reading. After more than a minute of scanning, he gave them the bad news.

"He's got something in the basement, but I can't get a readout on this thing. It might be a vault or a bomb shelter of some kind, but whatever it is, it's too thick for me to see through."

"Keep us posted if anything changes."

"I will."

After switching channels on his radio, Payne tried to get an update from Shell, who was in charge of knocking out Kotto's power lines with a small explosion. He remained silent until the device was set and he had repositioned himself in the nearby trees.

Once there, Shell turned his radio to an all-inclusive frequency and spoke to the entire squad, using the tone and mannerisms of a commercial airline pilot.

"Ladies and gentlemen, this is your lieutenant speaking. In exactly thirty seconds, we will be experiencing some violent turbulence, so I would advise you to prepare your night vision and put your firearms into their locked and loaded positions." Shell smiled to himself before finishing. "And as always, thank you for choosing the MANIACs."

Twenty . . . fifteen . . . ten . . . five . . . BOOM!

The earth shook as the explosion ripped through the power station, tearing the generator to shreds in one blinding burst of heat and light. Payne and Jones were tempted to glance at the display of sparks but realized it would ruin their night vision for the next several minutes. So they waited patiently, until the shower of orange light subsided and Kotto's entire estate fell under the blanket of darkness.

When the moment felt right, Payne pushed the button on his transmitter and growled into the microphone. "Gentlemen, don't let me down."

With phenomenal quickness and stealth, the soldiers converged on the stone mansion and crawled across the structure's moat in groups of two and three, using wooden boards that they carried with them. Windows, doors, and skylights were points of entry, and the MANIACs breached them effortlessly in a series of textbook military maneuvers.

"So far, so good," Payne muttered as he watched the

assault from Kotto's yard. "I'd like to be inside, though, where all the action is."

Jones nodded his head in agreement. "Yeah, but there's no way you could've climbed over the moat with that arm of yours. And you know it."

"Actually, I *don't* know it. I think if I was given the chance, I could've—"

Jones squeezed his friend's injured biceps in order to prove his point.

"Jesus!" he grunted in agony. "You didn't have to do that!"

But Payne was thankful that Jones had, because it reminded him that he'd made the correct decision by sitting this one out. If he hadn't, he would've slowed down the team, and that was something he wasn't willing to risk. At this point the only thing that mattered to Payne was Ariane, and everything else—his soldierly pride, his lust for action, and his desire for revenge—paled in comparison.

"I hope you realize there's no reason to feel guilty. We've accomplished more in the last week than anyone, including myself, could've ever imagined."

Payne didn't respond, choosing to keep his attention on the mission instead.

"Plus, you set a good example for the squad by letting them take over. A man has to know his limits, and when he reaches them, he shouldn't be ashamed to ask for help."

"I know that. In fact, I might ask for some more help right now."

"Really?" The comment surprised Jones. "Why's that?"

Payne took a moment to adjust his night vision, then calmly pointed over Jones's left shoulder. "If I'm not mistaken, I think our targets might've found a way out of the house."

Jones turned in the direction of Payne's finger and had a hard time believing what he saw. Levon Greene was standing outside Kotto's iron fence, helping Octavian Holmes climb out of a well-concealed passageway—a tunnel that wasn't mentioned on the blueprints Jones had downloaded from a local database.

"Get on the comm," Payne said, "and tell Sanchez to send half the team out to secure the periphery. Have the others continue their sweep for the slaves, but warn them about the tunnel. I don't want Greene doubling back inside if we can help it."

Jones nodded as he reached for the radio. "And while I do this, what are you going to do?"

Payne smiled as he grabbed his Glock. "I'm going to play hero."

CHAPTER 61

USING the darkness as his ally, Payne moved quietly toward the mouth of the tunnel, hoping to eliminate Holmes and Greene before they even knew what hit them. But as he approached the tall iron fence that surrounded the estate, he soon realized that there was more going on than a simple escape. Instead of slipping away from the house unnoticed, Holmes and Greene were trying to smuggle several slaves out of Kotto's house as well.

"D.J.," Payne whispered into his headset. "What's your position? I need your input up here."

A few seconds later Jones slipped into the bushes next to him. "You rang?"

"Take a look at them. Does this make any sense to you?"

Jones watched closely as the duo pulled two cloaked slaves from the tunnel and shoved them forcibly to the ground. Then, when Greene was satisfied with their positioning, he went back to the tunnel while Holmes hovered over the first pair with a handgun.

"No sense at all," Jones answered. "They must have something up their sleeves, otherwise they'd be heading for the hills by now."

"That's what I figured, but what?"

Jones shrugged. "I don't know, but it has to be something creative. They aren't going to hold us off all by themselves."

"Something creative, huh? See, that's what I can't figure out. What the hell could these guys come up with on such short notice? I mean, it's not like they have a lot of experience with . . ."

Experience. The word sent shivers down Payne's spine, for he suddenly remembered what Holmes and Greene were experienced with. Of course! It made perfect sense. The reason they weren't leaving was because they *needed* to stay nearby in order to complete their plans—just like when they blew up the Plantation.

Without delay, Payne hit the button on his radio and spoke directly to Sanchez. "Juan, get out of the house! Do you read me? Clear the area, now!"

"But, sir, we haven't completed our objective. Do you understand? We haven't—"

"Screw your objective, Juan! The house is hot. Get out at once!"

A few seconds passed before Sanchez replied. "But, sir, Ariane might still be in here."

The notion hit Payne like a sucker punch. God, how could he have forgotten about her? How was that possible?

It took him a moment to shake off the guilt—for forgetting Ariane in her time of need *and* for the command that he was about to issue—but once he thought things through, he realized he couldn't allow his personal feelings to interfere with his duties as squad leader. No matter how much he loved Ariane and how willing he was to give up his life for hers, he knew he didn't have a choice. This wasn't *Saving Private Ryan*. He couldn't risk the lives of several men to save one person. That just wasn't acceptable, especially since they were here as a personal favor.

After taking a deep breath to clear his mind, Payne turned his radio back on and said the most painful thing he'd ever had to say. "What is it about my order that you don't understand? Get out of the house now!"

* * *

LEVON Greene helped Hannibal Kotto to his feet before giving Edwin Drake a much-needed hand. Neither of the businessmen was thrilled with sneaking to freedom through the escape tunnel that started in the mansion's basement, but once they were assured that it was the only way to get away from the MANIACs, Kotto and Drake relented.

"What now?" asked Drake as he dusted off his white cloak. "Do we make a run for it?"

Greene chuckled at the thought. "A run for it? Do you actually think we can outrun an entire platoon of soldiers? Fuck that! There will be no running from anything."

Kotto heard the comment and moved forward. "Then how are we going to escape? Is someone coming to meet us?"

"No," Greene assured him, "there's no one coming to meet us. Octavian and I are going to take care of the MANIACs all by ourselves."

"You're what?" Kotto turned toward Holmes, looking for answers. "How are you going to do that?"

Greene answered cryptically. "Well, *we're* not going to do anything. Your house is."

"My house is? What kind of rubbish is that?"

Greene smiled as he reached into his pocket and pulled out a small detonator. "Not rubbish, *rubble*—because that's what your house is gonna be in a couple of seconds. With a touch of this button, your house and our problems are going bye-bye."

PAYNE was relieved when the first wave of MANIACs made it across the moat, but they weren't the men that he was truly worried about. That group was team two, the soldiers who were looking for the secret tunnel. Since they were ordered deep within the bowels of the basement, Payne knew it would take them much longer to evacuate.

He just hoped it wouldn't take too long.

"All out," declared Shell, who was the leader of the first

team. "Should we secure the periphery as ordered, or lag here to assist the others?"

"Your orders still hold." Payne wanted everyone as far away from the house as quickly as possible. "Be advised that six people have been spotted outside the fence. Repeat, six outside the fence. And some of them could be friendly."

"Half dozen on the run: some cowboys, some Indians." Shell waved his men forward before continuing his transmission. "Don't worry, sir. We won't let you down."

Payne nodded as he turned toward Jones. "What can you see?"

He answered while peering through his night-vision goggles. "The two people on the ground seem to be slaves. Greene just kicked the one on the right."

"Can you make out their faces?"

Jones shook his head. "Their cloaks prevent it. But if I were a betting man, I'd say the one getting kicked is a man. He's way too big to be a female."

Payne cursed softly. That meant the odds of Ariane being inside the house just increased. "And what about the other?"

"No idea. It could be Ariane, but I really don't know."

"Keep me posted," he said, rising to his feet. "I'm going forward to help Sanchez's crew."

"You're what?"

"I'm going to give them a hand. I'd lend them two if I could, but all I've got is one."

Before Jones could argue, Payne sprinted full speed toward the moat. He wasn't sure what he'd be able to do once he got there, but there was no way in hell he was going to sit passively while some of his men were still in danger. His men were his responsibility, and he was going to do everything he could to guarantee their safety—even if it meant risking his own life.

Once Payne reached the edge of the moat, he cast his eyes downward and studied the fifteen-by-twelve-foot trench that extended for several hundred feet around the base of the entire mansion. The walls of the pit were made of seamless concrete and had been laid with a steep slope to impede the climb of possible intruders. To discourage unwanted visits even further, Kotto had filled the bottom of the chasm with a freshwater stream and a family of Nile crocodiles that hissed and snapped like a pack of hungry guard dogs anytime humans approached.

"Knock it off," Payne growled, "or I'll make shoes out of your ass."

Captain Sanchez heard the comment as he emerged from the house. "I hope you weren't talking to me."

Payne instinctively raised his weapon but relaxed when he realized who it was. "Sorry to disappoint you, Juan, but I don't want to do *anything* with your ass."

Sanchez smiled as he traversed the narrow plank with the ease of a tightrope walker. He'd risked his life way too many times to be worried about heights or a bunch of hungry reptiles. After reaching Payne's side, he said, "I don't want to sound disrespectful, but what are you doing here? You should be back by the fence, where it's safe."

"And let you play with the crocs by yourself? Not a chance. Besides, you know how I am on missions. I'd rather do jumping jacks in a minefield than sit around, waiting."

"But, sir, aren't you just waiting up here, too?"

Payne was tempted to lecture him on the basic concept of leadership—never put anyone in a situation that you're not willing to be in yourself—but before he could, a second MANIAC exited the house.

The soldier immediately said, "Four more behind me, but I don't know where."

Payne nodded as he got on his radio to find out. "Team two status check, team two status check. What's your twenty?"

"I'm coming out now," answered the first, and a moment later he stepped outside.

"Making my way up the stairs," replied another. "About fifteen seconds 'til daylight."

Payne waited until the second soldier arrived before he went back to the radio. "Team two status check . . . What are your positions?"

Unfortunately, the remaining members of team two didn't reply.

Confused by their silence, Payne asked Chen, the soldier who had just emerged from the house, if he knew anything about their whereabouts.

"It's tough to say, sir. That basement is a labyrinth of empty jail cells and twisting corridors. There's no telling where they are or if they can even hear you. The walls are pretty thick."

"Damn!" Payne growled. He knew if he didn't get his men out of the house immediately, they were going to die. It was as simple as that. Out of sheer desperation, Payne used their real names over the airwaves. "Kokoska? Haney? Do you read me? Squawk if you can hear me."

But the only noise that followed was the foreboding sound of silence.

CHAPTER 62

THE sound of Payne's radio disrupted the quiet of the Nigerian night, but the message didn't come from the missing MANIACs. It came from Jones, and his words were ominous.

"The Posse's taking cover. Prepare for detonation."

Without delay, Payne ordered his men from the area while he dropped to his knees to secure the wooden plank with his good arm. After locking it in place, he yelled to Chen, the soldier on the other side of the moat. "Run for it!"

The young MANIAC did as he was told and started across the temporary bridge. Unfortunately, as he neared the halfway point, the first explosion erupted and its shock wave knocked him forward with the force of a hurricane. He instinctively tried to regain his balance using his arms as counterweights, but the jolt was way too powerful to overcome.

As Chen started to fall, Payne was tempted to lunge for him but knew it wouldn't do either of them any good. Even if he'd managed to latch on, there was no way he would be able to maintain his own balance. So, instead of doing something impossible, Payne used his energy to yank the board off the far side of the moat while holding on to his end the best that he could. Agony gripped its claws into his injured biceps as the plank slammed into the water below, but he didn't have time to suffer. If he didn't get to the bottom of the chasm immediately, Chen was going to be the only human in a battle royal, and he wasn't about to let that happen.

Grabbing his Glock, Payne sat on the smooth plank, which rested at a forty-five-degree angle, and started his descent on the kiddie slide from hell. He'd gotten a third of the way down the slope when he spotted Chen, who was injured and struggling to get out of the shallow water by the far bank, and the twelve-foot crocodile that was chasing him.

With the confidence of a big-game hunter, Payne aimed his weapon at the croc's head and fired. The bullet struck his target directly below its eye, causing the reptile to roar in anguish and thrash its tail like a flag in a violent storm, but that wasn't good enough for Payne. He realized that wounded animals were often the most dangerous, so the instant his feet touched liquid he finished the job by depositing two more rounds into the angry beast.

"Holy shit!" Chen gasped from the nearby shore. "That was unbelievable."

"Not really. I practice that move in my swimming pool all the time."

"Seriously, that was awesome!"

But Payne shrugged off the praise. After all, Chen was there to do him a favor. "Are you hurt? Can you make it back up the plank?"

"Doubtful, sir. I messed up my knee pretty bad when I landed."

Payne nodded as he scouted the waist-deep water for more crocs. Thankfully, the others huddled lazily on the opposite shore. "But you'll live, won't you? I mean, I shouldn't just leave you here as an entrée, right?"

Chen smiled through his pain. "No, sir. I don't think I'd like that very much."

"Good, then let's figure a way to get you out of—"

Before he could finish, a second explosion ripped through the house, one that lit the surrounding sky with a massive ball of flame and hurled chunks of wood and metal high into the air. To escape the falling debris, Payne shoved Chen under the lip of the concrete ledge and sheltered him with his own body while waiting for things to calm down.

JONES covered his head as another blast shook the earth but refused to take his eyes off the enemy. They had settled behind a rock formation near the escape tunnel, and he figured they'd stay there as long as there were more charges to detonate. At least he hoped that was the case, because while they sat on their asses watching the fireworks, his team was moving in to finish them off.

A static-filled message trickled over Jones's radio, but he was unable to make out the voice.

"You're breaking up," Jones shouted into his mouthpiece. "Repeat."

There was a slight delay. "This . . . Payne. Can . . . me?"

"Jon?" He cupped his hand over his earpiece so he could hear better. "Is that you?"

"Of course . . . me! I can't . . . you've already forgotten . . . fucking voice!"

Jones was thrilled that Payne was bitching at him. That was his way of saying that he was fine. "Where are you, man? I was told you got caught up in the pyrotechnics."

"I did. Thankfully, Chen and . . . were . . . the moat during . . . big blast. The concrete shielded . . . getting hurt."

Jones did his best to make out the words, but the tumult and the static made it difficult. "Are you hurt? Do you need me to get you out?"

". . . banged up, but I'm . . ." Dead air filled the line for a few seconds before Payne's voice could be heard again. ". . . word on Ariane?"

"We're still not sure where she is. Shell called in and claimed he could see a female with the Posse, but that report is unconfirmed. Repeat, that is unconfirmed."

". . . about . . . oska . . . Haney?"

"No word from Kokoska or Haney. But we aren't giving up hope. Those two have been through worse."

Several more seconds passed before Jones could hear him again, and when he could, Payne was in the middle of a long message. ". . . is a hole up . . . it might be . . . way into . . . I'm going to . . . Chen . . . it out."

"Jon," he shouted, "you're breaking up. I can't understand you. Please repeat."

". . . hole . . . moat . . . a way into the . . ."

Unfortunately, nothing but static came across the line.

PAYNE wasn't sure if his message had gotten through, but he realized he couldn't waste any more time on the radio trying to find out. He and Chen were currently sitting ducks, and he knew if they stayed put, it was just a matter of time before something—an explosion, a crocodile, or an enemy soldier—took them out.

"I know you're banged up, but how does a long walk sound to you?"

Chen looked at Payne in the flickering firelight and grimaced. "You tell me, sir. How does a long walk sound?"

"It's just what the doctor ordered." Payne slipped his good arm around Chen's waist and helped him to his feet. "Don't get any wrong ideas. This isn't going to be a romantic stroll. That last blast opened a fissure in the wall, and I'm hoping it'll lead somewhere safe."

The duo trudged through the waist-deep stream for several yards while keeping a constant eye out for crocs. Luckily, the giant reptiles were just as uninterested in a skirmish as the MANIACs were, and they did their best to stay far out of the humans' way.

"Okay," Payne said once they had arrived at the crevice. "Let me check things out before we get you in there. Will you be all right for a few minutes on your own?"

Chen nodded as he slumped to the ground, exhausted.

"Just holler if something starts to eat you."

"Don't worry, I think that's probably the natural reaction."

Payne grinned as he checked his weapon then leaned inside the cavelike opening, which extended from water level to nearly three feet above his head. The darkness of the interior prevented him from seeing much, so he was forced to use one of the chemical torches that he carried in his belt. After breaking the cylinder's inner seal, he gave the liquids a quick shake, and the phosphorescent mixture filled the manmade grotto with enough light to read a newspaper.

"I'll be right back," he told Chen. "Don't go anywhere."

By using the green glow of the high-tech lantern, Payne was able to figure out what he had stumbled upon. It was the tunnel that the Posse had used for their escape. The cylindrical shaft started somewhere to his right, deep within the bowels of Kotto's basement, and continued to his left, ending somewhere outside the fence on the western flank of the estate. Or at least it used to. Due to all the recent explosions, Payne had no idea if the route was still passable. He hoped it was, since he and Chen were looking for a way out of the moat, but he realized he wouldn't know for sure until he explored the mysteries that lay farther ahead.

CHAPTER 63

HOLMES and Greene laughed with childlike enthusiasm as the first few explosions tore through the house. In their minds every blast meant a few less soldiers that they'd have to deal with, and if the second part of their plan was going to be successful, they had to keep the number of MANIACs to an absolute minimum.

"Are you sure this is going to work?" Drake wondered from his position on the ground. "If these troops are as skilled as you claim, will they really be fooled by something so simple?"

The comment knocked the smile off Holmes's face. He had known Edwin Drake for less than a few hours but had learned to despise the man. "I'll tell you what, Eddie. If you don't want to participate in phase two of my plan, you can take off your cloak and start walking. It won't make a damn bit a difference to me."

"I didn't mean to offend you," he insisted. "But—"

"But what? You call my plan *foolish*, then claim you didn't mean to offend me? Fuck that, and fuck you! If you keep it up, I'll put a bullet in your ass myself."

The smile on Greene's face got even wider because he

disliked Drake as well. "So what's it gonna be? Are you in or out? We gotta know now."

Drake glanced at Kotto for some moral support, but none was forthcoming. Kotto had just watched his house detonated for the sake of the plan, so he wasn't about to give up on Holmes and Greene's idea anytime soon.

"Fine," Drake relented. "What would you like me to do?"

"Just lie there quietly until Levon and I change our clothes," Holmes ordered. "When it's time to do something else, we'll let you know."

AFTER helping Chen inside the tunnel, Payne headed west in hopes of finding the exit but found something more exciting.

Payne traveled less than twenty yards down the concrete shaft when he noticed the artificial light of his lantern start to burn brighter than it had just seconds before. At first he figured the chemical compound in his torch was simply heating up, but after a few more steps, he realized that the added radiance wasn't coming from him. The extra burst of light was shining from somewhere up ahead.

Concerned by the possibilities, Payne hid his light in his pocket and inched silently toward the source of the phantom glow. With weapon in hand, he crept along the smooth edge of the wall until he came to a strange bend in the tunnel. For some reason the passageway turned sharply to the left, then seemed to snake back to the right almost instantly—perhaps to avoid a geological pitfall of some kind. Whatever the reason for the design, Payne concluded that the epicenter of the light was somewhere in that curve.

Pausing to collect his thoughts, Payne reached into the leather sheath that hung at his side and pulled out a nine-inch hunting knife that had once belonged to his grandfather. Even though it was nearly fifty years old, the single-edged bowie knife was sharp enough to cut through metal and sturdy enough to be used in hand-to-hand combat. In this case, though, it possessed a less obvious attribute that he hoped to take advantage of: a mirrorlike finish.

By extending the weapon forward, Payne hoped to see what was lurking around the corner without exposing himself to gunfire. Sure, he knew he wouldn't be able to see much in a simple reflection, but if he was able to get a small glimpse of what was waiting for him, he'd be better prepared to face it.

"Show me something good," he whispered to the knife.

And surprisingly, it did.

Payne couldn't tell how many people were gathered up ahead—they were huddled too close together for him to get an accurate count—but he had a feeling he knew who they were. They were escaped slaves, part of the *original* Plantation shipment that had been sent to Nigeria several weeks before Ariane had even been abducted. People who—

Wait a second, he thought. If these were actually escaped slaves, what were they doing *sitting* in this tunnel? If they'd somehow gotten free from Kotto's house, why weren't they running down this passageway toward the outside world? Common sense told him that was what they should be doing. And what was keeping them so damn quiet? Were they afraid to speak, or was there an outside factor that was keeping them silent? Something, perhaps, like an armed guard? That would explain a lot, he reasoned. Plus, it would clarify the presence of their light. Payne figured if the slaves were hiding, then they wouldn't be dumb enough to use a lantern. That would be an obvious giveaway in this deadly game of hide-and-seek.

No, the slaves' silence, coupled with their ill-advised use of a light, suggested only one thing: Someone was trying to get these people noticed.

Thankfully, Payne was way too intelligent to fall for the ploy—especially since he'd taught the maneuver to many of his men during their initial training. And since he had taught the tactic, he knew exactly how to beat it.

"Yoo-hoo!" he called loudly. "Come out, come out, wherever you are!"

Several seconds passed before Payne heard the reply he was expecting.

"Captain Payne?" shouted Haney, one of the missing MANIACs. "Is that you?"

"It sure is, princess. I've come to rescue you from the evil dungeon. Are you alone?"

"No, Kokoska's with me, but he's unconscious. He took a bump on his head during the first blast. He's been fading in and out ever since."

Despite the conversation, Payne moved forward cautiously, just in case he was overlooking a foot snare or something more diabolical. "And the prisoners? Where'd you find them?"

"In a basement cage. Can you believe that shit? They'd be buried under tons of rubble right now if we hadn't gotten to them. The assholes were just planning on leaving them in there with tiny bombs strapped to their legs."

"Tiny bombs?" he asked. "Were they silver?"

"Yeah!" Haney showed his face and held up one of the devices to prove his point. "How'd you know their color, sir?"

Payne grabbed the explosive with disgust. "They used the same thing on the Plantation."

After taking a few seconds to examine the mechanism, Payne smiled at the hostages, trying to reassure them that their lives were about to return to normalcy. None of them smiled back, which wasn't surprising. As a group, they'd been through so much in such a short amount of time that Payne knew it would take more than a smile for any of them to start trusting the world again. He realized it would take love and friendship and a shitload of therapy to get them back on track, but he hoped that they'd be able to get over this eventually.

"Sir?" Haney blurted. "What's the status topside? Did everyone make it out okay?"

Payne shook his head. "Chen's resting in the tunnel behind me. He took a nasty fall into the moat, but he'll live."

"What about Ariane? Did she get out all right?"

Payne took a deep breath. "Unfortunately, that still remains to be seen."

"Sir?" he asked, slightly confused.

"Don't get me wrong. I'm confident she made it out before the blast. But my guess is there are still some loose ends that need to be taken care of before she'll be completely free." Payne paused in thought. "Thankfully, loose ends are my specialty."

JONES tried to reestablish contact with Payne but met with little success. With no more time to waste, Jones decided to change his priorities and forge ahead without him.

"Team one," Jones uttered into his headset, "what's your status?"

Shell answered. "We've got the Indians surrounded. We can move on your word."

"What's the risk to the cowboys?"

"Higher than it was a moment ago."

The comment bothered Jones, who had lost visuals on Holmes and Greene a few minutes before. "Please explain."

"Everyone's dressed the same. Long white cloaks with hoods that cover their faces."

"Give me the numbers, Lieutenant. How risky are the odds?"

"I wouldn't bet my dog on 'em, sir." Shell paused to speak to one of his men before he continued his transmission. "By our count we're looking at three black and three white, and one of the whites is definitely a woman. And two of the blacks are supersized."

"The big ones are probably Holmes and Greene. They're the ones we want the most."

"Maybe so, but there's a problem. Their size doesn't stand out anymore."

"Why not?"

"The six have gathered in a tight cluster, so it's tough to tell where one person ends and the next begins."

"In a cluster? How badly do they blend?"

"They look like a giant marshmallow, sir."

Jones cursed before he spoke again. "What are you telling me? No go on the snipers?"

"That's affirmative, sir—unless you can put out the fire. It's messing up our ability to see."

"How so, Lieutenant? It didn't bother my sightline."

"That's because it's at your back, sir. The frontal glare prevents our night vision from working properly. Without 'em, our snipers don't have enough light to shoot."

Jones couldn't believe what he was hearing. Each man was equipped with enough optical equipment to see a lightning bug fart from a half mile away, but they couldn't see a 275-pound man in the light of a raging inferno. "Let me get this straight: You're telling me it's too bright and too dark for you at the *exact same time*?"

Shell grinned at the paradox. "Ain't it a fucked-up world we live in?"

WHEN Payne reached the end of the passageway, he gazed through the thick wall of vines that had obscured the tunnel's presence from the outside world and studied the scene before him. The six people who had escaped through the corridor were now dressed identically and standing in a compact huddle—their arms around each other's shoulders and their heads tilted forward in order to obscure each other's height.

"Damn!" he growled. Even from point-blank range, there was no way he could risk a shot.

"D.J.," he whispered into his radio, "where are we positioned?"

Jones smiled at the sound of Payne's voice. He knew his best friend would pop up eventually. It was just a matter of when. "We're in a semicircle with a radius of twenty yards. We'd surround them completely, but the fence cuts off their route to the east, so there's no need."

"Have they attempted to make contact?"

"No, which is kind of puzzling. They obviously know

we're out here, but they haven't come forward with any demands."

"That is kind of strange," Payne admitted. "Almost as strange as their formation. I've never seen anything like it before."

"Me, neither . . . Out of curiosity, where are you right now?"

"Me? I'm about ten feet to their rear, watching them from the door to the escape tunnel."

"Did you say you're *in* the tunnel?" Jones shook his head in amazement, stunned at Payne's ability to turn up in the damnedest of places. "How did you pull that off?"

"Long story. Oh, and just for the record, I stumbled upon our missing brethren. They're a little banged up but very much alive."

"Thank God! I was worried about them. Any need for emergency evac?"

"Nah, they'll be fine until this crisis is over. By the way, how are you planning on ending it?"

Jones laughed at Payne's choice of words. Both of them knew who was going to put an end to things, and it certainly wasn't going to be Jones. "Thankfully, that's not my decision, Jon. Now that you're back as team leader, I can sit back, relax, and watch you work your magic."

"It's funny you should mention magic, because that's exactly what I had in mind. With a little help from you, I think we can make the Posse disappear."

CHAPTER 64

JONES waited for Payne's go-ahead before he walked toward the enemy. Jones continued forward while doing nothing to conceal himself. In fact, he so desperately wanted to be seen by Holmes and Greene that he fired his weapon into the air just to get their attention.

"You know," he exclaimed, "you guys are pretty damn bad at taking hostages. For this tactic to work, you're *supposed* to issue a crazy list of demands. I've been waiting for several minutes now, and I haven't heard a peep."

Greene's bass-filled voice emerged from the center of the huddle. "That's because we've been waiting for you. Now that you're here, I guess we can start this shit."

"Oh, goody!" Jones mocked. "But before we begin, I think it's only fair if I introduced the rest of my negotiating team. Fellas, why don't you come out and say hello?"

Like ghosts emerging from a sea of fog, the MANIACs simply materialized out of nothingness. One second they weren't visible to the naked eye, and the next they were standing with weapons raised, like Spartans waiting for an approaching horde.

"As you can see," Jones continued, "we outnumber you by a large margin."

"What, is that supposed to scare us?" Holmes screamed, his head bobbing ever so slightly as he did. "You might outnumber us, but there's no way you can shoot us without endangering the hostages. And trust me, if you guys come any closer, I'll kill one of them myself."

Jones smiled at the threat while taking another step forward. "I don't believe that for a second. Why? Because if you hurt anyone, you'll be killed. I know it, and you know it. Hell, everyone here knows it. So why even bother to threaten us? It's just so clichéd."

"Maybe so, but it's the truth! I wonder how Payne would feel if I sliced up that tasty bitch of his? How do you think he'd like that?"

"That's a good question. Why don't you ask him yourself?"

"I would, if he showed his face. Where's that pussy hiding?"

Payne answered the question by tapping Holmes on the shoulder. "Right behind you."

Like a well-orchestrated magic trick, Payne had used his assistant to lure everyone's attention forward while the key maneuvering was being done in the background. Of course, now that the deception was over, Payne needed to finish the performance in grand style. He did so by sliding his knife across his enemy's throat with assassinlike perfection. Crimson gushed from Holmes's carotid artery, staining the front of his cloak like a wounded deer in the snow, but that wasn't good enough for Payne. He immediately tossed Holmes over his shoulder and finished him off by falling backward and slamming his elbow into the bridge of his nose. The maneuver drove Holmes's nasal bone into his brain with brutal efficiency.

Death was instantaneous.

With his first rival vanquished, Payne sprang to his feet and searched the huddle in front of him for his next target.

Unfortunately, despite his speed, Payne was still too slow for Greene, who had latched onto Ariane's throat at the first sign of trouble. He was currently shoving a .45-caliber pistol against the side of her head.

"Stay back!" Greene demanded as he dragged her toward the tunnel. "I swear to God, if you come any closer, I'll kill her."

"Calm down!" Payne pleaded. "Don't do anything stupid. Just relax."

But Payne knew that would be tough, because he was having a difficult time doing it himself.

He had been a rock—poised and relaxed—when he crept up on Holmes, but some of his composure disappeared when he got his first real glimpse of Ariane since this ordeal had started.

One look and his heart started racing.

"Are you all right?" Payne asked.

"Been better," she mumbled with her swollen jaw. "And you?"

"Pretty damn good," he lied. "I've been trying to get ahold of you for a while. You're a difficult girl to track down."

"Sorry about that. I've been doing some traveling."

"Traveling?" Payne took a step closer, looking for an opening. "Come on, why don't you just admit it? You'll do anything to get out of an ass-kicking on the golf course."

"Darn, you finally figured me out. All of this has been—"

"Will you shut the fuck up?" Greene yelled. "Your lovesick banter is driving me *crazy*." To prove his point, he tightened his grip on Ariane's neck, nearly cutting off her airway. "This is my time to talk, not yours! Do you got that, Payne? My time!"

"Okay, okay, I'm sorry. Go ahead and talk. I'm listening. I swear."

Greene took a deep breath. "First of all, tell your men to get back. When I get anxious, my muscles start to contract, and if that happens, I'm liable to break her fuckin' neck!"

"Not a problem, Levon. But first you gotta ease up just a little bit. Let her breathe, my man. Just let her breathe."

"I'm serious, Jon. Get them back!"

"I will, I promise, but only if you stop hurting her." Payne took another step forward, trying to get as close to Greene as possible. "Come on, Levon, why don't you just put down your gun and walk away from this? If you do that, I promise we won't kill you."

"Great! So, what are you going to do? Cart me back to the U.S., where I'll be viewed like Michael Vick times a million? Screw that! I get out of this free, or I get slaughtered right here! There's no quit in me! You should know that. I don't quit!"

Another step forward. "It's not quitting, Levon. It's simply doing the smart thing."

"Stay where you are, or I'll kill her! I mean it!"

Payne threw his hands up in acceptance. "I won't move from here, okay? I just want to talk to you. Don't do anything stupid. I just want to discuss things."

"Then tell your men to back off! If all you wanna do is talk, there's no reason to have them so close!" The tension in his voice proved that he was close to losing it. "What difference is it gonna make if they back up? They'll still be close enough to kill me if I make a move, so get them to back up!"

Payne looked at Jones and reluctantly nodded. "Not too far, but ease the grip slightly."

"You heard the captain," Jones told the men. "Give them ten more feet of breathing space. But if Greene even sneezes, take him out with everything you've got."

The men followed their orders, dropping back several steps but never taking their aim off Greene. When they reached their mark, Jones shouted for them to stop.

"Is that better?" Payne asked. "I did like you wanted, as a sign of good faith. I didn't have to, but I did. Now, why don't you do the same for me? Why don't you give me something?"

"Like what? The only thing you want is the girl, and do

you know what? I can see why she means so much to you. I had a chance to check her out in the shower, and let me tell you, she's one tasty piece of ass."

Normally, Payne would've gone after somebody who made a comment like that, but in this case he all but welcomed it. He realized it was an opportunity that he could use to his advantage.

"Jeez," he said to Ariane, "you should consider yourself lucky! You've always wanted to hook up with an NFL player, and he sounds pretty interested. This might be your big chance."

Calmly, as if she wasn't in a life-or-death struggle, Ariane turned her attention to Greene. She wasn't sure why, but she knew that she was supposed to distract him with conversation. "You played in the NFL? Oh, my God, that is so cool! What's your name?"

But before Greene could speak, Payne answered for him. "That's Levon Greene. I told you about him, remember? He's the linebacker I met while playing basketball. You know, the one with the bad left knee."

"You have a bad knee?" she groaned. "How horrible! That's one thing I always hated about sports. The moment a player gets hurt, their opponents take advantage of it."

And then she proved her point.

Slowly, she lifted her left foot until it was directly in front of Greene's knee. Then, she thrust it backward with as much strength as she could, ramming it into his kneecap at a perfect angle. The pain from the blow caused Greene to howl in agony, but more importantly, it caused him to loosen his grip on her neck, which gave her the chance to get away.

The instant she dove to the ground Payne raised his weapon like a quick-draw artist and fired. Jones did the same from farther back, and the two of them filled Greene with enough bullets to take down a polar bear. Shot after shot entered his chest and neck, causing his body to dance to the rhythm of gunfire. It continued to do so until both of them had emptied their entire clips into the man they had once considered a friend.

When the firing stopped, the MANIACs charged forward to deal with Kotto and Drake and the slaves that remained in the tunnel, but Payne wasn't worried about any of them. His only concern was Ariane, and he ran to her side to see if she was all right.

"I'm so happy to see you."

"I love you so much," she insisted, crying tears of joy on Payne's shoulder as they sat on the ground. "I can't believe that you found me." She sobbed for an entire minute, clinging to him like a favorite stuffed animal. "But what took you so long? I thought you were supposed to be like Rambo or something."

Payne laughed loudly, thankful for a girl who was able to keep her sense of humor despite all that she had been through. "Hey, you said you were looking forward to the long weekend, so I figured I should take my time in getting here."

"A long weekend is one thing, Jonathon, but an entire week is quite another."

He smiled, wiping away her tears with the cloth of her cloak. "Look on the bright side. It's already Friday, so by the time we get back to America, it will actually be the weekend again."

Ariane sighed as she pulled him against her chest.

She never wanted to let go of him.

Jones was hesitant to break up the tender moment, but he needed Payne to decide what they were going to do with Kotto and Drake. "If you don't mind," he said, "I'd like to borrow Jon for a minute before you two start shagging on the damn ground."

Ariane glanced at Jones and gave him a warm smile. She knew that he'd risked his life on several occasions during the past week and wanted him to realize how much she appreciated it.

"He's all yours, D.J. There'll be no shaggin' until I get

cleaned up." She stood from the ground and dusted herself off. "Besides, I wanted to check on someone."

Payne raised his eyebrows. "Did you make a friend in prison? How cute!"

She smiled again, despite her sore jaw. "I think his name's Nathan, but that's all I really know. He doesn't talk too much because of all the torture."

"Big guy, lots of scars? He was in the Devil's Box before me. Hakeem said he'd left him in the device for several weeks. Unfortunately, I have no idea who he is, though."

"I do," interjected Sanchez, who'd been listening to their reunion. "I'm from San Diego, so I should know who he is."

All three turned toward him, looking for information.

"His name's Nate Barker, and he plays for the Chargers. According to ESPN, he's been missing for a few months now, simply disappeared from his house one night."

"Are you sure?" Payne asked. It seemed risky for the Posse to kidnap someone who was famous. "Why would they grab a high-profile guy like that?"

Sanchez offered an explanation. "If I remember correctly, he's the player that hurt Levon's knee. Snapped it like a twig up in Buffalo."

Payne glanced at Barker and studied his haggard appearance. He certainly had the height to be a football player, even though it was painfully obvious that he'd lost a lot of weight during the past several weeks. "This was all done for revenge? My God, what a sick bastard Levon turned out to be! I would've never guessed it before all of—"

"Sirs!" Shell shouted urgently. He was on his knees near Greene's body, and the look on his face suggested that something was wrong. "Get over here, sirs!"

Payne, Jones, and Sanchez dashed forward while Ariane chose to stay behind.

"It's Greene," Shell said. "He's still alive. He was wearing a vest under his cloak."

"Are you serious?" Payne sank to the ground next to Shell and looked into Greene's eyes. They were open and, considering his current condition, fairly active. "Levon, can you hear me?"

Greene nodded his head slightly, as blood gushed from the wounds in his neck and shoulders. "You got me, Payne. You got me good."

"I didn't get you, Levon. You got yourself. I can't believe you did all this shit for revenge."

Greene closed his eyes to escape the agony but managed to turn his lips into a large smile. "No regrets," he groaned. "I got no regrets."

Payne was ready to lecture him further when he suddenly sensed a large presence hovering behind him. Looking up, he was surprised to see the battered body of Nate Barker.

"Levon," the lineman croaked. His throat was dry and cracked from severe dehydration.

Greene reopened his eyes and stared into the face of his enemy.

Barker leaned closer, letting Greene see his face. "That play," he said. "That play where you got hurt? I didn't try to hurt you. I swear, I didn't."

But Greene wouldn't accept it. He closed his eyes and shook his head in denial.

It wasn't something that he'd ever believe.

"Honestly," Barker continued. "I've never hurt anyone on purpose in my entire life. I swear to God, I haven't." Then suddenly, without warning, he placed his foot on Greene's left knee and anchored it with his body weight. "That is, until now!"

With all of his remaining strength, Barker grabbed Greene's lower leg and pulled it upward, tugging and yanking on the limb until the weakened joint literally exploded from the excess stress. The loud popping of tendons and cartilage was quickly accented by Greene's screams of pain, which sent shivers down the spines of everyone in the area.

But Barker was far from done. With a devious grin on his face, he lifted his foot off of Greene's knee and slammed it into the middle of Greene's throat. He'd been put through so much over the past several weeks that there was no way he was going to stop. No fucking way.

Not until *his* revenge was complete. Not until *he* felt vindicated for *his* pain.

And no one in the area had any desire to stop him.

EPILOGUE

THE door was closed and the room was dark, but that didn't stop Payne and Jones from entering. They'd broken so many laws in the past few weeks that they weren't about to let visiting hours—or the heavyset nurse at the front desk—stand in their way.

Not with something as important as this to take care of.

"So," Payne growled as he approached the bed, "did you actually think we were going to forget about your role in this?"

The injured man didn't know what to say, so he simply shrugged his shoulders.

"You can't be that stupid!" Jones said. "What, are you a buckwheat or something?"

The comment brought a smile to Bennie Blount's heavily bandaged face. "I haven't known what to think," he whispered. "I haven't seen you guys since my accident."

Payne placed his hand on Blount's elbow and gave it a simple squeeze. "We're sorry about that. We would've been here *much* sooner, but we've been tied up in red tape. Of course, that tends to happen when you sneak into a foreign country and kill a bunch of people."

Jones shook his head in mock disgust. "The Pentagon and all its stupid policies. Please!"

Blount laughed despite the pain it caused in his cheeks.

Payne said, "I hear the swelling around your spinal cord has gone down. How's your movement?"

"Pretty good. I'm still a little wobbly when I walk, but the doctors think I'll be fine."

"That's great news, Bennie! I've been worried sick about you."

"Me, too," added Jones.

"Now my biggest concern is my face. That crazy dog did a lot of damage."

Payne gave Blount's elbow another squeeze. "Well, stop worrying about it. I'm flying in the world's best plastic surgeons to treat you. They'll have you back to your old self in no time."

Jones nodded. "Unless, of course, your old self isn't good enough. They could make you look like Denzel, or Will Smith, *or* give you a nice set of D-cups. Whatever you want."

Payne frowned. "Do you think his frame could support D-cups? I'd say no more than a C."

"Really? I think he'd look good with—"

"Forget the tits." Blount laughed. "My old self would be fine, just fine. But . . ."

"But what?" Payne demanded. "If you're worried about the money, don't be. All of your hospital bills have already been taken care of."

"What?" he asked, stunned. "That's not necessary."

"Of course it is! After all you've sacrificed, I wouldn't have it any other way."

"Listen to him, Bennie. Even with a truckload of insurance, you'd still have tons of out-of-pocket expenses."

"Yeah, but—"

"But, nothing!" Payne insisted. "Furthermore, you'll never see another tuition bill for the rest of your life. As soon as you're feeling up to it, you can head back to school, compliments of the Payne Industries Scholarship Fund. We'll take care of everything—including a monthly stipend for beer and hookers."

Blount shook his head. "Jon, I couldn't. Seriously."

"Hey," Jones added, "that's not all. We have one more surprise for you, something that's more valuable than money."

"Guys, enough with the gifts."

"Hang on," Payne insisted. "You'll really like this one. We saved the best for last."

Then, with his typical flash of showmanship, Payne threw the door aside to reveal the most attractive woman Blount had ever seen.

Dark brown hair. Dark brown eyes. Unbelievable figure. Simply dazzling.

She stood there for several seconds, speechless, unsure of what to do next. Finally, with her composure regained, she grabbed Payne's arm and glided across the room to meet the family member she'd never even known she had.

"Bennie," Payne said with a lump in his throat, "I'd like to introduce you to someone who's very special to me. This is your cousin Ariane."

Author's Note

While conducting my research for this novel, I read hundreds of journal entries that detailed the ungodly horrors that occurred on many nineteenth-century plantations. And *not* just the accounts of ex-slaves. In order to keep my research as balanced as possible, I studied just as many narratives from slave owners as I did from the slaves themselves. And do you know what? I'm glad I did, because it wasn't until I read the firsthand accounts of these brutal men that I started to understand how malicious and sadistic some of them really were.

Sure, it was unsettling to read about the sting of a bullwhip from a slave's point of view, but not nearly as disturbing as the words of one overseer who described the process of whipping his workers in near-orgasmic terms. "The delicious crack of leather on flesh fills my hand with delight and sends my body a shiver."

Chilling, indeed.

It was those types of quotes that convinced me to include the graphic sequences that I did, scenes that are so full of carnage and torture (the Devil's Box, the Listening Post, etc.) that some readers have complained to me about nightmares. Well, I'm sorry for your loss of sleep. But if I didn't stress the gore and bloodshed of plantation life, then I would have been the one losing sleep. Because my story would have been less than accurate.

And now a special excerpt
from Chris Kuzneski's

THE LOST THRONE

Available from The Berkley Publishing Group!

PROLOGUE

Christmas Day 1890
Piazza della Santa Carità
Naples, Italy

THE greatest secret of ancient Greece was silenced by a death in Italy.

Not a shooting or a stabbing or a murder of any kind—although dozens of those would occur later—but a good old-fashioned death. One minute the man was strolling across the Piazza della Santa Carità, pondering the significance of his discovery; the next, he was sprawled on his stomach in the middle of the cold square. People rushed to his side, hoping to help him to his feet, but one look at his gaunt face told them that he needed medical attention.

Two policemen on horseback were flagged down, and they rushed him to the closest hospital, where he slipped in and out of consciousness for the next hour. They asked him his name, but he couldn't answer. His condition had stolen his ability to speak.

The man wore a fancy suit and overcoat, both of which revealed his status. His hair was thin and gray, suggesting a man in his sixties. A bushy mustache covered his upper lip.

Doctors probed his clothes, searching for identification, but found nothing of value. No papers. No wallet. No money. If they had only looked closer, they might have noticed the secret pocket sewn into the lining of his coat, and the mystery would have ended there. But as hospital policy dictated, no identification meant no treatment. Not even on Christmas morning.

With few options, the police took him to the local station house, an ancient building made of brick and stone that would shelter him from the bitter winds of the Tyrrhenian Sea. They fed him broth and let him rest on a cot in an open cell, hoping he would regain his voice.

In time, he regained several.

Starting with a whisper that barely rose above the level of his breath, the sound slowly increased, building to a crescendo that could be heard by the two officers in the next room. They hurried down the corridor, expecting to find the stranger fully awake and willing to answer their questions. Instead they saw a man in a semicatatonic state who was babbling in his sleep.

His eyes were closed and his body was rigid, yet his lips were forming words.

One of the officers made the sign of the cross and said a short prayer while the other ran for a pencil and paper. When he returned, he pulled a chair up to the cot and tried to take notes in a small journal. Maybe they'd get an address. Or if they were really lucky, maybe even a name. But they got none of those things. In fact, all they got was more confused.

The first words spoken were German. Then French. Then Portuguese. Before long he was mixing several languages in the same sentence. Dutch followed by Spanish and Latin. English layered with Greek and Russian. Every once in a while he said something in Italian, but the words were so random and his accent so thick that they made little sense. Still, the officer transcribed everything he could and before long he noticed some repetition. One word seemed to be repeated over and over. Not only in Italian but in other languages as well.

Il trono. Le trône. El trono.

The throne.

This went on for several minutes. Language after language from one man's mouth. Like the devil speaking in tongues. Then, just as quickly as it started, it stopped.

No more words. No more clues.

The man would never speak again.

Two days later, after he had been identified, newspapers around the globe reported his death. Yet there was no mention of his strange behavior. Nothing about his ramblings or the throne he kept describing. Instead, reporters focused on the colorful details of his life—his wealth, his accomplishments, his discoveries. All the things that made him famous.

Of course, if they had known the truth about his final days, what he had finally found after years of searching, they would have written a much different story.

One of fire, deception, and ancient gold.

One that wouldn't have an ending for two more centuries.

CHAPTER 1

Present day
Saturday, May 17th
Metéora, Greece

THE monk felt the wind on his face as he plummeted to his death, a journey that started with a scream and ended with a thud.

Moments before, he had been standing near the railing of the Moni Agia Triada, the Monastery of the Holy Trinity. It was one of six monasteries perched on natural rock pillars near the Pindus Mountains in central Greece. Known for their breathtaking architecture, the monasteries had been built two thousand feet in the air with one purpose in mind: protection.

But on this night, their sanctity was breached.

The intruders had crossed the valley and climbed the hillside with silent precision. They carried no guns or artillery, preferring the weapons of their ancestors. Swords stored in scabbards were strapped to their backs. Daggers in leather sheaths hung from their hips. Bronze helmets covered their entire heads except for their eyes and mouths.

Centuries ago the final leg of their mission would have been far more treacherous, requiring chisels and ropes to scale the rock face. But that was no longer the case—not since 140 steps had been carved into the sandstone, leading to the entrance of Holy Trinity. Its front gate was ten feet high and made of thick wood, yet they breached it easily and slipped inside, spreading through the compound like a deadly plague.

The first to die was the lookout who, instead of doing his job, had been staring at the twinkling lights of Kalampáka, the small city that rested at the base of the plateau. Sadly, it was the last mistake he ever made. No questions were asked, no quarter was given. One minute he was pondering the meaning of life, the next his life was over.

No bullets. No blades. Just gravity and the rocks below.

One of the monks inside the church heard his scream and tried to warn the others, but before he could, the intruders burst through both doors. Brandishing their swords, they forced all the monks into the center of the room, where the holy men were frisked and their hands were tied.

Seven monks in total. A mixture of young and old.

Just as the intruders had expected.

For the next few minutes, the monks sat in silence on the hard wooden pews. Some of them closed their eyes and prayed to God for divine intervention. Others seemed reconciled to their fate. They knew the risks when they accepted this duty, what their brotherhood had endured and protected for centuries.

They were the keepers of the book. The chosen ones.

And soon they would be forced to die.

With the coldness of an executioner, the leader of the soldiers strode into the church. At first glance he looked like a moving work of art: muscle stacked upon muscle in statuesque perfection, a gleaming blade in his grasp. Unlike the others who had entered before him, his helmet was topped with a plume of red horsehair, a crest that signified his rank.

To the monks, he was the face of death.

Without saying a word, he nodded to his men. They sprang into action, grabbing one of the monks and dragging him toward the stone altar. Orthodox tradition prevented the brethren from trimming their facial hair after receiving tonsure—a symbolic shaving of their heads—so his beard was long and gray, draping the front of his black cassock like a hairy bib.

"What do you want from us?" cried the monk as he was shoved to his knees. "We have done nothing wrong!"

The leader stepped forward. "You know why I'm here. I want the book."

"What book? I know nothing about a book!"

"Then you are no use to me."

He punctuated his statement with a flick of his sword, separating the monk's head from his body. For a split second the monk's body didn't move, somehow remaining upright as if no violence had occurred. Then suddenly it slumped forward, spilling its contents onto the floor.

Head on the left. Body on the right. Blood everywhere.

The monks gasped at the sight.

"Bring me another," the leader ordered. "One who wants to live."

CHAPTER 2

Sunday, May 18th
St. Petersburg, Florida

THE phone rang in the middle of the night, sometime between last call and breakfast. The time of night reserved for two things: emergencies and wrong numbers.

Jonathon Payne hoped it was the latter.

He rolled over in the hotel bed and reached for the nightstand, knocking something to the floor in his dark room. He had no idea what it was and wasn't curious enough to find out. Still feeling the effects of his sleeping pill, he knew if he turned on a light he would be awake until dawn. Of that he was certain. He had always been a problem sleeper, an issue that had started long before his career in the military and had only gotten worse after.

Then again, years of combat can do that to a person.

And he had seen more than most.

Payne used to lead the MANIACs, an elite special forces unit composed of the top soldiers from the Marines, Army, Navy, Intelligence, Air Force, and Coast Guard. Whether it was personnel recovery, unconventional warfare, or counter-guerrilla sabotage, the MANIACs were the best of the best. The boogeymen that no one talked about. The government's secret weapon.

Yet on this night, Payne wanted no part of his former life.

He just wanted to get some sleep.

"Hello?" he mumbled into the hotel phone, expecting the worst.

A dial tone greeted him. It was soft and steady like radio static.

"Hello?" he repeated.

But the buzzing continued. As if no one had even called. As if he had imagined everything.

Payne grunted and hung up the phone, glad he could roll over and go back to sleep without anything to worry about. Thrilled it wasn't an emergency. He'd had too many of those when he was in the service. Hundreds of nights interrupted by news. Updates that were rarely positive.

So in his world, wrong numbers were a good thing. About the best thing possible.

Unfortunately, that wasn't the case here.

SEVERAL hours later Payne opened the hotel curtains and stepped onto his private veranda at the Renaissance Vinoy in downtown St. Petersburg. Painted flamingo pink and recently restored to its former glory, the resort was a stunning example of 1920s Mediterranean Revival architecture. The type of grand hotel that used to be found all over Florida yet was quickly becoming extinct in the age of Disneyfication.

The bright sunlight warmed his face and the sea breeze filled his lungs as he stared at the tropical waters of Tampa Bay, less than ten miles from many of the best beaches in America. Where the sand was white and the water was turquoise. Where dolphins frolicked in the surf. Born and raised in Pittsburgh, Payne rarely got to see dolphins in his hometown—only when he went to the aquarium or when the Miami Dolphins played the Steelers at Heinz Field.

In many ways, Payne looked like an NFL player. He was 6'4", weighed 240 pounds, and was in remarkable shape for a man in his late thirties. Light brown hair, hazel eyes, and a world-class smile. His only physical flaws were the bullet holes and scars that decorated his body. Although he didn't view them as flaws. More like medals of honor because each one stood for something.

Of course, he couldn't tell their stories to most people because the details were classified, but all of the scars meant something to him. Like secret tattoos that no one knew about.

The droning of a small aircraft caught Payne's attention, and he watched it glide across the azure sky and touch down at Albert Whitted Airport, a two-runway facility on the scenic waterfront, a few blocks away. It was the type of airfield that handled banner towing and sightseeing tours. Not large commuter jets. And certainly not the tactical fighters that he had observed during the last forty-eight hours. They required a lot more asphalt and much better pilots.

Every few months Payne visited U.S. military installations around the globe with his best friend and former MANIAC, David Jones. They were briefed on the latest equipment, and they offered their opinions to top brass on everything from training to tactics. Even though both soldiers were retired from active duty, they were still considered valuable assets by the Pentagon.

Part expert, part legend.

Their latest trip had brought them to Florida, where Mac-Dill Air Force Base occupied a large peninsula in the middle of Tampa Bay—eight miles south of downtown Tampa and nine miles east of St. Petersburg. All things considered, it wasn't a bad place to be stationed. Or to visit. Which is why Payne and Jones always looked forward to their next consulting trip.

They picked the destination and the military picked up the tab.

"Hey!" called a voice from below. "You finally awake?"

Payne glanced down and saw David Jones standing on the sidewalk, staring up at him. Jones was 5'9" and roughly forty pounds lighter than Payne. He had light brown skin, short black hair, and a thin nose that held his stylish sunglasses in place. Sadly, the rest of his outfit wasn't nearly as fashionable: a green floral shirt, torn khaki cargo shorts, and a pair of flip-flops.

"I'm starving," Jones said. "You want to get some chow?"

"With you? Not if you're wearing *that*."

"Why? What's wrong with it?"

"Honestly? It looks like Hawaiian camouflage."

Jones frowned, trying to think of a retort. "Yeah, well . . ."

"Well, what?"

"Maybe I'm looking to get *leid*."

Payne laughed. It wasn't a bad comeback for a Sunday morning. "I'll meet you in the lobby."

TEN minutes later the duo was walking along Bayshore Drive. The temperature was in the mid-seventies with low humidity. Gentle waves lapped against the stone wall that lined the harbor while palm trees swayed in the breeze. Payne wore a golf shirt and shorts, an outfit considered dressy in Florida, where many people wore T-shirts or no shirts at all.

As they turned onto Second Avenue NE toward the St. Petersburg Pier, Payne and Jones spotted a parked trolley-bus called the Looper. It was light blue and filled with tourists who were taking pictures of a tiny brick building with a red-tiled roof. A senior citizen tour guide, wearing a beige Panama hat and speaking with a Southern drawl, explained the building's significance over the trolley's loudspeaker system. They stopped to listen to his tale.

"You are looking at the fanciest public restroom in America, affectionately known as Little St. Mary's. Built in 1927 by Henry Taylor, it is a scaled-down replica of St. Mary Our Lady of Grace, the gorgeous church he built on Fourth Street that we'll be seeing soon. Both buildings are typical of the Romanesque Revival style, featuring several colors of brick, arched windows, and topped with a copper cupola. This one's approximately twenty feet high and fifty feet wide."

Cameras clicked as the tour guide continued.

"As the legend goes, the local diocese offered Taylor a large sum of money to build the octagonal church that he finished in 1925. However, for reasons unknown, they chose not to pay him the full amount. Realizing that he couldn't win a fight with the church, he opted to get revenge instead. At that time the city was taking bids to build a comfort station, a fancy term for bathroom, somewhere near the waterfront. Taylor made a ridiculously low bid, guaranteeing that he would get the project. From there, he used leftover materials from the church site and built the replica that you see before you, filling it with toilets instead of pews."

The tour guide smiled. "It was his way of saying that the Catholic Church was full of crap!"

Everyone laughed, including Payne and Jones, as the Looper pulled away from the curb and turned toward the Vinoy. Meanwhile the duo remained, marveling at the stone-carved columns and the elaborate tiled roof of Little St. Mary's.

"Remind me to go in there later," Jones said. "And I mean that literally."

LOVE ME
ALL THE
WAY

Simona Taylor

ARABESQUE

**★BET
BOOKS™**

BET Publications, LLC
http://www.bet.com
http://www.arabesquebooks.com

For my grandmother, Vas Rowley Carrington,
for the strong Tobago blood that flows in my veins.

For my Tobagonian friend, Erva,
for telling me about the pearl thing,
thus getting this whole book rolling.

For my little Trini-American friend, Safiya,
I love you, sweetie.

But most of all, for Rawle,
you're still my favorite romantic hero.

"Beware of a man who gives you pearls;
He will one day make you cry."
                    —Tobagonian saying

One

The mid-sized twin-engine plane shuddered as it hit an air pocket, sending a chorus of murmurs through its passengers, and a tremor of disquiet through Sarita. She clutched the arm of her seat, nails sinking into the yielding upholstery, unable to prevent a sharp cry of surprise from escaping her lips.

"Nervous?" The kindly minister in the seat next to her smiled, teeth as white as the collar that encircled his throat. (As if embarking on a fraudulent mission were not enough, she'd groaned to herself as she boarded, she was going to spend the entire five-hour flight from Miami seated next to a man of the cloth! Would that make her more or less vulnerable to divine judgment?)

She shook her head vigorously, sleek black pageboy haircut swinging and emphasizing her denial. "Not really. I'm not afraid to fly. It's just that I—er—I'm just not too sure of what I'm going to meet when I get there. I don't think I'm *nervous,* though. Not exactly."

The minister smiled again, pale gray eyes crinkling at the corners in amusement. His over-long salt-and-pepper hair stuck up in shocks all over his head, and the deeply ingrained rosy hue of his leathery face made him look more like an elderly outdoorsman than a man of religion. "Well, you *feel* mighty nervous to me," he said. He pointed with his free hand to the arm that lay along the armrest of the seat between them. She realized that the "soft upholstery" she had been so anxiously clutching with her long, well-manicured nails was, in fact, the poor man's forearm. She let him go as if she had touched hot metal.

She felt like an idiot. "Oh God—," she began to apologize, but then slapped her hand over her mouth. "I mean, *oh my!*" Now she *sounded* like an idiot!

The minister grinned as though he'd heard *that* blunder a few times before.

She covered up her embarrassment by voicing her concern. "Is your arm okay?"

He dismissed her anxiety with an amused wave of his hand, which was as richly freckled as that of any sporting fisherman. "Don't worry about it. Glad I could be there for you to lean on. Part of the job."

She smiled, grateful for his attempt to put her at ease. He was speaking euphemistically. She hadn't exactly been "leaning on" his arm; what she'd been doing was a lot more painful than that. But he did look rather grandfatherly, not like the type to hold a grudge, and besides, clawing a minister's arm to shreds probably didn't rank very high on the celestial hierarchy of sins.

At least, not as high as lying did.

Sarita was very bad at lying, which is why she didn't do it often. As a matter of fact, the last time she'd attempted it, she'd failed miserably, winding up with a lasting reminder that accused her every time she looked in the mirror. The intervening years had not been enough to blur the memory, and the fact that she had, in a moment of insanity, taken it into her head to break her usual hard-and-fast rule of "truthfulness until it hurt," served to bring the shadow of the experience back to her with all the pleasantness of a nagging toothache.

It'd been a common enough story: a teenage girl breaking curfew, sneaking out to a party she had been forbidden to attend—promised her devout Baptist parents she wouldn't attend—and trying later to cover up her crime by clambering up the family apple tree and into her bedroom window at two in the morning. There'd been a slip, a fumble, and a moment's panic. The next thing she'd become aware of was waking up in her own bedroom, in broad daylight, faced with two very angry parents, and the discovery that her fall had left her with a small cut that was to leave a permanent scar across her upper lip.

So, at seventeen, she'd learned the hard way that lying led to trouble—very bad trouble—and that it was an activity for people made of sterner stuff than she. Which is why, fifteen years later, airborne aboard Flight 337 from Miami to an island she had heard much about but had never seen, she wasn't exactly calm. She wasn't afraid of flying, or of visiting strange countries. What made her nervous was the knowledge that she had managed to make up for her many years of chronic truthfulness by telling a whopper of a lie, one that couldn't help but lead to trouble, and that the consequences of her actions would be waiting for her when she landed.

Those consequences would not be pretty, of that she was sure, but she'd come this far, and she sure wasn't backing down now, nerves or no nerves. *Get a grip,* she reminded herself. *You've got a right to be here. You've been part of this project from the start. It's your baby, too, as much as it is . . . his. And nothing he says or does can change that.* That reassurance stiffened her spine like a flat strip of metal laid along it, and she felt her nervousness ebb.

The minister beside her leaned closer, still smiling. "So, tell me what brings you to Tobago. It's a gorgeous island; I've been guest-pastoring in churches there for years. Let me guess. Vacation, right?"

Sarita shook her head, finding it hard to drag herself away from her little internal pep talk. If she tried to explain the long and convoluted story that had set her en route to the island, she wondered, and to a minister to boot, would a bolt from the blue strike them?

He didn't seem the type to need a response in order to keep up a conversation. "Visiting family? Migrating?" His eyes flickered over her left hand, to the fourth finger, and instinctively she shoved it out of sight to protect her wedding ring from exposure. "I'd guess honeymoon, but then, if that were the case, you'd be sitting next to someone other than me."

She nearly grinned at that one. Traveling alone, being alone, had almost become second nature to her. She almost didn't notice it. Almost. "None of the above." Her reasons for flying to Tobago weren't exactly something she wanted to get into in detail right now, but he really was charming, and the last thing she wanted to do was offend such a gentle-looking seatmate. But, gentle as he was, he was also persistent. Evidently, the in-flight movie hadn't succeeded in holding his interest, and he found in her more intriguing entertainment.

He went on, enjoying his little guessing game. "Buying land? Selling land? Meeting an old love?"

Ouch, she thought. *That hits home*—or near enough. "Meeting an old love" wasn't exactly what she would call it. More like catapulting headlong into a hurricane of emotions with nothing to protect her from the elements but a wish, a prayer, and stubborn determination to do the job she'd come to do before it was too late.

The minister's quick eyes saw her flush, and he registered his victory with a slight incline of his graying head. Before he could probe any further into the uncomfortable truth onto which he had stumbled, Sarita rushed to divert him. "Actually, I'm a marine biologist. I specialize in reef environments. I'm flying in to join a small team that's studying the reefs there."

He recognized the red herring for what it was, and graciously let the issue slide. "Ah, my dear, then you've come to the right place. Tobago has some of the most stunning reefs in the entire Caribbean—perhaps the world." He turned briefly to peer out of the window. They were nearing the end of the flight, and already the decreased altitude was allowing them to fully see the brilliance of the jeweled water beneath them. "I try to visit them as often as I can myself, at least once every time I make a trip there."

She nodded, trying not to think of him wading out into the deep blue in baggy shorts and snorkels, because that image might make her laugh out loud. He looked like he would be the first man into the water and the last man out. Glad that his attention had been diverted from her personal life and toward the reefs, she said, "The reefs are gorgeous, I'm told, but they're in trouble. I am—that is, the team I'm joining is—especially interested in Tobago's Buccoo Reef. It's one of the best known reefs in the region, but it's, well, dying."

He frowned. "Dying?"

She nodded sadly. "It's been suffering for years, through poaching, pollution, siltation and, of course, the bombardment of hundreds of thousands of clumsy tourists' feet tramping over it every year. I mean, I know the islanders haven't got much of a choice; most of the people earn their living from tourism, and the tourists all want to visit the reef. But all that has taken its toll, and the reef is gasping its dying breath. Or will, if someone doesn't do something about it."

His eyes, serious for a change, were fixed on her with no glint of their former mischief left in them, only deep contemplation. "And you think you're that someone?"

"I know I am," she declared simply. It was not a boast. For her, it was the truth.

The minister looked at her for a long time, a cool, evaluating look that made Sarita shift in her seat. She lifted her eyes to meet the piercing gaze with as much honesty as she could, and more than she would ever have thought of allowing a stranger. After a long moment, he spoke again. "You just might be. You have the passion for it. People can dream all they want, and have the best of intentions, but unless they can believe in their hearts that they are destined to achieve something, they fall short of the target."

He looked away, and Sarita felt like a mealworm being let off a hook. He fished about in his bulging black briefcase, shoving aside a mass of crinkling candy wrappers—"Got to give those up," he grinned apologetically—and slid his big hand behind a huge, worn Bible before withdrawing a small white business card.

"Here," he said, handing it over to her. "My name's Reverend Colin Constantine. I'll be in Tobago for the next six weeks or so. I'll mainly be ministering out of the Mount Moriah Moravian Church—"

Her brow wrinkled. "Moravian?"

"First cousin to the Lutherans," he explained. "I'm a Lutheran myself but we have a good relationship with the Moravian Church. Many Tobagonians are Moravians, so I get lots of invitations to preach whenever I'm in town. If you feel like you want to come in out of the reef for a few hours," he smiled again, "drop by and tell me how you're getting along."

"I'm—uh—Gwen Davis." She took the card and slipped it into the pocket of the loose cotton dress she was wearing in anticipation of the sweltering Caribbean heat. She felt like a fraud—no, she *was* a fraud! Giving a man of God a made-up name like that! But, she rationalized, if she was going to be palming herself off as someone else, she would do well to start practicing. There was little chance of her ever making it to his church anyway. Colin Constantine might be able to read passion and determination in her, but what he couldn't read was the likelihood that if her reception in Tobago was as catastrophic as she expected it would be, she could very well be making use of her return ticket on the next available flight.

Negative thoughts, she reminded herself. They weren't her style. She was staying, and that was that. Not even the Devil and a team of frenzied dray horses were dragging her back. That wasn't part of the plan. She pinched her upper lip between thumb and finger, letting the pressure on her own flesh force her to focus on what *was,* not what *might* be.

Colin, misinterpreting her reluctance to promise him a visit as a dread of going to church, shook his head sadly, and settled back into his seat. The conversation ended.

Feeling badly, but unable to explain further, Sarita tried to concentrate on the movie being projected on the small screen overhead, but they were on the last leg of their journey, and the film credits were already rolling. It wouldn't be long before they were on land.

There was a painful popping in her ears as the plane began its sharp descent, and she swallowed hard to relieve the pressure imbalance she was experiencing.

They had moved swiftly below cloud level, and the brilliant sunshine was turning the bright green water into gold. Even from this height, she could see the sparkles winking off the surface, and the bug-sized ships dancing on the waves. She craned her neck to see past her seatmate.

Colin Constantine was apparently not the kind of man who could withdraw from anybody for long. His smiling eyes were on her again. "Want to get a better look? I've seen it dozens of times."

She would have killed for his window seat, but as it was, she could only try to inch a little closer and peek around him.

That wasn't enough for Colin. He leaned in toward her and in a dramatic stage whisper, said, "Listen, Gwen. We aren't supposed to do this, but if we move really fast, we can switch seats. Quick, while the flight attendants aren't looking!"

This time, she *did* laugh out loud. His raspy whisper had been loud enough to be heard two rows down. The idea was tempting though; the emerald coast was already in view. But the Crown Point airport was so close to the sea that day-trippers who flew in from the sister isle of Trinidad routinely left the airport and literally strolled down to the water's edge, so before she could take the quirky older man up on his offer, the runway rose to meet them. With a whining of the engines and a slight bump, they were on the ground.

Colin clicked his tongue. "Too late. You missed quite a view."

She smiled back at him. He looked genuinely disappointed at having lost out on the chance to play switch-the-seats in mid-air. "Maybe next time," she offered.

He nodded. There was a rising chatter and a chorus

of clicks as the passengers, simultaneously, popped open their seat belts and stood up, glad to be on their feet again after a long, cramped flight. Sarita and Colin joined them, squeezing into the corridor and hauling their hand luggage out of the overhead storage bins.

With a pneumatic sigh, the airplane doors slid open, and passengers began to disembark. The first thing that struck her was the scent of the air: it was perfumed with sea salt and seaweed, and something else that was indefinable, but clean and sweet. It sent a ripple through her that almost felt like hope. She stopped short with her heavy bag in her hand, allowing passengers to brush past. She tilted her head back and stared up at the most awesome blue sky she had ever seen. For the first time, all the many stories she had heard about Tobago, island of magic and fantasy, of flowers, trees, and endless sea, had become a reality. Tears prickled at her dark brown eyes, and she wiped them away with the back of her hand.

Colin was already striding ahead purposefully, but, realizing that she hadn't kept up with him, he stopped and turned his head to her. "You okay?"

She nodded mutely.

He didn't look as if he believed her, and hesitated briefly before saying, "Don't forget. Mount Moriah Moravian Church. Wherever you're staying, it won't be far away. Nothing in Tobago is far from anything else, anyway. So pop in if you can. And I don't always preach," he paused, giving her another shrewd look, "I listen, too."

Sarita acknowledged him with a wave of the hand, not wanting to make any verbal promises she couldn't keep, and then he disappeared. She followed the huddle of tired travelers across the sunny open tarmac and into the immigration hall.

"Dr. Sarita Rowley?" The white-shirted immigration officer peered at her passport, turning it over in his hand as if something about it didn't quite click.

She nodded, frowning slightly. Was something wrong? She might have made up her mind to pass herself off as Gwen Davis, at least until the inevitable—and imminent—moment at which her cover would be blown, but that subterfuge had just served to get her the job that had brought her to the island. She hadn't been reckless enough to attempt to travel under an assumed name. That would have gone beyond deception into the realm of sheer stupidity.

"And you're American?"

She nodded in the affirmative. "Born and raised in Miami," she added, emphasizing her accent in case there was still any doubt.

The man, perched on a low pedestal behind the counter, shrugged, and handed her back her passport. "I asked because Rowley is an old Tobago name. Well-known on the island. Good people, the Rowleys."

"That's what I've been told." Sarita smiled in relief. So that was all it was, just mild curiosity.

"Who knows, maybe you'll discover you have relatives on the island."

She tried not to let her smile falter. "Maybe I will," she said evenly, and took back the documents he stamped and handed over to her.

He didn't seem ready to let her go yet, even though her entry had been approved. "So," he looked as if he was trying to assess if she was actually old enough to hold a degree. "You're a medical doctor?"

"No, I'm a marine biologist. I'm here to do some studies on the reef."

That did it. His entire body relaxed, his posture becoming more open and friendly. The initial, probing curiosity was replaced with sudden radiant warmth. "Ah, the reef! Tobago has some of the most beautiful reefs in the world!"

Sarita had heard that gleeful boasting before, every time she mentioned the island to anybody who held it dear. There was something about Tobago that inspired great pride in anyone who laid claim to it. The officer, now brimming with hospitality, waved her past enthusiastically, and soon she was headed for the main doors of the airport, with her single suitcase on her trolley, and her hand luggage and laptop computer balanced on top. The double doors were thrown open by the family walking ahead of her. She slipped through behind them—and was thrust into a world she had heard much about, but almost hadn't believed really existed.

There she was, a traveler arriving in an international airport that catered to major Western airlines, and unlike any other airport she had been to, this one seemed to have fallen into a snooze. It looked more like a Club Med shopping pavilion, and one in which many of the shop owners didn't seem too concerned with actually luring customers into their stores.

Sunny floral-print dresses hung in the windows of a row of airy booths, half hidden by sandals, snorkels, magazines, candy, and suntan oil. Spicy food smells struggled for dominance with the scents of sand and sea, and a handful of people strolled around, some in shorts, sandals, swimsuit tops, and sun hats. They weren't in much of a hurry to get anywhere. Families chattered happily among themselves, poked through the cluttered items on sale, and eventually headed in the direction of the sea that stretched out to her left. The airport was not just a transit point; it was a place to hang out.

Even the khaki-suited security guards looked unflustered. They stood around in small groups and chatted between sporadic bouts of directing the traffic that moved along the single roadway running through the center of the airport.

But Sarita was only briefly affected by the sleepy sense of calm that pervaded the island. She was faced with a question that was too pressing for her to let her guard down and allow the island to flow into her veins.

What should she do next?

"Taxi?" A white-jacketed, elderly man approached her on her left, smiling encouragingly, already laying his hands on her baggage, probably thinking that if he started ushering her to his car, she wouldn't be prepared to turn him down.

She hesitated. All she had for her new employer, Reef Rescue, was an address and a telephone number. Should she call to let them know she had arrived, or should she just take the taxi and go to them?

The taxi driver noted her hesitation, and tried to put her at ease. "Where you going, Miss? You lost? Anybody coming for you?"

Was anybody coming for her? She wasn't sure. She supposed taking a taxi might make the most sense. Hanging around the airport would do nothing more than delay her eventual arrival, and the best way to handle that was to get it over with. She drew in a lungful of air through her nostrils—there was that sweet, sweet scent again—and flexed her shoulders, easing the tension in them while making her feel confident and more capable.

She was about to hand over her possessions when another thought struck her. What if she took the taxi, and someone did come to fetch her? That would be rude, leaving them standing around, wondering if she'd even gotten off the flight. She hesitated. The man was motionless, patient, still smiling. She turned her eyes, which were part apologetic, on him hoping for a sign to tell her what to do.

Then suddenly there was one. Not a sign from heaven, though—no divine finger piercing the clouds—but a real sign, a physical one, written in black felt marker on white cardboard, and carried by a slender, dark-skinned young man who was sauntering in from the direction of the road with it held up across his chest.

Dr. Gwen Davis, it read.

The dilemma solved, she gave the patient taxi driver a brave smile. "Thank you, but I think that young man is here for me."

He bowed slightly. "As long as you'll be okay. Have a nice vacation. You'll love Tobago so much, you'll never want to leave."

She hurried in the direction of the sign, wondering if the taxi driver's face would be the last friendly one she would meet on the island. She lifted her hand to catch the attention of the man who had come to meet her, calling out to him. He looked in her direction, slowly, unhurriedly, and then his mouth fell open in exaggerated admiration. "You Dr. Davis?" he asked.

She looked him square in the eye and lied. "Yes, I am." The crescent-shaped scar on her full upper lip, the one she had received falling out of the apple tree all those years ago on her curfew-breaking caper, the one she thought of as her "lying scar," twitched slightly, like a built-in conscience.

The young man looked about twenty, maybe as old as twenty-two, but surely no more than that. He was taller than she, with hair cut close to his head, and a blinding grin that made his teeth seem a little too large for his mouth. He clutched at his chest in a mock heart attack. "They didn't warn me you were related to Queen Latifah!"

She laughed out loud at his outrageous compliment, not offended in the least by his effrontery. West Indian men were unabashed in their flirtation with women, and lacked the circumspection of their metropolitan counterparts. Sarita didn't mind one bit. She looked away as he took his time examining her, taking in her cocoa skin and round, dark eyes, trying not to giggle under his scrutiny.

His heart seemed suddenly all right again; he let his chest go and instead stuck out his hand in greeting. "I'm JoJo. I'm the Reef Rescue driver, diver, boatman, everything."

"Hi." She grasped his hand. "Nice to meet you."

He remembered his manners and tried to gather up all her bags at once. She hastened to stop him, but he only allowed her to hang on to her laptop.

He began walking in the direction from which he had come, carrying her bags as if they weighed nothing, so she assumed she was expected to follow him. They walked past a small alcove lined with wooden tables that were piled high with an array of multicolored sweets, most of which she had never seen before. Hundreds of little packages spilled to the edge of the tables: pink, yellow, green, candy-striped, and caramel-colored.

As they came into view, there was a uniform clamor from the women selling behind the tables, and their voices were like music.

"Darlin', you buying candy today?"

"Honey, any sweeties for the children?"

"Sugar cake over here! Over here!"

Sarita had to stop and stare. It was like something out of a glossy tourist guide-book, almost a West Indian cliché. The women were clad in bright-colored floral prints and stripes, with ruffled, oversized aprons that covered ample bosoms. Equally colorful squares of cloth were wrapped around their heads.

"Want something?" JoJo noticed her hesitation.

She shook her head vigorously.

"Come on. These are all handmade. We make very nice candy here in Tobago, you know," he cajoled.

She patted her hip, which swelled like a wave on the open sea and pressed against her jeans. Under her plain green shirt, soft full breasts bubbled up, threatening to overflow her low-buttoned collar. Sarita wasn't exactly what anybody would call slender. "I really don't think that would be a good idea."

"Ah." His frank black eyes flicked over her body. "Don't tell me you're one of those women who're always on a diet! Don't tell me you're one of those Americans who are always starving themselves to get skinny! Because you're in the West Indies now, and we like nothing better than a woman with curves." He gave her a slow, lazy grin. "No, there's nothing wrong with you!"

Sarita decided she was going to like this guy. She felt the warm flush rise under her skin, and was so pleased at his flattery that she didn't bother to explain that the last thing she was here for was male attention. She hadn't had much of that in a while and, frankly, that was the way she preferred it. She stood aside as he quickly completed a transaction with one of the candy ladies. He returned with a handful of plastic bags filled with sweets.

"That's sugar cake," he told her, pointing to little clusters of shredded coconut covered with pastel-tinted boiled sugar. "And those are nut cakes, and those are *bene* balls. Toasted sesame seeds in brown sugar. Enjoy."

"I will, but this looks like a week's supply." She tucked them away in her bag, eager to try them, and followed JoJo out to the roadside. He led her directly to a bright red 4X4 parked on the edge, and she watched in amazement as he threw open the unlocked doors and tossed her luggage in the back. Through the window she could see the keys glinting in the ignition.

"Didn't you lock the door when you came to get me?" she asked, stunned.

He shrugged and ushered her into the passenger seat. "No. Why?"

She strapped herself in. "I don't know. Car thieves, maybe?"

He didn't answer until he had started the engine and pulled onto the road. "This is Tobago, not Miami. Here, you leave your car, you find it when you get back. It's the way we are."

"I wish more places were like that," she murmured.

"More *places* wish they were like this," he countered.

They were on the road for two or three minutes before she spoke again. "We're going to Black Rock, right? Is it far from here?"

JoJo flashed what was already becoming a familiar grin. "Gwen, the island is less than thirty miles long. Trust me. *Nothing* is far from *anything.*"

He had a point. The minister, Colin Constantine, had said pretty much the same thing. "And the others on the team got here a few days ago?"

"Well, so far, the 'others' are just the doctor and me. The project doesn't have much money for staff, and we don't know how long the reef study is going to take. But you came at the right time. Nothing's set up yet, not even headquarters. You get to take part in the fun of unpacking all the equipment and getting the computers set up."

"Sounds lovely." She paused, wanting to ask a question but afraid that a tremor in her voice would betray her. Finally, she found her tongue and her courage. "And the doctor. Do you like him?"

JoJo nodded enthusiastically, taking his eyes off the road to look at her. "It's only been a few days since he arrived, but already I think he can help us. We get people all the time who come down and make a lot of noise about helping cure the reef, spend a lot of money, and do very little. But he, well, I think he's smart enough and passionate enough to make a difference."

Sarita turned her head and stared intently at the grass-flanked roadway that slowly moved past, afraid to let JoJo read what was written in her eyes.

He went on blithely. "And he's not exactly a foreigner, you know. He was born here. He grew up in the States, and this is his first time back. So he's one of us."

"Is he?" Her voice was barely perceptible.

JoJo might have been a great admirer of women, but he fell short when it came to sensitivity to tension, because hers had doubled within the past two minutes, and yet he prattled on with no sign of noticing.

"I can't wait to show you the reef. And the beaches. Tobago has—"

"Some of the most beautiful in the world," she supplied.

"Oh. You heard," he seemed disappointed at having his boast interrupted.

"Couple of times," she answered dryly. "Today."

There was no more time for further conversation. The truck slowed and turned into a short drive with much grating of gravel.

"This is it," he informed her unnecessarily. He

hopped out and trotted around to her side, holding open the door and waiting for her to descend.

She didn't move a muscle. Instead, she stared ahead at the pretty lemon-colored bungalow, with its scattered palms and mango trees and garden that was ankle deep in weeds. Beyond it, she could see the glint of the sun, now low in the sky, bouncing off the sea that came up almost to the front border of the yard.

JoJo was right. This *was* it. She had plotted and planned for weeks, making her way here by any means necessary, and traveled all day, just so that she could be part of Reef Rescue, the cause she believed in more than anything else. And now she was here, but her legs had turned to rubber and wouldn't let her out of the vehicle.

She felt panic claw its way through her insides, and the blood in her veins ran cold.

JoJo looked concerned. "Gwen? Are you all right?"

She didn't have the energy to say yea or nay. She struggled to draw a breath, eyes still focused on the little house as if she expected the door to be thrown open any second, and her worst nightmare to come striding out.

"Scared?" he asked with a sudden spark of perceptiveness.

She didn't bother to respond.

Gently, he urged her out of the vehicle and shut the door behind her. "Listen, if you're afraid of meeting the doctor, don't be. He's real smart, and he's written lots of books and been on many projects. But he's real people. He doesn't bite."

That's what you think, she wanted to argue, but still, she said nothing.

"Look," he offered kindly. "Let's leave the bags here

for a while. I'll take you in and let you meet him, and then I'll come out and get your things. Okay?"

She nodded and mutely followed him into the house.

Everything was in disarray. Boxes were piled high against the walls, and packing straw was scattered on every inch of the floor. The walls could do with a lick of paint, but apart from that, once everything was set up and running, the little house would be quite pleasant.

JoJo laid a hand on her arm and tugged her down a narrow passageway to an arched doorway at the end. She knew without having to be told what lay within those walls. She stopped short on the threshold.

He eyed her, slightly amused at her reticence, but concerned, too. "Come on, I'll walk in with you."

And let someone else witness the explosion that was waiting for her inside? Fat chance! She declined quietly. "It's okay. You go ahead and get the things. I can do this."

"Sure?"

"Sure."

"Okay, Gwen." He lifted his shoulders in elaborate resignation. "Good luck."

"Right." She waited until he was back out the front door, then inched toward the doorway. It was the only room so far that bore any semblance of order. It looked like it was to be used as a den; the walls were lined with shelves, many of which were already stacked with books. A plain wooden table stood in one corner with a desktop computer perched on top. Piles of papers were weighted down with large stones that looked as if they had simply been snatched up from the garden.

There were more boxes on the floor, and Sarita didn't have to be told that they were also filled with books. A figure knelt over one of the boxes, long arms delving into it. Sarita froze, wanting to turn tail and run, but unable even to tear her eyes away.

The man in the room was tall; his height was evident even as he knelt. He was wearing a simple white undershirt that clung to his torso, revealing powerful arms. Tufts of dark brown hair were sprinkled across his chest and peeked out from the hollows of his bare armpits. As he searched in the box, his biceps flexed and relaxed fluidly, like ripples on the ocean surface.

The awesome broad shoulders made his already narrow waist seem even more narrow; his sides plunged sharply inward to an abdomen that would have graced a dancer, and the exquisitely drawn lines of him went on to hips that balanced perfectly with his shoulders. Battered jeans, worn to threads in places, embraced his thighs, allowing his muscles the freedom to bulge as they pressed up against the coarse fabric. His long feet were bare.

Sarita let her eyes travel upward along his body, taking in the healthy golden glow of his skin, which all but shone like a freshly minted copper penny. The face she could see in three-quarter view: high forehead, long, straight nose and a mouth which, though pursed in concentration, lost little of its full sensuality. A pencil-thin moustache drew attention to his upper lip, and the dark brown color of those carefully trimmed hairs was picked up in the hundred or so finely twisted locks that fell to his shoulders, drawn back at the nape with a black piece of string. The rapidly setting sun, which was dropping out of the sky like a heavy ball, struck fire off everything in the room, including the golden threads that nature had woven among the darker hair on his head, leaving him with a halo that would be the envy of any angel.

She stared, taking him all in—every line, every muscle,

and every lock of hair, which she knew was soft and springy to the touch and smelled like citrus and rainwater. She couldn't understand why her chest was hurting her so much, and it took her several agonizing seconds to realize that the pain was due to her having stopped breathing ages ago. She opened her lungs and let the air rush in, hoping it would calm the pulse that slammed in her temple, throat, and wrists like storm water battering a seawall.

"God," she breathed, unable to find anything more fitting to say. She had almost forgotten that her husband was so beautiful.

Two

Dr. Matthias Rowley shifted position on the bare floor, easing his weight from one knee to the other. Sarita was sure that he had heard her movement in the doorway, and yet he didn't look up. "JoJo, have you brought Dr. Davis with you?" he called in her direction.

The rumbling baritone sent a shiver along her skin, as if light fingers had been gently and unexpectedly drawn down her nape. She hadn't heard that voice in close to a year, but remembered it well. It was the voice that had haunted her dreams, echoes of it in her ear, coupled with memories of hot breath against her cheek, an astounding vocabulary of lascivious words being whispered hoarsely in the half-light. That voice alone had always been enough to bring her to arousal so fast that painful shocks of expectation had shot up and down her spine.

This man had known what to do with that voice of his. During their marriage—at least during the parts of it that she wanted to remember—whenever their jobs separated them for more than a night, he had always called her up on the phone, sometimes rousing her out of sleep in the early hours of the morning, using that voice to stimulate her, soothe her, help her forget that the space next to her in bed had been empty. The heated instructions whispered over hundreds of miles of cables and wires had brooked no opposition; her compliance was always joyfully given, and had always brought them both solace and release, appetizers for when they would be reunited.

But then again, that voice had the ability to become harsh and cold, with an edge like a shard of ice, slashing through her emotions with uncaring ease. That same voice, given the right motivation, could freeze the soul. And the last time she had heard it, there had been no warmth in it, only rage. The anger it expressed was so powerful that it had traveled beyond the realm of heat and entered a cold, cold, wretched landscape.

Matthias, not hearing a response from her direction, looked up. Intense green eyes that were so dark they could be mistaken for brown in the dimming light fixed on her, and the wide, beautiful mouth fell slightly open. Gold wire-framed glasses slipped down his nose in almost comic surprise, and Sarita felt like a flightless bird suddenly caught in the sights of a huge, very hungry eagle.

"What the devil are you doing here?" The roar hit her like a physical blow, knocking her backward, and she was forced to throw out her arms to regain her balance.

He seemed frozen in position, too stunned to rise. The dark eyes were round with shock. "Well?" he asked finally. "Sarita?"

Her name on his lips. She hadn't heard that in a year. When they made love, he used to call her Sari, and in his voice the name took on the wonders of India, whence the name had come. That whispered *Sari* held in it the scent of spices, sandalwood, and crushed herbs, and the sound of it was like the rustling of the silken eastern dresses that bore the name.

But *Sa-ri-ta*, now, that was different. On his angry lips,

it was clipped and harsh. Three syllables, thrown like darts against a wall. She opened her mouth to speak, her every resolution to face his ire when it eventually came melting like sugar in the rain.

He found his feet, and advanced upon her, two steps, then three, but suddenly halted. His copper skin was mottled with anger, and he looked as if he had stopped approaching her because he was unsure of what he would do if he were to come any closer. He steadied his glasses on his nose and stood in the center of the room, hands on hips, eyes holding hers.

"I—asked—you—a—question," he said, spitting out the words as if they were bitter in his mouth.

She inhaled deeply, straightened her shoulders and looked him in the eye. If he thought he was going to intimidate her he was wrong. "I think it's pretty obvious what I'm doing here, Matthias."

His lips twisted. "It may be obvious to you, but it certainly isn't to me. Where's Dr. Davis? What did you do, con her into bringing you along?"

She said nothing.

He waited for an answer, but her silence told him all he needed to know. "No—" he shook his head, unbelieving.

She didn't need to confirm for him what he already understood, so she waited while the truth sank in.

"You didn't," he said, still unwilling to believe.

"I did," she burst out. "You got a problem with that?" Enough was enough. She wasn't going to stand there and wait for him to come to his senses, take aim, and fire.

"Don't tell me you passed yourself off as Davis!"

"I don't have to tell you," she countered. "Do you see anybody else here?"

"Have you lost your mind?" He slapped his head in incredulity and shook it as if there were water in his ear.

"No, I haven't lost my mind. But I was losing my project. Reef Rescue is as much mine as it is yours, Matthias, and don't you deny it!"

"I do deny it! I founded it—" he stopped, head jerking up to look past her shoulder. Sarita spun around in time to see JoJo appear in the hallway behind them, a puzzled frown on his face. He looked as if he wasn't too sure if he had actually heard shouting, but he knew that something wasn't right.

Matthias struggled to steady himself, passing one hand down his neat locks and then slipping it behind the nape, stroking the tight muscles there. "JoJo," he said eventually, and Sarita stared quickly down at her feet to avoid the young man's puzzled gaze. He was too nice to be drawn into this unpleasantness.

"Yes?" came the wary response.

"Just give us a little time alone, okay?"

JoJo nodded. "You want me to go back into town to get you something for dinner? I still haven't had the time to get that regulator for the stove, so—"

Matthias nodded distractedly. He slipped a hand into the back pocket of his jeans, counted out some of the country's brightly colored currency, and handed it over. "Thanks, buddy." Sarita felt his eyes flicker over her face, and then he added, "And I could do with a couple of beers."

JoJo took the money and withdrew without looking at her. Both she and Matthias stood silently until they heard the sound of the engine outside. The sun was fully gone now, in the way that the night had of swiftly falling in the tropics, and each could barely see the other.

"You planning on standing here in the dark for the rest of the night?" she needled him.

He took long steps across the room and punched the light switch so hard Sarita was afraid he would break the panel.

"Better?" he grated.

"Much," she countered.

He went on as if they had never been interrupted. "I founded Reef Rescue, Sarita. It was my concept, my baby."

She could have pointed out the irony of his use of the word, "baby," to describe what the project meant to him, but that would be asking for trouble. That one little word lay at the center of the firestorm their marriage had become. Better to let that one pass. Better to pretend he hadn't said it, or one of them, well, *she*, would end up in tears before the night was out. Instead, she responded, "But I worked as hard as you did on it!" She dropped to her knees and burrowed wildly into the box nearest her, coming up with handfuls of hardbound notebooks. "These," she waved them wildly under his nose, "are mine." She flipped them open, pointing at the cramped handwriting inside. "This is my writing. These are my notes."

She dug in the box a second time, hands closing around a CD in its hard jewel case, and threw it at him like a Frisbee, causing him to fumble to catch it. "I typed everything on that disk. I got all your files in order. When you went diving off Florida gathering your precious information, I was underwater next to you. And the UN grant that's funding this whole Tobago leg of the operation? I helped you draft the proposal that won it for you. Or did you forget?"

"I haven't forgotten." He stuffed the CD back into the box, hesitated, and took it out, slipping it into the three-tiered CD holder on the table next to the computer. "I'm not denying the work you did on this. But you were paid for that work. Leave it alone now, I don't need you coming here and ruining this for me."

Ruining this? For *him?* Oh, he never ceased to amaze her. Everything was about him; he saw every person's actions in terms of how they affected him. "Matthias," she spoke slowly, to make sure he understood. "Listen to me. I didn't come here to ruin anything for you. I came here to do the same thing as you, to see this project through. Do you hear?"

"No, *you* listen. This is my lifelong dream. I've worked all my life to get back to Tobago to do this. And I plan on doing it right; no mistakes, no slipups. So I'm not sure if you're the right person to help me." He paused, cruelly waiting a few seconds for effect before delivering his coup de grace. "After all, how do you expect me to work with you if you can't be trusted?"

She flinched. He couldn't have hurt her any worse if he'd slapped her across the face. That was unfair. Now, he was getting personal, alluding to circumstances in their marriage that had nothing to do with the fact that they worked well together, and had compiled a huge body of research in a short space of time.

She put her hand on his bare arm, trying to hold his attention long enough for what she had to say to sink in. "That's not fair. You know that. What happened in our—" the word "marriage" couldn't make it past her lips. She tried again. "What happened between us has nothing to do with what we have to do here. Besides, where do you get off with this 'lifelong dream' bull? Don't you think it's mine, too?"

Matthias was much too angry to allow her to touch him. Grasping her hand firmly, he threw it from him, making her feel like a leper. "I," he responded slowly, "belong here."

Sarita groaned. She'd heard *that* one a thousand times. "Please, Matthias. You're as American as I am. Just because you were born here, doesn't give you some kind of franchise over the place—".

"Yes, it does," he interrupted hotly.

She ignored him and went on. "And don't give me that old 'island boy returns home to save the day' routine, because it just doesn't wash with me."

"It's not a routine. It's the truth."

He looked so hurt that Sarita almost regretted her barb. She remembered the many sunny days on the Florida Keys, near the end of their last project, when Matthias would point eastward and dreamily tell her that the next stop on their program would be Tobago, his mother's island, the place he knew as a boy and had spent his entire life planning to return to. His love for the island was genuine, and it was unkind of her to mock it. She felt the fight drain out of her, shoulders becoming heavy. It had been a long day, and she was exhausted.

He didn't look prepared to go on fighting anymore, either. He let out a gust of breath and stared down at his feet, tugging a single lock from the bundle at the back of his head and twirling it between his fingers. His mind had left the room; where it had taken him, she couldn't say.

"Sarita, please," he said finally, "just leave now."

She was dumbfounded. Leave? Walk out of the house in the middle of the night on an island she didn't know? He had to be kidding. "And go where?" she stammered.

His eyes were on hers, their pupils wide black circles

rimmed with deep green. "Anywhere. A hotel. I'll get JoJo to take you there when he gets back."

"And then what, Matthias?" she challenged.

"Then you catch the next flight out of here. Go. There are a lot of projects out there. You're a good biologist—"

"Thank you," she cut in sarcastically.

"You can find work anywhere in the world. Just go, okay?"

Her eyes stung with tears of frustration. She'd known it was going to be bad, but she had never expected this. The silent treatment for a few days, maybe, but to be tossed out the door like a beggar maid? Never in her wildest dreams would she have imagined this.

Resignedly, she turned and walked out of the room, trying to get her eyes accustomed to the darkness in the rest of the house. She stubbed her toe on a box filled with something that was as heavy as rocks, but sensing him close on her heels, she bit her tongue to prevent herself from crying out.

JoJo must have placed her bags somewhere. The problem was, where?

"Off to the left," Matthias informed her, reading her mind. He flicked on the lights in the spacious living area and sidestepped her, then led the way to a room on the other side. He turned that light on, too.

The room was nowhere near as cluttered as the others she had seen. There was a single bed pushed up against the far wall, a wooden table and upright chair, and an over-stuffed visitor's chair in faded chambray. Plain white curtains screened the windows from the beachfront outside. Sarita knew that the Reef Rescue project didn't have much money for amenities. She and Matthias had always believed that every penny should be pumped into the project itself, rather than into making themselves at home. But the little room had been carefully cleaned, polished, and laid out in readiness for the new biologist who was supposed to join the team. She was grateful for his attempts to make her comfortable.

Or to make Dr. Gwen Davis comfortable.

JoJo had placed her suitcase on the floor next to the bed, her traveling bag on the clean bedspread, and her laptop on the table. Resigned to her fate, she walked over to her suitcase and tried to lift it. Her many hours of flying, coupled with her trepidation at meeting Matthias again and the eventual awful fallout of that meeting, left her exhausted. She was too tired even to make it budge.

She threw a covert glance at Matthias, hoping that he would at least do the gentlemanly thing and offer to help her get her suitcase back outside, but he was leaning against the door frame, arms folded across his chest, doing nothing but staring at her. His beautiful face, with its elegant planes and finely drawn features, was expressionless, a fact that scared her even more than his rage had before.

"What?" she asked, lower lip trembling. Was he preparing for another attack?

He shook his head, still impassive. "Nothing."

She dropped into a sitting position on the edge of the bed, letting her head fall into her hands heavily. "Matthias," she began, voice muffled by her intertwined fingers.

No answer.

"Please." Why was he punishing her like this?

He shifted his long body, changing position uneasily, but was silent.

She took her hands from her face and turned to him, eyes seeking him out. At the front of the house, the sound of wheels crunching on gravel made him turn his head fleetingly, but then he was looking at her again.

"Let me stay, please. Let me finish this with you. Then I'll be out of your life. I'll sign those damned divorce papers you sent me, and then I'll go. But *after* we finish the project. Not before."

The door of the 4X4 opened and slammed shut, and then the door to the bungalow creaked.

He shook his head. "I can't let you."

JoJo's footsteps sounded in the kitchen.

"Why not?" she whispered.

"It's too—" he paused.

"Too what? Too risky for your precious ego? Are you afraid that if I stay, you'll reconsider and see that you were wrong to send me away the first time? Is that what you're scared of?"

He closed the distance between them and sat on the bed next to her, alarmingly close, and his face was level with hers. His eyes held many mysteries. "Don't do this to me, Sarita."

JoJo was moving through the house, calling for Matthias.

"Don't do this to *you?*" Was he kidding? "What about what *you're* doing to *me?* You wouldn't throw a living creature out into the night. You would rather die than see a sea turtle or a bird tossed to the elements. But you have no problem shoving me out at this hour, telling me to 'find a place to sleep,' as if I never meant anything to you. Hate me all you like, that's fine. But I'm surprised that even you would deny me a bed for the night. What kind of man are you?"

Ah, Sarita noted with satisfaction. That did it. An attack on his manhood. He stiffened and stood up, a near-smile on his lips. "Fine, my dear wife. As you will.

Far be it from me to cast you to the wolves tonight, although one could hardly speak of this island as being unsafe. But it's my island," he paused to ensure that she noted the irony in his voice, "as much as you would seek to deny it, and as such I suppose I should be hospitable. So come and have dinner. You must be starving."

Relief! Her heart suddenly felt a thousand times lighter. She ran to him and put a hand on his shoulder; her face eager. "You mean, you're letting me stay?"

"Sure, I'm letting you stay," he told her coolly, unaffected by her enthusiasm. "Tonight. Tomorrow, I call the travel agent and see how soon I can get you on a flight back home." And with that, he walked away and left her standing there.

Even with the windows thrown wide open and the curtains pulled all the way back, the bedroom was intolerably hot. Matthias tossed restlessly in bed, his sheets dampened by perspiration. They clung to his bare skin, making him sticky and miserable. Even though he always slept in the nude—the fact that his bedroom windows were about chest level to anyone who might happen to be passing by outside didn't stop him—the habit gave him little comfort tonight.

He didn't need to glance at the glowing face of his watch to know that he had been awake for several hours. That wasn't good. He was a man who valued his sleep and knew that if he didn't catch a few hours, he'd be useless in the morning, with blunted wits and a raging headache. And he needed all the fortitude he had to contend with Sarita.

He ground his teeth. The nerve of her! Showing up like that, forging her résumé and other documents, and fraudulently applying to a job he advertised for on *his* project. How long did she think she could get away with it? Obviously, only long enough to get her on the island in the first place. She was mulish enough to think that once here, she could badger or wheedle him into letting her stay.

Well, that's where she was wrong. She wasn't welcome anywhere near, not while he was in charge. His wife simply could not be trusted. He bit his lip as the painful memories rose inside him like the tide. Sarita had made their marriage a lie, and no amount of pleading for him to see things her way would make things better. No matter how she tried to throw the blame into his lap, nothing could change that. She had deceived him. She had looked him in the face, day after day, and made love with him night after night, with a lie in her heart. She'd been like a siren, drawing him into her arms with the power of her enchanted song, but like those mermaids of old, her enticements had been nothing but trickery, designed to lull him into passivity until she could drag him, unresisting, under the waves. For that, he couldn't forgive her.

He slipped his hand to the base of his neck, feeling it damp under the fine dreadlocks. He was sweating beads, but it had nothing to do with the weather. It was the wellspring of anger and resentment bubbling up inside of him and searching for an outlet. That crack about "island boy returns home to save the day" had hit hard, and hours later it still rankled.

As much as she didn't understand his motives, and as much as she thought them ridiculous, they were valid and vitally important to him. As she had said, he was as American as she was, but although his adopted country would always have his allegiance, this tiny Caribbean island on which he was born would always own his soul.

He thought of the old wives' tale that held that wherever your "navel string," as they called it, was buried, there your heart would always be. As a matter of fact, many mothers deliberately buried the umbilical cords of newborns in their yards to ensure that their children would always remain close.

Well, Sarita might mock him for it, but his own "navel string" had been buried in the gentle hills of nearby Bethel, his mother's village, and for him that old country magic must have worked; throughout his life, never a day had passed without his thoughts being invaded by images of emerald hillsides dotted with cows, coconut trees swaying, mango trees heavy with gold- and rose-tinted fruit, and the blue sea a haze in the background.

He thought of his mother, Mavis Rowley, with her skin like a seal's: supple, black, and glowing with health. His poor mother, who had longed to leave the confines of the tiny island as much as Matthias had always yearned to return to it. More than anything, she had wanted to sing, to be on stage in New York or Las Vegas hypnotizing audiences with the power of her song. She had a voice that sounded like sunshine splitting the clouds and heaven opening up. But she had been forced to be content with calling down the angels from the altar of the small Moravian church she attended and at which her father had been minister. Mavis never did leave the island as planned, largely, Matthias thought bitterly, because of his own arrival on the scene.

Poverty had been, and still was, an ever-present concern for Tobago. Lacking the natural resources of her sister island, Trinidad, she turned to tourism to make a living. And with tourists came other ills. . . .

Like many other local girls, Mavis had harbored the

hope that one day a handsome stranger from some far-off land would whisk her away so that she could pursue her dream. Visitors to the island, from northern countries such as the United States, Britain, and most of Europe, knew this well, and both male and female tourists strolled across the island as though in a giant orchard, plucking the proffered fruit for their own amusement, only to discard them at the airport on the day they returned home.

The young islanders who were willing to play that game knew the risk: that their companionship might only be desired temporarily. But every so often they watched friends luck out and be invited by their lovers to return home with them. Some of the young Tobagonian women and men were fortunate enough to marry their foreign lovers; others were content to remain as concubines and companions for as long as the liaison lasted, staying several months or years in far-off countries before the dissolution of their relationships forced them home again.

Mavis had been less fortunate than most. She had found her handsome stranger and he had been entranced with her flashing brown eyes and glowing skin, and the voice she had stolen from heaven. But she had broken the rules. Mavis had fallen in love.

She had first seen the tall, blond Swiss-German on the beach at Black Rock, and had been as instantly smitten with him as he had been with her. She had often told Matthias that his father had been one step short of being a god. He had been the most beautiful man she had ever seen; slender, graceful, strong, and fast. "You have his eyes," she always said to Matthias, "as green as the heart of the ocean."

But the man didn't stay around long enough to witness for himself the color of his son's eyes or anything else, for that matter. The six-month romance had ended in heartbreak for Mavis. The man she had fallen deeply in love with explained to her that it was time for him to return home and that he was going alone. He told her he had enjoyed the time they had spent together, but an island wife didn't fit into his plans. And with that, he walked out of her life.

Matthias grew up in Bethel with his mother, set apart from the others because he was the son of a preacher's unmarried daughter and because of his coloring. The burnished copper of his skin made him stand out from the other children in the village, who were, for the most part, the color of sea-buffed black coral. The shock of curly, golden hair he was born with had brought him much teasing, and he was eternally grateful when almost all of it, except a few strands that glinted like highlights spun into a tapestry, darkened over the years to a rich deep sable.

He grew up determined that he would not be shunned or ridiculed for being different by his darker boyhood friends. He forced his presence upon them by swimming harder, running faster, and learning to hunt and fish better than they, and finally, far from being the outcast, he became the ringleader of a band of ragamuffins whose every free hour was spent roaming the narrow country roads, barefoot, looking for more mischief to get into.

And then tuberculosis took his mother. The beautiful voice, never heard beyond the boundaries of the island, was suddenly stilled. His grandfather, aging by then, and unable to care for a young boy, found the only solution to his dilemma: a distant cousin in New Jersey, who had emigrated over twenty years before, and who, being childless, was willing to take him. So there he was—in his ninth year, bereft of a mother, and never having known a father—being shipped to a cold and unfamiliar land, a place where there were no reefs and where there would be no swimming in the rivers, no scooping up crayfish to cook in tin cans, no waving palms, and no perfume in the air.

Of course, he was of hardy stock, as were all the Rowleys: he had thrived and learned fast in order to adapt. But the reefs of Tobago were in his heart, their salt was in his blood, and nothing ever swayed him from his determination to return to them one day to make a difference. Sarita could scoff at him all she wanted, but for him, that was his mission in life.

Matthias sat up in bed, frustrated, and threw his legs over the side. He strode to the window and leaned forward to take the cool breeze on his face and bare body. To his surprise, the distant glow told him that dawn was approaching. Had he really been up all night? He shook his head. Only Sarita had the power to make him upset enough to lose an entire night's sleep.

That settled it in his mind: her presence would only be distracting. He had been right about her talents: she was a good biologist, and he could have made use of her skills, but he knew they would never be able to work without going over the same old tired ground they'd gone over before. That would cause the project to suffer. As soon as possible he was going to call the travel agency and book Sarita a flight back, and then he would start looking for a replacement. Next time, he would be more careful and actually check the references he had been sent. He wasn't making the same mistake twice.

Like it or not, his wife was going home.

Three

Sarita felt like there was sand in her eyes. She'd tossed in her bed throughout the night, even after having thrown the thin cotton sheets off her hot body and onto the floor. The stress of travel, added to the awful fight she and Matthias had had on her arrival and the knowledge that if he had his way her departure would be imminent, were all enough to keep her eyes wide and staring for hours. She had lain there, straining her ears for any sound coming from the bedroom next to hers, but in vain.

She looked at him across the table from under her sooty lashes. He was attacking his plate of cheese, butter, and coconut bread from the nearby bakery, and washing it down with sweet coconut water, totally unconcerned. He'd probably slept like a rock, whereas she had finally tumbled out of bed at dawn feeling like she'd been out horseback riding all night—or rather, that the horse had ridden *her*.

But him, oh no, he looked great; freshly showered and wearing a lightweight gray T-shirt and the same jeans he had been wearing yesterday, smelling faintly of soap, eyes bright as ever, clean-shaven, feet bare. She, on the other hand, looked like she had slept in her clothes, and her eyes were so puffy that not even her skill with makeup could hide her bad night.

She watched him as he ate, surprised to see him so calm after yesterday, but glad that at least they weren't shouting at each other. The night's rest must have done him some good. An image flashed across her mind, riding on the tail of a fleeting question: did he still sleep naked? It was enough to make her choke on her drink. Coconut water shot up the wrong way, burning her nostrils as it went.

Matthias gave her an inquiring look, but chose not to speak.

"So why doesn't JoJo sleep here at the house?" she asked when she had recovered enough to breathe normally, if only to break the silence and hide her embarrassment.

He lifted a brow. "JoJo lives on the island. He has his own home. Why should he want to sleep here?"

Stupid question, she chastised herself. But all the same, she wouldn't have minded another presence in the house apart from the two of them. Last night, she had been horrified when JoJo had left two hot take-out meals on the kitchen table and informed Matthias that he was leaving for the night. That left her facing the prospect of having to eat dinner alone with her husband, and in view of the tone that had been set an hour earlier when she had first walked into the house, she didn't expect it to be pleasant.

So she had bowed out of dinner, claiming fatigue and jet lag, even though it was still early. With a raging hunger, and knowing without looking that Matthias had trained his hard, ironic smile on her—he hadn't bought her story for a second—she had retreated to her room and shut the door. Her torment had only been made worse when she had had to listen to the sounds of his knife and fork scrape against china as he did justice to the food, the tempting scent of which had pervaded the house long after he had finished. She made do with the handful of sweets that JoJo had bought her at the airport, and discovered to her dismay that huge helpings of sugar at that hour of the night was not a good idea.

Candy notwithstanding, she was starving this morning. She wished they had that gas regulator JoJo had spoken about so they could at least have a functioning stove. Matthias might be okay with coconut water and bread and cheese for breakfast, but as for her, she was a big girl and liked her breakfast piping hot. Besides, if she didn't have her morning coffee, she was nothing.

Matthias seemed to want to cut into the silence as much as she did. He spoke again, after a while. "JoJo is finishing up his Bachelor's degree in biology. He's working on this project as research for his thesis. He doesn't live too far down the road—just in the next village—and he's usually here by eight."

"Fine," she replied, for lack of anything else to say.

He leaned forward, face inquisitive. "Tell me something, Sarita."

"What?" she asked cautiously. His voice was deceptively soft, and she knew him well enough to know that this was a warning signal.

"Who's Gwen Davis?"

She frowned, immediately on her guard. "What do you mean?"

"I mean, where'd you get the name? Is she an actual person, or did you pull the name out of a hat? What about all those qualifications you sent on your résumé? Where'd those come from?"

Her lips twisted. Who was Gwen Davis? That just went to show that he was, as usual, so taken up with things that were important to him that he failed to see anything else. "If you recall," she began, unable to keep the sarcasm out of her voice, "that is, if you had ever listened to anything I said that didn't include the word 'reef,' Davis was my mother's maiden name. And Gwendolyn is my own middle name. I thought it was pretty obvious; I half expected you to pick up on it, but evidently, you were much too busy."

She was telling the truth: she *had* expected him to pick up on it. She knew deep down, even as she chose such a ridiculously flimsy pseudonym, that he might have seen through her ruse, almost hoped that he would—anything to induce a reaction from him. A furious transatlantic phone call would have been easier to handle than his persistent cold silence. But he hadn't even batted an eye.

Matthias was at least honest enough to look embarrassed. "Oh, yeah. That's right. I'm sorry."

"What for?" she asked stoically, pretending that his ignorance of her life didn't hurt.

He opened his mouth to speak, hesitated, and closed it again. He seemed to be waiting for more.

"You want to know how I came up with the qualifications on Gwen Davis's résumé, right?"

He nodded silently.

Again, another hint she had consciously or unconsciously given him as to her true identity, one he had never spotted, much to her chagrin. She put her butter knife down and pushed her plate away. "Every one of those qualifications, Matthias, is a qualification that I already hold. I just changed the names of the universities and the dates. But I have done everything I said I did on that document, and you know it. You helped me work on my doctorate when we first—" she paused and swallowed, unwilling to call to mind those golden days before anything had gone wrong.

He filled in the space for her. "When we first met,

down on the Great Barrier Reef. And after we were married." He shook his head as though astounded at his own cluelessness. "I should have recognized the subject matter."

"But you didn't," she said bitterly. She picked up her heavy tumbler and stared down into it at the small white flecks of pulp that floated in the coconut water. Probably a million calories in there, she thought idly, and each one of them headed for her hips.

He sounded less contrite than surprised at himself. "No, I didn't." Gracefully, he got to his feet and came around to her side of the table, scooping up her plate and heading for the kitchen. As he did so, she noticed that the ring she had once placed on his left hand was gone. There was not even a pale ghost of it on his skin to suggest that it had been removed recently. Probably tossed it away the same day I walked out, she thought wryly. It irritated her to think that she had never screwed up the courage to do the same with her own.

"I can handle my own dishes," she said irritably.

His answer was short. "Don't be silly." There was some clanking, and the sound of the refrigerator door opening and closing. "I've put your breakfast in the fridge," he told her. "In case you find your appetite again."

Hello, hunger. "Thanks."

He came back into the dining room and cleared up his own plate, on which there wasn't so much as a left-over crumb. "Do you know that supplying a fake Social Security number is a federal offense?"

Sarita stiffened. What was he up to now? "You planning on reporting me?"

"You planning on leaving quietly?" he answered without the slightest inflection in his voice, but the implied threat was like a hammer to her heart.

She wasn't going down like that. Matthias might be a fighter, but she would prove a worthy opponent. "You wouldn't."

"Oh no?" He was standing right next to her, looming over her, and so close that she could see the rough weave of the battered jeans and the way they were rubbed white in places. And oh, those places. . . .

She bit her lip and forced her gaze upward. "No. Not even you would do that to me."

"'Not even' me?" he echoed, sounding almost amused.

"No." She leaned back in her chair, regretting that her seated position gave him so much of a height advantage, but not bothering to get up because to do so would be to betray the sense of intimidation she felt. He was a head taller than she anyway, so standing wouldn't exactly make much of a difference.

She held an ace up her sleeve, one that had the power to stop him in his tracks, and from the looks of the situation it was time to play it. "And to answer your question, no, I don't plan on leaving quietly."

The look on his face was so precious, she almost smiled. "No?" he was making an effort to keep his voice steady.

She shook her head purposefully. "No."

"And may I ask why not?"

Now she allowed herself to smile. "Because all that work, all those heaps of disks and reports and data, is as much mine as it is yours. I worked on them jointly with you, so I hold joint copyright. So whatever you were planning to do with them, you can only do on my say-so."

Matthias let his breakfast plate fall onto the table with a clatter. His shapely lips compressed into a thin line, and his eyes grew cold behind his glasses. "That's blackmail."

"Darn right," she asserted. "And my terms are simple. I stay and finish the project, and we publish our findings together. I go, and you'll find yourself tied up in court with an intellectual property lawsuit that'll bury both you and Reef Rescue under a heap of legal documents for years." There. She had him over a barrel. Her mouth curved into a confident smile as she held his eyes, unwavering.

To her dismay, Matthias did the unexpected; he threw back his head and laughed loudly, voice booming. Her self-confidence took a hit. What was so funny? This wasn't a laughing matter! She was serious!

"Oh, Sarita, my dear girl." The chill had passed from his eyes and was replaced with cynical amusement. "Tell me. Do you remember those idle afternoons we passed, playing chess and sipping brandy out on the veranda at our apartment?"

She nodded mutely. Was he crazy? What did that have to do with anything? Sometimes they had played for penny-ante stakes—three or five dollars; sometimes they had played for sexual favors, backrubs, and foot massages. . . . The blood flooded her face with the memory.

He leaned forward, mouth so close to her ear—so close that she could feel his breath on her face—that instinctively her chin tilted slightly, mouth moving toward his, anticipation making her incautious. In her mind, the man was poison, but her body hadn't forgotten how to respond to his proximity.

Her brain, clouded with confusion, struggled to understand what he was saying.

"Remind me, Sarita. Tell me if I'm wrong. But you've never beaten me at a game, have you?"

She was poleaxed. Her mouth was burning with his nearness, and all he could talk about was *chess*? "I don't understand . . ." She didn't finish. Her mouth was dry.

"All those months together, dozens of chess games played. We played for, uh, indulgences." He smiled smugly. "But you never beat me. You might have tried to check, but I would always, always . . . mate." The last word was laden with meaning. She might have consistently lost to him, but although the responsibilities of making good on the bet had always been hers, they had both ended up winning.

She wasn't going to sit around and let him drag her down memory lane like this. Jerking back her head, she broke away and leaped out of her chair. She was threatening him, holding her legal power over his head in a bid to make him allow her to stay, and he was babbling on about chess and getting her hormones in a twist? She passed her trembling hand over her smooth hair.

"I don't know what chess has to do with this, Matthias. I'm saying that if you try to send me back—"

The tiny, temporary bond between them had snapped for him, too. He cut her off before she could finish. "Chess has everything to do with it. Never pit your strategy against mine; however you play it, you'll lose. Your little threat is full of hot air, and you know it." He gathered up his breakfast things again and walked over to the kitchen to deposit them in the sink.

Fists curled, nails grazing her palms, she followed him. "What do you mean, 'hot air'? So help me Matthias, I swear . . ."

He didn't even afford her the courtesy of turning around to face her. Instead, he lathered up a big sponge and began attacking the few dishes. "Swear all you like. But you love the reefs, and your heart breaks to see them dying. You'd sooner cut off your own arm than stall a project as important as this one. You and I both know that if it came down to the crunch, you'd never throw anything in the way of Reef Rescue." He paused, and then turned her own words against her. "Not even you would do something like that."

She was struck dumb by his accuracy. He was right. She would never use the project to get back at him. It was too important. The marine environment couldn't be allowed to suffer because of her. She hung her head in defeat.

Matthias saw the gesture, cocked his head slightly, and smiled his victory. "Checkmate, my sweet."

Before she could speak, a cloud of dust announced JoJo's arrival. He'd left the 4X4 that he'd picked her up in at the airport, but had taken the project's other rented vehicle, a sleek silver motorcycle that he was now parking in the driveway next to the van. She couldn't take the discussion any further, not with JoJo here. It was bad enough they had confused him with their obvious animosity last night.

She stood by quietly as the men exchanged greetings, avoiding eye contact with either of them. JoJo looked fresh and cheerful, as if he had forgotten all about the tension of the night before. He walked into the kitchen, showing that already familiar grin.

"Hey, Gwen. How was your first night in Tobago?"

She'd forgotten about the "Gwen" thing. She groaned inwardly. "Lovely," she lied.

"Ready?"

"To do what?"

"We're going down to Buccoo Reef this morning, to have a preliminary look around. We're not actually getting into the work yet, but my sister's renting her boat to the project. Matthias is going over to have a look at it. You're coming with us, right?"

She threw Matthias a covert glance. Was she under house arrest, or would she actually be allowed out with them until he decided her fate?

Matthias read the query in her eyes and seemed to consider the odds briefly before saying to JoJo, "Of course she's coming." He turned to her. "Go get ready. You've got five minutes. If I were you, I'd take some sunscreen. We'll wait for you outside."

She didn't have to be told twice.

Sarita could smell Buccoo Bay long before she saw it. The scent of salt and seaweed was overwhelming, hanging low in the air like a curtain. Buccoo wasn't as sandy as most of the other beaches on the island; instead, its rough coastline was broken up by rocks jutting out of the sea, and the shore was coarse and gravelly, the result of being slammed repeatedly by the many hurricanes that assaulted Tobago year after year. As they walked down the grassy mud flats that led to the murky beach, she had to step carefully to ensure she didn't get a foot stuck down any one of the huge crab holes dotting the landscape.

The Tobagonians had taken great pains to make the beach attractive to tourists: there were tiny blue and white wooden gazebos along the beachfront, and a small clubhouse offered the amenities of a bar, restaurant, and changing rooms. Loud reggae music blared from a tinny stereo system over antique speakers strung up over the bar; Sarita struggled to resist swinging her hips to the persistently cheery beat.

She turned to the water, and her gaze fell upon an astounding sight. Half a dozen young men stood in

waist-deep water with large goats, which, far from looking put out at getting wet, seemed to be enjoying
themselves. Some were swimming and others were up
on their hind legs, patiently allowing their owners to
stretch their forelegs like massage therapists pulling
kinks out of their clients' shoulders.

She heard the sound of her husband's footsteps
crunching next to her, and asked the question she was
itching to, not caring whether she would be rebuffed
or not. "What the devil are they doing with those
goats?"

To her surprise, he chuckled. "It's Easter time, and
that's the biggest religious festival in Tobago. In a few
days, the island is going to be chockablock with
tourists. In some of the villages, there's going to be goat
racing. The jockeys are getting their goats into shape.
The water helps relax their muscles, and swimming
makes their legs strong."

She gaped. *"Jockeys?* You mean, they *ride* them? Isn't
that sort of mean? Those goats look pretty big, but not
that big!"

He laughed. "No, silly. They don't ride them. They
run alongside them. Numbers are pinned to their
chests. Sometimes, the goats wear little halters with
numbers on them, too."

"Numbers on the goats," she muttered.

"They don't seem to mind. As a matter of fact, they
usually look like they enjoy it."

Sarita couldn't help but be intrigued by a people
who raced their goats. She stared at the goat-stretching
procedure for several minutes and murmured, bemused. "Goat racing. Now I've heard everything."

"You should see the crab races."

She squinted up at him in the bright sunlight.
"You're putting me on, right?"

"Nope."

"And do the crabs wear little halters with numbers on them, too?"

He seemed to be thinking hard about that one, and then answered, "No, but if you like, I could suggest it to the organizers. Ought to pull a crowd."

"Lots of fun for the crabs, huh?"

"I doubt that. Loser gets turned into curry. As a matter of fact, they all get turned into curry. With dumplings."

"Not fair. I'm calling the crab rights people."

"You do that."

They fell into a silence that seemed to go on endlessly, and the tenuous warmth that their exchange had sparked between them died.

"Not good," Matthias muttered after a while, frowning slightly and staring down at his feet.

She followed the direction of his gaze, their banter forgotten. "What's not good?"

Right at the edge of the shore, where lazy waves lapped at his sneakered feet, was a wide belt of coral smithereens, which stood out starkly against the ground. The stubby fragments looked like crushed fingers on a skeleton's hand, some bleached white by the sun, some grayer and fresher-looking, and some having lain so long at the edge that hairy filaments of dark green seaweed had become attached to them.

Sarita knew what he meant. Any beach enclosed by a reef would demonstrate signs of old coral and other reef debris: the coral was living, and it was only natural that pieces of it would break off and die, eventually being carried landward by the tide. But this heavy sprinkling of smashed and broken coral, obviously having accumulated over a long period of time, added to the murkiness of the water and the pungent scent of decay in the air, could augur nothing good for the reef that lay a mile or two off the coast. It was evidence of rapid decline in its health and integrity. Sarita felt a quiet sadness descend upon her.

She glanced up at Matthias's face again, intently watching his profile and the way his jaw worked to hold back the emotion. He was shaking his head, a screenplay of disaster spooling behind his eyes, and the tension made his shoulders taut under the cotton of his T-shirt.

Without considering the consequences, she slid a hand around his forearm, warm flesh coming into contact with warm flesh, mouth open to express her empathy, but sound was suddenly not forthcoming; the unplanned touch brought with it a jolt that stole her voice.

It seemed as if the longing and loneliness she had fought over the year they had been apart had been stored within her like some kind of electric energy, creating a hiding place for itself in her bones, her spinal cord, her lungs, and her heart. Contact with the cause of all that energy was all it took to set it free.

They were both standing in water, salty water that soaked their feet, grounding them in a worse way than trees in a lightning storm. Power flowed from him into her and back again, surging so forcefully she was almost convinced she heard a crackle and smelled the singed air. She tried to tear her hand away but it was suddenly nerveless.

Matthias wasn't immune, either. His head snapped toward her, green eyes wide with shock behind his glasses, sable brows arched in surprise, and hair bristling from the charge that shook them both.

"Sarita," he managed to say after painful seconds.

Overcome, she opened her mouth and shut it again.

Energy transferred from him to her, from her to him, forming a live, supercharged loop, and on the wake of that energy came the memories, of him and her, together before the debacle that had destroyed their marriage. The images flipped by as fast as pages in a photo album: the two of them in the brilliant blue waters of Australia and Florida, or sunning themselves in the nude like lizards on rocks near secluded beaches, often daring to risk discovery, or huddled together during long afternoons in their lab, mulling over piles of research. But in every disturbing image, they were both smiling, entranced by each other, crazy in love.

How things had changed.

The sobering thought was enough to shut the power off, and the leaping current between them died. Finding her hand free to move again, Sarita snatched it away from his arm and glanced down at it; against all rational thought, she was sure that she had been burned.

Matthias nudged his glasses up over his nose and continued to stare at her. By the flush in his cheeks, she knew he was as deeply affected as she.

"Now you understand," he told her softly, in a voice that came from deep within his chest and was wobbly with emotion.

"Understand what?" she asked, knowing, but not wanting to admit it.

"Why I can't—" He threw a glance over his shoulder. JoJo, who had left them since their arrival to chat with the lifeguards seated in one of the nearby gazebos, was making his way toward them determinedly, stepping boldly without looking down, yet somehow managing to avoid the many crab-hole traps along the way.

"Why you can't let me stay?"

"Your presence would be too—" He broke off, licked

his lips, and let his eyes flicker over her, from her eyes to her mouth, which was now slightly parted and revealed the gap between her front teeth that he had teased her about since the first day he had met her, and down past the open collar of her simple shirt; he looked away quickly. "Too disruptive," he finished miserably. "I'm here to do a job, remember?"

She shook her head, almost in contempt. "You're such a coward, Matthias," she managed to say before JoJo came within earshot.

The young Tobagonian was smiling broadly. "Ready? My sister's boat is over there, out on the pier." He turned and pointed to the concrete pier that jutted off to the right. "She's probably waiting for us."

Between the two of them they seemed to have come to a silent agreement not to bare their tension in front of JoJo, and so the subject dropped, as if it had never even been raised. They quietly followed JoJo along the wide pier, which was lined with brightly painted glass-bottomed boats with cheery sounding names that were waiting to be filled with their daily complement of eager tourists ready to go reef watching. Boatmen sat idly about, waiting for the tide to go out, thus making the reef shallower and more accessible.

"Looking to take a trip?" one of them called out, smiling, hoping for an early boatload of passengers. "I could take you, cheaper than all the rest."

Another one cut in before he could finish his pitch. "No, me! Mine is the pretty one over there!" He pointed to a bright red, gold, and green boat moored a little way out. The name *Happy as Pappy* was hand-painted unevenly along the side.

Before either Sarita or Matthias could answer, JoJo raised an arm. "They're with me," he said, sounding proprietary. In response, the boatmen nodded and let the matter drop.

Near the end of the pier, JoJo halted, coming abreast of a red, flat-bottomed boat that bobbed on the water. The name *Spanish Dancer* was scrolled in white along the side. That made Sarita smile. A Spanish dancer was a soft-bodied sea creature, similar to a large, colorful slug, that maneuvered through the water by unfurling its body behind it like a dancer's billowing skirts. Stunning to look at, and quite harmless, it was one of Sarita's favorites. It was a delightful name for a sea-going craft.

The boat was perhaps a little smaller than some of the others—it was not designed to hold twenty or thirty people as they were—but was still a comfortable eighteen feet in length. It looked in better condition than the others, too. The paint was fresh, and one glance at the motor that hung over the edge told her it would be fast. Faster than necessary, actually. If she wasn't mistaken, the outboard motor was designed for a speedboat—a racer, even. Weird, she thought. But maybe JoJo's sister liked speed.

Sarita stooped to peer down into the boat, excited, as she always was, by the prospect of being on the water. As she did so, it rocked a little, and she found herself face to face with a woman who was about to climb up the short ladder onto the pier. She almost fell over backward trying to avoid a collision.

The longest pair of legs she had ever seen extricated themselves from the boat. The woman stood next to Matthias, sleek as an eel, shorts barely covering her bottom and white tank top striking against her dark skin. She wore neither swimsuit nor bra under the top, and Sarita saw his gaze flicker downward to the bold impressions of the woman's nipples before rising to meet her dark eyes.

"Matthias," the woman said. Her teeth were like white pebbles against the blackness of her skin: straight, even, and perfectly formed. She shifted her shades to rest on the top of her head, revealing long-lashed brown eyes that held his green ones boldly. She was as tall as he and her taut body was as lithesome and strong. Sarita felt shorter and plumper than ever.

Matthias held out his hand in greeting. "Janelle." He was smiling. Sarita didn't like that smile; she knew it too well. The glimmer of naked male interest was undeniable. Uncomfortable, she examined the concrete beneath her feet.

Then JoJo brushed against her as he moved to embrace the woman, and Sarita looked up again to see his face a wreath of smiles. "Sis." He indicated Sarita with a small gesture. "See, I brought the new biologist to meet you. She's going to be on the team. Her name's Gwen."

Sarita flushed at hearing her counterfeit name on the young man's lips, and flashed Matthias a covert glance. It was met with an ironic one that only she and he understood.

"Hello." The handshake Janelle offered was over in a second. It was like briefly grasping a dead, boneless fish. "You had a nice flight in? How d'you like Tobago so far?"

Sarita would have replied, but Janelle's eyes were back on Matthias again, and she was sure that the other woman didn't really care about an answer. "You going out this morning then? The tide's on its way out; the reef will be just right." Janelle indicated the boat with a tilt of her head. "Let's take your new employee for a ride. Get her used to the island." Without waiting for an answer, she stepped into the boat. "I saw nurse sharks out there last evening. Maybe we'll see them again. That is, if . . . um . . . Gwen, is it?"

Sarita nodded mutely, trying not to look at Matthias for fear of the wry smile she would surely find there.

Janelle shrugged. "If Gwen isn't afraid of sharks." She laughed. There was island music in her voice.

"I'm a marine biologist," Sarita said. The acid in her voice took her by surprise. So what if the woman was giving Matthias the eye? He didn't look like he minded, so why should she? "I've swum with sharks before." She didn't have to add that nurse sharks, although large and awesome to look at, were gentle, almost friendly, and rarely launched attacks on humans. Obviously, the woman knew that.

"How nice," Janelle murmured. She stepped aside to let the others follow her in.

"After you, Gwen," Matthias said loudly enough to be heard by everyone. "Maybe we *should* take a trip out to the reef this morning. I can see how the boat runs, and *Gwen* can have a first look at the reef. That way, if she has to go back to the States suddenly, at least she can say she's seen some of Tobago."

Sarita could feel three pairs of eyes upon her: JoJo's startled, Janelle's amused, and her husband's inscrutable. Without bothering to answer, she tossed her small duffel bag onto a seat and climbed in, trying her best not to come into contact with Matthias as she did so. Face hot, she went over to the end of the boat farthest from the controls and sat down. JoJo hurriedly loosed the moorings before hopping in. After a few moments of consultation with Janelle, Matthias took the wheel and turned the key in the ignition. The engine came awake.

Sarita crammed a baseball cap down onto her head,

pulling the brim down to shield her face from the sun and to hide the glare that was directed at the back of his head. The wretch wasn't even looking at her, having long dismissed her from his mind. Instead, he was listening carefully to whatever Janelle was saying, pointing at dials and asking her questions. The tall, sleek woman stood closer to him than she needed to, touching his arm with one hand while smoothing her close-cropped hair with the other.

"What did he mean?" JoJo plopped down next to Sarita. His young face was full of concern. "What did the doctor mean by 'if she has to go back to the States'? Something wrong?"

He was so nice; she didn't want to lie, but if she were to tell the truth, how much could she tell him and where would she start? "Maybe," she finally managed to admit. "Maybe something's wrong." She didn't know what else to say.

"What? Visa problems? Work permit? Didn't you get everything cleared up at the airport? Because if that's the problem, I've got a cousin who works in Immigration. My mother's cousin, actually. I can always give him a call—"

She cut him off. "Not that."

"What, then?"

She tried to find an easy way to say this. "I might not be the right person for the job after all."

He frowned. "But you were perfect for the job. The doctor said so. All he could talk about yesterday was how anxious he was for you to get here, and how good you would be for the project. He picked you out of dozens of applications. He chose you personally, and if he says you're right for it, you're right for it."

"If he says so then it's so, huh?" Sarita smiled ruefully. JoJo was showing all the signs of hero worship. It was easy to recognize: when she had first started working with Matthias she'd been bitten by it, too. Matthias had a way of making people think he could still a storm with a wave of his hand.

"Yes," JoJo replied earnestly. "Don't worry. You don't have to be afraid of him. You'll do okay."

"I'm not afraid . . ." she began, but it didn't seem worth arguing about. She shrugged. "You mind if we drop it?"

His eyes were serious. "Okay, but . . ." He looked away and focused on the wake of white foam curving out behind them.

They were coming into drastically deeper water now, and the coast was a hazy green line. Sarita had been right: the boat was fast. Smooth, too; it barely rocked under them. A fairly high, flat roof sheltered about half of it, and a single padded bench ran around it on all sides. It was expensively trimmed in deep burgundy leather—real leather—and cupboards under the seats and above their heads kept ugly trappings out of sight. The *Spanish Dancer* was a beauty, all right. Matthias had chosen well. He did just about everything well, when it came to business, and she could admit that without grudging him the kudos. She turned a little in her seat, rather than deal any further with JoJo's probing, and instead focused on the water that had changed from green to navy. "Are we far from the reef?"

JoJo hesitated, and then graciously allowed her to change the subject. "Ten minutes, maybe. The water gets real shallow, real fast." He pointed at the center of the boat. Three large wooden boxes sat there, neatly fitting into holes that had been cut into the boat's floor. She leaned forward to peer into them. The bottom of each box was sealed with glass, effectively preventing water from entering the boat but offering a clear, wide-angle view of the churning water beneath them. Bubbles stirred up by the motor frothed against the glass, like soapsuds swirling against a washing machine window.

"You'll see it through here," JoJo said. "One second it's dark and blue down below and the next, we're in four feet of water and you can see every fish, every crab, and every speck of coral so close up you feel you can touch it." He relaxed a little, happy to be given the opportunity to boast about his island again. "You're going to see the Nylon Pool, too. Nothing but white coral sand, and the water's warmer than your bath. If Dr. Rowley says it's okay, we can get out and have a swim. It's smooth as glass, and nothing you have ever experienced. You can stand in water up to your chest, miles out in the middle of the ocean, with only sky overhead. It's like God's own swimming pool."

She listened to his voice as he went on about the fish in the area, and all the types of coral she would find, excited in spite of herself. She was in paradise, after all. Years of hoping and wishing, and now she was here, and she was damned if Matthias and his threats would spoil it for her. As he had said: even if she were only to be here for one day, at least she would have experienced the glory of the Buccoo Reef.

As if to taunt her, Matthias laughed from the other end of the boat, and Janelle joined him, making Sarita jerk her head in their direction. The woman was still draped so far over the controls that Sarita wondered how Matthias managed to see to handle the wheel. If he thought he was tipping the boat over just because this woman chose to throw herself at him while he was manning the controls, he was wrong. And as for JoJo's sister, wasn't she a professional sailor? Didn't she know that standing on a boat this small was dangerous? The backwash from a boat passing nearby could be enough to send her flying.

A woman could quite easily topple over on legs that long. The idea was almost delicious. Sarita barely had time to master her sudden grin before JoJo interrupted her thoughts. "Look!"

The dark, bubbly water beneath them cleared, and through the glass bottom, the sandy ocean bed came into view. It was like cruising over a mountain range at low altitude: hillocks and valleys undulated under their gaze, and coral mountains hundreds of years old loomed. Bright parrot fish with painted-on clown faces flitted by, fins spread out, fluttering in the current, and making the mountaintop image even more real as they swooped like pretty birds. Larger fish, brown ones with bull-dog faces, lurked in the darker corners waiting to snap up unsuspecting fingerlings.

She couldn't keep the excitement out of her voice as a long shadow unfurled past like a dark ribbon. "Sea snake!"

"Eel." Matthias was leaning over her shoulder, hands on his knees, looking into the glass-bottomed boxes with her. She flinched at his proximity. How did he always do this, approach without a sound? "You wouldn't want to go into the water with a sea snake that size around. Venom, remember?"

He was right. Sea snakes were among the most lethal creatures on Earth; some had bites worse than any mamba or rattler. "Eel then," she allowed. "But a big one. Gorgeous." She couldn't keep the pleasure of the sighting out of her voice.

He sounded amused by her excitement.

She looked up into his face, surprised by the warmth in it. Half an hour ago he was publicly threatening to throw her off the island. But the creatures of the sea were his purview, and when the subject of them came up, he couldn't help but talk about them, whether it be to friend or foe.

She hadn't noticed when he'd yanked his shirt off; his bare chest gleamed in the sun. She wondered briefly if he'd used the sunscreen he'd warned her to use earlier, and had the urge to offer to apply it. She hadn't felt those dark gold chest hairs crinkle under her fingers in a year. She remembered which lotion he preferred, it soothed with aloe vera and smelled of avocado. She had some in her duffel. Maybe she could—

He stood up abruptly, turning his head to yell across the boat to Janelle, who was standing at the controls but glancing over at her and Matthias rather than looking where the boat was going. "Around here will do just fine, Janelle."

Janelle nodded, and the throttle died. Then there was nothing but a silence broken by soft grunts as JoJo tossed the anchor overboard. "Gwen," JoJo said, when he was done, "the snorkels and rubber sandals are in a cupboard right under your seat. Kit up, and then I'll take you on a tour."

Matthias knelt and opened the cupboard before she could get to it, rooting around and yanking out snorkeling gear, handing her a mask before choosing one for himself. His presumption irritated her. "I can pick one out on my own," she told him, keeping her voice low.

He lifted his eyes to her face. "Why? That one will fit you perfectly."

She glanced down at it. It looked about right, but that didn't mean she had to back down. "Maybe so, but there are lots of types. Maybe I wanted to go through them and see which one *I'd* like to use on *my* face."

He came to perch next to her on the bench and carefully put his sandals on before he answered. "Suit yourself, my dear." He scooped up a handful of assorted bits and pieces of gear and poured them in her lap. To JoJo, he said. "It's okay, JoJo. I can take Dr. Davis around. You stay here."

JoJo didn't protest.

It only took Sarita a few moments of searching through the masks on her lap to realize that Matthias had indeed chosen the best one for her, but damned if she was going to let him know that. She chose the second best and ostentatiously put it on, trying not to think of the small space at her temple where the mask failed to make a perfect seal. It would begin filling up with water the minute she submerged, but she'd rather have to go back to the surface every few minutes to drain the mask than admit that, as usual, he'd been correct.

By the time she was stripped down to her swimsuit and had strapped on her sandals to protect her feet from coral shards, he was waiting for her at the ladder. He grinned at her as she struggled to keep the mask straight. "That one fits better, huh?"

"It does." She didn't look at him or take his offered hand as she slid into the water. JoJo had been right. It was warmer than bath water. She sighed audibly as the water came up over her hips, and kept on rising until it reached her nipples, which stiffened immediately against the fabric of her swimsuit. As the water pushed up against them, her generous breasts swelled and floated gently on the surface.

Whereas previously Matthias had scarcely allowed himself to glimpse Janelle's smaller, firmer breasts on the pier before looking away, now he took his time, leisurely letting his eyes roam from Sarita's bosom to her throat, and then to her face, which, she was sure, was flushing madly under her ill-fitting mask. In an instant, the space between her legs was warmer than the water they were standing in. Curse him for doing that to her with nothing but a look!

"You put on two or three pounds?" He asked indelicately.

More like five, but that was none of his business. "You were taking me on a tour?" she reminded him pointedly.

She might just as well not have spoken. "Looks good on you," he said. "There was always this wonderful softness about you. . . ."

Her belly flipped over. He was so good at that, making a woman feel she was everything a man could desire. She'd always known she carried around a few more pounds than she should for her height, but with his words and his loving he had made her feel not plump but lush and generous, like an acre of hilly, fertile land spread out and waiting to be watered. He'd been the man who taught her she was beautiful, and back in the time when he still loved her, he'd spared no effort to make her feel proud of her womanly body.

He'd done it then and he was doing it now. He filled his eyes with her for a few long moments before slipping his own snorkeling mask into place, and then beckoned for her to follow.

Lovely, she groaned inside. He set this ache in her groin and this hot yearning in her belly, and now he wanted her to *swim!* He struck out confidently, putting distance between himself and the boat, and there was nothing to do but paddle after him. She drew near and stayed close, following his lead as he expertly avoided contact with the jutting bits of coral, which were sharper than glass and could inflict a cut that took forever to heal. Fire coral was the worst: not only did it cut, but it injected a venom into the wound that, though it would not kill, would cause violent and agonizing swelling. These she gave the widest berth of all. She wasn't like Matthias, who was freakishly immune to their attacks: his skin bore innumerable scratches and scars from encounters with the living rocks, but he never seemed to suffer any ill effects.

His immunity seemed even more bizarre in the light of his hypersensitivity to venom from many creatures on dry land. Even a bee sting was enough to shut his system down, and the risks were so high that he never went anywhere without a small emergency medical kit. If ever there was proof that a man was born for life in a marine environment, surely that was it. When they lived as man and wife, Sarita took pains every day to ensure that he never left the house without his kit, as the man was prone to being absentminded about anything that didn't involve the water. She wondered what he did to remind himself about it now. Then she grunted dismissively. Matthias was a grown man. He could take care of himself only too well.

She shoved him from the center stage of her mind and peered down into the water. As her body grew used to being wet, it cooled and relaxed, and although she remained intensely aware of his proximity, she let herself focus on her surroundings. Curious fish wandered near enough to brush against her; after years of seeing the tourist boats come and go, they were used to the sight and scent of humans, and were not bothered by the invasion. Although she was glad for their company, it hurt her heart to see them so trusting. Their very courage made them easy targets for illegal spearfishers. She remembered Matthias telling her that in spite of stiff penalties, poachers raped the reef with impunity, taking home the brilliant jeweled fish to cook or stuff and sell to the tourists. It was a crime against nature.

Ahead of her, Matthias stiffened and held out a hand, signaling her to stop. She did so abruptly, bumping against his leg.

She held her hands open to him, asking without words for an explanation.

He popped the snorkel from his mouth; silently, his lips formed a single word—shark.

Her body jerked convulsively, an instinctive reaction to such a terror-instilling word. Although she knew that the sharks in question would no doubt be the demure nurse sharks that Janelle had mentioned—great whites and makos found the island's warm, shallow water less comfortable—her body trembled.

Matthias slipped his snorkel into his mouth again and reached for her, pulling her nearer and gently coaxing her back under the water with him. It was slightly deeper here: they were at the fringe of the reef, at the point where the atoll upon which they stood plunged sharply back to the depth of the rest of the sea. All that kept them from falling off the edge was a barrier of rocks that rimmed the reef. White waves broke over them with a sound like thunder. If sharks were within the barrier, they would be trapped until high tide came in, making it safe for them to swim over the chain of sharp rocks once again.

Sarita blinked into the darker water looking for the creatures, her heart pounding as much in anticipation of seeing them as from the grip in which Matthias held her hand. Then she saw a shadow move, almost directly below them. The huge beast's dappled hide had provided perfect camouflage on the ocean bed; it could have been a rock or a ripple in the sand. And then another moved against it, and another. Three sharks. Each was larger than Matthias, even the smallest, just a pup, was longer than he by a good few feet. The slow creatures sensed their presence and roused from their rest.

She felt his eyes on her as she watched them rise, and the knowledge that he was there gave her courage. What she had said to Janelle was true: she'd swum with sharks before, but that had been from behind the safety of a steel cage. And as friendly as the nurse sharks were by nature, they *did* have teeth. Lots of them.

She could hear her heart in her ears. A large one, which she quickly identified as a male by the pair of genital claspers under its tail, swam past, its expressionless eye fixed on her. Whiskerlike filaments grew at the sides of its huge jaws, wafting gently in the current and picking up their scent. It turned and passed by again, and then she could feel Matthias touch her lightly in the small of her back, calming her and telling her everything would be all right. There was a battle between fear and excitement, and excitement won out.

How glorious! Alone, she and this beautiful man, in the silence and hugeness of the ocean, were swimming with some of the oldest and most magnificent creatures of the sea. She was pressed so close to Matthias she could feel the rise and fall of his chest as he breathed: rhythmic and regular, the way he'd taught her to do underwater. She matched her breathing to his: inhale for a count of six, hold for three, and exhale for six. As the slow, meditative breathing soothed away the fear from her soul, she reached out her hand to touch the long dorsal fin of the big fish that swam next to her, feeling a jolt of excitement at the contact. Its skin was leather-tough, yet delicate and alive.

When he finally led her away, she felt not relief but

regret. As soon as the sharks had slipped from view, they both stopped and stood again. Matthias was behind her, against her. She could hear her breathing in the tube of the snorkel that ran against her ear, and there was no six-three-six rhythm here. It was erratic, chaotic, harsh. He was so close, up against her bottom, and the hard bulge against the small of her back told her his blood was pumping as fast in his veins as it was in hers. The rough denim of his cutoffs rubbed against her, stirring up trouble in her thighs and the warm place between them.

Water streamed from the long, loose hair that had floated in the water like strands of algae. He brushed the locks from his face, flipped up his mask, and popped the mouthpiece from his mouth so that he could say: "You were always a danger junkie, Sari."

He called her Sari. The name he'd used when they made love. She couldn't look around.

"The water thrills you. The dark, unknown places beneath the surface. Remember? I'd have to drag you back, because you would always push it and go beyond the boundaries. You loved the prickle of your skin when danger was near. And you loved sharks."

She removed her own mask, fiddling with the strap to avoid looking at him. She knew his eyes would be as deep as the water behind the rocky barrier that kept them safe. At least physically safe, because his presence and his words were a greater threat to her equilibrium than any many-toothed beast could ever be.

He kept on talking, his sonorous voice low, as if he were afraid that the fish would hear and tell on them. "You used to slip into a shark cage and take photos of them as they came at you, knowing full well that every time they rammed the cage it could burst open and leave you . . . naked. You liked to go up against something bigger than you and win." His hand came out to trace a line down the length of her arm, and his touch burned worse than fire coral.

He kept on talking. "And when you got out of the cage and you were on dry land, you were still . . . wet. Inside, where it matters. And your pupils were all dilated and your pulse was up. The sharks, the power, and the danger, excited you. And then, you remember what always came next?"

She remembered. Damn him, she remembered.

"Sarita?"

He couldn't seriously be waiting for an answer! What did he expect her to say: that in her excitement she would inevitably seek him out, wherever he was, even if he was in the lab, and either drag him back to their room or demand that he make love to her right there, wherever "there" was: the porch, the shower, even his office back at the marine research center where they'd both worked for a while? When she was aroused like that, their loving was always intense, almost rough, leaving them winded and feeling as though they'd scoured each other with their own bodies. Surely he didn't need to hear her tell him about that!

"I think you remember as well as I do, Matthias." She tried to be cool even though the bulge against her back was bigger and harder than it had been a few seconds before. Pulling away from him was like yanking a hunk of metal away from an electro-magnet, but with effort she was free and clear of his devastating influence. She began wading to the boat, being careful of where she stepped, and glad that in the spot where they now found themselves the water was only chest high again.

He followed, still close. "Tell me something."

"What?" She didn't bother looking around.

"Does what you did to get here excite you, too?"

She stopped dead and spun around. "Excuse me?"

"Faking a job application and lying your way onto the island. Toying with me. Flirting with danger. Did it excite you?"

She couldn't help but laugh. "Don't tell me you see yourself as a shark!" That was just too egotistical. "Believe me, Matthias, even at your most cussed, you're nowhere near as dangerous as a great white on the other side of a steel cage. Where do you get your ego?"

"Then you aren't afraid?" He was smiling, unaffected by her dismissal.

"Of what?" She tried to force disdain into her voice, but she knew what he meant, and that made it quiver.

"Of another night in the house with me. In all that heat. We might need to leave the bedroom doors open to catch a stray breeze. Will it feel as if your little steel shark cage is open?"

She remembered the wretched night she'd spent in the hot little room. They'd be getting back onto the boat, and soon they would be on shore again, headed for the little cottage by the beach. Maybe they'd work the rest of the day and maybe not, but either way, JoJo would leave them, as he had the night before. Then they'd be alone again.

And her cage door would be open. Matthias must have spotted the chagrin on her face, as much as she tried to hide it, because when she looked at him again, he was showing all his teeth.

Four

"That's it, JoJo. Let's call it a day." Matthias got to his feet, trying not to feel the stiffness that extended from the middle of his back all the way down his legs. He'd been hunkered down for most of the afternoon, going through box after box of documents, sorting them, and packing them away in his study. All that was left was to dispose of the cardboard boxes, sweep out the bits of packing popcorn and dust, and mop up, and he would have a useable office. A thrill ran though him at the thought. Reef Rescue was up and running, and after half a lifetime of yearning, he would finally be able to fulfill his commitment to the land of his birth. He owed Tobago a lot and, come tomorrow, he would start paying it all back.

JoJo sneezed and then excused himself. "Dust," he smiled. "You'd never think this little house could be so dusty."

Matthias walked him through the study door and into the living room. "It'll soon be all under control," he promised. "We're nearly there."

As they entered the room, Sarita, on her knees working at a dark stain on the hardwood floor, looked up. Even in her crumpled T-shirt and old jeans, with her hair tied up with a bandanna to keep the dust out of it, she looked cute. For a second, Matthias was distracted from his conversation. He never understood how she did it: other women spent an hour at a makeup table getting dressed. When they were done, they definitely looked good, but Sarita had the kind of allure that radiated from her no matter what she was wearing or how messy she looked. It was there in the eyes, the full, round mouth with its little scar, and the breasts that pushed up against her shirt. He thought again of the few pounds she had put on and how good they looked on her. He had always loved the feel of her in his arms and how solid she used to be under him. She was all flesh, all woman.

A buzz in his head warned him that if he thought any further in that direction, there would be a repeat of his astonishing and embarrassing arousal out there on the reef that morning. Where had that come from? He was mad at her, and she deserved every iota of his anger, but out there swimming with the sharks, with the awesome surge of excitement looping between him, Sarita, and the terrifyingly wonderful, primitive beasts that had made curious circles around both of them, he'd felt something that definitely wasn't anger. Perhaps it was the memory of the hunger she had always brought home with her from a day out at sea, or perhaps it was a response to the shock of being so close to her again, in the water, after a brutal year apart. Whichever it was, he'd wanted her so suddenly and so badly that he hadn't been able to stop himself from pressing his body against hers. They had not been close enough to the boat for JoJo and Janelle to see what was going on, surely, but the fact remained that he had practically accosted her in public, and public displays had never been his thing. She'd only been here one day, and in that one day, he'd lost control. She had to go.

JoJo was saying something. He struggled to listen. "I was asking what you wanted me to get you to eat tonight.

We didn't have any lunch, so I was figuring you'd want something heavy." JoJo waited for an answer.

Matthias struggled to clear his head, shunting aside the memory of Sarita's wet, near-nude body against his. In spite of himself he glanced down at her. She was still kneeling on the floor, but she'd stopped her cleaning, and the rag rested limply on her thigh. Her eyes were fixed on them, with an almost agonized look. He was worried briefly. Was she sick? Then he remembered: she'd had no dinner last night and had barely touched her breakfast. They'd all been so busy getting the Reef Rescue office and the rest of the rooms set up that they'd blithely worked through lunch. Poor Sarita probably hadn't had a meal since she'd consumed whatever mush the airline had fed her more than twenty-four hours ago. She must be ready to faint.

Quickly and decisively he slipped JoJo some twenties. "Whatever you get, get it fast. She must be starving. I'm pretty hungry myself."

As JoJo left, Sarita threw Matthias a grateful smile. He walked over and squatted next to her. "Why didn't you say something at lunch time? Just because I forget to eat doesn't mean you have to. I wouldn't have minded stopping to get you lunch."

She gave him one of her prideful looks. "We big girls can skip a meal just like anybody else," she said hotly.

"Technically, that was three meals in a row. And don't get up on your high horse with me, young lady. We both know you like your food, and there's nothing wrong with that. Don't treat me like a monster who'd try to starve you out."

"You mean you wouldn't? Starve me out, I mean. If you had the chance."

He wasn't sure if she was serious or not, but he gave her a straight answer instead of a bantering one. "No,

Sarita, I wouldn't. I'm not an unkind man. I'll deal with you on the level. I've already told you how I feel about you being here, and I've made my decision very clear. This project is mine: I sign the checks, I make the major decisions, and I have the power to hire and fire. I'm grateful for the elbow grease you put in today, and I'll make sure you get compensated for it. But you *are* going back home. Escorted out through the front door, not starved out through the side. Understand?"

He was glad that looks couldn't kill. The glare she shot him would have nailed him to a wall. "I don't need your money for a lousy day's work. Consider it a donation to a worthy cause." She stood up and dusted off the back of her jeans. Matthias tried not to listen to the sound of her bare hands slapping against her round bottom. There was only *so* much a man could take.

She headed for her room. "And as for sending me home, well, what do you want me to tell you? I tried logic, and I tried to barter. Neither worked. I love this project as much as you do. I believe in it as much as you do. And I can *help*. If you're willing to lose all the time it would take you to go out and search for another biologist, when you have one right under your roof, well, fine. But while you drag your feet, the reef will continue to suffer. I never thought you'd sacrifice it just to make your point."

He grabbed her arm before she could escape through her doorway. "It's not about sacrificing the reef. I'm here to help it. But I can't do it with you here."

"Why not?"

"You know why not." Did she really want him to spell it out for her? Again?

She smiled ruefully. "What, because you can't trust me?"

"That's right."

"Can't trust me to do what? Have I ever left you alone underwater? Have I ever neglected my duties at the helm, when it was my turn to handle the boat? Have I ever damaged a specimen or let one of your precious creatures die? Lost a file? Botched an experiment?"

His answer was taut. "No."

"Then what, Matthias? Our marriage is over. You decided that, not me. It's over because you can't or won't understand my side of the story, never took ten seconds to ask why I did what I did. If that's the way you want it, then go right ahead. But trust is not this big blanket you can throw over everything. Even if you don't trust my . . ." She wrung her hands, agitated, unable to look him in the face. "If you can't trust my love . . . ," her voice cracked over the word, ". . . there's nothing I can do to change your mind. But you can trust my work. Can't you?"

His head throbbed. This woman, his wife, was making far too much sense. She was a good worker, an excellent one. He had trained her, and she knew how to do things the way he wanted them done. But she failed to understand that her work was only part of it. He wasn't worried about the time they'd spend working, but the time they'd have on their hands when they weren't: the nights they'd spend under the same roof and the meals they'd share each day.

Ever since he'd met her, on that trip to Australia, she'd insinuated herself into his life so deeply that he knew within days he'd never be free of her influence. She was like a magnet placed near his compass, destroying the control he had of his own destiny. It had taken all of five weeks for him to decide he didn't want to live without her. They'd fallen into each other, rushed in too fast without stopping to think or talk; at the time, it had made perfect sense.

All that he had done during the meager twelve months of their marriage he had done for them. His plans had always included her. The house he'd dreamed of one day building was designed with her in mind. Even when he was working alone, the foretaste of being with her again, of kissing her and touching her, was almost real. Did he need that kind of distraction? No.

"It's not just about that," he answered weakly. He could explain further, but he'd probably trip himself up, so he decided not to bother. He'd be a fool to tell her how much their separation hurt, and how much he still yearned for her, in spite of the grievous wound her lies inflicted on his soul. To admit that would give her more bargaining power than he was prepared to allow.

"What, then?"

He took in the anger and disappointment on her beautiful face, and suddenly felt exhausted. "Look, Sarita, let's set it down for the moment, okay? We're both tired and hungry. And dirty. Why don't we both have a shower, and by the time we're done, JoJo will be back to drop off the food, and we can eat and have a good night's sleep."

She snorted. "Walk away from it if you like, Matthias. As you always do. If you want to turn your back on it, on *us*, go ahead." She left the doorway and walked into her little room; he had no choice but to follow. Without looking at him, she shucked off her jeans and yanked her T-shirt over her head; in her haste, she almost got it caught in one of her earrings.

"It's not about walking away. It's about giving it a rest."

"It's had a *year's* rest."

"That's because every time we get into it, this happens. We end up screaming at each other. Aren't you tired of it?"

She popped the hook on her bra and tossed it overhead onto the back of her desk chair. That she was willing to undress before him came as a surprise, but she was probably too furious to care. That was Sarita all over. When she got mad, she got reckless. He averted his eyes. The last thing he needed to be confronted with right now was Sarita naked, cocoa skin gleaming, soft breasts—much more than a handful each—bobbing as she walked, and those dark, delightful nipples, like small seedless grapes . . .

She laughed mockingly. "You've seen them before."

"Not . . . recently," he managed to say.

She took off her panties unconcernedly, as if he were not even in the room, and walked through to the bathroom. He heard the shower turn on, but she didn't get into it. Instead, she came back into the bathroom doorway and said, "Go take a cold shower, Matthias." Then she was gone.

She'd let it drop. He should be glad for that, but he was strangely unsatisfied. He stood in the center of her room, something compelling him to follow her, but fear holding him back. Going back into the past would only cause them both anguish. Every time he brushed against her he got hurt, and he knew from deep within himself that that hurt would be more than he could bear.

It was good to be clean. Sarita had been wondering if she'd ever get the grime out from under her nails and the grit out of her skin, but a half-hour shower in Tobago's sweet, soft water had cured a number of ills. Even her hair was clean, rinsed free of salt. Her hair care regimen was especially important in such a climate: sun and seawater could easily turn straightened hair, even hair as strong, healthy, and professionally done as hers, into a thatch of reddened straw. She lavished it with brazil-nut oil and pinned it up on her head. She felt energized, in spite of the argument she and Matthias had had.

She found him around the back of the house, sitting on the low porch wall and facing the sea. The sun's last rays were fading from the sky, leaving a purple glow that barely distinguished it from the darkening water. He'd washed his hair to get the salt water out, and it hung loose about his shoulders, drying slowly in the warm night air.

Two white food boxes were perched on the wall, and Sarita's belly leaped for joy. Food! It would be her first real meal in ages. The lure of it brought her to sit next to him, without any thought for their earlier fight.

He held out a bottle full of enticing golden liquid. "Local beer. It's called Carib. It's very good."

She took it gratefully. The outside of the bottle was frosted, and there were tiny specks of ice forming in the neck. She brought it to her lips thirstily, but he stopped her before she could drink.

"Eat first. At least a few bites. Get something in your stomach before the booze." He chuckled. "Wouldn't want you keeling over on me."

He was actually making a joke! She threw him a covert glance. Maybe there'd be a cessation of hostilities just for tonight. She set the beer down on the wall and took up one of the boxes, eagerly opening it. As she did so, a puff of heat and aroma hit her in the face: spices and pepper. In her famished state, it smelled like heaven.

"What is it?" she asked. As if she cared. She was hungry enough to eat road kill, if it was cooked right.

"It's jerk chicken. There's a place up the road that makes the best jerk I ever had. And those," he pointed to three or four long, golden dumplings upon which the chunks of chicken nestled, "are called 'festival.'"

She looked at him. "You're kidding, right?"

"Nope. That's the name. Fried cornmeal dumplings. They fill you up like bricks: three of those and you're set until breakfast." He took a bite of his, but she was still curious.

"This is Tobagonian?"

"Jamaican," he managed to say with his mouth full. "Eat."

Sarita ate. The jerk chicken set off a glorious fire in her mouth, but the Carib beer soothed the burn. He looked as hungry as she felt; neither of them said a word until the last of the festival crumbs were cleared up and the final drop of beer drained. She let out a satisfied sigh.

He turned his head toward her and smiled. "You okay?"

"I'm *real* okay." She could feel the energy return to her bones. She put her hands up over her head, stuck her feet out before her, and stretched languorously. "I'm so full. In about twenty minutes I'm going to be asleep where I sit."

He got to his feet, cleared up the boxes and bottles, and disappeared into the house with them. He was back in moments. "It's barely eight o'clock." He pointed to his watch as if to back up his statement. "You fall asleep now, you'll be up again at three in the morning and you won't know what to do with yourself."

"But there's no TV, and I don't feel like reading."

He thought for a second and then said, "Come."

"What?"

"Let's walk it off." He jerked his head in the direction of the beach.

She smiled dryly. "Ah, an opportunity for me to see a bit of the place before I get shunted home again, huh?"

He flushed. "Sarita, let's keep it pleasant, all right? It's a lovely night, and we've just had a great meal. We could round out the evening amicably—"

"Show the way," she cut him off. No sense in letting things get nasty again.

He relaxed visibly and kicked the door shut. He held out an arm, which she didn't take. Instead, she frowned at the door. "Aren't you going to lock it?"

He smiled, and there was pride in his answer. "Why? This is Tobago. Everything in the house is safe."

She surprised herself by smiling back at him. "You sound like JoJo."

He fell into step next to her and they walked out onto the sand. "We're a proud people."

There he was again, identifying totally with the blood that ran through his veins. Whatever his weaknesses, he had a loyal and noble spirit that would never allow him to let his ancestors down. She had to admire that.

The détente they had called during dinner lasted through the stroll. Sarita let Matthias prattle on about the island as they walked, listening intently to stories she'd heard before about his childhood on the island, and the wild and restless vacation days he'd spent as a boy roaming the hills and diving off the Scarborough jetty into the murky waters of the main port. The moon and stars lit their way, giving them just enough light to keep them walking above the high-water mark. The scent of salt was thick in the air, coconut trees waved overhead, and crabs made way for them as they passed.

"Grab a couple of those," Matthias joked, pointing at the fat-legged blue crabs that raced sideways into the water, "they make a mean curried crab here. We could have a feast."

"I'm too full to chase crabs," she laughed back. "Maybe tomorrow night."

Matthias had the grace to hang his head.

She bit her tongue. "I forgot."

"Sorry."

"So you already got me on a flight, huh?" She was hoping for an overbooking at the airline to win her at least an extra day or two to fight her case.

He stopped walking. "Yes. After breakfast tomorrow."

She dropped into a squatting position on the sand, and he followed suit. "Why?"

"You know why," he began. "We've been over it and over it—"

"No, I mean why bother wanting a nice evening? Why bother taking me for a walk? You fed me, so you know I won't die on you. Why not just go about your business for the rest of the night and leave me be?"

The question seemed to puzzle him. He reflected on it for a long time, and then, instead of answering, said, "Sarita, listen to me. I promise you this: as soon as I'm done here in Tobago, or maybe in a few months when everything here is up and running and I can afford to take a little time off, I'll come back to Miami, and then we can talk."

"Talk? About what?" Something dark inside her told her she already knew about what.

The word was so ugly that not even his beautiful, sonorous voice could soften it. "Divorce."

She drew her knees up, propped her elbows on them, and let her head fall into her hands. Didn't he know by now that this was the last thing she wanted? As much as he loathed her, and as angry as he still was, even after all this time, couldn't he look at her and know that she still loved him? That no matter what had passed between them, all she had ever felt for him was love?

Somewhere at the bottom of her suitcase, which she hadn't bothered to unpack, was a large manila envelope. In that envelope was a sheaf of papers with words couched in lawyers' jargon, bearing the weapon that would, once it bore her signature, blow their marriage to smithereens like a firing squad's bullets slamming into the red square pinned to a condemned man's chest. Divorce papers, sent by Matthias half a year ago. She had read them many a time, removing them from their nest and poring over them until the black print blurred, but had never had the courage—or the cynicism—to sign them. That, she was still unable to do.

Her voice was muffled. "You asked already, and I said no. What makes you think I'd change my mind?"

"I don't know. Time, maybe. A year's worth of water has passed under the bridge. Maybe you've had the chance to think it over. All we ever do is hurt each other. We grind against each other like misfit gears."

"It wasn't always like that," she protested.

"It's like that now," he said firmly. "If we end this sooner rather than later, you'd have ample time to move on with your life. You could meet someone new who'd give you what you need."

Meet someone new? Didn't that thought even make him a tiny bit jealous? She remembered the knife that had turned in her gut when JoJo's sister, Janelle, had flirted so blatantly with him this morning. The elixir of love was always flavored with the tang of jealousy. Did he feel none for her? "Would you like that? To see me with someone new?"

"I don't know if 'like' is the right word. But it would be fair. You'd be able to start over, have children—"

A groan burst from her lips. What an unkind cut. Children! The idea of starting a family had been the field upon which they had fought their final, terrible battle, and the casualty of that awful confrontation had been their marriage . . . better not to think about it. Her lashes prickled and dampened. "That was cruel."

"It wasn't meant to be. Sarita, please believe me, I don't mean to hurt you. But I know that there's nothing you want more in life. And you know that I can't—"

"You *can,*" she shot back. "You just choose not—"

"I can't," he ground out. "I won't."

Now the tears were seeping through her fingers, and she was unable to stifle the sob that tore up from deep inside her. Instantly, his hands were over hers.

"Sarita? Are you crying?"

"What does it look like?" She knew she sounded petulant, but she didn't care.

He was pulling her against his chest, trying to tug her hands away from her eyes and replace them with his own. "Don't cry. Please."

So much hurt! She let her hands fall away and let her body go limp as he pressed her face into his long, springy hair. The soft dreadlocks, which fell loose around his shoulders, soaked up her tears, but not even his murmurings could soothe her anguish. Still, he whispered low words that made no sense, his arms a tight circle around her. Her body softened as he rocked her against him in the rhythm one usually used to calm a fractious baby.

Too much time had crawled by since she'd last been held. His body was hard, but at the same time warm and yielding. After her tremors slowed, he tilted her backward onto the sand. Small stones, shells, and bits of coconut husks poked her in the back and stuck in her hair, but she didn't mind. He cradled the back of her neck with one hand, and let the other run down along her side, from under her arm to her hip, over and over. Then, as his hand slid across her belly, her hips rose of their own accord, pressing against it.

Matthias lifted his head. His thin glasses did nothing to shroud the hunger that sprung to his eyes, taking them both by surprise. The tip of her tongue slid up past the space in her front teeth to moisten her lips in preparation for his kiss, but even so, when it did come, she was not prepared for it.

Mouth to mouth after so, so long. There were the faintest traces of spices, and a whisper of the beer they had shared, but overwhelming these was his own personal, manly scent. Salt, shampoo, and warm skin. His moustache lightly tickled her upper lip. She put her hands up to grasp his long hair, enjoying the roughness of it, twining a lock around her fingers and bringing it against her own cheek, stroking it against her face from temple to chin.

Without breaking their kiss, he shifted his weight, bringing himself up over her until he half lay upon her body. The hand that explored her hip moved to her breast, insinuating itself under her shirt to slide under the full curve before letting the nails graze the outer perimeter of the aureole, shocking her into crying out. His lips stifled her cry as he took the sound into himself.

Then it was her turn to touch. She released her hold on his hair and brought both hands down along each side of the triangle that was his back, letting them turn abruptly inward to his waist, and then out again slightly against his hips. His hard, sculpted buttocks grew rigid as she clutched them, responding to the pressure of her sharp nails even through the tough denim. She'd put many a scar there when passion had driven her past caution to an insane place where neither he nor she could feel the skin being broken by her fingernails.

"Matthias," she whispered. Her insistent hands pressed him closer to her. He responded with barely a grunt. He was as hard as an iron rod, and every molecule of her body was riveted by the sensation of the pressure he was bringing to bear against her pubis. She was so close. . . .

Rather than thrust up hard against her, his motions were barely perceptible, an increase and release of slight pressure. Blue jeans against blue jeans, and that hand making crazy circles around her nipple. His tongue probed farther in, past her willing lips, letting her suck briefly on the tip of it before whipping away. Then her body went rigid and she squeezed her eyes shut against the explosion of color. Her head hurt.

"Breathe, baby, breathe," he whispered.

"Huh?" she struggled past the giddying pain to ask.

"Inhale."

She realized she'd forgotten to draw in air. She opened her mouth and sucked hard, welcoming in the oxygen, until the pinching at the base of her skull let up. His face came into focus. He was smiling at her without any of his previous rancor. "You're amazing. It's been such a long time since I've been able to touch you. You felt so good."

He was amazing. How he could draw a response from her with so little effort! Far from easing her need for him, bringing her so swiftly to a peak had only left her dying for more. It was like having the icing without the cake. She responded to his smile with one of her own. "Matthias, take me back to the cottage. This isn't the right place for this."

The dark brows pulled together. "What do you mean?"

Was he being coy? "I mean we should take this inside. To your room, or mine. Whichever you prefer. Out here is so . . . exposed." She laughed. "We were a lot of things, but we've never been exhibitionists."

His smile faded. "Is that your idea of an offer I can't refuse?" He shot to his feet and put a few paces' distance between them. "Is this a new deal on the table, Sarita? You let me sleep with you, and I let you stay?"

She couldn't believe what he was implying. He had it all wrong! The pounding in her head was coming back. She scrambled up. "No! Matt . . . Matthias, I wasn't thinking about that. I was wondering . . . if you and I . . ." He'd wanted her too, hadn't he? His own body had told her so. She knew him, and knew how he responded. He couldn't lie to her about that. "I'm your *wife*, dammit. We aren't strangers, and we aren't virgins. There's nothing wrong with us seeing this through. We know our way around each others' bodies. And it's been such a long time . . ." Her voice trailed off when a disturbing thought assailed her. Maybe it had been a long time for her, but Matthias was stunning to look at, the kind of man who could stroll into a room and have any available female he chose. In the year they were apart, had he chosen?

He didn't give her the time even to voice her question, had she a mind to do so. His reply was cutting. "Long time or not, it doesn't matter. This isn't why I brought you out here. I didn't plan any of this; it just happened. And no, I don't plan on 'seeing it through,' as you put it. I only wanted you to feel better. I'm not inhuman; I couldn't bear to just sit there and watch you cry."

She couldn't be hearing right. Make *her* feel better? The sheer arrogance bowled her over. "Oh, so it was all for me? Charity? You give me a little solace like you hand a baby a pacifier?"

"It sounds ugly when you put it like that."

"It *is* ugly."

"It wasn't meant to be. I was trying to help."

Oh, so he was being Dudley Do-Right, rescuing her from sexual famine. "Do me a favor. Don't try to help again." She hoped the hurt in her voice would be masked by the ferocity of her answer.

He touched her lightly on the shoulder. "I'm sorry. I didn't mean it like that." He stepped in front of her, blocking her path to escape. "I felt it too, okay? You know me well enough to sense that. I . . ." he paused, as if the admission gave him pain. "I wanted you. But even if I wanted to take you into my bed tonight, and a part of me does—"

She snorted. "And we both know which part."

He went on unfazed by her barb. "Even if I wanted to be with you, it wouldn't be practical. We have no contraception. I never envisioned it would come to this, and I sure as hell never came here expecting to need any."

"And God forbid I get pregnant." She forced that final word out of her mouth, the "p" making a popping noise, as if it were reluctant to be realized by sound. This is what it always came down to, the stumbling block upon which their marriage always fell.

His cold voice told her that his anger was quickly rising to match hers. "You knew when you married me how I felt about that. You said you understood. You promised that we'd be careful and that we wouldn't try to have any children."

She tried to explain, to justify her reneging on their unholy deal, both to herself and to him. "I barely had time to think about it before we found ourselves married. Just a few weeks, remember, from the moment we met to the time we took our vows. And I know you said it, I remember you said it, and I said okay, but half of me didn't think you were really serious, and the other half wanted to have you so badly that I thought I didn't care. Because back then I thought that all I wanted was you. I thought I'd be happy just as we were: you, me, and all those damn fish. And then I realized I wanted more. And you wouldn't give it to me. You were so stubborn."

"I wasn't being stubborn. I kept up my side of the

bargain. I was a loving husband. I was faithful. I gave you everything you ever wanted. And then you went behind my back—"

"I did not go behind your back! Not at first. I begged you. I pleaded with you for just one child. I'd have been happy with just one."

"And then you let me down. You promised to love and honor, and what you did wasn't honorable." There was raw emotion in his words.

Her head dipped in shame. She'd admitted her guilt a hundred times over, and still he had not seen fit to forgive her. She felt exhausted; all she wanted was to crawl into her bed—alone. Whatever desire she had been feeling moments before was history now. It was a long way back to the cottage and she realized she better get started. "You're a hard man, Matthias," she told him as she stepped around him and began to walk.

He was at her side in an instant. She stopped abruptly, glaring at him. "Where d'you think you're going?"

"Walking you back home, wife," he answered with hard civility.

"Don't bother. It's not like I'd get lost. We walked a straight line here; I can walk a straight line back. I follow the bright lights and stay out of the water; it's hardly complicated."

"I'm not letting you walk home alone."

"Why not? *Your island* is safe, isn't it?"

"It's not that I'm worried about your safety. It's common courtesy; I brought you here, I take you back."

"Oh," she sneered, "spare me your macho sensibilities." She spun around to face him and pressed hard against his chest with the flat of her hand, pushing him back a few paces. "Don't you get it? I want to be alone. Or, at least, I don't want to be with you."

He looked resigned. "What do you want me to do, then?"

"Give me a fifteen-minute head start. Chase crabs. Sing to the fish. Whatever floats your boat. Just leave me alone." Without waiting for his agreement, she stalked off.

Well, he'd botched that good. That wasn't how he'd planned for things to go tonight. Matthias watched Sarita's receding back as she picked her way along the beach. The tide was at the high-water mark now, and the moon had slipped behind some clouds, so it was hard for her to see where she was going. She'd certainly get her feet wet. He felt an urge to sprint after her and escort her home whether she wanted it or not, but he knew his wife well enough to know that such a gesture would probably win him nothing more for his trouble than a slap in the face. He would have to content himself with keeping an eye on her all the way back home; luckily, he had an unobstructed view.

He looked around for a fallen coconut tree to sit on, found an old almond stump, and sat on that instead. There was a slight chill picking up in the wind and the water lapping at his sneakers wasn't exactly keeping him warm. The ache of denial in his groin was nothing compared to the dull thudding between his eyes. For the first time in ages, he fervently wished he hadn't given up smoking.

He screwed his eyes shut, trying to go over the evening scene by scene to spot exactly when it had turned into such a disaster. He knew he'd been cruel, and he felt ashamed of himself. But at the time, he'd wanted to hurt her. The hurt she'd inflicted on him on the day their marriage ended was wider and deeper than the ocean near which he sat, and he'd thought that maybe if he passed some back to her, his would be less. He'd been wrong. Hurting her had only caused her pain to rebound on him, tenfold.

What would have happened, he always asked himself, if he hadn't walked in on her in their bathroom back in their apartment in Miami? What if he hadn't stumbled in to find her in her bathrobe, standing over the toilet with a little round packet in her hand, carefully pushing that day's birth control pill out of its plastic bubble and into the water? What if he hadn't made her confess, amidst her tears and his furious shouts, that she'd been tossing her pills away, one a day, and leaving the pill packets on the bathroom counter, leading him to believe that, as she had promised, she'd been taking them? Would he still be happily married? Would the child that she'd desperately sought to conceive without his agreement have eventually come along?

To be honest, if she had become pregnant, he'd simply have assumed that the pill had failed—that happened sometimes. Maybe after he'd recovered from the shock he would be happy, and try to do well by his child, even though babies were never in the cards for him.

What had stung was her lying. Not verbal lies; he didn't remember ever having stopped to ask, "Sarita, did you take your pill today?" and hear her answer "Of course." But leaving the packets on the counter! Making love to him, night after night, with the full knowledge that deep in her belly, a little egg might be waiting to be transformed by his gift into a tiny replica of himself and Sarita.

She'd used him, turned him into an unwitting supplier of genetic material. Wanting a baby more than wanting to be honest with him. That . . . *burned!*

Standing barefoot in the bathroom, caught red-handed but still defiant, she'd raged back at him, calling him selfish for refusing her the one thing she desired more than anything else. But she'd agreed to abide by his decision before they were married, he had answered. She knew from the start that Reef Rescue would have to come first. How could he fulfill his obligations to the reef if he had even greater obligations to a child? Gone would be the endless nights he stayed up gathering data, and the weekends spent underwater, photographing, cataloging, learning. A man couldn't devote his life twice over: a choice had to be made. And he'd chosen.

Besides, how could he, who knew no father, ever be a good one? His own father had hopped on a plane and returned to Switzerland without knowing or caring that his child's heart beat under a woman's ribs. Matthias had grown up under a mother's care, but he had never experienced the caring guidance of a man—only the rigid and disapproving control of the minister who'd been his mother's father; a man who believed that to love the child he had been would have been to condone his mother's sin and who thought that a harsh, un-pampered upbringing would make him a strong man. What kind of father would that make him? Would it be just and right to inflict his bumbling ignorance upon an infant? Would it be fair for him, with all his faults, who had never held a baby or read a bedtime story, to cause a child to be brought into this world?

He followed Sarita with his eyes until she faded from sight before answering his own question: No, it wouldn't.

Five

"I can carry my own suitcase," Sarita informed Matthias tartly.

"I'm sure you can. But I'll do it for you anyway." He lifted it, and carried it out of the room.

Twisting her lips, she took up her carry-on luggage and her laptop and followed him. She was glad that he had at least sent JoJo out on a contrived mission, so the young man wouldn't be around to witness her humiliating ejection. Whatever he chose to tell JoJo about her sudden disappearance was up to him.

"And I don't know why you're even bothering to take me to the airport. If you'd let me call a taxi, I could spare you the burden of my company on the way over there."

"No big deal," he responded dryly, as if the sarcastic tone in her voice had not penetrated. "It's just a few minutes away. Nothing in Tobago—"

"Is far from anything else," she finished for him. She got in on the passenger side of the 4X4 and slammed the door. "So I've heard. Endlessly."

He started the engine, but made no move to drive off. Instead, he tapped his glasses back up on the bridge of his nose and turned to look at her. She met his inscrutable gaze with a glare.

He opened his mouth, but she stopped him. "Whatever you're about to say, Matthias, I don't want to hear it. You've made your decision; live with it. Don't try to explain it away or soften me up out of guilt. Just drive."

He stared at her for several long seconds, debating whether to comply or buck her demand, and then the truck lurched onto the road.

Such a sunny day, she thought. *So much peace here.* The landscape rolled past her window: small houses and stores, roadside vendors selling fruit off trays, and pastures in which untethered cows and goats roamed. Some even wandered along the roadsides, most of which had no paved sidewalks. She worried briefly for them, close as they were to the roadway, but they seemed unflappable. They determinedly headed off in whatever direction would take them home, eying passing vehicles with disdain. Everything here was so calm. She thought of busy, bustling Miami and groaned. Home and unemployment were eight hours away.

Better to try to be philosophical. She'd known from the start that she'd been taking a risk, that Matthias might not let her stay. She'd gambled, and she'd lost. She'd gambled with her marriage, and lost that, too. She'd been sure that all she'd have to do was conceive, convince him that their contraception had failed, and he'd accept it. Surely his passion for all living creatures would have extended to his own child forming in his wife's womb, whether or not he'd planned for its arrival! But he'd caught her before she could prove her theory right, flown into a rage, and accused her of being untrustworthy, of using him. Using him! Did he think she'd wanted a baby just for her and her alone? She'd wanted it for them, to make their circle complete! Was he so blind that he couldn't see that?

Well, she had to admit, completing their circle had only been part of the motive. The other part had been

finding a way to assuage her loneliness, to fill the endless empty hours in which his obsession held him
captive and her sole companions were the television
and his locked study door. Some women were football
widows; Sarita thought they should consider themselves
lucky. The football season eventually came to an end.
For Matthias, work went on forever.

"This is it." His voice cut into her thoughts.

Sarita blinked. They had already pulled up at the off-
loading zone in the small airport, and she hadn't even
noticed that they'd been approaching it. Things were
busy this morning: taxis, tourists, vendors, and idlers all
milled about, spilling onto the roadway.

Before she could get out, he spoke. "Sarita, you know
this isn't about last night, right?"

She kept her face blank. "Did something happen last
night?"

He ignored the jibe. "It's not personal. It's about
work. I need to do my job, and I can't if my head isn't
clear, okay? I'll mail you a check for the time you put in
at the cottage."

"I told you yesterday, I don't want your money. Save
it to pay for your new help wanted ad when you start
looking for someone to replace me." She popped open
the door and slid her legs out. Before she could stand,
he put a hand on her shoulder to stop her.

"And I meant what I said to you. As soon as I get a
chance I'll fly over, and we can see about ending this
marriage that's not doing either of us any good."

He'd rather end it than save it. That hurt so much!
"You just can't wait to cut me loose, can you?"

He shook his head. He looked almost sad. "I'm not
cutting you loose. I'm setting you . . . both of us . . . free.
We're trapped in something that causes us pain—"

"And you think ending it will hurt less?"

"It'll hurt for a while, and then you can start over again, maybe find someone who could give you—"

"Stop trying to throw me into some other man's arms! Doesn't the thought of that make you the least bit uncomfortable?" Couldn't he be just a *little* possessive? She thought about the large manila envelope in her handbag, wedged in with her ticket and travel documents, and for one brief, insane moment, considered digging it out and, without ceremony, signing it right there on the dashboard and tossing it into his face. If he wanted it, he could have it, and let him be damned a thousand times for his insistence.

Her teeth barely budged as she asked, "Got a pen?"

He looked briefly puzzled. "Why?"

"Do you have one?" The question didn't bear answering.

He leaned over a little and rummaged through the glove compartment, fishing out a plastic ballpoint. He held it out to her without another word.

One signature, she told herself. *A few black scratches on white paper. Do it, and walk free.* She stared at the pen as if it were a cyanide pill, as if they had both been shot down behind enemy lines and the only thing that remained was for them to do the honorable thing.

Reach for it . . . But her hand wouldn't move. Her brain made one or two feeble attempts to nudge it along, but her recalcitrant muscles resisted. Her wedding ring weighed a thousand pounds.

"Do you want it?" Matthias asked impatiently.

Did she?

A tap on the glass put her conundrum to a merciful end, and they both twisted their heads around to see the source of it. A lady security officer in a beige uniform was bending over and peering into the window.

"I'm sorry, sir," she said in her melodious accent.

"But you causing a little traffic pileup behind you. You not allowed to park here, you know."

Matthias glanced up into the rearview mirror to take in the jam he was causing and apologized profusely. "I'm sorry, ma'am. I wasn't parking. I was just dropping off a passenger."

The lady's eyes ran briefly over Sarita and returned to Matthias's face. She was unable to disguise the open admiration in them. "That's okay. You can let her off here and then park in the lot around the side. You aren't leaving the island as well, are you?" She gave him a flirtatious smile.

Matthias smiled back. "Not for a while."

Sarita rolled her eyes, leaped out, and ran around the back to haul her luggage out of the car before Matthias could come around to help her. She could do this herself.

"I'll go park and then come back in to see you off, okay?" he told her. He tossed the pen onto the dashboard.

As she watched it roll, she felt a painful popping in her ears as the pressure around her suddenly changed. "Don't bother," she snapped. "I'm a big girl; I know how to check myself in. I can make it all the way through to the departure lounge on my own. Why don't you get back to the office? The reef needs you more than I do." She wondered if the irony of her last few words would penetrate his thick skin, but he had a hide like the carapace of a leatherback turtle. He didn't even blink at the taunt.

He shook his head adamantly. "I'm coming to see you off, Sarita. Wait here." Before she could say anything back to him, he drove off.

She stood at the curb, arms folded, scowling. How he fancied himself a gentleman in all the small ways: open-

ing and closing doors, lifting her heavy bags, and seeing her off on a flight he'd forced her onto. But in the
big things, the things that mattered, he was stubborn
and implacable. Well, if he thought he could park and
take his sweet time coming back, and still find her waiting at the curb like a waif, he was sorely mistaken.

Heroically, and driven by pique more than anything
else, she managed to get her suitcase, carry-on bag, and
laptop to the check-in line. Things were even busier
here than they were out at the roadside: harried clerks
tagged baggage, punched in data, and tore off tickets
at a quick pace, all the while managing to smile warmly
at each passenger. The line moved slowly.

Strangely enough, she'd made it all the way to the
counter and Matthias still hadn't returned. Sarita
frowned, looking around, trying to see out to the parking lot to spot him coming. After all, it wasn't that far
away.

"Ticket, please." The slender girl behind the counter
gave her a strained, tired smile and held out her hand.

Numbly, Sarita handed it over, murmuring answers
to the usual questions about who had packed her bags
and whether they'd been out of her sight at any time.
The young woman glanced at her passport. "You came
in only three days ago. Leaving so soon?"

Sarita shrugged. "It was a business trip. A brief one."

The girl squinted at the name on the passport. "Dr.
Sarita Rowley. Any relation to the Tobago Rowleys?
They're very well-known on the island."

"No," she snapped. If she heard that question *one
more time* . . . The girl's smile slipped a little, which
made Sarita feel bad. She hadn't meant to be so curt.
She took her boarding pass and stepped out of the line
with an unspoken apology. International flights were
checked in three hours in advance, and Matthias had

evidently been so anxious to get rid of her that he'd brought her here dead on time. She had more than two hours left to kill, and still no sign of him.

She wandered back out to the roadway, frowning. Had he really been so mean as to drive off without saying good-bye? True, she was the one who had demanded it, but that didn't mean he actually had to *do* it! Trust him to be so contrary!

She paced the length of the drive, turned around, and paced back, with her carry-on over one shoulder and her laptop cutting into the other. The combination of irritation and anxiety made her stomach numb. She hated flying; boats were so much more pleasant. Matthias knew that planes made her nervous. Surely he hadn't run out on her!

With each passing minute, her unease grew. Maybe she should go on through to Departure and get it over with. Still, there was a lingering hope that Matthias was toying with her, waiting until the last minute, letting her sweat before turning up . . . but that would be petty. As much of a pain as he was, he was a man who stood on principle, and whose word was as good as gold. He prided himself on that, and no matter how down and dirty their fights became, he had never deviated from his sense of honor. If he said he'd be there to see her off, he'd be there.

Unless, of course, something was . . .

. . . wrong.

The acute and painful feeling that something *had* happened to him assailed her. But what? The parking lot was at best a few hundred yards away. He couldn't have had an accident: she would have seen the commotion. A holdup? Didn't he say the island was safe? It wasn't that, but it was *something*. Years of loving this man, and of carrying him around inside her in a pri-

vate, special place, told her she was right. Matthias was
in trouble, and he needed her.

"Oh, God." Her bag banged painfully into her side
as she ran the length of the driveway and over to the
unguarded parking lot. Wasn't there supposed to be security here, or was there so little car theft on the island
that nobody bothered to watch over the lot? Apart from
one or two motorists retrieving or leaving their cars,
the place was quiet. She spotted the Reef Rescue 4X4
at the far end of a row of cars and raced over to it, heart
pounding.

The window was down on the driver's side, so she
headed there first. Matthias was sitting there, silent and
unmoving. One arm was draped over the steering
wheel, and his head lay upon it.

"Matthias!" Sarita let her bags fall, and a tinkling
sound upon impact told her the laptop had met with
an untimely end. Without stopping to pick it up, she
yanked open the front door, and Matthias almost
flopped out onto her. It took all her strength to shove
his dead weight back up onto the high seat.

Frantically, she ran her hands over his body, searching for a wound. No blood. Nothing. Holding onto his
long hair, she lifted his head, letting it fall back onto
the headrest. What she saw chilled her to the bone.

His face was swollen into a shapeless mass: eyes
puffed shut and his normally high, fine nose a potato
that spread across his face. His lips were so fat and thick
that barely a sound escaped them, and his throat
bulged so much she was sure she wouldn't be able to
span it with both hands. The awful sight of him told her
all she needed to know.

There was no wound. This was an allergic reaction: a
bad one. Something must have stung him, and, as always, as resistant as he was to corals and the occasional

sea urchin venom, land-bound stinging creatures were his kryptonite. A single sting could shut his system down. What had done this? She searched his face, looking for a bite or left-behind stinger that she could pull out, but his skin was too swollen to reveal anything. His hand slipped off his lap, and as she caught it, she had her answer. A small, brown winged insect lay crushed in his palm. He'd managed to swat it, but not before it had done its damage.

She flipped open the glove compartment, rooting about for the little red case of emergency hypodermics that Matthias always carried with him. It held enough epinephrine to get his haywire system back under control, and would keep him alive long enough to get him medical attention.

Nothing there.

She tried to tilt him over onto his side to search the pockets of his jeans, but found only his wallet, a penknife, and keys. Where was the kit?

"Matthias, listen to me!" She slapped his face, willing him to remain conscious. "Where's your kit? You need a shot. Where is it?"

There was a soft, liquid burble from his lips, and then a hoarse rasp. She sucked her teeth in frustration. Maybe he was in such a hurry to get her out of the house this morning that he'd forgotten to stow it in the glove compartment. Was he crazy?

She looked at him again and to her horror noticed that his skin, which had been bright red from the reaction, was slowly turning blue. She put her ear to his lips, listening for his breathing, but there was none.

No air! His airways were swelling shut, denying him breath. She tore down the front of his shirt, letting the buttons pop, eyes fixed on his chest, willing it to rise and fall, but there was nothing. With one hand clamped over his nose, she pressed her lips to his, blowing into his mouth, and then looking down to see if his chest would rise.

Panic now. He'd gone into shock, and the problem with the air lay not in his nose or mouth, but lower down, deep in the throat, where his muscles had gone into such a spasm that they would not relax, even when not doing so would mean certain death.

Sarita hopped out of the truck and ran to the entrance of the lot. She needed a doctor! Matthias was going and going fast. This was an airport. There'd be ambulances about.

But if her geography was correct, the hospital was half an hour away. Not far in real terms, but Matthias didn't have half an hour. Three minutes, four minutes, tops, was all the brain had before it started to die. Even if she did manage to get him to a hospital alive, that precious, brilliant mind would be . . . something else.

"God." Her only prayer was that divine name, whispered over and over again. "God, God, God." She was begging an entity Matthias didn't even believe in to save his life. Even in her terror, the irony was not lost on her. Her husband was not a praying man. He had never sneered at her when she sought solace in her staunch Baptist upbringing in times of strife, or when she reveled in it in times of joy, but he had never joined her either.

Too bad. She would have to have faith enough for both of them. *She* believed, and that was enough. "Tell me what to do, Father," she murmured. "Help me save him. Find me a doctor!"

Then she remembered: *she* was a doctor! Not a physician, but she'd done her share of anatomy. Marine biology was a specialty; to practice it, you first had to be a biologist, plain and simple. She'd dissected quite a few cadavers. She knew the human body as well as she knew any other living organism. If someone had to help Matthias now, it was she. She ran back to the truck.

He was silent, not even struggling for air anymore, and sinking fast. The base of his throat pulsed frantically, Adam's apple bobbing, and the indentation below it was sunken like a tiny valley. There was only one thing to do. If she couldn't get air in through his nose or mouth, it would have to get in through his throat—via a hole she'd have to make.

She snatched up his penknife and flicked it open. No time to sterilize it: he was in far less danger of dying from any future infection he could pick up off the knife than he was of dying of suffocation right now. With a hand on his forehead, she pushed his head back, baring his throat to her. She pressed the point of the knife to the little well there.

Then she hesitated. She loved this man. They'd gone through a lot together in the past: made love, fought, and made up again. She'd said unkind things to him and he to her. But could she cut him?

She could, if his life depended on it. Shunting aside fears of accidentally hitting a vein, slitting his throat, or going too deep, she set the tip of the blade against his tortured skin . . . and pushed it in. Past skin, past muscle, past cartilage, until the knife popped through into empty space, and then she withdrew.

Blood spurted and rolled down his neck, dribbling onto his chest and down until it was soaking into the fabric of his shirt. It made her hands slippery. The incision was barely an inch wide, but it was a slit, not a hole, and would be of no use to her if she couldn't widen it somehow and hold it open long enough to force air in.

On the dashboard—the ballpoint pen! The one she'd almost used to sign away her love. She tore off the small cap on the end with her teeth, and drew out the nib and inky strip from the other, leaving her with a hard, plastic tube that was perfect.

Gently, she eased it in through the slit, into that open space in his throat just below the barrier of contorted muscle, her own fear escaping through her teeth in a frantic whine.

"Breathe, Matt." That was what he'd told her last night, out on the beach, after she'd gone limp under him. "Breathe, baby." She placed her lips on the other end of the tube and blew.

And his chest rose under her hand. Sarita almost sobbed in relief. She blew again, and again, maintaining that rhythm that he liked: six seconds in, pause for three, and six out. He showed no sign of consciousness, but two or three minutes had passed and then he was breathing on his own, air whistling in through the narrow tube. Slowly, the blue tinge began to fade from his lips. She threw her arms around his limp body in relief.

But he wasn't out of the woods yet. His body's defense system had gone mad because of the wasp's invading venom, and the swelling would not go away without medical help. After making certain he was breathing fully on his own, she carefully propped him up against the seat, strapping him in with the seatbelt to make sure he wouldn't slump forward again and dislodge the breathing tube, and ran for help.

A man and woman were on their way out of the parking lot, headed for the main terminal. She caught up with them and grabbed onto the man's arm. "Please," she panted. He stopped and stared. It took her a few moments to realize what a sight she must seem, hair wild, eyes frantic, blood smeared on her hands and dress. "I need a doctor," she explained. "My husband needs help. Please, please, can you get me an ambulance?"

The man took in the fear in her eyes, dislodged himself from her anxious grip, and then said, soothingly, "Wait here. I'll be back."

Six

Matthias felt like an idiot. Of all the stupid, stupid things: leaving home without his epinephrine kit. He knew how anaphylactic shock worked: it was fast, and it could be lethal. Running out of the house without checking to make sure his kit was on him was near suicidal. It wasn't enough to tell himself that Sarita had so annoyed him that day that all he wanted to do was get her to the airport. That was a cop-out. He'd been careless and had almost paid for his mistake with his life.

And to think she had been the one to save him. He would never know what had made her come out to the parking lot to look for him. She had, after all, told him to go away and let her depart in peace. She could just as well have boarded the plane, assuming that he'd acceded to her request, leaving him to die an ignominious death in that hot, lonely lot. But the fact was that she had come back, and he would always be grateful.

Not that he'd shown it. She'd watched over him for five days, and for five days he'd been growling at her like a bear with a sore head, hating his confinement, even while admitting that his body needed rest. But in spite of his bad mood, she'd been nothing but nice: caring, gentle, and concerned, and seeing to his every comfort. She even patiently sat next to him while he griped, groused, and demanded his laptop so that he could work from his bed. Embarrassing, and unfair. Next time she came to see him he'd try to be more gracious, even though his throat hurt like the devil.

He patted the small bandage at the base of his throat lightly, comforted by the thought that it would soon come off and all that would be left to remind him of the ordeal would be a small scar. He grinned. Sarita was handy with a scalpel. Good thing she had majored in biology, rather than philosophy or French!

As if he'd dreamed her up, she was there, pushing aside the door with her bottom and backing into the room, trying to keep a tray steady with both hands. From where he stood, he could see a bowl of lentil soup sloshing about, and next to it, a tall glass of one of those hideous nutrition drinks she insisted was going to give him all the vitamins he supposedly needed. She set it down on the desk and turned to him and smiled. "Hungry?"

"Not for more soup," he growled, forgetting his promise to be nice. The puncture wound in his throat hurt with every word. "Why are you so insistent on pouring so many liquids down my throat? By the time you're done with me, I'll be a hundred and three percent water!"

She shrugged, facing him. "You want to try swallowing solids with that hole in your neck? Be my guest. I'll get you a nice heaping plate of whatever you wish. What'll it be? Baby back ribs?"

The very thought of it made him cringe. He took the bowl and sat by the window. "Well, maybe I'll pass on the ribs for another day or two. But no more. If I starve myself any longer, I'll get awfully skinny."

"You already are skinny."

"I'll be worse." He sniffed at the soup. "Smells good." She clapped her hands together, mocking him. "Oh my God, is that a compliment? Next thing you know, you'll be saying 'thank you.'"

He was dying for a spoonful of the soup, but he set the bowl down carefully, and came to stand near to her, taking her hand in both of his. "I haven't thanked you yet." It wasn't a question.

She shook her head gravely.

"I owe you my life, Sarita. There's nothing I can ever do to make up for that. You came looking for me. You didn't have to. And when you found me, you didn't freeze. You knew what to do. It took a lot of guts, too. Cutting into a living person. You and I were never trained to do that, and you could easily have panicked. But you didn't." She was smiling shyly at his words, looking almost bashful. Her hand was warm in his. As his gratitude deepened into something else, he had the urge to put his arms around her, sit down, and pull her onto his lap so he could hold her close. But he didn't want to startle her, so instead he kept on talking, even though the effort hurt.

"And then you stayed on and kept everything going these past five days. The cottage looks great. And everything's all filed away and in order. You didn't have to do that."

Mere mention of the contentious issue of work made her pull her hand away. "I wanted to. At least I got to make some sort of contribution to Reef Rescue: what I did, I did for the project, not for you."

"I'm grateful anyway."

She turned to go, but he stopped her before she could disappear.

"Sarita."

She halted, but didn't bother to turn around. "What?"

"Stay."

"*What?*"

He wanted to close the space between them, but didn't dare, lest she run away. "You can make a bigger contribution to the project if you stayed." He tried to make light of his invitation. "Haven't you heard? I'm in the market for a good biologist."

She looked puzzled. "You want me to stay on for you until you're better? You're practically good as new. Knowing you, you'll be out on the boat in another day or two. So why bother? Can't JoJo do whatever needs to be done until then?"

"No," he explained patiently, unsure whether she was being deliberately obtuse or if she really hadn't understood. "I wasn't talking about hanging around until I'm better. I meant the research assistant position. The job you came here to do." He waited for understanding to sink in. She'd be so happy, getting to work on the project at last. The thought of making her happy, of putting a smile on her lovely lips, made him feel warm all over.

She scowled, taking him by surprise. Her voice was gruff. "What's that all about? Why offer it to me now? A few days ago you were adamant that I couldn't cut it. Why the change of heart? Is this some sort of reward for . . ." She waved her hand at his neck. "For punching a hole in you?"

She made him feel so clumsy! He was trying to thank her properly, but she wasn't letting him do it with grace. "It's the only way I know how to give back something of what you gave me. Isn't staying what you wanted all along?"

"Not if you're only doing it because you think you're beholden to me. I want you to give it to me because I'm the right person for the job, not because you feel guilty."

"But you *are* the right person for the job."

"That's not what you said before."

He tried to explain. "No, I never had any doubts as to your abilities. I just didn't want our personal baggage causing problems with our work."

"I can keep our personal *baggage*, as you call it, out of this, if you can."

"I can."

"Good." She walked away.

He followed her into the living room, not wanting her to go yet, even though she was angry with him. The fact that he was dressed only in light cotton shorts, and that the front door was yawning open and facing the road, didn't even warrant a second thought. "So you'll stay?" He wished he didn't sound so anxious.

She nodded mutely.

"And will you stay for lunch, too?" he pointed at the bedroom. "It's awful hard sitting there eating soup by myself." He had to resist the urge to cross his fingers. She'd been very good at pandering to his needs—and if he were honest, he'd admit he made a demanding invalid—but she'd never stayed more than a few minutes, just long enough to bring him his meals, lend him a book or the paper, or offer him a cold drink when the afternoon grew hot. He was starving for company, and, to his surprise, *her* company was at the top of his list. He'd brought his chessboard with him to Tobago; maybe after he'd eaten. . . .

The grin on her face made his blood chill. "Sorry," she told him. She didn't look sorry at all. "I have plans for lunch."

Tell me I didn't hear you right, he wanted to say. "Plans?" What plans could she possibly have? She'd been on the island a week. Had she met someone in that short space of time?

She was deliberately nonchalant. "Yeah. Plans. You know, for a meal with another person? As a matter of fact, I'll be gone for most of the afternoon." She schooled herself into a look of fake concern. "Will you be all right on your own?"

It was only then that he noticed she wasn't wearing her usual denim shorts and T-shirt, but instead wore a pretty lemon sundress and leather sandals. Her hair, which she'd tied in a red-and-white floral-print bandanna to keep the dust out as she worked, was freshly washed and smoothed down, curling slightly at her nape. She was wearing *lipstick!* He shifted a little so she couldn't see his chagrin.

Who was she going out with? Was it a man? And if so, who was he, where the devil had she met him, and what were his intentions? He felt like a surly, protective old uncle, and she was . . . unconcerned. He wondered, briefly, if she were taunting him. If she was, he wouldn't give her the pleasure. "I'll be okay," he said, shortly.

"Good," she said. She gave him a cheery wave and a sweet smile. "Take care, now." With that, Sarita shouldered her bag, scooped up the keys to the 4X4, and walked out of the house.

Sarita pushed her sunglasses up onto her nose, which was a little slippery from sunscreen. Her sandals made a hollow noise on the stone path. She couldn't resist a giggle at the memory of the stunned look on her husband's face as he learned she was going out to lunch. He'd looked so thrown that she hadn't bothered to ruin the effect by telling him that her "date" was with a minister, and one who was old enough to be her father at that.

She had to admit that she hadn't given much thought to calling Colin Constantine at all, even though he'd been so kind to her on the airplane. But after a few days of Matthias storming around his room, whining about his liquid diet, grousing about the hours of work lost, and complaining about where she chose to put this filing cabinet or that piece of equipment, she was desperate for anyone, *anyone*, who would offer her distraction from her homicidal impulses. Her mother used to tell her that there was nothing more ornery—or more childish— than a sick man. She made a note to tell her mother, in her next postcard home, that she was right.

When by chance she lit upon Colin's card, she'd shrugged and made the call. He'd sounded delighted to hear from her, and immediately invited her over for a late lunch at the rectory, after the Sunday morning congregation had left for home. "I'm cooking," he had informed her, sounding mighty pleased with himself. "A Tobago specialty. Flying fish and coo-coo." She wasn't sure if she dared ask what coo-coo was, but it sounded better than another afternoon in her husband's company, so she happily accepted. Besides, she hadn't been any farther than the hardware store to buy a regulator for the stove, so she leaped at the chance to go exploring. She checked her purse one last time to ensure she hadn't forgotten the directions to the Mount Moriah Moravian Church, and stuck her keys into the door of the vehicle.

A spray of gravel left her coughing, and the thump of dub music pounding from a monster sound system almost obliterated the squeal of brakes. Sarita wiped the dust from her eyes in time to see Janelle leap from a trendy car that looked like it cost a whole lot more than Janelle's boat—her main source of income—was worth. Sarita blinked fast, willing her eyes not to tear up under the assault, as the woman approached her.

"Gwen." The smile didn't hang around long enough to be returned. "Going out?"

Since the truck door was open, and Sarita already had one leg inside, she didn't think she needed to confirm what was a pretty accurate guess on Janelle's part. Instead, she prodded her lips into a smile and asked. "How are you doing?"

Janelle shrugged without answering, her eyes not holding Sarita's for more than a second. She patted her hair and smoothed down imaginary wrinkles in the white tank top and shorts so brief, that she looked like a page torn out of an underwear catalog. Sarita recalled that the island had decency laws that forbade appearing on the streets in swimwear, but from what she could see, the lawmakers had been a little shortsighted. Swimwear Janelle's getup was not, but it was briefer than any bathing suit Sarita owned. The over-friendly shorts revealed half her small, muscled butt—making Sarita feel like a double-wide parked next to a Ferrari. The stark white fabric, of a brilliance not often found in nature, set off the woman's skin tone to perfection. Janelle glowed like a black pearl. Sarita tried not to snort. *Why*, she wondered, *does this woman rub me the wrong way so much?*

"How's Matt?" Janelle asked. She raised a laden basket and waved it before Sarita's nose. "I made him some cow-heel soup, with lots of cornmeal dumplings . . ."

Cows have heels? Sarita wondered.

". . . Got to keep his strength up." A curve of Janelle's brow telegraphed how important it was for that particular man's strength to be maintained.

That's why, she answered her own question. Janelle had been by at least once a day, bearing all kinds of concoctions, bottles of coconut water, hand-squeezed orange juice, and bowls of chilled watermelon chunks, and served them to Matthias with much concern and simpering. As if Sarita couldn't take care of him herself! It brought her great comfort to know that Matthias was all souped out and one bowl away from springing a leak. Besides, cow-heel soup sounded revolting. She wondered if the whole hoof was in there but tried not to dwell on the image. She was sure that the island boy in the cottage would be delighted for some good old grass-roots food, the way his mother used to make, instead of her boring old lentils and cream of chicken. And if the concoction left him further *strengthened,* to anyone else's advantage, well . . . A pain like a kick in the stomach kept her from going down that road.

"Feel free." She waved at the door to the house. "I'm sure your soup'll just make his day."

Janelle dismissed her with another split-second smile. "Sure." She took a few steps and then turned to glance at her car. "Am I blocking you?" she asked. Her voice was honey.

Sarita glanced at Janelle's shiny chrome bumper, and then at her own. If there was a foot between them, that was about it, and there was only one way out of the drive. She pursed her lips, but decided that a bullet to the gut would be a lot more desirable than admitting to the other woman that wriggling her way out of that tight fit would take quite some skill, not to mention elbow grease at the steering wheel. "Not at all," she insisted, and watched Janelle throw open the door and saunter inside.

Sarita hopped into the driver's seat and started the engine. She was making it out of there without Janelle's help even if she drove into a ditch trying.

Seven

"You made it!" Colin Constantine's florid face was beaming with pleasure as she spun into the narrow drive at the front of the small church. He was, not surprisingly, clad in ancient, baggy jeans and a stained T-shirt, looking as if he'd spent half the afternoon digging trenches. In fact, he was trailing a shovel behind him, making an unholy clatter on the rough bitumen driveway. Four or five small children, barefoot and with little more than a shred of clothing on their backs, left his side and trotted to meet her, arriving alongside well before he did.

Sarita was startled at the spike of delight she experienced at seeing him, but reminded herself that his was at least a genuinely friendly face, the face of someone who was truly glad to see her. He tugged off his heavy leather work glove and held out his hand to assist her down from the truck. She took it, pleased at his courtesy.

"Gardening?" she asked, as she shut the door and placed her bag over her shoulder.

He nodded. "Molding up the pigeon pea trees. They'll be ready for harvest any day now."

"Part of your duties as minister?"

He grinned. "Not exactly. Actually, we do have a groundskeeper. But fiddling in the garden gives me a good excuse not to be inside working on my sermons.

Too nice an afternoon to be thinking." He looked her over, as if trying to realign whatever memory he had of her face with what he was seeing now.

"You look flushed," he observed. "Had trouble finding the place?"

She wiped away a few droplets of perspiration at her hairline and whistled. "No, but I have to admit just driving—driving *anywhere* on the island—is a trial in itself. I think I sprouted a gray hair every five minutes, for every time I had to remind myself they drive on the left here. And another gray hair for every time someone *else* seemed to forget!"

Colin circled her once, pretending to examine her for silver streaks. "Looks perfectly black to me." The wrinkles around his eyes deepened.

"It'll probably be a delayed reaction," she responded dryly.

"Come then," he motioned for her to follow him. "Maybe a hot lunch will head it off at the pass."

By now, the children were crawling all over the 4X4, unabashedly peeping inside, tooting the horn, and chattering among themselves. One even slipped her little hand into Sarita's and smiled up at her, showing perfect white teeth. The child sported the first three or four inches of baby dreadlocks, her thick hair rolled into twists that could not agree on a direction in which to point.

Sarita felt a pang deep in her soul, and her mind flashed at once on Matthias, and the children they couldn't have, wouldn't have, because of his refusal. She touched the small girl's cheek lightly, wishing she'd thought to bring candy with her. But from the thinness of the children's limbs, she wondered, fleetingly, if they didn't need something more filling than sweets.

"From the neighborhood," Colin explained as he

walked. The children detached themselves from the vehicle and followed. "Most of them are home alone all day, or in the care of older siblings. Parents out working, or looking for work. Even on a Sunday. Poverty doesn't really take a day off."

"What about school?"

He scratched his head, and his eyes grew sad. "Some are enrolled, some aren't. Places are limited, especially in more rural areas. And for those who have a place, most of them can't afford the books, or shoes or clothes. Some can't afford the transportation to get to school, and some who make it there don't get breakfast at home, so they wander away because they're hungry."

"So what do they do here?"

"The church tries its best. We give them something to eat, and take turns teaching them basic things, like reading, writing, and a few other skills, like gardening." He gestured toward the rows of fat bushes that ran the length of the far wall. "They're the ones that planted the peas. I'm just giving them a hand with the heavy work. And when the crops come in, they either eat them here or take some home to their families."

The little girl was still clinging to Sarita's hand, sucking her other thumb and happily humming to herself. Sarita had to stifle the urge to grab her and run, to take her somewhere and buy her pretty clothes, and feed her something fattening to put some meat on her bones.

Colin saw the wistfulness on Sarita's face. "That's Lisa. Her mother died of AIDS last year. It's pretty prevalent on the island, thanks to the heavy tourism. Employment is low, and every plane brings visitors with foreign currency. Some of the young people don't think they have much of a choice, so they take their chances. Sometimes they win, sometimes they lose."

She thought of Matthias and the circumstances of his birth. It seemed that little had changed in over thirty years. "And her father?"

He shook his head. "None that I know of. She lives with her grandmother, who's blind in one eye. The church sends the old lady a food basket once a month, but that's the best it can do. It's a small church, living off offerings and grants. If it could, I'm sure the church would set up a more formal system to help them." He paused. "Maybe soon, I hope. For the children's sake."

Sarita was unable to drag her eyes away from Lisa's cherubic face. The little girl stared up at her, mouth open, a smile hovering around the thumb she was sucking. "This little one doesn't say much," Colin explained. "Goes for days without so much as a peep."

"Hello, sweetie," Sarita said encouragingly.

The thumb popped out. "Hello." The girl chortled, surprised at herself, and clapped both hands over her mouth in a bid to keep any more wayward words from straying.

Colin made a great show of pretending to look put-upon. "Well," he harrumphed. "That's made a liar out of me."

Sarita laughed. "Nonsense. That's her quota for the day." She was probably right. Thumb back in place, Lisa lapsed back into her contented humming.

Colin led Sarita around the side of the church; it was the smallest she had ever seen. As she glanced through the open door, she wondered if it could even hold a hundred people. A faded sign above the doorway told her it was established in 1927, and the wooden building with the sloping roof looked every day of it. He stopped and turned to the children. "Run along inside, now." He waved his arms like someone shooing baby chicks. "Reverend Owens has lunch for you. We'll finish up in the garden later, okay?"

With laughing good-byes, the children parted their company. Little Lisa hesitated, staring up into Sarita's eyes with her own round black ones, but the lure of food was too great, and it was only when the little hand tugged to be released that Sarita realized how tightly she had been holding on. Alone with Colin, she faced him, feeling suddenly shy.

He held out his hand to beckon, and she followed him through a small doorway. It led to a utilitarian but spotless kitchen, which was filled with the smells of fried fish, onions, and garlic. He washed his hands at the sink, carefully soaping up to the elbows, then dried them on a tea towel.

"Have a seat, Gwen. Let's see if a plate of my cooking counteracts the trauma of your ride over here or makes it worse."

Her heart sank to the level of her growling belly. Gwen. That was how she'd introduced herself to him on the plane. A prickle at the back of her neck made her feel as though astute, condemning eyes were trained on her, and that was not surprising. They might only be in the *kitchen* of a church, but they were in a church nonetheless. It was not the best place for keeping up a charade.

When she didn't return Colin's smile he set about serving them both, laying out whole flying fish, which had been fried with their heads on, onto big, old-fashioned china plates, and placing large yellow balls that looked like speckled dumplings next to them. They were the size of oranges and looked as if they would sit in the stomach like a brick.

"Coo-coo balls," Colin smiled. He seemed proud of his culinary skills. "As promised. Cornmeal and okra. Good.

Sticks to the old ribs. One of those and you're all set until dinner." He handed her a plate, sat opposite her, and bowed his head. "Shall we say grace before we eat?" Before she could answer, Colin began, "Father, I want to thank you for bringing Gwen here today safely. . . ."

That was enough! Guilt propelled her hand up to halt him before he could continue with his prayer. "Colin, wait. I can't . . ."

He looked down at the plates and then up at her, puzzled. "What, you don't eat fish?"

"I love fish. It's just that—"

"Is the coo-coo too strange-looking for you? I promise you'll like it. But if you don't, I could make you some rice."

His anxiety to be a good host embarrassed her. "They look delicious." As a matter of fact, they smelled good, and her stomach protested her delay. "It's just that I can't let you say grace like this. . . ."

His brows lifted. "You got something against Protestant prayers? I assure you, we're all praying to the same—"

"No!" The last thing she wanted to do was offend him. "*I'm* Protestant." She thumped her chest. "Baptist, to be exact. But even if I weren't, it wouldn't matter. It's got nothing to do with—"

"Would you like to say grace instead?" he offered.

"Colin!" If she could only get a word in edgeways! "Let me speak. Please."

"Okay." His hands were still clasped, but he was silent, expectant.

She wet her lips. How was she to admit to this kind, friendly man that she'd been lying to him? The only way to do it, she supposed, was to do it. She held her breath and plunged in. "I don't want you to think . . . I want you to know that I'm not who I said I am."

"Oh?" His face reflected not the slightest reaction.

"I'm not Gwen. Not really. I mean, Gwen is my name . . . middle name. But it's not really my name. Not what everybody calls me."

"Okay."

"And my last name isn't Davis."

Colin eyed her gravely, still betraying nothing. Not chagrin, not surprise. "And what is your name, Gw . . . uh . . . dear?"

"Sarita." She exhaled in a gust.

"Sarita," he repeated contemplatively. "Pretty name."

"Thank you." She waited. Wasn't he going to ask why? Instead, he held her dark eyes with his steady, unflinching gray ones; what she saw in them was not condemnation, but patient expectation.

She drew a steadying breath. "I'm really Sarita Rowley." Before he could query the island origins of the name, she rushed on. "My husband was born here. His mother was a minister's daughter, and she died when he was very young. He was just like . . ." she pointed in the general direction of the yard. "Like those children, straying and half lost. Something a tourist left behind. He's American now, but all he's ever thought about, all he's ever dreamed about, has been coming back to make a difference."

"With the reef?"

She smiled. "You remembered."

He inclined his head in confirmation, but waited for more.

"I took the name so I could follow him. Well, not follow *him*, exactly." She felt heat in her face. There was a Freudian slip, if there ever was one! "So that I would join his team, work on the reef project with him."

"Couldn't you just . . ." He waved his hand, not needing to finish.

She shook her head, her glossy hair swinging against

her cheeks. "We're . . ." The word "separated" was too painful to voice, so she tried another tack. "He wouldn't have wanted me here. He wouldn't have hired me if he knew I was the person applying for the position. I really *am* a doctor." This last she said defensively. It was important to her that he know that not *everything* she'd told him on the plane was a lie.

He seemed to understand. "So you made up a name, just long enough to get you hired."

"Sort of."

"And when you got here?"

She smiled ruefully. "Lightning and thunder. Sound and fury." She could see clearly in her mind the incredulous look that had preceded the tempest that Matthias had unleashed upon her that first night, and the memory alone made her shiver.

"But you're still here."

"I'm still here." She inclined her head toward her plate. The food was smelling better and better by the second, and seemed a darn sight more pleasant than the bitter taste of pain that was flooding her mouth. "He changed his mind. He'll let me stay, for the while. So I can help, too." She sighed expressively. "It's a long story."

Colin caught her longing look and said crisply, "Too long to hear on an empty stomach, I'll bet. You can tell me more, if you like, or you can keep it for another time. But whatever you choose to do, do it on a full tummy, okay?"

"Okay."

He bowed his head again. "Grace first. Then, we eat."

When Sarita got back, Matthias was at the door waiting for her. It was already growing dark, in that rapid, unexpected way it always seemed to, even though it was barely six. The lights were already on inside, and his tall, lithe frame filled the doorway. The light behind him made his hair glow as it hung loose around his shoulders, and she didn't need to get very close to know that he had shaved for the first time since his illness. The only tell-tale sign of the horror that nearly took his life—or rather, of the drastic measures she was forced to employ to save it—was a small, beige fabric bandage at the base of his throat. He looked squeaky clean and right as rain, and so good that she had to remind herself she'd spent the better part of the drive back from the church being mad at him.

After lunch, she'd unburdened herself to Colin, saying as much as she dared, leaving out the reason for their break up and trying to hide, as well as she could, the hurt and longing she still felt for her husband. To his credit, Colin didn't rush to offer any advice, because she was sure that there was little he could say that would help her surmount the terrible, unreachable wall Matthias had built around himself in the past year. Instead, he'd offered her a sympathetic ear; after such an awfully long period of hearing her own pain ricocheting in her head—words unspoken because there was nobody around to listen—Sarita was overwhelmed with gratitude.

After their meal had come a tour of the grounds. By then, the children were also finished eating and had returned to their playful meddling in the garden. Sarita had joined in, delighted by the sound of their laughter and their willingness to help. Now, she was grimy and hot and her limbs sore and heavy. She was suffused with the feeling of self-satisfaction and accomplishment that could only come after a hard afternoon's work getting dirt under the fingernails.

On the short drive back, with the voices of the children still ringing in her ears, she had been assailed by the sensation of being thrown back in time, of being given a glimpse of what life might have been for Matthias when he was a child. The stories he used to tell her of his life, as they lay entwined on the chaise lounge on the balcony of their Miami apartment watching the sun go down, came back to her: catching crayfish in milk tins; skipping school to watch the fishermen fix their nets; stealing cocoa pods off the plantations and cracking them open on sharp stones to suck at the sweet white pulp covering the seeds inside. Her heart had warmed at the image of him, and she felt almost sorry she hadn't known the little boy he had been.

Then the warmth was replaced by a chill wind. That little boy had grown into a man who had everything: the brains and education to make something of himself and the wherewithal to provide a good, stable, loving home to a child. No child of theirs would be exposed to want, need, or neglect. No child of theirs would be a latchkey kid, a stray, who would have to grow a tough layer of skin under his feet in order to compensate for a lack of shoes. And yet he refused. Not simply refused, insisted, that there would be no children. He bucked against the idea like a shark on a heavy hook. It was a shame, an outrage. Downright selfishness. The reef was an excuse. His sputtering about needing to concentrate, needing to devote all his time to it, was a diversion to steer her away from understanding the truth. Matthias was a selfish coward, and that was all.

As she approached him, she felt his eyes on her grubby dress.

"My mother had a recipe for taking out grass stains," he said dryly. He folded his arms, further filling the space between her and the indoors. "If you give me a moment, I'll try to remember it."

She looked down at herself ruefully. It really was a pretty dress—or rather had been. Now she looked as if she had been hiding in a foxhole during a shelling attack. Apart from grass stains, there were smears of rich, black earth, spreading patches of sweat at the armpits and the small of her back, and a smudge of dried blood where she'd absently wiped a cut finger. "I think it's beyond redemption, actually." Then she lifted her eyes to his face. He was relaxed, half smiling, but bristling with curiosity.

"Your date make you sing for your supper? Did you have to dig up your food before you could cook it?"

She tried to squeeze past, but he flexed his shoulders, thwarting her. "Can I pass?" She expected further resistance and prepared herself for a battle.

Surprisingly, he stepped aside, allowing her entry. "Don't tell me," he said as he followed her to her room. "He didn't warn you it was a hiking date and you were too stubborn or too proud to beg off."

"It wasn't a date," she grunted as she kicked off her shoes. They'd definitely need cleaning. Their soles were also caked with sweet-smelling black earth. She reminded herself that the next time she visited Colin she'd toss some old jeans and a pair of boots into the back of the truck. That way, when she offered to work in the garden, she would be prepared.

Then she went rigid, taken aback by her thoughts. She hadn't planned to be back, not in any concrete way, but before the idea could solidify she realized that she'd made that decision long before, while she was still in the churchyard trying to keep her sweaty grip on a huge gardening fork while making sure she didn't accidentally spear the feet of the children who were skipping to and fro like kittens venturing outside for the first time. She smiled at the idea of going back to

chat with Colin again and listen to his soothing, unruf-
fled voice. To see the children. . . .

Matthias saw the smile, and his eyes narrowed. "A
non-date put a smile like that on your face?"

She threw him an exasperated look. "You wouldn't
understand." She nudged open the door to the bathroom and gave him a meaningful look. He chose to
ignore it, so she elucidated it in plain English.
"Matthias, I'm hot, I'm tired, and, Lord knows, you can
see I'm filthy. I could do with a shower."

He gestured gallantly. "Feel free. Don't mind me. So
who was this non-date with? He local?"

"I—want—to—get—undressed," she said slowly. She
pointed at the door.

"Aw, come on, Sari. I've seen it all before. Plus, we'll
have to be friends if we're going to be working together. It's a small house. Not a whole lot of privacy in
a house this small."

"It's not that small," she huffed. "And it's got doors."
But sheer obstinacy made her strip, peeling off the of-
fending garments and kicking them away from her. If
he thought being naked would make her uncomfortable, he had another thought coming. She turned her
back to him, faced the mirror above the sink, and
began removing her watch and rings—all except her
wedding ring, which she was damned if she was removing without a decree from the court. Part of her
kept it on because, deep down, she was loath to relinquish her hold on the wonderful memories she still
had of their all-too-brief marriage before it went sour.
The other part of her kept it as an act of resistance,
knowing that the thin band of white gold, and the
bond it represented, probably annoyed the heck out of
Matthias. That alone was worth her perseverance. She
ran her finger along the edge of it, enjoying its solidity

and the backbone it gave her when she felt hers soft-ening. All the while, she cast covert glances at him in the mirror to see if he was watching her.

He was watching, but his eyes never drifted above her waist. They were narrowed, riveted on the roundness of her full, brown bottom, and concentrating, like an artist trying to decide where to begin his first brushstroke. She felt her skin heat up and the irritation that had fueled her trip home slipped a notch. Matthias was always an unabashed aficionado of her rear end. He had often teased her that it was the first of her many delightful features that he had noticed on the day they met in Australia, as she was clambering out of the water and back onto a boat. *Well,* she thought. *Let him watch. Let him remember what he could have had, but threw away. And let him see what he won't be having now, not even if he begs.*

At that point she stopped. Honesty reminded her of the last time he'd touched her, out there on the beach, the night before he'd driven her to the airport. That night, when he'd left her wet and shaking and starving for more, more, more, *she'd* been the one doing the beg-ging, and *he'd* been the one turning her down. She cursed, shoved aside the shower curtains, and stepped in.

"I'd give my right arm to know the sequence of thoughts that just skittered across your face," he told her. "You looked like a roller-coaster ran through your head. Up, down, up . . . ."

She turned on the water and tilted her face upward, closing her eyes, glad for the coolness on her skin and the distraction it provided. The pressure was heavy tonight, so powerful that the showerhead vibrated with a low hum. "That's funny. I hadn't realized you were looking at my *face.*"

He seemed amused. "I was looking at you *all over.*"

"Evidently." She tried to shut him out, to pretend

he wasn't there, but Matthias wasn't the kind of man you ignored.

"Well?"

"Well, what?" She squeezed body gel onto her bath puff and concentrated hard on lathering it up. Rosemary and citrus filled her nostrils. She smoothed the suds onto her skin, trying not to think too hard about the time when such a task often fell to Matthias. In that direction lay trouble.

He didn't take the hint. "Who's this guy? And what did he have you doing all day?"

"Why?" she shot back. "Jealous?"

His lips thinned the slightest bit, but there was no emotion in his voice. "No, just curious."

"What did Janelle have *you* doing all day?" she countered. He wasn't the only one who could ask questions.

"Why?" he mimicked. "Jealous?"

She sucked her teeth in derision. "No, just nauseated."

He laughed, deep gusts of sound rising from his chest. "She fed me, she hovered, she got bored, and she left." A lift of his shoulders dismissed the question.

"Yeah, fed you. Cow-heel soup, if I remember correctly. Did it get your *strength up?*"

He watched her with amusement. "I'm up and around, aren't I? Bright-eyed and bushy-tailed. Ready to hit the reef in the morning."

She squinted at him through the torrent of water. "You're getting back to work tomorrow?"

"Why not?" He stepped a little closer, and Sarita amused herself by ensuring he was accidentally splashed. "I'm much better now."

"Three cheers for Janelle and her soup. And all her other charms."

When she looked at him again, he wasn't smiling. "No need, Sarita."

"What?" She was genuinely puzzled.

"For jealousy. There's no need for it."

Was he deaf? Had he not been listening? "I told you—"

"I'm telling *you."* His voice left no room for rebuttal. "I don't know what you thought could have gone on in here today with me and Janelle—"

"I know what *she* was thinking—" If there was one thing a woman could sniff out, it was the scent of another woman on the prowl. Not that she cared. She grabbed a nailbrush and began furiously scrubbing at the soil under her fingernails. It made her feel cleaner and gave her a good reason not to look him in the face.

"But nothing happened. And nothing's going to." His lips took on a cynical twist. "I'm a married man."

"Huh," she snorted. Did he really expect her to believe that a man like him, who liked sex and liked it often, would let their marriage—defunct, interrupted, torn to tatters, however he wanted to describe it—stop him? Was she really to swallow the idea that a man like him, alone and unfettered for a year, would be willing to turn down who knew how many invitations from the women who had surely drifted into and out of his life, just because he had a wife stashed away somewhere, with whom he wasn't even on speaking terms? She wasn't that naive.

"You look as if you don't believe me."

She didn't answer but lifted her eyes to meet his. "Why should I?"

"Because I say so."

"So if you say it, it's so?" She was staggered at the possibility that he might actually be telling the truth.

Matthias? Celibate? For a year? She was calling up National Geographic and reporting a flying pig.

"Correct." His voice held not even the merest quiver.

Sarita stared, her mind churning. A ridiculous sensation that felt a lot like delight bubbled inside her, but it was dashed away by an ice-cold bucket of reality. She couldn't call what he had been "faithful," because, if truth be told, there was nothing to be faithful to. But the possibility of him being with other women during that time, and giving them what he had given her so ardently, had always burned away at the pit of her stomach—like a glowing coal rolled into the corner of a fireplace, waiting to be blown into flame—on cold, lonely nights when his face came to her mind. Now, with his revelation, the slow burn went out.

But if celibacy was so easy for him to assert, why was it so hard for him to believe the same of her? She asked him as much, fighting to keep her irrational relief at his so-called fidelity out of her voice. "So, you've been a good boy. You must be very proud—"

"I am."

"So why is it so important for me to believe you, when you won't believe me when I tell you I wasn't on a date today?" She searched his face, waiting for a glint of something that would tell her that, as far as he was concerned, her one little lie—well, a few big ones—made her a liar for good. If she saw even a glimpse of that thought, she was ending the conversation, throwing him out, and slamming the door.

He seemed to know what she was thinking and to anticipate her dread, because barely a moment passed before he nodded. "Okay, Sarita. I believe you. I'm proud of you—"

"Don't patronize me!"

"I'm not. Do you think I don't know what it's like?

Do you think temptation hasn't fallen into my path, and that I haven't lain awake at night, making lists of reasons in my head for not giving in, if only to make the hours before the dawn that much more bearable? And if it was like that for me, why shouldn't it be like that for you? You're a woman who needs a lot of loving. . . ." His words were like suede: soft, but with a rough edge to them. "Often, and well. . . ."

Was it getting hotter in the shower stall? She glanced at the hot-water tap. She didn't remember turning it on. Desperate to drag the conversation away from the direction in which it was heading, she pounced on the subject of Colin again: she was forcing Matthias back to the original question if she had to lead him there at gunpoint. "He's a minister," she sputtered.

"What?"

"My friend, Colin. The one I had lunch with today. He's a Lutheran minister. And he's my daddy's age if he's a day."

Matthias made an elaborate show of stepping away from her, slamming into the bathroom wall, and throwing his arms up in surrender.

Sarita was confounded. "What the devil . . . ?"

"Just getting out of the way, honey. In case lightning chooses to strike. Which will be . . ." He consulted his watch ostentatiously. "Any minute now."

She laughed, glad for the diversion. "I've been telling you all evening, Matthias, that it never even crossed my mind. . . ."

"I know." He approached the shower stall again, grinning. "I was only teasing you."

She was glad to see him so relaxed and glad that the conversation had taken a turn for the more innocuous. Anything to melt the butter-thick tension that had filled the house for so long. Happier still that Colin's calling hadn't drawn any sarcastic comments from him; Matthias wasn't fond of the ministry. For the most part, though, he kept his deep-seated antipathy to himself, so much so that he had never really let her get to the bottom of it. At least, to his credit, he had never attempted to foist his negative view of the Church upon her. Live and let live, he'd always said, as far as that was concerned; he just didn't want her to try to drag him into it.

"I'm glad you found a friend," he told her. He seemed to really mean it. "At least you haven't died of boredom. I can't imagine how you had time to meet him, though. You've only been on the island a week and most of that time you've been holed up in here."

"Listening to you gripe," she pointed out tartly.

He looked justifiably sheepish. "Oh, yeah. Sorry about that. I'm better now, you'll be glad to know."

"Even if you weren't, I'd have resigned from the post of nurse anyway. Too much work, too few benefits, and absolutely no recognition."

The bath puff was spirited from her even before she felt it go; suds engulfed his slippery hand as he smoothed them on her skin. "Sorry." His voice was in her ear, soft, but as deep as it always used to be, undiminished by the soreness he must surely still be feeling in his throat. "I don't want you to think I'm not grateful. I'd have died without you. And these past few days, I needed you, and you were there. I'd have been all alone without you. Sarita . . ."

Weren't they laughing with each other seconds ago? Like friends? When did it all veer in this direction once again? And *he* was accusing *her* of having a mind like a roller coaster? She was getting giddy just trying to keep up. Then, soap under her breasts and down around the mound of her belly; she found herself barely able to think at all. Her muscles quivered.

"Sari, turn around."

She obeyed without hesitation. Suds on her back, down her spine, to her hips. His chest was against her back. He was in the shower stall, shoes and all. Surely he had to be soaking. . . . *Oh, Lord.* One hand on her waist; the other, slippery as an eel, slithering between her thighs like a living shadow seeking shelter between underwater rocks. Emerging out front, not invading, not trespassing, but cupping her, and then, stillness. He didn't move. She couldn't. The cool water beat down on them both.

This is what it's like to drown, she thought. *Air cut off, and you fight and fight for more but your lungs refuse.* They said a drowning death was a peaceful one and that the mind and body, the limbs, and the heart were filled with a sweet lassitude that engulfed you, taking you under. They said it beckoned, becoming something not to be feared but to be welcomed. *Couldn't be much different from this,* she thought. She realized that she had reached down with her own hand to cover his cupped fingers, pressing them against herself. Between her legs her flesh swelled and burned, like jellyfish stings, the pain hot and anxious, and demanding to be stroked away, even though that stroking brought greater heat. He began to comply.

"Oh! Oh! Ow!" She could barely hear her own voice through the cascade in her ears. Cool water? It all but hissed and steamed as it hit her tortured skin. Then the water was shut off and he spun her to face him. No less drenched than she, he wound his arms around her, dipping his head to her mouth. The fine hairs of his moustache felt magnified a hundred times against her swollen lips, rasping. Torture! Enamel against enamel,

the clink of teeth meeting teeth like champagne glasses
toasting the prospect of a night of giddy pleasure.

With a thick towel, he squeezed the water out of her
hair and patted her down gently, and before she could
protest, or think of a good reason on which to base any
such qualms, he led her from the drenched bathroom
into her bedroom. The bare tiles felt blessedly cool to
her feet. He peeled off his wet clothes and left them
where they fell. He was splendidly naked and aggres-
sively erect. She goggled. The reality of him was as
accurate as her memory had been, and then some. The
rock-hard muscles of his abdomen quivered as droplets
of water rolled down them and disappeared into the
thatch of dark brown hair below. Her hand reached for
him, unbidden. Velvet and bronze. Her tongue flicked
out, moistened her lips, and disappeared again.

Seemingly unconcerned about the fact that he was as
wet as she was now dry, he gathered her back against
him, hands against her bare behind.

"Matthias! You're still wet!"

The fact seemed to hit him for the first time, and he
laughed. "I'm as wet outside as you are inside," he said
pointedly. "Don't worry. I wouldn't do that to your
sheets." Her belly flip-flopped at the idea of him in her
bed. She almost told him she didn't care about the bed,
or if he was wet or dry, she only wanted him prone.

He let her go, and she felt brief panic that he
wouldn't pick up where he'd left off once he was dry
again. Sarita watched as he grabbed the same towel
he'd used to dry her, even though it was almost too
damp to do the job. She was about to tell him there
were dry ones in the cupboard in the hall but to suggest that he leave her sight at a time like this would be
stupid beyond belief.

He dried himself hastily, carelessly, threw the towel

over a chair, and took his glasses off, setting them on the bedside table. "Come," he commanded.

Without false pride, she complied. The bedsprings creaked under their combined weight, but she didn't hear: what with the screaming of her skin as he kissed trails along it and the squeaking of her conscience—her last shred of rational thought, Jiminy Cricket hopping frantically on the bedpost issuing warnings—there was very little else that reached her ears.

Isn't he the one who thinks that the heat between them will be a distraction? the little voice demanded. *Isn't he the one who thinks their physical attraction will get between them and their work?* Reluctantly, and only to silence the wretched voice, she repeated its questions aloud. If Matthias came to his senses and walked away, she assured herself, she was whacking that darned cricket all the way into next Wednesday with her shoe.

"I must have been raving out of my mind," he lifted his head to say. As he spoke, his breath made warm puffs of air on the moistened nipple where his mouth had been. "This isn't about the sea. This is not about coral. We just admitted it: it's been a year for both of us. We're both hungry, and we can feed each other. We're grown-ups. Tomorrow, the sun will come up, and we'll go about our work like the professionals that we are. But let's not talk about tomorrow yet. Let's not even think about it. I want this. You want this. Okay, Sarita?"

She wasn't a fool. She knew what he was telling her. What happened here tonight would stay here. Tomorrow, under the beating sun, it might as well not have. And he wasn't only talking about their work, he was talking about their marriage, too. This wouldn't mean anything had changed. Their marriage was still a wreck; this wasn't even a bandage on a gushing wound.

It was separate, unconnected. This was about want and need, pure and simple.

"Okay, Sarita?" he asked again, more gently now, sensing her hesitation. He made to sit up.

"Don't go!" She grasped his hair, fingers twisting into the locks. They wrapped around her hand like damp seaweed.

He took that as assent and stretched the length of her again. His hands moved slowly, along her ribs and her belly, stoking a fire that needed no coaxing. His kisses were hallucinogenic, setting off firecrackers of color in the darkness of her mind. She could feel him hard against her belly, and she ached to feel him inside, filling the space that had been void too long.

There was one thing that stood in the way. She squeezed her eyes shut, trying to do quick mental mathematics, adding and subtracting dates, and then panted in relief, "I'm safe." She reached between them to hold him in her gentle grasp, letting her thighs fall open.

His voice was that of a drunk man, slurring. "What, sweet?"

"I'm safe," she said more clearly. "It's a good time. You don't have to worry." They had no protection; that night on the beach he'd told her so himself. There was no fear of disease between them, they'd married healthy and had both been celibate since. She knew—Lord, did she know!—that the only issue would be possible pregnancy, but she understood her own biology, and the risk right now, tonight, was so negligible that surely. . . .

He shook his head to clear it. "Don't do this to me, Sari. You know, you've always known—"

"Then what are you doing here? Why are we doing

this?" Even to her, her voice sounded shrill with frustration and disbelief.

"What we're doing here is making love. There are other ways. You know there are." He didn't sound angry, only persuasive. "I know your body. I know every trigger, every button, every sensitive spot. And you know mine." To demonstrate, he took her hand and slipped two of her fingers between his lips. He gently sucked on their tips, tongue touching and moving away, a warning of what he could do, and intended to do, farther down. He placed her hand between her own legs, and moved her fingers for her, sending sledgehammer jolts up her spine. "See?"

He was right. There were other ways. And right now, quite a few came to mind. Before she could dredge up a response from her drugged brain, he went on.

"We're not teenagers. This isn't prom night. We don't delve in, cross our fingers, and hope for the best. No stupid risks. Our future is not a . . ." He cast about for a metaphor. "A crapshoot. We have our pleasure, but we have it responsibly. There may be other nights, and by then we'll be better prepared, but right now, we make do with what we have, and what we have is plenty." He was firm but not unkind. It was up to her; he made that very clear. He kissed her cheek, not sensually but gently, and said in her ear, "Take it or leave it, Sari. The choice is yours."

She took it.

Eight

Matthias opened his eyes reluctantly. Dawn had painted the room lilac, and in the stillness only the birds stirring outside and Sarita's puppy snores could be heard. She was warm against his naked skin, her soft, full figure like an eiderdown bolster, and he felt that if he lifted his arm from around her waist he would never be that warm again. The tranquility he felt completely sideswiped him, taking him by surprise and leaving him with a glow inside that rivaled the paling sky.

As loath as he was to get to his feet and leave her side, another part of him wanted to get up and rush out to the bakery and buy her croissants, lay out the butter and jelly, and set the table with linen and good china, although he knew that this wasn't Miami; there were no croissants to be bought, no linen in the closet in the hall, and the project budget only allowed for discount-store tableware.

But until last night he hadn't realized how much he had missed female company—no, not just any female company, *her* company. How the tough, impenetrable strands of control he had wound around himself were a sham. In one night this woman, his wife-but-not-a-wife, had undone it all, leaving him to taste the bitterness of his own loneliness, and making him painfully aware of how empty the last year of his life had been. And that made him mad as hell.

"Damn fool," he muttered. He allowed the vehemence of his self-recrimination to propel him away from her side and onto his feet, steeling himself not to look back at her. He was sure that, like Lot's wife, he'd remain riveted where he stood were he even to glance one last time at the place where he longed to remain. He walked to the door, naked, not even thinking to gather up the clothes that he had tossed aside the night before. His survival instinct told him that maintaining his sanity meant getting as far as he could from the source of the disturbance.

He strained to remember what he had said to Sarita last night when, propelled by an ache in the groin and blinded by his own arrogance, he had assured her that they were adults and could do this and return to normal the next day, could slake their thirst with each other's bodies, and then wake up, get dressed, and go to work. *Like professionals.* That's what he'd said. His head hurt. There was nothing professional about how he felt now. He felt undone, disarmed.

He stepped into his own shower, letting the water run cold, hoping that lower temperatures would mean a clearer head. Once dressed, he set about making breakfast, smiling ruefully to himself at the thought that sweet coconut bread, with raisins falling from it as he sliced, would have to take the place of the longed-for croissants. There was butter, though, and guava jelly, and he set two places.

He heard movement in Sarita's room and felt the floor drop from his belly. What would she be like this morning? Regretful? Embarrassed? What if, like he, she awoke to the recognition of her own loneliness and he saw in her eyes even the tiniest spark of hope that somehow, some way, they could disentangle themselves from the dreadful mess they'd made of their lives? He wished to high heaven there was some way to erase the awful crisis that had put an end to their marriage. If only it had never happened!

The door creaked open, and he froze. He realized that he was standing at the table with a butter knife in his hand, not moving, staring at the corridor waiting for her to make her appearance and looking like a fool, but he couldn't move a limb.

She was dressed for work: jeans and T-shirt, running shoes with Velcro tabs (easy for her to slip off when she needed to hit the water, and put on again). Her hair was neatly combed, held back with a series of pins to keep it out of her eyes as she swam. She was ready for the reef. She gave him a brief, unfaltering smile, and then her gaze fell to the table.

A second's acknowledgment, maybe less, and that was it. She hadn't held his gaze a moment longer. Was that a good sign or a bad one? "I made breakfast," he said stupidly.

"Thank you." Not a tremor.

He searched her face, marveling at her coolness. Just one spark, he prayed. Just a glimpse of something that told him that last night had touched her, too, and that there were fragments of hope and longing left, like flotsam bobbing on the waves after the shipwreck of their marriage. He wanted to run around the table and confront her, grab her by the chin and tilt her face to his, the better to read her eyes. But fear of seeing nothing kept him where he was.

She was waiting for something. "You going to sit?" she asked after a while.

He sat opposite her, watching in amazement and spiraling dismay as she helped herself to a hefty serving, and began chatting about what needed to be done today. Question followed question: Was JoJo coming here, or was he going ahead to Buccoo Bay? When were they meeting Janelle at the pier? Did he want her to pack the cameras? Were they taking any water samples? Coral samples?

He heard himself answer, like someone speaking through a swim mask: muffled and distant. He had the uncanny feeling of being thrown back to his college days, when, after a night of intense sex with a beautiful woman he'd met at a party, he would wake up to the discomfort of breakfast with a complete stranger. What happened? Last night, she'd been the one craving intimacy, and he'd been the one who'd sworn that they could do this and emerge unscathed. Today, their roles had changed with dizzying speed.

Or had they? Had anything changed for her, or was it simply his perception of her? At the beginning of their breakup she'd pleaded for another chance; he'd been adamant that too much damage had been done and that it wouldn't work. The year had passed with minimal contact between them, and she'd only been back a week and a few days. She'd made it quite clear that she was here for the reef, not for him, and since his illness, he'd spent half the time drunk on painkillers and the other half griping and feeling sorry for himself. He couldn't claim to have spent any time assessing her or how she felt. Was the pragmatic reservation he'd professed, but discovered to be a sham, really hers?

"I'll do the photography," she was saying. "And download all the shots afterward. I was toying with the new camera while you were sick. It's a beauty."

He struggled to focus on what she was saying, training his eyes on her mouth and watching the words take shape. The "lying scar" on her upper lip winked at him as she spoke. He cleared his throat and found it too dry to put forth a response, so he took a swig of water before he answered. "I'd appreciate it." He was astounded to find that his voice sounded normal.

She put her knife and fork together and leaned back in her chair, looking satisfied. "Ready?" she asked. "There's sunshine going to waste."

That's it then, he thought. *You're keeping our deal. Stay professional. Get up, move on, and do the job.* His resignation was tinged with defiance. If she could do it, so could he. Maybe she was right. A night's pleasure didn't mean all was well with them. It couldn't repair the damage done. It was a stupid thought, anyway. Hope fueled by the afterglow of sex. Like morning dew, it would dissipate in the blaze of the sun; then he'd be all right again. He pushed away his untouched plate and stood up. When he looked at her, his eyes were guarded and his face without expression. "Ready," he agreed. "I'll load up the truck. Meet you outside in five?"

"No problem," she told him.

Sarita was sure that if she got any tauter she would snap. When she was in eighth grade she had taken up the violin, albeit for a short time, as the enterprise had been more her mother's idea than hers. She remembered her first music school recital: a sea of parental faces and all the other children watching her from the wings. She had lifted her bow, nestled the violin under her chin, and begun. Her quavering rendition of *Für Elise* had been interrupted by a *twang* that, in retrospect, only she had probably heard, but which, at the time, she was sure had reverberated throughout the small hall. Snapped violin string. The E string, to be exact. She'd remained on stage, rooted to the spot by stark terror, her piano accompaniment fading away and eventually stopping, until her teacher had waddled onto the stage and ushered her off, whereupon she had fallen into a heap of anguished tears, the kind only a twelve-year-old could generate.

If she lost the taut control into which she had steeled herself, right here on the boat in front of Matthias, JoJo, and the dreadful Janelle, would the snap be audible? She'd sooner lose an arm than find out. She was seeing this through if it killed her. If Matthias wanted professional, professional was what he would get.

That look on his face this morning! Like a rabbit in the headlights: morning-after regret if there ever was. The kind a confirmed bachelor got when he woke up after having spent the night with a woman he liked enough to bed, but not enough to have to go through the charade of actually being interested in. Hoping that things wouldn't get "complicated." Watching her face for any sign of weakness, any sign that she would renege on the pact that they'd made in her bed last night. Pleasure for its own sake, for the sake of their starved sexuality, and then in the morning: business as usual.

Complicated? It couldn't get any more complicated than this: being in love with a husband who was in love with the ocean; a husband who didn't trust her, couldn't forgive her, but seemed honor-bound, gratitude-bound, to let her work with him. In order to keep her eyes from straying across at him, she twiddled with the buttons on their underwater digital camera. At least, there was one thing she could prove to him: that regardless of their messy private life, she was an asset to his operations. If he was a man, he would one day admit it.

"Didn't do too badly for your first day back on the job, Matt," Janelle was purring.

Matt! Sarita was sure that she'd only ever called her husband that in bed. Where did the woman get off thinking it was a diminutive to be bandied about as she chose?

Janelle was letting JoJo sail the boat for a change, the better to concentrate her efforts on fatter fish. Matthias was standing near the prow, leaning against a post, with arms folded, hair tied back, and eyes squinting against the glare. He looked amused rather than irritated by the proximity of the woman. As she spoke, she actually had the temerity to run her forefinger along the small fabric bandage at the base of his throat. He neither flinched nor moved her hand away.

Sarita shot mental daggers at both of them. In spite of the claims Matthias had made about not being interested in the creature, he certainly made no effort to disabuse her of his availability. Even without Janelle's amazing ability to brush against, touch, be thrown into, or otherwise make contact with Matthias at least a dozen times over today's six-hour trip, Sarita would not have liked her. She was patronizing of her and her abilities, and almost seemed to question the validity of her presence on the project. Even when she was being nice to Sarita, which was rare, that niceness was more for show than anything else.

But Sarita's dislike went beyond that to the realm of the instinctive, the intuitive. Janelle was beautiful and lithe and smart, and acted as if nothing in the world meant more to her than the health of all God's little creatures on the reef, but still Sarita wasn't buying it all, even if Matthias was. Something about the woman rankled, something that went beyond female competitiveness.

There was a counterfeit quality to her. A brittleness lay beneath.

"How long before you take the bandage off?" Janelle wanted to know. Her voice dripped concern, like honey poured over aloe.

"A day," Matthias answered. "Maybe two."

Tell her to stop touching you, Sarita telegraphed. *Before I throw up.*

Matthias didn't pick up on her mental admonition, or ignored it.

"Wonderful." Janelle squeezed his arm encouragingly. (*Ha,* Sarita thought.) "Then you'll be back to your totally handsome self: no blemishes, no bandages."

"Actually," Matthias said calmly, "I'm going to have an ugly scar, most likely for the rest of my life. A penknife certainly isn't a precision surgical instrument. But I'd rather have a hundred of those than contemplate the alternative." This time, his eyes caught and held Sarita's, and the smile he gave her was genuinely grateful.

Janelle's wasn't. "Thanks to Gwen, we still have you around. Where would we be without her?" The fake grin wavered in Sarita's direction for a nanosecond before her eyes were on Matthias again.

Try as she might, Sarita was unable to stop her eyes from rolling. She had never been prone to seasickness, but she was sure she was going to have her first taste of it any minute now. But then as her gaze circled upward, something caught her attention. The ceiling of the small boat was, like the rest of the upholstery, made of leather that was the color of ox blood. As with any marine vessel space was at a premium, so shelves protruded below it; this was where emergency life vests were stored.

But the padded ceiling looked odd, somehow. It

didn't seem to sit right. Sarita glanced at the edge of the roofing and then back at the ceiling again. She could have sworn that the ceiling was several inches lower than it should have been, rather than being flush with the roof. Facing her, on the opposite side of the small boat, she spied a wrinkle in the seam where the leather met the wall, and a slip of—what, clear plastic?—protruded like a small, mocking tongue. Idly, more for the sake of diversion than anything else, Sarita stood and leaned over the row of glass-bottomed crates that ran down the center of the vessel. Maintaining her precarious balance, she grasped the small piece of plastic and gave it a gentle tug. Three or four inches more slid out from the now obvious groove between ceiling and wall.

Bad upholstery? Sarita wondered. Cheap padding job? Whatever it was, it was a space. She wondered if—

"What the hell are you doing there?" Janelle's bark was startling in its vehemence.

Still balancing, stretched over the middle of the boat, Sarita jumped, her hand closed around the protruding plastic. "Just looking at this . . . this strange piece of . . ." The awkwardness of her position made it difficult to speak. She was aware of all eyes on her now and was beginning to feel foolish. After all, if Janelle had had her interior upholstery done by a clod, who was she to—

"Let it go!" Before Sarita could anticipate the attack and turn to defend herself, Janelle was upon her, grasping her around the waist and trying to tear her away from the ugly breach in the ceiling that held her interest. JoJo must have been distracted; at that moment their ride became decidedly less smooth. The boat hit a swell head-on and bucked like a bronco, sending the two women sprawling.

Sarita released her grasp on the jutting piece of plastic, the only thing that was helping her maintain her equilibrium, and lurched forward. She landed painfully on the glass-bottomed crates in front of her, banging her ribs hard enough for the impact to rob her of her wind. It was only the flexibility of their construction that spared them from being shattered. The crates swayed but held. Janelle hit Sarita's body a glancing blow as she fell on top of her and was immediately caught and set on her feet by Matthias.

"Sorry!" JoJo yelled. "I don't know what—"

"Concentrate on sailing," Matthias shouted over the noise of the engine.

When Sarita was able to focus again, and see past the stars of many colors that collided into each other right before her eyes, she looked up to see Matthias ensuring that Janelle was uninjured. She braced her arms against the wooden crates and dragged herself upright, just as Matthias saw fit to come to her aid.

"You okay?" he asked. His face was clouded by concern.

Sarita shook herself free of his grip. *Nice of him to be worried. Nice of him to check on me* after *he makes sure Janelle is unharmed*. She pushed him away. "Don't," she snapped. Her ribs hurt like the devil. Only pride prevented her from allowing the threatening tears to flow. She touched her chest gingerly, running her fingers along the ribbons of pain that wrapped around her. Anything broken? Maybe not, but . . .

"I just want to know—"

Whatever Matthias wanted to know, Sarita would never hear, because Janelle was forcing herself between them, face contorted. "Don't you ever go messing around with my boat, you hear?" she shrieked. Her mouth was inches from Sarita's face.

"I wasn't messing with anything," Sarita objected. She

THE "THANK YOU" GIFT INCLUDES:

- 4 books absolutely FREE (plus $1.99 for shipping and handling).
- A FREE newsletter, *Arabesque Romance News*, filled with author interviews, book previews, special offers, and more!
- No risks or obligations.

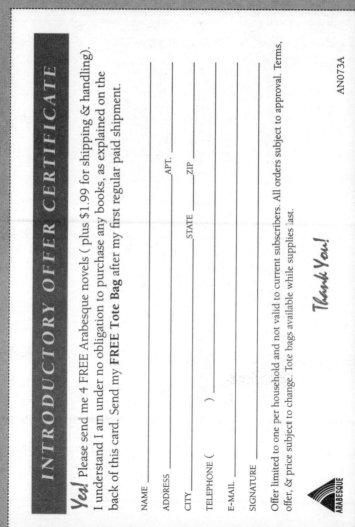

INTRODUCTORY OFFER CERTIFICATE

Yes! Please send me 4 FREE Arabesque novels (plus $1.99 for shipping & handling). I understand I am under no obligation to purchase any books, as explained on the back of this card. Send my **FREE Tote Bag** after my first regular paid shipment.

NAME _____

ADDRESS _____ APT. _____

CITY _____ STATE _____ ZIP _____

TELEPHONE ( ) _____

E-MAIL _____

SIGNATURE _____

Offer limited to one per household and not valid to current subscribers. All orders subject to approval. Terms, offer, & price subject to change. Tote bags available while supplies last.

Thank You!

AN073A

ARABESQUE

THE ARABESQUE ROMANCE BOOK CLUB
P.O. BOX 5214
CLIFTON NJ 07015-5214

PLACE
STAMP
HERE

tried to wriggle away. Her head hurt, her pride hurt, her everything hurt, and here was this woman making everything worse. Janelle was too close for comfort and irrationally upset. It was a stupid little thing, what she had done. Tugging on the plastic out of mild curiosity. No big deal. Why was she making something out of nothing?

"I never gave you permission to touch the boat. Don't you touch my boat!"

This was too much! "I'm *on* your boat!" Sarita tried to explain. The stupidity of the demand almost floored her. "I've got to *touch* it to be *on* it!"

"Well, sit still, enjoy the ride, and don't touch anything that doesn't concern you. How's that?" Janelle's finger poked her in her tender ribs.

"Ouch, that hurts!" Sarita's hands came up to protect herself, banging into Janelle's hand.

Janelle retaliated, tenfold. "What about this, does *this* hurt?" A mighty shove sent Sarita in the opposite direction this time, back against the wall. The impact was like getting slammed onto the mat in a wrestling ring. She heard a curse fly from her mouth as she flailed about, struggling to stand. There was heat in her head and blood red stark rage blurring her vision. If that was the way Janelle wanted it—

Matthias snatched her up before she could charge, his arms like restraints, his chest hard against her back. "Sarita! Sarita! Stop!" She struggled, but was no match for his strength. A sob of sheer anger and frustration burst from her lips.

"Me, stop?" She was incredulous. If there was a villain in the piece, it certainly wasn't her! "What about her? She's the one was started it. She came after me! I was only trying to—"

"What you could try to do is mind your own business!" Janelle spat like a wet cat.

For the first time, Matthias was stern toward Janelle. "That's enough." His voice invited no opposition and received none. "Both of you. Let it rest." When he spoke to Sarita again, his voice was several measures softer than it had been before. "Sari, honey, take it easy."

"What did you call her?" JoJo asked. He looked bewildered, squinting at Sarita, and she could see his brain churning as he tried to reconcile the "Gwen" that he knew with the "Sarita" that Matthias was now trying to bring under control like a recalcitrant child.

Matthias ignored the question. "Take us in."

JoJo stared in surprise. There was much more on the agenda and many hours of daylight left. "But what about—"

"Take us in, JoJo."

Stung by the curtness of his idol's response, JoJo dipped his head and concentrated on operating the boat. If Sarita hadn't been so upset by the whole debacle, and furious with every tear that burned behind her eyelids right now, she would have felt sorry for him.

"Sit," Matthias said, and unceremoniously plunked her down on a bench. The fact that he sat next to her was no comfort. His attitude was more that of a guard ensuring his captive did not flee than a concerned friend sitting near to offer reassurance.

Janelle was pacing nearby, restless, arms flexed, and body taut, like Laila Ali spoiling for a brawl. "Matthias." There was no sugar in her voice this time. "Instruct your employee not to mess with my boat."

"She didn't mean anything by it," Matthias said soothingly. "She was only—"

"I can speak for myself!" The nerve of the man!

Speaking about her as if she were a small, naughty child, as if she'd broken something in a toy store and he was trying to placate the shopkeeper.

He turned toward her. "Sarita, please." There was anguished pleading in his eyes and in his voice, and Sarita realized with pique that his anxiety was not for her or her bruised pride—not to mention body—but for the preservation of peace on the job. As always, the job came first. She looked away, hoping that staring into the water would numb her until JoJo could get them back onto land and she could get off this blighted vessel once and for all.

Janelle snorted. "Gwen, Sarita, Sarita, Gwen. What, you hired someone who isn't even sure of her own name?" Feeling better after her parting shot, she retired to the farthest corner to glower for the rest of the journey.

Once on land, Sarita wrenched the keys from Matthias and stalked toward the truck, where she sat and simmered, and watched him in the side mirror as he faced Janelle, his arms folded across his chest, listening intently as she spoke. Whatever she was saying, he seemed to be buying it, as he nodded from time to time. Eventually, just as Sarita was half considering starting up the engine and heading home without him, he wrapped things up. When he shook her hand briefly, the woman was giving him her kitty-cat smile, looking satisfied and assured. He turned to JoJo, who had been hovering anxiously at his sister's elbow, and shook his hand, as well. JoJo's face brightened considerably.

There was a crunch of gravel, and Sarita straightened up and turned her head quickly, so he wouldn't know she had been watching him in the mirror. The door on the driver's side creaked open, and the truck gave slightly under his weight. "It's all fixed," he said. He sounded satisfied with himself.

"What," Sarita rejoined dryly. "You fired her?"

Matthias fixed his eyes on her face, not sure if she were joking or not. "You know I can't do that."

She supposed she *had* been joking, but a very small part of her wanted to hear that he had. It would have, at the very least, told her that he was as outraged as she was over Janelle's behavior, which had gone beyond the pale today. Flirting was one thing, snide comments another . . . but today she'd been the victim of a direct physical assault, and Matthias didn't seem to give a rat's—

"She was paid in advance, you know that." Matthias interrupted her disgruntled thoughts. "With project money. If I let her go, how would we pay for another boat?"

She threw up her hands. "The project, the project, the project. Lord knows we wouldn't want anything to get between us and *that.*"

"The project is why I'm here. It's why you're here." He nailed her to the seat with a steely stare. "Isn't it?"

A school of starving barracuda couldn't tear any *other* reason from her lips. She shrugged. "Why else?"

"Good. So we're agreed on that." He set the vehicle in motion. "Besides, she apologized."

Sarita couldn't believe what she was hearing. "She hit *me* and then apologized to *you?*"

"I don't think she meant to hit you. It was an accident. She was trying to protect her property."

"And what, I was a threat to it? Because somebody did a lousy job on the trim?"

"Some people are just defensive."

"Some people are just insane."

The road was fairly busy with tourists, fishermen, and

Tobagonians going about their usual business, and Matthias concentrated on the road for such a long time that Sarita was sure that the subject was closed. But then, he opened his mouth to say, "So, no more cat-fights, then?"

Catfight? She sputtered, unable to give shape and form to the indignation bubbling up within her. Before she could choose between giving him a piece of her mind and demanding that he let her out right here, right now, because she could find her own way home, thank you, his hand closed over hers.

"Just joking," he grinned.

She pulled her hand away and hid both of them in her armpits. "Not funny," she snapped.

Matthias wished he knew what to say to Sarita. He knew, without having to be told, that she was angry with him, even disappointed. He wouldn't disagree with her there: he was disappointed in himself. When he played and replayed the scenario on the boat in his mind, it seemed so ludicrous. It was like a spat between children in a sandbox, something that got out of hand too fast. He'd spent enough time on boats to know that con-fined spaces drove people to act in ways that they would never dream of otherwise. He remembered once see-ing a sailor slash open a man's face, just because the man had moved the sailor's knapsack from one bench to the other.

He supposed that with Janelle, it had been pretty much the same thing. Territorialism gone amok. And yes, she had been the aggressor. But a good leader shouldn't choose sides in a dispute, unless there has been a more serious life-threatening or mission-threatening transgression. He'd done what he'd had to do: poured oil over the troubled waters. He just hoped that things would quiet down between the two women enough for them to work together, so that they could all get the job done.

Still, every time he caught Sarita's dark, resentful eyes upon him, his belly clenched and shame filled him. Once—it seemed so long ago!—he'd vowed to protect her. And he supposed that as a husband the right thing to do, the noble thing to do, would have been to intervene, speak up on her behalf, and cut them loose from Janelle and her boat. Find another crew if he had to, and damn the consequences. But as project director, he knew this wasn't feasible, if not impossible. The project ran on a UN grant, and UN money had to be accounted for: every last copper penny. His hands were tied and he knew, with every shred of his rational mind, that he had made the right decision. But if he had, why did his heart ache so badly?

This past week had been an object lesson in diplomacy. Janelle was even more cutting with Sarita, if such a thing were possible, and in turn, Sarita was even more determined to prove that she wasn't the incompetent Janelle implied that she was. Doubly motivated, he supposed, by her determination to prove to him that she could be all about the job, and nothing else, she had worked like a demon. Most of the time, he had been the one to beg her to call it a day, and remind her that the reef would still be there, and needing her, in the morning. The two women barely spoke to each other, and only when strictly required by their respective jobs.

The undercurrents left both women resentful of each other, JoJo distressed by the turn things had taken, and Matthias burdened by the added responsibility of managing the personal grudges that hampered with project. To say that it was not an ideal situation would be putting it mildly.

Today, he watched as Sarita bent over in the hallway to put on her sandals. She was dressed demurely in her Sunday dress, a green one this time, after ruining her yellow one the week before doing whatever she had been doing to become encrusted in dirt up to her eyeballs while visiting her minister friend. He assumed she was going to see him again. He was happy that at least she had someone on the island to talk to . . . because she certainly wasn't talking to him.

He hoped she wasn't discussing their personal affairs with the man. Growing up the grandson of a minister, the kind of minister his cold, judgmental grandfather had been, had left him with an abiding sense of caution, and a ruthlessly guarded need for privacy. If the little church garden was all there was on their conversation agenda, well, she was welcome to it. If Sarita invaded his right to privacy, and he found out about it, then that would be another story.

He approached her. "Hope you're not planning on doing another hike today." He tried to keep his voice light and keep out the quaver that had come to him recently whenever he braved the cold front she had erected around herself. "Not dressed like that."

She regarded him steadily, not in an unfriendly way, but not warm either, and not welcoming of conversation. "Gardening, not hiking, and you know it." She held up her tote, which was stuffed to the seams. "And I have a change of clothes here. Work clothes and boots. Don't worry about me. I'll come back home almost as clean as I am now. You won't need to help me get showered tonight." Her last statement was almost accompanied by a smile. Almost.

He tried to steady himself. It had been a whole week

since they had spent that night together in her bedroom. A whole week since he'd touched her, since she'd been anything but cool, distant, and *professional* toward him. It was one of the longest weeks of his life. "What are you planting?" he asked politely. What he really wanted to say was: *Stay, Sari. Come play cards with me, or chess. I promise that by the end of the day I'll make you smile.* But he knew she thought him a dictator, a controller, and he'd re-open the healing wound at his throat with a rusty spoon before he sought to constrict her movements while she was on her own time.

"Last week, we were molding up pigeon pea trees, not planting. This week, I don't know. I don't even know if Colin will be in the yard today. I just wanted to be prepared." She swung her tote over her shoulder and rattled the keys to the 4X4, almost unaware that she was doing it. Her face was blank, but her body was screaming that she wanted to go.

As she opened the door, he blurted: "What time are you coming home?"

One soft, feathered eyebrow lifted. "Excuse me?"

"I . . . I just wanted to know if you'll be back . . ." Shame on him, he thought. A grown man, stuttering. He didn't dare say "home" again. ". . . in time for dinner. I could make us something really nice. Some of the shops are open today, and I'm sure I could scare up a decent bottle of wine or at least a few beers." He swallowed hard. The indignity of begging his own wife to have dinner with him dimmed in comparison to the horrific prospect of another deathly silent night in the house.

He tried to sweeten the pot. "I could teach you to play All-Fours." He smiled. "We have cards, and we have a box of matches." All-Fours was a local game he'd learned growing up in Tobago. Matches were used for keeping score.

She softened, but only a little. "There's just two of us. Didn't you say you need four to play?"

"We could think of something." He waited, not flexing a muscle, knowing that to push Sarita was to find resistance.

She seemed deep in thought, and then nodded. "Okay. We can do that."

Her lips didn't curve, but it was a start. He tried not to look jubilant. "I'll see you later then."

Without another word, she exited, crossed the small yard in the front of the cottage and hopped up into the driver's seat of the 4X4. She eased out onto the roadway. Matthias stood in the doorway and watched as she disappeared at the end of the short access road. "Take care," he murmured.

"She criticizes my every move," Sarita railed. She stabbed the earth with her pitchfork. It amused her to imagine herself doing the same to a certain well-muscled part of her antagonist's anatomy. "She acts like I found my degree at the bottom of a Cracker Jack box! She doesn't like the way I work, doesn't like the way I swim. If I sit on one side of the boat she wants me on the other side. And if I so much as touch one of her cupboard doors . . ."

Colin's attention, to all outward appearances, seemed wholly concentrated on digging up huge cassava roots, but she knew he was listening patiently. The air around them was perfumed by the rich, sweet scent of cassava, which rose to their nostrils if they accidentally cut the roots with their pitchforks, or even if the tall stalks aboveground snapped.

Several yards away a handful of children kicked a basketball up and down the drive, having long grown bored with "helping" in the garden. Lisa was among them; it had taken Sarita several minutes to disentangle herself from the child's welcoming grasp, although she had to admit that she was probably equally loath to let go. All the children had white lollipop sticks poking out of their mouths, a present from Sarita, and as she worked with Colin, she made sure to keep a watchful eye on them, as she was half afraid that they might stumble and choke on a lollipop as they ran.

She went on. "The woman is violent and unpredictable. And she hates me. She downright, flat-out, doesn't like the best bone in my body. I can't go anywhere on her stupid boat without her watching me like I'm a sneak thief or a snoop. And when I'm in the water and I look up, she's still watching me. I get the feeling that if it wasn't for JoJo and Matthias, she'd like nothing better than to sail off and leave me there, in the middle of the ocean, with the tide coming in. . . ."

"What's she protecting?" Colin asked at last.

"What do you mean, what's she protecting? She's just a mean, spiteful little b—"

Before the epithet could leave her lips, Colin lifted a warning finger, and nodded his head toward the huge crucifix that dominated the church wall above the main entrance. "Shush. We've got company."

She felt her face go hot. "Sorry. No offense."

"None taken." He placed a large fragrant cassava atop the pile they had already accumulated and paused from his labors, leaning on the handle of his fork with both hands and resting his chin on them.

"But you know what I mean."

He laughed. "I do indeed." His face became a shade more serious. "So, what's she protecting?"

She frowned, and, in turn, paused from her labors. "I don't understand."

"People are always protecting something. Whether it's themselves, or something else that means a lot to them. And if they're behaving irrationally—"

"Which she is!" Sarita snorted.

"—it probably means that there's something at stake. Something big. The question is, what?"

Sarita realized that she had unconsciously imitated Colin's pose, hands folded over the handle of her tool, chin on hands. It was a good position for being pensive, so she reflected upon Colin's question for several moments before trying to answer. Janelle, protecting something? What, apart from her astounding ego? She hadn't thought of that. "Well," she said at last, "maybe it's just the boat. She's real finicky about it. I know it's her only source of livelihood. And I know she and her brother have always lived off the sea. But she treats it like men treat their precious cars. She's got a speedboat engine on that thing, can you imagine? It's got more horses on it than a professional racer."

"Go on."

"And she's always whining about the Coast Guard patrols. She's afraid of them, like a little girl afraid of cops. They patrol the reef every day."

"I know."

"And whenever they appear on the horizon she freaks out. Gets out her binoculars and watches them until they leave again, like she's watching a big, hairy spider crawling along the ceiling. And that's when she's at her worst: yelling at me to get off the prow because the Coast Guard doesn't like it and might stop us; yelling at JoJo to slow down, even though half the time we're practically crawling. Fat lot of good her speedboat engine does us. She never seems to open it up on the water. I don't understand," she ended in frustration. "What's she afraid they're going to do to her? Give her a ticket?"

Colin appeared deep in thought for a few seconds, before he eventually advised, "All I can say is: be careful. Trust your instincts."

She let out a short, cynical laugh. "Colin, if I'd trusted my instincts in the first place, I probably wouldn't be here. I wouldn't have gotten mixed up in all this nonsense, faking a job application—playing Matthias for a fool—to get him to hire me. He doesn't want me here. He might *need* me here, for his precious work, but he doesn't *want* me." Saying the words made her aware of how true they were; how sad they were.

Colin's eyes were on her, steady. He made no attempt to say anything, just let her talk.

"And I'm probably the only one around here who has any instincts as far as Janelle is concerned. Matthias either doesn't notice or doesn't care. He's a bright man, a brilliant man, but he's only got space in that big brain of his for the world that exists underwater. On dry land, he's hopeless: couldn't read a situation if you paid him; wouldn't recognize a threat if it slapped him in the face and ran on down the street. He barely even sees Janelle. He looks at her and all he sees is a means to a boat. Although, Lord knows, she's been trying to change that. She sure does a whole lot of bending over when he's around."

Colin tried not to grin.

"And I don't like the way she looks at him. It's as if she wants nothing more than to spear-gun him, stuff him, and glue him to her wall on a big, tacky wooden plaque."

Colin gave up trying to contain his amusement. His laugh rumbled. "She likes him," he stated.

"I'll say."

"And that bothers you."

She was about to explain that it was Janelle's hunting technique that she found distasteful, not her choice of prey, but before the words could leave her lips she realized they were a lie, so she opted to say nothing.

"So if your marriage is as over as you say it is, why are you bothered? If it's simply a matter of signing a few papers, then shouldn't you be happy for him that it looks as if he'll be able to get on with his life, at least where women are concerned?"

Their marriage *was* over, she wanted to protest. It probably shouldn't have begun, not with the two of them having such diverse ideas about how their lives should be lived. But, lost cause that she knew it to be, it was still, for the moment, very real and very binding. And though she had sworn to Matthias a week ago that jealousy over Janelle was the furthest thing from her mind, she could smell it now: a faint but definite stench, like a dead rat entombed within a basement wall. She wrinkled her face in disgust. "Don't, Colin."

"Don't what?" he asked innocently.

"You know very well, don't what. Don't push me there."

"Why not? Because it hurts?"

She swallowed hard. "Yes."

"And doesn't that tell you something?"

"What's it supposed to tell me?" she pretended not to know.

"That dead flesh experiences no pain. You can cut it away and let it fall, and feel nothing. Living flesh, on the other hand, is still fed by blood, and still run through with nerves that tingle and respond. . . ."

"Okay, already!" she grumbled. "I hear you."

"And what are you doing to do?"

"What *can* I do? I knew when I married him how much he loved his job. I just didn't know how much it would affect our lives as husband and wife. I love my job too, but . . ."

"But he takes it too far?"

"Yes. It swallows him up. He talks of nothing else. He *wants* nothing else, not even me, if I get in the way. That fight we had, the last one, over . . ." She hesitated, reluctant to discuss the agonizing subject of her deception with their contraception, and instead said, "That fight we had over having a child, that was an excuse. He says he doesn't trust me, and he swears it's why he doesn't want me in his life, but the real reason is that he wants to be alone; the more time he has to himself, the more time he can spend on his precious reef. If he could sleep an hour or two every day, and give up eating altogether, he'd do it just so he'd have more time to work."

"I see," Colin murmured encouragingly.

"So there's nothing I can do about it. I dream of babies. He dreams of . . . of . . ." she waved her arm in the air, searching for a corresponding thing. "Of fish!"

"Why?" was all Colin asked.

"Why what?

"Why is he willing to give up everything for the reef? He gave you up and the chance of having a family. For a project? For a dream? I don't think so. There's a saying in Tobago: There's more in the mortar than the pestle."

She wrinkled her brow quizzically.

He clarified. "There's more to it than meets the eye. More to your man than you think. Find out what it is and then you'll really know him."

"Then what?" she asked bitterly.

Colin retrieved his fork and began digging again. "Then it's up to you."

Sarita looked at her own fork and considered following suit, but she felt suddenly tired and totally drained. Instead of digging, she laid it down on the ground and began filling her arms with cassava to take into the kitchen. She didn't want to talk about Matthias any more. "Stop it, Colin. You're . . ." She searched for a word. "You're *counseling* me."

He shrugged, and the look on his face was wicked. "You're friends with a minister, my dear. Didn't you see it coming?"

"Hang Jack!" Matthias shouted triumphantly. He slapped a Queen of Hearts onto her timidly proffered Jack, and the sound of his palm hitting the table cracked in the air. "That's four points for me . . ." He helped himself to four more matches and neatly added them to his collection. The matches had to be set out in a specific order, she learned. Three rows of four, and then the final two stood alone. "And that makes fourteen. Game over."

"You win again," she said dryly. "Hooray." Frankly, the game was too complicated, and she had more than an inkling that playing a four-person game with only two people left it wanting. If pressed, she'd freely admit she preferred gin, by a long shot, but Matthias seemed eager for her company, as if he thought that a game and a few beers would help smooth away the bad week they'd had. She knew he needed to make amends over that awful scenario with Janelle last week, and she was so tired of the issue, so fed up with being mad at him, that she was willing to go along with it. So, good naturedly, she conceded defeat gracefully and let him gloat.

"I won again because you're not even trying to learn the game," he chided.

"You won again because I've only been playing this game an hour and you've been playing your whole life," she countered.

He shook his head. "That's where you're wrong. I haven't played it since I left home and that's more than twenty-five years. They don't play All-Fours anywhere else in the world, except in the Caribbean. I'm rusty, and still I whupped you good. You're lucky we weren't playing for money. . . ." When he realized she was staring at him, and not even taking part in the banter, he stopped. "What is it? Don't tell me you're upset. It's only a game, Sari."

"You said 'home,'" she said softly.

"Did I?" He seemed surprised at himself.

"You did," she confirmed. "Is that what Tobago is to you?"

He didn't have to think long. "It is. It always was. Didn't you know that?"

"And the States, isn't that your home?"

Matthias gathered the cards on the table and placed them in a neat pile, halfway between them. "Of course it is. I'm a U.S. citizen. I've got a U.S. passport. If America went to war and needed me, I'd be there—"

"I'm not talking about your passport, Matthias. I'm talking about your heart, and your mind."

"My mind is wherever I choose for it to be. I focus my attention wherever I need to."

"And your heart?"

He watched her quietly, green eyes full of puzzlement at the strangeness of her question. "You know the answer to that. Why ask it again?"

Why indeed? She thought of Colin's words this afternoon. Understand the motive, and you understand the man, or something to that effect. She tried to explain herself. "Colin said that if I knew what it was that drew you here, I'd finally understand you."

He frowned. "'Colin said' . . . ?"

"Yes, why?" She wasn't sure where he was going with this.

"You talked to him about me?" His voice had lost all of the mirth of a few moments before, growing hard and dangerous.

Sarita protested. "Not a whole lot. I just wanted to bounce things off of somebody. I've got nobody else to talk to and he was there. I didn't tell him anything really private, I just . . ."

"You just went blabbing to a do-gooder in a robe about our personal affairs." Matthias shot to his feet and took several steps away from the table. He folded his arms, scowling. "Don't you know better than that?"

Now she was getting agitated. As always, he was making a mountain out of nothing at all. "What's wrong with you? You knew from the start that I grew up in the Church. Maybe I haven't been to it as often as I should have in the past year or two, but when I've got a problem, it's the first place I look to. It's the first place I go for solace. Besides, Colin is my friend. You do *allow* me to have friends, don't you?" She threw the last remark in for good measure. If there was one thing Matthias hated, it was being told he was controlling, even when he actually was.

"Talk all you want with your friends, my dear, but I'll thank you not to talk about me."

"Your name doesn't fly from my lips every second sentence, you know," she snapped.

"Keep it that way," he shot back.

Why did it always have to end like this? Why did their every encounter always end in tension? Was it some sort of curse? She tried to placate him. "It was no big deal, Matthias. Believe me. Please. And don't let's argue again." She pointed at the remains of their meal and the card game that followed. "We were doing so well. We were having a good evening. Can't we once, just once, have a conversation without winding up shouting at each other?"

It seemed to work. He tried to massage the tension out of the back of his neck. When he spoke next, much of the edge was gone. "So, your friend thinks you need to understand me better?"

"Sort of," she played it down. She didn't want him flying off the handle again.

"And you don't think you understand me enough already?"

Her shoulders lifted and fell. "I don't know. I thought I did when I married you. Or maybe, I was so taken up with you—how much you knew, how smart you were, the way you looked, and the things you did to my belly every time you walked into the room . . ."

Her embarrassment was pushed into the background by the knowledge that there was nothing Matthias ever did to her that he didn't already know about. It wasn't as if her attraction to him had ever been a secret!

She pressed on. "Maybe all that, the romance and the sex, the whole big whirlwind that sucked us in, made me not care. I didn't need to know who you really were. I didn't need to know what you cared about. All I wanted was you. All I wanted to be sure of was that you were mine, mine, mine, and that alone made me happy."

Matthias came around the table to stand next to her.

Becoming aware of how his height dominated her, he dropped onto his haunches; with her seated, they were level. He cupped her chin in one hand and Sarita knew that, although there was no pressure there, there was no sense in trying to turn her face away from his. "But the happiness didn't last," he stated.

She didn't have to admit it. They both knew it to be true.

"We got married very fast," he murmured.

She smiled wryly at the memory: a hot afternoon at the registrar's office in Miami; Matthias in his only suit, off the rack but as sexy on him as any Armani would be, and she in lemon yellow, clutching a handful of pansies, mere days after their return from Australia. No relatives; for her, there hadn't been time, and for him, he had none living. Only half a dozen exuberant friends to bear witness. "Six weeks," she reminisced.

He corrected her. "Five. Not a lot, not even by today's standards. But I wanted you for myself. Fast. Too fast. Not enough time for us to really talk."

"Not enough time to warn me that I'd always come in second." *Deny it,* she challenged silently. *Deny it, you coward. Tell me I was never second to your work, even if it was just for the two meager weeks of our honeymoon. Lie to me if you have to. Let me hear it once, so I can pretend to believe it. Make me feel more than second best, just this once.*

She didn't know whether to be relieved at his honesty or devastated by reality when, instead of protesting, he hung his head. "I warned you, before I asked you to marry me, about the children. You agreed."

He was right. She *had* agreed. "I thought it wouldn't matter. It didn't, not at the time."

"And you knew about the work. About the hours I kept. About my dream—no, not a dream. A mission.

My compulsion. To come back here and do what I'm doing now. I never lied about that."

"Why?"

He was flummoxed. "What do you mean, why? I can't believe you're asking me that question. You're committed to the cause, too." He pointed at the room behind them. "Reams and reams of paper. Stacks of books. Gigabytes of data, all pointing to the same problem and the same solution. How can you ask me why?"

"I'm not talking about Buccoo Reef. Damn Buccoo." In frustration, her voice raised. He flinched. If he thought her condemnation of his precious bay was blasphemy, well, tough. "I mean why here? Why Tobago? This island is not unique, Matthias. It's just a big lump of coral, with fish swimming around it and people living on top. There are bigger lumps of coral in every ocean in the world, and all of them are under threat. What's so special about here?"

"I was born here," he answered levelly. He showed no outward offense at her provocation.

"So what? Lots of people are. Practically everybody we meet every time we step outside was born here. You don't see them living out your obsession. You don't see them sacrificing everything to save a few lousy square miles of water and sand!"

"Somebody has to!"

"And that somebody is you?"

"Yes!" His voice raised to the level of hers, but it was fired by passion, not anger.

"Why you? Were you appointed? Were you anointed? Did you fall flat on your face before a vision of God, like Joan of Arc, and receive a divine directive—"

"Don't bring God into this conversation! Don't mock me!" He shot up again and began pacing. "I don't believe in visions, and there's no such thing as a divine directive."

"I'm not mocking you! And it's a pity you *aren't* doing this thing under divine directive; if you were, at least I could console myself and feel that my happiness was worth the sacrifice! So if not for the love of God, then, why?"

"I don't understand why you're being like this, Sarita. What can I possibly tell you that I haven't told you before? What is it that you need to know?"

The sheer force of her response propelled her to her feet. Her words were hot in her throat as they rushed out unchecked. "I need to know exactly what it is I lost out to and one thing's for sure: it's more than the reef. I need to know what you gave me up for!"

They faced each other, barely a few feet between them, with the dying boom of her words still hanging in the air. She watched him as he stood rock still, and emotions flickered across his face like an old reel-to-reel film projected onto a wall. She felt the irrational need to hang onto something to prevent herself from being sucked into the vortex of time that had him in its grip. Instead of spinning around to clutch the table to steady herself, she dug her nails into her palms and waited for several long, agonizing minutes.

Without answering, or bidding her to follow him, he abruptly strode to the porch. She stuck close to his heels; nothing would deter her from hearing what he would say next.

It was long since dark outside, but she didn't dare reach to turn on a light for fear that any distraction would interrupt his introspection and bring it all to naught. He sat on the short wall that surrounded the porch, and she sat nearby, turning her body to face him. In the still night he was a moving silhouette, a living mass that was denser than the space around him. She squeezed her eyes shut, partly to help grow accustomed to the darkness and partly the better to listen.

"You never understood," he began.

"You never explained it to me," she pointed out.

"Maybe I didn't understand, either. Maybe I didn't know."

"Explain it to me now, and we'll both understand."

He exhaled heavily and began talking. "You know about my mother. I told you. About how young she was, and how my father left her and went back to Switzerland."

"Yes."

"Try to imagine what it was like growing up a half-breed, and an unwanted one at that. Nowadays, nobody notices and nobody cares, but that was more than thirty years ago. It's a small island, and things were very different then. My skin color, my eyes, and my hair: everybody knew just by looking at my mother and me that my father was white and, at that time, white meant foreign. Everybody said my mother had conceived me whoring after tourist dollars.

"And she was a preacher's daughter. Because her father was well-known in the village, a well-respected man, people smiled at her, at least to her face. But behind her back the rumors flew. They said she probably couldn't even identify my father, that she wouldn't even know which of the many tourists she supposedly slept with had actually begot me. They wondered aloud how much my father had paid to bed her."

"That's not true!" Sarita protested, indignant on his behalf. Her eyes flew open.

"I know that. I know my father's name. And I know she was in love with him. I hate him for leaving, though, and what it did to her. And me. I remember going to school without shoes and all the children laughing, even though they didn't have any, either. They used to ask me what use it was to have a rich white man for a father if I didn't have any money for shoes. They used to tell me there was a cruise ship in the harbor and ask why I didn't tell my mother to go down there and make us some money."

She could see better now, as her eyes grew used to the dark. He was sitting with his head back against the wall, eyes staring out over her shoulder across a span of time and to a place she could only see and hear through him. The repetitive shushing of the waves on the shore behind them lulled him more deeply under, like a hypnotist's soothing voice. She touched the back of his hand lightly. It was cold.

"And my grandfather! You'd have thought he'd have done something to stop it. People were saying things about his own daughter! I kept waiting for him to stand up and shout at them, and tell them they were wrong. Defend the family honor." He grunted.

"He didn't?"

"The scandal shamed him, or so he said over and over. But he was a resourceful man and knew an opportunity when he saw one. He relished the chance to showboat before his congregation and to prove he was such a fair man that not even his own daughter should be spared the sharpness of his tongue. Every once in a while, every two months or so, he'd drag her down out of the choir and make her stand at the pulpit, in front of his whole congregation; he would throw out his hands and shout to the rafters: 'Behold! The face of sin!'" Matthias threw his arms wide in an imitation of the old man's grandiose posing.

"And before she was done crying, he always made me join her, so he could parade me around, and shout:

'Behold! The result of sin!' I hated Sundays, and I hated church. He made us come to every service; it wouldn't do for the minister's family not to be there. And every Sunday I sat and waited, and wondered if this would be the day he forced us up there again. An object lesson for the good Christians who sat there and fanned themselves and *tut-tutted* and mocked us, and clapped their hands and shouted *Amen!* All this to impress your God, Sarita."

"My God isn't impressed by that," Sarita responded defensively. "And you know it. One spiteful old man hurt you, but that's not what God is about. It's not what His Church is about. If you met Colin, you'd see. The Church isn't all about fire and brimstone. It's kindness and gentleness, too. And understanding."

He shook his head. "It's your personal choice to believe that. I'd never try to persuade you otherwise. Just don't bother trying to foist it on me. Hear?"

"It certainly couldn't make things any worse," she shot back. She shredded her thumbnail in agitation.

"It's not going to make them any better," he responded passionately.

She wished desperately for a way to argue even harder, but words failed her. She knew now, at least, why he'd refused her a church wedding and why he'd balked at a suggestion she'd once made, when he'd first demanded a divorce, that they try to find arbitration in the Baptist church in Miami she'd attended once or twice a month, but always alone. But surely that was only half his story?

"Okay." Her voice was placatory. "Now I understand why you feel the way you do about the Church. I don't agree with it, but I understand why. It still doesn't explain—"

"What brings me back here?" he cut in. "What makes

me think I'm the chosen one? I sure as hell don't think I'm Joan of Arc. I'm here because I made myself a promise when I was a little boy, after my mother died. After she escaped and left me behind to face the music alone. And every day I tolerated the vileness that spewed out of my grandfather's mouth, and the narrow-minded vindictiveness of the people who valued his opinion over the innocence of a little boy, I renewed that promise."

"And that was . . . ?" She was almost afraid to ask.

"That one day I'd be back. And show them. And prove that every spiteful thing they said about me, and every prediction that I'd grow up to be nothing, wasn't true. I'm here to show him he was wrong."

The fierceness in his words scared her. His passion was on the frontier between sanity and delusion. "Your grandfather's *dead*, Matthias! And so's half his congregation, most likely. Since you've been here, have you found anyone, *anyone*, who remembers you?"

"I know he's dead. It doesn't matter. Somehow, in some way, he's going to know. This whole island is going to know that I made something of myself. I didn't fall like they all said I would. I left because I had to, but now I'm back, and next time I leave here, I'll leave something behind that they can't deny, that they can't ignore. I'll leave them a living monument miles wide, that will still be there, and alive, fifty years from now. A hundred years after I'm dead."

"So is that what it's all about? Your ego? The new and improved Buccoo Reef is going to be a monument to you?" She took her hand away from his. She'd been trying to comfort him but that had been foolish of her. She'd been offering her sympathy, but now she understood that it all came down to himself.

"It's *not* about·ego," he denied. "I love this island."

He pounded his chest with his fist. "I love it with everything in me. All I want is for it to love me back." His voice cracked with the admission.

Silence stretched out agonizingly. He slumped a little, fatigued by the force of his outburst. Sarita watched him as his face worked, trying to bring those powerful emotions back under control. Now that she knew how huge her competition was, it made her almost laugh out loud to think that she had once seen Janelle as a threat. The object of his affections was greater than a mere woman, bigger than the reef, and huger, even, than the noble purpose of their mission. It was a whole island, and tangled inextricably therein was the whole idea of birthright and self-worth, vengeance, and vindication. What sort of fight could she put up against that?

"Now I know," she said softly.

He closed his eyes.

"Matthias," she called his name after a while.

He focused on her. His eyes were more honest than she had ever seen them. She was sure that whatever she asked him now would receive nothing but the whole truth. She steeled herself. "We made a mistake, didn't we? Getting married." It was only partly a question.

There didn't seem to be a need to answer, so instead he said, "I loved you."

"Did you really?" She needed so badly for him to affirm it.

"Yes."

She wanted to hug him, if only to use his body to still her trembling. "Just not enough, huh?"

His hands slid along her arms and pulled her closer, as if he'd read her need. "It wasn't a matter of *how much*. It was a matter of *when.*"

"Bad timing?"

"Yes."

"You needed to do this first."

"Yes."

She ached to ask him if he loved her less than he had a year ago but it was a stupid question. Just because her love was still as strong as it ever was, in spite of all they had gone through, why should his be? Instead, she asked, "Is there anything left? Some little spark, maybe?"

When he smiled, his face took on the softness of the Matthias she had fallen in love with. "That spark will never die. No matter what happens."

At least there's that, she thought. *For what it's worth.* Now that she had so much more information about what made him who he was, she needed to confirm for herself that their breakup over her deception with the Pill had been more of an excuse for him to disentangle himself than true outrage at her behavior. She broached the subject delicately. "You understand why I was so desperate to have a baby? When I sensed our marriage slipping away, I thought—"

"That it would hold us together."

"Yes."

"Children aren't glue, Sarita."

"I know that. Do you forgive me, for lying?"

"Of course I do. I pushed you to it. I was wrong." His arms around her squeezed tighter. "Now I need you to forgive me."

She tilted her head so she could see his face. "For what?"

"For using one stupid little incident as a means to escape. I saw a good excuse and I took it. And made you feel all year that this . . . wreck of a marriage was all your fault. I feel like a monster."

"You're not a monster." Her voice was muffled

against his shirt. It was funny how she hurt so badly, yet could drum up no anger toward him. All she could feel was a profound sadness, and a pain that she knew would never be dulled. "I forgive you."

"Oh, sweetheart." His hands were in her hair, and his own long locks brushed her face. "I wish I could have spared you this."

Grief and loss were sucking at her energy. She needed to turn in, or she would never make it to her bed, and she knew if she fell asleep in his arms out here she would die of heartbreak. Something stayed her, a stubborn ray of hope. Without daring to look at him, she asked, "If I came back to you, if we agreed to put all this behind us, and just keep each other company, would you?" She rushed on, trying to clarify before he could say anything. "Could you just be my lover, and I be yours? And forget the marriage, forget the pain, and see where the wind takes us?"

"I thought we could. A week ago, I could have sworn it was possible. But now I know it isn't. You'd only get hurt again."

"Why?"

"Because you would only be . . ." He couldn't force himself to say the rest.

"Second," she finished for him. "Like always."

"Yes."

It would be so easy. Second wasn't bad, if you really thought about it. It was still ahead of most of the pack. She'd have Matthias, and he would treat her with kindness and respect. He was a kind and imaginative lover, and would see that her needs were taken care of, so she wouldn't have to worry about that, either. She was sure that she could prod him, persuade him, even seduce him, right here. And by morning he'd change his mind and let her in, and her place as second in his life would be assured. If she were willing to take it.

Problem was, she wasn't. She wanted more. She knew she deserved more. She wanted to be first in his mind, and first in his heart, as he had always been in hers. Anything less wasn't good enough. With terrible sorrow and regret, she rose. He made no attempt to prevent her from going.

"I'm tired," she mumbled. "I think I'm going to bed."

"Wait!" He looked as if he just remembered something.

She spun around. "What?" Her pulse boomed like African drums. He'd called her back. . . .

He fished in his jeans pocket and pulled out a small box. "I forgot this. I got this for you today, as an apology over the whole thing with Janelle and the boat. I know I was a pig about it. I wanted to say I'm sorry." He handed it to her.

She took it, slightly disappointed, though greatly curious, but all the while protesting. It was surreal. Something inside her had just died, like a faithful pet put to sleep at her own hand, and here he was, giving her a forgotten gift. It was a plain box, unwrapped, and under the lid was a puff of cotton. He reached up and turned on the light so she could see better.

In the box was a pair of gold hanging earrings, two slender chains on small posts, and attached to each one was a luminous pink object the shape of a grain of rice, its undulating surface catching the light.

"River pearls," he said. "I remembered you like them."

She held the box tightly; the cardboard gave slightly in her grip. She felt ridiculous. She loved river pearls; she had bracelets, pendants, and necklaces of them. Matthias could be so kind sometimes, so thoughtful.

And yet what he had placed in her hand were two tiny punctuation marks at the end of a dead marriage. She wondered if she would ever have the heart to wear them.

"Thank you," she choked. She wanted her room, and she wanted it now, but before she left, there was one last thing she had to say to him. "Matt?"

"Yes?" His eyes glowed like the pearls. She briefly wondered if what she read in them was his sadness, or simply hers, reflected.

"Those divorce papers you sent me. You know I brought them with me, right?"

"I didn't know that."

"I did."

He waited, stock-still. Even the house fell silent, and the night outside, as all of Nature paused and waited with bated breath for what she would say next.

Courage, she told herself. *Courage.* "I'll sign them in the morning." There. It was done. Decision made. Before he could say another word, she ran.

Nine

Sarita Rowley. Two little words, neatly written on the dotted line. Sarita set her pen down and looked at them, feeling strangely numb and a little bit disoriented, the way she would feel if she had just come from a trip to the dentist with a head full of gas and a lip full of Novocain. She remembered the first few weeks of her marriage, when she was still getting used to the strange sound of her new name and when she would fill page after page with it, trying it out, wanting to see if her signature looked better with a large loop on the "y" or if it was best to leave a straight, sharp tail on it.

Now, the name had become a part of who she was. She tried to think of herself as she could soon become, once the divorce became final, if she chose to revert to her maiden name. Sarita Sanderson. Weird. She had carried around the name all her life, and yet it didn't ring true. If she spoke it out loud, would her tongue trip over it? The name had only a vaguely familiar ring to it; she couldn't shake the feeling of knowing this person, in the distant past. It was like knowing there was a girl by that name in your homeroom in junior high, swearing that you once took a class together, two, maybe, but not quite being able to recall her face.

She grunted dismissively. It was so stupid; lingering over something as trivial as what she would be called once Matthias was through filing the papers she now held in her hand. Did it matter what people called her? Would it make the huge distance between her and her soon-to-be ex-husband any greater? Such a thing could hardly be possible.

She folded the papers along their original creases and slid them into their envelope. They slipped inside without so much as a rustle, worn soft by constant handling. In the many months since she had received them, she had often taken them out and spread them on her bed, pored over them, sighed over them, prayed, vacillated, and, in fits of frustration, even seized a pen and tried her best to sign them, but before she could bring herself to make that first black mark, her heart had always failed her.

Not today. A promise was a promise. A coffin nail was a coffin nail, and her signature was nothing more than the last formality, a hurried incantation over something that was long dead, but had refused to lie down. She rose, straightened her spine, and walked carefully, one foot placed deliberately before the other so that she wouldn't give in to the giddiness that assailed her.

Matthias was waiting in the small room that served as the Reef Rescue office. For a change, his head wasn't bent over a notebook, nor was he engrossed in the information blinking and flashing across his computer screen. He was dressed for work, but was sitting in the lone armchair in the room, an old wooden affair that Sarita herself had painted in matte white and padded with an overstuffed cushion. He had positioned himself to face the doorway, and his eyes were on her as she walked in.

"Good morning," he said.

"Good morning." *That's how we're going to play it,* she thought. *Civilized. Adult.*

His gaze dropped to the envelope she held tightly in her hand, and there was a glimmer of recognition on his face. She neared him, and her arm rose, stiffly and straight out, like that of an animated department store mannequin. She couldn't think of anything appropriate to say at such a time, so she handed it to him without another word. He gently took the package.

She stood and waited as he stared at it. He read her name and address off the envelope, slowly turned it over and read the return address of his lawyer, and then turned it face up again. He didn't open it. He looked unsure of what to do with it at all. Eventually, he bent over and slipped it into the pocket of his knapsack.

"You can drop it off at the courier in town this morning, if you like, before we head off to Buccoo Bay. Or anytime that suits you. It'll be at your lawyer's office in three days, give or take, and he can do whatever it is he needs to do. And then, well . . ." She threw up her hands. The tension was so weighty upon her that she wanted to make some stupid joke, utter some line that would parody the finality that would result from dispatching the document: *then, "th . . . th . . . that's all folks!"* or *then, "goodnight, Gracie!"* Instead, she spoke a crueler truth. "Then you'll be free, like you always wanted." She waited to be thanked.

When he lifted his eyes to meet hers again, there was concern in them. "How do you feel?"

She was temporarily disarmed. He was concerned? Her whole life, her love, her faith in happy endings had just been signed away by her own hand. How did he think she felt? And what was it to him anyway? She made an inarticulate sound.

He tried again. "Did you sleep okay?"

Enough was enough, she thought. He was feeling bad, and he deserved to, but she wasn't standing around while he tried to assuage his own guilt by being so solicitous, and so darn nice to her. She held up her hand, signaling him to stop. "Look, Matthias, don't bother. It's not worth the effort, okay?"

He looked pained. "I just—"

"Drop it. I don't want to talk about it because there's nothing left to say. As soon as you're ready, I'll be waiting in the truck."

"But don't you want breakfast?"

She wondered if there would ever be a time when she would look at food again without her stomach roiling. "No," she said shortly, and left.

There was something different about the island today. It was as lazy as always; almost eight o'clock, and less than half a mile from the capital city, and there was nothing she could remotely call a traffic jam. It was beautiful as always; hot April sun bleaching the walls of the houses that flashed by, big-headed purple morning glories bobbing in the breeze at the roadside. But still, somehow, different.

The other woman, she realized. *Tobago. My competition is an island, and she beat me to it. Took my man right from under my nose, and there was nothing I could do about it.* She couldn't even challenge her to a duel, a battle of the wits, pit her charm against the other woman's and see who was the smarter, the prettier, the better cook, the better lover. The game had been lost before it had begun. There was nothing she could do to fight: after all, the island had him first. She was just a Jane-come-lately, a stopgap to help him pass the time until he could find his way back home to his true love. Her mind ran to the memory of Matthias jokingly calling the spat she had had with Janelle a catfight, and a bubble of laughter popped out of her mouth.

Matthias shot her a curious, almost alarmed look, as though he suspected she was on the brink of hysterical collapse. "Share the joke?"

"You wouldn't get it," she shot back. She might be willing to smile with herself, even at a time like this, but she wasn't up to smiling with him. She folded her hands in her lap, frowned, and looked out the window.

Before he could speak again there was a sharp crack, immediately followed by a curse from Matthias. He put on his indicator and pulled onto the shoulder.

"What?" she asked.

"Sounds like I ran over something. Sounded like a bottle exploding, or a stone under the wheel. I want to check the tires."

He hopped out and squatted at the front, near the driver's side, and peered under the wheel well. She wondered whether she should join him and offer to help, but figured she wouldn't have known what to do anyway. So she waited where she sat.

"No dice," he hollered. "Nothing's wrong with the tires. Maybe it's something else." He threw open the hood and peered in. Moments passed, and then she heard him suck his teeth in that long, drawn-out way, that very West Indian way that she couldn't imitate if she tried. He cursed again, and that was enough to get her out of the door and standing next to him.

"What?"

"Power steering pump. It's busted." He gestured vaguely at the tangle of wires and hunks of molded metal, as if she was supposed to spot the problem at once.

"And?" She wouldn't know a power steering pump if she tripped over one.

"And we've got to get a new one before the steering seizes up," he answered irritably, and then relented long enough to explain. "See the liquid that's squirted all over the engine?"

She nodded.

"It's supposed to be inside of that," he pointed at a small contraption. "Keeps the power steering working. Lose the juice and the bearings start grinding." He studied her blank face and then added helpfully, "and that's not a good thing."

"I figured as much," she replied dryly. A twinge of irritation penetrated her melancholy. She'd been looking forward to the solace of the water to help wash away her ache, but now it looked as though they wouldn't even be making it that far. "So we're stuck here?"

He made sure her fingers were free from harm's way and then slammed down the hood. "Not stuck. It wouldn't be a very good idea to keep heading toward town, so I'm turning us around. We should try to make it as far as the bay. Then JoJo and I'll have the chance to take a better look, see what we can do." He walked back to the driver's side. "Hop in."

She did.

They made it to Buccoo Bay, but not without the accompaniment of the engine's painful grinds and groans, and considerable effort from Matthias, whose biceps bulged as the steering began to stiffen up. Once there, Sarita left the men to it, seeking refuge at the water's edge rather than in Janelle's boat, which was moored and waiting nearby. The boat's owner sat in the shade of a tree and glowered at Sarita, like a dog protecting its bowl. Sarita decided that a hurricane would touch down before she approached either the woman or the boat without Matthias or JoJo nearby.

Instead, she concentrated on the young men exercising their goats, as they had almost every morning since she arrived. Some of them swam alongside the goats, which seemed quite proficient in the water, paddling around like big happy dogs. With Easter a week away, she was sure the sense of competition was getting keen. The tourist population was swelling, and even at this early hour, sunburned visitors in flowered shorts strolled along the rocky beach with cameras and camcorders, as interested in the goat-training routines as she was. She felt the merest twinge of excitement. Maybe Matthias could take her to the races.

She gave herself a mental slap to help her overwrought imagination return to clarity. "Maybe not," she said aloud. She looked around. Matthias and JoJo had abandoned their tinkering with the engine and were now passing the cellular phone from one to the other, speaking earnestly. Eventually, Matthias hung up and approached her.

"Good news or bad news?" she asked before he could speak.

"A bit of both. The pump won't be that hard to replace. We can probably do it ourselves."

"Good."

"But we can't find anyone on the island with that particular model in stock."

"Oh."

She looked so crestfallen that he smiled a little. "Don't worry. We've got a supplier in Trinidad willing to take one up to the airport over there and get it on a midday flight. The flight's only about twenty minutes, so we'll have it soon enough. In the meantime, I guess we wait."

Wait? Today? When all she wanted was the splash of the boat's wake and the feel of the aquamarine water lapping up around her to soothe her frazzled nerves? Not likely. "You wait," she told him firmly. "You and JoJo wait for the part, and then have fun tinkering with your toys. I came here to work, and I'm going out today."

He frowned. "Alone?"

"I won't be alone." Simultaneously, they both looked across at Janelle, who seemed to sense that they were talking about her. She rose from the spot where she had planted herself and began to approach slowly, lazily, hips swinging, as though she had all the time in the world, and as though she knew how good she looked when she walked like that.

"You want to go out alone with Janelle?" he repeated. He squinted at her as if she were wearing coveralls that had the words "Psych ward" stenciled across the front.

"I don't *want* to," she corrected, not forgetting her vow of a few moments ago to not even approach the woman unaccompanied. "I'm *willing* to. There's a difference. Reef Rescue has a crisis, and as an *employee,*" she stressed the last word, "I'm willing to bite the bullet and do what needs to be done."

By now, Janelle was upon them. She looked only at Matthias, and spoke only to him. Sarita might as well have been air. "What's the status, Matt? Are we going out, or aren't we?"

"I'm going out," Sarita said evenly. She spoke these words to Janelle's back, as the woman had managed to insinuate herself between her and Matthias.

Janelle didn't even glance around. "Matt?" Her voice said *I'm waitinggggg. . . .*

Matthias settled his glasses firmly on his nose and shifted a little so that he could see Sarita better. It didn't take him more than a few seconds to make up his mind. "You two wait here," he said and walked back to the truck.

After a hurried conversation with JoJo, he returned with his knapsack slung over his shoulder. "JoJo will take the motorcycle to the airport when the flight gets in and pick up the part. By the time we get back this afternoon, he should have it installed."

"And you?" Sarita wanted to know.

"I'm coming with you ladies." He turned to Janelle. "Let's go.

The radio crackled. Sarita paid no attention; Janelle usually spent a great deal of time on it, speaking to one or two people who always seemed interested in where her boat was and how far the Coast Guard was from her. She assumed it was some kind of relay system between boat owners, pretty much like truckers back in the States who were constantly watching for Smokey.

She rubbed herself with a towel, feeling the stickiness of the drying salt water and the grit of the coral sand that always found its way into the folds and creases of her swimsuit. The sun was beginning to dip, and it was about time to head home. With luck, she thought, JoJo had solved the problem with the pump doohickey. The cottage would mean a shower, a change of clothes, and, most importantly, food. She was already beginning to regret her decision to forego breakfast this morning, even though she knew that, at the time, her stomach wouldn't have been able to take it.

As expected, the day of vigorous swimming had brought her the solace it had promised, even though for most of the day the source of her turmoil had been swimming right beside her, or seated close to her as they pored over pages of notes and charts, trying not to get them too wet as the water dripped out of their hair. Throughout the day, he had seemed uneasy, cautious around her, obviously still suffering the effects of last night's conversation, and the signed papers in the inner pocket of his bag. They'd never made it to the courier in Scarborough to drop them off: the breakdown of the truck had cut short that venture. She wondered if he still intended to send them to his lawyer later today. If he did, he'd be making that trip alone. *She* was getting out at Black Rock.

Involuntarily, she glanced at him, half hoping that she would catch him looking back at her, and read the same turmoil she was feeling reflected in him. But he was staring at Janelle, body rigid, one shoe on and the other grasped in both hands, poised above his bare foot.

Sarita felt a twinge of foreboding. What could Janelle possibly be saying to attract his undivided attention? She struggled to listen to the hissed, anguished conversation.

"I can't head back in," Janelle was saying. Then she said something that sounded like "I'm carrying, you know that!" But that couldn't be right. Janelle wasn't carrying anything other than two clients, and a load of expensive marine equipment.

"Get rid of it, or get out." The crackling of the radio did little to diminish the decisiveness of the voice on the other end.

"I can't ditch it! The receivers, you know what they'd do to me if I did. I can't! You're asking me to put my life on the line. Besides, I've got . . ." Janelle looked around her for the first time and seemed startled to notice them staring back at her. She faltered, and then her face took on a determined set. "I've got company. The Americans. You don't expect me to—"

"Dump it or leave. Head east, and lay low."

Before Sarita could get her brain around what was going on, Matthias was moving. He snatched the radio from Janelle's hand and barked into it. "Who is this?"

Nothing but static. The connection was cut. Frustrated, he slammed it down and faced Janelle. "Dump what, Janelle?"

She was resolutely mute, unflinching.

He repeated his question, grasping her by the arm until she yelped. "Dump what? What's on the boat?"

"None of your damn business!" Janelle snapped. She wrenched herself away and regained control of the wheel, grabbing hold of the throttle and throwing it into high. The boat lurched as it changed direction, almost throwing Matthias off his feet and sending Sarita sliding to one side until she banged her knee on the hull.

Matthias regained his balance quickly and had both hands on the wheel, trying to right the boat as Janelle struggled to keep it on its new course. "Where're you headed?" he shouted.

"East. Didn't you hear?" There was no trace of the sugar and molasses that she usually dipped her voice in when she spoke to him. It was stripped bare, cold, and very angry.

Still a little baffled by Janelle's mad antics, but keenly aware that Matthias was trying to right something that had gone very, very wrong, Sarita leaped to his aid. She threw her arms around Janelle and tried to drag her away from the controls, long enough for him to take over. Although Sarita outweighed her, Janelle was strong, and wriggled strenuously, trying to throw her head back to hit Sarita in the nose. *This is what it's like to wrestle a gator,* Sarita thought.

"Coast Guard! Coast Guard!" Janelle panted. "Didn't you hear?"

"They're always around," Sarita pointed out. The woman was crazy. "So what?"

"They're . . . they're *boarding!* Routine checks. Mandatory compliance. Every boat. Every . . . single . . . boat."

Sarita managed to force Janelle into a seat and

brought the brunt of her weight on the still-struggling woman's chest. *Pays to be a big girl,* she thought proudly. If the situation hadn't been so serious, she would have laughed.

"Headed our way!" Janelle added, "Don't you understand? How stupid can you be?"

The penny dropped. It took her a while, Sarita admitted to herself sheepishly, but the penny finally dropped. Janelle was afraid of the Coast Guard for a bigger reason than a simple fear of authority. There was something on the boat besides Reef Rescue property. Something worth running for. Her shock made her slacken her grip on Janelle, and she turned her head toward Matthias, who was frowning, concentrating on returning the boat to its homeward course. "Matthias?"

"She's carrying, Sari."

"Carrying . . . what?" There were so many types of illegal cargo a person could get into trouble for. A long jumbled list scrolled through Sarita's mind. What were they sharing a boat with?

Janelle took the opportunity to wriggle free, and Matthias braced himself for another attack. Instead, she hopped to her feet and looked agitatedly from one to the other. "They're headed right for us! Matthias, Matthias, stop! For the love of God!"

"Carrying what, Janelle? What exactly?" Matthias sounded so uncompromising, so authoritarian, that even Sarita at her angriest would not have been able to oppose him.

Janelle looked stubborn, hands grasped behind her back and glaring at him, like an unruly teen summoned to the principal's office, but determined not to let him intimidate her. Her black eyes had lost their fluttering flirtatiousness.

"Don't make me tear this boat apart," Matthias

threatened. "Tell me, or I find out for myself. Either way, you're deep in it. You know that."

Still rebellious, she spat out a one-word confession. "Weed."

Sarita's jaw dropped. Marijuana? Janelle had drugs on the boat? How much? Certainly not a loose joint or two, not the way she was behaving.

Matthias asked the question for her. "How much?"

"Eighty kilos, high quality, compressed."

Sarita felt her stomach lurch. There were eighty kilos of compressed marijuana on the boat. But where? She knew the boat by heart, every inch of it. She and Matthias had been in and out of it a dozen times, stored their equipment, and taken turns at the wheel. Where did one hide close to a hundred and eighty pounds of . . .

She saw Janelle's eyes swivel skyward and had her answer. She followed suit. The ill-fitting padded leather. The same trim she had gotten into so much trouble with Janelle for touching. She'd been right all along. There *was* a space between the ceiling and the roof, and not because of an incompetent workman. It had been deliberately designed. And now that space was filled with a substantial quantity of drugs.

Matthias figured it out, too. "Pull out the padding, Sari," he instructed, not wanting to leave the wheel for a second with Janelle in her present state.

"No!" Janelle protested. She was about to lunge forward when a shout from Matthias stayed her.

"Don't!" was all he said.

She froze but glowered.

Sarita stood and lifted her arms above her head and gingerly began inserting her fingers along the seams. She found the place where she'd spotted the stray tongue of clear polythene peeking out from the edge.

It taunted them to decipher its message and neither of them had. The truth was bizarre, unexpected, but yet, made so much sense. Her fingers found purchase in a narrow crease and she pulled.

A whole section of padding gave way, almost three feet square of it, and dozens of hard, dark bricks rained upon them like toads in an ancient Egyptian plague. Janelle clapped her hands over her mouth and moaned. Sarita picked one up gingerly. It was hard-packed, rectangular, and tightly wrapped in clear plastic, and then heavily secured with duct tape. It was lighter than she would have expected, weighing no more than one of those extra-large packs of dried oregano or basil one could buy at a warehouse outlet. There had to be quite a few of those crammed into the double ceiling.

She stared at it, a part of her curious. She remembered some of her friends doing the occasional joint back in college but that was as close as she ever got to an illegal drug. To be surrounded by so much of it was an entirely different story. She handed the package to Matthias, who turned it over and sniffed at it. "Ganja, all right," he confirmed unnecessarily and then tossed it back onto the heap. "How long has this been on the boat?"

"Couple of days," Janelle answered sulkily. "I was getting rid of it tonight."

"Getting rid of it, how?"

Sarita found her head jerking back and forth between the two, like a spectator at a tennis match. She was happy to let Matthias have control of the questioning. She, for one, had no desire even to speak to the woman.

"Taking it out a few miles off, into international waters. It only takes a few hours. Then someone picks it up from there and heads farther on up north."

"To the States?"

"Yes."

Matthias looked disgusted. "Who picks it up?" Janelle was silent, and a mulish set to her jaw told him she wasn't answering that one anytime soon. Matthias tried another tack. "Where'd it come from?"

"Trinidad. Where else? What, did you think all they grew down there was sugarcane and oranges?"

"You pick it up there?"

"Yeah. Easy work, if you can get it, and it's not exactly brain surgery, even though it pays better. An overnight sailing to the south coast and voila. Half a million dollars' worth of goods. Not bad for a few hours' work."

She was getting cocky and that was exasperating. Drug-running required a fast, agile, low boat. This baby's engine packed an unusually large wallop, a fact that had always puzzled Sarita, until now. But even so, this was not the usual sleek, black cigarette racer that drug couriers favored, ones that sat low in the water and could hide among the waves. Even one of the Coast Guard's oldest and heaviest patrol boats would catch up to this eventually. What had Janelle been thinking?

Matthias voiced her thoughts. "Why this boat?"

Janelle smiled slightly, looking proud of her own ingenuity. "It's a tourist boat. Supposed to be slow and doesn't go far. Who'd suspect it? The Coast Guard doesn't have time to bother much with stupid tourists on vacation, trampling around on the reef and taking photos. Half the time, the only thing they think about is your safety, and as long as we're not going too fast and you're not trying to steal the coral or the fish, they're happy."

"So we're your cover. They see us on the boat and sail on by."

Sarita didn't have to know Matthias as well as she did to read the anger and revulsion on his face.

"Yes."

"Except for today."

Janelle's cockiness melted away, and her worried look returned. "Spot checks. I can't do anything about that. Except stay out of their way. Matthias, listen to me. We can't go back. Bear with me for an hour or two. Turn around, let us lay low for a while. Then I'll set you back ashore and you can forget all about this. I'll refund your money and you can hire another boat."

She might as well not have spoken. He picked up the radio.

"What are you doing?" Janelle screeched.

"Calling the Coast Guard," he answered reasonably.

"Are you crazy?"

He paused and turned to answer her. "I'm perfectly sane. But what else do you expect me to do?"

"Have you got any idea how much time I can do for this?"

"You should have thought about that before," he responded grimly, and began setting the relevant channel on the radio.

Janelle wasn't giving up without a fight. Her voice dropped; it was less frantic but even more dangerous. "Have you any idea how much time *you* could do for this? Both of you?"

Sarita broke her silence. "What's she going on about, Matthias?"

Matthias was frowning at Janelle. "We have nothing to do with this. We've got nothing to fear."

"You think so? They board us and find that quantity of drugs, you think they're going to just let you walk away once you touch dry land? They're handing all of us over to the police."

"And we'll tell them our story, and they'll let us go."

"And I'll tell them *my* story . . . about the part you two

played in this whole thing. About how Reef Rescue is nothing but a big front for your operation. About how you threatened me into carrying your goods for you," Janelle rejoined.

"You wouldn't!" Sarita gasped.

Janelle's only response was a taut smile. Sarita's mind reeled at the implications. She turned pleadingly to her husband. "What do we do?"

He was reassuring. "Don't worry. There's not a court in the world that would buy that story. We don't have to prove our innocence; they have to prove our guilt."

Janelle, sensing that Sarita's resolve was weaker, turned to her and tried to press her point home, speaking to her for the first time in ages. "Tell him that just because you don't belong here doesn't mean they're going to take it light on you. Tell him the jails are full of foreigners. What do you think they're in for? We're smack in the middle of a major trafficking route; there's cocaine and ganja coming in and out of these islands in large amounts, and the law doesn't take kindly to people abusing our island hospitality and using our waters for hauling drugs. You think they'd be nice to you?"

Matthias seemed to sense Sarita's fear because his next words were soft and soothing. "Sari, if we run like she wants us to, and they catch up with us, that's an affirmation of our guilt, before we've even begun to defend ourselves. To my mind, the best thing to do is to end this, face up to them, and explain what happened. This isn't Wild West justice. We'll have our say, and they'll listen."

What an awful, awful choice! They were caught between the devil and the deep blue sea. To run like cowards, and either escape or compound their current difficulties, or to sail home straightaway and face the inevitable interrogation.

They were well within sight of land. Matthias prodded her. "I'm not making any decision without you, Sari. What's it to be?"

Running would mean lying, and a liar she was not. She desperately wanted to prove that to him. Her decision didn't take long. "Keep on heading home," she said.

Matthias half smiled and gave her an admiring look, leaving her feeling vindicated and proud that she'd made the hard choice rather than the easy one. He looked like he was about to speak, but whatever he was going to say was cut off by a howl from Janelle. She lunged. Matthias steeled himself, but she didn't go for him or for Sarita. Instead, to their bewilderment, she threw herself at the large emergency kit that was securely fastened near the stern. She flung open the lid and reached in, grabbing something in her hand.

"What is she—" Sarita began to ask, but her words were drowned out by a high-pitched whine that sounded awfully close. There was a blinding flash of light, and an intense heat seared past her as something exploded in the hull behind. She spun around.

A blazing emergency flare was wedged in the hole into which Janelle had shot it. Designed to fly hundreds of feet into the sky, it had hit the hull with tremendous force. The blue-white flame hissed like a Fourth of July firecracker for several seconds more, spraying sparks on her and Matthias before petering out.

And when Sarita turned to face Janelle in horror, there was a flare gun—a loaded flare gun—aimed at her head. Sarita felt her knees go weak.

"Drop it," Matthias demanded. "Don't make this any worse."

Janelle sneered. "It can't get any worse than this. Either way, I do time, and at least this way I've got a fighting chance. Hard to starboard, Matthias, and head east. Now."

"It *can* get a lot worse," he argued. "You hit Sarita with that thing and it's . . ." He couldn't finish.

"Murder," Sarita breathed. She wasn't stupid. She had used flare guns before, and knew that the cartridges were no laughing matter. They were bona fide weapons, and Trinidad and Tobago even required boat owners to have a license to carry them on board. She couldn't resist looking over at the large, blackened hole left by the burned-out flare and tried not to think of what one of those would do if it hit her. They gave off a light so intense that not even water could put them out. She'd heard that if they hit you, they lodged in the flesh and kept on burning. . . .

"Hard to starboard, Matthias," Janelle insisted. "Move it!"

Sarita anxiously searched his face, pleading with him to comply, even though to do so would only prolong their ordeal. At least the immediate danger would be temporarily averted. Maybe there would be another way out of this mess, if only she and Matthias had the chance to think. He seemed to read her thoughts and nodded. The boat shuddered as it changed course. The setting sun was now at their backs, rather than in their eyes.

Janelle didn't lower her arm. "It doesn't have to be murder," she clarified. She addressed Sarita, but her words were meant for Matthias. "Not if he keeps us steady. If you're lucky, I'd only hit an arm or a leg. If he tries to pull any stunts to throw me off balance, well, then your life will be on his head." To Matthias she said, "Full throttle! What are you waiting for?"

Matthias opened up the throttle without another word.

"Sit," Janelle gestured at Sarita. Sarita thought it best

to comply. Janelle sat facing her, and still keeping a firm grip on the trigger of the flare gun, let it rest in her lap. "Don't think that just because this thing isn't pointed at you, I'm no longer willing to use it. It's locked and loaded, and I can fire it off before either of you can take it away. And if you think you can wait until I fall asleep, good luck. I've made my share of night trips and still managed to be at the pier each morning, haven't I? I don't need a lot of sleep."

Maybe that was why Janelle was always so mean, Sarita thought ironically. She was suffering from sleep deprivation. But then she corrected herself. Janelle was mean because she was a mean person. She'd known it all along; something was wrong with Janelle, but it had never struck her that things could be *this* wrong. Colin Constantine's words to her on her last visit came to mind. "Be careful," he had told her. "Trust your instincts."

Her instincts had been right, but neither she nor Matthias had listened. And now they were in deep, deep trouble.

Ten

The sun was sinking worryingly low—and so was the fuel gauge. Matthias had already topped up once using the large container of extra fuel that Janelle had kept on board, but that wouldn't take them much farther, and it certainly wouldn't take them back home. They hadn't even set out with a full tank this morning, and he kicked himself for not bothering to check before they had left Buccoo Bay, even though the maintenance and seaworthiness of the craft was Janelle's responsibility. For a project leader, he'd slipped up in his duties. For a criminal, Janelle wasn't much of a planner.

He spoke up. "Running out of fuel, Janelle. And we lost sight of land long ago. Don't you think we should stop? The Coast Guard operation must be over by now. It'll be totally dark in half an hour. It's hard enough to see as it is." He tried to sound reasonable and non-aggressive. The woman had hair-trigger nerves, and he didn't want to do anything that would set her off again, not unless he had to. He hadn't forgotten the very real threat she still posed to Sarita.

For the length of the journey, the women had been seated face to face across the narrow boat, each staring the other down. He had to admire Sarita for her steely nerves and ability to unswervingly hold Janelle's gaze, even while she held a lethal weapon that was loaded and ready to go off. From time to time Janelle had even amused herself—and reminded Matthias that she was serious—by raising the gun and training it dead center of Sarita's face. Each time she had done that, it had been all he could do not to abandon the helm and leap on Janelle and throw her to the floor. Only the sickening fear that she could actually manage to pull the trigger before he took her down had stayed him. Besides, he'd never hit a woman in his life. Could he do it now? The answer came to him after little more than a moment's pause: if Sarita's life depended on it, he would damn well try.

"Janelle?" He hadn't got an answer.

"I heard you," she answered calmly.

"And?"

"And you keep going until I tell you to stop."

He shoved his exasperation down into a deep, private place and tried to keep his tone free of hostility. "Janelle, we're miles from the coast. We can't even *see* the coast from here. We're headed into open waters, and the only thing facing us is several thousand miles of Atlantic. And do you know what the next landfall ahead is? Africa. There's nothing between us and Africa. We have no food, and maybe a day's worth of water. This is suicide. Do you really want to die out here on a boat?"

She took her eyes off Sarita for the first time and looked directly at him. "I don't plan to die, Matthias."

"What do you plan to do, then?" His frustration made asking difficult. "Tell me, so I can help."

"Eat us," Sarita giggled. She clapped her hand over her mouth to stifle the sound.

Matthias shot her a searching look. Under any other circumstances that would have been funny, but he had little means of assessing her mental state after being under the gun, literally, for so many hours. So how did he know if she really was joking, or if she had begun to crack? His only reassurance was the fact that he knew her, had loved her, and accepted that she was a strong woman. She was just trying to ease the tension, he assured himself. She had to be.

Janelle even saw the funny side of Sarita's comment. She half smiled. "Hardly, dear. Although in a pinch, there would certainly be a lot of *you* to go around. . . ." She waited for Sarita to bristle at the barb about her weight, but she didn't even flinch, so she continued, "Although I'm sure your friend here would make a tastier morsel."

"Husband," Matthias corrected, surprising himself in the process. He was aware of both women staring at him, both amazed, but each for a different reason.

"Come again?" Janelle said.

"I'm her husband, not just her friend. I want you to know that." At least for now. He thought of the signed papers in the bag he'd left on the bench a few feet away. His status remained true until those found their way to his lawyer, and until then, he was responsible for her. He'd do whatever he had to do to keep her out of danger, even though saving her from the real and immediate threat of the flare gun meant taking her, temporarily, he hoped, into the possible—No, who was he fooling? Increasingly likely—threat of being stranded.

"You two are putting me on, right?" Janelle blustered, looking from one to the other.

Sarita was smiling at him, a broad, stunned smile, and that made him feel ashamed. Since the moment she'd landed, he hadn't claimed her as his wife to anyone. How his denial of her must have hurt! He wished he could rush over and hug her, and tell her how sorry he was for his behavior, but that was impossible given their predicament. Instead, he smiled back reassuringly.

Janelle still seemed fascinated by the concept of them as a married couple. "When did it happen? Here? In Tobago?"

Sarita answered in triumph. "Long before you came into the picture, I can assure you."

"Well," Janelle shot back scornfully, "at least *one of you* got a bargain."

Janelle was distracted, and she was drifting off the urgent point at hand. He was the one who had set the conversation on a tangent, so he was the one who had to drag it back. "Janelle," he called her name sharply and her head snapped around. "I'm stopping. Right now." He was done asking. He'd already eased off on the throttle by degrees, so gradually that she hadn't noticed. That had served to slow them down a little, reducing the distance they could cover, but it didn't help much. They were still far from land. It was time to take back some control. "We'll wait until morning and then find a way back home. Understand?"

She seemed to think about what he said. "Stop. Stop if you like. But you don't have to worry about getting back. My friends will come and get us."

"Your drug-running friends?" Sarita was tired of being meek to suit Janelle, and she was speaking up. Matthias felt a glimmer of pride. That was his girl. Never backing away from a good fight.

"Yes, them. My friends. They'll come for us."

"In the middle of the ocean?"

"It's part of the plan." Janelle tried to sound sure of herself. "If there's trouble, we head east, away from land. And then the others come looking for us."

Matthias killed the throttle and the engine went silent. He thought it was a stupid plan, a slipshod plan, and he didn't mind telling her so. "East is a big place."

"Wonderful, we're going to get rescued by drug pushers," Sarita said at the same time. "So you call them your friends, huh? The ones who left you out here to face the music on your own? They sound real dependable."

Before Janelle could come up with a retort, Matthias asked, "Do you have any particular coordinates? Do you have a meeting point?"

She shook her head slowly. "No, but all I have to do is get them on the radio and tell them where I am. Then they'll come get me."

Matthias unhooked the mouthpiece of the radio from its cradle and held it out. "Give me your channel, and I'll set it for you. Call them, and tell them to come get us."

"No."

Patience, patience, he reminded himself. *Our lives depend on it.* "What do you mean, 'no'?"

"Just that. No. I'm not calling them."

"And why not? You just said—"

"I'll call them when I'm good and ready. Right now, the channels are probably being scanned. We keep radio silence until I tell you." The next thing he knew, the flare gun was aimed not at Sarita but at his bare chest. "Understand?"

His shoulders ached. The taste of defeat was like bile rising in his throat. This lunatic had the upper hand and there was nothing, but nothing he could do. Carefully, he replaced the radio mouthpiece and abandoned the helm. He dropped anchor, but there was little the anchor could do to prevent them from drifting, as they were in deep waters now, and it would hardly touch bottom. He was getting nowhere with Janelle, so the only intelligent choice to make now was to concentrate on helping where he still could: Sarita.

Gingerly, he edged around the glass-bottomed trays in the center of the boat, and the haphazard pile of plastic-wrapped packets that still lay scattered among them, moving slowly so as not to spook Janelle, who had lowered the gun but was still alert and baleful. He settled down next to his wife. Her dark, anxious eyes were on his face, pleading, searching for a sign that he had a plan, that he would rescue her.

Nature would eventually take its course and Janélle would grow tired. It was simply a matter of waiting her out. The battle would be lost by the first to fall asleep, and he was determined that it would not be him. But until then, the best they could do was keep a level head and wait, drawing as little of Janelle's ire as possible. With a heavy heart, he opened his arms. Sarita settled against his chest without hesitation.

"We'll be all right," he whispered. "Don't you worry."

Her silence let him know she didn't believe him.

He laid his jaw along the side of her head and felt her hair brush his lips. "You know I'd never let you get hurt, don't you?"

Again, she didn't respond, and that bit. Instead of coaxing her further, he just held her. Never in his adult life had he felt so useless, so impotent. Not even last night, when she'd challenged him to put her first, and he'd confessed that he would not been able to do so, had he ever failed her so badly.

Sarita had been right about Janelle all along. She hadn't liked her from the get-go, had insisted that something was wrong about her, that something didn't fit. And he'd been vain enough to chalk it up to jealousy and female competitiveness. Surely, that had been there, but it had been only a veneer, the thinnest layer that had masked the solid truth: Janelle was rotten to the core and he'd been too obtuse to see it. A thousand purgatories would not be long enough for him to expiate that grievous transgression.

After a while, he heard her murmur something. "What?" he asked.

"I'm so hungry."

"Bet you're sorry you didn't have that breakfast now, huh?" He tried to lighten the moment.

She actually managed a chuckle. "I'm almost ready to bob for jellyfish."

"Oh, we won't have to. We'll sit out the night, and then tomorrow, we'll find a way out of this mess." She needed to hear that, so he told her, whether or not he believed it himself.

She twisted a little so she could get a better look at him. Her eyes were deep, black, and shiny. He wasn't prepared for what she said next. "Pray with me, Matthias."

He hadn't heard right. "What?"

She repeated herself clearly. "Pray with me. For once in our lives. Let's you and me talk to God about this. He's the only one who can help us. He'll help us, if we ask."

Pray? He didn't know how. Even if he believed that such an undertaking was anything more than an empty, ritualistic gesture, he didn't know if he could. He hadn't done so in more than twenty years, not since he had left the condemning, stifling confines of his grandfather's church in Bethel. He floundered for a way to turn her down. There was a delicate way to do it, wasn't there? "I don't think—"

"Don't think. Just do it. We don't have to say anything fancy. We don't have to remember any special words. Just talk to Him with me." Her voice was low, urgent, and he admired the unshakable faith with which she made her assertion. "He'll listen. But two voices are better than one."

"I can't," he managed.

"You can," she insisted.

"I don't want to, then. I won't. I don't believe in your God, and I can't talk into thin air and hope for a miracle. You knew that about me all along. You know I can't just change my point of view, not like that."

"The air's not thin," she insisted. Her eyes and her voice were pleading, distressed. "It's full of wonderful sounds; you choose not to listen."

His stomach hurt. Where he had felt no real fear under Janelle's gun, he felt it now. Real, manifest fear. She was asking the impossible. How could she expect him to look past all the miserable years of his young life, when he was shoved to his knees to beg forgiveness of a harsh and vengeful God, one who was outraged by his very existence? Did she really expect him to purge himself of his grandfather's poison, and forget what he and his mother had suffered, just so that she could have a conversation with this same God?

He couldn't. It was impossible. He wanted to get up and get as far from her as he could, but she was his wife, and she needed to be held. Physical support was all he could give her. *Please,* he begged her silently. *Please don't hope for anything more.* His mouth was dry when he spoke next, and it was not just due to their limited water supply. "You go ahead, love. You pray, and I'll hold you."

Hurt drew her eyebrows together in the center. "You don't believe," she said, part accusing, part disappointed.

"I believe that *you* do," he responded. "That's all that I can offer you right now."

She held his gaze for an uncomfortable eternity, before clasping her hands around his and closing her eyes. "Shut your eyes, then."

He glanced across at Janelle, who, though unable to hear their conversation, kept them in her unwavering view. He cringed at the thought of what she might do if they both shut their eyes, but steeled himself and complied, for Sarita's sake. Maybe her God would cut them some slack in those few unguarded seconds. He divided his attention between any possible movement from Janelle's corner and the sound of Sarita's words.

"Father, it's me, Sarita. And Matthias. We're in trouble. We're stuck and we're scared and we're in trouble, and we need your help . . ."

Matthias listened to the soft whisper, feeling vaguely embarrassed, as if he were eavesdropping on an intimate conversation. His surprise grew as he listened. This was not what he remembered prayer to be. This straightforward, unabashed conversation with a friend was light years away from the ostentatious racket that haunted him in his dreams, the one where he found himself trapped, engulfed by the perpetual dimness of his grandfather's church. The women around him in their starched linens and rustling taffeta, who threw their hands heavenward and shouted praises while looking out of the corners of their eyes to see who was watching. The long, rambling, unending diatribes that served more to impress the audience of fellow worshippers with the diligence and dedication of the speaker. It wasn't one of those prayers that shouted "Look at me! See how pious I am?" It was pure and simple and straight from Sarita's heart, and listening to it touched his. It almost made him want to join her.

When she was finished, her body relaxed against his, and he let her be quiet for as long as she wanted. He looked up at the deepening purple of the sky, and the narrow red line that separated the dying day from the predatory night. The moon had risen, a round, bright, full Easter moon. The sky was so flawless he could see the dark shadows of its rivers and lakes. He was half convinced that if he strained to listen, he would be able to hear the wonderful sounds she spoke of. Cowardice prevented him from trying.

Sarita shivered. He was still bare-chested, not having realized before now how chilly it had become. Even in the tropics it was cold out on the open sea, as the wind rushed unimpeded over the surface of the water. He looked down at her arms. Goose bumps had appeared on her skin.

"You're cold," he observed unnecessarily.

"Didn't know I'd be needing a jacket," she answered wryly. "Shoulda warned me about this whole kidnap and chase scenario, I'd have come prepared. I'd even have brought along a few beers."

"And chocolate."

"Mmm. Chocolate. That's the ticket." She licked her dry lips.

"Sit up." He slid from under her, rummaged around until he found his shirt, and made her put it on. It was short sleeved, more was the pity, but it would create another thin layer of air around her, and that, once warmed by her own body heat, would make all the difference.

"You think they'll really come for us?" she asked anxiously. She hugged his shirt against herself. "Her friends, I mean." Her eyes flicked in Janelle's direction to ascertain how much attention she was paying. Not much, it seemed: the basilisk stare was now fixed on the void around them.

"I don't know," he admitted. The possibility of Janelle's cohorts not turning up was not his greatest fear. In fact, he was far more anxious about what might happen if they *did*. How high was their tolerance for living witnesses?

Sarita lowered her voice even further. "And if they come, would they hurt us?"

"I was wondering the same thing," he admitted honestly. Lying to her would have been an insult. She was too smart not to have thought about the possibility that if Janelle's friends came by for a visit, not everyone was necessarily making the trip back home. She was too strong to wilt at the suggestion. He trusted her to keep it together. She had to.

"Maybe the Coast Guard will get to us first," she suggested hopefully. "Maybe JoJo called in a report when we didn't come back. . . ." She halted, and Matthias knew without having to be told that the same thought that entered his mind had popped into hers.

JoJo. Was he friend or foe? Did he know what his sister was up to? Was he part of the whole mess? Even if he were, would he raise an alarm, or was he willing to sell them out for the continued security of his sister's operations? The possibility of such treachery coming from the young man whom he had grown to like so much made him deeply sad. He liked JoJo, enjoyed being a mentor to him, even tolerated with indulgence the growing hero worship that had been evident in JoJo's every interaction with him. Under normal circumstances, Matthias would be willing to put his neck on a block for the young man's integrity, but now he wasn't so sure. The events of the day had proven to him that he was a pretty lousy judge of character.

She sensed his distress, and now it was her turn to comfort him. "He's a nice guy. I'm sure. . . ." She hesitated, and glanced over at the silent, motionless Janelle before lowering her voice even more, so that the only way to hear her was to press his ear to her lips. "JoJo loves you. He idolizes you. He thinks you're Batman, the thirteenth apostle, and a Jedi Knight all rolled into one." She halted, and he felt the laughter vibrate in her belly.

"What?" he whispered, his spirits lifting slightly in spite of the horror of their predicament. The laugh had so much of the real Sarita in it. They could almost have been back at the cottage, sitting on the porch on a cool Tobago evening, sharing a joke. They could almost have been completely out of mortal danger.

"I had this image of you in a gown and sandals, with bat ears and a cape, and a light saber in one hand." The laughter kept on bubbling, softly, almost stifled by the proximity of his cheek, but it was real, genuinely amused, and infectious. He grinned.

"I wish I could see that image."

She shook her head. "No, you don't. It's not a pretty sight." They giggled like schoolchildren.

"What's so funny?" The harsh, agitated tone of the question brought them crashing back to the reality that surrounded them. *Janelle.* "What're you two laughing at?" She was fully alert, her agitated body a dense black silhouette in the darkness that was now as thick and absolute as the belly of a whale.

"Nothing," Sarita answered tartly before Matthias could stop her. "I was sharing a joke with my *husband.*" She stressed the word. It was full of hard-won victory. "You got a problem with that?"

Matthias fully expected Janelle to start brandishing the flare gun again but she didn't, which was just as well because the gesture was beginning to get tired. Instead, she said sourly, "Whatever. Keep each other company. Laugh all night. I don't care. Just don't cross the middle of the boat. I don't want either of you coming over onto my side, if you know what's good for you." She may have imagined that she sounded tough, Matthias thought, but to him she sounded like a petulant six-year-old staking out territory on her half of the backseat of Daddy's car.

"And you," she pointed at Matthias. "Don't let me catch you near that radio. Or the controls. As a matter of fact . . ." She crab walked around to the front and snatched the keys out of the ignition. Her hand drew back.

She's bluffing, Matthias thought. *She won't.* . . .

The back-flung arm kept moving, at the same time quick and slow. His stunned mind had the faintest impression of his body being propelled forward to her, trying to catch the arm before its momentum could do its worst, but even as he grabbed hold of her, he was too late. In the faint glow of the boat's lights, the keys glinted once before they plinked into the black sea.

Eleven

"No!" Frustration met anger, then panic. Sarita found herself next to Matthias, who by now had taken advantage of the distraction and thrown himself at Janelle. The flare gun catapulted from her grip, and immediately he pinned Janelle's arms to her side and forced her into her seat. Never mind they were on the "forbidden" side of the boat, the side Janelle had claimed as her own.

Sarita didn't give the gun a second glance. All she cared about was the depth of the Atlantic, and the fact that their ticket back was slowly sinking to the bottom of it. "You stupid . . . !" Her rage was too great to allow her to find a suitable name to call this demented woman.

"It's okay." Matthias was surprisingly calm, even though the muscles corded in his back and arms as he struggled against Janelle's insanity-fueled strength. But sheer size advantage won out over Janelle's demons, and it was not long before he had her in total control, her fists curled against him but unable to deal him the punches she so obviously wanted to. Her lips were drawn back like those of a rabid dog, perfect white teeth gnashing and curses of frustration being ground out between them.

"Get the flare gun, Sari," Matthias said. He didn't even sound winded.

Sarita's ears so burned with the names she and Matthias were being called that she could barely hear him. She stood rooted.

"Get the gun," he said again. He didn't raise his voice.

She looked wildly around for it. In all the commotion it had slid across the floor and now lay in the middle of the boat. Before today, she had always thought of it as a routine piece of equipment, a tool of survival that, much like life insurance, you knew you had to have but dreaded the day when you would ever need it. Now, it had forever been transformed in her mind. It had morphed from tool into weapon. She gingerly picked it up by the barrel.

A surge of something ran through her; something violent and ugly. Colors flashed on the movie screen at the back of her brain. This was the gun that Janelle had threatened her with, for hours, forcing Matthias to take them on a one-way journey away from dry land, safety, food, and water. No, not just threatened. Her eyes drifted to the blackened hole in the ship's interior, where Janelle's warning shot had shattered and sat, burning brightly and menacingly, a gruesome forewarning of what they could do to human flesh. In Sarita's hand, the flare gun felt warm, inviting. Turning against their aggressor with her own weapon . . . now, *that* would be poetic justice. . . .

Matthias called her name, snapping her out of her dark reverie. "Take the flare out," he instructed her softly.

Was he crazy? Take the flare out? That was like disarming themselves, leveling a playing field that should, by all rights, be tilted in their favor, had to be, if they ever intended to emerge alive from their predicament. She could keep the gun loaded, hook it into the waist of her shorts, and patrol the deck like a sentry, in case

Janelle chose to strike again. They had seen for themselves what she as capable of, and forewarned was forearmed. Forearmed was, well, protected.

Then, another quiet voice in the back of her mind whispered to her. This violent impulse was not like her. It was not the kind of woman she wanted to be. She knew in her heart that she could never fulfill her desire to exact retribution against Janelle in her own currency of violence. Wasn't she the same woman who, half an hour ago, had closed her eyes in prayer, imploring the Lord, *believing*, that they would all be kept safe? If so, then what was she thinking? Wasn't this newfound thirst for blood more about avenging her hurt pride than about their own protection? And if that were the case, didn't that make her justification of self-defense a flimsy excuse?

She looked at Matthias, who was staring at her, waiting for her to absorb and respond to his last instruction. Mutely, hands trembling, she complied. The chamber of the flare gun released the unspent flare with a soft click.

"Good," he said soothingly. "That was good. Now, put the flare into your knapsack. Slip it into the pocket and zip it up. We'll know where it is when we need it. As a matter of fact, get all the flares from the emergency kit and put them in your bag."

She did as she was told. All the while, Janelle cursed and taunted her. "Coward! You don't even have the guts to do to me as I did to you. You're not only useless, you're yellow to boot."

"That's enough now, Janelle," Matthias said sternly. "I don't want you talking to Sarita again. Do you hear me?"

"Her conversation isn't that interesting anyway," Janelle sulked. She lapsed into disgruntled silence.

"Now," Matthias said. His tone was soft once more. "Put the gun in my bag. And put mine as far from yours as you can. On the other side of the boat. That's right. Now, if a craft sails by, we know where to find them. It won't take us too long to load up and fire off a few."

She unzipped the front of his bag to slip the gun in, and as she did so, her fingers encountered the thick manila envelope within: their divorce papers, still unsent. If they never made it back to land and one day someone found them, or what would be left of them by then, floating somewhere, they would know that all had not been right with them. The possibility embarrassed her, as it would to know someone was rifling through her underwear drawer or flipping through the pages of her adolescent journal. Marital trouble was such a private pain. Divorce dragged all one's dirty linen out in public. She flinched and hesitated, but then chided herself for allowing her mind to wander. There were far more pressing matters at hand. She shoved the gun down to the bottom of the pocket and zipped it shut decisively.

"Good, sweetheart. Well done." He could have been talking to a skittish animal.

"I don't know why you're so calm," Sarita snapped. The anxiety of the day kept her emotions in flux, and although she knew he was not to blame for any of this, she was frazzled and irritated by his unflappable self-control. "Didn't you see what she's done?"

"I know what she did. I saw what you saw. But don't worry. Try not to let all this get to you. It's okay," Matthias repeated.

"You keep saying that!" She was so frustrated and he was so annoyingly unfazed! "She threw away the keys, Matthias. To the boat! Don't you understand? Are we on the same page here?"

His smile was so infuriating that she wanted to throw something at him. "It's just a bunch of keys," he told her. "They aren't worth much. If you can hot-wire a car, you can hot-wire a boat. Don't make it a problem."

"Well, can you?"

"Can I what?"

"Hot-wire a boat. Don't play dumb, Matt. Do you want to just sit here, floating, waiting for our fate? Do you want to sit here, surrounded by water, and die of thirst? This is *serious!*" She knew she was shrieking. She didn't care.

He nodded in agreement. "Yes, sweet, I know it's serious, but I'm trying to be levelheaded. One of us has to," he added meaningfully.

She felt ashamed. He was right. They only way out of this was to use their heads. Getting frantic wouldn't help. Her vengeful, murderous urges toward Janelle would help even less. She knew and accepted that but was still glad that the gun was no longer within her easy grasp. Even worse, her despair was making a mockery of the very faith in divine deliverance that she had been trying to impress upon Matthias moments earlier. She'd sworn to him that they would be saved. Shouldn't she believe it, too?

Before she could tell him how sorry she was for her outburst, he spoke again. "But we're not going to die. I'm as hungry as you are and as thirsty. But we won't die here. We'll get help. It's that simple."

"Simple?" she echoed incredulously.

"Simple," he reiterated. He pointed in the direction of the radio with his chin. "Call for help. Go ahead."

Sarita turned her head in the direction of the radio. It was a small and rudimentary model, no bells and whistles, but to her it was like a magic machine that held the power of life and death over them. There was no weapon trained on her anymore, nothing to keep them from making that distress call. Salvation! For the first time that day her spirits soared. She headed toward it.

"No!" Janelle screamed. She struggled against the binds of her captor's strong arms, but they held her fast.

"Keep going, Sari," Matthias advised.

Sarita felt the smooth plastic of the mouthpiece in her hand and began twiddling with the controls, trying to find an appropriate channel.

"Don't, don't, don't!" Janelle begged. "Have mercy!"

Sarita stopped and stared. "What?"

"I'll die in jail. I will. I can't face it. I can't, I can't!"

"You should have thought of that," she responded. There was no sympathy left in her for the woman. "You brought it on yourself, remember?" There was static in her ear as she began calling, asking anyone to come in. Crackles and hisses were her only response. She tried again.

Matthias spoke directly to Janelle. "There's a way out, you know."

"There isn't! There isn't! I can't go to jail, I won't! I'd rather die out here than let them take me in." Janelle was shaking, hunched over as far as she could given the powerful hold Matthias had on her. In the muted light wet streaks were visible on her cheeks.

"Get rid of it," Matthias suggested. "All of it. Toss it into the sea. You do that and you'll be free."

"Are you crazy?" Janelle shrilled.

"Matthias!" Sarita was shocked. She was momentarily distracted from her task. "That's evidence of a crime! You can't tamper with it!"

"This is about survival," Matthias answered. "We do what it takes to get through this."

At the same time, Janelle cried, "You're mad! This

isn't mine to toss away! I'm just a courier. I have no right—"

"If you want to save your skin, you'll do it," he retorted. "We toss it all away, make that call, and wait. Tell them we got lost. Tell them something. We make it back to land and nobody's any the wiser."

"And when I get back, what do I tell my clients? What do I say? How do I replace half a million dollars' worth of goods? I don't have that kind of money! We toss it away and I'm dead. No, Matthias, no!" Janelle was near hysteria, her contorted face screwed up into a mask of terror and tears. Out of pity, Matthias released one of her hands to allow her to wipe her dripping face. All evidence of the belligerent, contemptuous virago was gone. In her place was a sniveling, frightened heap. "I'd rather die here!"

"Well, we're not dying with you," Matthias said firmly. "We toss the stuff, and you deal with your clients. Get your so-called friends to back you up. Either that or keep it on board and you face the police; either way, this whole farce is going to end. Now. We're going home." He turned his attention to Sarita. "Making any progress?"

Sarita spoke into the mouthpiece. "This is the *Spanish Dancer*, out of Tobago. Do you read me?" Her nervous hands were damp on the buttons. "Static. I don't know . . ."

"At least turn the beacon on. They'll be able to track us down that way."

Sarita complied and clicked on a switch. The beacon would emit an inaudible signal, a distress satellite call that any monitoring station could detect and respond to. With the right equipment, the source of the beep, and their stranded boat, could be located fairly accurately. The only evidence of its being in operation was a tiny, flashing green light.

"Keep trying with the radio, too," Matthias advised.

Janelle shrilled like a wounded banshee. The sound was beginning to get on Sarita's nerves. Even Matthias seemed to be on the brink of losing his patience. "What's it to be?" he asked her. "Toss it or keep it on board? Your choice."

"I can't. I can't choose." Janelle moaned like a person in agony.

Still holding Janelle fast with one hand, Matthias reached forward and grabbed one of the plastic-wrapped packets of contraband and flung it as far as he could. It made barely a splash.

The effect on Janelle was galvanic. She writhed like an eel, her bones becoming fluid, and twisted against him, bringing her heel sharply down on his foot. He yelped, more out of surprise than pain, but the brief distraction was enough to make him let her go. She lit out of her seated position like a sprinter out of the starting blocks. Sarita braced herself. Surely, the woman was coming after her, or was perhaps bold enough to try to go for the flare gun again. She was glad now that Matthias had had the foresight to separate weapon from ammunition. Even if Janelle went for one, she wouldn't have the time to get the other before the two of them could stop her.

Just then, a voice. Not hers. Not belonging to anyone else on the boat. A man's voice—distant, distorted, breaking up badly—but it was a human voice and it was on the radio.

"Hello!" Sarita shouted. Relief made her head light.

Matthias had righted himself. He was moving. Janelle was moving.

"We're stranded!" Sarita yelled. "We've got no fuel.

We headed east, past Charlotteville. We lost sight of land."

Crackle. ". . . your coordinates?" *Crackle.*

Janelle had something in her hands. Out of the corner of her eye, Sarita clearly saw that it was large and red, but her brain was unable to process anymore information.

Sarita began to recite them but the crackling drowned out the sound of her voice.

Janelle, the dark eel, slithered near, grunting with effort. Her movements were blurred but promised trouble all the same. Matthias, a flash of light, bare skin bright in the shadows, threw himself at her feet, arms locking around her legs, and brought her down, like a last-ditch tackle in the end zone.

"Hello?" Sarita banged on the radio. The crackle was fading. She cursed the wretched machine. "Can you read me?"

Before Janelle hit the deck, she released the red object in her hands, hurling it in Sarita's direction with all her strength. Half a second before it struck Sarita square in the abdomen, she recognized it as the fire extinguisher. It was standard issue and not all that heavy: easy to lift, easy to use. But the momentum with which it traveled, and the force with which it had been flung, were enough to knock the wind from her and make her lose her balance.

Time went on and on and on. There was more than enough time for her to realize that she was airborne and time enough to look up into the sky and think, once again, about how huge and perfect the big, full Easter moon was. There was even time to marvel at how bright the sky could be when you were far from land and the omnipresent artificial light that always dulled its fire.

And then her time was up. The wonder of the

sparkling sky was thrust from her mind as her body struggled to adapt to a new sensation. Water so cold she thought her heart would stop. Stinging in her nose as it rushed in, filling her wide-open, surprised mouth. Salty. It should be holding her up but it wasn't.

Why not?

It should be supporting her, or, at the very least, she should be fighting it: kicking, striking out, swinging her arms in an arc, anything to keep her head above it; swimming, like she had done without effort since she was five. But strangely, alarmingly, she wasn't sure how. There was some sort of coordination involved, some sort of rhythm; arms and legs moving in repetitive order, one, then the other, over and over. But which limb did you move first and which next? How did you move them? Surely she hadn't *forgotten*? These things didn't happen. Swimming was like riding a bike. You got started, found your flow, and went with it.

She tried, throwing her arms out at her sides, kicking frantically, cycling her legs. Ungainly. Floundering. The water grabbed her ankles, like the hands of long-drowned sailors longing for company, unwilling to let others escape the fate they had suffered. Jealous of the air in her lungs, when theirs held only water. They grasped, insistent and unrelenting, and tugged her downward.

Dog-paddle, she told herself. *You don't need to be taught that. You just know. It's natural. Even babies can . . .*

She couldn't. Why couldn't she?

Mermaids' hands, wrapping around her waist. Drawing her into their lair. Water blacker than the sky above. The twinkle of the stars dimmed. Too far away for her to see them, now. Water in her eyes, burning. She squeezed them shut.

Twelve

Over the edge! Matthias wasn't sure he'd seen what he thought he had. It was unthinkable, a sick parody of his worst nightmare. His wife had been standing there, right there, calling for help on the radio, trying to save them all, and then there was this blur of red being hurled across the boat, and her mouth opened in a soundless mask of confusion.

And then she hit the water.

Matthias tried to shout but his throat was sandpaper. Janelle was half under him, panting, kicking him wherever she could land a foot, yelling incoherently, squirming. He let her go as if she were a live wire snaking along on the floor. He scrambled to the spot where Sarita had fallen, hauled himself up to the edge of the boat with both hands and looked out.

All around him there was utter blackness.

Beside him, Janelle was tearing at the radio and beacon, clawing at the wires and ripping them loose from their moorings, but he was barely aware of it. The beacon was designed to function even if it was in the water—but it wouldn't work if it was off. The small green light, and with it the signal that had flashed out their distress message, was dead: Janelle had disabled it, an putting end to any hope of detection, but he did not care.

Sarita was in the water.

And for the life of him, he couldn't see her.

There was no hesitation. He didn't take the time to remove his glasses or his shoes. He hit the water awkwardly, raising up a tremendous splash, he, who so prided himself on his diving skill, his ability to cleave the water like a blade dropped point first. He cannonballed into it like the clumsiest child at the community pool, and as soon as he found himself submerged, he stuck his arms out, searching. He put his hand to his face and realized that he'd lost his glasses as he'd fallen. That made it all the more difficult; unaided, his vision was not the best.

She'd been wearing his shirt, a gray one, and denim shorts. Dark colors in a dark ocean. Why couldn't he have brought a white shirt that day?

She can swim, he told himself. *She's a good swimmer. A strong one. She'll pop to the surface any second now and fill her lungs with air. She's got to.*

But she didn't.

"Sari?" he yelled. He could see nothing six inches below the surface. Even that wonderful full moon didn't have the heart to penetrate that dark water. He spun around to face the boat. "Shine the light over here, Janelle! I need light!" If she didn't obey, so help him. . . .

There was a sound right next to him, a splash that froze the blood in his veins. Half of him wanted to believe that it was Sarita, breaking the surface. The other half was too afraid to find out what *else* it could be. This was the Atlantic and the open waters were chilly. Open waters meant sharks. It was perhaps not cool enough for great whites, or even makos . . . but tigers and bulls liked the warm waters, and those beasts were nowhere near as complacent as the nurse sharks he and Sarita had been thrilled to swim with before.

Staving off panic, he followed the sound with his eyes, only to realize that it was their vandalized radio, which dallied on the waves for the merest moment before it began to sink.

He didn't have time to grieve its loss. The radio meant nothing if Sarita couldn't be found. Loudly, he called her name again and pleaded for light once more. "Light, Janelle, dammit! Turn the spotlight on the water!"

A beam cut through the blackness and his gratitude knew no bounds. He widened the arc of his search, reaching all around him. He took deep breaths and went down as far as he could, expelling the air to make himself less buoyant. He tried to resist his body's demands for oxygen; every time he rose for another breath was a few more seconds that Sarita lost.

He was almost sobbing with terror and frustration, even though he knew that the resultant upheaval in his body and his quickened respiration would do him no good. He was sure that in his entire life he had never endured such a sickening sense of hopelessness. Each time he reached out and drew only empty hands to himself, his faith shrank.

Faith.

An ironic word. A word Sarita often used. She was a woman of so much faith, even in the face of his derision. Even in the face of impending disaster she had held fast to her faith. Just . . . how long ago? Half an hour? An hour? She had prayed to her God, asked Him with the pure faith of a child asking a favor of a parent, to spare their lives. And now she was in the water and he couldn't find her.

It had to be some kind of cruel joke. A god with a warped sense of humor.

Not so, Sarita would have said. A god willing to test you. A god willing to make you risk everything you hold dear, just so that you have no other choice than to turn to Him, so that you can see for yourself, and wonder, at how great and magnificent He truly is.

Rubbish. The only person he ever had to rely on was himself, and he'd find her if he drowned trying.

"Matt!"

The voice almost caused him to lose his stride and sink. Could it really be she?

"Matt!"

There was water in his ears. He shook his head and tried to find the source of the sound.

"Here!" Janelle was hanging over the edge of the boat, one arm outstretched, backlit so that he couldn't see her face. "She's gone, Matt. Come, take my hand. Get back in the boat."

Sharp disappointment wrenched in his gut. That voice was not the one he longed to hear, and what it was saying was obscene. If Janelle was right, and Sarita was gone, logic would dictate that he return to the boat. But if Sarita were indeed gone, his heart argued, there was nothing to return to. The way out that Janelle was offering wasn't an option. It couldn't be. He turned his back on her and kept on looking. As he did so, the presence of Sarita's God loomed larger, refusing to be ignored.

I don't believe in you, he insisted. *I'll find her on my own.* He went down again, back into the black ink, reached for her and grasped at nothing. He came up empty.

He was so weak, powerless in the face of this huge and awesome ocean. He felt terrified, alone, and ashamed. "God," he breathed. "My God, my God." His own words shocked him so deeply that he went still, and only the need to maintain his buoyancy propelled him into movement once more.

Somebody heard him. He knew in his heart that

Someone was listening and that he was far from alone. There was a storehouse of favors to be granted him, if only he would ask. How did you pray? What did you say to someone you hadn't spoken to in twenty years? "Our Father," he began. Then he stopped. He was sure he'd remember the rest, if he were calm and on dry land and had the luxury of time to think, but here, adrift and with Sarita's seconds slipping through his fingers, he couldn't remember what came next.

But Sarita hadn't relied on prayers that were written down and learned by rote. She'd talked to Him. Opened up her heart and asked for what she wanted. Sarita was a smart woman and her faith was as huge as the hills. If she believed that would work, well, so did he.

"Help me," he prayed. "I know I haven't believed, and I know that I've walked away from You for too long, so I don't deserve any favors, but help me find her. Do it for her, not for me. Help me find her. Help me bring her back." The wind-whipped waves broke over him, bowling him over like a living enemy that was growing stronger with each passing moment; with Sarita's faith in his heart, he dove again.

Nothing.

And again.

Empty hands.

He submerged once more, kicking hard and forcing the air out from between his lips and nostrils, down where it was far too black for human eyes to see. The pressure of the water weighed upon him, making his skull feel as if it were about to explode. His lungs screamed, begged for one last breath. Even when his body was threatening to save itself and return up top, his mind and heart propelled it forward, outvoting it two to one.

Then something bumped into him.

His oxygen-starved brain screeched *shark-shark-shark,* over and over again. All he wanted to do was get away, but before panic could rob him of his last shred of sanity, he held out his hand and touched it, preparing himself to encounter rough, sandpapery skin, a sleek, powerful tail, or multiple rows of long, jagged teeth.

He touched fabric.

Thank you, Lord. His soul shouted out his gratitude, even as he grabbed her. She was still. He tried to reorient himself, dizzy now that his own brain was slipping into sleep. Which way was up? He'd read of sailors who'd drowned because they'd become confused, due to oxygen deprivation, and had been unable to find their way to the surface. He did the only sensible thing. Grasping her securely, as if she were the most precious pearl that the depths had ever surrendered, he went limp . . . and floated.

As his body broke the thin membrane that separated the ocean from the sky, he gasped, and the air tasted better than he had ever imagined it could. He clutched Sarita, holding her head above the reach of the waves and expecting her to suck in air as he had, but she didn't. Fear as cold as death surrounded his heart. How long had she been under? How many moments had gone by since she had hit the water? Things had happened in such a disembodied, distorted manner that he had no way of knowing whether it had been sixty panic-clouded seconds since he had gone in after her, or ten life-robbing minutes. His only hope was to get her to the boat.

He tried to locate it, even as the waves around him pitched him onto their mountaintops and tossed him into their valleys. It was a full thirty yards away; either he had swum away from it or it had drifted from him. Thirty yards on an ordinary sunny day in calm water was nothing; he could do that a dozen times over without effort. Tonight, the darkness that sucked him in and the dead weight of the woman in his arms would make it tough going.

The rescue hold he'd learned during survival at sea training came to him without his having to search his memory for it. He propped her back against his chest, making sure her face could not slip below the water, and brought his legs up around her hips, grasping her firmly. He then began a slow and determined backstroke, letting his arms do the work for both of them. It was simple, practical, and it worked. In moments he was butting against the boat's hull; and all he had to do was get her into the boat.

This would be hard. Lifting her overhead would be near impossible since he was in the water. If he dared release her long enough to climb aboard himself, he might lose her again, and he simply was not willing to chance that. He looked up. Janelle's face was a shadow above him.

"Hold out your hand," he shouted at her. "Hold her and help me get her into the boat."

Janelle's stare was blank, uncomprehending.

His patience snapped. "Woman, listen to me. Reach out and grab hold of her. I'll push and you'll pull. When you have her, lay her down on the floor. You let her go, just once, and you will have to deal with me, and I promise you that I'll make every single day of the rest of your life unbearable. Understand?"

Without speaking, Janelle reached down and grasped Sarita by the shoulders. Matthias had nothing against which to brace his feet, so relied solely upon the power of his arms. The effort was superhuman, but between both of them, Sarita slid up and over the side. In a flash, he joined her, snatching her from Janelle's arms even before she could set her down.

"I didn't mean for that to happen," Janelle whined. She was hopping around, wringing her hands. "I'm sorry. I'm sorry. All I wanted to do was stop her. . . ."

Concentrate, Matthias said to himself. *Don't let her distract you. Focus.* He tried to tune Janelle out and knelt over the limp form beneath him. She wasn't dead. He knew this because his own mind rebelled against the idea; it was so abhorrent to him that such a possibility could not become concrete.

So, she was still alive, because she had to be, because he *said* so. And since she was alive, how was her pulse? He touched the side of her neck with two fingers, concerned by the clamminess of her skin. He knew exactly where her pulse should be, but he couldn't . . .

There it was. Like a drum muffled by goatskins and being tapped lightly by a hesitant drummer. Soft. Irregular.

Good. Now to have her breathing again.

Her wet clothes clung to her, constricting her chest, so without any thought for false modesty on her behalf, he stripped her of the shirt he had lent her, along with hers, which she wore beneath it, and then reached around to undo the clasp of her swimsuit so that he could pull the top down to her waist. Tilting her head back straightened her airway and let him hold her mouth open. He pinched her nose shut, sealed her lips in a life-giving kiss, and blew. Her chest rose and fell, but apart from that, nothing happened.

Janelle was still singing her tiresome song, sobbing now. "I'm so sorry, Matthias. She's not dead, right?"

He was so focused on Sarita that his mind barely acknowledged that Janelle had spoken. She could just as well have been on the other side of a wall. He breathed for Sarita, feeling her chest swell under him, coaxing her, until—thank God—there was a cough and a sputter, and he swiftly rolled her onto her side so that she could spit up the water that had filled her lungs. He was shocked at the volume she had swallowed. But each gasp thrilled him: for her it meant life. He sat her up and held her tenderly until she stopped coughing.

She opened her eyes for the first time. "Dark," she said in horror.

"Yes, it was." He wanted to grab her and pull her close and hug her and never let her go, but she needed air and space, so he had to forbear. "But we're in the light now." He realized he was crying. The salt of his tears tasted like the water that dripped from his hair.

It was beyond comprehension how close he had come to losing her—and how bleak and meaningless his life would have been if he had. "I missed you," he told her. She hadn't been gone long but he spoke the truth. He had, terribly. She shivered against him.

"You're cold!" He felt so stupid. She was naked from the waist up, wet through and through, and the wind whipped at her. He left her just long enough to grab one of their still-damp towels and bring it back to her. He stripped her down completely, shielding her body from Janelle with his own, even though by now Janelle had folded into herself and was a limp, tearful heap on a bench. He started with her hair, knowing that this was the spot through which the most body heat escaped. Then he moved to her back and chest, and her belly and legs, and when he had reached her feet he made his way up again, trying to compensate for the dampness of the towel by the friction of his movements. After several passes her skin was warm and once again kissed by life.

She wouldn't remain that way for long. There wasn't a single dry garment left on the ship, and her nakedness left her open and vulnerable. He squeezed the water as best as he could out of the few articles of clothing and then hung them from the rafters, hoping that the wind would make them serviceable by morning.

She might be breathing on her own but wasn't out of the woods yet. There was still the possibility of hypothermia. A musty, rolled-up sheet of canvas stowed near the prow provided a grubby but valuable covering, and he gently drew it over her like a blanket. That might hold her for now, but if he was to help her make it through the night, he'd have to be vigilant—in more ways than one.

Cold wasn't the only danger they faced. Janelle had proven herself untrustworthy, unstable, and violent. Matthias cursed the innate sense of right and wrong that prevented him from returning Janelle's aggression in kind. If she had been a man, this problem would have been settled long ago with their fists. But punching a woman wasn't, couldn't be, the right way to go about it. He glanced over at her, and what he saw surprised him.

Exhausted from her tears and perhaps even the nerve-wracking events of the day, she had slipped into an uneasy doze. She had curled herself up into as small a package as possible and wedged herself against the hull. Her lips moved, as she repeated some litany that only she understood, and her body rocked in small, rapid movements. She didn't look as if she would be posing much more of a threat to them tonight.

Another miracle. It had been a night full of them. But the blessings delivered by the hand of God sometimes needed to be affirmed by the hand of Man. Matthias knew he had only been given a brief respite. He moved quickly.

A strip of nylon rope, found in one of the cluttered

cupboards under the seats, was ideal. He looped it several times around Janelle's hands, tying them together but making sure his knots were not tight enough to cut off the flow of blood. She didn't even protest, or seem to be aware of his actions. He gave her three feet of leeway so that when she woke she would not be completely constrained, and tied the ends off at a post. Then he searched around her, ensuring there was no blade or sharp object that she could use to free herself from her bonds; only then was he satisfied.

He returned to Sarita. She was still awake, watching his every move. Her voice was raspy as she called his name.

"You shouldn't be talking," he chastised her. "Save your breath."

"I'm okay . . . really."

"Save it anyway," he advised, although nothing made him happier than to know that she was lucid, alert, and able to converse—a far cry from her condition not too long ago!

"Tyrant."

"A concerned one," he defended himself. "Bullying you for your own good."

She followed him with her eyes as he approached her, a half smile playing on her lips. She must have seen his bemused look because she tried to explain, "I was thinking how hard that must have been for you."

"What?" Everything had been hard tonight!

She let a hand crawl out from under the canvas that covered her and pointed at Janelle's crouched, restrained form.

He appreciated her understanding. "I had to do what I had to do to keep you safe. She's dangerous. She's a threat to you. You knew it all along, sensed it. You tried to tell me and I wouldn't listen." He apologized humbly. "I'm sorry."

"It's okay. You made an . . ." She tried to find the right word. ". . . executive decision. Arbitration between employees to keep the project going. It's understandable."

"Damn the project! You nearly died."

"I didn't."

He looked at her for a very long time and then peeled off his own clothes. When he was down to the buff, he hung up his clothes much as he had hers, and settled next to her, lifting the canvas and sliding into their makeshift sleeping bag. "Body heat," he explained. "It'll help us make it through the night. Besides, I forgot to bring fresh bed linens with us and you have the only set in the house."

She didn't complain.

The rough wood of the boat floor was harsh against his skin. "Maybe we should get up onto the bench," he suggested. "At least that's padded."

"Maybe we should," she agreed. She made no move to get up.

He felt her warmth infuse his own chilled skin and wondered if *he* was supposed to warm *her,* or if *she* was supposed to warm *him.* Although her bare flesh was pressed against his, his response was not sexual but more like the deep satisfaction one felt when snuggling down with a fluffy bathrobe that fit just right. She made him comfortable, even in a circumstance of extreme discomfort. After a while, he made his confession. "You know, tying up Janelle wasn't the only hard thing I had to do tonight."

"No?" she asked softly.

"When I was down there, and looking for you . . . when I couldn't find you, I thought my heart was breaking." Even the memory of the ordeal was hard to talk about. He hesitated.

"Go on," she encouraged. He could have sworn he felt her hand touch his.

"I thought you were lost. My imagination was full of a thousand sea monsters. I was convinced the sea was alive with them. Boiling with them. Sharks. Things with tentacles."

"I thought there were mermaids. Drowned sailors, dragging me under. Hands all over, clinging to my ankles . . . ." She shuddered against him.

She'd felt the same fear! It made him feel less alone. "And all my body wanted to do was get out of the water. My mind and my heart were searching for you, but my body was saying *save yourself.*"

"That's normal," she tried to comfort him.

"That's so . . . un-heroic. I'm ashamed."

"You were scared. That's nothing to be ashamed about. You were scared, but you stayed. *That's* what makes you a hero. You stayed and you found me. You don't have anything to feel guilty for."

He was so grateful for her understanding. Here he was, feeling so much less of a man, but she understood and forgave him.

"And that was your hard decision?" she asked.

"One of them."

"And the other?"

He was almost embarrassed to share the next with her. It wasn't often you had the feeling of being sucked down into the mouth of Death, and then cried out to the God you had denied and abandoned and had Him save you and the one thing you had been willing to face that death for. "I couldn't find you. Everything around me was black, and I couldn't tell up from down. And all the while, I kept insisting that I was going to do it on my own. I was going to save you on my own. But I couldn't. I wouldn't have."

"So, how did you?"

"I prayed."

She tilted her head so she could look into his eyes. A delighted smile played upon her face. "You did?"

"At first I couldn't remember how. I didn't remember the words—"

"You don't need any special words. All you have to do is talk."

"That's what you've always said. I remembered you on deck this afternoon, when Janelle was making things hard for you and everything seemed to be getting worse and worse. And then you talked to Him. And then you seemed so . . . calm."

"So you talked to Him."

"Yes."

"And did He listen?" Her smile was broader now.

He kissed her damp hair. "You're here, aren't you?" His lips moved from her hair to her throat to her mouth, and when she kissed him back it was like the sky opening up; something in his chest did the same. He felt full to breaking point, splitting at the seams with a wonderful glow and the assurance that everything was all right. He'd made peace with his estranged God, and his woman was safe and alive and he loved her, loved her, loved her.

He broke the kiss and pressed her head into his shoulder. "Sleep," he said softly. "We have a long day ahead of us tomorrow. And don't worry: I'll watch over you."

As she fell into a snooze, her shivering having long since stilled, he looked up into the sky. It seemed brighter now, less threatening, and the stars were so radiant he was sure he could count each one of them.

At least he was going to try.

Thirteen

No sunrise had ever been that beautiful. No dawn so perfect. As Sarita lifted her lashes she almost expected to hear the twittering of birds and the stirring of the creatures of the day. The sky was slashed in two by a blade of gold in the east. Directly above them, the blackness had mellowed into Prussian blue, and the moon was a mirage, a semi-transparent hologram of its former self. She was awed by the beauty all around her. Then she remembered where she was, and exactly what predicament she was in, and her pleasure at awaking popped like a balloon.

"Good morning," Matthias rumbled at her back.

She lifted her head from his shoulder and shifted her weight, unable to prevent an *ungh* of discomfort from escaping her lips. "My butt is dead," she groused.

"That's a pity. I was a great fan of it. I'll miss it, now that it's gone," he joked. "We'll have to hold a requiem for it when we get back."

His humor was almost enough to distract her from the stinging of pins and needles in her legs as she tried to get up. "That's hilarious," she said, still a little grouchy but glad he was able to see the lighter side of their situation; or at least, to manufacture one where none existed.

She pushed the blanket aside. "Yuck. Smells of fish."

"Canvas found on boats tends to do that."

She grinned. "You can be such an idiot."

He responded with a grin of his own. "I'm guessing fish won't be a huge part of your diet for a while, once we get back."

"Got that right!" She didn't want to ruin the moment by asking the question that sprang to her mind: *exactly when did he think that would be?*

He stood up next to her and began stretching, raising his arms above his head, rotating his torso in circles, and grasping his ankles and lifting his feet to his bare behind to stretch his hamstrings. She wished he wouldn't do that. He was very, very naked indeed. She wondered if her cheeks were deepening in color. More for the distraction that conversation would bring than for the need for information, she asked, "Did you sleep?"

"Not a wink. I was on security detail."

She knew exactly what he meant. She remembered the person responsible for their problems and looked around for Janelle. A silent human bundle was wedged into a corner facing the hull. A short bit of rope emerged from under her; it was tied to a pole. Janelle's hunched position and refusal to look around, even when the conversation was about her, were scary. "Is she . . . alive?"

"Of course. I gave her some water an hour ago. She just . . . doesn't feel like talking right now."

She eyed him. "You went over there?"

"Yes. Why?"

"Like that?" She gestured at his nakedness. The idea of another woman benefiting from such a visual treat, and especially the idea of that woman being Janelle, made her fiercely territorial.

"Yep. Like this." He grinned, seeming to enjoy her

chagrin, but then relented enough to let her off the hook. "I don't think she noticed, though. She's a little out of it, as you can see."

She'd better not have noticed. Sarita thought, but instead she said, "Then she's further gone than we thought."

He looked down at himself, amused by her chagrin. "I'll take it as a compliment."

She tried to be casual about it. "If you like." Better not to let him get any more cocky than he usually was. Especially when, considering their marital situation, she wasn't sure if she had any right to be territorial in the first place. She added snippily, "But savor that compliment. It's the last you'll be getting today. I wouldn't want you to get a swelled head."

"It's not my head I'm worried about."

"Don't tempt me," she murmured, but too softly for him to hear, she hoped. She tried to divert the conversation from its hazardous course, using the old magician's trick of misdirection. "I'm sorry you had to stay up all night. We could have shared the duty."

He looked amused at her ham-handed attempt at changing the subject, but let her get away with it, and dismissed her suggestion. "Who's being the idiot now? You were half drowned. You needed the rest more than I did."

"But . . ." she protested.

"It's nothing. Forget about it. I'm a chronic insomniac, remember? What's one more night?"

She accepted this without any further protestations.

He fished into his bag and brought out a bottle—she was prepared to take the pessimist's stance that it was half empty, not half full—of water. "This is all we have left. Have just a few sips. We'll be needing it later when it starts to get hot."

Water! Her parched throat ached for some but the

pressure in her bladder made her groan. The *Spanish Dancer* didn't have a toilet. She had to admit to being fleetingly envious of the anatomical advantage that Matthias had over her when it came to seeing to their bathroom needs over the side of the boat. She was sure that if Sigmund Freud were alive he'd be chortling in self-vindication. "I . . . uh . . . think I'll pass."

Matthias was adamant. "This is life and death. You never, *ever* pass on water."

"I know, but . . ." Now that she was aware of her problem, it became pressingly urgent. She squirmed. She could perch on the edge, she supposed, but losing her balance would mean another unwelcome dunking in the ocean. And right now, she and the briny weren't on the best of terms.

He deduced her predicament. "I'll hold you, if you like. You won't fall in."

Have him hold her? That would be way too embarrassing. "That's okay," she said hastily, even as her body protested in outrage at her betrayal. "I'll hold it a little longer."

"You hold it any longer, you'll pop." He grabbed her hand and was already leading her to the edge and taking her in his arms. "This is no time for false modesty. Come on, we shared a bathroom for almost a year, remember? I'm your *husband.*"

It was a losing battle, so she surrendered, but clung to him for dear life as the water loomed closer. She wondered, quite seriously, if she would ever have the courage to swim in deep water again.

When both their needs were seen to, he took their clothes down from the rafters. After a night of flapping in the stiff breeze, they were fairly dry. Sarita dressed, glad for the barrier between her skin and his eyes. She drank the water he offered, without protest this time, trying to hold it in her mouth for as long as possible before swallowing it regretfully. "What happens when we run out of water?"

He looked grim. "We hope for rain, and in the meantime, distill some sea water."

"How?"

"I'll show you, in a while. But for now, sit with me. We have to talk."

She sat beside him on the bench, not close enough to touch but not exactly on the farthest end, either. Across from them, Janelle stirred briefly, and then lapsed back into immobility. Sarita couldn't take her eyes off the rope. As pleased as Sarita was that Janelle's confinement meant that she probably wouldn't be tossed into the drink or shot at a second time, she felt sorry for her. The hellion who had stormed the deck, cursing and threatening—the woman who had tried to drown her—was a shivering wreck. Sarita wondered if she would ever be normal again—at least as normal as Janelle could be.

"She's terrified," she said softly.

"Yes."

They both stared at the woman in the corner for several moments. "Can we help her?" Sarita asked.

"That's what we need to talk about. She's facing three very hard possibilities and none are pleasant." He counted them off on his fingers. "One, we continue to drift, and, well, never make it back to shore."

"Let's not even think in that direction," she said decisively. "That's defeatist. That's not the way I want to go down."

"Good. I agree. On to option two. We could dump the drugs and let her clients deal with her. But drug pushers aren't the most understanding people. It probably wouldn't be pretty."

"You wanted to dump it last night," she reminded him.

"In exchange for the use of the radio. Now the radio is gone. But you were right. Dumping it would be illegal. It's evidence of a crime, and if we got rid of it, we could be accused of complicity."

"Not to mention find ourselves on the top of some drug lord's hit list," she shuddered.

"Exactly. And we wouldn't even know who to fear, or when and where the retribution might come. We'd be afraid for the rest of our lives . . . and how long that would be is anyone's guess."

"We could go back home. To Miami. Safer there."

He nodded. "Yes, we could run, but we'd always be hiding. And Reef Rescue would be . . . over."

She knew he wouldn't be willing to even consider that. "And the other option?"

"The other option is that we keep the stuff on board, and Janelle will have to face music of a different kind when we're rescued."

"And us? Won't we be suspects?"

"We will."

"So can't we just explain to them that we're innocent?"

His lips curved ruefully. "I'm sure the police have heard *that* before."

"But we are!" she said hotly.

"I know. But I can see that we'll have some heavy explaining to do. But I think that's the best choice. The only choice. The justice system will have to work in the favor of the innocent. There's nothing to implicate us. They'll have to let us go, eventually."

"Eventually," she repeated slowly. That sounded like it could be a long, long time.

"Yes." He squeezed her shoulder. "Scared?"

"Aren't you?" She threw back at him.

"Yes. But we have to trust—"

"The system. So you said." She hated to admit it but they didn't seem to have any other choice. "The drugs stay, then."

"Until we're rescued."

"And if her friends find us first?"

His tone was light, but his eyes told her he was dead serious. "Well, then, we're armed with a flare gun and half a dozen flares. I'm not exactly a lousy shot. We fight."

It was strange; now that they both knew the enemy, and were agreed on how they would face it, she felt calm, even upbeat. He'd watch her back and she'd watch his. "Shake on it, then." She held out her hand.

He didn't take it. "No, kiss on it." Before she could resist, or even consider whether she wanted to, his mouth was on hers. It was a far cry from the insistent, hungry kisses they'd shared since she'd come to the island. This one was not passionate but intense. Slow, it spoke of a covenant. She had the fleeting illusion that the man she was kissing was not the same man she'd boarded the boat with yesterday. The fear and anxiety of the day and night before, and the danger that they still faced, seemed to have completely erased the bitterness that she had harbored in her heart toward him.

It was so funny. For all the time that she had known him, her image of him had always been clouded by her desire, her passion, her love for him, her fear of losing him, and her anguish over their many ferocious battles. Now, though her love was no less, she was seeing things in him that she had been too close to see before: his strength, his determination, and his nobility of spirit. What was even stranger was that this new discovery of him, far from making her more frantic to hang onto him in spite of all his protests, made her more prepared to relinquish him, as he had been asking for for so long. Finally, at last, she was willing to . . . able to . . . let him go.

She put her hand up to his cheek and felt the day-old stubble there. Either she broke the kiss or he did, and when it was over he was the first to speak. "I don't think we've ever kissed like that."

"No. We haven't."

He looked about to say something, and then changed his mind. "We'll survive this. And more." He got to his feet and offered her a hand to help her up. She took it. "We can talk when this is all over."

He was right. They would be able to talk and part ways amicably. She searched deep inside herself for any trace of the endlessly increasing anger and resentment that she had nurtured inside her like a serpent's egg since their marriage had begun, but all she could feel was a benign warmth. She wished him well. Maybe he felt the same way about her.

"Until then, we need water." By moving away from her he broke their connection, and then he was all business. "Help me with this." He bent over one of the glass-bottomed trays that sat in the middle of the boat, tossing aside the few plastic-wrapped packages that had fallen into it from the hole in the ceiling, and lifted it out of its frame. Beneath it there was only exposed water.

It would have made sense to think that given that there was now a hole in the middle of the boat, the water would come rushing in, but it was constructed so that the equal pressure within the hull didn't allow it to. As eerie as the hole looked, the procedure was completely safe.

"We have to get it up top, onto the roof. Into the

sun." With effort, he lifted it and hauled it onto the flat roof. As they went under for the second tray, Sarita noticed that Janelle was awake and sitting up, and watching them, almost disinterestedly. The dark eyes, so capable of catlike sensuousness and equally catlike malice, were hollow and staring. Blank. She didn't seem aware of what they were doing. She didn't seem to care.

Pity made Sarita ask, "Are you thirsty?"

"She's already had enough for the morning. We're not scheduled for another sip until noon. Remember, we have to ration . . ."

"I know, Matthias, but she looks so . . . awful."

He thought about it for only a few seconds and then gestured to their last bottle. "Okay, go ahead, but just a little. I'll get these other trays up top." He busied himself.

Sarita uncorked the bottle and held it out to Janelle. The other woman made no effort to take it from her. Gently, she put the bottle to her mouth and tipped it, so that she could force a few sips past unwilling lips. It was like feeding a reluctant child. When she was done, she covered the bottle and put it away. She checked to make sure the rope bonds at Janelle's wrists were still secure, but not too tight, and joined Matthias again.

He had already assembled his paraphernalia on the flat rooftop. The three glass-bottomed trays were spread out and he was busy filling them with seawater, hopping down from the low roof with a plastic bowl—the one kept in reserve for emergency bailing—and dipping it in over the side in the ocean. She would have liked to help with the filling, but there was only one bowl. Instead, she squatted next to the trays, rested her hands on her knees, and watched him work.

In no time, all three trays held two or three inches of

water. Carefully, he placed a swim mask, face up, in the bottom of each. She was amused to notice that he had selected, accidentally or deliberately, the ill-fitting mask she had insisted on using against his advice on their first trip out to the reef.

"At least it's good for something," she joked.

He grinned. "With any luck, and lots of sunshine, they'll be full of distilled, drinkable water by the end of the day." He squinted up into the brilliant sky. "And we have a whole lot of sunshine; let's hope we can rustle us up a smidgen of luck." He completed his arrangement of the face masks. "Come, help me with the plastic."

By now, she had deduced what he was trying to do, so she helped him stretch the thin sheets of polyethylene that had been keeping Janelle's marijuana cache dry and odor-free, and which he had dragged down from the ceiling. They sealed it as best as they could by tucking the ends under the trays, but left a little slack on top.

"This is the best I could come up with for weights." He showed her an assortment of small items: pocket change, house keys, and the knobs from the cupboards on the boat. A few items on the top of each sheet of plastic weighed it down just enough so that the plastic sunk over the masks. When they were done, they sat back with satisfaction, admiring their handiwork. When the heat of the sun caused the seawater to evaporate, it would condense on the inside of the plastic sheets. The weights would cause the droplets of water to roll toward the middle of the trays where they would eventually become heavy and drip—right into the waiting, upturned face masks.

"We should each have a cup of water by nightfall," he said, satisfied.

She didn't like the sound of that "nightfall" business. She wondered how many of those dreadful, lonely, black nights they might have to endure. Facing them without fresh water would be a whole lot worse, she reminded herself, and tried not to let her spirits sink. She admired his ingenuity and his determination to remain positive, so she said, "If I'm ever stranded again in the middle of the ocean, with no radio and no water, I'd want to be stranded with you."

He smiled at her, surprised at the compliment. "And if you're ever stranded again," he returned in kind, "I'd want to be stranded with you, so I could be there if you ever needed me." Then there was a catch in his voice. "Because if you ever went off on a trip like this, and didn't make it back . . . the world would lose . . . *I* would lose . . . a wonderful, unique person." He leaned forward and kissed her lightly on her sunburned nose.

She gaped in surprise, unsure of what she could possibly say to that. It had been a long, long time since Matthias had said anything that sincere to her.

She didn't have time to say anything, because he stood up and said briskly, "All right, let's break up this meeting of our mutual admiration society. I'm turning this boat around."

Turning the boat around! Her heart filled with hope. He couldn't have said more wonderful words. "Can I help?"

"You can stay close. Just stay with me. That's all the help I need right now."

"Do we have enough fuel to make a difference?"

"Not enough to make it home again but the nearer we get, the better our chances are."

She watched as he pried open the ignition housing and gently pulled out a bird's nest of colored wires, muttering to himself all the while. Once again, she was glad he seemed to know what he was about; she was sure that even if she tried to hot-wire a boat, she'd wind up touching the wrong two wires and blow herself out of the water.

"Never stole a boat," he said, "but it's times like these I wish I had." He pulled two wires out of the tangle and peered at them. "These should be the ones."

She crossed her fingers.

He stripped the ends of their plastic casing, tapped them lightly against each other—

—and the engine roared.

"Oh, thank You, Lord," she was unable to stop herself from clutching her chest like someone in the throes of a heart attack. Her knees were weak with relief.

"I second that." He deftly twisted the wires together to maintain the connection and took the wheel. "Home?"

"You bet."

The boat lurched and then the sun was at their backs, and, with all the blessings of heaven, Tobago was dead ahead.

Sarita perched near him, not wanting to speak and risk breaking the wonderful good-luck spell that had been cast upon them. Instead, she laid one hand lightly on his arm, to keep him charged with her positive thoughts.

In an hour's time something wonderful happened. Out of the blinding haze on the horizon, a faint shadow appeared.

Tobago.

"Land!" she shouted deliriously and clapped her hands.

"My land," he added.

She didn't even feel a twinge of resentment. Yesterday morning the island had been her competition, and she was half on her way to hating it as a jealous woman hated her husband's mistress. Today, it was life to her—to them—and his devotion didn't rankle.

Just then, as if sensing that it had done its best in trying to deliver them and now, mission accomplished, could give up the ghost, the engine coughed.

"Oh, no!" Sarita exclaimed.

"Oh, yes," Matthias frowned. "That's about it, love. We've been sailing on fumes these last twenty minutes."

The boat lurched and the engine gave its last death rattle, falling silent. So close and yet so far.

"What now?" she asked dejectedly. Disappointment set in, even in the face of her prior knowledge that there had been no chance of making it much farther.

He put his arm around her shoulders. "Now, we keep out of the sun, try to stay hydrated, and wait."

"What would you like for dinner, dear?" Sarita asked. They were sitting on the roof, glad that it was once again becoming cool enough to allow them to emerge from the claustrophobic confines of the covered area and Janelle's silent, heartbreaking presence.

Sarita saw Matthias look at her with concern and knew exactly what he was wondering. Was she suffering heatstroke? He'd done his best to keep her in the shade, even made her reapply her sunscreen every few hours, and advised her to throw a dampened towel around herself when the afternoon heat had become unbearable. It was late afternoon now, and the air was cooling a little . . . and now she was babbling about making him dinner.

"Are you okay?" he asked suspiciously.

"I'm great, thank you," she said pertly. She could

have stopped him worrying right then by explaining what she was up to, but it was amusing to string him along a few moments more. "Just rustling up some dinner. What're you having?"

"Honey . . ." he began gently.

"I'm starving!" she protested. "I haven't had a bite to eat in almost two days!" She patted her belly. "If this keeps up, my tummy will actually get *flat!*"

"And I wouldn't want that," he smiled and pressed his hand on the mound of her belly, and, though it was completely empty seconds before, it instantly grew full of butterflies and all manner of tickly creatures in response to his touch. "I kind of like it the way it is." Then he grew serious again. "We can go for weeks without food, if we have to, you know . . . all we need is water."

Typical man. Always thinking they could deal you information you already had! "I know that," she groused. "You don't have to tell me that! But I'm still hungry."

"So am I. But what's all this talk about what I want for dinner?"

She wanted to sock him one. Him and his prosaic sensibilities. He was one of those people who thought a scientist shouldn't have an imagination. You had to be patient with people like that. "You play fantasy football, don't you?"

"Sure, sometimes. When I have nothing better to do."

"Well, let's play fantasy dinner. I'm cooking. What would you like?"

"Oh." He still looked bemused. "Okay."

"I'll start," she offered. She closed her eyes. "For openers, I think I'll have some soup."

"What kind of soup?"

"Oh, something creamy and expensive. Asparagus, maybe, or something with truffles in it."

"You know how to cook cream of asparagus soup?"

She opened her eyes long enough to shoot him a black look. "I do in my dreams. Do you mind not taking potshots at my cooking at a time like this?"

He chuckled. "No, not at all. Go ahead. And while you're at it, pour me a bowl."

"Asparagus?"

"Um, no. Smells funny."

"It does not!"

He ignored her protest. "Make mine tomato. With those little round pasta 'O's in it. Or alphabet bits. Yes, that's right. Tomato soup with alphabets. I can spell our names in the spoon."

"Tomato soup is so *ordinary!*" she protested. Her eyes popped open again.

"Hey, it's my fantasy. I can have anything I like and right now, that's what I'd like. Make it a double."

He was still stroking her belly, and the good vibrations that stirred up were enough to make her receptive to any suggestion he chose to make. "Tomato it is," she said decisively. They spent a few moments savoring their starters. "How was yours?" she asked after a while.

"Lovely, but I thought your hand was a little heavy on the basil."

She punched him on the arm, hard. "What's next?"

"Me, I could eat a twenty-four ounce steak, grilled Texas style, well-done, with roasted jalapeños and thick-cut fries. And about half a gallon of frosty beer."

Even in his fantasies, he was annoying. "I was thinking of something more stylish. Wouldn't you prefer a chateaubriand?"

He shrugged. "Beef is beef. I just want lots of it."

"How about stuffed lobster tails?"

"Honey, right now, I don't think I could eat anything

that came out of the sea." He pretended to gag. "Trust me on that."

They might have to, she could have reminded him, if things got any worse, even though Reef Rescue equipment didn't include fishing rods or nets. But she didn't even want to think about the absurdity that would be involved in finding food from the ocean without tools. It was fantasy time and that was much more fun. She nodded. "Okay, I'll stick with the chateaubriand. And a nice cabernet. You can keep your beer if you like."

"Thank you."

She ignored the irony in his tone. "You're welcome. And stuffed potatoes with mushroom sauce. *Truffle* sauce."

"You sure like those truffles."

"I do. And sweet Vidalia onions, rings of them, on top."

"I can't kiss you after dinner if you have those onions."

She smiled at him. "Okay, hold the onions." She ran her tongue along her lips. She could taste the mushroom sauce smeared there. Her stomach growled in response. After long moments in which they filled their minds, if not their bellies, she asked, "Ready for dessert?"

"I am if you are."

"And don't say ice cream."

He looked injured. "You mean I can't have any ice cream?"

"Matthias! You can have anything you want! Think big!"

"All right, all right. I hear you." He pretended to think hard. "I think I'll have cinnamon apple crumble, hot from the oven."

"Mmm! Sounds good! Cut me a piece!"

"With that sticky raspberry puree thing you like so much. What's it called?"

"Coulis."

"Yes, that. And three scoops of ice cream on top."

In spite of her protests, she had to admit that ice cream *did* sound good, especially in this heat. "Feed me," she said softly. "I'll have a spoonful."

The tip of his finger was at her mouth and she parted her lips slightly to allow it in. She tongued it, surrounding it with wetness. Now it was his turn to say "Mmm."

"Good?" she asked.

"Very." His lips were close to her cheek.

"I see you put the music on," she murmured as the low thump of a bass drum filled the air and beat out a sensuous bossa nova, like an orchestra playing just for them.

He stiffened. "What music?"

"Latin music." She was near drunk with the taste of his fingers against her lips. "Drums. Don't you hear it?"

He was galvanized, on his feet, jumping down onto the deck and racing across the boat, leaping without effort over the empty receptacles in the middle where the glass-bottomed trays had been. "Get the flare gun!" he shouted. "I'll get the flares!"

She followed him, bemused, dragged from her fantasy abruptly. "What?"

His lips formed one magical word that she read rather than heard. "Helicopter!"

Even Janelle seemed alert, sitting up ramrod straight in her seat, eyes bugging, straining to look up into the dimming sky. Her face was a mixture of anxiety and alarm.

Sarita grabbed her bag and rummaged through it.

The butt of the gun seemed to leap into her hand—a sentient thing, eager to be used. She handed it over to Matthias, whose hands were already filled with flares. He clambered back onto the roof and she kept close upon his heels, watching him slam a flare into the barrel and lift his arm.

By now the hum of the rotors was louder, and she spun around and around, neck craned, trying to see where it was coming from. With another half an hour to go before sunset, visibility was a little low for them to spot it. Conversely, it was not yet dark enough for the helicopter to easily spot the flares, but it was their only chance.

Matthias pulled the trigger and an arc of light sliced the sky. They both trained their eyes on it as it reached its peak height of several hundred feet, and then began its descent. Too soon, even before it hit the water, it died.

"Do you think they saw it?" she asked urgently.

"I don't know. But I can see them. Look." He pointed to the northwest and she could see the small black dot suspended like a bee. Was it approaching or retreating?

"Shoot off another one!"

"I don't want to use them all up before they get closer into range," he explained. "Let's give them a minute."

"Thirty seconds!" she haggled.

"Thirty seconds," he agreed. When the time had elapsed, he shot off another. It, too, fizzled out quickly. They kept their eyes fixed on the craft suspended in the distance.

"It's . . ." Matthias had to squint, because he'd lost his glasses when he jumped into the water to rescue Sarita.

"Coming this way!" Sarita threw her arms around

him, giddy with relief and happiness and imaginary wine. "We're saved, Matt!"

He clutched her to him in mute response. The water around them rose with the wind as the helicopter neared, spinning blades creating a mini-tornado all around them. It loomed lower, near enough to allow them to see the silhouettes of the two men on board; their round-helmeted and goggled heads turned in their direction. Matthias and Sarita waved, exuberantly. The men waved back—and then the craft made a rapid turn and headed in the opposite direction.

Fourteen

"No!" Matthias heard Sarita scream. Before he could stop her, she lurched toward the edge of the roof, arms windmilling frantically in a desperate attempt to recapture their attention. He tried to restrain her but she dodged him, grabbed the flare gun, loaded it, and squeezed off another round in the direction of their departing hope.

He wrenched it from her grasp. "Are you trying to shoot them down?"

"They're leaving!" He was surprised to see tears drenching her cheeks. "They aren't picking us up!"

She hadn't understood what was happening. The panic on her face moved him, and he pressed her against his chest in an effort to console. "Baby, baby, they'll be back. They've radioed for help. Someone'll come get us."

"But I want to go *now!* It's not fair! To get our hopes up . . ."

"Honey, it's a two-seater. Didn't you notice? I'm sure they wanted to take us, it just wasn't physically possible."

She stopped struggling and seemed to be thinking about what he had said. Then she passed her hand across her forehead and said slowly. "You're right."

"Yes, I am."

She looked a little embarrassed, rubbing away her tears like a schoolgirl. He tried to help her, lifting up the bottom of his shirt and dabbing at her cheeks, gently, as she was a little sore from sunburn. When her face was dry, she said sheepishly, "I freaked, didn't I?"

"You did. But I won't tell anyone."

"You're so kind," she murmured dryly.

"Come, let's go tell Janelle they're coming." He took her hand and helped her down from the roof, making sure to bring the flare gun and flares with him as well.

He didn't even have to broach the subject with Janelle. When he got onto the deck she was on her feet, her face ashen, dark eyes like anguished pinholes in her face. "They left," she croaked.

"But they'll be back. Someone will be here soon."

"Oh. . . ." She looked as if she were standing at a door and the hounds of hell were snarling on the other side of it.

Pity filled him and he lied to make her feel better. "You'll do okay."

She didn't accept it and shook her head vehemently. "I won't." Her lip trembled. "Twenty years. That's what I'll get."

The mere idea of it horrified him, even though she had brought it on herself. He wished there was something he could do to comfort her. Her hands were still bound, and had been since last night, so he thought he could start with that. He withdrew his utility knife from its holster on his belt and glanced across at Sarita. She read his question. It was a calculated risk to release Janelle, even as meek as she appeared to be now. A desperate person could be unpredictable. At this stage, though, he was less concerned about her trying to do *them* any harm. Right now, she was an even greater threat to herself. But he didn't want her to suffer the humiliation of being found tied up like this, and if he cut her free, he would just have to watch her like a hawk.

Sarita nodded her agreement with his decision, so he slid the blade under the rope binds. "If I let you go, will you behave?"

Surprise at his decision to release her registered on her face, but nothing else did.

He pressed the point further. "Don't do anything rash, okay?"

Slowly, she promised. "Okay."

The lengths of rope hit the deck and Sarita quickly scooped them up and tossed them overboard. Matthias tugged Janelle back into a seated position and sat right next to her, ready to act if it seemed necessary, but Janelle barely seemed to notice, or to care, that she was free. She rubbed her wrists absently, didn't thank him, and lapsed back into her sullen silence.

Sarita sat opposite him. Her face looked tired but her mouth was set in a determined line, and he felt himself brimming over with compassion for her. After all that she had been through—being shot at, half starving, and then near drowning—she was still bearing up. She was so strong, this woman he loved—and if there was one thing this ordeal had revealed to him, it was that he *did* love her, even as angry as she made him and as frustrating as she could be. There was nothing he wouldn't do for her, and he would stop at nothing to convince her to put their awful mistakes behind them and start afresh.

But that would come later, with dry land and the assurance of safety. Right now, all he could do for her was be strong.

Once again, he briefly thought about the discussion he had had with Sarita about dumping their cargo. If he were to change his mind, now would be their last chance . . . but the packets would float; he'd learned that yesterday. It would be a macabre joke for their rescuers to return and find them adrift in a sea of small, bobbing plastic packets, even if they decided to make that last-ditch effort in the face of the overwhelming arguments against such a rash action. So, with half a million dollars' worth of contraband heaped between them, they waited to be rescued.

They didn't have to wait long. Before the last light faded from the sky, the gray outline of a vessel appeared. Soon, he could identify the austere bulk of a Coast Guard launch. Sarita could not contain herself. She let out an ecstatic whoop that he came close to echoing, and then leaped onto the bench. Matthias watched her bottom wiggle as she did a dance of sheer joy, snapping her towel in the air above her head. When he discovered she was singing her old college football cheer, he laughed out loud.

"You're crazy, girl."

"Happy-crazy!" She laughed back, and danced even harder.

"Well, don't fall in!" he warned, but he was still chuckling. He half wished he didn't have to stick close to Janelle, for everybody's security, or he would have joined her. The warning was enough to get Sarita down from her precarious position on the bench, but she kept up her victory dance on the deck until the launch drew abreast of them.

Then things started happening. Fast. Men in blue military uniforms swarmed the *Spanish Dancer*, and everyone shouted questions. Sarita threw her arms around each one in turn, bubbling over with gratitude. Janelle fell into a dead faint, collapsing to the floor in a crumpled heap. Then the men noticed the pile of plastic-wrapped packages in the middle of the boat. One man picked up a package and sniffed at it. He peeled back the plastic covering and identified it for what it was.

Men yelling instructions at their colleagues still on the boat, radio calls being made. Guns being drawn and the friendly greetings being transformed, as in a nightmare, into barked questions and demands for explanations.

One of the men, whose epaulettes bore more stripes than those of the others, holding an incriminating package out to Matthias, right under his nose—too close, in fact—and asking loudly, "What's this all about?"

Matthias put his hands on his hips and sighed. "It's a long story," he said. "But could we tell it on land?" *Maybe the hard part isn't really over,* he thought. *Maybe the hard part has only just begun.*

Sarita had a headache, the kind four cups of coffee didn't even come near to quelling. She was exhausted. Worse than that. She felt as if she'd been run over by a three-ton truck. More than once.

Three days.

Three long, arduous days since she had seen Matthias, or been allowed any information about him. The first had been spent in a hospital in Scarborough, where sympathetic nurses in crisp white linens treated her for sunburn and dehydration, and filled her up with hot food. She had been glad for the respite, grateful for their kindness and the luxuries of a functioning bathroom, clean clothing (even though it was just one of those dreadful standard-issue backless hospital gowns), and a bed.

But after being given a clean bill of health by a harassed-looking doctor, she had yet another tribulation to face: the next day the police arrived to take her away.

Two days are too much, she thought, to be asked the same questions over and over. Where did the drugs come from? Did she buy them? Was she contracted to sell them? Who was her supplier? Who was her client? Where had she been taking them? And what role did her husband play in all this? And to each question, her response was a denial, an insistence upon her innocence.

The interrogation room was small, hadn't been painted in too many years, and lacked ventilation. Even a working fan would have earned her undying gratitude. But instead, she had been subjected to stale air and claustrophobic conditions . . . and here was better than the small holding cell in which she had spent the past two terrifying, uncomfortable, sleepless nights.

A single, low-wattage light bulb was barely enough to see by, and that was just as well, because what she could see depressed her even further. It was late afternoon, Good Friday, a day she usually spent in church spiritually preparing herself for the celebrations of rebirth that she would enjoy come Easter Sunday, and she was in her sixth hour of interrogation for the day.

"More coffee?" one of her tormentors asked, as polite as he could be under the circumstances. His accent was soft, his tone civil, and his dark face almost seemed sympathetic. Maybe he was tiring of the interrogation, too.

The thought of the tepid, over-sweetened dishwater made her gag. She almost longed for the distilled water that they'd left percolating on top of the *Spanish Dancer*'s roof on the evening of their rescue. They'd never had the chance to even taste the results of their contraption, but she had no doubt that their home-made water would definitely have tasted better than station-house coffee!

"No, thank you," she said, grateful that their belligerence had dimmed. She let her head fall into her hands, her shoulders slumping. *One more question,* she told herself, *one more, and I'll snap.*

And then, just then, the questions stopped. There was a knock on the door of the interrogation room. One of the officers rose and opened it, and Sarita caught a glimpse of two men who had come to exchange whispers from time to time during her prolonged interrogation. She didn't know why but she was convinced that they were the officers who were interrogating Matthias somewhere else in the building. The thought of him being so near, and yet denied to her, increased her loneliness a thousandfold.

But something was different this time. All four men kept glancing over at her, and their heated, whispered conversation became more intense. When she was sure that one more agonizing second of suspense would just about kill her, one of the men, the eldest and most senior of the bunch, and whom she had come to know as Sergeant Andrews, came over, towering above her.

"Mrs. Rowley," he began.

That's Dr. Rowley to you, she wanted to snap irritably, but she quelled the impulse. She was in more hot water right now than a lobster at a beach cookout, so it was in her interest to keep a civil tongue. So instead, she acknowledged him with a simple, "Yes?"

"We've decided not to file any charges against you or your husband—at least for now."

She gaped. "Why?" As soon as the question was out of her mouth she wanted to kick herself. Instead of grabbing the opportunity to leave, she was asking questions? She really was sleep deprived!

His face was almost kind. "So far, you seem to be telling the truth. We don't have any reason to believe that you or Dr. Rowley are involved in this."

Incredible. Matthias had been right. The justice system had worked in favor of the innocent. Her face split in a wide grin. "Thank you!"

Then, he added hastily, "What I mean is, investigations will continue, of course, and we may or may not have further questions for you. But we can't hold you much longer without charging you with a crime, and at this time, we have nothing to charge you with. You're free to leave but we'd rather you stayed in Tobago, at least for the time being."

Her heart struggled against the force of gravity, which was doing its best to drag it back down again. That was just the cop's way of covering his bases, she tried to convince herself. If they came back with questions, that would be all they would have: more questions. It didn't mean they were still under suspicion. Did it?

She clung to the relief she had felt mere seconds before and shot to her feet. She was halfway to the door when another sobering thought intervened. "And Janelle?"

The officer's face returned to its usual doleful expression. "I'm afraid that Miss Jeffries is still assisting us with our investigations."

"Oh." She knew that was cop-speak for being under interrogation and the officer confirmed it by adding, "We expect to be making some arrests regarding this case very soon." He gestured toward the door. "Come with me. We'll have you processed and out of here as quickly as possible."

Sarita scurried after him. There was a whirl of paperwork, things to sign, documents handed back to her, and then she was swept toward a door. . . .

Matthias was standing in the lobby. Even on a religious holiday like today, the station was packed with people, but in spite of the bustle, she spotted him immediately, and everyone around them melted away.

She was glued to the spot, unable to take another step. He looked as bad as she felt: grubby, exhausted, and anxious, but she had never beheld a more beautiful sight. She was so tired, so miserable, so drained, and there he was, like a towering tree, and all she wanted to do was curl herself up at his roots and sleep in his shade. She held her arms out to him, but still couldn't move.

"Sari," he mouthed her name—or may have spoken it aloud, but she couldn't hear it above the noise and the ringing in her ears. He crossed the distance between them in two long strides and lifted her into his arms. "Are you okay?"

She felt embarrassed by his proximity. She had surrendered the awful hospital gown before she was taken into the station and hadn't been given a change of clothes since. She still wore the now-filthy shorts and T-shirt that she had left their bungalow in five days before. Her hair was a tangled nest. She longed for sweet-scented soap and skin-softening body lotion. "Don't," she protested. "I'm a mess. I'm dirty. I smell like a troll's armpit. . . ."

"So do I." He refused to set her down. "But we're alive and free, and I just want to hold you. Do you mind?"

She discovered that she didn't. She twined her fingers around his neck. "Did they treat you right?" they asked simultaneously. He set her down and they stood, inches apart, staring at each other solemnly.

"I did okay." She tried not to think about the terrible claustrophobia that came with seeing a cell door slam shut, or about the regimentation, the bad food, and the hostile stares from other women in communal areas, like the mess hall. But all the same, she shuddered visibly.

"Let's just say that if I ever entertained any thoughts of breaking the law, I've changed my mind." He took her hand. "You know we did the right thing, don't you? In not dumping the stuff?"

She'd asked herself that question dozens of times during her short but harrowing spell in captivity, but she was proud of the fact that she, too, even in her darkest moments, had clung to the same belief. "Yes, we did."

"And it all worked out okay in the end."

"Yes. I think. The cop said there might be more questions." The idea still worried her.

His tone was soothing. "Don't worry. They told me the same thing. If they've found no reason to charge us yet, they won't unearth anything else. If they come back, it will only be for more information. We're out of danger. I promise you. Okay?"

She wished she could be as certain as he was that they were free and clear, and in the face of her own disquiet she made his assurance her own, but she didn't answer.

He pressed her for a reply. "Okay?"

She gave in. Just as, in his darkest moment, he had relented and shared her belief that God could and would pluck them from danger, so too could she share his belief that justice would prevail, and that the innocent would go free. Everything was going to be normal again—it had to be. "Okay."

He released her from his python embrace and grasped her hand. "Let's go."

He didn't have to repeat himself. She was ready and willing to shake the dust from this place off her feet—but their means of escape was still undecided. "How do we get home?"

"I don't care. We walk. We get a taxi. A bus. Anything. Let's just . . . *go.*"

They didn't even make it to the door. "Sarita!" A voice rose above the chatter in the lobby.

She whirled around, recognizing it at once but trying to locate its source.

A large, hairy hand rose above the crowd and Colin Constantine shouldered his way over to them. He was clad in his minister's robes, white collar stark at his throat. He seemed as relieved to see her as she was to see him. His friendly face was red and wrinkled, and creased with smiles as he pulled her to him and wrapped her in an enthusiastic bear hug. Matthias watched, bemused, but did not release her hand.

"My dear girl! How are you! I've been so worried! I'm so glad to see you! Have you eaten?" Colin was, as usual, talking a mile a minute. Before she could answer, he stuck out his hand at Matthias. "Reverend Colin Constantine. You must be the good doctor. Pleased to meet you." The men quickly shook hands, and then Colin was chattering again. "Excuse my work clothes but I just did a Good Friday service. I was supposed to do another one but I got somebody to fill in. Come, kids, the car's this way."

"You came for us?" She could barely believe it.

Colin looked about to say "silly question," but instead he chose a more polite route. "Of course, why?"

"I just . . ." She was so overwhelmed by his gesture. She'd seen nothing but hard, cynical, disbelieving faces within the station, and now to have her only friend on the island actually go out of his way . . . "How'd you know we were here?"

He laughed, sounding like a big dog coughing. "Are you kidding? You're all over the news. Front page and first story on the seven o'clock broadcast!"

"Oh." She hadn't really thought of that. She wasn't used to being the center of attention, especially negative publicity. She wondered what sort of things they had been saying about her and Matthias, and which way the tide of public opinion flowed regarding their guilt or innocence. She ventured to ask, shyly. "So you heard about the . . . uh . . . stuff on the boat?"

For a change, Colin wasn't smiling. "Yes. Nasty business."

"And you believe we didn't have anything to do with it?"

He patted her shoulder heavily. "Of course I do, child. I'm a very good judge of character. You don't survive long enough to be my age if you aren't. And from what you've told me of that other young lady, well, I have no doubt that your story is the more credible one."

By now they were at Colin's car, and he opened up the back door to allow them to crawl in gratefully. It was a battered Ford, well past its prime, with vinyl that was cracked in places, but it was taking her home, and to Sarita that made it better than a horse-drawn chariot. Colin started the engine and they pulled onto the road. She was so tired that she wondered if she would manage to stay awake for the short ride. She let her head fall onto her husband's shoulder and murmured, "You warned me about her."

Colin shrugged, and didn't respond directly to her comment. "I couldn't sleep the night your boat didn't come back. My soul couldn't rest. I stayed up, praying for your safe return."

Matthias, who hadn't spoken since the two men had exchanged greetings back at the station, spoke now. "And we're more grateful for your intervention than you'll ever know, Father."

Colin laughed again. "Actually, I'm not a Father, I'm a Reverend. But you'll have to call me Colin, if you call me anything."

"Colin, then. My wife and I owe you our lives."

"You're welcome," Colin said modestly. "But I'm not the source of the power, only a conduit for it."

Sarita threw Matthias a look of stark surprise. He'd not only admitted his newfound belief in the power of prayer to another person, but he'd once again called her his wife! What were the chances of that, she mused. Miracle was spilling over upon miracle. She caught Colin's amused gray eyes in the rearview mirror and they exchanged smiles. She didn't think there was anything else she needed to say.

They were at their door in a mercifully short space of time, and Matthias helped her out of the car and led her to it. He unlocked it, stepped aside for her to enter, and then turned to Colin. "Would you like to come in?" he asked politely, but the fatigue was visible in his eyes and Colin shook his head.

"You're both tired. You need sleep and a lot of time to recover from your ordeal. I wouldn't force the presence of a guest upon you at a time like this." The men shook hands warmly.

For the first time, Sarita released her grip on the hand that had held hers throughout the journey, and rushed to throw her arms around Colin again, kissing him on the cheek. "Thank you for believing in us." That simple gift of faith meant so much! Before she embarrassed herself by snuffling like a baby, she broke away and disappeared into the house. She heard the muffled exchange of good-byes, and then the rattle and bang of Colin's car as it disappeared. Matthias closed the front door, turned on a light, and they stared at each other.

Alone.

The last time they had been alone here, this house had been filled with the smell of defeat and the pain of love lost. Now, she only cared that they were both alive, both delivered from their ordeals, and free.

He somehow looked older. She wondered if she appeared the same to him. He looked tired, but there was a light shining somewhere inside. He'd changed. The change in him was barely perceptible, but radical, like someone in one of those old-fashioned sci-fi movies, who had been sucked into some tremendous field of energy and been taken apart molecule by molecule, and then reassembled, to all external appearances exactly the same as they had been at the beginning except for one small variation that turned them into a completely different being.

She watched him silently, wondering what they could say to each other now after all they had endured.

He seemed to be wondering the same thing. He coughed. "JoJo was at the station today."

She was half disappointed, half relieved that he hadn't said anything more personal about them. But he had her attention anyway. "JoJo?" Had he been there to see his sister, she wondered, or had he been entangled in the police dragnet to find Janelle's accomplices? She ached to know but waited for Matthias to go on.

"I didn't see him, but I was told they questioned him for three hours."

"And do they think . . . ?"

"They don't think he had anything to do with it. As a matter of fact, he was the one who alerted the Coast Guard when we didn't come back."

It was a relief to know that they hadn't been *completely* surrounded by conspiracy! Besides, she genuinely liked the young man. "You think we'll see him again?"

"I think so. No reason he shouldn't want to keep working. Unless he can't forgive me for tying up his sister."

"You didn't have a choice," she reminded him.

"I know, but I'll probably feel bad about it for a long time to come."

"But he'll be okay, right?" She needed to know that.

Matthias thought about it for some time. "I think he will."

"I'm glad. He's a good person. He doesn't deserve to be caught up in all this mess."

"Amen to that." He pressed his fingers into his temple. "Four days without glasses. I feel like I got a sledgehammer to the skull."

"Don't you have your spares?"

"Somewhere inside. In a drawer, maybe." He made no move to go look for them.

"Need any headache tablets?"

"Probably have some inside, too." Then, as an afterthought, "Hungry?"

Surprisingly, she wasn't. "Too dirty to be hungry."

"Got that right." Matthias dragged his filthy shirt over his head and balled it up. This," he said, "gets burned in the morning."

She smiled at him. She wasn't keen on wearing anything she had on again, either. "Let me know when you're lighting up. I've got a thing or two to add to the blaze."

He began heading in the direction of his bedroom, stripping as he went, and kicking his clothing ahead of him disgustedly. "I think I'll stand under the shower for an hour. I don't know if being clean again is even physically possible. I shudder to think what sort of cooties that place must have been swarming with."

The image alone made the hair on her arms crawl. "I think I'll do the same." A gallon each of shampoo and bubble bath was calling her name. Her skin could prune up permanently; she wouldn't care. She headed in the opposite direction.

"Sarita?"

She stopped and turned back to him.

"Sleep with me tonight." It was phrased as a command, but she could see that he was all but shaking at the possibility of a refusal. "I promise, nothing will happen. I just want you near me. I'm tired and I haven't slept in days, but I don't think I'll be able to fall asleep tonight if I have to face the whole night alone. Please."

She swayed a little, partly from fatigue and partly from the realization that she needed the same comfort that he did. Clean sheets and fluffy pillows might ease the ache of her body, but the emptiness of her bed would bring no consolation to her soul. She barely hesitated. "Yes."

"Thank you." He looked like he was about to say more but instead, hastily backed away and disappeared into his room.

After an hour-long shower she padded over to his room, struggling to quell the mild trepidation that she felt. All they were doing was sleeping. He'd made that promise, and she knew he would keep it. They'd slept in each other's arms that hideous night on the boat, in spite of all that was going on between them, and there was nothing that said that they couldn't do it again.

He was sitting on the edge of the bed with a large towel, vigorously drying the long, thick locks that he had subjected to a relentless shampooing. She smiled when she noticed he was wearing clean navy blue shorts. If she remembered correctly—and there was *no reason* to forget—he slept in naked splendor. He'd no doubt dressed for bed as a signal to her that he intended to keep his word.

The bed sank slightly as she sat next to him. "All free of jailhouse cooties?" she teased.

He grinned. "With any luck, the little monsters are running for the hills. How are you feeling?"

"Squeaky clean." She squeaked like a mouse to prove it.

He tossed the towel down. "Good." Without another word, he got up, crossed the floor, and turned off the lights, and then unerringly found his way back to bed in the dark. The bed creaked and he stretched out, pulling her against him.

She fit perfectly into the curve of his body—always had. He offered his arm as a pillow, and even as hard and muscled as it was, it made a cradle for her head. He smelled, as he usually did, of lemons and rainwater.

He pressed a light kiss at the back of her head. "Sleep," he whispered.

Sarita woke up alone.

"What the . . . ?" She'd slept like the dead, she knew, but she'd been aware of his presence, even in her dreams, and when they'd turned sour, when the ghosts of drowned sailors had threatened to drag her down once again, she'd felt his grip around her waist tighten, and the nightmares were sent galloping off into the darkness once more. Now the sheets next to her were cold. Bright sunshine streamed in through the windows, an assault on her eyes, and her arm rose to shield them.

"Matthias?" She walked out in the living room and became aware of a muted, one-sided conversation. It was coming from the study. She followed the sound of Matthias's voice, arriving in time to see him release the phone. He did not set it back down into its cradle but let it fall from his fingers. His shoulders were hunched and his head hung down. Even with his back to her, she could read dejection in every line of his body.

"What is it?" She felt real but unidentifiable fear. Was it the police on the line? Had they changed their minds about setting them free? Were more doubts about their innocence arising? She reached his side, put her hands on his shoulders, and turned him around, almost shouting her question into his face again. "What is it? Tell me!"

His skin was sallow, and his eyes were darkening like storm clouds gathering. He opened his mouth to answer her, but all that came out was a low, anguished groan. Matthias stumbled toward an armchair and fell into it.

Sarita dropped to her knees before him, eyes searching his, wanting to beg for an explanation one last time but not having the heart do so. She placed her hands on his thighs and kept her gaze on his face.

He rubbed his brow like a man with a migraine, and then he began to explain. "That was our UN rep., calling from New York." He motioned blindly at the phone, which had begun its off-the-hook howling.

"Yes?"

"Calling about Reef Rescue."

Get on with it, she wanted to yell. The suspense was tearing her apart. But she held her tongue.

"And about our little . . ." He floundered and then tried again. "Our little run-in with the police. And the drugs."

"We haven't been charged," she said immediately. "Didn't you tell them that?"

"They know that. But we haven't been cleared, either. The police haven't ruled us out a hundred percent. They said . . . they implied . . . that they'd be back, if they need to. Their investigation is far from over. And besides, she said that policy is policy . . ."

"And?" The howling of the phone grew to a frenzied pitch.

"And the UN will need to conduct an investigation of its own. A thorough one. A complete procedural audit, to decide if we were—if *I* was—complicit, negligent, or just plain *stupid.* . . ." He hammered his forehead with the palm of his hand.

"You weren't any of those things. It could have happened to anybody. We needed a boat, and Janelle was willing to rent one to us. You have no control over what she did with it in her spare time, and you couldn't have had any idea what she was up to."

"Maybe, but they'll have to determine that for themselves."

Why did she feel as if she didn't want to hear what would come next? "How long will that take?"

He shrugged. "Months, maybe. I don't know."

"And until then? They'll let us go on with our work, right?" Hanging on to her hope was like trying to grasp an octopus with her bare hands. *"Right?"* She stepped away from him, crossed the room, and slammed down the phone receiver, ending its cacophony. Then she was back before him again, kneeling at his feet and looking up into his face.

She read the answer in his face before he put it into words. "Reef Rescue's been shut down. Indefinitely."

Fifteen

Sarita made breakfast, but it sat on the table untouched. From time to time she walked to the balcony and looked out at the beach, where she could clearly see Matthias, sitting on the sand at the water's edge, not caring that the tide was rolling in and soaking him. The usually square shoulders were bent under the burden of all the cares in the world. It broke her heart.

It was much like being the cuckolded wife who, after having wished all manner of ills and curses upon her rival, learns that her husband's mistress has been run over by a bus. Where there should have been relief that the rival had been laid low, leaving her husband free for her again, all she could feel was grief and a deep sense of unfairness. Reef Rescue might have been a rival, but it was a worthy project and didn't deserve to be strangled by red tape. Matthias didn't deserve it.

She longed to go out to him but wouldn't have known what she could possibly tell him that would make him feel any better. Furthermore, something told her that whatever grieving he needed to do, he would want to do on his own.

The sun had already crossed its high point by the time he came inside, damp and bedraggled. She watched him anxiously, waiting for him to acknowledge her, waiting for him to say something, but he walked straight past like a blind man. Long moments later he emerged from his room, having exchanged his sandy clothes for his favorite jeans and a T-shirt. This time, he walked right up to her.

"Will you come with me?"

Anywhere, she wanted to tell him. *I'd go anywhere with you.* But instead she asked "Where?"

"I don't know." He showed her the 4X4's keys in his hand. "Just driving. I couldn't bear to spend one more minute in this house. Just ride with me. There's something I need to say to you."

Curiosity propelled her forward. What could he possibly have to say to her? His career was listing to the side like a leaky rowboat, his reputation and integrity in question, and his pet project, his life's work, was drowning in a bureaucratic sea. If he needed to unburden himself, she'd try to lend him a sympathetic ear. She hurried to her bedroom to get her bag.

It was on the old wooden dressing table where she always left it. She slung it over her shoulder, and as she was about to leave the room, something caught her eye. It was the small box containing the pearl earrings that Matthias had given to her on the night she'd decided to sign the divorce papers, the night he'd told her that she came second in his life, not first. She'd never had the chance to wear them; she wasn't sure she ever would, given the pain that was associated with them. But some vague superstition made her reach out for the box, to touch what could be a talisman of some kind.

"I've been living on a little island too long," she muttered to herself as she pocketed it. "Half beginning to believe in magic." She patted her pocket to make sure it was safe and joined Matthias by the truck.

They headed toward Scarborough. From time to

time, Sarita cast him sidelong glances, as every silent minute made her more anxious to know what he needed to tell her and if it would be something she wanted to hear. Every time he drew breath she braced herself, preparing for his words. But he remained focused on the road, both hands gripping the wheel and staring through the window like a first-time driver afraid of straying across the white line. His intensity scared her.

She tried to concentrate on what was going on outside the window in an effort to distract herself from the tension that expanded within the truck's cab and threatened to crush them both. Along the roads people scurried, well dressed and looking excited. It was Gloria Saturday, the day before Easter, and she deduced that there would be much going on; nobody seemed prepared to miss it. Many of them were dressed up in their best: colors bright, shoes shining, and hair neatly combed.

They passed a park crowded with people, and an excited cheer erupted. "What's that?" she blurted.

Matthias skated to a stop. "You want to see?"

His voice almost startled her, as he hadn't spoken in so long. She wasn't sure if stopping was a good idea, but the distraction might prove good for him, so she nodded her assent. Matthias spun around in the road and turned onto the grass, edging as close to the action as possible. From where she sat, she had a fairly clear view of the source of the excitement.

In a clearing she could see a racetrack, and straining for all their worth toward the finish line were half a dozen goats. They each wore a bright fabric bib with a number on it and by each one's side ran a young, barefoot man, spurring on his goat with a small stick. Turf flew under the sharp hooves, and as the racing creatures drew closer to the finish line the fans screamed, encouraging their favorites. In seconds it was over, and the ecstatic crowds surged in to congratulate the victorious jockeys.

"Amazing," she exclaimed. Even though she had watched the goats practicing, actually seeing them in action was unexpectedly intriguing.

"It is. And see those kids over there with the boxes?" Matthias pointed.

She looked in the direction he indicated. Young children hugged cardboard boxes to their chests, looking expectant. From time to time they peered into the boxes and poked at whatever was unfortunate enough to be in captivity there. She remembered what Matthias had told her once and hazarded a guess. "Crab races?"

"Yes, they've probably laid out a crab racetrack somewhere nearby. I raced them when I was a boy, too."

Forgetting the pain that had led them there, she was mesmerized, enthralled by the noise, color, and charm that surrounded her. For a brief moment, she was convinced she could see the ghost of Matthias past on the field, clutching his own box, making soothing noises to the large, angry blue crab inside. He was barefoot, unable to afford shoes, and his fair hair was closely cropped, as would have befitted the grandson—unwanted or not—of a village minister.

And in that moment, she saw the island through his eyes and was able to feel, for the first time, a little of the love he had for it. How he must be in pain right now! She reached out and took his hand, squeezing it, trying to offer comfort.

"Everything I've ever wanted is now gone," he said. "And I don't know if I'll ever get it back."

"We can start a new project," she said immediately. "We can get new funding. Or we can take out a loan and fund it on our own, for the time being, until we're cleared. The UN investigation will be over, and then they'll know we're innocent. Then they'll let us start again."

He didn't seem to hear her. "Tobago always came first. Reef Rescue always came first. I gave up everything for this."

Including me, her heart said. But for the first time, she understood. Her lack of resentment shocked her.

He reached over. She was half convinced he was about to kiss her and closed her eyes. But he opened the glove compartment in the dash on her side and rummaged within. Her eyes popped open to see him holding the dreadful, omnipresent manila envelope, the one whose contents she had vacillated about signing for half a year, the one she handed over to him last week. Intervening events had prevented him from ever making it to the courier's office, and now, like a bad penny, it was showing up in her life once again. He held it out to her.

"I want you to do something for me."

She didn't take the package. Her lips barely formed the word, "What?"

"Tear this up."

"What?"

"They're our divorce papers."

"I know what they are."

"And I don't want them anymore. I can't not be married to you. I don't want to be anything other than your husband. Tear them up, Sarita, please. And let's try again."

She knew her mouth was open, dumbstruck, but she was powerless to close it. The package in his hand tantalized her, and she could almost hear the satisfying sound of paper tearing under her fingers. She could rip it up and toss the pieces about like confetti, celebrating the resurrection of a marriage she had believed was dead.

But that would be cheating. She would have won this race unfairly, breasting the tape only because her opponent had stumbled. He'd said himself that he had never loved her first and that she would always come second to his mission. Now that his mission had been scuttled he was turning to her. She couldn't live with that.

The envelope was still in his outstretched hand. Puzzled, he called her name, softly.

She didn't respond. The brown package blurred, and it was only then that she realized her eyes were filled with tears. *How humiliating,* one part of her thought. *To be second best and to know it.* To be second best and to be willing to accept it, was far worse. The other part of her screamed, *Take it! Take it! Tear it to shreds, erase it from your life, and be with the man you love, the only man you could love. Second best is still good enough if it allows you to have him. He's a good man and always has, always will, treat you right. Maybe there wouldn't be babies, if he was still against the idea. Maybe you'll change his mind, and maybe you won't. But you'd have him. Wasn't that all that mattered?*

It wasn't. For one thing, the project wouldn't be frozen forever. In a few months, when those that held the purse strings were convinced that she and Matthias were guiltless, Reef Rescue would get a second lease on life. Then, no matter how well things would be going for them, she would once again find herself in the same situation she had been in a year ago: married but still alone.

For another, her pride told her that second-best-winner-by-default just wasn't what she deserved. She wanted to be loved first and foremost, the way she loved him. She wanted to be his center.

The words of an old song came back to her: *"If somebody loves you, it's no good, unless they love you all the way."* No truer words had ever been sung. If he couldn't give her that, she wanted nothing less.

"Sari?" Puzzlement and nervousness. "I'll tear it up for you, all you have to do is give me the okay."

Even in their most heated arguments, nothing she had ever said to him had hurt *her* more. "No, Matt."

An agonized, rasping sound escaped his chest. "I don't understand what you're saying. . . ."

"I'm saying you should send it off like you planned. Like we agreed. Send it off and let's try to build our own lives again. Separately. And when Reef Rescue is back on track, you can find somebody to replace me because I won't be staying." She blindly fiddled for the door handle, scrunching her eyes closed against the bitter sting of tears. Mercifully, the door sprang open. She fell out onto the grass, backing away from him even before he was out and coming after her.

She held her hands up in front of her to ward him off. "Stop. It's over! It's over!" People had begun to stare, but she didn't care.

"It can't be!"

"It is!" Then, in her confusion, her foot sank into a crab hole hidden by the grass, and she tumbled down. Before she could right herself, Matthias was helping her to her feet.

Don't touch me, her mind screamed. *If you touch me, I'll relent. I'll give in and then I'll be undone.* "Let me go, Matt," she said quietly.

She didn't have to say another word. His hands fell to his sides. His eyes were clouded, dark with pain, and holding hers steadfastly. She was immobilized by his gaze, and then she dragged herself out of his thrall, turned, and began running. Mothers snatched up their children to get them out of her way, and the crowd parted for her, closing behind her like the Red Sea behind the last of Moses' people. She broke through the barrier of racing spectators—and found herself on the field, in the path of huge, thundering goats and their jockeys.

Chaos as runners tried to stop their goats, and goats swerved to avoid her. Some fell over into the dirt, and others, disoriented, veered off the field and into the crowd, sparking excitement as onlookers ran after them. A large black-and-white billy goat, panicked and confused, lowered its head; through her mist of tears Sarita saw nothing but a whirl of churning hooves and curved horns fast approaching.

She felt herself go airborne as a pair of powerful hands hoisted her out of the way and a rush of air as the maddened animal blew past. Then she was being set down again on the other side, held steady by the man who had rescued her. He was as tall and as wide as a refrigerator, but his face was kind and concerned.

"You all right, Miss?" the man asked, and did not release her until she nodded. "You going to be okay?" he asked again, to make sure.

She found her voice. "Yes. Thank you." She took a few uncertain steps away, trying to put as much distance as she could between her and the scary animals on the racetrack. She was on the other side of the track now and that side was even more crowded. When she found her bearings, she looked around, shading her eyes from the sun with her hands. She searched faces, squinting to see the roadside.

There was no sign of Matthias.

Sixteen

Sarita had always liked Easter Sunday, even when she'd grown too old for egg hunts and bunnies. There was something fresh and clean about the day: it smelled of promise. When she was growing up, church on Easter Sunday morning was a major family outing; she and her mother got new dresses, gloves, and hats, and her father bought wrist corsages for them and a boutonniere for himself.

Last Easter, the only one she had spent with Matthias, she had tried to persuade him to join her, but he had gone surfing instead. By then their marriage was already foundering: in weeks it would have received its deathblow.

This morning, Colin's little church was crammed to the seams as the Tobagonians, religious almost to a fault and never willing to miss an event, turned out in their finery. The seats were all taken, and the aisles were awash with brightly colored silks and taffetas. Huge, elaborate Easter bonnets competed with each other; some were adorned with silk or fresh flowers and others with large, loopy bows with ends that trailed down their wearers' backs. Sarita stood at the rear, feeling almost shabby in her short-sleeved sundress and sandals. It was about as much as she had been able to buy in town yesterday, as most of the stores had been closed by the time she'd gathered her wits and left the playing field where she and Matthias had parted company. She even wore in her ears the pearls he had given her, her pearls of tears. When she'd put them on she'd told herself they would help her look more dressy, but even then she knew that she was wearing them because they were a tangible link to the man she was trying to escape.

She'd spent an awful sleepless night at a small hotel, having endured the suspicious glances of the check-in clerk as she arrived without so much as an overnight bag, with very little cash, and only a credit card with which to buy her way past the door.

Colin's vigorous voice chased away her fatigue and depression. As he spoke of the season of hope and rebirth, she struggled to believe him. There would come a time when she would be able to emerge from the hurt and loneliness that now held her prisoner, heal herself, and be able to function as a whole person again. Never mind that without Matthias she felt as though she were missing a limb or that a vital organ had been torn from her body, leaving a gaping wound from which blood never stopped flowing. Life went on, even after tragedy. It did! It had to!

Didn't it?

"Excuse me."

She was sure she heard the voice, a soft whisper several feet away, but it was only her imagination, so she didn't bother to look around. She was conjuring up Matthias everywhere. Last night, he'd invaded her fitful sleep, a poltergeist who didn't like to be ignored, shattering her emotions against the wall like plates in a haunted kitchen. The crowd around her parted obligingly, as if an angel had flown low and rushed through the congregation like a wind over the transoms.

A new hymn began. It was an old one, one she had loved since childhood, and one she even remembered her grandmother playing over and over on an old gramophone when she was a little girl. There were not enough hymnals to go around, but Sarita knew the words by heart. They came to her lips without effort:

Christ the Lord is risen today,
Sons of men, and angels say;

She closed her eyes and sang, loudly if not melodiously: music had never been her strong suit.

"Excuse me," she heard again. It was a little closer now, still soft, barely perceptible. Movement, a presence beside her. Then, a deep baritone, resonant, rumbling like the stone being rolled away from the mouth of an ancient tomb:

Raise your joys and triumphs high!
Sing, ye heavens, and earth reply!

Sarita almost choked on the lyrics, and her eyes flew open. She wasn't sure which shocked her more: finding Matthias standing at her elbow or hearing him sing out the lyrics without faltering. Perhaps growing up in a church left its *positive* mark upon his memory as well. She tried to weave her voice into his, inspired by its strength and forcefulness, but she found that she was trembling, unable to hold a note, shaken by his mere presence. As the final strains of the organ faded, she glanced up again and found him smiling down at her. Her frozen facial muscles didn't allow her to smile back. When his hand came down to engulf hers, it was as warm as hers was cold.

Her thoughts were like spinning Catherine wheels, careening off each other, leaving trails of bright sparks behind. What was he doing here? Okay, it would have been a cinch to deduce where she would be: finding her in church on Easter morning didn't require great detecting skills. But *why* had he come? She'd rejected him in no uncertain terms, turned down his invitation for her to be a second-class citizen in his life. If he were to try to repeat the same offer, her response would be no different. It was all or nothing, and Matthias was a driven man. He didn't have all to give because it had already been pledged elsewhere. She waited for him to speak.

He didn't say a word, apart from the required responses as Colin moved through the liturgy. The sermon was gibberish for Sarita, but even as she cast covert glances up at Matthias, he seemed spellbound, hanging onto every word, feeding an abyss inside him that had been unfilled for over two decades.

She vaguely remembered being led up the aisle for the Communion, with Matthias gently guiding her by the elbow, and then, later, a babble arising as the service came to an end. The congregation, after having been confined in the small church for over an hour, spilled out into the yard, chattering and laughing, hugging each other and greeting friends. Sarita didn't move from her spot at the back of the church.

"Fresh air?" Matthias asked, after a while.

"I . . . guess," she mumbled. She let him take her outside. From where she stood she could see the pigeon peas trees she had tended with Colin bobbing in the breeze. She tried to focus on those, in an effort to mute her confusion.

"Will you at least look at me?" he asked gently.

She struggled with the *No!* that rushed to her lips but didn't dare leave them. Instead, she dragged her gaze up to his face and fought to bring it into focus. He had the same glow about him that she had perceived that night when they'd come home from the police station. An intangible sign that told her something about him had changed. What it was, she couldn't put her finger on.

"I just want to make sure that you know I'm here," he explained.

Know he was here? How could she not? He was like a signal from a powerful transmitter that interrupted everything else, shutting down her systems and leaving her confused as to which way was up. "Oh, I know you're here," she answered wryly.

Before either of them could say another word, Colin approached. "Sarita! Matthias!" He kissed her cheek and shook hands with Matthias. "So nice to see you." He gave Matthias a meaningful look. *"Both* of you."

"Nice to see you, Colin." Her mouth was dry. She would be embarrassed to let Colin know that they hadn't arrived together. That they would not be leaving together either was almost a given. Then Matthias blew her mind.

"Father . . . uh . . . Reverend," he began.

"Colin," he was reminded sternly.

"Colin," Matthias started over.

"That's better." Colin was smiling broadly.

"Is there a place where my wife and I can talk privately?"

Sarita gasped. "Matthias!" She felt her cheeks run hot, but she was not sure if her flush was motivated by surprise, annoyance at his forwardness, or nervous anticipation about whatever would come next.

Colin's florid face grew even pinker. "Oh, I see." He hemmed and hawed awhile, thinking. "Well, my office is about the quietest place around." He began to lead them there, even before he finished speaking, beckoning with two fingers. "Come, come."

"Colin, it really isn't . . ." Sarita began.

Matthias cut across her. "Come, Sari. Hear me out. Give me that much. Just listen. Okay?"

Her protests were stillborn. Between the two men, she found herself being railroaded back into the church, past the main area, and into a small, yellow-painted room with a desk, a few filing cabinets, and rows of books on overburdened shelves.

"Take as much time as you need." Colin's eyes crinkled with impish glee. "I'm here all day, and I don't have another service until six." Wickedly, he flashed Matthias the victory sign and disappeared.

She scowled at her friend's receding back. Traitor!

Matthias shut the door and then stood before her. Unable to bear his gaze, she looked past his shoulder at the bookshelves, perusing the titles. Most of them were religious texts, but there was also a wide range of classics, both ancient and modern, ranging from *Moby Dick* to *Jaws*.

"Look at me," Matthias appealed. "Please."

"I . . . can't," she managed.

"Look at me," he asked again. His voice was neither louder nor more intense but simply patient. Waiting.

She lifted her eyes to his face. It was taut, anxious, and had the near-haggard look of one that had not had the solace of sleep in a long time. The storm green of his eyes was washed aside by a troubled amber, like sand being churned up from the ocean's floor.

"You turned me down," he said. There was no accusation, just puzzlement and hurt.

"Yes."

"Why? You were the one who fought against the divorce all the way. I thought you loved me."

I do would have been a more honest reply, but she couldn't risk it. So she said, "I did."

It could have been her imagination, but he seemed

to flinch at the past tense. "I thought you wanted us to be together," he persisted.

"Not like that."

His brow furrowed. "Not like what?"

Didn't he know? Had he forgotten their conversation on the night before they were set adrift? "Not second," she tried to explain, but the humiliation of knowing that that was what she was wouldn't allow her to go any further.

"What do you mean, second?"

She had to put some distance between them! She ducked around to the other side of Colin's desk, bracing her hands on the back of his overstuffed brown leather chair. "Did you forget? How could you forget? You admitted it. You told me yourself—"

"Told you what?"

"That I'd never be anything other than second. That Tobago came first. The reef came first. You told me, Matthias . . . !"

He struck his forehead, hard, with the palm of his hand. "That *is* it, then! I knew . . . I knew that's what scared you away. I thought you'd understood, or I'd have explained. . . . That was a long time ago."

"That was a week ago today."

"And a whole lifetime has passed since then. Baby, we've been through so much this week—"

"And then you lost your project. They took Reef Rescue away from you, and then, with that gone, you decided that since I was here, and you didn't have anything else to do, you might as well give the marriage you so recently wanted out of a second try." She knew her tone was accusing, angry, but he'd hurt her and she wanted it to show.

"That's not how it happened! You are *not* second, Sarita!"

She rushed on, not giving him a chance to deny what was so patently the truth. "Well, if I'm not, I happened onto first place because the runner ahead of me tripped up!"

"No! You're first because I love you!"

"Matthias, don't do this to me," she pleaded. He wasn't a liar. That had been her crime, not his. She didn't want him to start now—not in desperation, and not to make her believe in something that wasn't real.

"What am I doing to you, other than telling you the truth?"

"You don't love me. You can't."

"Why can't I?" He had pursued her behind the desk and insinuated himself into her sanctuary. Now she had no means of escape.

She put her hands over her face to hide her anguish. "Even if you do, it's still not enough."

"Why isn't it enough?"

"Because you only think you do since you lost what you really love. I'm first by default, and I don't like it!"

He tried to pull her close, but she resisted. He gave up and let her go. "Don't say that. I'm not here because I lost the project."

"That's not true, Matt!"

"Well, not entirely," he conceded. "But it's not the way you think. When I heard about it, I was upset. I was devastated."

"No kidding." Her churlishness protected her from all that rehashed hurt.

He pressed on. "But then I sat down and tried to sort through my feelings. And I made some discoveries." He paused. When she didn't respond, he asked. "Don't you want to know what they were?"

She waved him on, grudgingly, unwilling to admit,

even to herself, that she really did. "Tell me if you want to. I'm just so tired of all this. . . ."

"Hear me out, then."

"Okay. Say what you have to say, and then . . ."

He rushed to speak before she could change her mind. "After I got over the shock, and sat down and thought about it, I surprised myself. I thought my world was going to collapse when the project slipped through my fingers. It didn't. It was supposed to be my one chance to prove myself to my people, and to my grandfather. When it was gone, I realized that I didn't have to after all. Not like that. I realized that building a new reef to avenge my mother and myself against a cranky, mean old man was an ugly motive. And I didn't even need vengeance anymore. I didn't hate my grandfather anymore. He's dead, and I kept him alive in my heart just to blame him for every bad thing that ever happened to me in my life. And once I understood that, I let him go."

"Good for you," she said gruffly, but she was listening.

"The only people I really need to prove myself to are me and you. And if you give me a chance, I'll do just that."

He took her left hand in his and rubbed his thumb along the band of gold that sat there. She looked down and gasped. The ring she had placed on his finger, which had been missing from it since their breakup, was back. The gold glowed against his deeply tanned skin and the dark hair on his knuckles.

"Losing Reef Rescue didn't mean the end of my life's dream. That didn't even occur to me in any real and tangible way. What it meant was that you and I didn't have an excuse to be together anymore. And that scared me. I know I rushed you yesterday. I didn't take the time to explain myself, but I was terrified that once you didn't have a reason to be here, you'd be on the first plane out. I tried to railroad you. It was bad timing and I was clumsy. I startled you and scared you away. I'm sorry."

She wasn't sure if she believed what she was hearing. Did he really not mind losing his project? Could keeping her here really have been his motive for getting it back?

"I was so busy trying to make you stay, I don't think I had the good sense to convince you how much I love you. And need you." He was almost shaking with raw emotion.

There was an awakening belief in her that he *did* love her. He had before, once, when they had first married. She'd believed it then, why shouldn't she believe it now? The question, then, was not whether he did, or didn't, but how much. She wanted total commitment, all of him, not something that waxed and waned with his other interests. She spoke slowly, clearly, ensuring that he understood every word. "If you love me, Matthias, love me all the way. Don't leave any room for chance. If you know that three months from now, or four, when our names are cleared and you have your funding back, you'll shunt me aside again, squeeze me out of your life like you did the first time, tell me now. Tell me, and we'll part ways, because I can't bear to—"

"I love you all the way, and then some. I never stopped loving you, I just lost my direction. I've found it again. You're like a beacon throwing light onto the rocks. You've helped me find my way back to shore, and now I want to drag my boat above the high-water mark, stow my oars, and be with you. My love for you is all I have, and all I have is everything. Every day it's grown, and if you give me a chance, it will grow and grow and push its own boundaries aside, like an expanding universe. Just give me the chance, Sari."

She so wanted to believe him! His fingers had not desisted in their gentle caress of her hand. Under his touch, they lost their chill. "Are you sure?"

"I'm sure. Sure as God made little blue crabs." His lips twitched slightly at his joke. "I give you my word, sweet. I lived without you for a year, and my life will never sink so low again. I spent hellish moments in the black ocean thinking you were drowned. I was half convinced that I'd rather have water fill my own lungs than climb back into that boat without you."

His arms felt so good around her! Her tears stained the front of his shirt. He'd spilled everything before her, and she gathered up every word, not wanting to ever forget them. But he was not the only one responsible for the downfall of their marriage. She wasn't blameless in all this. "I'm sorry." Her voice was muffled against his chest.

"For what?"

"It takes two to make a bad marriage. You're not the only one to blame. I fought you, provoked you, nagged you to spend more time with me. I can only guess how tiresome I must have become after a while."

His fingers toyed with her hair. "You did that because you were lonely, but your loneliness . . . that was my fault." Then, his kisses followed his fingers against her scalp. "I promise that I'll never let you feel abandoned again."

Her mouth was jealous, so she lifted her face so it could get its share of kisses, too. No kiss that ever passed between them at any time before, not even on their wedding day, had ever been that sweet. Her hands curled into his locks and his slipped down to her bottom. She was aware of the heat of his skin through the thin fabric of her dress. Only the recollection that they were in a church stopped her from removing the barrier. In fact, it was the steady gaze of the small, beaten bronze figurine on a cross above their heads that made her bring their kiss of eons to a halt.

"What, love?" he murmured, half drugged with want.

"We're, uh, being watched." She pointed with her chin to the figure staring down at them.

He looked up and then laughed. "Oh, well, we're married. And we're back together again, after a separation that should never have taken place. I'm pretty sure He's happy for us."

She looked a little closer. She was almost certain the small bronze face bore a smile. "You're right."

"I usually am."

"Don't start!"

They faced each other, hands clasped between them, feeling energy circle from one into the other and then back again. Bitterness, hurt, and anger were a vague memory, washed away by a wave of reborn love.

"Heart?" Matthias spoke.

"Yes?"

If she didn't know that Matthias was not a shy man, she would have sworn that the expression he now wore was a bashful one. "I think He'd be a lot happier for us if we were married with His blessings. I mean properly, in a church. This church."

She giggled. "Are you proposing to me? I'm a married woman!"

"I'm sure if we explained the special circumstances to Colin he'd make allowances for that fact."

"I'm sure he would," she conceded. She was afraid her smile would split her face. "Let's ask him."

"Let's do that." He followed her to the door, but before she opened it, he leaned forward to whisper in her ear.

"I'll tell you something else."

He was a veritable fountain of information today. "Tell me."

"There's a saying on my island that children conceived in Tobago can have special magic powers. You know, a sixth sense. Talk to the animals and all that."

Her eyes rounded. "Really?"

He looked sheepish. "Well, no. I made that up. But no harm in testing the theory."

She was stunned. "You mean that?"

"I mean that. Sincerely. I'm a new man, Sari, and the man that I am wants everything: you, family, the works. We have so much to give a child. It'd be a damn shame to keep it all to ourselves."

Sarita wondered if anything could wipe the delighted grin that spread across her face. "I'm willing to try, if you are. And try, and try. . . ."

He looked at his watch. "If I drive under the speed limit, we can make it home in about fifteen minutes. If I drive like a man ravenous to make love with his wife, we can make it home in five, seven tops. After all, nothing in Tobago is very far from—"

"—anything else!" She cut him off, delightedly.

"Right. You game?"

She squeezed his hand, and her body thrilled in its response. "I'm game."

Outside, the sunlight hurt her eyes. Most of the congregation had already dispersed, rushing off to enjoy their huge, traditional Tobagonian Easter lunch. Colin was standing in the company of a large woman whose ample body was adorned in swathes of lilac shantung, and whose entire face was hidden under an ungainly straw bonnet laden with real fruit. She was energetically waving her arms as she spoke, pleased at the opportunity to express herself at length to her audience of one.

Colin tilted his body slightly to one side in order to see beyond the woman's girth, looked across at them as they stepped out of the church, and raised his brows in inquiry. Sarita slid her arm around Matthias, pressing her hip into his waist, and returned the same victory sign her friend had flashed to Matthias back at the office.

Elated for them, and to the astonishment of his companion, Colin whooped like a sports fan at a winning game, punched the air in victory, and cheered.

Dear sisters and brothers in romance,

I did not set out to write a romance that was so heavily influenced by the spiritual needs of my characters; in fact, my initial purpose in writing *Love Me All the Way* was to reveal lovely Tobago, the island of my grandmother's birth, for the delightful island that it is. Reverend Colin Constantine, as funny and as warm as he is, was never intended to be a recurrent presence in the book, but simply a kindly gentleman who would help distract Sarita during her nervous flight before exiting stage left after his only scene.

However, as I grew to know and feel for Matthias and Sarita, I realized that their marital difficulties were caused as much by a disparity in spiritual beliefs as by their dissimilar priorities. Sarita kept gravitating toward Colin, seeking comfort and spiritual grounding; Matthias was so damaged by his early suffering through misguided and misapplied religious dogma that I began to be afraid that they would never find their way toward each other . . . and then where would I, their creator/mentor/friend, be?

Fortunately, like Matthias and Sarita, I do believe in miracles, and the greatest one is that they managed to blunder onto the path to healing pretty much on their own, with very little prodding from me. The result is, for me, a charming story of two people who were meant for each other, and who overcame their own personal stumbling blocks long enough to realize that, in spite of all their mistakes, they just might have a marriage made in Heaven.

ABOUT THE AUTHOR

Roslyn Carrington, who writes romance as Simona Taylor, just can't believe her luck. She was born and raised in the Caribbean twin-island state of Trinidad and Tobago, and if ever there was a setting created for romance, this is it! By day she puts her creativity to work as a Public Relations Officer for a major state enterprise, and by night, enjoys the company of the fantastic parade of characters who people her imagination, and who come alive on her screen and on these pages as she hammers away at her keyboard.

When she is not writing, she is a passionate and inquisitive cook, and an avid but lazy gardener. She shares her life with an imperious and domineering cat (the notorious Simona the Lizard Killer, from whom she stole her pen name), two deranged dogs, and a warm, wise, and wonderful man whose patience knows no bounds.

You can write to her at:
      7311 NW 12th St.
      Suite 14/T-926
      Miami, Fl 33126

You can also visit her Web site at
      www.roslyncarrington.com

Or e-mail her at
      simona@roslyncarrington.com

LOVE ME ALL THE WAY

Sarita watched him as his face worked, trying to bring those powerful emotions back under control. Now that she knew how huge her competition was, it made her almost laugh out loud to think that she had once seen Janelle as a threat. The object of his affections was greater than a mere woman, bigger than the reef, and huger, even, than the noble purpose of their mission. It was a whole island, and tangled inextricably therein was the whole idea of birthright and self-worth, vengeance, and vindication. What sort of fight could she put up against that?

"Now I know," she said softly.

He closed his eyes.

"Matthias," she called his name after a while.

He focused on her. His eyes were more honest than she had ever seen them. She was sure that whatever she asked him now would receive nothing but the whole truth. She steeled herself. "We made a mistake, didn't we? Getting married." It was only partly a question.

There didn't seem to be a need to answer, so instead he said, "I loved you."

"Did you really?" She needed so badly for him to affirm it.

"Yes."

She wanted to hug him, if only to use his body to still her trembling. "Just not enough, huh?"

His hands slid along her arms and pulled her closer, as if he'd read her need. "It wasn't a matter of *how much*. It was a matter of *when.*"

"Bad timing?"

"Yes."

"You needed to do this first."

"Yes."

She ached to ask him if he loved her less than he had a year ago but it was a stupid question. Just because her love was still as strong as it ever was, in spite of all they had gone through, why should his be?

BOOK YOUR PLACE ON OUR WEBSITE AND MAKE THE ARABESQUE ROMANCE CONNECTION!

We've created a customized website just for our very special Arabesque readers, where you can get the inside scoop on everything that's going on with Arabesque romance novels.

When you come online, you'll have the exciting opportunity to:

- View covers of upcoming books

- Learn about our future publishing schedule (listed by publication month and author)

- Find out when your favorite authors will be visiting a city near you

- Search for and order backlist books

- Check out author bios and background information

- Send e-mail to your favorite authors

- Join us in weekly chats with authors, readers and other guests

- Get writing guidelines

- AND MUCH MORE!

Visit our website' at
http://www.arabesquebooks.com